SORROW BOUND

DAVID MARK

Quercus

First published in Great Britain in 2014 by

Quercus Editions Ltd
55 Baker Street
7th Floor, South Block
London
W1U 8EW

A CIP catalogue record for this book is available
from the British Library

ISBN 978 1 78206 313 1 (HB)
ISBN 978 1 78206 314 8 (TPB)
ISBN 978 1 78206 315 5 (EBOOK)

10 9 8 7 6 5 4 3 2 1

Typeset by Ellipsis Digital Limited, Glasgow

Printed and bound in Great Britain by Clays Ltd, St Ives plc

For my children, George and Elora.
I hope you never stop being seriously frigging odd.

Oft have I heard that grief softens the mind,
And makes it fearful and degenerate;
Think therefore on revenge and cease to weep.

Henry VI, Part 2, 4.4.1–3

PROLOGUE

Keep going, keep going, it's only pain, just breathe and run, breathe, and fucking run!

He skids. Slips on blood and ice. Tumbles into the snow and hears the sound of paper tearing. Feels the flap of burned skin that was hanging, sail-like, across his chest, being torn away on unforgiving stone.

His scream is an inhuman thing; primal, untamed.

Get up, run, run . . .

Sobbing, he bites into the fat of his hand. Tastes his own roasted flesh. Spits blood and skin and bile. Petrol. Somebody else's hair.

Not like this. Not now . . .

He tries to pull himself upright, but his naked, frozen toes fail to respond to his commands. He thrusts his ruined hands into the snow and pushes his body up, but slips again and feels his head hit the pavement.

Stay awake. Stay alive.

His vision is blurring. From nowhere, he finds himself remembering the television in his old student flat – the way the picture disappeared down a dwindling circle of colour in

1

the centre of the screen, creating a miniature whirlpool of swirling patterns and pictures. That is what he sees now, his whole world diminishing. His senses, his understanding, are turning in a shrinking kaleidoscope of crimsons and darks.

Half-undone, almost broken, he raises his head and looks back at the grisly path his feet have punched in the snow. Miniature ink-bombs of blue-black blood, scattered haphazardly among ragged craters.

'There! There he is! Stop him. Stop!'

The voices force him upright, boost his vision, his perception, and for a blessed moment he gathers himself and takes in his surroundings. Looks up at the Victorian terraces with their big front windows and bare hanging baskets: their 'vacancies' signs and joyless rainbows of unlit coloured bulbs.

His own voice: 'Bitch, bitch.'

He realises he can hear the sea; a crackle of static and sliding stones, slapping onto the mud and sand beyond the harbour wall.

And suddenly he is adrift in a symphony of senses.

Sounds.

Scents.

Flavours.

He smells the salt and vinegar of the chip shop; the stale ale of a pub cellar. Hears the scream of gulls and the wet kisses of rotting timbers knocking against one another as bobbing fishing boats softly collide. Doors opening. Sash windows sliding up. Glasses on varnished wood. Faintly, the triumphant song of a slot machine as it pays out. A cheer. The rattle of coins . . .

Up. Run!

He has taken no more than a dozen steps when his strength

leaves him. He slides onto his belly. Feels the snow become a blanket. Deliriously, tries to pull it around himself. To make a pillow of the kerb.

Running feet. Voices.

Up. Up!

A hand around his throat, hauling him to his feet. An impact to the side of his head. Perhaps a fist, perhaps a knee.

'Bastard. Bastard!'

His teeth slam together: the impact a blade biting into wood.

Stars and mud, snow and cloud, boots and fists and the kerb against his skull, again, again, again . . .

He is drifting into the tunnel of shapes, now. Disappearing. Everything is getting smaller. Darker.

All over. All gone . . .

The snow so soft. The dark so welcoming.

Fresh hands upon him. Hands, not fists. Soft. Firm, but tender. Flesh on flesh.

A face, looming over him.

'Look what you've done to him.'

A moment's clarity, before the black ocean pulls him under . . .

'Let him die. Please, let him fucking die.'

Part One

1

Monday morning. 9.16 a.m.

A small and airless room above the health centre on Cottingham Road.

Detective Sergeant Aector McAvoy, uncomfortable and ridiculous on a plastic school chair, knees halfway up to his ears.

'Aector?'

He notices that his left leg is jiggling up and down. *Damn!* The shrink must have seen it too. He decides to keep jiggling it, so she doesn't read anything into his decision to stop.

He catches her eye.

Looks away.

Stops jiggling his leg.

'Aector, I'm not trying to trick you. You don't need to second-guess yourself all the time.'

McAvoy nods, and feels a fresh bead of sweat run down the back of his shirt collar. It's too hot in here. The walls, with their Elastoplast-coloured wallpaper, seem to be perspiring, and the painted-shut windows are misting up.

She's talking again. *Words, words, words . . .*

'I have apologised, haven't I? About the room? I tried to get another one but there's nothing available. I think if we gave that window a good shove we could get it open, but then you have the sound of the road to contend with.'

McAvoy raises his hands to tell her not to worry, though in truth, he is so hot and uncomfortable, he's considering diving head-first through the glass. McAvoy was dripping before he even walked through the door. For two weeks it has felt as though a great wet dog has been lying on the city, but it is a heatwave that has brought no blue skies. Instead, Hull has sweated beneath heavens the colour of damp concrete. It is weather that frays tempers, induces lethargy, and makes life an ongoing torture for big, flame-haired men like Detective Sergeant Aector McAvoy, who has felt damp, cross and self-conscious for days. It's a feverish heat; a pestilent, buzzing cloak. To McAvoy, even walking a few steps feels like fighting through laundry lines of damp linen. Everybody agrees that the city needs a good storm to clear the air, but lightning has yet to split the sky.

'I thought you had enjoyed the last session. You seemed to warm up as we went along.' She looks at her notes. 'We were talking about your father . . .'

McAvoy closes his eyes. He doesn't want to appear rude, so bites his tongue. As far as he can recall, he hadn't been talking about his father at all. She had.

'Okay, how about we try something a bit less personal? Your career, perhaps? Your ambitions?'

McAvoy looks longingly at the window. The scene it frames could be a photograph. The leaves and branches of the rowan tree are lifeless, unmoving, blocking out the view of the university across the busy road, but he can picture it in his imagination clearly enough. Can see the female students with their bare midriffs and tiny denim shorts; their knee socks and back-combed hair. He closes his eyes, and sees nothing but victims. They will hit the beer gardens this afternoon. They will drink more than they should. They will catch the eye and, emboldened by alcohol, some will smile and flirt and revel in the sensation of exposed skin. They will make mistakes. There will be confusion and heat and desire and fear. By morning, detectives will be investigating assaults. Maybe a stabbing. Parents will be grieving and innocence will be lost.

He shakes it away. Curses himself. Hears Roisin's voice, as always, telling him to stop being silly and just enjoy the sunshine. Pictures her, bikini-clad and feet bare, soaking up the heat as she basks, uncaring, on their small patch of brown front lawn.

Had he been asked a question? Oh, yeah . . .

'I'm not being evasive,' he says, at last. 'I know for some people there are real benefits to what you do. I studied some psychology at university. I admire your profession immensely. I'm just not sure what I can tell you that will be of any benefit to either of us. I don't bottle things up. I talk to my wife. I have outlets for my dark feelings, as you call them. I'm okay. I wish my brain didn't do some things and I'm grateful it does others. I'm pretty normal, really.'

The psychologist puts her head on one side, like a Labrador delicately broaching the subject of a walk.

'Aector, these sessions are for whatever you want them to be. I've told you this. If you want to discuss police work, you can. If you want to talk about things in your personal life, that's fine too. I want to help. If you sit here in silence, that's what I have to put in my report.'

McAvoy drops his head and stares at the carpet for a moment. He's bone-tired. The hot weather has made his baby daughter irritable and she is refusing to sleep anywhere other than on Daddy. He spent last night in a deckchair in the back yard, wrapped in a blanket and holding her little body against his chest, her fingers gripping the collar of his rugby shirt as she grizzled and sniffled in her sleep.

'The rowan tree,' says McAvoy, suddenly, and points at the window. 'They used to plant them in churchyards to keep away witches. Did you know that? I did a project on trees when I was eight. *Sorbus aucuparia*, it's called, in Latin. I know the names of about twenty different trees in Latin. Don't know why they stayed in my mind but they did. Don't really know why I'm telling you this, to be honest. It just came to me. I suppose it's nice to be able to say something without worrying that people will think I'm being a smart-arse.'

The psychologist steeples her fingers. 'But you're not worried about that at this moment? That's interesting in itself . . .'

McAvoy sighs, exasperated at being analysed by anybody other than himself. He knows what makes him tick. He doesn't want to be deconstructed in case the pieces don't fit back together.

'Aector? Look, is there somewhere else you would rather be?'

He looks up at the psychologist. Sabine Keane, she's called. McAvoy reckons she's divorced. She wears no ring but would be unlikely to have been saddled with a rhyming name from birth. She's in her early forties and very slim, with longish hair tied back in a mess of straw and grey strands. She's dressed for the hot weather, in sandals, linen skirt and a plain black T-shirt that exposes arms that sag a little underneath. She wears no make-up and there is a blob of something that may be jam halfway up her right arm. She has one of those sing-song, storytelling voices that are intended to comfort, but often grate. McAvoy has nothing against her and would love to be able to tell her something worthwhile, but is struggling to see the point of these sessions. He's grateful that she learned to pronounce his name the Celtic way, and she has a friendly enough smile, but there are doors in his head he doesn't want to unlock. It doesn't help that they got off to such an inauspicious start. On his way to the first session, he had witnessed her involvement in a minor incident of cycle rage. It's hard to believe in somebody's power to heal your soul when you have seen them pedalling furiously down a bus lane and screaming obscenities at a Volvo.

McAvoy tries again.

'Look, the people at occupational health have insisted I come for six sessions with a police-approved counsellor. I'm doing that. I'm here. I'll answer your questions and I'm at great pains not to be rude to you but it's hot and I'm tired and I have work to do, and yes, there are lots of places I would rather be. I'm sure you would too.'

There is silence for a second. McAvoy hears the beep of an appointment being announced in the waiting room for the main doctor's surgery downstairs. He pictures the scene. The waiting room of sick students and chattering foreigners, of middle-class bohemians waiting for their malaria pills and yellow fever jabs before they jet off to Goa with their little Jeremiahs and Hermiones.

Eventually, Sabine tries again. 'You have three children, is that right?'

'Two,' says McAvoy.

'Youngest keeping you up?'

'Comes with the job.'

'It's your duty, yes?'

'Of course.'

'Tell me about duty, Aector. Tell me what it means to you.'

McAvoy makes fists. Thinks about it. 'It's what's expected.'

'By whom?'

'By everyone. By yourself. It's the right thing.'

Sabine says nothing for a moment, then reaches down and pulls a notepad from her satchel. She writes something on the open page, but whether it is some clinical insight or a reminder to pick up toilet rolls on the way home, McAvoy cannot tell.

'You've picked a job that is all about duty, haven't you? Did you always want to be a policeman?'

McAvoy rubs a hand across his forehead. Straightens his green and gold tie. Rolls back the cuffs on his black shirt, then rolls them down again.

'It wasn't like that,' he says, eventually. 'Where I grew up. The set-up at home. The script was kind of written.'

Sabine looks at her notepad again, and shuffles through the pages to find something. She looks up. 'You grew up in the Highlands, yes? On a croft? A little farm, I believe . . .'

'Until I was ten.'

'And that's when you went to boarding school?'

McAvoy looks away. He straightens the crease in his grey suit trousers and fiddles with the pocket of the matching waistcoat. 'After a while.'

'Expensive, for a crofter, I presume.' Her voice is soft but probing.

'Mam's new partner was quite well off.'

The psychologist makes another note. 'And you and your mother are close?'

McAvoy looks away.

'How about you and your father?'

'Off and on.'

'How does he feel about your success?'

McAvoy gives in to a smile. 'What success?'

Sabine gestures at her notes, and the cardboard file on the floor at her feet. 'The cases you have solved.'

He shakes his head. 'It doesn't work like that. I didn't solve anything.' He stops. Considers it properly, shrugs. 'Maybe I did. Maybe I was just, well, there. And when it was just me, on my own, when nobody else gave a damn, I ended up thinking I shouldn't have bothered. Or maybe I should have bothered more.'

There is silence in the room. McAvoy rocks the small plastic chair back on two legs, then puts it down again when he feels it lurch.

After a moment, Sabine nods, as if making up her mind.

'Tell me about Doug Roper,' she says, without looking at her pad.

Involuntarily, McAvoy clenches his jaw. He feels the insides of his cheeks go dry. He says nothing, for fear his tongue will be too fat and useless to make any sense.

'We only get the most basic details in the reports, Aector. But I can read between the lines.'

'He was my first detective chief superintendent in CID,' says McAvoy, softly.

'And?'

'And what? You've probably heard of him.'

Sabine gives a little shrug. 'I Googled him. Bit of a celebrity policeman, I see.'

'He's retired now.'

'And you had something to do with that?'

McAvoy runs his tongue around his mouth. 'Some people think so.'

'And that made you unpopular?'

'It's getting better now. Trish Pharaoh has been very helpful.'

'That's your new boss, yes? Serious and Organised Crime Unit, is that right? Yes, you mentioned her last time. You mention her quite a lot.'

McAvoy manages a faint smile. 'You sound like my wife.'

Sabine cocks her head. 'She means a lot to you?'

'My wife? She's everything . . .'

'No. Your boss.'

McAvoy's leg starts jiggling again. 'She's a very good police officer. I think so, anyway. Maybe she isn't. Maybe Doug Roper had it right. I don't know. I don't know anything very much. Somebody once told me that I would drive myself insane trying to understand what it's all about. Justice, I mean. Goodness. Badness. Sometimes I think I'm halfway there. Other times I just feel like I'm only clever enough to realise how little I know.'

'There's a line in the report we have that says you take the rules very seriously. Can you tell me what you think that might mean?'

McAvoy holds her gaze. Is she making fun of him? He doesn't know what to say. Is there something in the file about his adherence to the rule book? He's a man who completes his paperwork in triplicate in case the original is mislaid and who won't requisition a new Biro from the stationery cupboard until his last one is out of ink.

He says nothing. Just listens to the tyres on the bone-dry road and the sound of blood in his ears.

'The report says you have lots of physical scars, Aector.'

'I'm okay.'

McAvoy tries to be an honest man, and so does not reproach himself for the answer. He is okay. He's as well as can be expected. He's getting by. Doing his bit. Making do. He has plenty of glib, meaningless ways to describe how he is, and knows that were he to sit here trying to explain it all properly, he would turn to ash. At home, he's more than okay. He's perfect. With his arms around his wife and children, he feels like he is glowing. It is only at work that he has no bloody clue how he feels. Whether he regrets his actions. What he really feels about the corrupt and pitiless detective superintendent whose tenure at the head of Humberside CID only ended when McAvoy tried to bring his crimes into the light. Whether noble or naïve, McAvoy's actions cost him his reputation as rising star. This gentle, humble, shy giant of a man was made a distrusted, despised pariah by many of his fellow officers. He was dumped on the Serious and Organised Crime Unit as little more than accountant and mouthpiece, expected by all to be chewed up and spat out by the squad boss, Detective Superintendent Trish Pharaoh, with her biker boots, mascara and truckloads of attitude. Instead she had found a protégé. Almost a friend. And at her side, he has caught bad people.

The burns on McAvoy's back and the slash wound to the bone on his left breast are not the only scars he carries, but they have become almost medals of redemption. He has suffered for what he believes.

Sabine puts down her pen and pulls her phone from her bag. She looks at the display and then up at McAvoy. 'We have half an hour left. You must want to get some of this off your chest.'

McAvoy pulls out his own phone to check that she is right, and sees that he has had eight missed calls, all from the same number. He pulls an apologetic face and before Sabine can object, rings back.

Trish Pharaoh answers on the second ring. Spits his name the only way she can pronounce it, with a mixture of sugar and steel.

'Hector, thank fuck for that. We've got a body. Tell the shrink to tick your chart and let you go. You're in fine shape. Let's just hope your gag reflex isn't. This one's going to make you sick.'

Tick-tock, tick-tock, indicator flashing right. A bluebottle buzzing fatly against the back window. Horns honking and the drone of a pneumatic drill. Shirtless workmen lying back against the wall of the convenience store on the corner, egg-and-bacon sandwiches dripping from greasy paper bags onto dirty hands.

The lights turn green, but nobody moves. The traffic stays still. Two different radio stations blare from open windows. Lady Gaga fights for supremacy with The Mamas and the Papas . . .

A city in the grip of a fever: irritable, agitated, raw.

McAvoy checks his phone. Nothing new. Tries to read the sticker on the back windscreen of the Peugeot two cars in front, but gives up when the squinting makes his temples sweat.

Looks right, at the Polish convenience store: its sign a jumble of angry consonants. Left, at the gym with its massive advert for pole-dancing fitness classes. Wonders if any of the immigrants in this part of town have become champion Pole dancers . . .

He's at the bottom of Anlaby Road, already regretting his decision to turn right out of the doctor's surgery. He's driving the five-year-old people-carrier that he and Roisin had settled on a month ago. There are two child seats in the back, leaving

McAvoy constantly worried about being asked to chauffeur any more than one colleague at a time.

The lights turn green again, and he noses the car forward, into the shadow of a boarded-up theme pub. He remembers when it opened. A local businessman spent more than a million on revamping the building, convinced there was a need for a sophisticated and luxurious nightspot in this part of town. It lasted a year. Its demise could serve as a mirror for so much of this area. The bottom end of Anlaby Road is all charity shops and pizza parlours, cash-for-gold centres and pubs where the barman and the only customer take it in turns to go outside for a cigarette. The streets are a maze of small terraced houses with front rooms where a man of McAvoy's size would struggle to lie down. Once upon a time, the people would have been called 'poor but honest'. Perhaps even 'working class'. There is no term in the official police guidance to describe the locals now. Just people. Ordinary people, with their faults and flaws and wishes and dreams. Hull folk, all tempers and pride.

The lights change again, and McAvoy finally edges into Walliker Street.

Second gear. Third.

He is at the crime scene before he can get into fourth gear. There are three police cars blocking the road, and a white tent is being erected by two constables and a figure in a white suit. Pharaoh's little red convertible is parked next to a forensics van, outside a house with brown-painted bay windows and dirty net curtains pulled tight shut. Next door, a woman in combat trousers and a Hull City shirt is talking to a man in a dressing gown in the front yard. McAvoy fancies they will have already solved the case.

He abandons the car in the middle of the road and reaches into the back seat for his leather satchel. It was a gift a couple of years ago from his wife, and is the source of endless amusement to his colleagues.

'Hector. At last.'

McAvoy bangs his head on the doorframe as he hears his boss's voice. He looks up and sees Pharaoh making her way towards him. Despite the heat, she has refused to shed her biker boots, though she has made a few concessions to the weather. She's wearing a red dress with white spots, and has a cream linen scarf around her neck, which McAvoy presumes she has placed there to disguise her impressive cleavage. She is wearing large, expensive sunglasses, and her dark hair has a kink to it that suggests it dried naturally on the hot air, without the attentions of a brush.

'Guv?'

She looks at her sergeant for a moment too long, then nods. 'No suit jacket, Hector?'

McAvoy looks at himself, neat and pressed in designer suit trousers, waistcoat, shirt with top button done up and his tie perfectly tied in a double Windsor. 'I can pop home if . . .'

Pharaoh laughs. 'Christ, you must be boiling. Undo a button, for God's sake.'

McAvoy begins to colour. Pharaoh can make any man blush but has an ability to transform her sergeant into a lava lamp with nothing more than a sentence or a smile. He has refused to wear a white shirt since she told him she could see the outline of his nipples, and has yet to find a way of looking at her that doesn't take in at least one of her many curves. He raises his hands to his throat but can't bring himself to give in to slovenliness. 'I'll be fine.'

Pharaoh sighs and shakes her head. 'All okay at the shrink?'

He spreads his hands. 'She wants me to have more problems than I have.'

'That's what she's paid for.'

'Came as a relief to get your call.'

'You haven't seen the poor lass yet.'

Together they cross the little street, passing a closed fish and chip shop that appears to have been built in the front room of one of the terraced houses. The row of houses stops abruptly and behind the wall of the last house is a large parking area, its concrete surface broken up and pitted, and the beads of broken glass on its surface testament to the fact that this is no safe place to leave your car.

The forensics tent has been pitched on a patch of grass beyond the car park, behind a small copse of trees that stand in a dry, litter-strewn patch of dirt. Behind it is the railway bridge that leads over the tracks to another estate.

'Brace yourself,' says Pharaoh, as she lifts the flap of the tent and steps inside.

'Guv?'

'Take a look.'

A forensics officer in a white suit is crouching down over the body, but he stops taking photographs and backs away, crablike, as McAvoy enters the tent. Breathing slowly, he crosses to where the corpse lies.

The victim is on her back. The first thing that strikes him is the angle of her head. She seems to be looking up, craning her neck so as not to see the ruination of what has happened to her body. Even so, her expression is one of anguish. The tendons in her neck seem to have stretched to breaking point and her face is locked mid-scream. Her mouth is open, and her blue eyes have rolled back in her head, as if trying to get away.

McAvoy swallows. Forces himself to look at more than just the wounds.

She is in her late fifties, with short brown hair, greying at the roots. She is wearing black leggings and old, strappy sandals that display bare toes with nails painted dark blue. Her fingers are short but not unsightly, with neatly clipped nails and a gold engagement ring and wedding band, third finger, left hand.

Only now does he allow himself to consider her midsection.

His bile rises. He swallows it down.

The woman's chest has been caved in. The bones of her ribs have been snapped, splintered and pushed up and into her breasts and lungs. Her upper torso is a mass of flattened skin and tissue, black blood and mangled organs. Her white bra, together with what looks like the remains of her breasts, sit in the miasma of churned meat. For a hideous moment, McAvoy imagines the noise that will be made when the pathologist disentangles them for examination.

He turns away. Takes a breath that is not as deeply scented with gore.

He turns back to the horror, and flinches.

Though it shames him to have considered it, McAvoy finds himself in mind of a spatchcocked chicken; split at the breast and flattened out to be roasted.

He feels Pharaoh's hand on his shoulder, and looks into her face. She nods, and they step outside the tent.

'Bloody hell, Guv,' says McAvoy, breathlessly.

'I know.'

He breathes out, slowly. Realises that the world has been

spinning a little, and waits for the dizziness to pass. Forces himself to be a policeman.

'What sort of weapon does that?'

Pharaoh shrugs. 'I reckon we're after a bloke on a horse, swinging a fucking mace.'

'That can't have been the cause of death, though, can it? There must be a head wound, or a stab somewhere under all that . . .'

'Pathologist will get to all that. All I can say for certain is it wasn't suicide.'

McAvoy looks up at the sky. It remains the colour of dirty bathwater. He feels the perspiration at his lower back and when he rubs a hand over his face it comes away soaking. Although he knows nothing about the life of the woman in the tent, the little he knows of her death makes him angry. Nobody should die like that.

'Handbag? Purse?'

Pharaoh nods. 'The lot. Was only a few feet from the body.'

'What time?'

'She was found a couple of hours ago. Bloke on his way to get the morning papers. Saw her foot sticking out and phoned 999.'

'Regular CID can't have had a look, then . . .'

'Came straight to us.'

'Guv?'

Pharaoh makes a blade of her fingers and waves them in front of her throat, suggesting he cut short his questions. As head of the Serious and Organised Crime Unit, Pharaoh is used to the infighting and internecine warfare that pollutes the upper strata of Humberside Police. Her unit was established as a murder squad, set apart from the main body of detectives, but budget cuts and personnel changes have left the team with no clearly defined role. At present, Pharaoh and her officers are loosely tasked with investigating a highly organised criminal outfit that appears to have taken over most of the drugs trafficking on the east coast. Its emergence has coincided with a marked spike in the incidents of violent crime, and both McAvoy and Pharaoh know for certain that the gang's foot soldiers are responsible for several deaths. Their methods are efficient and brutal, their favoured weapons the nailgun and blowtorch. Pharaoh's unit have locked up three of the outfit's significant players but so far the information they have managed to glean about the chain of command has been pitiful. Ruthless, efficient, single-minded and worryingly well informed, each tier of the gang seems to be insulated from the next. The soldiers have little or no knowledge of who gives them their orders. It is an operation based on mobile phones and complex codes, which has recruited a better class of muscle through a combination of high reward and justified fear.

'This is down as gang-related?' asks McAvoy, incredulously. It is the only way the crime would have come straight to Pharaoh.

Pharaoh gives a rueful smile. 'She runs a residents' group. Spoke out at a recent public meeting about street dealers ruining the neighbourhood.'

McAvoy closes his eyes. 'So what do we know?'

Pharaoh doesn't need to consult her notes. She has already committed the details to memory.

'Philippa Longman. Fifty-three. Lived up Conway Close. Past Boulevard, near the playing fields. There's a uniform inspector from Gordon Street with the family now. Philippa worked at the late shop that you passed driving in. Was working last night, before you ask. And this would have been on her way home. Somebody grabbed her. Pulled her behind the trees. Did this.'

'Family?'

'Our next stop, my boy.'

'Bloke who found her?'

'Still shaking. Hasn't got the taste of sick out of his mouth yet.'

'And we're taking it, yes? There won't be a stink from CID?'

Pharaoh looks at him over the top of her sunglasses. 'Of course there will. There'll be a stink whatever happens.'

McAvoy takes a deep breath. 'I'm supposed to be prepping for court. Ronan Gill's trial is only a month away and the witnesses are getting jumpy . . .'

Without changing her facial expression, Pharaoh reaches up and puts a warm palm across McAvoy's mouth. He smiles, his stubble making a soft rasp against her skin.

'I have a hand free for a kidney punch if you need it,' she says sweetly.

McAvoy looks back at the tent. Sees, in his mind's eye the devastation within. He wants to know who did it. Why. Wants to stop it happening again. Wants to ensure that whoever loved this woman is at least given a face to hate.

He wishes the bloody psychologist were here, now. It would be the only way she could ever understand what makes him do a job he hates. Wants to tell her that this is what he is. What he forces himself to be. Here, at the place between sorrow and goodbye.

'Okay.'

2

'Poor lass.'

'Aye.'

'You can hear it, can't you? When it goes from panic, to something else . . .'

'Bloody terrifying is what it is. They should play that to anybody who thinks about leaving the house without a pitbull terrier and a spear.'

McAvoy is holding Philippa Longman's mobile phone to his ear, still inside the polythene evidence bag. He is listening to her voicemails. There are ten of them, starting with a gentle enquiry from a man with a West Yorkshire accent, wondering if she is on her way home, and progressing through an assortment of sons and daughters, increasingly desperate, asking where she is, if she's okay, to please call, just please call . . .

'Out of character, least we know that,' says McAvoy, switching off the phone and putting it back in Pharaoh's red leather handbag, which he is holding between his knees in the passenger seat of the convertible.

'Getting murdered? Yeah, it definitely hasn't happened to her before.'

'No, I mean—'

'I know what you mean.'

McAvoy looks out of the window. He doesn't really know this part of Hull. They are on an estate towards the back end of Hessle Road, where those who made their living from the fishing industry used to make their homes. It's pretty run down, but in this grey light, nothing would look pretty.

'Tenner for the first person to spot an up-to-date tax disc,' mutters Pharaoh.

None of the cars that are parked on the kerbs and grass verges looks younger than ten years old, and Pharaoh's convertible draws stares as they pass a group of people lounging by a low wall that leads to a fenced-off storage yard. They are of mixed ages. Two youngsters, shirtless, with buzzcuts, lounging over the frames of BMX bikes. Three men, tattoos on their necks and roll-ups in their fingers. A woman in her late sixties, with grey hair and tracksuit bottoms, sipping from a can of lager and telling a story. One of them says something, but the convertible's roof is up, and the words are lost in the sound of tyres on bone-dry road.

They pass a sign declaring that they are on Woodcock Street, and he vaguely remembers reading that the army had used this neighbourhood to practise their tank manoeuvres before being deployed to Afghanistan. He wonders if that was true.

'Up here. Playing fields.'

Ahead, several acres of untended grass stretch away: a play park in one direction, and some form of stone memorial in the other. A police car sits abandoned in the road, among half a dozen vehicles parked haphazardly around a corner terraced house. The cars look as though they have arrived at speed and been abandoned.

Pharaoh and McAvoy step from the car. As McAvoy arranges his clothes and makes himself a little more presentable, he peers over the wall that marks the boundary of the park. Old gravestones have been laid against the far side of it, their inscriptions mossed over and names lost to wind and time.

'Shall we?'

McAvoy takes a deep breath. He has done this too many times. Sat in too many rooms with too much grief; felt too many eyes upon him as he made his promises to the dead.

They head towards the house. It sits on the far side of a low flower bed which carries nothing but dry earth and hacked-back stumps. Beyond that is a footpath, its surface a camouflage pattern of different tarmac patches.

'Poor lass,' says McAvoy, again, pushing open the gate.

The house where Philippa Longman lived is the nicest in the row. Freshly painted black railings edge a driveway of neat bricks, upon which sits a tastefully varnished shed, with double locks, and a child's plastic playhouse. There are two hanging baskets by the double-glazed front door, and the front window carries posters for a charity coffee morning and a reading initiative at a local nursery.

Pharaoh reaches up to knock on the door, but it opens before she can do so. In the hall is a Family Liaison Officer that McAvoy remembers having met before. He is pushing forty, with receding hair and slightly crooked teeth, set in a face that always looks to be squinting against harsh light. He's a nice enough guy, who understands what he is there for. His job is not to heal these people or make sense of things. He's just there to show that the police are doing something. That these people matter. That this death is important . . .

26

'They're in the lounge,' he says, his accent broad Hull. 'Husband. Jim. Nice old boy. Two sons, one furious, one falling apart. Couple of daughters-in-law. A neighbour. A sister, too, if I got the family tree straight. Eldest daughter bolted about twenty minutes ago. Took the nippers to the park, I think. Boy and a girl. A cousin, too. Was all too much. Inspector Moreton and PC Audrey Stretton are holding the fort. Family know Mum isn't coming back. They know that we found a body that matches her description. They had called her in as missing about five this morning.'

Pharaoh nods, turns to McAvoy, and without a word passing between them, he turns away from the house. The FLO opens the door to the living room and as Pharaoh continues inside, McAvoy hears the soft patter of emotionless conversation, pierced by a wet, choking wail . . .

He makes his way over to the entrance to the playing fields and follows the footpath through the long, straggly grass to the play area beyond a line of oak trees. *Quercus robur*, he remembers, unprompted, and has a sudden image of sitting at the kitchen table, breathing in peat smoke and wood shavings, mopping up potato soup with a hunk of soda bread: his dad washing pots at a deep stone sink and softly imparting facts over his broad shoulder at his eight-year-old son. *They call it "petraea" in some places. Flowers in May and leaves soon after. Sometimes they have a second flush of leaves if it's been a bad year for caterpillars. They call it Lammas growth. Can you spell that? You write it down and I'll check it. Best charcoal for making swords, the oak. Burns slow. They use the bark for tanning, Aector. High-quality leathers, especially . . .'

He shakes himself back to the present. Looks ahead. It's a modern swing park, with a protective rubber surface and plenty of padding. He remembers mentioning to Roisin that parks seem a little too safe these days. Said he couldn't see the point of bubble-wrapping all of the equipment when children have such a habit of banging their heads into one another. He had predicted crash helmets becoming compulsory on roundabouts within five years.

There are several adults in the play park but McAvoy spots Philippa Longman's daughter straight away. She is pushing a child on a swing, and between each shove she is raising her hands to her face to cuff away tears that have turned her fleshy cheeks red and sore. She is wearing a denim skirt and a green vest top, her hair pulled back in a ponytail to leave a severe fringe at the front. It doesn't suit her. Hers is a warm, open face that looks as though it hides a pleasant smile.

She sees McAvoy approaching. Immediately identifying him as a policeman, she gives a slight nod and then grabs the swing to halt its momentum. She lifts the toddler out and gives him a gentle pat on the bottom, before pointing at a climbing frame where an older child is dangling upside down. She tells him to go play with his cousin. He wobbles off, and the woman extends her hand.

'Elaine,' she says, and her voice catches. 'Elaine,' she says, again.

'I'm Aector,' says McAvoy, taking her hand in his. It's cold, tiny and birdlike in his large, fleshy palm. 'I'm a detective.'

'The house is over there,' says Elaine, waving, vaguely. 'They're all in there. Crying and bloody carrying on. I couldn't take it.'

McAvoy recognises her voice from Philippa's answering machine. She had left the most messages. By the last, her voice was just a staggered breath, broken up around the word 'please'.

'People are different,' says McAvoy, leading Elaine to a bench that overlooks the park. 'Some need company, others needs space. It's agony whatever you do.'

Elaine meets McAvoy's eyes. Holds his gaze. He watches as tears spill afresh.

'I don't know what to do,' says Elaine, looking away. 'Last night I had a mum. The kids had a grandma. It was all normal, you know? I watched a DVD and had a bottle of white wine and I tucked in my son and I went to bed. Dad woke me up, ringing. Mum hadn't come home. Was she with me, had I heard from her, did I know where she might be. I rang her, as if he hadn't already tried that. Nothing. Phoned her work and there was nobody there. I got Lucas up and we went to her shop. Walked her route. Christ, I must have walked right past where she was bloody lying . . .'

A shudder racks her body.

'What if he was doing it as I walked past? What if I could have saved her . . .'

Elaine dissolves. She shrinks inwards, a creased fist of pain and despair. Her head falls forward, tears and snot pouring unimpeded down her face, and it only takes the slightest of touches on the back of her head before she is steered into McAvoy's arms, where he feels her shudders like those of a dying animal.

McAvoy had not meant to hold her. He knows officers who have no difficulty with the professional detachment encouraged in the national guidelines, but he cannot witness pain without providing comfort.

'Oh my God, oh my God . . .'

He senses her words as much as hears them, whispered against his skin. Gently, as if she is made of shattered porcelain, he lifts her back into a seated position and tries to raise her head to look in her eyes. She ducks from his gaze and then, unexpectedly, gives a little pop of laughter.

'Your shirt, I'm so sorry . . .'

McAvoy looks down at his waistcoat, and the mess of mucus and tears.

'It doesn't matter.'

'Here, I have a tissue . . .'

'Your need is greater than mine.'

She stops talking then. Just looks at him. Then she uses her wrists to dry her eyes, and pulls a paper tissue from the pocket of her skirt. She dabs her nose.

'Don't. Give it a proper blow,' says McAvoy.

Elaine blows her nose. Folds the hankie. Blows it again.

'You're a dad, then?' she asks, tucking the tissue away. She manages a smile, at a memory. 'My dad always speaks to me like that. Still takes my arm when we cross the road. What you got?'

'Boy and a baby girl.'

She looks him up and down. 'Bet the lads won't give her any trouble when she's older, eh? You could snap them in two.'

McAvoy smiles. 'She'll be able to look out for herself. That's what you want for your kids, isn't it? That they're good people. Responsible. Able to take care of themselves.'

Elaine nods and presses her lips together. 'I think Mum did okay with us. Did her best, anyway. There's me and my two brothers. Two grandkids now. Mine and Don's. Don's the middle kid, if you need to know that.' She stops herself. 'What is it you need to know? Really? I'm no good back at the house. Don's wife's such a bloody drama queen. If I go in there I'll say something. Dad doesn't need all that around him. He doesn't know what to bloody do either, but once he's stopped making everybody cups of tea this is going to kill him too. They were together thirty-three years, you know. Got married as soon as she found out she was pregnant with me. Dad could have done a runner, couldn't he? But he didn't. Married her in a flash. Last time they agreed on anything was when they both said "I do" but they loved each other.'

Elaine falls silent. She doesn't seem to know what to do with her hands so just holds them in her lap. McAvoy looks past her. The other parents in the park have drifted together and the pair of them are receiving repeated glances. McAvoy wonders if they already know what has happened to Philippa, or whether they think he is some hulking great brute of a boyfriend who has just made his girl cry.

'Mum helped get the funding for this park,' says Elaine, gesturing at the assemblage of brightly painted swings and slides. 'Badgered the council until they couldn't say no . . .'

McAvoy looks around him. Wonders whether it is too soon to suggest they name it after the dead woman. He tries to find something to say but finds his gaze falling on Elaine's son, sitting on a roundabout and hoping somebody will come and give him a push. His cousin seems to have wandered off. McAvoy stands up and walks over to the roundabout. He smiles at the toddler, and then gently gives it a push, walking around at the same speed in case the child topples over and falls. He feels a presence beside him and turns to see Elaine, smiling weakly.

'What am I going to do without her? What will he?'

McAvoy reaches down and picks up the boy. He tickles his tummy, then under his chin, and is rewarded with a delicious peal of laughter.

31

Still holding the boy, he chooses his words carefully. 'Elaine, the unit I work for deals with organised crime. There is some suggestion that your mother was a little outspoken about some of the more unsavoury elements in the neighbourhood.'

Elaine's expression doesn't change. 'Is that something to do with this?'

'We don't know.'

She turns away and stares across the grass in the direction of her mother's home.

'I don't live around here,' she says, after a time. 'I live up Kirk Ella. Nice little place, just the two of us. I didn't grow up here either. We're from Batley. West Yorkshire. Dad came over here for a job about fifteen years ago and they bought this place. I can't say I thought much of the area but Mum said the people seemed nice. She made it a lovely home. Well, you can see that, can't you? And she was never one to keep herself to herself. Couldn't help but get involved. She'd lived here a year and she'd started a neighbourhood association. Even ran for the city council as an independent. The papers used to come to her for a quote and she was always good value. Told them this was a nice neighbourhood but that a few rotten apples were spoiling it for everyone. She meant that too.'

'Did she ever name names?'

'I don't think she knew any,' says Elaine. 'Everybody on this estate knows how to buy a bit of this or that, but Mum was no threat to anybody's business. Not really. She was probably a nuisance, if anything. She used to give your lot hell about the lack of police patrols and not seeing any policemen on the streets any more but it was busybody stuff, really. She wasn't some supergrass. She worked in a bloody late shop, for goodness' sake . . .'

'And she always walked home? It's quite a hike.'

'That's my fault,' says Elaine, kicking at a clump of grass that is pushing through a crack in the spongy surface of the park. 'We started this health challenge a couple of years ago. You have to do a certain amount of steps each day and enter the number on this website and it tells you how far around the world your team has got. She was well into it. They gave us pedometers and we both lost a bit of weight chalking up the miles. I packed it in when I got pregnant but Mum stuck with it. Said she wanted to be able to say she had walked to Mexico. Worked out that if she walked to and from work for her shifts and did a big walk on a weekend, she could be there before she was sixty.'

'So anybody who knew her would know she always walked, yes? Anybody waiting for her would know.'

Elaine reaches out and takes Lucas, holding him like a teddy bear.

'This isn't anything to do with drugs or gangs,' she says, softly. 'It can't be.'

'Do you know anybody who would want to harm her?'

'She was a good person. My best friend . . .'

'Elaine, this is a very early stage in the investigation but we need to build up as clear a picture of your mum as possible. Did she have any enemies? Had she ever been threatened?'

The dead woman's daughter shakes her head. 'She was everybody's friend. She was a lifesaver. There was . . .'

Elaine stops herself, her hand raised to her mouth.

'Darren,' she says, softly.

'I'm sorry?'

Elaine puts down her son. Tells him to go play.

'My ex.'

'Elaine?'

She grabs a handful of her fringe, eyes suddenly alive with more than tears.

'Shit, I didn't think . . .'

McAvoy takes her shoulders and turns her eyes to his. Tries to make it okay.

'Elaine, you can tell me.'

She sobs, and covers her mouth with her hand.

'He said if he ever saw her again he would kill her. That he would tear her heart out the way I tore out his . . .'

3

'Lemon-scented.'

Helen Tremberg walks back to the car and pokes her head through the open window.

'Sorry, Ma'am?'

Sharon Archer punches the steering wheel with the flat of her hand. When she speaks, it is through bared teeth and unmoving lips, and for a moment, she takes on the look of a psychotic ventriloquist.

'I said lemon fucking scented.'

Tremberg nods, pressing her lips down hard on the smile that is threatening to become a snigger. It is an act as hard as calling a woman two years older than herself 'Ma'am'.

'Sandwich, or anything?'

Archer's eyes flash fury as she turns.

'Do I look like I'm in the mood for a fucking snack?'

Tremberg turns away and heads for the pharmacy that represents the only high-street name on this little parade of independent shops and salons. She pauses for a moment to look at the display of cupcakes in the window of a bakery, but an angry blaring of the car horn indicates that Archer is watching her in the rear-view mirror and is not in the mood for waiting.

'Okay, okay,' she mutters, accepting that for now, there is no time for cake.

It's cool inside the brightly lit store and for the first time in days, Tremberg's skin goose-pimples as the sweat turns cold upon her bare arms. It's rare that she exposes any flesh while on duty but today she has acquiesced to a short-sleeved blouse, which she has not tucked into her pinstripe trousers.

'Wipes, wipes . . .'

She finds the right shelf, and pretends she can't see the lemon-scented ones. She picks the packet with the most overtly chemical smell, then heads to the counter, where a short Asian lady gives her a bright smile.

'It's two for one,' she says, conspiratorially. 'Special offer.'

Tremberg shrugs. 'They're for my boss. She can make do.'

The lady grins, and Tremberg hands over the five-pound note Archer has given her. 'Put the change in the charity box,' she says, crumpling the receipt.

'We don't have one.'

'Then get yourself an ice cream.'

Tremberg heads for the exit, catching a glimpse of her reflection in the mirror behind the make-up display as she leaves. She's at ease with what she sees. At thirty-one, she's happily single and rarely lonely, and though she may be a little more broad shouldered than she would like, there is nothing offensive about her round face with its narrow features, or her simply styled brown hair.

He'll like it, she tells herself. *Get up the courage to suggest a drink. And stop checking your phone!*

For the past few weeks Helen has been receiving increasingly colourful messages from a solicitor she met while waiting for a court case. His emails are the favourite part of her day and she has taken to checking her phone almost obsessively. Although she is no stranger to relationships, she is nervous about being the first to get in touch each day. It seems important to her that she is the respondent to his overtures, rather than making the running herself.

Helen emerges back into the muggy air and takes in the view. She's never got out of the car on this stretch of road before and wonders if she ever will again. It's no shabbier than anywhere else, and there are only a few untenanted shops. Each of the parking spaces by the side of the road is taken, and there is a steady procession of shoppers wandering from store to store, filling shopping bags with fruit and veg, bread rolls, sliced meat, saying hello over the noise of the traffic and thinking about how best to jazz up the salad they are considering for tonight's tea. It reminds Tremberg of the Grimsby neighbourhood where she grew up. Normal folk. Normal people. Bit skint by the third week of the month, and a week in Benidorm each June. Fish and chip tea on a Friday, and six-packs of supermarket lager in front of the Grand Prix on a Sunday. The people she became a copper for. The people worth protecting.

Tremberg tries to get her bearings. Works out where she is. She's half a mile from the prison on the road that leads to the Preston Road Estate. She has only been working in Hull for a year and has not had time to familiarise herself with every neighbourhood, but knows the PRE by reputation and is grateful that it was never her beat when she was still in uniform. More Anti-social Behaviour Orders have been handed out here than on any other estate in the city boundary, and barely an edition of the *Hull Daily Mail* is published without it containing some report or another about teenage gangs making life miserable for 'decent' people.

Tremberg rarely troubles herself with the politics of her job or the social background to the crimes she investigates. She does what she's asked, and enjoys catching villains. She's good at it too, even if she is currently feeling less than happy in her work. As one of four detective constables on the Serious and Organised Crime Unit, she has little say in which of her senior colleagues she is paired with, but she enjoys her working days considerably more when helping McAvoy or Pharaoh. At the moment, she is working for Detective Inspector Shaz Archer, and loathing every moment of it. Archer and DCI Colin Ray are effectively leading the unit's investigation into the spike in organised crime. Pharaoh is overseeing, but her day is so filled with paperwork and budget meetings that Ray and Archer are running the show, revelling in being top dogs.

This morning, Ray had told Tremberg to accompany Archer to HMP Hull because there was a good chance that the man they were seeing would warm to two women more than he would to Ray himself. Tremberg had seen the logic in that. It is impossible to warm to Colin Ray. He's a walking sneer, all yellow teeth and nicotine-stained fingers; all curses and spittle and ratty little eyes.

Tremberg had accepted Ray's orders with good grace, even though she had despaired at the thought of spending the morning with the snotty detective inspector who seems to be the only female that Colin Ray has any time for. The two are pretty much inseparable, though they make for unlikely friends. Archer is part of the horsey crowd and spends her free time playing polo and knocking back Pimm's with people called Savannah and

Sheridan. Ray coaches football in his spare time and spends his money on greyhounds, lager and ex-wives.

Tremberg is not the sort to be jealous of her female colleagues and does not object to the fact that Shaz Archer is extraordinarily attractive. It's her personality she bridles at. She puts Tremberg in a mind of a California high school bully in a film for teens. She holds everybody and everything in open contempt, and uses her looks to manipulate colleagues and crooks alike. Her arrest record is impressive, but Tremberg finds the way she flaunts herself distasteful. While she admires Trish Pharaoh for just being herself – for being sexy and mumsy and hard as fucking nails – with Archer it's all strategic. Every time she purses her lips or blows on her perfect fingernails, she's doing it to get a reaction out of somebody. She keeps miniskirts and crop-tops in her desk so she can get changed into something exotic if she's interviewing some easily led pervert, and there are rumours she has traded her affections for confessions in the past. Tremberg knows police stations to be termite mounds of malicious gossip and had originally decided to ignore such slander about a female colleague. Then she got to know Archer herself, and decided the woman was, if nothing else, a bitch of the first order.

Still, she didn't look quite so well groomed this morning . . .

As Tremberg passes the cake shop, she has to bite down on her smile again. The morning's interview at Hull Prison had been fruitless in terms of information, but Tremberg wouldn't call the day a waste of time. It's hard to think of any morning as a write-off when it involves watching a drug dealer chuck a polystyrene cup full of piss over your boss.

'How did he even do it?' Archer had spat, furious, as the guards led the laughing Jackson away, and her waterproof mascara began to prove it wasn't piss-proof by running down her cheeks.

Tremberg had had no answer. She had thought Jackson was just ignoring them. Instead he was busily urinating beneath the desk, waiting for the right moment in proceedings to demonstrate his strength of feeling about their questions. It had worked, too. The interview was terminated without him even confirming his name, let alone who had paid him to be at the wheel of the marijuana-filled Transit van that had been pulled over by traffic officers eight weeks before. Tremberg had been planning to tell the middle-aged convict that it was in his interests to talk to them; to point out that his employers had lost money, and face, because of his decision to drive at 53 mph on the bend of the A63. She wonders if Jackson will learn the hard way.

Tremberg turns her head away from the cake shop as she passes, avoiding the temptation to stop and drool. Across the busy street, an attractive, pink-haired woman is hanging a special offers poster up in the window of a nice-looking hair salon. Inside, a pretty young blonde looks as though she may eventually stop talking for long enough to cut some hair. Next to it is a smaller shop that looks as though it has not been open long. 'Snips and Rips' says the sign, and the lettering on the large front window declares it to be a specialist in clothing repair, dressmaking and curtain alterations. Tremberg, who has a nasty habit of pulling buttons off shirts and snagging the turn-ups of her trousers on chair legs, makes a mental note to remember that it is there.

'It's Helen, isn'it?'

Tremberg turns, startled. Police officers are rarely pleased to be taken by surprise.

'It is! Jaysus, how are you?'

The girl is stunning, in a mucky kind of way. Petite, tanned and toned, she is wearing a purple bikini top, jogging trousers and Ugg boots, and is pushing a stroller in which a dark-haired baby is chewing on a sunhat. She has a tangle of golden necklaces at her throat, and several earrings in each ear.

Tremberg tries not to frown as she struggles to remember where she knows the girl from. Is she one of the travellers from the Cottingham site? Has she tipped them the wink on some stolen goods, maybe. But *Helen*? Not 'Detective Constable'? Who the bloody hell . . .

'Roisin,' says the girl, helpfully, in an accent tinged with Irish. 'Roisin McAvoy.'

Tremberg finds herself flustered, suddenly embarrassed at not having remembered her sergeant's wife. They have only met once, and then only briefly, but McAvoy had once opened up to her about the circumstances of his meeting Roisin, and Tremberg hopes her face does not betray her as the memories flood in. This is the traveller girl that McAvoy saved. The girl who suffered agonies at the hands of attackers when not yet a teen. Whom McAvoy revenged, and to whom he later gave himself completely.

'Roisin, of course, I'm sorry, it must be the heat. How are things? Warm isn't it? And goodness, who's this little thing? Lovely, lovely.'

If Roisin finds Tremberg's gabbling amusing, she hides it well. She smiles at the constable and then crouches down by the stroller. 'This is Lilah,' she says, proudly. 'Our youngest. Seven months now. Hasn't she got her daddy's eyes?'

Tremberg is never comfortable around children, but as she bends down she does at least appreciate the sloppy, gummy grin

41

the child turns her way. Lilah's eyes, as promised, are brown and innocent, looking out at the world in confused fascination.

'She's a stunner,' says Tremberg, and then winces as she hears Archer honk the car horn.

'That for you?' asks Roisin. 'Tell them to hold their horses.'

'It's my boss. Well, one of them. Bit of an incident at the prison this morning.' Tremberg holds up the packet of wipes by way of explanation. 'She needs these, fast.'

'Have an accident, did she? Scary places, prisons. There's some Sudocrem in my bag if she thinks she might get a rash . . .'

Roisin says it with a smile, but her accent is pure traveller, and Tremberg finds herself wondering how difficult it must be for this young girl to be married to a policeman when she grew up thinking of them as the enemy. There must be times when the worlds collide, she thinks, and remembers the night Ray and Archer put the cuffs on the drugs outfit's enforcers up at the traveller site. There had been rumours that McAvoy was there too: bloodied and dirty, his great fists grazed to the bone.

There is another angry blast on the horn.

'Patient woman,' smiles Roisin.

'Oh she's a love,' says Tremberg. 'What brings you up this way, anyhow? Kingswood you live, isn't it? Or did your husband tell me you were moving?'

Roisin nods, like a teenager about to tell a friend what she is getting for Christmas. 'We're living out of boxes at the moment but we should exchange contracts next week. Aector's taking care of all that. Lovely house though, down by the foreshore, under the bridge. Old cottages, done up a treat, so they are. I've got a load of ideas. I've spoken to Aector about having a few people over when we get moved in, so it would be lovely to see you. Bring a friend or two. Maybe not whoever's honking that horn, though . . .'

Tremberg smiles. She can see how McAvoy fell for this girl. She's not just beautiful; she has some inner light, some warmth. She is a soothing presence. *This is what McAvoy comes home to*, she thinks. This is what keeps him upright. Keeps him good. Keeps him alive . . .

'Oh, before you rush off, can I give you one of these?' Roisin reaches behind the stroller and hands Tremberg a flier for the alterations service across the street. 'My friend's place. Mel. Met her at salsa not so long ago. Such a nice person. This is her dream, running her own place. She's dead good, too. I'm just here for a bit of moral support because she feels a bit daft sitting there when there's no customers. No air conditioning in there either, so she'll probably have me wafting the door! Anyway, I'll let you go but it's lovely to see you again.'

To Tremberg's surprise, Roisin reaches up and gives her a clumsy kiss on the cheek. Tremberg gets a whiff of sugary pop, of expensive perfume and hand-rolled cigarettes, then gives a vague wave as she heads back to the car. She stops after a few paces, when she remembers that she owes Roisin a thank you. A few months back, Tremberg had been badly cut during the hunt for a killer, and through McAvoy, Roisin had sent her a pot of some herbal remedy that had helped take the sting out of the wound. At the time, Tremberg had tried to make a joke of it, and asked her sergeant if his perfect wife was a white witch as well as everything else. McAvoy had looked hurt, and Tremberg had ended up scolding herself for being mean and feeling like she had just punched a rabbit in the face.

'Next time,' she says, under her breath, opens the car door.

'Could you have taken any fucking longer?' demands Archer, as she snatches the packet and begins pulling out fistfuls of wet-wipes. She scrubs at her tanned brown arms, her made-up face, down into the cleavage of her pink tennis shirt. 'No lemon?'

'They were out of lemon,' says Tremberg, wincing as her sweat-soaked shirt presses against the skin of her back as she sits down. She looks into the rear-view mirror and watches Roisin waiting for a gap in the traffic, singing gently to baby Lilah.

Archer scoffs, and then reaches into her designer handbag and starts pulling out lipsticks and assorted blushers.

'Who was that, anyway?'

'Ma'am?'

'The tart? Tits out. Fat arse. Asking the world to fucking look at her.'

Tremberg opens her mouth to explain, then changes her mind. 'Just somebody I know from a case.'

Archer loses interest as she begins applying eyeliner. 'On the game, is she?'

Tremberg looks at her boss and lets a little temper bubble to the surface. 'I think you've missed a bit.'

11.44 a.m.

A taxi office off Hull's Hedon Road, halfway between the prison and the docks.

In the back office, Adam Downey is sipping whisky. It's an expensive bottle. Japanese. It came in a metal casket with a samurai on the front. It's supposed to be one of the finest spirits in the world and he's drinking it from a crystal tumbler that weighs as much as his head. To Downey, the tipple tastes like

44

petrol and heartburn, but he reckons he looks good while sipping at it, so tolerates the bad taste.

Downey is in his early twenties. He's a handsome lad who takes his appearance seriously. He's in good shape, with muscles built for showing off rather than for lifting anything heavy. He looks like he should be auditioning for a TV talent show. He has a pop-star appearance. He's a vision in designer white trainers, slashed-neck T-shirt and £100 haircut. The diamond in his earlobe cost him a mint and the little stars he has tattooed behind his ear show he can take a bit of pain if the reward is worth it.

He's flicking through a porn mag. He likes black women best of all. Usually he looks for something stimulating on his top-of-the-range mobile phone but the reception here is terrible so he has resorted to old-school thrills.

Out front, half a dozen drivers sit snacking and sweating, waiting for the phone to ring. Three of them are Turks. Dominating the scene is Bruno, a mountain of muscle and dreadlocks. They're his team. His boys. They do what he fucking says.

For the past few months, Adam Downey has been somebody to fear. He has been a drug dealer since his teens. He was always going to be trouble. He grew up in a nice house with a stable family unit, but he was never any good at living the quiet life. Downey wanted to be respected. Admired. Feared. He had put himself in harm's way from an early age and by his mid-teens he was running drugs for the punk rocker who used to run the trade in the east of the city. Orton, his name was. He didn't look like much of a drug dealer. He had little in the way of style. He was all tattoos and combat pants, lace-up boots and piercings. But for the best part of fifteen years he was responsible for most of the gear that came through the docks. Downey was never his muscle or the brains, but he was reliable and ambitious and soon became one of Orton's confidants.

It was when Downey got sent to prison that things changed. He showed up on somebody's radar. He got headhunted. A phone was pressed to his ear as he lay in his bunk and a man with a refined accent and perfect diction told him he had been talent-spotted. A new outfit was safeguarding the interests of a number of established crime organisations on the east coast. Orton was refusing to see the benefits of following suit. They were seeking somebody young, ambitious and capable who could step into the gap that would be left by his imminent departure. Would he be interested in the position? It hadn't taken Downey long to make up his mind. For as long as he could remember he'd secretly thought of himself as the prince of the city. He daydreamed about people doing his bidding. He fantasised about dispensing mercy and justice in equal measure. He wanted to point, nod, and know that whoever had wronged him was going to learn just how very special he was.

Downey had said yes.

Soon after, his sentence was inexplicably cut. He found himself back on his own streets. A grateful, oblivious Orton came to pick him up from the prison gates. He had Big Bruno by his side. Orton handed over an envelope full of cash, which Downey pocketed. Then Bruno drove them to the woods. They were barely free of the city when Orton began to realise things were not going as he had planned. He began asking Bruno where he was going. Asking him who had been in his ear. Offering him cash and blubbing about his family.

Ten miles from Hull, Bruno pulled Orton from the car. He

smashed the old punk's head open with a hammer. Then Downey joined in too.

Downey likes being a drug dealer. He likes the fact that the police don't seem to know anything about him but know that somebody like him must exist. He likes that the men he has recruited to his cause are so international. It makes him feel sophisticated and cosmopolitan. He likes the occasional phone calls he gets from his employers, praising him for his initiative and tenacity. He likes feeling like a somebody.

The taxi firm is the perfect front for his operation. His drivers rarely pick up real fares. They just attend the addresses they are given and hand over the packages that Downey has carefully weighed out for them. Their customers are all approved and trusted. It's a slick operation with a huge turnover. Downey doesn't have to worry about how to get the gear into the country. His job is to get it from Point B to Point C, where it will be cut, packaged, and passed on to other people in the chain. Downey's drivers know what they are involved in. They get paid handsomely for it. It's a system that works, and that makes Adam Downey feel blissfully fucking untouchable.

He sips his whisky again. Grimaces.

It's hot here, in this small, bare office, and Downey wants to go and sit out the front with the lads. They're a good crowd and seem to respect him. But he believes that being aloof adds to his image, and Downey loves image. He watches himself in the mirror, and plays with the grenade.

Downey had nicked the grenade when he was picking up a wholesale delivery. Among the crates of white powder were half a dozen handguns and a leather holdall full of grenades and plastic explosives. Impulsively, Downey had wanted one.

He knew the guns would be missed were he to help himself, but the grenades seemed deliciously inviting. They didn't look the way he had seen them in war films. The one he holds in his palm is black and square: no bigger than his mobile phone. It has a pin through the top and Russian lettering down its side. He likes to hold it. Likes to play with the pin. Dares himself to throw the grenade in the air and catch it again before it can detonate.

Downey hears the front door of the taxi office bang. There is a muttering from beyond the door to his office, then it is pushed open by a tall dark man in a football shirt and camouflage trousers.

'We knock in this country, Hakan,' says Downey, over the lip of his glass. 'Remember? We flush toilets too? None of that folding up the bog-roll and putting it in the bin. We're not keen on shit samosas.'

Hakan doesn't seem to understand. His English is good but he seems too flustered to pay attention.

'What's the matter?' asks Downey.

Hakan closes the door behind him then leans against it. He's quite a good-looking guy, though he is hairy enough to blunt a lawnmower.

'I fuck up.'

Downey spreads his hands. He's not worried. There's nothing he can't handle.

'Police,' says Hakan. 'I think they follow me. I not know what do. I park. Put parcel in coat. Take coat seamstress. Seamstress has coat.'

Downey sits forward in his chair. He spits his whisky back in the glass.

'Again, Hakan. In fucking English.'

Downey sinks lower in his seat as the driver tells him what happened. He'd been delivering a wallet-sized package of white powder to the address that had been phoned through just an hour ago. He'd been driving normally, doing as he was told. Then he saw the flashing lights in his mirror. Panicked. Started seeing a conspiracy. Every parked car was suddenly a plain-clothes officer. Every van was a surveillance unit.

'I have coat with me. I see shop, yes? Southcoates Lane. I have idea. Put package in coat. Take coat in shop. Ask for them to fix zip. She nice lady. We talk. I go back when all quiet, yes. I do right, yes?'

Downey chews on his lip.

'You gave the parcel away, Hakan. You gave it to a stranger. What if she looks in the fucking pocket?'

Hakan waves his hands.

'She say she busy. I say "No rush." I go back for it in a week, perhaps. Tell her I not need work done at all . . .'

Downey throws his glass at the wall. It shatters in a rain of jagged crystal.

'Ticket,' he says, furious.

'Ticket?'

'The fucking ticket, you Turkish prick,' says Downey. 'The ticket for the alterations shop. I'll go for it. Christ, if she finds it. If we lose that parcel . . .'

Downey doesn't finish the sentence. Everything he has could be yanked away from him with one swift tug. Being prince of the city depends on staying in the good graces of the powers behind the throne.

He drains his whisky. It burns, and tastes like shite.

He snatches the ticket from Hakan's hand. Looks at the words.

'Snips and Rips – alterations a speciality'.

Downey grunts.

'Story of my fucking life.'

4

'If you weren't such a pansy you would be a hell of a Romeo.'

'Guv?'

'Women. They bloody love you, don't they? One look at those big sad eyes and they're pussy in your hand.'

'Putty, you mean.'

'I know what I mean. It's just funny. They don't know what they want to do with you, do they? Don't know whether they want you to throw them around like a ragdoll or put them in the bath and wash their hair.'

McAvoy keeps his eyes on the road. He swallows, and is aware of his Adam's apple rubbing against his shirt collar.

'Do you do that? Do you wash Roisin's hair?'

He can feel his boss staring at the side of his face. Senses that she is shaking her head slightly, and smiling with only one half of her mouth.

'Paint her nails? Read her bedtime stories? Cut her fish fingers up for her . . .'

McAvoy turns in the driver's seat and looks into Pharaoh's blue eyes. She's gone too far, and she raises her hands, acknowledging it. She does this, sometimes. Teases until she feels bad. He has come to understand her pretty well these past months. He knows all about so-called 'gallows humour' – cops cracking off-colour gags so the misery of their jobs has to work harder to reach their souls. With Trish it's different. Her job does affect her. The sights she sees make her cry. She never makes jokes about the dead. She just performs with the living the way she has learned to in two decades of policing. She's Trish Fucking Pharaoh: brash and seductive, loud and maternal, hard as fucking nails. She gets the job done, and then she goes home to her four kids and crippled husband and drinks until the screaming in her head goes away.

'Sorry. It's the heat.'

He nods. Turns back to the road. Tries to be jolly British about the whole thing and move the conversation on to the weather. 'It's just so sticky, isn't it? Back home, there would be clouds of midges in this heat. You rub your hand over your face and it comes away black with the little sods.'

'I've heard. Coming back with bites is not my idea of a holiday. Not unless they're on your thigh, anyway.'

McAvoy gives the tiniest of laughs, and that seems to satisfy her. She goes back to reading her phone.

Home, he thinks. Why did I call the Highlands 'home'? Roisin is *home*. The kids are *home*. What did I mean by that? What would Sabine make of it . . .

McAvoy gets annoyed with himself and curtails the train of introspection. Concentrates on driving, his hands where they should be at a precise ten-to-two on the steering wheel. Looks out through dead flies and dust. It's a boring road, all bland fields, four-house hamlets and dead farms. It seems popular with boy racers intent on risking their lives on hairpin bends, and McAvoy has winced several times in anticipation of a horrific smash as

52

souped-up Vauxhall Corsas and Subarus tore past him at 90 mph.

The journey is giving him the beginnings of a migraine. He's been squinting for half an hour. The windscreen wash is empty. He is staring through grease and dirt, smeared into a khaki, blood-speckled rainbow by the wipers that squeak across the glass.

'I'm getting a stuffy nose,' says Pharaoh, giving a sniff.

'It's the rape fields,' says McAvoy, waving a hand in the direction of the luminous yellow crops either side of the winding B-road.

'*Rape Fields*? Think I rented that from Lovefilm . . .'

'Rapeseed, Guv. A lot of people are allergic to it. Really, you should plant a blue crop called borage nearby to counteract it, but the European Union didn't insist, so nobody does. A lot of people think they have hay fever when they don't. Gives you runny eyes, a stuffy nose . . .'

'You seem fine.'

'I'm not allergic to it. Penicillin and coconut, that's me.'

'Yeah?' Pharaoh takes a handkerchief from her bag and tries to blow her nose. 'Fuck, one nostril's blocked.'

'Sea air will help.'

'So will a vodka.'

A minute later they are drifting through the centre of Hornsea, a seaside town half an hour from the outskirts of Hull. It's not really a resort. Holidaymakers head for Bridlington and Scarborough, and though the place does have a few guest houses and some amusement arcades jangle and bleep on the seafront, they're more for listless local teens than to satisfy any deluge of tourists. It's a presentable, quiet place that's doing okay for itself and doesn't make much noise. It's a jumble of coffee shops, curiosity shops and estate agents, with ornate awnings and

Victorian roofs, huddling together between the new all-night mini-supermarkets and chain pubs.

McAvoy parks outside a strip of attractive townhouses, opposite a large white Art Deco building with huge bay windows. He can tell they'll offer awesome views of the bay. Having spent the past few weeks mired in real-estate dealings, he instinctively wonders how much the view adds to the asking price.

'He'd better be bloody in,' says Pharaoh, getting out of the car.

McAvoy purses his lips, blows out a stream of silent concerns, closes his eyes, and becomes a detective again as they walk up to the red-painted front door. Darren Robb lives in Flat 3, and works from home as a website designer. Elaine has given them a brief sketch of his background; told them he's a bit of a useless lump who likes computer games and crisps. A quick search of the police database has come up with nothing exciting in his file. He once got a caution for urinating in a side street off Holderness Road, but having been to Holderness Road, McAvoy finds it hard to think of that as much of a crime.

It is Pharaoh, as the senior officer, who is allowed the honour of leaning on the doorbell. She does so for a full ten seconds. McAvoy turns back to the street. There are houses both to his left and right, but directly in front of this building is a swathe of stubby grass. The view to the sea is unimpeded. Some kids are kicking a football around. A mum with a pushchair is lying on the grass reading a magazine. The kids who were leaning by the sea wall are now squatting in a rough semicircle, eating chips from polystyrene cones. Normal people, normal day . . .

'Hello.'

The voice is made tinny by the intercom.

'Mr Robb?'

'Aye.'

'This is the police. Can we come up?'

There is a pause.

'I didn't do it.'

Pharaoh gives a little laugh. Rolls her eyes.

'Okay then, we'll be off.'

After a moment, the door clicks open, and both officers step into the wide hallway. The corridor is bare brick and linoleum, leading down to a ground-floor flat with a black front door. To their left is a set of stairs with a black handrail.

'Up,' says McAvoy, needlessly, and begins to climb.

Darren Robb is standing in the doorway of Flat 3. He's shaking with so much nervous energy that he puts McAvoy in mind of a stationary car with its motor running. The information they have on him suggests that Robb is forty-one years old, but there was nothing in the files about him having put on a stone each birthday. The man is enormous. Grotesquely fat. He's wearing grey jogging bottoms and a black T-shirt which is stretched almost to breaking point over fleshy arms, tits and belly. His skin has the mottled, waxy hue that makes McAvoy think of bodies pulled from water. His round head is bald on top and close-cropped at the back and sides, while his face, locked as it is in a mask of worry and annoyance, is all fleshy lips and blackheads. McAvoy briefly pictures Elaine, and wonders how the hell she fell for this monstrosity. Pharaoh is clearly thinking the same thing. As she reaches the top of the stairs, he hears her laugh.

'I wouldn't have picked you out for living on the second floor, Mr Robb. Can you imagine if you were a ground-floor guy? You might lose your figure.'

If Darren Robb is offended, he gives no sign of it. He just stands in the doorway, all but blocking out the light, jiggling up and down like he's driving over cobbles. He turns his gaze on McAvoy, realises he has no chance of getting past the big man, and seems to sag. He steps back into the flat, vaguely waving them in.

The door opens into a tasteful apartment. The floor is natural wood and the sofa is cream leather. A black-and-white cowhide serves as an island between the pine coffee table and the large flat-screen TV, and the walls are decorated with colourful landscapes, all purple mountains and shimmering lakes. The big bay window gives the kind of view that would cost a million in Brighton, and McAvoy crosses to it, looking out over the grassed area and down past the sea wall to the grey ocean. It moves as if being sifted for gold in a prospector's pan. As he hears the sound of Pharaoh plonking herself into the sofa, he gently moves aside one of the velvet curtains that hang to the floor, and spots the binoculars that sit on the windowsill. McAvoy looks again at the sea, wondering whether Robb enjoys watching the waves and the gulls, following the spirals of the kittiwakes and the razorbills. Then his gaze falls upon the woman with the pushchair on the grass. McAvoy decides not to make up his mind about the man until later.

'I didn't do it.'

Robb is standing by the far wall, between the door to the kitchen and a closed serving hatch set into the brickwork.

'Didn't do what, Mr Robb?' asks Pharaoh, sweetly.

'Philippa. I didn't do it. I couldn't.'

Pharaoh looks up at McAvoy. Pulls a theatrically confused face. 'Has the body been formally identified, Sergeant?'

56

McAvoy shakes his head.

'Identity released to the media?'

'No, Guv.'

'So, Mr Robb, what the fuck are you talking about?'

Robb raises his hands to his head. If his hair were long enough, he would be pulling at its roots. His breath is shallow and ragged. Suddenly, he starts forward and drops onto the arm of the chair, his T-shirt rolling up to reveal a stomach that appears to have been boiled in onion skins and leaves.

'Elaine's Facebook. Somebody posted how sorry they were. It's had five "likes" . . .'

Pharaoh runs a hand through her hair and scowls.

'And you put two and two together? Big leap.'

He shakes his head, frantic now. 'Radio said there'd been a murder, near where Philippa worked. I used to do that walk with her, now and again, when we were together like. Me and Elaine. I started that whole weight-loss thing with her. Couldn't keep it up–'

'Get to the point, Mr Robb.'

'Elaine's brother, Don. He has a Twitter account. Said this morning his mum was missing. Was asking for help on there. He only has a few followers so I don't know what he was expecting –'

'Oh for fuck's sake.'

'And I tried to phone Elaine and some copper answered. Family Liaison, or something . . .'

Pharaoh kicks out, a biker boot catching the corner of the coffee table. There is a bowl of glass beads at its centre, and they give a little tambourine sound before settling back.

'Don doesn't know I follow him. On Twitter, I mean. I use a different name. Same with Elaine's Facebook. And her friends.

Shit, I know all this sounds shite for me, but, look, I haven't done anything wrong . . .'

Pharaoh waves a hand to silence him. She looks at McAvoy then rubs her hand across the back of her neck. It comes away damp.

'Mr Robb, if you sit quietly for a moment, we can get this over with quickly. Now, as I should have said at the door, we are investigating the murder of Philippa Longman. Her body was found this morning, not far from where she works. Somebody had caved her chest in and left her for the birds. It was one of the most unpleasant things I've ever seen, and though I never met Mrs Longman when she was alive, my sergeant and I have just been sitting with a family that is so broken, they'll never be whole again. And your ex-partner, Elaine, has given us reason to believe you had made threats against Mrs Longman. She told my sergeant here that you threatened to rip out her heart. Now, we couldn't tell whether anybody had ripped out her heart because it was too much of a fucking mess. We'll have the post-mortem results back this evening. But I think that means you have some questions to answer, okay? I don't want to hear about Facebook, or who's following who, or who's been Tweeting or Twatting or whatever it is people do for fun when they should be drinking and watching *X-Factor*. Just tell me where you were last night, where you were in the middle of the night, and why I shouldn't get this big bugger here to slap the cuffs on you while I kick you in the knackers. Got it? On board? Fire away.'

Robb looks from one detective to the other. McAvoy has crossed his arms. Framed by the window, the light defines his muscles and casts a shadow across his eyes, leaving only the set of his jaw illuminated. Robb has no friends in this room. He looks down at his feet, stuffed into dirty white trainers, then addresses himself to Pharaoh.

'We were together, yeah? Elaine and me. Three years, all in all, off and on.'

'How exactly did you meet?' asks McAvoy, unable to hide his surprise that the two were ever a couple.

'Her brother. We were mates. Still would be if things turned out differently. He introduced us.'

'So you were a friend of the family?'

He shakes his head. 'No, just Don. He's a delivery driver. Dropped some stuff off at the office where I used to work. He's a rugby man. Bradford Bulls. We hit it off.'

'And?'

'His sister came to a match with us. Her and a friend. We hit it off too.'

Pharaoh looks Robb up and down. He sees her looking and can't help but let his annoyance show on his face. 'I've put weight on since we split.'

'Comfort eating?'

'Yeah, if you like. I was slimmer. Better-looking. Less bald.'

'Sorry I missed out on you. You sound a catch.'

Robb looks down at the wooden floor. Sees himself, blurred and colossal, in the polished surface of the wood. 'You see any mirrors in this room? There are none in the flat. I know what I am. You don't have to remind me.'

Pharaoh looks at the side of his head until he looks up and meets her gaze. She nods, and while it is short of an apology, it is at least an acknowledgement.

'You fell for her hard?' asks McAvoy.

'She was everything I wanted. I've had a few girlfriends over the years but I never thought it would feel the way it did with Elaine. She just made the world better, you know?'

'You lived together?'

'Yeah. Lovely place. Bought it cheap and did it up. I like all that stuff. Made it nice for her and the kids.'

'And you met her family.'

Robb doesn't seem to be able to cough up the ball of gristle in his throat. He swallows painfully. 'Philippa, you mean?'

'I mean her family.'

'Yeah. Nice family. Close. Proper family, you know? Don was well happy with the way things worked out.'

'And your relationship with Philippa?'

Robb looks away, past McAvoy, to the slate sea and stone sky. 'We were close. All those jokes about mothers-in-law? It wasn't like that. We were mates. She was a laugh. I helped her with her work on the council. Computer stuff. Research. I typed up her speeches. Set up a spreadsheet for her expenses. She used to make ginger biscuits for me as a thanks. Proper ones, with stem ginger.' He gives a tiny smile at the memory. 'It was all nice.'

'So what happened with you and Elaine?'

Robb blows air through his nostrils. Scratches at his throat. He seems to be about to stand up, to offer to make tea, to straighten a picture or move the rug, but he appears to see the actions for the distractions they are, and stays where he is. When he speaks, his voice is soft as tears falling on wood.

'Philippa was at our place. I was showing her how to use a website. Might even have been that walking challenge website. I can't remember. Anyway, I left her in my office for a bit. Went for a pee or a cup of tea or whatever. Next thing she's pulling on her coat and slamming the door behind her. I didn't know what was going on until I went back into my office.' He looks at the wall, shame creeping up into his cheeks. 'She'd clicked the wrong thing. Gone into my private files. Seen some of the things in there.'

Pharaoh gives a whistle. 'Worst nightmare, eh?'

'It was nowt weird,' he says, despairingly.

'Just good wholesome stuff, was it?' asks Pharaoh.

Robb doesn't reply.

'Mr Robb, I don't want to be crass, but everybody in the world has the occasional glimpse at stuff like that. She'd be embarrassed, sure, but she'd hardly cut you off for that, would she? These days? Really?'

Robb looks at her, quizzically, then his mouth opens wide as realisation dawns.

'It was drawings!' he splutters. 'Drawings I'd done. I like to draw.'

Pharaoh is getting frustrated. 'What?'

'I'd done some drawings. Portraits, if you like. Sketches. Some still-life. Some from memory. Other times, they'd sit for me . . .'

'Who?'

'The kids. Elaine's kids.'

Pharaoh's mouth drops open and she turns to McAvoy. 'Are you hearing this? Can you get a straight answer out of this bloke for me please, Hector, because I'm starting to get angry.'

McAvoy takes three steps to the middle of the room and looms over Darren Robb. Were he here alone, he would never consider using his size, would never threaten or intimidate, but in Pharaoh's presence, he knows his role. He is both her enforcer and gentle poet. His job is to keep the suspect off-balance. To become his friend, and then step into his personal space with the softest of snarls. 'Were they naked pictures, sir? The drawings you did of your girlfriend's children?'

Robb stares up at the big man. 'It's art. Like Rubens. Cherubs and stuff. I like all that. I scanned them into the computer so I could use some art software. I wasn't sending them to anyone. I wasn't doing anything wrong! It's just pictures.'

'Nothing that could be considered inappropriate?'

'Not unless there's something wrong with you.'

'But Philippa didn't like what she saw?'

'She wouldn't answer her phone. Wouldn't come to the door when I called for her. She just cut me off.'

'And Elaine?'

'She didn't understand. Her mum sent her this message, telling her that her boyfriend was sick. Twisted. Disgusting.'

'Did you explain?'

'I deleted the pictures as soon as Philippa left.'

'Why?'

'I panicked.'

McAvoy runs his tongue around the inside of his mouth. 'So when Philippa told her daughter that you had naked pictures of her children on your computer, you had no evidence to the contrary.'

Robb looks back at his feet.

'Elaine left you?'

He nods. 'She wouldn't listen.'

'Did you try and make her?'

Robb bites at his lip. 'Over and over. I tried to get Don to talk to her but he wouldn't take my calls either. I went to Elaine's work, to the kids' schools, I just wanted her to listen.'

McAvoy pushes a fist into his palm. 'You must have been frustrated. Angry.'

'Everything was ruined, over a mistake. A misunderstanding. I'd never hurt those kids. I loved those kids.'

'But Elaine didn't know you were drawing them naked, did she? If it was innocent, why not tell her?'

Robb is silent. He tries to find somewhere to direct his gaze, but finds nothing to his satisfaction. He gets up, and adjusts one of the pictures on the wall. 'It was just art,' he mutters to himself.

'And if we took away your computer, Mr Robb, would we find more art?'

A look of horror passes over Darren Robb's face, and McAvoy takes a step towards him, using his size to put the fat man almost into shadow.

'You've been stalking your ex, Mr Robb. You've been following her on Facebook with a fake alias. You've been making a nuisance of yourself. You've made threats about a woman who is now dead.'

Robb's lower lip trembles. He seems to be about to cry.

'Where were you last night?' asks Pharaoh from the sofa.

'I was here,' he says.

'Doing what?'

'I was on the computer. I'm often on the computer.'

'Doing what?'

Slowly, like a bouncy castle deflating, Darren Robb sinks to his knees. 'Same as fucking always,' he says, between sobs. 'Reading her emails. Reading her messages.'

'You hack her emails?'

'Elaine's. Don's. Philippa's. I just want to stay close to them. They were my family too. It was just a misunderstanding.'

'You can show us your search history, then. You can show us that you were here all night, I presume.'

'I stopped about 2 a.m. Then I went to bed.'

'Alone?'

'Of course alone.'

Pharaoh turns to her sergeant. 'We don't know what time she was killed yet. Not for certain.'

'If he's good enough with computers he could do his Internet browsing remotely and make it look like he was on his home terminal. But if he did that on his mobile, we can pinpoint the location from the signal. Will be easier once the forensics people have had their fun.'

'Aye, if he was there we'll probably have found a crisp packet in the vicinity.'

Robb looks at each of them in turn, as if they are passing his fate between them like a tennis ball.

'I can't drive,' he blurts out, as if the admission is the most important thought he has ever had. 'I haven't got a car. I don't have a licence. I work from home. How the hell would I even get there?'

Pharaoh lets the annoyance show in her face. 'You can't drive? How did you bother Elaine then? See her at work? At the kids' school?'

'I took cabs. Buses. I've only moved back to Hornsea the past few weeks. I kept this place on when Elaine and me moved in together. I don't go anywhere. I couldn't.'

Pharaoh looks at the fat man on the floor. 'Pathetic,' she says, and her sneer is an ugly, powerful thing.

McAvoy has been running his tongue around his mouth for the past few moments, his thoughts sliding into one another like coins inside a slot machine. 'The emails,' he says, at length. 'You've been reading them for a while?'

Robb nods, seemingly unsure whether to stay on his knees or get up.

'Did Philippa ever receive any threats of any kind? And I advise you to think carefully about this, because at the moment, we're staring very hard at you for the murder of Philippa Longman.'

Robb screws up his eyes, like a child pretending to concentrate. 'Philippa's emails were just council stuff. Vouchers. Special offers. Sometimes she'd get pictures from friends. I used to search under my name in her correspondence and there wasn't a thing. They'd just moved on. Cut me out like I was something disgusting.'

'And Elaine?'

'She mentioned me sometimes. After I'd been to see her, or sent her a letter or texted her or whatever, she'd message a friend about me. She never sounded cross with me, just sorry for me.'

'But you were cross with her. With Philippa too.'

'I said things I shouldn't have. I was just trying to shock her into listening.'

'You said you would cut out her mum's heart.'

Robb shifts his position, moving the fat around. 'I've never hurt anybody in my life.'

Pharaoh clicks her tongue against the roof of her mouth. She seems to be weighing things up.

'Hector?'

McAvoy looks at the morbidly obese specimen before him. He sees something pitiful, but he does not yet see a killer.

'Don't go anywhere,' he says, to Robb.

Pharaoh scoffs. 'He can't drive, remember?'

'Let's check that, eh?'

'And we'd better tell the boys in the tech unit to remotely access his hard drive. Make sure nothing gets deleted in the next few days.'

McAvoy manages to keep the look of confusion off his face. Pharaoh knows nothing about computers, but has a quality poker face and knows how to scare a suspect.

They turn away from the snivelling man on the floor and head for the door. Halfway across the living room, McAvoy turns back.

'Are you sorry she's dead?'

Robb raises his head. There is nothing but sorrow in his face, though most of that seems to be for himself.

'Did she suffer?' he asks, at length.

McAvoy nods. 'More than anybody should.'

Robb drops his head. The only sound in the room is the soft snuffling of a fat man crying into his T-shirt, and the distant peal of children laughing beneath the crashing of the waves.

5

3.28 p.m. Courtland Road Police Station. Hull.

A three-storey building, all bare brick and dirty windows, painted the colour of storm clouds, shielded from the estate it watches over by bent silver railings and untended grass.

First floor. Home of the Serious and Organised Crime Unit.

Flickering monitors, overstuffed folders and cardboard boxes cluttering the pathways between desks. Home Office posters on the walls and every window pushed open as far as it will go. Phones, answered with coughs and grunts; fingers bashing inexpertly on keyboards that are missing letters and patterned with crumbs. Bluebottles buzzing helplessly on dirty windowsills varnished in coffee stains and smudges of printer ink.

Helen Tremberg, wrist-deep in a packet of crisps, salt sticking to her damp fingers and chipped nails, sweat on her upper lip, fringe twisting itself in knots every time the fan turns in her direction and the edges of her paperwork lift their skirts.

She types, one-handed, on a keyboard that sits in front of a monitor garlanded with Post-it notes. They contain reminders. Phone numbers. Her passwords.

She's hunched. Furtive. Trying to stay below the plastic barrier that divides her desk from DC Ben Nielsen's. There is a tiny smile on her face.

Helen has been officially single for three years. She had two serious relationships before that, with men she was pretty sure she loved. Each ended within a year of them moving in together. In both cases, it was the men who made the decision to go, and Helen who had done nothing to change their minds. She enjoyed cohabiting, liked the intimacy of it all: the foot-rubs during the movie; the unexpected cups of tea; the feeling of slipping on a man's big cosy jumper to pad downstairs in the middle of the night and having somebody warm to spoon up beside when she worked a late shift. It was the other side of it that caused the rifts. Bills. Sensible stuff. Which electricity supplier to use. Getting the broadband to work properly. Whether to do a big shop once a month for freezable stuff, or pop out every night for perishables. Them, forgetting to keep the shower curtain inside the bathtub and soaking the floor. Her with her stubbornness. Her refusal to compromise. Even to be guided. Steered. Told. Sitting there with her fingers digging into the leather of the sofa as some great interloper held the remote control for her TV and decided what they should watch. Both of her failed relationships were so similar in their pattern and make-up that sometimes she forgets which was which, and has to consider the length of her hair in each snapshot of memory to know which lover she went where with, and when.

While she has enjoyed the company of a few blokes over the last few months, she has lacked any real enthusiasm for taking things further. She likes her own space, her own company. Has a few mates, both inside and outside the police service, and has years left before her biological clock starts trying to get her attention. She even has the odd Friday night out on Cleethorpes seafront. Has some fancy sequinned dresses and painful strappy shoes. Knows how to do her make-up and ruffle her short hair in a way that takes the attention away from her broad shoulders and weightlifter thighs. She's okay with herself.

So why are you so giddy, you silly girl?

Helen tries to focus on the half of the computer screen she gets paid to give a damn about. She's cross-referencing between two databases, trying to spot any familiar names among the owners of white, 2003-registered Land Rovers. Such a vehicle was captured on blurry CCTV, heading away at speed from a petrol bombing on the Preston Road estate. The target was an empty bottle shop, and the motive most likely insurance or boredom. It comes under Helen's purview because she is attached to Colin Ray's investigation into the spike in organised crime, and because there had once been a Drugs Squad raid on the shop amid accusations it was being used as a halfway house for cocaine coming off the nearby docks. That raid had proven fruitless, but with the top brass happy to throw resources at making the drugs problem go away before the end-of-year figures are collated, anything with even a sniff of organised criminality about it comes to Colin Ray, and anything he doesn't think is worth his time goes to Shaz Archer, who dutifully passes it on to the people she likes least.

Having already wasted a morning on the entertaining but fruitless trip to Hull Prison, Helen is resigned to a day of futility and irritation, made worse by the buzzing flies and oppressive heat. She had been gutted to hear that Pharaoh was looking into the murder off Anlaby Road. Tremberg is an ambitious woman, hoping to be put forward for the sergeant examination, and had cautiously celebrated when placed on Colin Ray's side of the squad not so long ago. That joy has faded now. She is on a unit that is making no progress, led by a man who is at best tenacious, and at worst, dangerous. Her immediate superior is a tart who doesn't rate her and the last bit of work Helen did that in any way helped make the east coast a safer place was when she put Colin Ray in the back of a taxi before he made good on his promise to cut DC Andy Daniells's head off with a glass bottle at the last CID quiz night.

Her computer suddenly beeps and Helen takes a deep breath. Her left leg bounces up and down.

Stop it, you silly girl . . .

She opens the email. It's him. Mark. The one she can't get out of her bloody head.

Couldn't wait another minute to hear from you. I have no excuse. Are we not past that? Do I need to pretend I have something work-related to discuss? I just wanted to send you a message. Honestly Helen, even seeing your name written down makes me excited. What are you doing to me? Tell me something personal. Can't wait. Xx

Helen smiles and exhales at the same time. She rubs the back of her hand across her face, and prepares to compose a reply. She's no poet. She wishes she'd read the Philip Larkin collection McAvoy had sent her when she was in hospital a few months back. Wishes, even more, that McAvoy himself were here. There are few moments when she is not second-guessing herself in his voice, wondering whether he would approve of her decisions, her police work, her heart. He has somehow become her conscience.

Her thoughts drift to his wife. Helen knows what McAvoy did for her. Remembers that day in the greasy spoon café when her senior officer opened up. Told her about the men who hurt Roisin when she was not yet a teen. McAvoy was just a constable then. A young man in uniform, called to a traveller camp. A man who heard screams and went to investigate. Who carried the crying girl from a burning building and did things to her attackers that scarred his soul. Helen has never asked him what he did to those men. Never asked how he and the child he saved came to be lovers as adults. She has not made up her mind whether she truly wants to know. Whether she wants to unpick the perfection of the image she carries of the McAvoys. She just knows his love for his family is a palpable, magical thing. When he talks of Roisin and his children, the air around him is thick enough to be scooped up with a ladle. She wants some of that. Some of that honesty. That perfect, powerful thing he carries inside him.

You don't need excuses. Message me whenever you want. I won't ever be disappointed to hear from you. xx

It's the best she can do. She makes sure the number of kisses she types is no more or less than the number he placed on his. She runs a quick spell-check, just to make sure she hasn't embarrassed herself, then sends it back, hoping she will not have to wait too long for a reply. She is using her personal email account on the work computer, which is strictly against the rules. She has heard of other forces where viruses have been uploaded simply by opening an unvetted file, but she is so eager to hear from the man that she is willing to take the risk.

Sort yourself out, Helen.

71

He's not her usual sort. She likes sporty, athletic types. She likes men bigger than her, who know their Grand Prix history and don't shave on a weekend. Mark seems the complete opposite. He's a lawyer with a local firm, dealing mainly in divorce cases and the occasional bit of blame-and-claim litigation. They got talking last month in the canteen at Hull Magistrates' Court, where Helen was giving evidence in a youth offending case she had dealt with in her first plain-clothes job. It had taken an age to come to court and Helen had been sitting there struggling to remember which little bastard had punched which other little bastard. Her mood had been foul, as a man in tracksuit bottoms, shirt, tie and baseball cap had discovered when he told his toddler son to shut the fuck up and cuffed him around the head. Helen, pretending to fall as she passed him, had found a way to tread on the man's instep and knee him in the groin at the same time, all the while apologising out loud – even as she nipped the skin beneath his armpit and whispered cold threats in his ear.

If anyone saw what she'd done then they had the sense to keep quiet about it, but she was soon the only person sitting in the waiting area with an empty chair beside her. Despite the chaos of the court, nobody had wanted to sit next to her. Nobody except Mark. He sat down with a smile, whispered 'Nice work' and waited for her to meet his gaze. He smelled nice. Clean, but not soapy. No aftershave, but somehow fresh, like line-dried laundry. He was small and wiry, his physique putting her in mind of a cyclist's. His sideburns were slightly too long for a man in his mid-thirties, but his designer, frameless glasses and blue pinstriped suit went well together, while the Maori-patterned leather strap around his wrist made him seem just intriguing enough to warrant further investigation.

She'd noticed, even then, that he wore no wedding band. Had it been mercenary? Predatory? Had she been eyeing him up as a potential mate? She didn't know. But he did not run a mile when she told him she was a police officer, which was a hell of a good start, and when he gave her his business card, she had waited less than an hour before sending him an email saying how much she had enjoyed their chat, even though not a word of it had stuck in her head. Since then their correspondence has grown more regular and passionate. She looks forward to his words and spends time thinking up her own. She wants to tell him about her day. Her life. She wants to look at him over the lip of a wine glass and smile as she offloads the dirt and sweat of the day. She wants to know whether his chest is hairy or smooth. Wants to look down on him as she moves . . .

Ask him. Make a date, girl . . .

Helen wishes she were brave enough to suggest a drink tonight. Hopes that in his next email he takes the initiative and does so himself. Oh Christ, how she hopes . . .

'Now then, children!'

The door to the office is already open but Trish Pharaoh still manages to make enough noise as she barges into the room to get everybody's attention. Like worried meerkats, heads pop up above monitors and phones are silenced. Ben Nielsen leans over and switches off the fan and a hush falls on the room. Helen sees them as canaries, their cage suddenly shrouded and silent. Pharaoh is rarely here. She has an office of her own, up another flight of stairs, where she does complicated and exasperating things with spreadsheets and budgets. She is one of CID's most senior figures, having got to a position where she can do little actual police work by being very good at police work.

Tremberg waits for McAvoy to come in as well, and is surprised by his absence. Pharaoh catches her looking at the door, and gives an indulgent smile. 'He's busy,' she mouths. 'We'll be okay without him.'

Helen nods. Joins the rest of the officers in watching Pharaoh stride to the far end of the room, where she starts rubbing Colin Ray's scribblings off the whiteboard. She doesn't even stop to read them.

'Right, you lot. I'm talking to the whole room here because I can't remember which of you lot are still mine and which are Colin's. So, if this is nowt to do with you, just be quiet. In a minute, some very efficient people are going to turn this part of the room into a murder suite. I've spoken to the brass and we've agreed that Philippa Longman's death should be looked at by this unit. Regular CID are about as happy about that as you'd expect, but it will be me that gets the earache and none of you, so don't worry about it. More importantly, don't go approaching any of this thinking that it's got anything to do with bloody organised crime. It hasn't. The gang we're all looking for wouldn't give a shit about some local community activist kicking up a stink about drugs. But by the time that information reaches the Assistant Chief Constable, we'll have found who did it and there will be champagne and cigars all round. Savvy?'

There are smiles and snorts of laughter at that. Tremberg finds herself turning around, half-hoping that Colin Ray and Shaz Archer return from whatever errand they're running and walk into the middle of the briefing.

'Colin and I will be having a chat about which officers stay on current cases and which assist me in the murder enquiry. For now, I've got uniforms doing door-to-door in the immediate vicinity.

It's bloody hot at the moment so people will be sleeping with the windows open and may well have heard something. You can't do that much damage to a person without it waking somebody. I've insisted the forensics be fast-tracked and the PME will be done this evening. McAvoy and me have already interviewed a suspect – the former partner of Longman's daughter. Document wallets will be going around when my secretary or whatever they're supposed to be called these days finishes trying to turn my handwriting into English.'

There are a few mutters at McAvoy's name. Some people are holding a grudge longer than others.

'We've got one lead that needs your immediate attention. Sophie, Andy, I'm thinking of you two.'

Helen lets the disappointment show on her face, but Pharaoh does not acknowledge it.

'We've got a footprint. Almost a perfect one. Size eight, big grips, heavy indent at the toe.'

'Work boots?' asks Helen, hoping to make herself noticed.

'Give that lass a gold star,' says Pharaoh. 'Yes, work boots. We've got plaster casts on their way over, so you need to be hitting the warehouses, the builders' merchants, trying to find a match, and see how widespread those kind of shoes are.'

'It could be anybody's boots, Guv,' comes a dissenting voice. Helen traces it to Stan Lyons. He was a detective sergeant before his retirement, and now works part-time for the unit as one of its complement of civilian officers. He's a nice old boy in his early sixties who takes tablets for his blood pressure and as such is always cold. Even today, in this heat, he's wearing vest, shirt and golfing jumper.

'It could indeed, Stan,' says Pharaoh, 'but given that he's trodden some of Philippa Longman's blood into the grass, I reckon it's worth thinking about, yes?'

'We got anything else?' asks Ben Nielsen, optimistically.

'Early days, my boy, and given you haven't read the paperwork yet, you'll forgive me if I don't hold your hand and baby-step you through every last detail.'

Ben smiles. 'Sorry, boss.'

She nods, looks at the expectant faces, then raises her hands to tell her team to get on with it. This is how she works. She doesn't micro-manage. Sometimes they go days without hearing from her. She hand-picked most of the officers on the unit, and trusts them to do their jobs. The only people she didn't want, and still doesn't, are Colin Ray and Sharon Archer, but she respects them enough to know they won't make waves when it comes to a murder investigation.

Pharaoh heads for the door, stopping only briefly at Helen Tremberg's desk.

'Sorry, Helen. I wanted you. It seems Colin can't spare you. The ACC mentioned you by name.'

Helen looks confused. 'Guv?'

'Seems you're doing a good job. Keep it up.'

With a warm, motherly squeeze of her shoulder, Pharaoh bustles away. For a brief moment, there is silence in the room. Then the fan is switched back on, and officers start to pick up phones. A middle-aged woman in pleated skirt and round-neck T-shirt enters carrying a pile of folders, which she begins to distribute to the team members like a teacher handing back homework.

Helen scowls for a while, then decides to accentuate the positive. Whatever it is she's doing, she's doing it well. She's essential to the ongoing investigation into a criminal gang responsible for countless deaths. That must be something to celebrate.

Quickly, before she can change her mind, she types Mark a new message.

Let's stop messing around. Drink. Tonight. I have so much I want to tell you. xxx

*

McAvoy pushes his hair back from his face and looks in disgust at the sweat on his palm. He feels like he's melting. His insides feel wrong. He's hungry but the heat of the day is making him feel sick. He wants something sweet and cooling but thinks it would probably be unseemly if he conducted his section of the murder enquiry while licking an ice lolly. He resigns himself to stopping in at a newsagent's for a bar of chocolate on his way back to Arthur Street, where he has another twenty-five houses to doorstep before his section of the house-to-house is completed. People are cooperating, as much as they can. Police are tolerated around here. It's not a bad neighbourhood, all told, and nobody wants to live in an area where the nice lady from the late shop can have her chest caved in on her walk home. The trouble is, nobody saw anything. Nobody heard anything. And while everybody that he and the uniformed officers have spoken to has been only too willing to take his business cards and to promise to call if anything comes back to them, they have yet to find a witness.

McAvoy puffs out his cheeks and lets out a sigh. In front of him, the traffic is still moving at a crawl. Horns are honking. Drivers are revving their engines and the music from competing stereos blends with the sound of a distant pneumatic drill. The whole scene throbs with grinding noise. He stares straight ahead, not really seeing, jolting slightly as he realises his gaze is fixed on a group of pre-teens who are making a nuisance of themselves on the single-decker bus in front of him. They see him looking and mouth a variety of insults, punctuated by fulsome use of mid-finger salutes. Banging on the window, they laugh as if they have just committed the century's greatest act of social disobedience, then sit down as the driver turns around and threatens to let his fraying temper snap.

McAvoy gives a little nod. Fair enough, he supposes. Makes a V-sign of his own in the pocket of his trousers and wishes that the rule book allowed him to show it. He pushes off from the wall, feeling his shirt sticking to his back. He's sick of this heat. Sick of the oppressive grey skies, and the fact that his palms are sweaty every time he proffers one to a potential witness. He knows his hair looks nearly black at the temples, slick with perspiration, and while he is wearing enough anti-perspirant to ensure he doesn't embarrass himself, he wishes he had listened when Roisin suggested this morning he use some of the powder she had knocked up from cornstarch and oatmeal, and which she swears by when it comes to avoiding heat rashes anywhere too painful. 'Too late for that now,' he mutters, as he crosses between two barely moving vehicles and jogs painfully back to the other side of Anlaby Road.

As he reaches into his pocket for the change to buy a bar of chocolate, he grips nothing but empty cloth. He's out of money. Shit. It's nothing new. Buying the new car cleaned out his savings, while every spare penny he can muster is going on the new house. He qualified for the mortgage without any problems.

On paper, he owns a small croft near Gairloch in the Western Highlands, five or six miles from his father's, though he has only visited it a couple of times and sublets to an arty English couple who make their living doing complicated things with seashells. As a crofter's son, he qualified for government subsidy and had bought the place for a steal while still a young man. The bank had considered the property sufficient guarantee to give him a larger than usual mortgage and he will be moving the family into the new house on Hessle Foreshore next weekend. He's paying for a removals company to do some of the hard work. Paying for a proper wooden summerhouse for the back garden. Paying out too much, truth be told, but each purchase is making Roisin squeal, and if there is a better sound in the universe, he has yet to hear it.

Over the noise of the road, McAvoy hears his radio crackle. The uniformed officers still prefer to use radios, while he and his CID colleagues have made the transition to mobile phones, but McAvoy has no issue with doing things the way the uniformed sergeant coordinating the majority of the house-to-house preferred, and had taken the radio without argument. The team know who to contact if they came up with anything useful.

'McAvoy,' he says, into the radio.

'Sarge, this might be nothing, but I think we have somebody for you to come talk to . . .'

Five minutes later, McAvoy arrives back on Granville Street. He had run the first 500 yards, then slowed when he came in sight of one of the patrol cars so he could catch his breath.

PC Joseph Pearl is waiting by the door. He's a tall, strikingly handsome black man whom McAvoy has only met briefly, but whom he seems to remember as coming from somewhere over

Lancashire way. When he had briefed the officers, McAvoy had felt like warning PC Pearl that his colour would barely provoke a comment in this relatively multicultural area, but that he should keep his Lancashire accent under wraps for fear of abuse. Yorkshire folk have complicated prejudices.

'Nice lady,' says PC Pearl, nodding into the open doorway. 'Hard to shut her up.'

McAvoy steps inside the nondescript terrace, two minutes from where Philippa Longman lost her life. He had intended to make this row of properties part of his own house-to-house, but for fear of being accused of cherry-picking, he had left it to uniform.

The nice lady in question is Lavinia Mantell. She's sitting with her feet drawn up in the corner of a large, squashy, three-seater sofa, which dominates the small living room. On the walls are framed posters of various local theatre nights, and the carpet is a maddening swirl of purples and golds. McAvoy takes a quick look around and decides it must be rented. Lavinia has put her stamp on the place but has not gone to the trouble of replacing the vile soft furnishings or the woodchipped wallpaper. On the table in front of her is a laptop and a pile of papers, held in place by a biscuit tin, which stops the half-hearted breeze from the open window from making a mess. McAvoy recognises the salmon-pink colour of Hull Council Scrutiny Committee reports.

'Miss Mantell,' he says, edging his way around the huge sofa and coming to stand in front of the TV. He introduces himself. 'My colleague tells me you may have some information that would help us.'

She nods, then holds up her hands, as if urging him to wait.

She is chewing on a biscuit. She reaches down beside her and takes a swig from the mug of coffee on the floor.

'Sorry, you caught me.'

He smiles. 'The day biscuits are a crime, I'll be doing life.'

She's in her late thirties, and attractive in a bookish and careworn kind of way. She has brown hair that was probably cut into a sleek and sophisticated bob a couple of months ago but looks a little wilder now. She's wearing Red or Dead glasses and has the sort of figure that men are perfectly at ease with, but women would like to tighten up.

'I presume you work for the local authority,' says McAvoy, indicating the paperwork.

Lavinia pulls a face. 'I'm freelance. I work for whoever.'

'Journalist?'

She shakes her head and laughs. 'Chance would be a fine thing! No, my spelling's terrible. Good enough for marketing though.'

'Ah, right. Press officer?'

'That's what they used to be called. I'm a communications consultant, I'll have you know.' She adopts a haughty tone as she says it, and makes herself giggle. She raises a hand to her mouth suddenly, as if deciding that she is being overly jolly, given the circumstances, and takes on a solemn expression to make up for it.

'I presume you've been told about the events of last night,' says McAvoy, sitting down on the centre cushion of the sofa. 'Did you know Philippa Longman?'

'Not personally. Not really. I knew her face when your mate showed me the photo, and I'd seen her in the late shop.'

'Did you ever speak?'

Lavinia rubs at the tip of her nose with an index finger, trying to be helpful. 'Well, only in the shop. I think she once said the wine I was buying was nice. Something like that.'

'Anything else?'

'I think this was her walk home. I sometimes have a cigarette if I've had a really shit day, and the landlord doesn't like me smoking indoors. I'll sit on the front step with a coffee and a fag and I've said hello to her once or twice like that.'

'And last night?'

Lavinia opens her mouth and sits forward, nodding even before she speaks. 'Sort of. I wasn't on the doorstep last night, I was having a fag out of the window upstairs. I hardly ever do that, but it was so bloody hot last night I couldn't sleep and sometimes a cigarette calms me down. I was sitting on the windowsill.'

'And what time was this?'

'Oh, some time around midnight. Maybe a little earlier. I was reading a book on my phone. There's just enough light from the street lamp for me not to have to put the bedroom light on, you see. I'm on an electricity meter—'

'And you saw Mrs Longman?' asks McAvoy, moving forward in his chair so he can maintain eye contact with her as she wriggles around on the edge of the seat.

'Definitely. She was walking that way.'

She points in the direction the murdered woman would have had to walk to get home, and where, a few yards further on, she was torn to pieces.

'Was she alone?'

'At first,' says Lavinia, reaching forward for a piece of paper from the coffee table then discarding it, distractedly. 'As she came past the window she was. I'd looked up to drop some ash out the window and saw her walking by. Then the next time I was dropping the ash she was with somebody else.'

McAvoy takes out his notebook from his waistcoat pocket. He will remember every single detail, but Lavinia seems the sort of person who will respond well to him taking her words as hugely important, and he holds his pen invitingly over a blank page.

'Were they walking together, or standing still?'

Lavinia appears to think. 'They were talking. It looked like he'd come from the other direction.'

'What makes you say that?'

'The way they were standing. She had her back to me. He was sort of facing me. It's the way you'd stand if you'd just bumped into somebody.'

McAvoy nods, a picture forming in his mind. 'This was at the far end of the street, you say. Near the car park where she was found?'

'Not more than a few feet away from the entrance.'

McAvoy makes a note, moving the notebook just enough for her to see that he is taking down her words in shorthand – the result of an intensive night class he paid for himself.

'How long did you watch them for?'

'It was literally a moment,' says Lavinia, sadly. She seems to be wishing she had seen the whole attack and then taken pictures of the killer.

'And the person she was talking to – it was definitely a man?'

'Definitely,' says Lavinia.

'Big? Small? White? Black?' He checks the door and sees PC Pearl lounging in the doorframe. Begins to explain himself to both of them. 'These questions are crucial, you understand . . .'

'I'd say average. White, I'm pretty certain.' Lavinia looks sorry to be able to offer so little.

'Age?'

'Not old. Not young, either.'

'And they were talking. Not arguing?'

She shakes her head. 'They didn't seem to be. They looked like they had just stopped for a natter.'

McAvoy closes the notepad around his pen. 'Could you show me your room, please, Miss Mantell? PC Pearl, could you please ask a uniformed colleague to stand at the point Miss Mantell has described? Thanks.'

Lavinia looks surprised, but also quite pleased that there is more of this rather exciting aspect of her day still to come. She stands up, straightening her flared pinstripe trousers and white strappy vest. She leads him through the living-room door and into an L-shaped kitchen, then up a flight of stairs, covered with posters from foreign films.

'You like the arts?' he asks, as he follows her up.

She turns back. 'I do a lot of work with theatre companies, and in a perfect world that's all I'd do. That, watch films and smoke cigarettes. Not a perfect world, is it?'

Lavinia pushes open the door to her bedroom and scurries inside, throwing the duvet over the unmade bed and picking up a few items of laundry from the floor to stuff in a wicker hamper next to an open wardrobe. It's a bit of a mess, but comfortably so.

'There,' she says, pointing, rather unnecessarily, at the window. 'You have to reach up to blow the smoke out or dock your ash.'

McAvoy crosses to the window. A young WPC is talking into her radio and crossing to the spot McAvoy has requested. Behind her, he can see the edge of the white forensics tent and behind that, the bridge across the railway lines that would have led Philippa Longman home. He sits on the windowsill and looks out through a single-glazed pane, smears on its surface and dead flies at its edges.

The WPC has come to a halt as instructed. McAvoy squints. He does not know the officer. Could not, now, pick her out of a line-up. He turns to Lavinia. 'Can I borrow you for a moment, Miss Mantell?' He pushes himself back against the wall and invites her to lean past him. He gets a smell of medicated shampoo and Impulse body spray. Could count the freckles on her bare right shoulder, should he so choose. 'Describe the officer for me, please.'

She squints, theatrically. 'It's a woman,' she says. 'Brownish hair. Young.'

'Anything else?'

'I can't tell you the colour of her eyes, no.'

They both stand, unsure whether to be pleased or not with how the past few minutes have gone. Eventually, McAvoy smiles and gives her a card. 'An officer will take a formal statement. In the meantime, if you remember anything else, please give me a call.'

She looks at the card with its variety of numbers. Work. Personal. Email. Home.

'Do you think you'll catch him?' asks Lavinia, looking up. 'It's not very nice, is it? That sort of thing happening where you live. I mean, you get yobs and boy racers and the odd fight after Hull Fair or the football, but somebody being killed like that? I mean, it could have been me. It could have been anyone.'

McAvoy holds her gaze, then breaks away and crosses back to the window. 'It couldn't,' he says, softly. 'He wanted her. She knew him.'

6

8.48 p.m. Hessle foreshore.

A wide strip of grey-brown water, separating East Yorkshire from Northern Lincolnshire; the bridge overhead a loose stitch of concrete and steel, holding two counties together.

Aector and Roisin McAvoy: standing on the strip of muddy shingle, smiling indulgently as their son throws dirty pebbles at the rotten timbers sunk deep into the sucking sands.

He breathes deep. Catches the scent of sun cream and citrus. Her skin lotion and cigarettes. He wants her, as he always wants her. Wants to wash himself, lose himself, in her movements, her affection . . .

He breathes in again. And there it is. That faint chemical tang. The merest whiff of disinfectant and grey steel, still suffusing his skin. The post-mortem. The mortuary. That ghastly tapestry of guts and innards made art by the precision of the incisions and stitches.

If Philippa Longman suffered in her final moments, the wounds are as naught compared with the indignities wreaked upon her corpse by Dr Gene Woodmansey. He was a lot more tender, more dispassionate about it, than whoever tore her ribcage open, but there is no tender way of slicing up human flesh, and McAvoy's hour at the mortuary had been vile. McAvoy has witnessed post-mortem exams before. He saw enough animal corpses and butchered enough cattle in his youth not to be rendered nauseous by the pathologist's work. He is not the sort of officer who would rather do anything than visit the mortuary. He has seen fellow officers volunteer to break the news of violent death to the victim's family rather than visit that anodyne, sterile cathedral of human deconstruction, with its grey walls and floors.

McAvoy is okay with blood. He had not raised objections when asked by Pharaoh to attend the autopsy on her behalf. But he had never seen a corpse like Philippa's before. Nor had he seen Dr Woodmansey give that tiny little shake of the head, that muted exhalation of breath, that suggested, he, too, was at once disgusted and appalled by what had been done to the woman who lay naked and mangled, scrubbed and exposed, upon the metal table before him.

As he holds his wife and watches his son throw stones into the water, McAvoy pictures the scene that played out before him just a couple of hours ago. Sees himself, wraith-like in his disposable white coat and with blue bags on his shoes, standing back against a wall so joyless in hue that it seemed to have been coloured in with a pencil. In front of him are two steel tables. Philippa Longman lies upon one – her face having settled into a curiously inhuman, characterless mask, so pale as to be almost translucent. Against the far wall is a hydraulic hoist and steel doors polished to a reflective gleam. To his right are sinks and hoses, a cutting board and specimen bottles. Next to McAvoy is a large whiteboard, the names of the recently dead scrawled upon it in doctor's handwriting. The numbers scribbled in the various columns record the weight of heart, brain, kidneys, lungs, liver, spleen. McAvoy takes them in, and wonders what he should feel. Cannot help but picture himself, on the slab. Cannot help but imagine Dr Woodmansey leaning over him, slicing the scalpel around the crown of his skull, lifting his hair away as if he has fallen to a tomahawk blow . . .

As he works, Dr Woodmansey wears a green apron over green surgical scrubs, topping off the outfit with white welly boots and rubber gloves. As she was brought in, Philippa Longman's body was wrapped in plastic sheeting, evidence bags secured over her hands and feet to preserve any microscopic evidence contained within. As he watched, sombre and silent, McAvoy wondered how it felt to be a policeman a half-century before. Wondered how he would have fared were he asked to catch a killer without knowledge of skin cells, hair fibres, DNA. As ever, he felt he would come up short.

Dr Woodmansey is a short, portly man with close-shaved hair and unashamedly old-fashioned glasses. He is businesslike in his dealings with both the living and the dead. He is not one for small talk. He makes no jokes over the body and appreciates silence as he works. McAvoy likes his manner. Likes that he knows nothing more about the man than the fact he is good at his job.

'Swing me, Daddy.'

The vision disappears as Fin gives his father an attention-grabbing kick on the ankle. He smiles indulgently at his son, who is a miniature version of his dad – all broad shoulders, red face and russet hair. McAvoy picks him up and gives him a quick spin around, enjoying the laughter it brings from his wife and his child. The boy is sticky with sweat, and McAvoy can see problems this evening when they try and get him to change out of the Ross County football strip he has worn every day since it arrived in the post on his fifth birthday. As presents go, McAvoy is not sure that turning a youngster with his whole life ahead of him into a Ross County fan is a tremendous gift. Still, Fin had been pleased, and is busy working on an elaborate thank-you card for his uncle in Aultbea. McAvoy wonders if the boy will still be as grateful as an adult, when he is nursing a consoling pint and wishing that he'd been raised to support Celtic.

Fin runs off, back to the wooden timbers. McAvoy reaches out for Roisin's hand. It's delicate and cold, despite the heat of the evening, and he takes it in his great warm paw, pulling her in. She rests her head against his chest and as one, they sink down onto the pebbles. It's still horribly muggy and warm and the sky is the colour of the pathologist's cutting tools, but at least here there is enough breeze for them to be able to hold one another without their clothing sticking to their skin.

'Every night,' says Roisin, raising her head and turning to look back at the row of properties 100 yards away across a strip of grass and a quiet road. 'We can do this every night, Aector.'

McAvoy kisses her on the forehead. 'You don't think you'll get bored with the view?'

'It changes every day,' she says, looking back at the water. 'I've never seen it the same twice.'

She's right. The Humber is one of the most dangerously unpredictable waterways in the world: a mess of contrary tides and shifting sands. Two millennia ago, the estuary managed to hold the Romans back as they marched north; a procession of slaves losing their lives as they failed to find a safe channel through the mud and waters. McAvoy has never worked out why they didn't just go inland fifteen miles and turn right at Goole.

'And you're sure it's what you want? There are those apartments in the Old Town. You'd be near the shops, the museums . . .'

She reaches down and nips his thigh, then slaps him across his chest. This is her way of telling him to shut up. She has told him endlessly how much she wants this: this house, with its views and big back garden; this place, this life. He believes her. The only part he struggles to comprehend is why she wants to share it with him.

McAvoy stretches out his leg and gives the baby-carrier a little rock. Lilah is sleeping soundly at last. The heat has been too much for her, and every time McAvoy opens her bedroom window, flies, moths and wasps begin to circle her cot. Her crying had been a torturous and heartbreaking thing and they had decided to all go for a drive. To get some fresh air. To head for the new house, and indulge in pleasant daydreaming about how their lives will be when they move their stuff in next weekend.

'Mel says she'll come,' says Roisin, into his chest.

'To what?'

'The housewarming, Silly. Suzie too. And a couple of the mums.'

McAvoy nods. He doesn't know what to say. He doesn't want a housewarming party. Doesn't want strangers in his home. But he will have one, and smile as wide as he can muster, to please his wife.

'The shop's doing well, apparently. Slow, but it takes time, doesn't it? And there are loads of shops closing down, so she's doing well even to be in business, you know?'

'Aye, it can't be easy.'

'She got a big order while I was there. Big bag of suits that needed taking in. I think the bloke had been on some sort of extreme diet. He looked thin but green, and his breath smelled like cat food.'

'Lovely.'

'Aye. She'll be good. She doesn't mind working hard. I just wish there was somebody to keep an eye on her. It's rough up there, and she's not really tough, is she? I might spend a bit more time up there until she's a bit more settled. I don't like thinking of her on her own.'

Roisin met Mel a few months before at a salsa class and the two have quickly become close friends. McAvoy finds her pleasant enough company, though is never truly pleased when he comes home to find her in his living room, three-quarters of the way through a bottle of red wine and planning to spend the night on his sofa. Roisin always asks him whether he minds her friends staying over. He always tells her it's fine. Tells her to do whatever she wants. Tells her to enjoy herself, and then he goes upstairs to read a book or fiddle with some new software on the computer in the bedroom. Lets her be. Lets her do whatever the hell she wants as long as she continues to love him.

'I had a look in the hairdresser's next to her shop,' she says. 'Nice people. They don't do nails. I was thinking I might see about offering my services.'

McAvoy has to force himself not to visibly react. In his mind, Roisin has already started work at the salon. She is chatting. Laughing. Living. A sales rep comes in to offer samples. Makes her giggle. Touches her bare shoulder as he leaves. Slips a business card into her hand. She looks at it, longingly. Weighs up her options. Pictures her daft, hulking husband and his big stupid face and picks up her phone.

He feels his heart, disintegrating, in his chest.

'That's a good idea,' he says, as brightly as he can muster. 'Would do you good. Would you be able to do just a few hours, either side of school runs and stuff?'

'It's only a thought at the moment. We'll see, eh? Anyway, they might want me to have all the certificates and stuff. I'm self-taught, aren't I?'

McAvoy squeezes her. 'You're naturally brilliant,' he says.

'You think?'

'I think.'

They sit in silence, just loving each other, and for a time, McAvoy manages not to picture anything dispiriting or gruesome. Manages not to fill his imagination with Philippa Longman, or the things he has seen being done to her corpse. Manages not to picture what was done to her in her dying moments, in the darkness, on a mattress of cracked stones and smashed glass.

He lets his mind spin. Presses Roisin closer to him. Tries to be a better man. Suddenly sees himself outside the mortuary, leaning against bare brick, fringe plastered to his forehead, strong mints wedged between teeth and cheek, phone to his ear and telling Pharaoh the pathologist's findings.

'She had a heart attack while it was happening, Guv. Her arteries were furred up and her cholesterol was above average so the shock of it all sent her into cardiac arrest. By that point though she was on the ground and she was getting hit in the chest. There's a bruise to the back of her head. She went down hard but not hard enough to knock her out. There's bruising around the hinge of the jaw that suggests pressure to the lower half of her face. Perhaps a hand, holding her mouth shut. Dr Woodmansey says she was pummelled with a large flat implement with a soft surface, whatever that may mean. Repeated strikes to the ribs and chest. Ribs broke under the stress and punctured inwards. Eventually the ribs punctured the lungs and then finally the heart. He says twenty minutes all in. Twenty minutes, pounding on her chest. No evidence of sexual assault. A few fibres, under her nails. Red and black threads, soft cotton. Some substance, as yet unidentified, but organic. Could be anything, but he's sending it off for analysis. Should have it back in a couple of days if we fast-track it. Dr Woodmansey says that it was furious but sustained. Whoever did it would have had blood spray on them, but wouldn't have been covered. Her breath was full of blood particles and the killer would have been in close.'

Here, now, McAvoy closes his eyes. Tries to put the day's findings into some kind of order. Tries to work out why somebody would kill Philippa Longman so brutally. Whoever killed her, it was important to them that she suffer. Somebody hated her. Was it a random stranger, hating the world? Or has she done something so terrible that her murderer wanted her to endure that much agony in her dying moments? He thinks of Darren Robb. Tries to imagine the pitiful fat man having that much rage inside of him. He struggles to see it. But he has been wrong before.

'Did I tell you I met your friend Helen? She was up by Mel's shop.'

'Helen Tremberg? Detective constable?'

'Yeah. Big girl. Nice. Got hurt when you were both in Grimsby . . .'

'Yes, DC Tremberg. Did you say hello?'

'Just briefly. She was with some snooty cow.'

'Detective Inspector Sharon Archer?'

'I dunno. She just sat there with her hand on the horn.'

'Yeah, that would be her.'

McAvoy wonders how he feels about his wife chatting to his work colleagues. Unbidden, a blush rises from his shirt collar up to his cheeks. He imagines her telling Tremberg about their new home. Their plans. He imagines her inviting her to the housewarming. Telling her to bring a friend. Imagines Archer asking her junior officer whom she was talking to. Sees Tremberg, spilling her guts. Telling her about Aector McAvoy's traveller wife. About what he did to the men who attacked her when she was young. Fuck. Fuck!

'The lady who died,' says Roisin, shifting position so she can look up at her husband. 'Why did they kill her?'

McAvoy gazes into her for a few seconds. Her eyes are innocent and guileless.

'We've got a few ideas. It may just have been a random nutter, but it doesn't feel that way.'

'Had she been putting it about or anything? Any affairs?'

McAvoy shakes his head. 'We don't think so. She was just a nice lady. Mattered to people. Did her bit. And somebody caved her chest in. Splintered her ribs like she was made of twigs.'

'What with?'

'We don't know that either.'

Roisin makes a face, mildly disappointed in the detectives of Humberside Police. 'They break easy, ribs. Even when you're doing CPR, you can break ribs. I think I saw that in an episode of *Holby City*, actually . . .'

McAvoy has gone still. He breathes out, slowly, through his nose, and without saying anything, sits up and rolls Roisin onto her back. He places one hand on her chest and the other on top of it. Roisin looks up at him, happy, but confused.

'We trying something new?'

He gives the slightest push. She winces, but doesn't stop smiling.

McAvoy rocks himself back, onto his toes. He stares at her, eyes unfocused.

He stands and pulls out his phone.

'Guv? I've had a thought . . .'

11.58 p.m. Barton-on-Humber.

The last town before North Lincolnshire hits the water. A decent, likeable place. Pleasant. Arty. A mingling of sturdy, centuries-old merchant homes and newly built estates. A place where cosy restaurants sit comfortably beside kebab shops; where slick Mercedes park next to rusted hatchbacks while the owners of both drink happily in real-ale pubs.

This wide road leading out of the town centre, up towards the roundabout and the last stretch of motorway that leads across the bridge.

A modern, detached house with neat front lawn and a sensible car parked on a newly tarmacked drive . . .

Yvonne Dale. Forty-six. Mother of two and gratefully divorced. She's lounging at the apex of an L-shaped sofa in a long, white-painted living room. The walls serve as a timeline of her children's lives. Above the flat-screen TV are baby pictures. Jacob, restless on the photographer's cloud of tousled silk. Andrew, two years later, placid and uncrying as the same photographer manipulated his chunky limbs and soft curls into a more pleasing pose. Above the fireplace, their first holidays, all muddy welly boots and rain-streaked cheeks. First days at school. Almond-coloured skin between grey socks and shorts. Their trip to Kefalonia three years ago. Jacob then six, Andrew four. Yvonne in some of these pictures, lounging by the poolside in the rented villa, large floppy hat casting a shadow on rosy cheeks and ample skin spilling out of a black swimsuit. Behind her, pixelated on a huge canvas, both boys laughing, Jacob's arm thrown carelessly over his little brother's shoulder as they sit cross-legged and side by side on Cleethorpes seafront reading the same book; Jacob patient with his younger sibling when he struggled with longer words.

Here, now, Yvonne is wearing a baggy American football vest and pyjama trousers. She is a large lady. Always was, even when she was slim. She stands nearly six feet tall and would be considered formidable by the primary school children she teaches were it not for her big smile and silly sense of humour. She has been a teacher most of her life. Had been working with kids for thirteen years before she had one of her own. Had been content enough, too, before a supply teacher took a fancy to her. She was wooed, wed, knocked up twice, and then divorced before Andrew's first birthday. Her ex is abroad now, teaching English as a foreign language to uncomprehending teens in Jakarta, the Child Support Agency proving bloody useless in making him cough up his maintenance payments with any kind of regularity. He phones the kids once in a while. Carries their pictures in his wallet. But they haven't seen him in over a year, and the weekend he visited had been awkward, full of stilted conversation and stored-up arguments.

She pushes her scruffy blonde hair back from her face and drinks the last of her hot chocolate. At her feet are the crusts from a meat-feast pizza. She has some garlic mayonnaise left in the fridge and half-heartedly thinks of going to get it. Then she imagines sitting up in bed dipping cold pizza crusts in a pot of fattening gunk, and doesn't like the image of herself, so decides against it.

A sigh: 'Bloody carbs.'

She takes another look at her phone. Decides it's time for bed. She put the kids down just after nine. They'd watched a few episodes of some light-hearted American drama, eating popcorn chicken and spicy fries, drinking pint glasses of orange squash, wriggling in their matching cotton pyjamas until the fleece blanket that covers their half of the sofa looked like a whirlpool. Yvonne hadn't given the show her full attention. The story on the local news kept slipping into her thoughts. The picture they showed. Older, certainly. A few more wrinkles. Shading beneath her eyes. But unmistakably *her*. So sad. Such a shame.

She looks again at her phone. At the address book on the arm of the sofa. It's an old one, as full of crossings-out and amendments as useful information. She uses her phone for such things now, but the number she sought earlier this evening had not made the transition from paper to memory card and she had been forced to dig through her old diaries and papers to find it. In all honesty, she had never expected to call it. She had only taken it for form's sake and because she is a nice person who favours the old-fashioned way of doing things. She likes sending Christmas cards and birthday cards. Likes little notelets and writing with a fountain pen. Makes jam tarts and maids-of-honour and hangs proper paper chains each December. Says 'fiddlesticks' when she is cross and 'gee whiz' when the kids show her something impressive. Sometimes in the staff room they tease her about such things. Suggest that she would have felt more at home in the 1950s, teaching lacrosse or hockey in an all-girls boarding school.

Yvonne reaches again for the address book. Stares at the old address, neatly scored out with a line of black ink. At the new number, scribbled in the margin. The Hull area code.

'What a waste.'

She chides herself for never thinking to pop over and say hello. To make the kids a flask and some sandwiches and plan a nice Sunday walk across the bridge. To arrange a play date at the Country Park, perhaps. To sit on a bench while children played with grandchildren and she and her old comrade could let their conversation drift to the night they met, to that evening of blood and adrenalin, of crimson splashes on virgin snow, beneath colourful bulbs and against the whispered threats of the waves . . .

Too late to try again, she decides, putting the phone back down on the arm of the chair. She wasn't even sure whether she should have rung. Poor lot will have been inundated with real friends, she thinks. Real family. What would I have said?

Making the grunt of effort that the kids tease her over, Yvonne pulls herself from the chair. Starts the little ritual she performs unthinkingly every night. Pulls the plug out the back of the TV. Closes the living-room door. Checks the front and back door, rattling the handles and moving the kids' discarded shoes from the bottom of the stairs so they don't trip during the rush to breakfast. She walks to the kitchen, bare feet on plum-coloured carpet. Puts an aspirin in a shot glass and adds two inches of water. Stirs it and listens to the fizz. Drains the glass and pulls a face. Takes a gingerbread biscuit from the biscuit barrel beside the microwave and pulls the kitchen door closed. Puts her right hand on the banister and hauls herself up two stairs. Carries on up the steps, biscuit now just a crumb on her lower lip. She visits

Jacob's room first. Takes the book from his unresisting hands and smooths his hair down. Kisses him on the side of the head and fans him a little with his summer quilt. Visits Andrew next. He's the wrong way round in bed, his feet on the pillow, a wrestling figure clutched in one hand, another protruding from beneath his face. She leaves him as he is. Blows a kiss, knowing that he'll wake should she disturb him further. She switches his bedroom light off and pulls his door half closed.

A whisper: 'Sweet dreams.'

Yvonne heads to her own bedroom. It's untidy, with half-unpacked luggage and unsorted laundry. The bottom of the bed is covered in loose socks, still waiting to be paired a week after being spat from the tumble drier. Carrier bags from discount stores litter the dressing table, full of labels and receipts, discarded packaging from hastily bought vests and underwear. The half-dozen books she has on the go are scattered loose by the bed and behind the curtains, the windowsill is covered in empty pop bottles and dusty DVDs, as is the top of the TV that sits precariously on a wall-bracket she put up herself and doesn't fully trust. It's the untidiest room in the house because nobody else ever comes in here, and Yvonne doesn't mind.

She pushes open the door to the en-suite bathroom. Slides down her pyjama trousers and sits on the pink plastic. Looks at her feet. Spots a place on her right knee that she missed while shaving. Reminds herself, again, to take the mound of toilet-roll cardboard to the recycling bin from its place beneath the sink.

She hears the familiar creak as the door swings closed. Looks up.

Had the situation been described to her, Yvonne Dale would have expected to scream. Perhaps to physically react. To leap up or shuffle back or reach for the glass she uses for rinsing her mouth after brushing her teeth and smash it into the intruder's face . . .

There is no time. Her heart does not find the opportunity to beat between her noticing the figure, two steps away, against the tiled wall, and their moving forward to where she sits, still pissing, face turning grey.

The intruder grabs her by the hair. Pulls, hard, and instinctively she stands – one hand upon her scalp and the other trying to pull up her trousers. Something slams up beneath her jaw and her teeth mash together. Her eyes fill with tears from the pain and then she is being pushed back, onto the windowsill behind the toilet; bottles falling, glass smashing. A fist slams into her left eye and then her head is being smacked against the tiled wall. She sinks forward, falling against the intruder. Her vision swims. What she sees and what she feels merge before her. And she sees her boys. Feels them. Lashes out with a mother's instinct, suddenly desperate to fight, to flee. To live.

A weight drops on her back. The attacker pushes her down to the linoleum floor, her face scraping against the wooden door, the wall, into the dust and the cobwebs of the skirting board.

And then she feels it. The sharp, cold, metallic agony at the back of her left thigh. She roars in agony; a masculine, guttural howl of pain, and then a hand is across her mouth. She bucks. Pushes back. Claws with her right hand at the figure that presses her down. Bites at the warm, gloved hand inside her mouth. Tastes plastic. Chemical. Feels wetness at her thighs and shame at having pissed herself.

Clarity, suddenly. A moment of comprehension. Feels the stickiness. The warmth on her bare skin. Feels blood, not urine.

Rolls, left and right, trying to dislodge the weight upon her, even as her strength begins to fade. Her hand slips in blood. Head hits the ground. And then the weight is rising. She is free to move. Free, yet unable. She has no strength. She feels empty. Hollow. Unchained and weightless.

In her last moments, her eyes focus on the figure on the side of the bath. Through the tears, she sees colours. Shapes. Red mixed with black; blood and dirt. Sees the perfect exclamation mark of steel. Sees a face that she half knows; features blurred, as though a child has dipped their fingers in a still-wet portrait and swirled the eyes, nose and mouth into insensibility.

And now her mind is all children. Little palms in her big warm hand. She sees Jacob, looking down on her, eyes of concern, stroking her hair back from her face. Sees Andrew, holding out a picture he has drawn. She tries to say 'gee whiz'. . .

Her lips flutter, but no words emerge.

'Sshh,' says her killer, watching. Then: 'Sweet dreams.'

Silence, here, in this room.

A dead woman on her bathroom floor. Her killer, head in palms, shoulders shaking and fists tugging hair.

Blood seeping into every corner, intractable as night.

7

'This is yours?'

Helen Tremberg waves her hand. 'Ssh. They're all quite old. The neighbours, I mean.'

He smiles, the street light adding shadow to his high, attractive cheekbones. 'I'm not surprised.'

Tremberg pretends to be offended and opens her mouth wide. 'This is a very desirable neighbourhood,' she whispers, a slur to her words. 'Handy for the shop. Good parking. Easy access to the main road . . .'

'Meals on wheels, ambulances available if you pull the orange cord in the bathroom . . .'

She slaps him, playfully, across the arm. Feels the definition of his muscles. Starts to pull a sulky face but is too full of wine to do it properly.

'I grew up here,' she says, as she pushes open the gate and closes it again behind them. 'I told you, didn't I? When Grandad went into care it came up for sale and I got it for a steal.'

Mark slips his arm back around her waist as they walk up a red-brick driveway to the back door. They have walked this way from the restaurant. She has rested her head on his shoulder and felt his breath behind her ear and on her neck. He kissed her on the crown of the head when she said something funny. She has yet to taste his mouth, but knows that she will do that and more when she gets them inside her bungalow home.

It has been a tender, romantic evening. She had been unsure whether to agree when he suggested the restaurant only half a mile from her own front door, but she remembers them discussing it in a previous email chat, so it made sense and hadn't felt like he was trying to manipulate her into going somewhere within easy reach of her bedroom. He doesn't strike her as that kind of man. He could be, if he wanted. He's handsome, charming, and has spent all night making her laugh, but he seems too easy-going to be duplicitous. She can't remember a time when she has felt so pretty. She hadn't been sure whether or not to wear the tennis dress that shows off her legs, or whether to pair it with the high, wedge-heel sandals, but she has received nothing but compliments and admiring glances all night and Mark had said she looked 'stunning'.

Of course, it had taken a couple of brandies to get herself out of the house and to walk past her neighbours in the uncharacter-istically revealing outfit. She had got through two more while waiting in the bar for him to show up. By the time he walked in, five minutes late and dauntingly handsome in cream linen suit and black shirt, she was pink to her earlobes and flushed from both the walk and the booze. But he had put her at her ease. He'd taken her hand as if to shake it, then turned it, delicately, palm side down, so he could kiss her knuckles. He'd looked at her, over the top of her hand, and she saw it tremble. Then he gave a grin and made a joke of the action and himself, and they had giggled together, setting the tone for the next few hours.

Tremberg fumbles in her little sequinned handbag and pulls out her keys. At the second attempt, she gets them in the lock and pushes open the back door that opens straight into the kitchen, switching on the light as she goes. The sudden illumination hurts her eyes and she raises a hand to shield her vision, stumbling back a little as she does so. Mark catches her, hands upon her waist, and helps her inside, laughing. He doesn't seem drunk, though he matched her drink for drink. Ordered the best booze, but didn't argue when she said she wanted to split the bill. He seems to know her. Seems to know how she likes to be treated. How she likes to think of herself. Didn't ask her about the scar on her arm. Waited for her to volunteer the information. Didn't push or try too hard. Just spoke to her as if she was interesting, and stared into her eyes in a way that made her blush. Even when she'd invited him back, he'd been a gentleman about it. Insisted that she think about it. That she decide whether she was sober enough to make that kind of decision.

'Don't be afraid to change your mind,' he'd said, stepping from the restaurant into the warmth and dark of the evening. 'I don't want to spoil things. It's been perfect. You've been perfect.'

As they walked, Helen had done most of the talking. She has done for most of the date. She'd recognised almost every other diner in the restaurant, and they had all given her encouraging looks as she sat opposite her good-looking companion and devoured her blade of beef. It had been a nice feeling, and helped her let go. She knows almost everybody in Caistor. She grew up here, twelve miles from Grimsby, on the road to Lincoln. She went to the local school. Used to walk her dogs in the vale. Got stranded, like everybody else, each winter. The town sits in one of the few valleys in the county, and whenever it snows, the roads become impassable. Her childhood memories seem to involve endless snowball fights and sledging down the sloping playing fields in the school grounds. She had her first kiss behind the Chinese takeaway. Once got knocked over in the Market Place as she crossed the wide road while engrossed in a bag of chips. Her dad had belted the driver. Given her a bloody good telling off, too, as he took her to hospital to have her leg plastered. She stacked shelves for a while in the Co-op, in her teens. Got drunk in the park on cans of Strongbow and let a county cricketer take her virginity on a friend's sofa at sixteen. It's home, and only half an hour from the city where she now tries to catch villains. She has no plans to move over the water to Hull. This is where she belongs. It's a town that likes her, and she lost no friends when she decided to become a copper. It's a town where the police are appreciated.

Here, now, she feels absurdly pleased that she has shown Mark where she is from. She likes that he has listened. She has told him her best stories. Told him a little about being a detective. She is proud of her job, and does not mind talking about work. She has asked him a few questions about his own job, but each time the conversation has steered back to her. She has rarely felt as interesting or desirable.

She giggles as Mark closes the door behind them, then puts a hand to her mouth. 'I'm not a giggler,' she says, primly. 'I hate those giggly girls. That just slipped out.'

Mark turns her towards him and gives her a warm, forgiving smile. 'It's nice,' he says. 'You can do whatever you want. Be whatever you want. I like whoever you are.'

Helen looks away, embarrassed. Thinks about making coffee, then decides to stop the charade. She pulls him to her, and opens her mouth for his kiss, eyes closed. When she opens them again, Mark's face is an inch from her own. 'Are you sure?'

She grabs him by his short, brown hair, and pulls his mouth onto hers, kissing him hungrily, wetly, drunkenly. She is ferocious and rough with him, forcing his mouth onto her neck, her shoulders, grabbing his hands and forcing them onto her breasts. She feels outrageous and wanton, wildly happy. He pauses, grabbing her wrists so as to be able to look at her properly. 'You're beautiful, Helen. Not here. Bedroom?'

She holds his gaze. Nods. Takes his hand and leads him to her room. It's not much different to when she used to stay here as a teenager. The walls used to be patterned with Formula one posters. Now the prints are in frames, and there is a little more order to her wardrobe, but it is still an unashamedly teenage room.

Mark doesn't comment. Just turns her to him and presses himself against her. She tears at the buttons of his shirt, but he smiles and does it himself. Lets the garment fall to the floor. Stands there, muscled and perfect. Tattoos, artful and expensive, upon his shoulders and chest; a mayoral chain of Italian lettering inked into his skin.

She presses her face to it. Traces the outline with her mouth. She doesn't care what it says. Just wants to consume it. To consume him.

Mark pushes her back onto the bed. Pushes up her dress. Kneels before her and pulls down her knickers. Smiles at her. Tastes her. Doesn't even wince as she digs her nails into his skin and wraps her strong thighs around his head.

Panting, breathless, he turns her over. Plants soft kisses on the back of her thighs.

She hears him removing his clothing. Feels tiny, delicate touches on her skin. Feels his warm hands upon her hips.

'Are you a bad girl?'

The words make her wriggle. She turns back to him. He reaches forward, puts his fingers to her lips. Lets her taste herself. She sucks on his fingers. Tastes something else, too. Bitter. Unpleasant. But it is gone in a moment, replaced by fresh pleasures as he uses his other hand on her.

'I'm such a bad girl.'

She hears him breathe deep. Inhale. Slide inside her. And then she is lost in pleasure. In his movements. In the warmth in her belly and the sloshing pleasures in her skull.

She doesn't see the camera.

Doesn't see the tiny lens, busily recording it all.

Doesn't imagine, as she loses herself in another climax, that she is being watched. Filmed. Immortalised electronically, having cocaine snorted off her arse and rubbed into her gums by a man who works for the very gang she is supposed to be trying to put away . . .

4.36 a.m. The A180. Five miles from Barton and two screaming boys.

She's doing 80 mph in the outside lane, Soul II Soul on the CD player and a mug of black coffee rattling in the holder; police radio on the passenger seat and a satnav set barking lefts and rights.

Detective Superintendent Trish Pharaoh, putting on make-up in the rear-view mirror and steering with her thighs, trying to remember the right word for what has been done to Yvonne

Dale. Ex-something. *Excoriated*? No. *Excommunicated*. Don't be fucking daft.

The glass of the convertible is misting up so Pharaoh swipes a hand across the glass. She clears a porthole, jewelled with droplets and streaks. Peers through at the pissy yellow street lights and the damp grey motorway; at the distant line of pyrite glow and the beginnings of a sepia sunrise through a sky of wire wool.

She snaps her fingers. *Exsanguinated*. Bled out. Emptied. Cut to the femoral artery and left to empty on the lino.

Pharaoh is too drunk to drive, but she's driving anyway. She does, sometimes. She lives an hour from her office and downs a bottle of wine and a few vodkas every night. Sometimes she's still over the limit when she leaves the house in the morning, though she gets her kids up, dresses them, feeds them and makes packed lunches, without any noticeable sign of intoxication. She doesn't plan on stopping drinking, doesn't think she would be able to if she tried. She's a drinker. Always has been. And she has to drive. She makes no excuse for it. If she gets caught, she'll take her punishment. She'll accept the headlines and the loss of her rank. That's life. You do what you want to do, or what you have to do, and you deal with the consequences. That's justice. That's police work. That's what she is for . . .

The radio crackles. A voice asks her whereabouts.

'I'm ten minutes away. See you in three.'

She's up two hours earlier than usual, so reckons there is no doubt that she is still technically over the limit She feels fine though. Better than she should.

Pharaoh was the first senior CID officer to answer the phone.

108

The uniformed constable who attended the house in Barton had immediately called in the duty inspector, and he in turn had alerted CID. The duty detectives had passed it up the line, and ACC Everett was woken at home. He bumped it back down again, and within half an hour of Yvonne Dale's body being discovered, the three most senior officers in CID were getting calls on their mobiles. Pharaoh answered on the second ring. Said she'd be there within half an hour. Pulled on leggings, boots, a smartish jumper and a light suit jacket. Phoned her mum and asked her to come sit with the kids. Made a strong coffee, took her anti-depressants and her antacid tablet, and jumped in the car.

Pharaoh lives in Scartho in Grimsby. She pronounces the word properly, though true locals insist on 'Scather'. It's happily middle class, with a couple of foodie pubs and the kind of swimming pool where people actually get out of the water if they want to go for a piss. A lot of the properties are set back from quiet side streets, all white paint and neat hedges. Pharaoh does not have the funds to even dream of such a home. She earns a good wage on a superintendent's salary but historic debts, costly childcare and her husband's condition mean she is grateful to scrape together enough each month to pay the mortgage on their three-bedroomed semi in the circle of a quiet cul-de-sac. Her name and hers alone is on the mortgage. Her husband lost everything when his business went bankrupt. Lost their big home on the outskirts of town. Lost their fancy 4x4s and Florida holidays. Paid the price for thinking too big, and then let the stresses and guilt squeeze his brain like a fist.

Five years ago, aged just forty-four, he suffered the stroke that has left him crippled down one side and a stranger to his children. Adapting their house to his needs took the few savings Pharaoh had kept back when he was trying to keep his business afloat. Her home life is hard. She feels half-widowed. She still has her man; still sleeps next to him in their remote-control, adjustable bed. But he struggles to make himself understood. Can't hold her. Can't get his lips to form the right shape for the word 'love'. The children know him as little more than a living ghost; some grunting, malevolent spirit of a man they half remember. They struggle to know how to love him, and she does not know how to teach them. She feels the loss of who he was more keenly than her kids. She remembers their life. Remembers the fire in him. The fight. The way he grunted, animal-like, as he moved inside her. Remembers, too, his temper. His hands on her throat. His spittle on her face. Remembers loving and wanting and hating him all at once. She never expected to pity him. And yet that is the emotion she now feels most keenly. Sorry for him, to be so reduced. Sorry for herself. Sorry that nobody kisses her properly. Sorry that while the bitches at work put about the rumour that she's some kind of slag, she hasn't been fucked yet in her forties.

Pharaoh spots the house as soon as she turns off the motorway and drifts down the steep hill into the town. There are two patrol cars on the road and a third in the drive. An ambulance is parked across the road and a police constable is wrapping blue and white tape around a lamp post. Lights are on in windows all the way down the road. Faces peer out through glass. Some doors are open: householders on doorsteps, wearing dressing gowns and drinking tea. The properties here are worth twice what Philippa Longman paid for her place, but the reaction of neighbours to death in their midst is the same in any postcode.

Pharaoh pulls up against the kerb, one alloy hubcab scraping the stone. She flashes her badge at a slim WPC and ducks under the tape. She spots a familiar face over by the garage.

'Guv.'

'Morning, Lee.'

'We got a call from DCI Barclay from Grimsby CID. Seemed to think this was his . . .'

'I'm sure he did. So, what have we got?'

Detective Sergeant Lee Percy is a twenty-year veteran, who started as a uniformed constable around the same time as Pharaoh. He made it into plain clothes before she did, but when she finally got the call into CID, her career took off, while his did not. They were sergeants together, and were both up for the same inspector job. It went to Trish. He took it okay, but Pharaoh fancies that after a few drinks he will lance his spleen and spew bitter rants about how he lost out to a token woman who shagged her way into the job. She hopes she is wrong, of course, but has been right too many times to hold out much hope.

Sergeant Percy weighs things up and then shrugs. Decides that all the arguments will be among people well above his pay grade. He started his shift at 6 p.m. and had been planning an easy night writing up statements and trying to persuade a reluctant eyewitness to a hit-and-run to make a statement. He hadn't been prepared for this. Hadn't been prepared for what he saw in Yvonne Dale's bathroom. He stands against the brick of the flat-roofed garage, hands in his pockets, short-sleeved, pale-blue shirt flapping around arms that lack muscle or definition. He's got the slightest of pot bellies and a weak chin, but has caught his share of crooks.

'Bloody horrible, Guv.'

'Tell me everything.'

Yvonne Dale's body was discovered not long after she took her last breath. Her neighbours had been woken by a furious banging on their door and had come downstairs to investigate, expecting to find a drunk or gang of difficult teens. Instead, they found the glass in their uPVC front door had been smeared in what they took to be red paint. They did not take it to be so for long.

'Tried to wash it off, Guv. Old couple they are. The sort who don't leave a job until morning. Filled a bucket of warm water and started soaping it off. It was only when they started doing it they thought it might be something a bit more sinister. Old boy licked some off his finger. Threw up in the azaleas.'

'How did it get there? Does that mean the killer banged on the door? Why? Did he want us to find her?'

'Your guess is as good as mine, Guv.'

Pharaoh presses her lips together and scratches her nose. 'Better, I would say. And then?'

'They phoned 999. Uniforms started an immediate search of the area. One bright spark found a footprint in the mud of next door's garden. Found another outlined in the gravel of the drive. Followed the trail next door and banged on the door. Got no answer so tried to get the householder's details. Phone rang for ages. Then a little kid answered. PC persuaded him to come open the door and the poor little sod did. Uniform went inside and did a search for Mum. Found her in the bathroom in more blood than I've ever seen in my life.'

Pharaoh screws up her eyes. 'Two kids, they said on the way over . . .'

'The youngest didn't wake up until one of the uniforms came and scooped him up. Little bugger went nuts. There was proper screaming. They're with one of the uniformed sergeants now, down the street at a neighbour's house. We're trying to get hold of any other family.'

'Dad?'

'Lives abroad. They're divorced.'

Pharaoh nods. 'How much did they see?'

Percy shrugs, but not unkindly. He just doesn't know.

Pharaoh says nothing for a moment. She turns, as if to say something to somebody behind her, then remembers he isn't here. She gives a nod to Percy and pulls out her phone. She is scrolling down to McAvoy's number when she stops herself. Thinks of the bags under his eyes and the teething, red-faced baby he keeps trying not to mention at work. She decides he deserves another couple of hours. Sometimes, when the world seems more ghastly than usual, she likes to think of him asleep. It soothes her. When she pictures him, he is peaceful, bare-chested and flat on his back, baby in one arm and Roisin in the other. She enjoys the vision for a second, then puts her phone away. She gives a wave and tells Percy to lead on. She pulls a pair of blue plastic bags from a pocket and slips them over her boots, then tucks her hands into her pockets to avoid the temptation of touching anything. Then she follows him into the house.

As she steps inside, she hears sirens, growing closer. She hears more tyres grinding to a stop by the road. It's beginning, she thinks. Won't be long until the press are here, waking up any neighbour still lucky enough to be asleep and asking them precisely how sad they are that a neighbour has been bled out on her bathroom floor.

'Body's upstairs. You need to see?'

At the foot of the stairs, Pharaoh pauses. She can already imagine the scene. She has seen scores of bodies in her career and accepts it as part of her job. She no longer shudders at the thought of flesh and bone torn open, and the only time she can't stop her eyes from filling with tears is when the corpse before her is that of a child. But this is a *mum*. A woman only a couple of years older than herself, who put her kids to bed, sat up for a while, then walked up these stairs for the very last time. She feels herself grow warm across her back and shoulders. Feels her cheeks flush.

Too much wine, she thinks. *For God's sake, don't cry.*

'I'll have a look downstairs first,' she says, running her tongue around her lips and scrubbing her mouth with the cuff of her jacket. 'Get the lay of the land.'

'Okay, Guv. I'll be around.'

Pharaoh enters the living room and the sheer normality of it all nearly brings her to her knees. The pictures on the walls break her heart, and it is all she can do not to mentally superimpose tears and open mouths onto the smiling faces that stare down at her.

She breathes out, slowly. Rubs her hand over her face and opens her mouth as wide as it will go. There is a satisfying click from her jawbone, then she shakes her head and gives an elaborate stretch. All of these movements represent a transformation: the putting on of another form. She is getting dressed. Becoming who she needs to be.

From the pocket of her coat, she feels a vibration.

'Pharaoh,' she says, into the phone.

'Detective Superintendent, this is Ken Cooper from the Press Association. We understand there has been a major incident—'

Pharaoh cuts the call. Switches the phone off. Looks at the wall and the pictures of Yvonne Dale with her two happy lads.

Feels a warmth for the woman. Decides this will be the picture she gives the press. Decides too that it will be the one she keeps in her mind, whatever she sees when she goes upstairs.

She turns, and sees the address book on the arm of the chair. The mobile phone, plugged in by the wall. Forensics will get to it eventually. Everything in the damn house will be printed and catalogued, photographed and entered into the system. Everything will be done properly, in time. Court cases are won and lost on whether the right serial number is entered into the right evidence bags. Murderers have walked free because the police have been unable to prove that key forensic evidence never left their sight on its way from the crime scene to the lab and the storage room. She takes a pair of polythene gloves from her inside pocket and rolls them on. Were McAvoy here, she would make a crack about him enjoying watching her do it. Might even insist he picture her wearing nothing but these and a pair of welly boots. She does it to get a reaction. She does it to warm him up. She does it because she knows that even for a fraction of a second, the image appears in his head. And she likes that. Likes it more than she should.

Pharaoh picks up the address book. It's full of scribbles and crossings out, probably only legible to the author. She puts it back down again and squats down by the phone. It's a similar make to her own, so she navigates its complex settings without too much difficulty. She finds the call log. Hull area code. She screws up her eyes, somehow already knowing what will happen when she hits redial.

The phone rings nearly a dozen times. Then a voice she recognises answers the call.

'Family Liaison. Longman household. This is PC Bob Tracy.'

'Bob?'

'Who's that?'

'This is Trish Pharaoh.'

'Sorry, Guv, didn't recognise the number. Half asleep, actually. What's happening?'

Pharaoh pauses. 'Have you had any phone calls this evening from an Yvonne Dale?'

'No, Guv. I've answered every call. But there have been loads of people ringing. Condolences, you know. Hang on . . .'

In the background, Pharaoh hears the Family Liaison Officer telling somebody not to worry. Tells them just to go back to bed. This is what the FLOs are for. It's what they're damn good at. They provide a little comfort and a lot of help. They answer the phones for a couple of days. They keep the press away. They sleep over and make tea and try to help the household forget that one of their number has had their chest caved in while walking home from work.

'Sorry about that. No, there's been no Yvonne. But like I said, the phone's barely stopped ringing. Why?'

Pharaoh doesn't answer. She's staring at the mantelpiece and the picture of the woman who lies dead and bled out in the bathroom above.

'I'll call you back. Don't worry.'

Pharaoh sits down on the carpet and leans against the wall, thinking hard. Two women. Two apparent innocents. Mums. Average, likeable, decent. Her mind conjures connections. Links. Bonds. She purses her lips, closes her eyes, then switches her phone back on. Her call is answered on the second ring, and in the background, a baby is crying. It sounds like it has been for some time.

'We've got another one,' says Pharaoh, by way of greeting. 'And they knew each other.'

8

Tuesday morning. 8.14 a.m.

Sky the colour of damp stone. Air fizzing with static, thick with dirty heat.

Aector McAvoy, both hands on the steering wheel, face and neck shaved and sore.

Buttoned up to the throat.

Sweating through grey shirt, old school tie, navy blue waistcoat and trousers.

He's pressing buttons on the dashboard to try and make the air conditioning blow out something other than this recycled warm air.

50 mph on Beverley Bypass. It's a 60 zone, but nobody else in East Yorkshire seems to know that, so he has to go at the pace of the Volvo driver in front. He takes a slow left into standing traffic, crawling past roadworks and cones. Drifts around three roundabouts. The windows are open but there isn't a breath of breeze to cool the gloss of perspiration that is already sticking his cowlick of ginger hair to his forehead.

Finally, a left turn, into a pretty village of old-fashioned, white-painted cottages and detached five-bedroomed homes: Audis in the driveways and Fiat 500s nose to bumper at the kerbside.

McAvoy likes Kirk Ella. It's a dainty, old-fashioned sort of place that looks as though it would be more at home thirty miles to the north. It feels like a suburb of York or Harrogate, but is only eight miles from the centre of Hull.

Elaine Longman lives on Hogg Lane, a tiny little street a stone's throw from St Andrew's Church and the centre of the village. It's a white-painted property with chunky sash windows and a red front door – one of a row set back from the road and which all share the same long picket fence. Elaine's has a hanging basket at the front, which looks well cared for.

McAvoy gives his policeman's knock; brisk and efficient, a pause between the fourth and fifth beats.

Elaine opens the door. She's wearing a simple white vest and a pair of linen trousers. Her eyes are so swollen and dark that it looks as though she has smeared coal dust beneath them, and the burst blood vessels and capillaries in her cheeks betray the fact she has been vomiting. McAvoy wonders if she opened a bottle or two last night, or whether grief just gnawed at her guts until she gagged on it.

'Aector,' she says, quietly. She manages a half-smile. 'Did I say that right?'

McAvoy nods. 'Very good, Elaine. Shall I try a Hull accent in return?'

'Order me a dry white wine,' she says, stepping back into the house and gesturing for him to follow. 'Or a vodka and coke.'

'Drar whart wharn,' says McAvoy, his mouth forming the syllables like a goldfish. 'Vodka and curk.'

'Arrived this morning. Talking on a mobile while driving. That's me up to nine points. One more and I lose my licence.'

McAvoy doesn't know what to say. 'It arrived this morning?'

She nods, then turns the action into a shake of the head. 'Just what I need, isn't it? I thought it was something to do with Mum . . .'

'It will have been sent out last week,' says McAvoy, aware that he is gabbling, unsure whether to defend the police or commiserate with her for the shittiness of the situation. 'They come second class. It's all automated. They wouldn't have known . . .'

Elaine shrugs and picks up her pen, filling in her details in the automatic guilty plea section. 'We weren't even moving. I was in a traffic jam. I phoned Mum to ask her to pick up Lucas.'

McAvoy says nothing. Just goes back to the tea and listens as she sniffs. When he returns to the table, her eyes are red and the backs of her hands are wet. He wishes he could make a phone call and tell her he will take care of it. Wishes he had that power, then realises that he wouldn't know what to do with it even if he did. Can imagine driving himself crazy trying to decide what is right and what is wrong. Here, now, he doesn't know whether giving Elaine a fixed-penalty notice for a minor driving infraction is *just*. But were he sitting in the kitchen of somebody who had lost a loved one in a road accident caused by somebody talking on a mobile while driving, he would be agreeing with their contention that blasé motorists should be strung up. He knows this about himself. Hates it, too.

Elaine gestures at herself and creases her face into a damp, half-hearted smile. 'Mess, aren't I?'

'You're doing great.'

'You think?'

'You're the one that Detective Superintendent Pharaoh and I thought we should see about this. You're the one holding it together and best able to assist in the investigation.'

Elaine gives him a puzzled look. 'There's been a development? Do you have someone?'

McAvoy raises his hands to slow her. Takes a sip of tea. After yesterday's meeting with Darren Robb he had called her and informed her that at this stage, her ex-partner was not being treated as a suspect. She had accepted the news with some relief, though she had immediately begun to ask where that left them. McAvoy had promised to keep her informed, even before he got the call from Pharaoh in the early hours and an instruction to get his arse over to the Longman house as soon as the sun came up. A call to the FLO suggested that nobody there was in any fit state to be any use to anybody, so he had elected to speak to Elaine instead.

'We haven't got anybody yet, no,' he says. 'But yes, there's been a development. Can I ask you if you know somebody called Yvonne Dale?'

Elaine squeezes her fist with her palm, thinking hard. 'Rings a bell, maybe. I don't know. Why?'

McAvoy takes a breath. 'She was murdered last night in her home in Barton. Cut with a knife. Bled to death.'

Elaine closes her eyes and puts both hands to her mouth, steepled at the fingertips. Her voice catches as she speaks. 'That's horrible.'

'Yvonne tried to call your mum's house last night, Elaine. Shortly before she died.'

There is silence in the room. Elaine simply looks at McAvoy, her bottom lip trembling, before she throws her hands up. 'I don't know! Were they friends? Why did she want Mum?'

McAvoy puts his hand on her shoulder again, as if trying to soothe a skittish horse. 'Ssh, just breathe for a second. Elaine, I need you to think hard about this. Here, I have a picture . . .'

Elaine pushes her chair back. 'I don't want to see. I can't let any more of this inside me . . .'

Fresh tears spill and McAvoy finds himself putting the picture away. He forces himself not to. Insists that he does his job as a police officer before he allows himself to become a human being.

'Please, just take a look.'

Despite herself, Elaine examines the image on McAvoy's mobile phone. At the large lady in the black swimsuit, floppy hat and sarong.

'She looks nice,' says Elaine, sniffing. 'I'm sorry, though, I don't know her. I don't know why she'd want Mum,'

McAvoy tries not to let the disappointment show on his face. He drains his tea. Begins to stand, then stops as he remembers the other thing that was bothering him.

'Elaine, last time we spoke you mentioned your mum was a lifesaver. Can I ask what you meant by that?'

Through the tears, Elaine gives a proud little grin. 'Means a lot of things, I guess. Means she was always helping people when they needed it most. She would do anything for anybody.'

'Oh.' McAvoy looks away. 'I thought you meant . . .'

Elaine opens her mouth. 'You mean actual lifesaving? Oh yeah, she was trained. Part of her job, I think. She went on a course, years ago. Came in handy, too.'

'Go on.'

'She never really told me much about it. She gave CPR to somebody though, on a long weekend in Bridlington. I think it was some drunk bloke bumped his head. She didn't speak much about it, to be honest.'

McAvoy's lips have formed a tight line. 'Do you know when this was?'

'Maybe fifteen years ago? A bit less? I'll have been at college, I think.'

'Would your dad know more?'

'Maybe.' She rubs a hand over her face. 'Why, is it important?'

McAvoy looks away, scratching at his cheek, tongue clicking at the back of his teeth. 'Did she save the person?'

Elaine nods. 'Oh yes. Apparently it took a while. That's all she really told me about it. Broke a few ribs . . .'

She stops herself. McAvoy sees goose pimples rise on her forearms, the colour bleaching from her face and neck.

'Is that . . . no . . . is that something . . .?'

She dissolves, all ghastly thoughts and half-imagined memories. McAvoy pulls her to him and holds her, her sobs trapped within his embrace. He closes his eyes, angry at himself, unsure how much he should have said, how much he should still say. He disentangles himself and tries to get her to look up. She fights like a child, one arm beneath her chin, another behind her head, face pressed into the grain of the table. He excuses himself and walks into the living room. Makes a quick call to the control room. Comes back to sit at the kitchen table. Answers his phone before it has a chance to ring.

He listens as the civilian officer relays the information he had sought. Hangs up, eyes closed. Insides churning.

'Elaine,' he says softly.

She looks up, eyes full of so much pain that McAvoy feels his stomach lurch.

'Elaine, we can't say with absolute certainty but it looks like your mum did know Yvonne.'

She blinks, twice, to clear her vision. 'How?'

'If the dates are right then your mother was an even more impressive person than we first gave her credit for. December, fourteen years ago. Bridlington seafront. Your mum saved a man's life. She gave heart compressions while another bystander applied a tourniquet to another serious wound. That person was Yvonne Dale. They both gave witness statements. The man didn't die so there was no inquest, but the person they saved was later charged with an incident and they were called to court to give evidence. As it happened, they didn't have to go into the courtroom, but I can only presume that is how they got to know each other.'

'So why was she phoning last night?'

McAvoy looks away. 'She probably heard what happened to your mum. Was ringing to offer condolences . . .'

His phone bleeps, alerting him to an email from control. The files he has requested are being electronically downloaded and will be with him inside the hour. The officer involved in the Bridlington incident is now retired, but still lives in the area. His phone number and address are included in the message.

McAvoy looks up. Locks his jaw.

'Your mum went to Bridlington a lot?'

Elaine gives a little nod. 'She was from West Yorkshire, wasn't she? They love it, the Westies. Look, should I phone Dad? Ask him about this lady? That night? I mean, her chest. Mum's chest. That's how she died, isn't it? And this other lady who died? You said she was cut. Did they say where she applied the tourniquet? Years ago, I mean.'

126

McAvoy shakes his head. They didn't say. But he reckons he knows anyway.

Elaine stands up, pulling at her hair. 'But somebody killed her. Hours after Mum. That can't be . . . I mean, it's too much of a coincidence. I don't understand,' says Elaine, lost and tearful.

McAvoy stares at his phone, a picture, all blurred edges and uneven patterns, swimming in his vision.

'Nor do I.'

'It should be a costume party,' says Mel, over the top of her takeaway iced coffee. 'Cops and robbers! Or tarts and vicars, maybe. No, no, Disney characters. I could make the costumes.'

Roisin laughs at the thought. 'Can you see Aector agreeing to that?'

Mel blows a raspberry derisively. 'He'd agree to whatever you asked. If you told him to run to bloody Land's End and bring you back a pebble he'd be out the door before you could tell him what type you wanted.'

Roisin pauses before smiling. She isn't sure if her friend is making fun of her husband. 'Just because he would do it, doesn't mean it's fair to ask. He'd hate it.'

'Who hates costume parties?'

'Giant ginger policemen,' says Roisin, grinning. 'He doesn't like being the centre of attention, you know that.'

'But we'd all be in costume. Oh go on, Ro, it would be awesome.'

Roisin shakes her head. 'No, he'd hate it. We'll have fun anyway. Just wear something nice.'

Mel pouts. 'Wouldn't get anything to fit him anyway,' she says, trying to get a laugh.

'Don't,' says Roisin, with a little shake of her head. 'Don't make fun.'

Mel opens her mouth to speak, but closes it again. Sips her drink.

They are sitting in Mel's alterations shop on Southcoates Lane, bakingly hot in the glass-fronted, airless room. To Mel's left is a rail of clothes in polythene covers, labels pinned to cuffs and lapels. Mel is sitting behind a sewing machine, looking pretty in a short skirt and a floaty poncho patterned with butterflies. She has her feet up on the desk, pieces of tissue paper stuck between each freshly painted toe. Roisin is sitting on the windowsill, lifting up her purple vest top to feed Lilah, the baby suckling contentedly on her left breast. Her beauty kit is open beside her, a rainbow of varnishes and treasure chest of files, clippers and emery boards. She's warm, but has not yet had to reapply her mascara, or stuff any loose and frizzy hairs back into her ponytail. Still, she's regretting her black leggings and wishes she'd gone for a skirt or pair of denim shorts. She feels sticky and a little irritable.

'Coffee's nice,' says Mel, to break the silence.

Roisin smiles. 'Place on Newland Avenue that does the good cakes. Took ages to get parked. You have to go in at such a funny angle.'

'I heard they got the plans the wrong way around,' says Mel, leaning forward to check whether her toes are still tacky. 'It's madness. You have to reverse into the space but there's never a moment when the cars aren't nose to tail. You go forwards, it's . . .' she counts on her fingers. 'It's like a 260-degree maneuver. Mental.'

Roisin nods. She'd parked on a side street because it was easier. Had thought about leaving Lilah in the car as she popped in to

Planet Coffee but decided the car was too hot and there were too many odd-looking people around to risk it. Besides, if Aector found out, he would want to go spare. He wouldn't actually do it, but he'd want to, and Roisin hates her husband suffering as much as she loves his flickering moments of true happiness.

Mel is about to suggest that they close for lunch and head to the pub near the fire station, but she stops herself when she sees the shape of a customer at the frosted glass door.

'Put it away,' hisses Mel at Roisin.

Roisin looks puzzled. 'What?'

'Your boob.'

Roisin laughs. 'Bugger that.'

The door opens and a good-looking lad in his early twenties steps into the shop, bringing with him the sound of the street and the whiff of liberally sprayed deodorant. He's wearing slouchy jean shorts and a white T-shirt with a slashed neck. He's in good shape, with a pop-star look; a diamond earring in his left lobe and three stars inked on his skin. His hair is neatly tapered at the back and stylishly ruffled at the front, and the headphones that he has taken off and looped around his neck are the most expensive model Roisin knows of.

'Hi,' he says, approaching the counter and enjoying Mel's legs as she hurriedly removes the tissue from between her toes. 'I was hoping for air conditioning.'

'We had a fan,' says Mel, hopping on one leg and blowing her fringe out of her eyes. 'It was blowing everything around.'

'I know girls like that,' he says, turning to Roisin. He gives her a quick once-over, sticking out his lower lip in a sort of gesture of admiration when he notices the feeding child at her breast. 'They do that in Amsterdam too, y'know.'

'What?'

'Shop window. Goods on display. You know how it is.'

Roisin stares at him, a half-smile on her face. 'You in here to have a few inches knocked off something?'

He grins back, playing ball. 'Nothing needs lengthening, I'll tell you that.'

Mel looks between the two of them, a little confused. Roisin is always better with the customers than she is. She has a way about her. She knows what to say. Mel always feels like she's a couple of sentences behind the conversation.

'Are you picking up or dropping off?' asks Mel, and he turns his attention back to her.

'Picking up. I've got my ticket here somewhere.' He starts patting pockets. Finds a couple of receipts in his T-shirt pocket and puts his car keys, complete with BMW keyring, down on the counter.

'When did you drop it off?' asks Mel, quizzically. 'What was it?'

'Puffer jacket,' he says. 'Dark blue.' He nods at the rail. 'That one?'

Mel turns. 'No, that was another man. He was wearing 501s. Proper Levi's. I remember because we talked about them. I think he was foreign. Turkish or Kosovan or something. Are you picking it up on his behalf?'

'Yeah,' he says. 'Mate of mine.'

Mel looks apologetic. 'I need to see the ticket. Otherwise . . .'

He shrugs. Checks his back pocket. 'I can tell you all about him, if that helps. Can give you chapter and verse.'

Mel looks at Roisin and receives a tiny shake of the head. 'We're a new business. Rules are rules. If he turns up tomorrow and I've given his coat to a stranger . . .'

The young man's face hardens. He pulls out a mobile phone. 'I can call him.'

'No, that wouldn't—'

'Look, I'm sure we can sort this out. His ticket must just be in another pair of trousers, or something.'

Mel tries her most ingratiating smile. This is becoming awkward and unpleasant. 'It's the same for everybody.'

The man stares into her eyes, hard. Runs his tongue around the inside of his mouth and bites his lower lip. He's getting pissed off. 'Come on, love. It's only a coat.'

Roisin interjects, her voice empty of patience. 'She said no.'

He gives a perceptible twitch. He's getting edgy, his gestures tense and nervous. Angrily, he reaches into his back pocket and pulls out a roll of notes, neatly bound. He throws the wad down on the table.

Mel's eyes flicker to Roisin, who is busy putting Lilah back in her stroller and tucking herself away. She looks at the pair of them, and the money on the counter.

'Your horse come in?' Roisin asks, her Irish accent suddenly more marked.

'Yours has, love. Now give me the coat.' He pauses. Adds, unpleasantly: 'Please.'

Roisin gently holds up her left hand, to indicate that Mel should do nothing. Her friend is looking at the money, and Roisin can see she is weighing up the offer. It's only a coat. She could buy the real owner a new one. It doesn't matter . . .

'I'm sorry,' says Roisin, leaning back against the wall. 'It's not worth the risk.'

He double-takes. 'What fucking risk?'

'Come on, fella, you want this coat that badly? Go buy yourself ten of the bastards. You could with that much cash. Don't be bothering us. My friend here's trying to run a business. I don't know what you want, but I'd go while you have the legs to carry you.'

As she speaks, her accent becomes so thick that Mel misses a few words. The man doesn't. He snarls.

'Who the fuck do you think you are? Do you know who I am?'

Roisin laughs, softly. 'I know what you are.'

He spits on the floor. Licks his lips.

'Out of the way.'

Without another word, he walks behind the counter. Mel gives a little squeal and tries to block his way, but he puts one hand on her face and pushes her backwards, hard, against her desk. Threads and needles and £20 notes fall to the ground.

'Silly fucking bitches,' he says, grabbing at the puffer jacket on the rail. He gives it a squeeze, as if testing fruit for freshness. Nods. Turns to Mel, who is pulling herself up. 'Didn't have to be like this,' he says. 'I just forgot the ticket. Nobody else is coming for it. Why did you make a fuss?'

He bends to her face.

Hisses: 'Bitch'.

Punches her in the stomach so hard that her feet leave the floor.

'You fucking bastard.'

Roisin is standing between him and the exit, a nail file in her hand and Lilah on her hip. She doesn't look scared. She looks like she wants to stick it in his eye.

'What you going to do with that? File and polish?' He laughs at her. 'What are you, seven stone wet through? I could throw you through the fucking window.'

'You could try.'

Mel gasps behind him. 'Her husband . . . he's . . . a policeman.'

The man laughs out loud. 'Coppers don't marry pikey slags, love. Well-known fact.'

'You're not leaving,' says Roisin, matter-of-factly. She reaches into her waistband and pulls out her phone. 'I've already called them. They're on their way.'

He peers at the screen. Can see she is connected to the emergency services. He gives a mirthless laugh and moves forward, ready to shove her bodily from the door. He does not think she will swing the nail file. Does not think for one second she will get in his way.

Roisin swings the nail file. The man sees it coming and instinctively raises his arms, still holding the coat. The file rips into the material of the jacket, and as he pulls away, a cloud of dust billows up from between him and Roisin.

'You stupid, stupid bitch!'

The man is frantically examining the coat, trying to find the patch of quilting that tore. He spins it around and a large white packet falls to the ground, spilling powder like a bag of flour.

'Jesus, no . . .'

He throws himself down, scooping the powder into pockets, looking up, sweat and fear on his face as he hears sirens.

'You don't . . . you don't know what you've—'

Roisin kicks him in the balls and he doubles over, mewling like a child, powder in his hair and on his clothes.

Behind the counter, Mel pulls herself up. 'What's happening, Ro . . .'

Through the glass, they see a patrol car pulling up beside the bread delivery van. See two officers running towards the shop, barking into radios.

Roisin only has a second to react. She bends down, and scoops up the fallen money from the floor.

Then she kicks Adam Downey in the balls again, grabs the stroller, and heads for the back door.

Part Two

9

Two days later, 10.44 a.m.

The health centre on Cottingham Road. The same, airless room. The same hum of traffic and the dark shadow of the rowan tree at the window.

The same school chair.

The same reluctance to talk.

Aector McAvoy, jiggling his leg like he's playing boogie-woogie piano.

Sabine Keane. Sweating like she's just finished dancing a flamenco, but trying to keep professional. Her legs are sticking together as she tries to shift them. Her high heels are sweaty and slippy, crushing her already painful toes. She wants to reach into the bag beside her and pull out her flip-flops. Wants to open her litre bottle of water and pour it onto the back of her neck, to shake her head in a mountain stream like she's advertising shampoo . . .

'Aector, would you like some water, perhaps? It's still so muggy, isn't it? I thought there would have been a storm by now. I thought I felt rain on the way in but no, it's holding back. The sky's so ominous though, isn't it? Just really eerie.'

McAvoy gives her a polite nod. 'So psychologists are as irrational as the rest of then,' he says, trying to make his voice light. 'You still see signs and symbols where there aren't any.'

'Human nature,' says Sabine, returning his look and tone. 'We have to accept some things about ourselves, don't we? We may want to be the best versions of ourselves and have good mental health, but you still can't look at a sky like this without expecting a wolf to howl.'

McAvoy considers it. Pulls his clammy pinstripe shirt from his skin and wafts it. 'Last wolf in Britain was killed in 1743,' he says, studying her to see if she's interested in the story or in what it says about him. 'Shot near Inverness. Everybody was delighted. Big celebrations and the hunter was a hero. Funny thing is that since then, the number of deer has exploded. Half of Scotland is barren and treeless because the deer just eat through everything in their path. Scotland doesn't look like it should and it's because the wolves have gone. There are people want to reintroduce them. Can you imagine? Reintroducing wolves. I guess that would mean reintroducing hunters as well. It all goes round and round, doesn't it? Interesting idea, though.'

Sabine taps her chin with the nib of her pen, leaving a tiny blue dot. 'What do you think?'

'Me?' McAvoy looks surprised. 'I don't know enough about it. Dad thinks it's a good idea.'

'People have opinions, even when they don't know all the facts.'

McAvoy pulls on his nose, as if it will help him articulate the thought better. 'I don't have many opinions worth listening to. Maybe if I read all the reports . . .'

'But what does your gut say, Aector?'

138

He sighs. 'Why does it matter?'

'Gut instincts are important. Do you never act upon them?'

'I have them, yes. But I don't have to give in to them. They're suggestions, not impulses. A lady told me she likes how I think the other day. What do I make of that? It's not like I can take pride in it. I didn't choose to be this way. It's just how I am.'

Sabine smiles. She's fanning herself with her notes and her blonde hair is clinging to her forehead. When she reached up try the sash windows, she had exposed unshaved armpits and the label on a Primark bra. McAvoy had looked away. He doesn't want to judge his psychologist any more than he wants her to judge him.

'You seem to hold yourself in quite close control, Aector. There must be times when you have given in to those suggestions. When you've let go. Your file suggests—'

A sudden buzzing interrupts the conversation. Somewhere between embarrassed and grateful, McAvoy pulls out his phone. He holds up a finger to suggest he will be quick.

'Sergeant McAvoy? This is George Goss. You've been ringing me. Can I help?'

McAvoy gives Sabine an apologetic glance. Decides to follow her advice and act on impulse. Gestures that he will call her to set up another appointment, and bolts for the door. He hears the psychologist calling his name, but tells himself that he doesn't.

'Mr Goss, yes, I wondered if I could come and see you . . .'

An hour later, McAvoy is pulling into the driveway of a terraced property on North Road, at the centre of the Gypsyville estate. It hasn't got the greatest of reputations and the house prices are through the floor, but McAvoy has always rather liked this little network of quiet roads a stone's throw from the old trawling hub. There's no litter in the gutters or dog shit on the pavement and the people who live here strike him as the sort who would take it upon themselves to scrub a neighbour's wall if somebody had spray-painted graffiti on the brickwork.

George Goss's house is the neatest in the row. There are roses in the front garden, the exact variety neatly labelled in blue ink on white labels, and there are no weeds growing in the cracks between the paving slabs that lead to the front door.

McAvoy is fumbling in a pocket for his warrant card when the door swings open.

George Goss is in good shape. He's mid-sixties, and though his face has the waxy jowls of a man who likes a cheese course after his dessert, he's not overly portly and has a full head of grey-black hair. He's wearing a pair of polyester trousers with a neat seam down the front, with a short-sleeved checked shirt. As he extends his hand, McAvoy notices the mottling of liver spots that starts at his knuckles and carries on halfway up his arm. He's a man who likes his drink, but McAvoy has never met a retired copper who doesn't.

'I phoned Tom Spink,' says Goss, brusquely, by way of greeting. 'He said you're not a dickhead.'

McAvoy gives a laugh, pleased that Pharaoh's old boss had vouched for his credentials. 'Praise from Caesar.'

'Spink's not a dickhead either.'

'I'm sure he'd be delighted to hear it.'

'Still writing, is he? Books and stuff? His house fallen into the sea yet?'

McAvoy nods. 'He's writing a book on some unsolved cases, I think. Just finished doing something for the top brass. History of

Humberside Police, sort of thing. I'm not sure about his house. That coastline's eroding fast . . .'

McAvoy follows the retired inspector into a comfortable square living room. He figures this is the family room. It's a nice space, all sand-coloured wallpaper and pictures of Whitby seafront in tasteful frames. There is a three-seat leather sofa and matching armchair, angled to view the small flat-screen TV beneath the window. Half a dozen different pairs of spectacles lie jumbled on the video recorder and DVD player on its fancy glass stand, and a picture of a boy in school uniform grins toothlessly from the mantelpiece, above an electric fire. There is a catapult on the windowsill, with some rolled-up pieces of Blu-tack. McAvoy gives the object some thought. Considers the pretty garden, with its neatly tended roses and wall-climbing ivy. Decides that either George Goss or his wife are not big fans of cats.

'Back in a sec,' says Goss.

McAvoy hears cupboards opening and closing. Water pouring on teabags. The chink-chink-chink of spoon on mug. Hears it again. Guesses he's getting a mug of tea.

'Here you go,' says Goss, handing him a giant cup. 'Guessed you took sugar.'

'I do.'

Goss spreads his arms and makes fun of himself. 'Once a detective, always a detective, eh? Sit down.'

McAvoy sinks into the sofa, careful not to spill his sloshing drink. Goss gives a tiny nod of appreciation. 'Missus is at Sainsbury's,' he says. 'Her daughter takes her once a week.'

McAvoy notes the use of the word 'her'. Goss smiles.

'Yeah, I said "her". Not mine. I've got two of my own from my first marriage. Any of that important?'

There is silence in the room for a moment while McAvoy decides how to play this interview. The old boy seems to swing between welcoming and brusque with every sentence. He wonders if it was his trademark when he was still in the force. Wonders whether the retired inspector liked to play both roles in the 'good cop/bad cop' game.

'Mr Goss, I . . .'

'George, please.'

'George, I'm attached to the Serious and Organised Crime Unit in Humberside Police. We're investigating two murders that took place within the space of twenty-four hours. Our enquiries have demonstrated—'

Goss takes a loud slurp of tea and gives an exaggerated nod. 'I know what it's about, son. You said in your messages. You want to know about Sebastien Hoyer-Wood, yeah?'

McAvoy pauses, not liking to be steered. He considers the man in the armchair opposite. Imagines his day-to-day life. Is he bored? How does he fill his days? Does he like to talk about past cases or does he hate being reminded of the things he has done and the bodies he has stood over during a thirty-year police career? McAvoy decides that he likes to talk, but likes to tell a story rather than answer questions. Sees him as a pub raconteur who doesn't appreciate interruptions. He decides to just let the chat play out. He nods, sits back in the sofa.

Goss settles back too, mug resting on his thigh, his other hand tapping on the arm of the chair.

'Hoyer-Wood,' he says, again. 'Nasty business.'

'Hmm?' says McAvoy, coaxingly.

'More people should have heard of him.'

'I read the file.'

142

DAVID MARK

Goss makes a scornful noise. 'File? Date of birth, date of arrest and a couple of witness statements? They don't know the half of it.'

'Why don't you fill in the gaps?'

Goss stares for a moment, then appears to come to a decision. 'Hoyer-Wood was a posh boy,' he says, sighing. 'Mid-thirties when we got him. Nearly qualified as a doctor, if you can believe that. Left university under a cloud four years into his training. Went abroad for a bit and trained as a sports physiotherapist. That's what he was doing when all this came out. Had a private practice at his nice big house out on the road to York. Nice gaff. Don't know who's got it now . . .'

'You found all this out in the background probe, did you? After he was arrested?'

Goss nods. 'I went to town on the bugger. Spoke to everybody who'd ever met him, it felt like. We thought the case was watertight.'

McAvoy waits. Drinks his tea. Listens to the silence and stares at the carpet. When he looks up, Goss is staring at nothing. Picturing things only he can see.

'We don't know how long he'd been at it. How many there were. He liked them to watch, you see. That was his thing.' He snarls. Swallows, as if there is something vile in his mouth. 'It wasn't the actual sex that he got off on. It was the look on their husbands' faces. Their kids'. Their mums' and dads' . . .'

McAvoy breathes out. 'Jesus.'

Goss nods. 'He'd wander about in crowds. Take a shine to a family. Maybe a couple. Maybe some middle-aged woman pushing her old dad in a wheelchair. And then he'd just choose. Pick who he liked, and follow them. He'd just bloody choose!'

Goss slaps the arm of the chair, then gives a joyless little laugh. 'First one we heard about was a young mum in a holiday cottage in Aldbrough. Little village on the coast there. Her and her two boys, up here for a little break. All she could afford, poor cow. Petrol station attendant reckons Hoyer-Wood was there at the same time as she was filling up her car, second day of her holidays, but they'd wiped the CCTV. Wasn't much good in those days, anyway. Reckon that's where he took a shine to her, though. Just caught his eye.'

Goss bites on his lip. 'He broke into her place the next night. Boys were sleeping in her bed with her. She said later they'd been scared. They'd heard noises the night before. Asked if they could sleep in with Mum. She woke up with a knife against her cheek. Him looking down at her. He wore a surgical mask. Can you believe that? Like he was carrying out a procedure. He woke the kids. Wasn't rough with them. Just told them to wake up. Told the oldest to put the light on. Then he raped her. Just like that. Held a knife to her throat and told the boys that if they tried to move he'd open her windpipe. Then when he was done he said that if she told anybody, he'd come back and do it again. And again . . .'

McAvoy stares at the floor. 'She reported it?'

'Not at first. Not until after. Not until we were investigating the one we got him for.'

'In Bridlington?'

Goss nods. 'This was a couple of years later. He'd got good at it by then. Perfected his technique, so to speak. Wasn't enough for just the kids to see. He was into husbands by now. Same MO. Breaking in when they were asleep. He added a bit more of a kick this time, though. Started playing with lighter fluid.'

McAvoy looks up. 'What?'

Goss nods, finding it hard to believe even as he relays it. 'When they were asleep, all curled together. He'd spray them with lighter fluid. Then he'd stand there with a lighter. Tell the bloke to stay still or he'd set fire to the three of them.'

'The three?'

'Oh aye, he'd be covered in the stuff himself. Blokes would wake up with this stranger in their bedroom threatening to set them on fire. And they'd do what he said. They'd stand against the wall and they'd cry and call him a bastard and threaten him with all sorts. But they wouldn't stop him. They wouldn't do a thing. When he was done he'd tell them the same thing – he would come back. And nobody wanted to report it, anyway. Not the blokes. Not the blokes who were too bloody scared to stop a stranger raping their woman in the middle of the night.'

McAvoy briefly imagines how the men felt. Imagines the fear and the rage and the helplessness. Then he imagines the women. Imagines their sheer, indescribable terror.

Goss gives a smile. 'I know what you're thinking, son. Thinking you'd never do what he asked, yeah? I thought that too. But these weren't cowardly blokes, lad. These were ordinary fellas. Blokes who would wade into a scrap if you asked them to. But there's something about fire, isn't there? Something that stops you dead. Hoyer-Wood knew that. He would have kept going if he hadn't messed up.'

'Bridlington, yes?'

Goss nods. 'Picked the wrong family, I'll tell you that. Locals, they were. Not holidaymakers . . .'

McAvoy sits forward. 'Sorry George, can I just ask, were these cases all seaside towns? Was that part of his thinking?'

'No, there were a couple in little towns as well. Or at least, we think there were. Half of this is guesswork, son. We put this together afterwards, based on where we knew he had been, and with a lot of promises that none of the information we received would ever be shared. No, we think he liked the seaside because it's where families and couples spend happy times. You know how it is when you see a family enjoying themselves at the beach. All that candyfloss and kiss-me-quick hats. That's what he liked.'

'But this happened in December, yes?'

'You can get cheap breaks in places like Bridlington in winter. You still find holidaymakers. Maybe he'd seen this family before and got a taste for them then and couldn't wait until the snows thawed. We don't know.'

'What happened?'

'Same thing,' says Goss, wearily. 'Woke a family up. Cromwell, their name was. But he hadn't done his research properly. Didn't know the Cromwells like we did.'

'Bad news?'

Goss opens his eyes wide to demonstrate his strength of feeling.

'He didn't cooperate? The dad?'

'Did for about five seconds. Did as he was told. Stood against the wall and watched Hoyer-Wood stick his cock in his wife, holding a lighter to her hair.'

'He intervened?'

'He hasn't got many gears, Johnny Cromwell. He's not one of life's thinkers.'

'And Hoyer-Wood dropped the lighter?'

'We don't think he'd ever have done what he threatened to. He just liked having the power. Soon as Johnny-boy came at him

146

he panicked. Tried to flick the wheel on the lighter and dropped the thing. Johnny threw him around like he was made of straw. Beat the shit out of him.'

'There was a fire, though, yes? The reports I read—'

'Johnny told us that Hoyer-Wood did it himself. Flicked the wheel on the lighter. That's bollocks. It was Johnny. Set the bastard on fire.'

McAvoy purses his lips. 'Was he naked? Hoyer-Wood? During the attacks?'

'Aye,' says Goss. 'Just the surgical mask. We found his clothes outside Cromwell's house. We reckon he used to get changed before and after.'

'Condom?'

'Yeah. Put it on before he came in.'

McAvoy considers it. 'That rather suggests—'

'That the anticipation of it got him hard? Yep. Sick bastard, like I said.'

'What happened next?'

Goss gives a laugh. 'Threw himself out the bloody window, didn't he? First floor, straight through the glass. Tore himself to bits and hit the ground like he'd fallen from an aeroplane.'

'Bloody hell.'

'He got up, though. Was thick snow that night. That took some of the impact out of his fall and put the flames out. Staggered a few hundred yards before Cromwell caught up with him again.'

'This was on the seafront, yes? There were people around . . .'

'That's what saved the bastard. People in pubs and chip shops, looking out as this battered and burned naked bloke stumbled past the window.'

'They stopped Cromwell? Stopped him from killing him?'

'Couple of blokes held him back. They didn't know what was happening.'

'And Hoyer-Wood?'

'Went into shock. Heart stopped. His leg had been cut coming through the glass. He'd fractured his skull, too.'

'And Philippa Longman? Yvonne Dale?'

Goss breathes out, slowly. 'I didn't realise when I heard about the poor woman in Barton. But yeah, I remember Philippa. She was up in Bridlington for a mini-break or something. Over from West Yorkshire. She pumped his heart. Blew in his lungs. Brought him back.'

'Yvonne?'

'I've brought her to mind since I got your message. Quick thinker, that one. Pulled off her tights and tied them around the wound. Tourniquet, it's called, yeah? Then she sat there in the blood and snow holding his hand until the ambulances arrived. They say you shouldn't do that now. Guidelines have changed. You should just hold a compress over the wound. But back then, she did the right thing.'

'They saved him?'

'For a while. His heart stopped again in the ambulance. They brought him back. Then they operated. Saved him, though.' He shakes his head. 'They should have let him die.'

McAvoy finds himself nodding and then stops himself. 'They didn't know. And even if they did—'

'The local uniforms turned up to arrest Cromwell. He told them everything. That's when we got the call. CID.'

'And?'

'And it unfolded, lad. What he'd done. What he liked.'

'How did you find out about the other incidents?'

Goss points with his chin, as if Hoyer-Wood's home is at the end of the garden. 'Searched his place. Found his appointments book. Had a look at his magazine collection. Proper police work, lad. Appealed for witnesses and got a call from the Aldbrough lass. She said she could never give evidence, but thought we should know what he did to her. I think she wanted to know, more than anything. Wanted to know if it was the same man. Why he'd done it. Who he was. Just couldn't bring herself to give a statement.'

'And the others?'

Goss closes his eyes. 'Hoyer-Wood liked to write. In court, they said it was just fantasy. It wasn't. He wrote it all down afterwards. Described every bloody moment of it.'

'What did he say? When he came out of surgery, I mean?'

Goss laughs. 'He didn't say much, lad. He was a wreck. Paralysed down one side. Couldn't walk. No motor skills in one half of his face.'

'But he was charged?'

'We charged him with what we knew for certain. One count of rape. Figured that when we got him for that, we could start to build a case around any others that decided to give evidence. The important thing was locking him up.'

'What happened?'

Goss grinds his teeth. 'His posh friends happened, that's what. A psychiatrist said he was unfit to stand trial. Judge bought it.'

'But you didn't?'

'He was an evil little bastard but he knew what he was doing. The shrink was an old university friend. They'd studied together. Half his old university chums sent the judge letters saying what a super chap Hoyer-Wood was. They said they didn't believe he had acted maliciously but was suffering from some mental disorder or something.'

McAvoy squeezes the handle of his empty mug. 'He was sent to a mental facility?'

'He was sent to his mate's place. Private healthcare facility, licensed by the Home Office to look after dangerous patients.' Goss sneers. 'Got the licence about a week after Hoyer-Wood was arrested. It was a holiday camp! Went to live there in bloody luxury.'

McAvoy rolls his head from side to side, his neck suddenly stiff and sore. He becomes aware how cool it is in here. Wonders where the chill is coming from. What is raising the goose pimples on his skin.

'And he's never stood trial? Never been brought to account?'

'No.'

'Cromwell?'

Goss shrugs, suddenly looking a little older. 'Got sent down a couple of years later for attempted murder. Row in a bar. He never did control that temper. Still inside.'

'So where is Hoyer-Wood now?'

'Went to stay at his pal's asylum, not far from here. Was there a couple of years then moved to another facility. He's still classified as unfit to stand trial, and there's no hunger to change that. I heard he suffered a major stroke a few years back that left him worse than ever. He's a cripple. Can't do anybody any harm and has to piss and shit in a bag. The thinking is that for a man with appetites like his, that's punishment enough.'

McAvoy considers it. 'No, it's not,' he says, finally.

'Tom Spink was right about you.'

They share a tired smile and McAvoy scratches at his eyebrows, trying to formulate his thoughts.

'The murders I'm investigating . . .'

Goss holds his gaze. 'Bloody big coincidence if it's nothing to do with this, but I don't know how it could be. How, or why . . .'

'They saved his life. Saved the life of somebody who did terrible things and ruined the lives of others.'

Goss nods. 'I don't envy you,' he says, ruefully. 'Bloody shame, all this. I only spoke to Yvonne the once and Philippa not much more than that, but they were nice ladies. Didn't deserve that. If somebody is punishing them, whoever they are, then they're as bad as Hoyer-Wood. And he was the fucking worst.'

McAvoy stares into the bottom of his mug.

Goss softens his voice. 'I made it with a bag, son. You won't find answers in your tea leaves.'

McAvoy runs his hands through his hair, wishing he had started taking notes when the conversation began. It would help him, now, to be able to read back through what he has discovered. To busy his mind, his eyes, his fingers, with something other than the thoughts banging like heartbeats in his head.

'The facility. The one his friend ran . . .'

'On the way to Driffield.'

'You ever go?'

'Tried to. His mate wouldn't agree to the interview. Said it would interfere with his treatment.'

'You push?'

'Had to apply to the Home Office. Orders came down to leave it alone.'

McAvoy reaches into his pocket and pulls out his notebook.

'I'll need some names and addresses. Whatever you can remember . . .'

Goss considers. 'I promised the people who came forward I'd never share.'

McAvoy says nothing. Lets the old man consider it.

He shakes his head. 'I'll see what I can rustle up. First thing you want to do is visit the shrink who got him off.'

McAvoy raises an eyebrow. 'You think?'

'There are questions to be answered, lad.' He stares hard at McAvoy.

'On the road to Driffield, yeah?'

Goss reaches into his shirt pocket and pulls out a scrap of paper. 'I wrote the address down before you arrived, lad. Figured it would be your next stop. I think it's in new hands, but there are some ghosts at that place worth exorcising.'

McAvoy starts to stand then stops himself.

'Does it get easier?' he asks, softly. 'Living with it. The ones that beat the system? Got away with it?'

Goss is silent for a second then lets out his breath in a hollow laugh. Shakes his head apologetically.

Come on, Mark, please, just a text, just a trio of kisses or a promise to call later . . .

Helen sits at her desk, staring at the screen, desperate for her email inbox to light up. She hasn't heard from Mark since he slipped away from her home in the middle of the night. She woke unsure if he had ever been there. The warm residue of pleasure and the stickiness between her legs were the only evidence that they had made love. That they had made love the way they do in the movies and in a way that she wants to be made love to again.

Her inbox flashes and she clicks on the screen. It's not him. Just a message from another police force about Adam Downey:

the little shit who's been saying 'no comment' for two days and who they are about to charge with possessing a large quantity of cocaine.

Colin Ray's team were among the last to hear about what had happened at the alterations shop on Southcoates Lane. The incident went to Drugs Squad, who held on to it for as long as they could. Their detective inspector, a fast-track university graduate by the name of Rick Breverton, had done the first interview with Downey. He had done some decent work on the basics. Got his name. A list of known associates. Even persuaded the lass from the shop to give a statement. Breverton didn't deserve to be called the names that Colin Ray threw in his direction when they both met with the Assistant Chief Constable and the head of CID to decide who was going to be given the case. Ray was adamant that it fell within his remit. He had no doubt that the lad was involved with the drugs gang he had been tracking for months. Breverton believed the young man was more likely linked to an older, more established outfit within the city, and therefore nothing to do with Ray's wild imaginings about the elite new organised crime outfit outmuscling the old guard. For an easy life, ACC Everett had given the case to Ray, who had briefed his team immediately. Given them chapter and verse on Adam Downey.

Downey is twenty-four, and lives on the Victoria Dock estate by the waterfront. The area was built with London's Docklands in mind and marketed as an 'urban village' but has failed to draw the middle classes away from the West Hull villages, and large chunks of the area have been bought up by private landlords to rent out at reduced rates. It's a mixture of hard-working families and dodgy bastards. Downey falls into the second category. He did his first stretch in a young offender institute at sixteen, having been caught using stolen credit cards. None of the other incidents on his record include violence, but he's no stranger to drugs. A year ago, he was arrested when a van on board the *Pride of Rotterdam* ferry was found to have packets of pure cocaine stitched into the upholstery. CCTV showed Downey getting out of the van when it boarded. He and the driver were both charged, but the case collapsed before it got to court. Downey had done a few months on remand in Hull Prison. Ray told his troops that he believed it was during his time inside that Downey joined the new outfit. The old punk rocker who used to have a hand in local supply and demand had disappeared not long afterwards.

'He's in the big leagues now,' Ray had barked, tugging at his tie as if involved in some auto-asphyxiation sex game. His face was greasy with sweat and his hair, slicked back from his ratty face, had only been combed at the front. It stuck up on his crown like an antenna and gave him the look of a crazed preacher as he stomped about in front of the whiteboard and scribbled illegible theories and scrawled lines between suspects' names.

'It was a handover, plain and simple,' he'd snorted in a spray of spit. 'They were trying something. One lad drops the coat off, pockets full of coke. Passes the ticket to our boy. Our lad's a thick piece of shit and loses the ticket. Reckons he'll charm the coat out of the shopkeeper. She says no and the next thing it turns nasty.'

Shaz Archer had chipped in next, sitting directly in front of the fan so her hair billowed theatrically around her and the lads could see her nipples through her white sleeveless blouse.

'The call to emergency services came from an unregistered mobile phone. The shopkeeper says she has no idea who called

154

it in. Must have been somebody passing by the window. We have our doubts. I think she has a friend who didn't want to hang around. We'll look into that. For now, Adam isn't talking and we're going to charge him. See who he calls. What he does next. We've got a chance here, people. They've fucked up. They've hired themselves a right bloody monkey, and if they don't want their operation going tits-up, they'll want to get him out of custody before he can talk to us. Col has a few friends inside who are going to make sure he doesn't enjoy himself too much. Let's shake the tree and see what falls out, yeah?'

Helen had registered only mild surprise that the incident had occurred in the shop she had stood outside only the other day. She had barely taken anything in. Her mind had been elsewhere. Had she gone too far? Should she have slept with Mark on the first date? She can't concentrate. Her mind is screeching with fears and uncertainties. Is he playing it cool? Should she play it cool too? Should she just write it off as one great night?

She is staring blankly at the PNC database. She can't find any connection between Downey and the driver who chucked piss over Shaz Archer, but she's hardly concentrating on the task.

Her email lights up. It's a message from an address she doesn't recognise.

Subject: **'Thought you might like to see this'**

The email contains a video clip. The file size suggests it's only a few seconds long, so she mutes the sound and opens it up.

She sees herself. Herself on all fours, bare arse and curved spine: her sex pointing catlike at the sky. Sees Mark. Naked. Face in shadow. He's drizzling a line of white powder onto her buttocks. Lowering his face. Snorting it up. Rubbing his fingers on her gums. She's looking back at him, lustful and dreamy, mouthing 'do it, go on' and then losing herself in pleasure, powder sparkling in her smile . . .

Here, now, she starts to shake. Feels her whole body tremble. Can barely control her fingers for long enough to close the video down before anybody else can see. Just stares at the blank screen, as sickness crawls up her throat.

Another email flashes up, from the same address.

With fingers that quiver, hands that do not feel like her own, she opens the message.

Blinks away hot tears as she reads the words.

We will be in touch. x

10

Friday. 9.46 a.m. The sky a dark shroud: crumpled and creased above a landscape of dying greens and browns.

Aector McAvoy's people-carrier heading north; dead flies on the windscreen and fluffy toys in the boot. A local DJ talking nonsense on the radio, and sweat on the inside of the glass.

'She was brave,' says Pharaoh, fanning herself with her notes. 'Standing up to him. Saying no. Lot of people would have filled their pants.'

McAvoy gives a grunt of agreement. 'You never know, do you? How you'll react?'

'She gave him a couple of good ones, according to Colin Ray. Was my grandma taught me that, as a kid. Go for the soft places. Eyes and bollocks.'

McAvoy watches the road. Nods along to the song playing in his head. It's a salsa number and always arrives, unbidden, in his skull, when he thinks of Mel. He'd been shocked to hear what had happened at her shop. Relieved, too, to hear that Roisin hadn't been there. More than anything he'd been impressed. He didn't think Mel had it in her. Apparently some drug pusher had turned up at her shop demanding a coat containing a bumper stash of pure cocaine, and she had refused to let him take it because he hadn't got his ticket. It had all got nasty, and according to Roisin, Mel had managed to call the police in her pocket then give him a couple of swift kicks to his tender places. He'd been crying like a girl when the uniforms arrived.

'Never said a word in the interviews,' says Pharaoh. 'Colin's doing his nut.'

Bored, listless and too bloody hot, she stares out of the window. There's not much to look at. It's all green fields and sparse woodland, overgrown footpaths and villages with names that were recorded in the Domesday Book. She's seen half a dozen lay-bys where swingers could get their kicks. Took great pleasure in pointing them out to her favourite sergeant.

'Detective Inspector Archer gave it her all, apparently.' McAvoy's voice is unreadable, his expression to match. 'In the interviews, I mean.'

Pharaoh turns to him, licking her lips. 'You could be a politician, Hector.'

'Guv?' he asks, innocently.

Pharaoh lets it drop. Were she to start criticising Shaz Archer, she would never stop.

For a time, she considers the Adam Downey case, and what a good result would mean for her unit in general, and her own position within it. Were Colin Ray to bring the new outfit down, she would be hard-pressed to justify remaining head of Serious and Organised. She and Ray have fought like cat and dog ever since she got the job. He had expected the unit to be his, and had planned to make Shaz Archer his second-in-command. Pharaoh got it instead. They have very different styles, but Pharaoh at least knows that her rival's style is effective and respects his record.

He, on the other hand, thinks Pharaoh is little more than a nice pair of tits in a stab vest.

'You all right, Guv?'

Pharaoh shakes it away. Concentrates on what she had learned in this morning's briefing.

'He's shit-scared,' she says. 'Downey. I reckon they'll charge him before the day's out, whether he talks or whether he doesn't. He won't get bail, so the next few days should be interesting for the lad. Pretty bloody obvious he works for the new outfit in some capacity, but it's all guesswork. Colin Ray's going to pop a vein.' She gives the matter some thought. 'Could be worse.'

'You don't want a crack at it yourself?'

Pharaoh raises her hands to point at herself and mouth the word 'moi?' Her bangles give a clank. 'I can't be everywhere,' she says, sighing. 'Ray brought in the only significant victories we've had with this lot. He's earned the right to run with it, and to fall on his face if he does it wrong. My only contribution so far has been getting one of the units firebombed down at St Andrew's Quay. I don't think it would be well received if I marched in and took over, no matter how much I'd like to. I've got some questions I'd like to ask that shopkeeper, I know that much . . .'

McAvoy says nothing. He finds himself uncomfortable talking about what happened on Southcoates Lane. It was pure good fortune that Roisin wasn't there when Downey tried to muscle Mel. He imagines his wife in danger. Pictures her, helpless and afraid. The thought makes the hairs on his forearms rise. He imagines her giving a statement to Colin Ray. Imagines the look on the bastard's face. Passing judgement on her. On him. On his family. McAvoy is not ashamed of his wife, or her heritage. He just doesn't want to give the people that he knows to be bastards any more sticks to hit him with.

'That's nice,' says Pharaoh, nodding at his left wrist.

'Thanks Guv,' he says, and can't keep the smile from his face. Roisin had given him the new watch in bed last night. She had told him it reminded her of him. 'Precious, with a big face,' she had said, giggling and sitting cross-legged in front of him, their bedroom piled high with boxes and bags, ready for the move to their new home, their new lives. He had hugged her and stroked her hair, said thank you time and again, even as the policeman's voice in his head screamed.

Where had she got it? Where had the money come from? Christ, we're up to our eyeballs in debt and she's splashing out on a watch for me, a new mobile phone for her, football boots for Fin . . .

'Thought you were skint,' says Pharaoh, guilelessly.

'I think she'd been saving. She's been doing nails . . .'

Pharaoh nods again, losing interest. She hums a song that sounds a little Motown in origin, then begins to root through the glovebox of the people-carrier. She is worse on long journeys than either of his children. She's a terrible passenger and can't seem to help giving him directions, urging him to slow down, speed up, change gear or indicate, even though she drives like a madwoman herself.

'How do you keep it so neat?' she asks, her tone critical.

He takes his eyes off the road for a moment and glances in her direction. She's wearing black today. Head to toe. Trousers, boots, blouse and biker jacket, which she is steadfastly refusing to remove, even though she is clearly far too warm. Her hair is sticking to her forehead and clinging to her hoop earrings, and she has a sheen of perspiration on her upper lip.

'Eclectic tastes, Hector,' says Pharaoh, examining his CDs and not waiting for him to answer her previous question.

'Some of them are Roisin's . . .'

'Yeah, I can see that. Shakira. Pink. Lady Gaga.' She eyes him. 'You sure you're not a closet pop fan?'

He gives a laugh. 'Mine's the depressing stuff. That's what Roisin says.'

Pharaoh holds up a CD with a picture of a woodland clearing on the case. 'This any good?'

'Emily Barker? Superb.'

Pharaoh puts the CD in the player. After a few seconds the car is filled with mournful accordion and sad guitar, vocals about love and loss, bleeding knuckles and flying crows. The song always hits McAvoy in the heart. He can't listen to it with his eyes open, which is why he rarely plays it in the car. Pharaoh gives it a minute, then switches it off.

'Fucking hell, Hector.'

'She's amazing.'

'That your thing? Folk?'

'It's not folk. Not really. And no, it's not my thing. I don't have a thing . . .' He stops himself, chewing his lip, embarrassed. 'There's some U2 in there. Oasis.'

Pharaoh holds up another CD. 'Prodigy?'

McAvoy shrugs. '"Firestarter" was a big hit when I was at university.'

She considers the image in her mind. 'I'm not sure I can imagine that without going insane, Hector. I can't see you dancing. Not properly. Maybe a Highland fling. In a kilt. Eating haggis. On the back of the Loch Ness monster.'

McAvoy pulls a face, scowling at the road, saying nothing as Pharaoh stuffs the CDs back into the glovebox with no consideration for the careful order in which they had previously been stacked. She goes back to staring out of the window, occasionally referring to the notepad in her lap. After a while she gets bored again. 'Are we nearly bloody there?'

McAvoy had been pleased when Pharaoh had told him she was coming with him to the mental facility on the road to Driffield. She had been interested in what he had told her about Sebastien Hoyer-Wood. She even remembered hearing about the case, though she had been a young sergeant working in another patch at the time of his crimes. McAvoy's discoveries are being thought of as a lead, though the exact direction is unclear. Back at the station, Ben Nielsen is trying to find a current address for the shrink who did the medical report on Hoyer-Wood and who worked at the private asylum that McAvoy and Pharaoh are on their way to visit. They have requested the old case files and already discovered that the psychiatrist was a man called Lewis Caneva. A Google search came up with a few old academic papers and a profile in some long-defunct medical periodical, but he has clearly not been thought of as a rising star in a long time. A quick check with his professional association showed Caneva is no longer practising, and as such, the association has no record of his current whereabouts. It had all struck McAvoy as worthy of some further digging, and he had suggested a trip to the facility, which has lain dormant and for sale for the best part of a decade. Another quick sweep of some property websites revealed that Abbey Manor had just been snapped up by some multinational healthcare giant, which is seeking planning permission to transform it into a luxury home for the rich and dying.

'It just all seems to point to something,' McAvoy had said, when he filled Pharaoh in. 'I don't know what.'

Pharaoh had agreed with him. She'd phoned him in bed last night and spent twenty minutes listening to his theories. It was a bizarre conversation because she was on his TV at the same time, busy appealing for witnesses to Yvonne Dale's death to come forward. Roisin had made a gun of her forefinger and thumb and pretended to shoot herself in the head. Sometimes, there is too much Trish Pharaoh in her life. By the time McAvoy hung up, Roisin was making a noose out of her dressing-gown belt. Still, he's pleased she's here. Her presence suggests he is doing things the right way. He is following the trail correctly. He has investigated murders on his own before and found himself constantly riddled with doubts and questions. Having Pharaoh here makes him feel like a policeman.

'Here,' she says, suddenly. 'Right.'

Dutifully, McAvoy turns the vehicle down a barely visible side road, hemmed on both sides with sycamore and ash trees. They follow the deserted road for half a mile, past a row of half a dozen houses whose occupants will probably be the last to hear about the end of the world.

'Pretty,' says Pharaoh appreciatively, as she glimpses the old church to her left. She succumbs to impulse and winds the window down, sticking her head out like a happy dog.

'Have I told you the story?'

'Yes,' says Pharaoh, abruptly. 'You have.'

They have arrived in the tiny hamlet of Watton. The nearest place with a post office or somewhere to buy milk is four miles away in Hutton Cranswick. The larger town of Driffield is a little further up the road. After that, East Yorkshire starts to become

North Yorkshire, and the house prices go up. McAvoy has never been here before, but plans to bring Roisin and a picnic. 'Bloody hell,' says Pharaoh, as they drive slowly through ornate brick gates and into a vast drive coated in round, shiny pebbles. 'Rather swish.'

The manor house is magnificent: all stone vaulting and turrets, tippy-topped towers and rounded, mullioned windows. In this light, it appears timeless, though McAvoy finds it hard not to imagine some medieval princess sitting at one of the dark windows, weeping and working on her tapestries as father and brothers practise swordplay in the grounds.

'Cost more than three million,' he says. 'I've requested a brochure.'

McAvoy parks the car in the shade of some tangled elderflower trees. He makes a note to tell Roisin the berries are coming early this year then steps from the car and listens to the silence. Wonders how one should knock on a door of this size. Whether he should go the kitchen entrance, like a tradesman.

Christ, Roisin would love this, he thinks.

It's a beautiful home, and yet carries with it an air of something vaguely unsettling. It is not so much the quiet, though the absence of noise is noticeable. It's the air. The heat seems more oppressive here. There is a whiff of something McAvoy recognises as rotting vegetation; like the bottom of a compost bin when it has been cleaned. Something remains here. Something lingering and powerful. McAvoy listens hard and can hear the sound of rushing water somewhere nearby. He hangs on to the sound. It seems to represent a place beyond the mansion walls. It represents escape.

As they approach the big front doors, a figure comes into

view. A young man in overalls and a lumberjack shirt is spraying the paved area in front of the giant front portico with what McAvoy takes to be weedkiller. A large canister of the stuff is strapped to his back and he has a hose in his right hand. He's whistling to himself, the wires from a pair of headphones dribbling out from underneath a dark baseball cap. McAvoy doesn't want to come upon him unaware so makes as much noise as he can as he approaches. Pharaoh has no such qualms, and merely yells 'Oi'. The man turns, startled. He's in his late twenties. Not bad-looking, but could do with a scrub. He pulls an earpiece out of one ear but leaves the other one in. He gives them a smile.

'Not open yet,' he says, and his accent is local.

Pharaoh pulls out her warrant card. Crosses the space between them. He gives her a quick once-over and his eyes linger on her breasts for no longer than anybody else's do.

'Superintendent,' he says, reading the card and looking impressed. He smiles, friendly and open. 'What's he?'

Pharaoh turns to look at McAvoy, trying to get his warrant card out of his waistcoat pocket and dropping his car keys all at the same time.

'Him? He's a defective sergeant. Don't try and pronounce his name. He's Scottish.'

The man looks at McAvoy, who is straightening his clothes. 'Rangers or Celtic?'

McAvoy pushes his hair back from his face. 'Ross County. I can only apologise.'

The man laughs. 'Better state than Rangers these days, at least. How the hell did they let that happen, eh?'

Pharaoh gives a wave of her hand, telling both men to stop talking about football. She looks up at the imposing building. 'Lovely place,' she says. 'You the groundsman?'

The man sticks out his hand and withdraws it when he sees the dirt on his knuckles. 'Groundsman? Nah. I'm a contractor. New owners have got a whole crew coming in next month to do the place up. I'm keeping it nice enough so that the MD can show his investors around as it stands. They're not short of cash, I'll tell you that.'

'I read on the Internet it had been sold . . .'

'Yeah, big company with a base in Sweden. Or Norway. One of those—'

'Sweden. Sceptre Healthcare.'

The man rummages around in the pocket of his overalls and finds a grubby card. He reads the name on it. 'Yeah, Sceptre.' He shows them the card. 'Bernt Moller,' he reads. 'He's my contact. Just told me to keep it nice, really. They've only been up here a couple of times but they had people in expensive suits with them. It's going to be fancy. I've seen the plans.'

Pharaoh looks at the card, and in the corner of her eye sees McAvoy taking down the name and number in neat handwriting.

'It's not going to house nutters any more, then?'

The man gives a laugh, showing slightly crooked teeth and silver fillings. 'Last of them were long gone by the time I got this contract.'

'And it's going to be an old folks' home?'

'Don't let them hear you say that! I've seen the brochures. They love their marketing speak, it's all respite care and quality of life and fancy words to try and get you to part with your cash.

166

Going to be lovely, though.' He gestures at the house. 'Couldn't not be, really. Gorgeous place.'

McAvoy looks around him. Through a line of lime trees he spots an outbuilding with a red slate roof. He can see a faint line of what looks like barbed wire above loose brickwork.

'Outbuildings come as part of the sale?'

The contractor looks puzzled. 'I just stop the weeds growing through the cracks and pull the leaves out of the gutters. Why do you ask?'

McAvoy shrugs, and then realises he doesn't like being the sort of person who answers a question without words. 'I heard there had been an incident here. When it was still in the hands of the old owners.'

'No idea, mate. Is that what you're here for?'

Pharaoh kicks a pebble with the toe of her biker boot. She seems to be mulling something over.

'I'm Trish, by the way,' says Pharaoh, with the practised ease of somebody who knows how best to get men on her side. 'You are?'

'Gaz,' he says, with a smile. 'Gary. Reeves.'

'A pleasure, Gaz. We were rather hoping to speak to somebody who used to work here. A psychiatrist. He was a very senior figure here a few years ago.'

Gaz rubs a hand over his jaw. His face implies that he would love to help but can't.

'There's still some of the old stuff in boxes,' he says, after a pause. 'Belonged to the old owners. May be some names and addresses. If you ring that Swedish bloke he would probably say to help yourself.'

Pharaoh looks at him for a moment, then swallows, letting a smile creep onto her face. 'Already phoned him, Gary. Just now. Nice chap, isn't he? Loves pickled herring, apparently. Got a poster of Freddie Ljungberg on his desk. Reads a lot of Wallander. Says it's fine. Just to go right in. You probably heard me.'

Gaz's smile matches Pharaoh's. He looks like the sort who enjoys giving the rules a slight tweak. He looks as though he had been expecting a boring day and now has the opportunity to give himself a story to tell in the pub tonight.

'Was he sitting in an Ikea chair?' he asks, enjoying this. 'Blond. Drives a Volvo . . .'

'That's the chap,' says Pharaoh. 'We good?'

Gaz nods. 'I'm going for a bacon roll in a bit anyway. Door's open. Load of cardboard boxes in the second office to your right. I'm sure he told you that.'

Pharaoh reaches out and puts a hand on his forearm. 'Word for word.'

Gaz crunches away across the gravel, towards a small blue Transit van parked in the shade of the far wall. A moment later, he's reversing out and heading through the gate.

'Coming?'

McAvoy has a finger in his ear and his phone to the side of his head. He's reading the dirty business card in his hand and having no luck getting in touch with Bernt Moller. He leaves a message with a secretary with a better English accent than his own and mentions that Gary Reeves had told them to go right ahead.

Pharaoh is standing in the doorway of the great stately home, leaning against the cool stone. 'Does it suit me?' she asks, gesturing at the mansion. 'Think I would fit in here?'

McAvoy stands beside her and turns to take in the view.

Examines the grounds, the church, the tumbledown outbuildings and the lime trees that veil the barbed wire.

'Lady of the manor,' he says, nodding. 'I can see it now. You married the owner and he died on your honeymoon night. Now you offend all the old-money posh nobs and have elaborate parties here with your husband's money.'

Pharaoh laughs appreciatively and plays along. 'And you can be a Scottish laird, visiting from the Highlands. You're here to persuade me to buy five hundred acres of quality sheep-farming land. This evening I'm going to get you drunk on old wine from the cellar and persuade you to do a handstand in your kilt.'

McAvoy busies himself putting his notebook away. 'It's always the kilt with you, isn't it, Guv?'

Pharaoh turns her back and enters the cool of the porch. 'You should wear one for work. Would be something to threaten the villains with during interviews. Can you imagine? "For the benefit of the tape, Detective Sergeant McAvoy just waggled his bollocks at the suspect. The suspect is crying."'

They cross a wooden parquet floor past the deserted reception desk. It's a cool, airy place with high ceilings and dangling chains that have clearly been used to support chandeliers. It has the air of a Tudor castle: its owner imprisoned for heresy and his buildings left to fall into disrepair. The light does not extend much beyond the open doorway but there is enough of a glow for McAvoy to investigate the black and white photographs that still hang in brown wooden frames upon the drab magnolia walls. He and Pharaoh spend a few minutes using the lights from their mobile phones to stare into crowd scenes, to examine pictures of agricultural workers long dead, standing by hay bales and scowling below hats and moustaches. The images are a joyless jumble, all pixels and dead eyes.

Pharaoh pushes at a pair of mahogany double doors that swing open as she twists the brass handle. It's dark and cold inside, and smells old.

'This place would drive you mental even if you were sane,' mutters Pharaoh, shivering. 'Shut down for years, you said. How come I can still smell cabbage and disinfectant?'

She reaches up to the long panel of light switches and flicks half a dozen of them down. After a slight pause, the chandeliers crescendo into life, pitching a yellow puddle into the chilly space, spreading in a flood down the corridor.

Pharaoh carries on down the hallway with its chessboard floor and burgundy walls, to the staircase, which sweeps elegantly upwards.

Peaches-and-cream little girls in velvet dresses.

Stern patrician types in curled wigs and uncomfortable robes.

The place may have been a hospital but it feels like an abandoned stately home. Pharaoh looks as though she is considering sliding down the banister, then gives a shiver and comes back down, heading businesslike to the door she had been directed to.

'This one,' says Pharaoh, twisting a door handle. 'Oh bloody hell.'

'Guv?'

Pharaoh pulls a face. The door that Gaz had directed them to is locked.

McAvoy lets his disappointment show. He wants to try the handle himself, just to feel involved, but forces himself not to.

'Worth looking around?' he asks.

Pharaoh angles her head to peer up the stairs. She doesn't

look keen to spend any more time here. It feels old. The walls have soaked something up over the centuries and seem to be silently screaming that this building will be here long after they, and everybody else, has gone. McAvoy wonders what the patients thought when they were brought here. Some were willing, asking for help. Others had been sectioned by their families. Half a dozen had been sent by the courts, trying to ease the workload of busier and better-known facilities like Rampton.

Pharaoh screws up her face. 'Load of empty bedrooms and the lingering smell of cauliflower farts? No thanks. It's okay, we weren't sure what we were looking for anyway, were we? We're just bloody fishing.' She looks a bit dejected, suddenly. 'Let's go, eh? Ben Nielsen will have an address for the shrink by now anyway. And it won't be hard to find out where Hoyer-Wood is a patient, even though I don't know what we're expecting to find there either. Bloke's a cripple, you said.'

Discreetly, McAvoy gives the door handle a shake, for good measure. Were he to allow himself to try, he would be able to kick the damn thing off its hinges. But he knows he will not try.

A sudden vibration in his pocket causes McAvoy to give a tiny shout and Pharaoh begins to laugh as her sergeant retrieves his phone and blushes furiously. He speaks softly and quickly. Lays on the charm. Hangs up, smiling.

'Bernt Moller,' he says, by way of explanation. 'Very polite man, but asked if we would mind submitting our request through the proper channels. Told us that our new friend had overstepped the mark a little.'

'Reeves?'

'Yeah. Moller employed him by pure luck when he was on a site visit. I hope we haven't got him in trouble. Seemed a decent sort.'

'Well, we better hadn't upset the Scandinavians any further,' says Pharaoh, and threads her arm through his own. 'Come on.' He feels the heat of her, the closeness. Smells her. Hairspray and wine, perfume and perspiration.

He doesn't know what to say. What to do. Just feels himself colouring, and the hairs on his arm rising to scratch the strap of his watch.

'Excuse me, this is private property.'

McAvoy looks up as the double doors swing open. Two men in uniform stand outlined in the soft light.

'We're police,' says Pharaoh, pulling out her warrant card. 'Sorry. The gardener said to go straight in . . .'

The nearest man takes the warrant card from Pharaoh's hand and looks at it closely, then at her. He's young. Too young to scare anybody but not old enough to realise it.

'I've grown my hair since then,' says Pharaoh, pointing at the picture on the ID. 'You like it?'

'You be quiet,' says the second man. He's got a round belly and receding hair and there are short bristles sprouting from his red nose. Up close, there is enough of a similarity about the two men's eyes for McAvoy to think that they may be father and son. The logo on their uniforms is a bearskin hat, and the words 'Tower Security' are stitched in yellow onto their grey short-sleeved shirts.

'Easy now,' says McAvoy, stepping forward. 'We were just hoping to speak to somebody in charge . . .'

'There's nobody here yet,' says the older man. His face softens a bit. He's clearly relieved that the intruders are nicely dressed and aren't carrying anything that could be used as a weapon. He instructs the younger man to give Pharaoh her warrant card back. 'Sorry, we get no end of bloody trespassers.'

Pharaoh is sucking her teeth, unsure whether to accept the apology or beat the man to death for telling her to be quiet. She nods.

'We'd best get some air, eh?'

The four of them walk back into the light, the heat feeling like a physical barrier as they emerge from the cool of the reception area. As one, they stare up at the grey clouds. They are shifting. Rolling. Taking shape. Taking on the hue of rotten fruit and crackling with barely contained energy.

'Going to be one hell of a bloody storm,' says the younger security guard, breathlessly. 'Will give us an easier life though, eh?'

'You get much hassle, do you?' asks McAvoy, showing his own warrant card and finding that nobody cares.

The older man blows out demonstratively. 'Ramblers are no bother. There's a public right of way past the church, even though it's all bloody nettles and thistles and cow shit, so you wouldn't head up there for a picnic. It's the house itself that brings the nutters out. You know how it is. They read on the Internet about this abandoned asylum and get all these images in their mind. We've had loads of photographers trying to get in. Lick of paint and it could still be a mansion. You should have seen it back in the day. We just chase them away.'

McAvoy considers. 'You're on site all the time, then?'

The older man shakes his head. 'Head office is York but we have regional offices here and there. Two-man teams look after a few different properties. Me and the lad are based in Driffield. Got a call on the radio about a couple of intruders. We weren't far off so shot on over.'

Pharaoh and McAvoy exchange a look, picturing Gary Reeves. *Little git.*

Something occurs to McAvoy. 'You saw this place in its glory days, then?'

The older man nods. 'We've had the contract to look after it for years. Tower has been in business for decades. You've probably heard of us. We try and help the police where we can –'

'Did you work here fourteen years ago?' McAvoy breaks in.

'Boy was at school,' says the older security guard. 'I was still working the oil rigs.'

McAvoy gives up. He is about to thank them for their time when the older man speaks again.

'I live just up the road though, mate. Hutton Cranswick. If you're talking about the fire, I know a bit.'

McAvoy scratches his face. Controls his breathing. Stares at the grey sky and the bare brick, the barbed wire and the lime trees.

'Fire?'

'Yeah, not a big one. Just the old groundsman's cottage. The doctors had access to it, you see, for when they stayed over. Not much of a place to live, in the grounds of a nuthouse, but the shrink who had it seemed happy enough. Was a shame what happened.'

McAvoy coughs, knowing that when he speaks next, he is at risk of sounding feeble.

'A shame?'

The older man nods. 'One of the nutters went nuts, mate. Held one of the doctors and his family at knifepoint. The owners called security instead of the police, but by the time our lads got here it was all over. Horrible for the family, though. I got all the gossip from one of the old boys in the village. Was a bit of a balls-up all round, apparently . . .'

'The doctor had family with him?'

174

More nodding. 'I can't remember much more than that. Was amazing they kept it out of the papers, really. That was the beginning of the end, I think. Old owners put it up for sale not long after. Took years before this Swedish lot showed an interest.'

Pharaoh nudges McAvoy. Indicates he should shut up. 'How did it end?' she asks. 'The hostage situation?'

'Don't really know,' says the older man. 'Nobody really wanted to go into it. Was all very embarrassing. Mental units are supposed to have strict security measures, you see. Tower were the outside contractors. The owners' own psychiatric nurses would have been the ones in the firing line if it had got out. I'm just surprised it's taken you so long. Bit late now, though, I reckon. Shrink's long gone. I reckon the locals will like the place more as an old people's home, don't you think?'

McAvoy closes his eyes. 'The incident,' he says, softly. 'The night it happened. Could you tell us everything? We're investigating a murder. Two.'

The older man whistles. 'More than my job's worth, mate.' He looks at the younger man, then the two detectives. Gives a naughty smile. 'But it's lunchtime in a couple of hours. We drink in The Wellington in Driffield. Mine's a pint.'

Pharaoh smiles, and McAvoy breathes out. He watches the other two walk away. Stands here, on the steps to the manor house, his back to the forbidding structure where Sebastien Hoyer-Wood was a patient because his university friends convinced a judge he was crazy.

'Sebastien Hoyer-Wood,' he shouts, at their backs. 'You know the name?'

The security guards looks baffled. Shrugs. 'I'll check with the lads who worked here.' He looks at his watch. 'Pint. The Wellington.'

And they are gone.

McAvoy nods. Tries to walk down the steps to where Pharaoh is waiting, looking at him strangely. Behind her, he sees the dark clouds of the coming storm.

Detective Chief Inspector Colin Ray turned fifty last night. He celebrated at home, alone, in his flat in Hull's Old Town. There were two cards on his mantelpiece, both from mail order companies that valued his custom and wished him a very happy day of celebration. He drank four cans of beer, ate a chicken bhuna, texted a filthy joke to Shaz Archer and then masturbated half-heartedly over a picture in the *Hull Daily Mail*. The lucky recipient of his attentions was a local MP, fronting a campaign for better street lighting, and there had been something about her smile for the camera that had struck him as mucky. Not mucky enough, as it happened. He had gone to sleep half-pissed and frustrated, fingers coated in garlic and grease, cursing the MP, his mobile phone discarded next to him on a yellow-stained pillow. The call he had been hoping for never came.

Here, now, he can still taste the curry on his skin. Can pick out the flavour of spice and cardamom, in among the heavier aromas of nicotine and old booze. He's chewing on the fat of an index finger, gnawing on it, like a dog with a bone, squinting at a computer screen and breathing noisily through his nose. When he sat down at the desk there were half a dozen other officers in the room. They have gradually drifted away, to speak to witnesses or check in with informants, or go for a walk around the car park. Nobody wants to be near Ray when he's in this mood. Even Shaz Archer is giving him a wide berth.

He should be pleased, of course. They've just charged Adam Downey with conspiracy to supply a large quantity of Class A drugs and the evidence is pretty damning against the pretty boy in cell 4. He'll be denied bail, come the hearing on Monday morning. He'll be found guilty, should he have the temerity to deny the charges. Should he plead guilty, he'll still get hit with a few years in view of his previous offences. Ray has got a scumbag off the streets. He's put away a villain. He should be drinking the cheap whisky in his desk drawer and slapping backs as people tell him he's ace.

Instead, Colin Ray looks like he is about to tear his own skin off and start throwing it at people in great wet clumps.

Adam Downey isn't enough. Not nearly enough.

A few months ago, Ray spoke to one of the senior figures involved in the new drugs outfit. At that time, the group had just taken over all cannabis operations on the east coast, and successfully outmuscled the Vietnamese gangs that had previously been responsible for growing the crop. The new lot had simply moved in, and told the Vietnamese that they now worked for them. Even more remarkably, the Vietnamese bosses had complied. The foot soldiers and farmers who did not like the new arrangement were dealt with swiftly: hands nailgunned to their legs, chests turned to tar with a blowtorch. A few physically imposing enforcers kept an eye on things, and a handful of bright young chancers looked after deliveries and shipments. During his conversation with the voice at the other end of the phone, Ray had realised that the new outfit had plans. They were never going to content themselves looking after a bit of cannabis production. They had moved in without any real resistance, and in Ray's mind that kind of victory could make an ambitious man feel invincible. The voice on the phone had warned Ray that it was in nobody's interests to look into their operations too carefully. He had made it plain that they were well informed, well connected, and had half of the Drugs Squad in their pocket. Ray hadn't given a damn. He'd ignored their bribes and gentle threats, and given the go-ahead on an operation that led to the unit's first significant arrest. Now he feels he has made another. It just hasn't had the domino effect that he'd hoped.

Last night, sitting in his boxer shorts and mismatched socks, he had expected his mobile phone to ring, expected threats or promises from a mysterious voice. But nobody had called. He is not given to self-doubt, but his conviction that Adam Downey is connected to the operation is starting to waver. Ever since the lad was brought in, he has been convinced that Downey is a mid-level operative for the new group. He's young, bright enough, and has met some proper villains while inside. He's been dealing in drugs since he was a teen, and the sheer quality and quantity of the cocaine found in his possession suggest to Ray that he is part of something big. But the bastard isn't giving them anything other than 'no comment'.

Ray pushes back his greasy hair and scratches at the psoriasis on the back of his neck, sending flakes of dead skin into the air. He sniffs and swallows the phlegm that appears in his mouth. He's fighting his instincts. Fighting the urge to go down to the cells and beat some answers out of Downey with his own shoes.

He is so wrapped up in his thoughts that it takes him a moment to register the vibration coming from his shirt pocket. At his age and with his diet, any trembling by his heart should be a cause for concern, but Ray is smiling as he pats at his chest, and removes the old-fashioned mobile. Number withheld.

'Colin Ray.'

There is silence at the other end of the phone, and then a familiar voice: accentless and perfectly enunciated.

'Mr Ray. A pleasure to speak to you again. Allow me to apologise for the unforgivable delay between our last conversation and this one. We have been extraordinarily busy and there has been no opportunity for indulgences.'

Ray sits back in his chair, a broad smile on his face. He's remembering their last chat, sitting in the front of an umarked car down Division Road, rain beating on the roof and steam rising from his clothes, Detective Superintendent Adrian Russell shitting himself in the driver's seat as Ray took the phone from his hands and put the call from his colleague's paymaster on loudspeaker.

'Now then, lad,' says Ray, warmly. 'You're right. It's been a while. And yeah, you've been busy. Onwards and upwards, I see.'

'A business has to expand or it stagnates, Mr Ray. Running water is so much fresher and more vibrant than a static pool, would you not agree?'

Ray sticks a finger in his ear and inspects what he finds, rubbing it on his suit trousers. 'Never thought about it, son. My mind's a bit busy right now. Just charged a young lad with conspiracy to supply. Seriously good quality, the stuff he had on him. Must be worth a fortune.'

There is a silence at the other end of the line. Then the slightest suggestion that the caller is taking a discreet sip of liquid. In the background, the softest of sounds – china on china, cup on saucer; the extinguishing of a cigarette into a clean ashtray.

'You have probably never seen the like, Mr Ray. Even during your time working in the Met. Even when you lived in that flat in Maida Vale with the Polish lady whom your senior officers did not know about and whom you met during a six-year undercover operation that ended in disaster. Not even when they moved you up to Newcastle to keep you out of the way and you beat a suspect half to death in the custody suite. Even then, you will not have seen a product like the one that was spilled all over the floor of the premises on Southcoates Lane.'

Ray shrugs, though nobody can see. 'My CV has its ups and downs. Like your lad. Downey.'

'Yes, indeed. My associates are of course aware of the young man to whom you are referring . . .'

'Whom?' says Ray, mockingly. 'Public schoolboy, you, I reckon. Definitely got breeding. That narrows it down a bit . . .'

'Mr Downey,' continues the voice, as though there has been no interruption, 'is a young man for whom we had some hope of future advancement. This week's development was most unfortunate.'

'Yeah, that's the word. Unfortunate. If I'd lost one of my main guys and a packet of pure coke, I'd call it a bit more than that, my lad.'

There is more silence. Ray wonders if this will be it. Whether there will be more. He suddenly feels empty at the thought of the call being terminated. He wants to talk. Wants to tell this supercilious bastard with his perfect vowels that he's worked it out.

'Shall I tell you something?' he asks, suddenly sitting forward in his chair. 'I've been thinking about you lot. Thinking about you a lot. Where you came from. What you do. I've been thinking about the way you marched in and turned every Vietnamese cannabis factory into your own personal operation. The way you kept the workforce. I've been thinking about what you did to those poor bastards who said they were going to talk. And I reckon I know how it works. It's a hostile takeover, isn't it? And you can carry those out with only a few guys. I reckon you look at which organisations are profitable, and instead of setting up a rival business, you just take over the one that works. You scare the shit out of the top dogs, and tell them they can carry on and pay you a handsome cut, or you can put them in the ground. It's a beautiful system, matey. I reckon with the right information and a few good lads you could have half the established gangs in Britain paying you protection money. How am I doing?'

There is a lengthy pause before the man speaks again. When he does, there is a note of humour to his voice. 'That sounds like a great deal of conjecture and guesswork, Mr Ray. But I admire the scale of your imagination. I'm sure my associates will too. However, if that is indeed the case and they are only a few individuals with vision and guile, why would they show any interest in the young man in your cells?'

Ray spits in the mesh waste-paper basket. Watches the phlegm slide down the inside of a polystyrene food carton. Sniffs, and scratches at his neck.

'I'll tell you that when you tell me why you are ringing,' he says, wetly, into the phone. 'If you're ringing to suggest that we somehow lose interest in Adam Downey, then I reckon it's because your organisation is bright enough to know that loyalty has to be earned. We already know that Downey worked for a dealer around here for years. He supplied on street corners then got a bit more of a reputation and started dealing wholesale. If your outfit has taken over the gang he used to work for, Downey will know about it. He might even have done the killing himself. I reckon his old boss is in the ground. I think during his last stretch inside, one of your bright things got in touch with him and promised him the earth if he showed a little ambition. That's how you lot work, isn't it? You look at the individual. You look at what they want. And you find a way to give them it. That's how it worked with Aidy Russell, I'm guessing. You realised he was an ambitious officer and you gave him enough information to get him some good headlines, and the price was that he left you alone.'

The caller breathes out, slowly. 'There are so many more people willing to assist us in our endeavours than your friend the detective superintendent, Mr Ray. As you say, my associates have an uncanny ability to find out what matters most to people. We are all about the individual. And Mr Downey is an individual who has demonstrated loyalty. We would not be particularly effective employers were we to then turn our back on him for making an error of judgement.'

'Storing his gear in a sewing shop, you mean?'

Another pause, then: 'He was demonstrating original thinking. We prize that, even when the results do not go as hoped.'

Ray taps his fingers on the phone at his ear, slowly, deliberately. He fancies it will be irritating to the man at the end of the line.

'So you're ringing to ask me to go let him out?' asks Ray, smiling wide enough to show the pastry crumbs in his back teeth.

This time, the man allows himself what could almost be called a laugh. 'No, Mr Ray. I am ringing to tell you that Adam Downey will be released within the week. He will not talk to you. Nothing you can do or say to him will change that. I am aware of the conversations you have had with some local hooligans with regard to Mr Downey's incarceration. I can assure you that Mr Downey's brief time at Her Majesty's Pleasure will not be the purgatory you envisage. Nobody is going to threaten him, Mr Ray. Nobody is going to lean on him. If you check your call log in around twenty minutes, you will see that two members of your CID will be on their way to Hull Prison, where one of the inmates of your acquaintance was found, moments ago, in the shower block, with nails through his hands and knees. A most unfortunate incident. I am ringing to tell you that while some people are resistant to change, others embrace it. These are changing times, Mr Ray. I am ringing out of courtesy, because there is something about your intractable demeanour that some of my associates find charming. More than anything else, I am ringing to apologise for not sending you a birthday card. You made a sad sight, sitting there alone. I do hope that by next year, you have somebody to share it with.'

Ray's smile fades. He clears his throat.

'Do you think I'm scared of you, son?'

The line goes quiet. There is a suggestion of a cigarette being lit.

'No,' comes the voice, finally. 'You have nothing for us to threaten. You have no money and no children. You have your pension and will be dead by the time you are sixty even without our intervention. You would not respond well to promises of remuneration and you treat your body far more poorly than anybody in our employ could.'

'So what are you going to do with me, eh, son?' Ray asks it with a laugh, but it sounds weaker than before.

'Nothing, Mr Ray. We will simply tolerate you. You are not important enough to care about.'

Ray's fist slams on the desk. The computer shakes, a coffee mug falls. The sound bounces off the walls of the empty room.

11

Monday morning, 9.18 a.m.

The same room in the same health centre on the same road.

Too hot to breathe.

Aector McAvoy: bone-tired and unshaven, aching across his shoulders and back. He has bags under his eyes and plasters on the backs of his hands, and the blue suit he is wearing was chosen because it has the fewest creases rather than none at all. He's spent the weekend lifting furniture in and out of a removals van. Has carried mattresses and bed frames up flights of stairs and climbed in through a first-floor window with a wardrobe on his back while a crowd gathered on Hessle foreshore and shouted encouragement. He has spent two days struggling with cardboard boxes full of books and shoes and pots and pans, wrestling with a sofa that wouldn't fit through the bloody front door, despite the careful measurements he had taken when they viewed the place. Spent an hour with his fingers in an ice bucket borrowed from the Country Park Inn, after Fin decided that tickling Daddy while he carried a washing machine would be incredibly funny. This morning he selected his clothes from a suitcase and a variety of bin liners.

He is trying not to dwell on the fact that his socks don't match. He has already made up his mind never to move house again. He's exhausted and sore and doesn't want to be back here. Not back in this airless room, with its traffic sounds and buzzing flies and stupid plastic chair.

'It went okay, yes? The move? It was this weekend, wasn't it?'

Sabine Keane is giving him an encouraging smile. He tries to return it. This could be his last session, if he plays nicely.

'Hard work,' he says. 'I didn't know we had so much stuff.'

'You didn't get removal men in?'

'Sort of. A man with a van. I thought he'd be more help than he was. He was very good at drinking tea and smoking cigarettes.'

'So you did it all yourselves?'

McAvoy gives a laugh. 'Roisin was more of a foreman. She's not built for lifting sofas. She and Mel kind of directed . . .'

'Her friend, yes? You've mentioned her before.'

McAvoy clears his throat. Stares at his tie for a while. 'She's been through a bit of an ordeal. There was an incident at her shop. Had a bit of a set-to with a drug dealer and helped the police nab him.'

Sabine looks impressed. 'So you're tolerating her more readily?'

McAvoy wonders if his answer will lead to another note in his file. 'I don't dislike her. I never said that I did. And Roisin thinks she's great. Is that important?'

Sabine shakes her head. She looks up at the ceiling. Looks down, into her open handbag. Appears to be working out what to say.

'This could well be your last session, Aector. If I count the last one.'

She says it with a smile. Warm and friendly. McAvoy nods, hopefully.

'Yes?'

She sighs. 'I'm not sure you've really told me anything.'

McAvoy looks frustrated. He opens his mouth and makes gestures with his hands, then breathes out as if this is all too much. 'What would you like to hear, Sabine? I'm fine. I'm investigating two murders. I'm doing my job.'

'But you feel better *because* you are investigating murders, Aector. What if there were no murders to investigate?'

He looks at her, perplexed. 'I don't think we need to worry about that. This is Hull. And people will always be horrible to each other.'

She persists. Sits forward in her chair. Adjusts the strap on her sensible sandals then gives him her full attention. 'How would you define yourself if not for your job? That's what I mean.'

He doesn't understand. 'But I *am* a policeman.'

'And what does that mean?' she asks, probing deeper. 'What does being a policeman mean to you?'

McAvoy wants to stand up. Wants to pace. 'Is this about duty again, because we've talked about that—'

'What I want to know, Aector, is whether you are a policeman first and a human being second, or whether there is room inside you for both.'

McAvoy turns to her, wondering what she is trying to get him to say.

'You've broken the law, yes? You've hinted at doing something bad when you and Roisin met. You have been present when people have been killed. You can talk about these things in here, Aector. You're safe.'

188

He looks at her, hard. Looks at this middle-aged woman in her cream dress and frizzy hair, her visible panty-line and her untended nails. He does not see her as a safe repository for his secrets. Were he to meet her in the street he would not take it upon himself to tell her what he did to the men who attacked Roisin as an adolescent. And yet, she is right in what she says. This room is safe. Her report to his senior officers will only declare that he is not suffering from any mental illness and is fit for duty. Were he to unburden himself, he would not lose a friend. He does not mind if she judges him harshly. This is a confessional. A place to give voice to the thoughts and feelings of guilt that sometimes threaten to eat him up.

'Aector, you're safe. I don't want anything from you. I want to help you. This case you are investigating now must be taking its toll. You have so much to think about. You can't rely on Roisin for everything.'

McAvoy looks away. She is right, of course. He expects too much of his wife, though she never fails to give him what he needs. She is his confessor. She is his sounding board. She is his whole soul. And yet he cannot tell her everything, for fear of reminding her of darker times. Cannot discuss how he feels about the day he found the farm boys raping a twelve-year-old traveller girl. Cannot tell her what he did to them for fear of changing the way she views him.

He rubs a hand through his hair. Sabine has begun talking again but he is not listening. He finds his thoughts turning back to Friday's meeting in The Wellington in Driffield. His chat over a couple of pints of real ale with the two security guards. The older man had introduced himself as Jimmy Forsythe. Taken a pickled egg from the jar on the bar and devoured it in a bite.

Took his pint, found a table, and gave McAvoy and Pharaoh the lot. Told them what the lads at Tower Security knew about what happened at the facility. There had been no dazzling revelations, but Pharaoh considered the cost of a couple of pints to have been money well spent. They are building up a picture of Sebastien Hoyer-Wood and his friend Lewis Caneva. It is becoming clear that the rapist was neither as injured nor as mentally ill as his old university friend claimed. He seemed to have lived with Caneva and his family more as a house guest than as a patient at the neighbouring asylum. And something had happened that had broken up this cosy arrangement and sent Caneva into a tailspin.

Caneva is the man they want next. Ben Nielsen has found an address for him and McAvoy will be heading there as soon as he has got this last session with Sabine out of the way. He's going alone. Pharaoh is back at the station, fighting fires. ACC Everett is attempting to suspend DCI Colin Ray from duty for beating the shit out of Adam Downey in the cells. Downey has spent the weekend in Hull Royal Infirmary and has a bail hearing this morning. The top brass are doing their damnedest to keep quiet what happened, but Downey's solicitor is threatening to blow the whole lot in his address to the court unless bail is agreed to. Ray has made an almighty balls-up and played into the hands of whoever pays Downey's wages. The case is likely to collapse before it ever gets before a judge.

'Aector?'

McAvoy sighs. Closes his eyes and tries to keep his breathing steady.

'She thinks I killed them,' he says, and is surprised to hear himself speaking. 'Thinks I put them in the ground.'

Sabine's eyes widen.

'And did you?'

McAvoy looks at the floor. Gives the slightest shake of his head.

Confesses his greatest sin and is surprised to discover that he still has tears to shed.

It's just before one o'clock, and on Hull's Princes Avenue a blue Peugeot 306 is sitting in stationary traffic, waiting to turn left. On its roof is a large sign, advertising the services of the man at the wheel. It boasts of a 90 per cent first-time pass rate and promises that the first two lessons are free. Godber Driving School is written in a sporty-looking font, though to call the company a 'school' may be an overstatement. Allan Godber has no colleagues, though he has plenty of students. Allowing himself this hour for lunch is a luxury.

As he sits waiting for a gap in the traffic, Allan Godber hits himself in the chest with the flat of his hand. He swallows hard, neck bulging like a bullfrog's. He makes his hand into a fist and strikes himself in the ribcage. Manages half a belch. He screws up his face at the taste and spits like a baby trying solids for the first time. He reaches into the pocket of his jeans and finds a loose antacid tablet among the coins. He takes his eyes off the road for a moment, checks the chalky pill for any obvious fluff, then pops it in his mouth. He chews it up and swallows, wishing he had a glass of milk to chase it down with. Then the weight settles back on his chest.

During his last visit to his GP, Allan had been told he was suffering with gastro-oesophagal reflux disorder. It was a more satisfying title for the condition than the 'heartburn' that his wife had diagnosed him with. Allan also discovered that he more than likely had something called a hiatus hernia as well. They won't know until next month, when he goes to Castle Hill Hospital for an endoscopy. He's not looking forward to the procedure. He still knows a lot of the staff at the hospital, and doesn't want to know which of his mates will be knocking him out and sticking a tube down his gullet. He knows them too well to believe that they won't take a liberty or two while he is unconscious. He imagines himself coming round from the procedure to find himself naked in a corridor with the name of his least favourite football team scrawled in permanent marker on his chest.

Allan misses his old job. Misses the camaraderie and his mates. He gave seventeen years to the Ambulance Service, but when the last voluntary redundancy scheme was announced he saw a chance to get out and retrain in something that didn't involve quite so much blood, guts and night shifts. He's been a driving instructor for four years now and doesn't hate it. The money's okay, he's patient enough to tolerate the pupils, and he hasn't had to pick up any body parts or restart someone's heart in an age. The only downside is the rather sedentary nature of his job. He spends all day sitting down. He's put on three stone since quitting the service, and the gastric problems are clearly linked to his increasing waistline. Still, he's not a bad-looking guy. Despite being bigger than he was, he's not noticeably fat and has most of his hair, which he keeps in a short and fashionable style. He wears T-shirts with the right logos and buys the kind of jeans that his two teenage sons don't sneer at. He's in okay condition, and smells of an aftershave that his female students have admired from time to time, while his prescription sunglasses carry the same designer emblem as his underpants. He looks like he's doing alright, generally speaking, though he

192

does not see himself as any kind of catch or Romeo. It's hard to woo women or charm your way into somebody's pants when there's a risk of you burping sick every thirty seconds.

Allan turns the car onto Park Avenue, his back to Pearson Park. On a hot, muggy day like this, the park will be full of foreigners playing football and students lying on towels, drinking bottles of pear cider and trying to feign interest in textbooks. Kids will be taking it in turns to laugh and cry in the swing park, grazing their knees on rocks, coming off the slide too quickly and spraining their ankles, bumping heads or falling from railings onto the woodchip floor. As a paramedic, he has been called to that park too many times to think of it fondly. He once had to pop a three-year-old girl's shoulder back into place after she grabbed hold of a spinning roundabout. He'd tried to be as gentle as he could but she had still screamed. Her dad had still stood there crying in front of him and saying it hadn't been his fault, it was just an accident, these things happen . . .

Allan burps again. Grimaces. Rubs his chest.

It's been a normal morning. He's given three hour-long lessons and navigated his way through the traffic from one side of the city to the other without messing up his schedule by more than a couple of minutes.

The car glides past the shabbily grand houses on the wide, tree-lined street. The Avenues is the Hull address that everybody wants if they choose to remain inside the city boundary and not head for the suburbs. The parking's a bloody nightmare and a few too many of the three-storey dwellings have been converted into flats, but these are still mightily impressive homes and he is proud to call one his own. Allan lives on Ella Street, which is not, technically speaking, an Avenue. But it's close enough for him to share a postcode with those in the slightly larger properties that run parallel to his own.

There are no other vehicles around, but Allan indicates his intentions anyway. He checks his mirror and his blind spot, then slowly turns, in first gear, past a large detached house and into a row of lock-up garages. On foot, he is three minutes from home, and believes the lock-ups are well worth the tenner a week he pays by direct debit to a landlord he has never met. His car is his livelihood, and while there is on-street parking on Ella Street, there is also the occasional gang of on-street teenage wankers to worry about, and he can't relax worrying that somebody will rip the wing-mirrors off or write 'knobhead' on his advertising boards.

Allan swallows again and gives another little shudder. He's sick of tasting his own insides. He had always presumed that the condition was a result of stress, but his current job is considerably easier than the one he did for seventeen years. He has a pretty easy life. He only has another nine years to go on the mortgage, his children are doing okay at school, he gets a fortnight in Majorca every August and he doesn't dislike his wife. They'll still get away at Christmas too, having recently earned a minor windfall. The money they had been saving up to repoint the brickwork at the back of the house had turned out to be far more than was necessary, after Allan found a contractor who would do the job for next to nothing, cash in hand. If Liverpool would buy a decent centre forward and Cheryl Cole could be persuaded to send him a picture of her in her knickers, he would have everything he could ask for.

The row of garages is deserted, as ever. There are half a dozen on either side of the central area, all with rusty blue doors and their numbers spray-painted freehand in their centre. Allan pulls up next to his own garage. He looks out and decides, once again, that the tenner a week is worth it. Sure, there are a few potholes in the tarmac and somebody has dumped a mattress on top of the industrial bin at the far end, but it's nice to have a little space to call his own and where he knows the car is safe. Sometimes, when the kids have friends over and the noise is too much, he'll come and sit here and read the paper, alone in the cool and the dark.

He steps out of the car, giving a grunt of exertion as he moves his right leg for the first time since he got in the vehicle at 8.30 a.m. He crosses the small patch of tarmac, pulling the garage key from his pocket. Puts it in the padlock and turns. Unhooks the padlock from the rusted metal loop. He raises the garage door, up and over, then reaches inside to pull the cord that brings the bare bulb on the far wall to life.

As he turns to head back to his vehicle, there is a movement in the periphery of his vision. A crunch of boot on broken stone. There is a moment in which he feels unbalanced, half-turning, feet in opposite directions, knee twisted, hands flailing. And then he feels a blow to the back of his head.

Allan pitches forward, into the empty garage. For a moment he wonders if the door has come down and struck him, but he cannot remember hearing the metallic clang. He wonders why he is considering this. Why here, now, he is giving it any thought at all.

There is another blow, and suddenly Allan is not thinking about much any more. He is on his face on a cement floor, smelling dust and diesel. Over the rushing of blood in his ears, he hears the distinctive grating of the garage doors closing. He tries to right himself, but his limbs don't seem to be responding to his commands. He feels fingers in his hair then hands upon his shoulders. Feels himself being turned over onto his back. His eyes flutter open, but then a fist closes around his short hair and his head is cracked back onto the floor. After that he keeps his eyes closed.

Allan feels as though he is swimming inside his own skin, oblivious and helpless. He feels his shirt being torn away, ripping from the buttons through the expensive logo. There is a pause. Nothing. No sound, no sensation, and then he feels a tightening of the skin on his chest. He wants to raise his head. Wants to see what is happening to him, but he can taste blood and his head feels too heavy and his body is not his own any more.

Suddenly, in the darkness, there is a voice. A robotic, inhuman thing. He cannot make out the words, but they seem familiar, somehow. He struggles up. Raises himself on his elbows. Sees a figure, crouching at his side, an open plastic box beside him. The figure is raising its arms, frustrated and angry. The metallic voice is calling for medical assistance.

Allan tries to speak, and the bubbling sounds that come from his lips cause the figure to raise its head. For an instant, the merest fraction of a second, Allan sees a familiar face. Sees features he knows, twisted into anger and madness.

Then words, bestial and screeching, echoing off the bare brick walls.

And the figure is upon him, the plastic box gripped in its hands, the weight and the cold and the tight sensation still upon Allan's skin.

Allan looks up, and sees the figure raise the object over their heads. For a second, he sees an image from a movie, playing in his mind. Sees an ape, holding a club in front of a blue sky, smashing a skull against uneven rocks.

The impact of the first blow breaks his nose and fills his eyes with blood.

After that, he is not really Allan any more.

Part Three

12

It started raining as McAvoy crossed the Pennines, a sudden downpour hitting the glass a mile before the Lancashire border. He passed into the storm as if driving into a waterfall, watching in his rear-view mirror as Yorkshire's green and brown slopes were abruptly snatched away.

The rain felt wonderful. It was good to open the window and let the droplets run in. He has baked in oppressive heat for weeks and the cool breeze and damp air had felt both cooling and healing as they touched his flesh and drenched his clothes. By the time he reached the Chester city limits, the novelty had worn off. The car was steaming up, he was shivering inside clothes soaked with both sweat and rain, and he had the beginnings of a headache from squinting through the wall of water at the brake lights of the car in front.

He rubs his temples. Kneads his forehead. Pinches the bridge of his nose. He looks like a Plasticine man trying to disguise his identity.

On the passenger seat, his mobile phone is barking out lefts and rights, and he is grateful for its help. With the windscreen made opaque by the deluge, he would have no chance of spotting the road signs without the metallic tones of the satnav. He's only been to Chester once before. Fin was still in a pushchair and he and Roisin had thought he might like to see the elephants at the impressive city zoo. The boy had slept the entire time. Roisin and McAvoy had enjoyed it just the same. They'd had a picnic in the bat cave and gone home owning one more okapi than they did when they woke up. Roisin had fallen in love with the curious striped creature, half-giraffe, half-zebra. She'd felt compelled to adopt one, and still receives monthly updates on its well-being. All in all, it had been a nice day.

'In 100 yards, turn left . . .'

The row of shops is a jumble of damp colours and swirled shapes. He glimpses a convenience store and a takeaway then turns the car abruptly into a quiet side road. He cruises past a school at less than 5 mph, nosing the people-carrier over a speed bump, then turns right twice more and finds himself edging down a quiet street of semi-detached homes. It's early afternoon, so most of the homeowners are at work, their empty driveways and unlit front rooms testament to the emptiness of each property. McAvoy squints and makes out a house number on the brick wall by a white-painted front door. Consults his notes and follows the curving road another hundred yards. He pulls in outside number 17 and leans across the passenger seat, opening the electric window as he does so. He stares through the rain at Lewis Caneva's home.

It's an unremarkable property. Three bedrooms, a small front garden screened by tall green trees, and a boxy Fiat on the brick drive.

Craning his neck he sees a face appear at the downstairs window.

Sees peach curtains moved by a timid hand.

Sees the bone-white of Lewis Caneva's skin.

McAvoy puts the window back up and switches the engine off. He looks at his phone, half-expecting there to be a message. There is none. Everybody back at the station is too bloody busy, fighting fires or trawling databases. Nielsen and Daniells have spent the weekend going goggle-eyed in front of computer screens, trying to come up with a list of anybody and everybody who had some involvement the night Sebastien Hoyer-Wood went through the window. They have managed to track down all the witnesses who gave a statement to the uniformed officers at the scene, and at McAvoy's suggestion, persuaded the Ambulance Service to give them the names of the paramedics who saved Hoyer-Wood's life. One is now living abroad and the other is a driving instructor in Hull. Daniells is trying to get in touch with him and two uniforms have been sent to his house, but so far he's off the grid. Were Pharaoh around she would no doubt be able to rustle up some extra resources, but Pharaoh is still locked away in a meeting room with ACC Everett, the Police Federation rep and Adam Downey's slick lawyer, trying to thrash out how best to play the case in the wake of Colin Ray's decision to beat the shit out of his client.

Downey is still in Hull Royal Infirmary and the legal situation is a mess. He has already been charged, but without a bail hearing he is in a state of limbo. It's likely that before the end of the day, magistrates will be instructed to give him bail, allowing him to walk free as soon as his injuries are healed. Where that leaves the case against him is anybody's guess. Pharaoh is trying to persuade Everett they should go ahead with the prosecution of Downey. Even Colin Ray has told them he is willing to take his punishment rather than let the little bastard go free. But Everett is unsure. He can see the headlines. He knows that Downey's legal team will tell the court all about what one of his senior officers did to him in the cells.

McAvoy steps from the car, his battered leather satchel above his head to try to block the rain. He slams the door and runs up the drive, sheltering against the wall as he raps on the wood. The colours change behind the opaque windows of the door and a moment later, Lewis Caneva is peering out.

From his file, McAvoy knows that Caneva is fifty-six years old, but the man in the doorway could be two decades older than that. He has a slightly Mediterranean look, but if he is as Italian as his name suggests, he has not aged like a Pinot Noir. He is bald on top, with a short horseshoe of white hair running from just behind his large ears. He's wearing dust-speckled glasses, and there are broken blood vessels and purple mottling across his cheeks. His skin puts McAvoy in mind of church candles. Small patches of grey hair sprout below his nose and below his jawline, and it looks as if he has shaved haphazardly or in the dark. For a moment, McAvoy wonders if this is true. Wonders whether Caneva struggles to look at himself in the mirror for any length of time.

'Sergeant McAvoy,' says Caneva, closing his eyes and sighing. 'You made good time. Please. Come in.'

There are long pauses between Caneva's words and he sounds breathless, his chest and throat bone dry. McAvoy rubs his boots on the plain welcome mat then follows Caneva down a short corridor with varnished wood underfoot. To his left is a staircase, a waterproof coat slung over the banister and two pairs of shoes on the bottom step. Caneva leads him into a small square living room. There is a two-seater leather sofa against one wall, facing an elaborate fireplace that houses an unlit, furnace-shaped wood-burner. The walls are decorated with what appear to be quality lithographs and sketches, all fine detail and pen-and-ink contours. There is no TV, but a variety of books lie scattered on the coffee table. As he stands in the doorway, McAvoy tries to glimpse their titles. They appear to be poetry books, though some of the text is laid out like prose. Caneva follows his gaze.

'Bit of a hobby,' he says. 'Analysing a few of the old Beat poets. Keeps me busy.'

McAvoy nods, unsure what to contribute. He vaguely remembers reading some Allen Ginsberg while doing his 'A' levels but fancies any attempt at demonstrating wisdom on the subject would end in tears.

'Please,' says Caneva, pointing to the sofa. 'Take a seat.'

McAvoy sits down awkwardly, watching as Caneva lowers himself painfully onto the seat next to him. It's an awkward position and McAvoy has to half-turn to look the man in the eye. This close, he can tell Caneva is not well. He's wearing two sweatshirts over a padded lumberjack shirt and still appears to be shivering. McAvoy wonders why he has not lit the fire. Notices, as he opens his mouth to speak, that his breath has begun to form crystals in the air.

'Dr Caneva,' he says. 'I'm grateful to you for agreeing to see me. As I explained on the phone . . .'

Caneva nods, telling him it's okay. 'You mentioned it was to do with a case I assisted with? As I explained to you, I am of course constrained by doctor–patient confidentiality . . .'

Now it is McAvoy who interrupts. 'I am fully aware, Dr Caneva. I appreciate you are in a difficult position and anything you say that breaches those rules would of course be inadmissible in court. However, I understand that you are no longer a practising psychiatrist, so at least you won't have the fear of breaching any professional code of ethics.'

For a moment there is silence in the room. McAvoy has decided not to make up his mind about the man who declared Sebastien Hoyer-Wood mentally unfit to stand trial. He does not want to prejudge him and therefore colour any information he gleans from this interview.

'It's very cold in here,' says Caneva, at length. 'I would have made up the fire but it wears me out. I'm not in the best of health, Sergeant.'

McAvoy looks at him, as kindly as he can.

'I could do it,' he says, shrugging.

'Could you?'

'No problem.'

McAvoy pulls himself off the sofa and kneels down in front of the fire. He does not speak as he twists newspaper into cones and assembles a triangle of kindling in the centre of the grate. He takes larger logs from the stack by the fireplace and a couple of pine cones, which he knows will burn like the devil as he touches a match to the paper. He wishes he had a little dried ragwort to add to the pile, the way his father taught him. The poisonous plant is one that fascinates him. Though it can kill horses, they seem to seek it out, nosing aside any quantity of verdant grass to nibble at the yellow-headed flower that can cause them an agonising death. McAvoy wishes he knew its Latin name, but never did that project at school. He makes a note to ask his dad.

'Lovely,' says Caneva, a slight smile on his face.

206

He sits back against the sofa cushions and watches the yellow flames take hold. Though it is not yet giving off warmth, the light in the room seems to have energised Caneva a little, and there is a healthier colour to his cheeks.

McAvoy returns to the sofa and prepares to speak, but Caneva beats him to it.

'Bowel cancer,' he says, unexpectedly, turning his head to McAvoy. 'Diagnosed six years ago. Two operations and a bout of chemo. They say I'm better now. Not cancerous, anyway. Not sure I feel it.'

'I'm sorry to hear that.'

'You imagine that once they've cut the cancer out everything will be back to normal, don't you? It's not like that. They messed about with me so much that my old life is gone. I don't mean to be rude here but I'm never off the toilet. Seriously. That's where they'll find me, when I go. I'll be on the toilet.' The smile drops. 'Not that anybody will be looking.'

McAvoy brushes the raindrops off his trouser legs. Rubs his hands through his hair. 'You don't get many visitors?'

Caneva shrugs. 'My daughter, couple of times a month. My son every few months. They'll ring. Birthday or Father's Day. But they have their own lives, I suppose.'

'Grandchildren?'

Caneva shakes his head. 'Not yet.'

They both sit and watch the fire, as if waiting for the other to spoil the nice warm glow that the policeman has brought to the room.

'You want to talk about Seb,' says Caneva, with a sigh.

'What makes you say that?'

'Just a feeling, I suppose.'

McAvoy looks at the older man. 'Is that something that psychiatrists believe in? Intuition?'

Caneva looks away.

'None of us are as clever as we think we are.'

After a moment, McAvoy nods. 'We're investigating two murders within the Humberside Police boundary. Both victims assisted in saving Sebastien Hoyer-Wood's life almost fifteen years ago in Bridlington. Our enquiries have led us to believe that Hoyer-Wood was a very dangerous man who was responsible for some very serious crimes. However, he has never been tried and never been jailed, and that was due in part to your testimony that he was mentally unfit to stand trial. At the moment, none of this makes a great deal of sense and we have no suspect and only half an idea, but I am of the opinion that you have some things to tell us about Sebastien Hoyer-Wood that may help. So, in essence, we're in your hands. It's very much a question of what you would like to tell me.'

Caneva looks away. Stares, through the net curtains, at the dark skies and the wall of water that beats against the houses and pavements of this quiet street. He looks back. At McAvoy. At the glow of the flame. At his books upon the coffee table, then down at his slippered feet on the peach carpet. His eyes close. He breathes, slowly, painfully. It is as if he is coming to an end.

'Dr Caneva?'

The older man turns to him.

'We were university friends,' he says, and has to cough when his voice comes out weak and reedy. 'Both studying medicine. Early Seventies, this was. I can't remember how we got talking. I think I was reading a book that he'd just seen the film of. Don't ask me what it was. But that was kind of typical of the pair of us.

Me, reading. Him enjoying the bright lights. Seb was kind of a big personality. He was a couple of years younger than me. I'd seen a bit of the world after finishing school and started university a little later than everybody else. Even so, we hit it off. We lived in different dorms for the first year but got a house together in our second.'

'And this was London, yes?'

Caneva nods. 'Yes, sorry. We're both southerners. I only moved up here to be near my son, after I retired and sold the house. I just live off the equity nowadays. The difference in prices . . .'

McAvoy waves a hand, and immediately regrets it. He should just let the man talk. To rattle on the way he wants. 'I'm sorry,' he says.

'No, no, you're right. You want to know about Seb. Well, we were friends. Best friends, if you can imagine such an old-fashioned concept. I was the quiet, bookish one, and he was all buzz and big bangs. He was very good-looking. Got a lot of attention from the ladies. Could have had anybody he wanted. I just don't think he wanted them. There was the odd girlfriend here and there but he wasn't really into relationships. Had a lot of female friends but didn't take advantage. I think that was partly what caused the incident.'

McAvoy's eyebrows meet. 'In Bridlington? Seriously?'

Caneva waves his hands. Seems to send his mind somewhere else. 'No, no. While at university. A girl. A fellow student. She tried it on with Seb. He politely declined. She was a real beauty, very vivacious and lively. She wore these little hippy dresses that drove people crazy. She wasn't used to being rejected. She went off in a huff and the next day she told her modern languages tutor that she had been assaulted. Sexually assaulted. I'm not saying she hadn't been, don't get me wrong. I'm just saying it wasn't Seb. He was with me all night. But Seb was the one she pointed the finger at. She didn't tell the police. Just told her tutor and he told the faculty of the university and Seb was brought in. He was shocked. Just didn't know what to make of it. It was like his whole world had fallen in. Seb's from an old family in Warwickshire. Military men, most of them. I think Seb had hopes of maybe serving as a doctor in the military when he finished his training. His dad was one of those really strict, distant types. I was with Seb when he called him to tell him what had happened. I had to listen in as he told his dad they were thinking of kicking him out and were advising the girl to go to the police . . .'

'What happened?'

Caneva rubs his hands over his face, pushes his cheeks back so it looks as though he is moving at speed. 'We changed courses.'

'We?'

'I wasn't doing very well in regular medicine anyway. I persuaded him to take the easy route and just get the hell out of there. Seb had shown a flair for physiotherapy. I felt psychiatry was something I could do well. The faculty were pleased to have the situation brought to a quiet conclusion.'

'And the girl?'

Caneva looks away. 'I don't know.'

There is silence in the room as each man absorbs the story. Finally, McAvoy speaks.

'You stayed in touch, yes? You both graduated and went on to decent careers?'

Caneva pulls a face. 'I did a little better than Seb,' he says, almost guiltily. 'I was a good psychiatrist. Got a job with a respected London firm straight out of university and specialised in several elite fields. I ended up as a partner in a practice in Bloomsbury. I married. Had two children. The right kind of life, or so they tell me.'

'And Seb?'

Caneva stares at the flame. 'He had his problems. I don't think he put himself back together really. He did okay in physiotherapy. Worked for a decent practice, met some interesting people. But there was a bit of him missing. That spark. We stayed in touch, of course. He spent a couple of Christmases with us. He was my son's godfather, though it took some persuading to get him to take the job.'

'He didn't want it?'

'Said he didn't deserve it. By then he had withered a little. He was drinking a little too much. I don't know whether he had started using drugs but I know that whenever we met, he would make jokes about him needing to see me for more than just my sparkling personality. Looking back, I should have seen that he was in trouble. I should have done more.'

McAvoy clicks his tongue inside his mouth. Thinks again of the crimes Hoyer-Wood went on to commit. 'You didn't think he was dangerous?'

'I wouldn't have had him near my family if I did,' he says, and his voice cracks on the word 'family'. He closes his eyes, tight. Controls his breathing. 'I knew he was depressed. I knew he was single and lonely. I should probably have had him to the house more often, but hindsight is a wonderful thing.'

'Your wife?' asks McAvoy, suddenly curious. 'How did she feel about your old university friend?'

'She knew him from university too. She liked him. Thought he was fun. But she saw the change in him too. Saw what a mess he was becoming.'

'And when you heard about his crimes?'

Caneva pinches the bridge of his nose. 'You have to remember that Seb was only ever charged with one incident. Despite the investigations of Humberside Police, there was no evidence he carried out any other crimes. So, when I heard about him breaking into a house in Bridlington and being viciously beaten by the homeowner, I had a very different picture in my mind from the one you currently hold. To me it was a cry for help. In my mind, he was the victim. Seb underwent surgery. He nearly died. And while he was under the knife, the police tried to build a case against him that would have put him in prison for a very long time. I visited him in hospital. He could barely speak. He couldn't move down one side of his body. They tried him with physiotherapy and he collapsed after every step. He had to defecate in a bag. This was not a man who needed prison. He needed help.'

McAvoy nods. 'So, you helped.'

Caneva breathes in, holds it, and then lets the air out of his lungs. 'For a while, my firm had been looking to provide a facility for the mentally ill. We wanted to set up a place for calm, quiet study that would be a relaxing, soothing place for the patients. I brought that initiative forward. I found premises in East Yorkshire. At that time, there was a high demand on existing provision for the criminally insane. It seemed obvious that there was money to be made for the company by getting Home Office approval to also take mental patients referred by the courts. Thankfully, one of our other partners had some old school connections that were able to fast-track the application. I was managing director and chief psychiatrist. I planned to maintain the Bloomsbury practice and provide a certain number of days at the premises in East Yorkshire.'

'And Seb?'

'He was still in hospital. Still barely able to communicate.'

'And yet you volunteered to compile the psychiatric report that went before the judge.'

McAvoy does not mean for his words to sound like an accusation, but there is little other way for Caneva to take them. He bristles a little.

'At that time, there was nobody better qualified in the country than me.'

'How did you conduct the interviews, given his difficulties?'

Caneva looks down. Begins to speak and stops himself.

'You didn't, did you? Didn't interview him at all?'

Caneva sniffs. Takes a handkerchief from his trouser pocket, but does nothing with it other than hold it in his palm.

'I'd known him for twenty years. It was obvious to me prison was no place for him. My facility was a healing place. A place where he would get well.'

McAvoy considers taking out his notebook, but decides not to. He wants to focus his gaze on the older man's eyes. 'And the judge agreed, yes? The criminal proceedings were thrown out.'

Caneva nods. 'We had the very best facilities. We brought in specialists to help with his physiotherapy, and obviously Seb's own skills and expertise were very handy with that. Once the court case was no longer hanging over him he could concentrate on healing. He made progress. He began to speak more freely . . .'

McAvoy nods. Runs his tongue around his mouth. Cracks his jawbone.

'Dr Caneva, I'm informed that you and your family eventually moved into the gamekeeper's cottage at your facility and that Sebastien Hoyer-Wood lived with you almost as part of the family.'

The accusation hangs in the air.

Caneva looks puzzled. Then he protests.

'That is simply not true, Sergeant. Yes, we had access to that lodge when I stayed in East Yorkshire for any significant time. Yes, I brought my family on occasion. And yes, after a time, I felt that Seb was well enough to begin a course of psychotherapy with myself, and we opted to conduct some of those sessions at my private residence . . .'

'But he was sent to a secure mental facility, Dr Caneva. That was the point. You can understand why some people may have issues with the idea of him spending so much time in a nice house with an old friend . . .'

Caneva raises a hand. He bristles. Scowls. His flash of temper has added some life to his features, and for the first time McAvoy can imagine this man in a sharp suit and designer glasses, sitting in a swish London consulting room.

'I had known him for twenty years!' barks Caneva. 'I knew best! The sessions were tremendously important and a safe, friendly atmosphere was crucial to that. People should leave it to the experts. People shouldn't judge . . .'

Now McAvoy pulls out his notebook. He flicks back a page and shows Caneva the date he has underlined twice.

'What happened that night?'

Caneva waves his hand again. Looks down at the floor. 'Without checking my diary, I couldn't honestly . . .'

McAvoy reaches across and puts a hand on Caneva's shoulder.

He forces the older man to meet his eyes. 'You know the date I'm referring to, Doctor.'

Caneva rubs his hand over his head. He takes off his glasses and holds them in his lap. McAvoy takes them from him, and cleans them with this cuff of his shirt. Wordlessly, he passes them back. Caneva nods his thanks. Purses his lips.

'It was just bad luck,' he says, at length. 'Seb was at the old gamekeeper's lodge with us. Our place. Tilia Cottage. We had been meeting once a week for several months. His therapy was going well. It was clear, at that stage, he had no memory of the incident in Bridlington or the alleged incidents before that. We were talking about his childhood. His relationship with his father. His dead mother. He had no siblings and grew up in a very isolated property. It was really quite surprising he was so gregarious by the time he came to university. It was obvious there was a lot of sadness in him. A lot of pain.'

'Anger?'

'There is anger in all of us. I am sure you know better than anybody that people are capable of things that come as a surprise to them.'

McAvoy gives an accepting nod. Wonders whether Caneva Googled him after he ended the phone call to arrange this interview. Whether the man has a computer and how he spends his time . . .

'And the night in question?'

Caneva sighs. 'One of the other patients made a run for it. I don't remember their name. They had a taste for arson, I remember that.'

'And Hoyer-Wood was at your home?'

'I received a call from the chief nurse. He told me what was happening. Told us to stay inside.'

'And then?'

Caneva breathes deeply. In the fireplace, a log cracks and the ash settles. A pine cone, half aflame, falls from the pinnacle of the fire to land in the grate. It burns, brightly and alone, then winks out.

Caneva lets his gaze drift to the ceiling then back to the fire. He closes his eyes.

'The house was set ablaze. We don't know why. The patient just wanted to see the smoke and the flames, I think. Just wanted to see some firemen.'

McAvoy sucks at his cheek.

'And Hoyer-Wood? Your family?'

'We got out. Seb was moving a little better. The nurses were able to talk the escaped patient into coming back inside. The fire was put out. Unfortunately it had already burned through a supporting wall, so it was declared structurally unsound and the property has since fallen into ruin and disrepair.'

McAvoy stares at him. Waits for more.

'Dr Caneva, it would seem that since that date, your life has taken something of a turn. Might I ask what happened?'

Caneva rubs his palm across his forehead. 'I had overextended the practice financially. We couldn't afford to run the facility and nobody wanted to buy it. At the same time my marriage was in difficulty. Things were hard at home. My wife's own mental health began to take a turn for the worse. It was a difficult time.'

'And your sessions with Hoyer-Wood?'

Caneva shrugs. 'I'm afraid that despite my best intentions and our long-established friendship, I had to curtail our sessions and find him alternative accommodation. A panel of psychiatrists declared that he was no longer mentally unstable but there was no appetite for reactivating the criminal case against him, and due to his physical difficulties he went to live at a private medical facility in the Lake District. We're no longer in touch, despite my best efforts. I know he suffered a major stroke some years ago. He began to suffer epileptic fits as a result of the damage to his brain, and one caused a severe stroke that left him paralysed.'

McAvoy has not taken his eyes off the side of Caneva's head. 'You went bankrupt?'

'I didn't have to, thankfully. The business did but I did not. I sold my home and moved to Chester. My son lived here, for a time. My daughter not too far away. She's doing very well in her career. A nurse, did I say? I had hoped to build some bridges.'

'There were problems?'

Caneva looks away. 'All children blame their parents, don't they? And they had a lot to blame me for.'

McAvoy looks at him, expectantly.

'Oh I'm sorry,' says Caneva, startled. 'I thought you would have that in your file. My wife died, Sergeant. It must be ten years now. More.'

'I'm sorry,' says McAvoy, and means it. Then, gently: 'How?'

Caneva closes his eyes. 'She took her own life, Sergeant. Pills. Enough pills to kill herself a dozen times over. She did not want to go on.'

He knows that Caneva is holding back but finds himself unable to bully this old, broken man. He wishes Pharaoh were here.

'Is that it, Sergeant?' asks Caneva, looking puzzled. 'Is that any help? I don't know anything about the incidents in Humberside.

I didn't know there still was a Humberside. I thought that all went with the boundary changes . . .'

McAvoy blinks, hard. 'We just kept the name,' he mumbles. 'Us and Radio Humberside. It's East Yorkshire on one side and North and North East Lincolnshire on the other. Bit unwieldy fitting that on a badge.'

Caneva manages a tired smile. 'So much pain,' he says, sadly, then looks at his watch, as though expecting the sergeant to say his goodbyes.

Instead, McAvoy gestures at the books on the table. 'This is just for fun, is it? You must miss the analysis. The sessions.'

Caneva looks a little more animated, sitting forward in his chair. 'I like getting inside people. Understanding them. Helping them understand themselves. Poetry is perhaps the human brain at its most exposed and honest.'

'Do you ever revisit old patients? In your mind, I mean.'

'Oh yes,' says Caneva, clearly thrilled to be talking about a subject he knows a lot about. 'I used to tape-record my sessions and have them transcribed. Sometimes, I will go through an entire transcript and something new will jump out at me . . .'

McAvoy swallows. 'Did you tape-record your sessions with Hoyer-Wood?'

Caneva stops, aware that his mouth has run away with him. Then he gives a half-laugh. 'I can't let you have them. It's not about never practising again. It's about your own code of ethics. Besides, I don't know if I could even find them . . .'

A sudden vibration in McAvoy's pocket alerts him to a text message. He opens his phone. Reads about the fate of Allan Godber. Beaten to death in a garage down the Avenues. A defibrillator machine found at the scene. Nothing left of his features save gristle and bone.

Suddenly, McAvoy's pity deserts him. His face becomes hard, his voice soft. Were Pharaoh to see him, she would not recognise him. Roisin would. She has seen him like this before. She was twelve, and bleeding, and the handsome constable with the ginger hair was smashing a wooden plank across the skull of a dying man . . .

'Dr Caneva,' he says, his jaw locked. 'Dr Caneva, it would be a tremendous help to me if you were to send the transcripts to the address on my card. I am not going to threaten you or appeal to your better nature. I am merely going to say that the doctor–patient privilege only extends so far. Sebastien Hoyer-Wood is alive. I am on my way to see him this afternoon. I feel he will make it clear that he has no problems with you sharing the transcripts with me. I know you have not been honest with me and I know that you are hiding many things, and I may never find out what they are. But people are dying and I feel that whatever sin you need to atone for could be atoned for now.'

McAvoy stands, placing a card on the coffee table. He towers over Caneva. Stares at the man until he looks away.

'Another man has died. The paramedic who saved Hoyer-Wood's life. This is no longer a theory. I know something happened that night and it cost you everything.'

He leans forward, his face in Caneva's, his breath upon his lips.

'Don't let it cost you anything more.'

Helen Tremberg has almost managed to persuade herself that she is suffering from a genuine virus. She has all the symptoms.

Sweats. Upset stomach. Sudden chills and uncontrollable shaking. She had felt almost unfairly treated when she phoned Shaz Archer this morning and said she was too ill to come in, only to hear her line manager give a snort of derisory laughter and tell her she was letting people down. It was only as she opened her mouth to defend herself that Helen remembered that her sickness is self-inflicted. Her mind, her heart, her conscience, are what is making her sick. She has spent the weekend crying, drinking, unsure who to tell or what to do next. Her thoughts keep turning to McAvoy. She wants to call him. Wants to tell him what she has done. Wants to ask for help. But McAvoy looks disappointed in her when she admits to taking the last chocolate biscuit. What the hell would he look like if he knew what she had done? The detective in her wants to send the footage to the science unit and have their boffins trace the origins of the email. But her face is clearly in shot. There is no denying that it is her in the film. It's her, gasping and moaning and slurping at the cocaine on her lips. It is her pushing back against the toned, tattooed man who never shows his face to the camera.

Helen has emailed him several times. She has asked him why. Asked him what he wants. Has called him every name she can think of. The emails have bounced back. The address she sent them to, and with which she shared such gorgeous flirtations these past weeks, no longer exists.

Here, now, Helen sits on her sofa, wrapped in a duvet, shivering as she drinks hot blackcurrant juice and stares at her phone. She has come up with a hundred different angles that could yet play out. Those in possession of the film could demand money. She has little, but has made up her mind to pay if that is what they want. They could demand information. She is willing to go only so far. Her fear is that they will simply keep her in their pocket. Her fear is she will become what she despises: a mole for the criminals she should be trying to catch.

Her phone rings.

Number withheld.

Helen's hands tremble as she answers.

'Hello.'

'Detective Constable Tremberg. Good morning. I am sorry to hear you are not in the best of health. Could I perhaps suggest that you take a couple of Ibuprofen and drink plenty of fluids? I am also led to believe chicken soup is good in these situations but can neither confirm or deny that from my own experiences. I have a very robust constitution.'

Helen says nothing. Just feels tears make tracks down her cheeks.

'Perhaps you are right,' comes the voice, after a moment. 'Perhaps we should not dilly-dally with pleasantries and chit-chat. Perhaps we should come to the crux of the matter. And the matter is this: I have in my possession footage of your good self, performing acts that are most unbecoming for a police officer. I have no doubt you would not wish for this footage to be seen by your superior officers, or any members of the popular press, or for that matter simply emailed to every one of your colleagues. If it is any consolation, I do not wish to see that happen either. You are not a very attractive woman and nobody really wants to open their emails to find footage of your large posterior bouncing up and down in front of them. So perhaps we could spare ourselves any unpleasantness. Perhaps you could help my associates and me.'

Helen swallows. Manages a few words. 'What do you want? Please, I don't have much—'

'Detective Constable, we know precisely what you are worth, and financially, your meagre savings are akin to the fluff in my pocket. No, I need one small favour from you, and then the footage in question will be destroyed.'

'What? What do you want?'

'At present, a young man of my acquaintance is unreasonably being held in custody. He is in Hull Royal Infirmary having suffered some rather nasty injuries at the hands of the intriguing and entertaining Detective Chief Inspector Colin Ray. I am optimistic that your ACC Everett will ensure that the charges against him are dropped. He is, after all, an accommodating man. However, there are those within the police force who will not roll over quite so easily, and to that end, it would be best if those who witnessed young Mr Downey's brief moment of embarrassment could be persuaded to alter their statements. There is a seamstress by the name of Melanie Langley who helped apprehend Mr Downey. I would be most grateful if she could be persuaded to alter her version of events. I have, of course, got many other ways to accomplish this goal, but your intercession would be least messy.'

Helen holds her stomach, feeling a fresh wave of nausea. 'I can't, I don't—'

'Please, Detective Constable, there is more. I am further led to believe that while Mr Downey was incapacitated, an associate of Miss Langley took it upon herself to relieve him of a sum of money. This money is neither here nor there, but the presumptuousness, the lack of respect, are unacceptable in light of the ongoing expansion of our enterprise. I would like the name and address of this person. If it helps, I am led to believe she is very pretty, was carrying a child, and is somewhat Romany in her appearance and deportment.'

The nausea stops. The pain halts. Adrenalin flows through Helen's body. She opens her mouth but is cut off before she can manage to speak.

'I am grateful for your assistance in this matter. I realise this is a lot to ask and it will be difficult for somebody with your sense of justice and morality. To this end we have deposited a large sum of money in your bank account. I would suggest, as you endure the sting of acting against your better judgement, that you remind yourself you are doing so to save lives. I would also encourage you to visit a general practitioner at your earliest convenience. Our mutual acquaintance is a carrier of any number of sexually transmitted infections . . .'

Helen drops the phone. It lands on the sofa without being switched off, and at the other end of the line the man to whom she was speaking hears her throwing up all over her living-room floor.

13

4.40 p.m. Chamomile House, in the heart of the Lake District: just two miles south of where William Wordsworth doomed the humble daffodil to a lifetime of overexposure.

Some 160 miles north of Hull.

Aector McAvoy is leaning on the desk in a brightly lit reception area, talking to a pretty young woman about the traffic he has endured on the three-hour drive up from Chester. He has passed through hail, rain and blindingly bright sunlight. He would not be surprised to see snow start to fall.

Here, now, the weather is dry but decidedly gloomy. Beyond the windows the clouds hang low: a damp hammock punctured by the tops of the trees that dot the woodland grounds of this expensive care home. It's a welcoming place; all slate roof and chunky brickwork, low roofs and climbing ivy. It is home to twenty-two patients with varying degrees of dependency, all of whom pay handsomely to enjoy the best possible facilities. This is a care home that smells of rhododendrons and roast dinners rather than boiled cabbage and bleach, and McAvoy, with his aching back and tired eyes, is considering checking himself in.

'I'm sure she won't be long.'

McAvoy is running out of things to say to the receptionist. She is strikingly pretty, and from his elevated vantage point he has inadvertently noticed both the tattoo on her chest, and the lace of her bra. Neither of these discoveries has helped him make small talk, or calmed him down after a difficult and tiring journey, made longer by constantly having to pull over to take phone calls from the office. Ben Nielsen is doing a superb job, following McAvoy's instructions and hunting down everything they have on the people who were patients at Caneva's facility the night of the escape. He is also seeking whatever is available on Lewis Caneva's family, and on a hunch, is doing a general search on the father of Sebastien Hoyer-Wood. McAvoy does not know what he expects to find but is certain the answers will be unearthed if they all just keep working hard and thinking positively. The thought of giving any kind of rousing speech to the troops terrifies him, but he fears that such a moment may yet be called for. Pharaoh has unofficially handed things over to him during her absence, and the two officers under his command are rising to the challenge of pleasing him.

He's pleased they aren't grumbling about being stuck in the office, giving themselves migraines in front of flickering computer screens, getting steadily unhealthier in sticky, fly-blown rooms. After all, it is McAvoy who has taken on the job that none of the others want. He's the one who has to sit down with a monster. It is a thought that scares him. He doesn't feel up to it. He has got better at believing in himself, but there are still times when he wants to run back to the office and hide in a cupboard while stronger personalities take charge.

A little shaky, a tremble in his voice, he turns his attention back to the young girl.

He is trying to think of something to say to her when a small, round-bottomed woman in her late thirties emerges from a corridor, smiling broadly. She extends a soft plump hand, which McAvoy takes in his. She is wearing what looks a little like a karate suit, but it is a livid blue and has the name of her employers stitched on the breast, next to an upside-down watch.

'I'm Evelyn,' she says, brightly. 'I'll be looking after you. Sebastien's waiting for you. He seems quite excited.'

McAvoy turns back to the receptionist, who appears to be checking that her blouse is sufficiently unbuttoned for a tall man to enjoy the view. He gives a smile that makes him look like a pumpkin lantern, and then scurries away. At six foot five, McAvoy is not built for scurrying. He looks like a giant in chains.

Evelyn leads McAvoy back out through the front door and across the car park where his people-carrier is still making a worrying whooshing noise. So far, he has driven well over 200 miles today and the car is as unaccustomed to long journeys as he is to squeezing his big frame into such a small seat for so long. Both he and the vehicle are suffering.

'You've caught us at an awkward time, Sergeant,' says Evelyn as she points him down one of the footpaths into a copse of trees. 'Problems with the drains. We have a septic tank here. Doesn't need emptying more than twice a decade, provided you use the right chemicals, but we rather forgot to inspect the chamber and it's really backed up. Not very nice. If we hadn't got it drained we would have been wading in sludge, and that isn't what you want when you're in a wheelchair.'

McAvoy, who stands a good head and shoulders above her, is surprised to find that he has to jog to keep up with her boisterous, bustling progress down the path. He can't think of what to say, so sniffs the air. Smells rhododendrons and damp grass. Smells earth. Gets a tiny whiff of Evelyn's anti-bacterial hand-wash and Avon perfume. He decides to make no comment on the septic tank.

'Sebastien's at the end there,' says Evelyn, pointing ahead. She has led them around the building and swipes a key card on a pad by the glass back door. Stepping inside, she ushers him down a wide, empty corridor, its walls illustrated with pictures of hot-air balloons and birds.

'I don't really know what you're expecting of him,' she says, neutrally. 'He can't communicate well at all. He can make emotions understood and we know when he's angry, but other than that, it depends whether you're on his wavelength or not. I've helped him write the occasional message on some website or other that has caught his eye, but you have to go through the alphabet with him for every single letter. It's very laborious, but that's what we're here for, I suppose. His computer is his lifeline. Very expensive piece of kit, but it means he gets to know what's going on in the outside world and I don't have to spend every moment reading to him.'

McAvoy stops in the corridor, several feet from the room that contains the man who used to enjoy raping women in front of their husbands. He suddenly doesn't want to knock. He turns to Evelyn.

'So you're his personal carer? Full-time, yes?'

Evelyn brushes her bobbed hair back from her pleasant round face. 'I'm his nominated staff member, if that's what you mean. Each of our patients has somebody who is specifically responsible for their well-being and standard of care. I oversee a team of nurses and health-support workers who then assist in taking care of him. Sebastien's one of our more challenging patients. A lot of our patients are relatively mobile. Sebastien needs round-the-clock care. We have a good staff though and can call on a central agency for support should we ever be short-staffed. He's well looked after.'

McAvoy nods. He's not sure he's overly concerned with how well they are looking after Hoyer-Wood.

'How much do you know about his case history?' he asks, delicately.

Evelyn appears to understand the magnitude of the question. 'To treat our patients the best way we can, it's important to know as much about them as we can. We have full access to Sebastien's case notes. He's been in the system a long time.'

'And the court case?'

Evelyn looks nonplussed. 'The file said he was charged with an offence while exhibiting mental health problems. That was when he suffered his initial injuries, I believe. Those injuries to his brain led to severe epilepsy, and I understand that in turn caused the stroke that left him like this. It was a double tragedy, really, as it appears that he was making good progress with his physiotherapy and speech therapy. Some people just have misfortune thrown at them.'

McAvoy studies the image nearest him on the wall. Admires the fine pencil strokes that have created the wicker basket, hanging below a brightly coloured balloon. It is an image that suggests freedom. Release. He doesn't want to take his eyes off it and step into the room of a man whom he cannot picture, but feels he is beginning to know.

'It's expensive here, I presume?'

Evelyn smiles. 'You get what you pay for.'

228

'And who pays for him?'

She spreads her hands, apologising for not being able to say. Then she leans in and whispers, as if this will be less of a breach of confidentiality: 'His father died. He inherited a lot of money.'

McAvoy nods his thanks.

Breathes deeply.

Coughs.

Blinks.

He can't put it off any longer.

He takes three steps and knocks on the pine. At his side, Evelyn turns the handle and pushes open the wide door.

Sebastien Hoyer-Wood sits in a low-backed chair at the centre of a large, green-painted room. In front of him is a computer monitor; to his right a low sofa facing a television. One wall is all glass, reflecting back the opposite wall, which is stacked with books, CDs and DVDs. The floor is linoleum, but with a wood-panel effect.

'Would you mind?' says Evelyn, pointing to a small patch of black matting by McAvoy's feet. 'You have to discharge your static on there or it can cause a fit.'

Flustered, McAvoy does as he is told, rubbing his shoes on the odd material, until Evelyn tells him he can stop.

'Do I take my boots off?'

'No, you're fine now. Anyway, this is Sebastien. Sebastien, this is Detective Sergeant McAvoy. He's come to talk to you.'

McAvoy extends a hand, as if to shake. He looks at the proffered palm. Feels appalled with himself. Drops it back to his side.

Up close, Hoyer-Wood is a melted waxwork, a handsome sculpture left too close to the fire. His face is bottom-heavy, locked open in a permanent yawn. A column of thin drool spills from his lower lip to puddle on the chest of his green sweatshirt. His clothes seem to conceal nothing but bones. McAvoy is put in mind of a pirate's skeleton. He half imagines pulling back the man's shirt to reveal bare ribs and a cutlass blade.

Evelyn beckons him forward.

'Please, take a seat. It's best if you're near him. It might help you better understand.'

Hoyer-Wood's expression does not change as McAvoy clumsily takes a wooden chair from beside the bookcase and places it next to the patient. He turns his head and looks at Hoyer-Wood's computer screen. A web page is open, the text-size triple the norm. McAvoy glances at it. Hoyer-Wood is reading an essay on a poem by Robert Browning. It is a verse that McAvoy recognises and admires; ugly language made beautiful. It is written in the voice of a jilted wife, planning to poison her husband's lover. McAvoy glimpses the words 'moisten' and 'mash'. Reads the phrase 'pound at thy powder'. It is a poem in which murder is coolly and deliberately planned and enjoyed.

'Browning?' asks McAvoy, turning to Hoyer-Wood, whose eyes are rolling back to stare at the panelled ceiling. 'I always enjoyed "Lost Leader". I like the Beat poets too. And the modern classics. Actually, a mutual acquaintance of ours is currently studying the Beat poets.' McAvoy looks at the side of the other man's face, trying to capture his gaze, before adding: 'Lewis Caneva.'

Next to him, Hoyer-Wood twists in his chair, his mouth opening and closing and a series of unintelligible noises coming from his throat.

'I don't think that's one of his favourites,' says Evelyn, sitting down on the sofa.

'No,' says McAvoy. 'I got that.'

230

'He's very fortunate to have this machine,' says Evelyn, indicating the computer in front of Hoyer-Wood. 'It recognises certain sounds. It has a keypad too that he can operate with his finger when the drugs have his muscle spasms under control. At the moment he's having quite a rough time. He can surf the Net quite easily. We loaded up a lot of favourite sites and he can scroll through them as he wants. He can spell out search words, though it's a hell of an ordeal. Still, it keeps him out of mischief, eh, Sebastien?'

McAvoy says nothing. He just looks at the man in the chair. The room is warm and bright, but it contains a scent, perhaps a colour to the air, that he finds unsettling. It is as though something has died in this room. He smells decayed humanity. Something nearby is rotting. It is a place of moist corruption and slow, damp death.

For a moment, McAvoy is unsure how to proceed. He doesn't know what he wants or what he expected. It is clear Hoyer-Wood is not faking his injuries. Before he entered the room he half-entertained the notion of tipping him from the chair and seeing if he put out his hands to break his fall. Now he sees how unnecessary that would be. Hoyer-Wood is a virtual skeleton. His body will not obey his commands. His mind is a prisoner in a bag of bedsores and rotting flesh. McAvoy feels a sudden rush of pity for the man. Tells himself that whatever his crimes, he is suffering punishments far greater than a prison sentence. He reminds himself that only one case was ever built against him and that the rapes he is alleged to have carried out are based on unsigned statements and guesswork. Perhaps the man in the chair was truly a victim. Perhaps he, too, suffered in his youth. Perhaps he acted as he did as a cry for help, and care facilities such as these are a better place for him than a jail cell. He is glad Pharaoh is not here. She would see the softening of his face.

'Sebastien,' he says, quietly. 'Is it okay to call you Sebastien? Thank you. Sebastien, I'm investigating two murders. Three, I suppose. I don't know whether you read the newspapers or have much interest in current affairs, but over the past week, three people in the Humberside Police region have been killed. You might remember these people. They saved your life. Philippa Longman gave you CPR the night you almost died. Yvonne Dale applied pressure to your leg wound. Allan Godber was the paramedic who restarted your heart. All of these people have been killed in manners that suggest somebody is not very grateful to them for saving you. I would ask you to think very clearly and carefully. Now, do you have any thoughts that might be of benefit to our enquiries?'

McAvoy licks his lips and breathes out, slowly. Behind him, he hears Evelyn let out a little exclamation of surprise. He wonders how long it will be before she goes and makes a quick phone call to her superiors. When he had rung to arrange to speak with the patient, he had been a little economical with the facts.

Suddenly, Hoyer-Wood begins to spasm. His right arm bounces up and down and his jaw jerks forward so suddenly that McAvoy half expects his neck to crack. His left hand clutches at his own trouser leg and his face suddenly looks pained and wretched. McAvoy turns to Evelyn, unsure whether to intervene. She gives him a quiet shake of the head. This is normal.

At length, the paroxysm subsides. Evelyn crosses to his side. She takes a pad from her pocket.

'Do you want to talk, Sebastien?'

A noise. A blink.

Evelyn confirms that he has given his assent. She starts to recite the alphabet. After he has picked four letters, McAvoy interrupts.

'Is he saying he's sorry?'

The noise Hoyer-Wood makes is clearly a 'yes'.

'Sorry they are dead?'

Evelyn looks at him, not understanding. Hoyer-Wood stays silent. Just drools onto his clothes.

McAvoy sighs. He wonders what he can possibly get from this.

'Sebastien, I spent an hour today with Lewis Caneva. You remember him, yes? Your best friend from university. The man who did you quite a good turn? He tells me that there was a time, back when you were a patient of his, that you were getting better. He tells me you were beginning to walk unaided. You could make yourself understood. I wonder, could you tell me exactly what happened to leave you in this condition you are now in?'

Hoyer-Wood's face stretches open. The top half of his head looks as though it could come off. McAvoy turns to Evelyn, and she begins the process again.

McAvoy does not want to interrupt. He crosses to the bookshelf. He examines the spines of some of the novels. There are some classics. A few thrillers. Poetry anthologies and biographies of poets. He tries to find anything useful. Any tome on voyeurism or domination. But there is nothing incriminating.

'Sergeant?'

He turns back. Evelyn is standing with her pad open.

'He says Lewis is his friend. His wife was too. He misses him. He hopes he remembers what good friends they once were.'

McAvoy waits for more.

'And?'

Evelyn gets up and walks over to McAvoy. Her voice drops to the conspiratorial whisper in which she had shared the details of his financial circumstances.

'He says I'm to tell you the rest from what I know of his files,' she says. Takes a breath. Rushes on. 'The epilepsy got steadily worse in the years after he left the home that you mentioned. The fits became so severe that even if the mental health authorities left him out, he would not be safe to live alone. Then he had what we call a "catastrophic" stroke. There was an incident involving a vehicle he was a passenger in and the stress of that event was almost certainly the trigger. He came to us shortly afterwards. It was such a shame because he had started writing. He was getting fitter. I think he entertained hopes of being allowed to go back to work some day . . .'

McAvoy crosses back to Sebastien Hoyer-Wood. It is impossible to read his expression. His face is too inhuman to convey his thoughts. But for an instant, McAvoy could swear that in that gory mask, between the damp eyes and the rictus set of his mouth, he sees a flash of life.

Unable to stop himself, McAvoy reaches out and touches Hoyer-Wood's computer screen. He takes the sensor that sits on the smooth plastic tray in Hoyer-Wood's lap, and quickly flicks back to the websites that Hoyer-Wood has been browsing before McAvoy entered the room. He looks at the screen for a moment. Swallows. Drinks in the gaudy colours. The lurid banner adverts. The image of the young girl on all fours, crying as a man in a mask holds her hair and fucks her roughly; another man tied to her bedpost with a belt and clearly begging the masked man to stop. He wonders how long it took Hoyer-Wood to blink out the word 'cuckold'. Whether his nurses allow this indulgence or if he has found a way to keep it to himself.

McAvoy flicks the screen back to the poetry as Evelyn moves back to his side of the screen.

'Erm, Sergeant, I'm not one hundred per cent comfortable with this. Would you mind if we took a temporary break while I contacted my superiors? I'm terribly sorry . . .'

McAvoy does not want to cause a scene or get her into trouble. Nor does he want to leave without understanding who the man in the chair used to be.

'You said he was writing again?' he asks, innocently.

'Yes, yes, some lovely poetry. A diary of sorts, all about his plans to get well again and the battle with his physiotherapy. It was all sent to us when he moved here, though I believe he asked for much of it to be thrown away during one of his darker days. I read a little myself. Very inspirational. He spoke about the staff at the last care home. How he imagined them at home, in their peaceful, pleasant lives. He wanted that. Wanted to share it with them. Very moving. Now, please . . .'

McAvoy turns his head to Hoyer-Wood. Slowly, softly, he bends down and places his lips by the crippled man's ear.

'You'd do it all again, wouldn't you? You'd get out of that chair and rape women and destroy lives and get off on the suffering. I know you would. Somebody else knows you would too. I think they are punishing those who saved you, Sebastien, because after you were caught, after your life was saved, you ruined somebody else's life too. They can't punish you, can they? What's to punish? There's nothing left of you. So they're taking out their rage on the people who kept you in the world. Whose life did you destroy last, Sebastien? Whose?'

McAvoy raises his head. Watches the brown of his own eyes swim in the blue irises of the man in the chair.

Slowly, as though using every ounce of his strength, Hoyer-Wood says Evelyn's name. She crosses to his side. Dutifully takes out her pen. Begins the alphabet afresh.

A moment later, McAvoy stomps from the room, moving as fast as he can. Were he to stay, he would not be able to stop any violence he began.

In Sebastien Hoyer-Wood's room, Evelyn looks quizzically at the letters on her pad. Reads again what he has told her in grunts and blinks.

'Tell me about your wife.'

Adam Downey is on his knees, spitting saliva and bile into the green water of the toilet bowl. He can taste blood. Can taste the three slurps of tea that he had managed for breakfast. He can smell the thick mucus that seems to have formed a wall in his sinuses behind his bruised nose.

He snarls as he wipes his mouth. Sneers at his own distorted reflection in the water of the toilet bowl. The act of retching has made his bruised ribs throb with pain and his already aching jaw now feels as though it has been opened with a car jack.

Fucking Colin Ray!

He pushes himself back from the toilet. Rinses his mouth and splashes water on his face. He looks at his reflection in the tiny mirror above the sink. He has cuts and bruises to his handsome face and a big scab on one elbow. The bandages and padding that cover the lacerations to his back form a slight bump in the outline of his T-shirt, but he doesn't look as bad as he feels. He uses his thumb to check, one more time, that none of his teeth are wobbly, then opens the door.

The smell of the hospital ward offends his nostrils, so his

actions are quick. He crosses to the bed where he has been a patient these last couple of days. He picks up his copy of his release paperwork, feeling a half-smile crease his face. He knew he'd get bail somehow. He just didn't expect to have to get his head kicked in to achieve it. Still, he trusts that his new employers had no alternative. He's just grateful they kept their promises. He always intended to keep his.

Downey takes another quick look at the room. He's pleased to be leaving. He doesn't like being cooped up, and the succession of uniformed constables who kept him company were not great conversationalists. Anyway, he hasn't really wanted to talk. His mind has been elsewhere. On getting out. On getting paid. On getting *her*.

The last uniformed constable has gone. Downey is a free man, for now. He can walk out the door and do what the fuck he likes. And he knows exactly what he'd like to do.

Gingerly, painfully, but refusing to yield to his injuries, he gets himself ready. The bin liner that contained the possessions he had brought with him from the custody suite is lying on the bed. The T-shirt he was wearing when they brought him in to A&E was too ragged and bloody to be kept, but he slips into the same jeans he had on when Colin Ray beat the shit out of him. The T-shirt he is wearing was torn fresh from a cellophane packet. It had been inside the bin-liner. He doesn't know if it is a present from somebody. Perhaps it is some kind of apology from the police for what happened to him. If it is, they can fuck off. He doesn't wear plain T-shirts. He likes a label.

Downey stands in the doorway to his hospital room. He takes a breath.

Young, fit and energetic, Downey would normally be able to walk the mile and a half to his Victoria Dock home, but he's feeling a bit banged up and doesn't fancy walking through the city centre wearing this T-shirt. He pulls out his phone to call a taxi. There's probably a rank of them somewhere around here, or a pay phone with a free link to a local firm, but Downey reckons there's no point running a taxi firm if you can't get yourself a lift. Besides, it will be nice to give the drivers a real job for a change. He might request Hakan. The lad will have been shitting himself these past few days and it will be better all round if his punishment comes quickly.

He opens his phone. He's surprised to find that it's already ringing. The number has been withheld.

Downey feels a tongue of nausea licking the inside of his throat. He knows himself to be able to hold his own in a fight, but his confidence has taken a little knock and he's weak as a kitten. If the call is from the man he thinks it's from, he knows he needs all his faculties, and right now, he's not himself. He's had his arse kicked twice in the past few days – once by an old bloke and once by a girl. It's the girl who's hurt him most. She took his money. Got him caught. Acted like he was a nobody. Oh, he has such plans . . .

'Hello,' he says, focusing on the call.

'Mr Downey,' comes a familiar voice. 'I hope you are well.'

Downey closes his eyes. He leans against a circular column that supports the front of the hospital, pleased to be outside. He looks around him. There are people in wheelchairs, people holding drips. On the grass, beyond the little shop, is an area where patients and visitors alike sit and smoke; some holding cigarettes in hands that are wrapped in bandages or skewered by a cannula. A husband and wife pass a cigarette between them. She's in a pink dressing gown, both eyes black. He's in jeans and a Man United shirt and his right hand is in plaster. To his left, Downey sees the maternity hospital. New life. New hopes. New customers, some day.

The vista of real life suddenly makes his head reel. He doesn't want to be a part of it. Of *them*. He's above it all. He suddenly reminds himself who he is. What he had to do to prove himself to these men. The voice at the other end of the line scares him. But he has earned their respect and they owe him a favour. He tells himself to get it together.

'I've been better,' he says, trying to sound casual. 'But fresh air feels nice.'

'Excellent. I can assure you that we had several stratagems for securing your release. The one that was successful came at a high price to your well-being. I trust that when the physical wounds heal, no festering resentment will remain?'

Downey finds himself smiling. He likes how this man talks. He wishes he could picture him.

'I'm out, that's what matters.'

'A pragmatic and sensible approach, Mr Downey. You repay our faith in you.'

There is a pause. Downey expects more, but nothing comes. Nervous again, he fills the silence himself.

'Look, what happened . . . at the shop. One of my lads thought he was going to get pulled over. He didn't want to lose the gear. The sewing shop was his idea. I did my best. It just got out of hand—'

The voice is placating and soft. 'Hush, Mr Downey. We fully understand that sometimes our employees do not represent us in the way we would represent ourselves. You have been an asset to us during your brief time in our employ. We have no inclination to rebuke you for this minor blot on your otherwise impressive curriculum vitae. I would, however, prepare yourself for some distressing news about one of your drivers. Hakan is no longer available for night shifts. Or day shifts. Or walking around and breathing. I trust you will not grieve too much for this loss to your staff?'

Downey screws up his eyes. He'd planned to give Hakan a slap. Maybe cut his take. He tries not to let himself picture what they did to him. He knows it will have involved a nailgun and a blowtorch. He knows his skin will have bubbled like sugar in a pan. *Fuck.*

A memory comes, unbidden. He and Hakan had talked about football. They'd watched a Champions League game together, Hakan's team trying to get past the group stages. They'd both cheered and laughed when they stuck one past Barcelona. They might even have bloody *hugged*. Christ, Hakan had given him a Galatasaray scarf to wear. They were never mates. But they'd laughed together. Shared a few cans of beer . . .

Downey gives a little cough, which becomes a retch. He swallows down what comes up.

'Mr Downey?'

'It's okay,' he says, and hopes it is.

'Excellent. Now, as you can see, we are calling on a mobile phone number that is open to abuses and eavesdroppers. I hope you do not distress yourself over this. We have taken steps to ensure that we can talk freely. However, there is always the possibility of the unforeseen hiccup, so I will keep the remainder of this conversation brief. You should know that Colin Ray is currently suspended and under observation by ourselves. The seamstress will soon be withdrawing her statement. The loss of our product is not of huge concern at this time. You will soon be free to resume deliveries. There remains just the one frayed thread for you to pick at.'

Downey focuses. Feels his lips twitch. 'The girl.'

'Precisely. I do not want you to feel too emasculated by her involvement in your predicament. However, you are a young man with pride and an ego, and I know you will not sleep well until you have demonstrated to this young Romany that you are not to be treated thusly. It would also be a useful PR exercise if you were to make an example of the penalty for such transgressions.'

'You've found her?'

'I am confident the information will be with us swiftly. For now, I would advise you to go and reassert your authority with your workforce and perhaps offer a little financial incentive to anybody who wishes to relieve their frustrations by assisting you in censuring the young lady.'

Downey bites his lip. Holds in vomit and a smile.

'How far can I go?'

For the first time, Downey hears the man give what might be considered a laugh. 'Mr Downey, you are a young and vigorous man, watched over by powerful friends. I should imagine that by now it has occurred to you that you can do whatever you want.'

The nausea subsides. Downey finds himself grinning. He likes this. Likes the feeling. He's untouchable. The sea of humanity may not part as he walks through, but here, now, it feels as though he can point and nod and dispense life or death as he sees fit. He matters. He's going to show his guts, that he's got what it takes . . .

'Blowtorch?' he says, softly.

The line remains silent, as if the man is weighing things up.

241

'Perhaps not. This is not our regular business. This is a perk. I leave it to your discretion. We will be in touch.'

Downey hears the phone being put down and stands, unmoving, for a moment or two. He looks around him. At the people. The *plebs*. He feels sick and decides he doesn't give a damn.

He decides to walk. Suddenly, he is a young man with energy and a sense of purpose.

More than anything, he is a man with a bitch to kill.

14

Everybody thinks the rain will come today. The sky is a mountain of cold ash but the sun still burns through, and the air is thick and greasy. Hull yearns for a storm. People watch the skies the way they used to watch the seas. Then, it was to glimpse a returning trawler. Today, it is in the hope that the clouds will finally part and the tensions that fizz and crackle across the city will be swept away in a flood of healing rain.

In his ten years in Hull, McAvoy has never known its residents to actively yearn for a downpour. On this flat landscape, rain is something to be feared. In 2007, the city was almost lost to floods. An extraordinary deluge left Hull half-submerged. The city had sloshed and skidded to a halt as an ocean of water tumbled from the sky onto bone-dry streets and poured into drains blocked by rubbish and leaves. McAvoy, in his last few days in uniform, had barely slept for three days as the city's emergency services worked round the clock to drain the water and help stranded motorists and residents make it to high ground. McAvoy was even shown on the local news, carrying a pensioner and her dog in his arms, the water up to his waist, a look of grim determination upon his red face. If it had happened in London it would have been a major catastrophe, but it happened in Hull, and barely made the national news. All these years later, there are still people living in mobile homes in the driveways of their houses, gradually repairing the damage to their properties. Every time it rains, there is a sense of mild panic in the city. Even so, most would risk a downpour now. It's just too hot. Too oppressive. Too bloody muggy by half. And with three murders in and around the city inside a week, Hull is feeling twitchy. It is as though the air is charged with something. People are aggressive, and scared.

McAvoy is feeling ill. He feels like he's coming down with a cold. His bones ache from yesterday's long drive, and though he made it home to Roisin by 8 p.m., there was unpacking to be done, and Lilah had not settled in her new bedroom, so there was little chance to rest and groan the way he had wanted to. The baby's cries began around five minutes after McAvoy's eyes finally closed, having spent restless hours trying to get Sebastien Hoyer-Wood out of his mind. Roisin had told him to stay in bed, to leave it all to her, but he couldn't be that kind of dad. He got up. Sat with his wife and child on the front step of their new home and watched the black waters and the distant lights. It had been nice, at the time. She had closed her fingers in his, and Lilah had been happy enough to sit in Daddy's lap and pull his chest hair. But it meant that he got little more than an hour's sleep. A breakfast of scrambled egg and home-made tomato sauce now sits uncomfortably at the top of his stomach, refusing to go down, and he doesn't know if it's sickness or the heat of the day that is making him sweat.

It's mid-morning and McAvoy is walking over to the small swing park that sits near the police station at the edge of the Orchard Park estate. The schools break up for the summer holidays in a day or two and soon the place will be packed with kids from the estate. Coppers looking for a place of quiet reflection will not be made welcome. It will be teeming with shell-suited yobs necking energy drinks, and younger kids trying to play games without appearing to act like children. McAvoy has chatted to a few of them in the past and knows the locals are far from all bad. Though some of the pre-teens can be obnoxious, most are just normal children who happen to have been born somewhere that offers more bad influences than good. There are good people here. They just seem to get swallowed up.

He couldn't have stayed in the office any longer. For the past couple of hours, McAvoy has been briefing his small team of officers on what he learned yesterday. As he spoke, he heard how half-hearted and far-fetched it all seemed, and he could see from their reactions that they were losing faith. It is clear that the victims are all linked to Hoyer-Wood, but McAvoy's half-formed idea that somebody is punishing those who saved the man's life is starting to be challenged by the team. While McAvoy mumbled and stumbled through his notes, the junior constables began to throw out fresh theories. Perhaps the victims simply *met* through Hoyer-Wood. Perhaps they became friends. Perhaps their deaths were nothing to do with him. Would it be worth checking their Internet histories to see if they were in some kind of relationship? Was there a weird three-way love triangle at the centre of it all? McAvoy had pointed out the nature of the injuries. He had tried to make them *see*. But when they asked him whom he had in mind as a suspect, he had nobody to offer. He'd agreed to let Nielsen run with the alternative theories. He told them that Trish Pharaoh would be back in charge before the end of the day and they would all meet up for another briefing at teatime. He had bolted for the exit like a frightened horse, not knowing what to do next.

He thinks, again, of the words Nielsen had so carelessly tossed into the pot.

'The thing is, you might see serial killers everywhere, Sarge. After what you've been through . . . after that shit at Christmas. Not everybody is killing for cosmic reasons, Sarge. Some people are just stupid or horrible or evil little bastards . . .'

McAvoy had stood there, face so sallow and motionless as to look halfway decomposed. He'd wanted to run. Wanted to sprint from the room before he was reminded of any more bodies from his past.

While he tries to get a hold of himself and fit some of the pieces of it all together, the basic police work is continuing. Door-knocking, fact-checking, forensics and CCTV may well provide the lead that they are seeking. The Allan Godber murder had clearly not gone as the killer planned. The team are working on the assumption that the killer had planned to electrocute Godber with the defibrillator machine, but that he had not reckoned with the complexities of the device. Constable Daniells had done a quick crash course on defibrillators yesterday evening and this morning told the team what he had learned. Over the past couple of years, a charity had seen to it that thousands of the damn things were given to community centres, leisure centres and various neighbourhood groups, for use in emergencies. The serial number of the device found with Godber's body showed that it had been stolen from a swimming pool in North Yorkshire. The staff there had presumed it was still locked safely away in the cupboard they had installed for it, and nobody had looked inside for at least three months. The reason that it had not been used

army man, of course. A proper old-school officer. He drank sherry in the officers' club and knew how to fasten a cummerbund. He'd seen service and got his scars, but it was all giving orders rather than fighting. He was a Rupert. That's what they call them, did you know? Posh officers. Expensive education and a stately home. That's what he was. I didn't know that, growing up, of course. He was a hero to me. He was still serving when I was born. Stationed in India, though I don't remember it. He had an accident of some kind and was invalided out. Mother, him and little baby me. Came back to the family home. I don't know how much of this I remember and how much I've made up, but he walked with a stick and always seemed to be in pain. Mother was from good middle-class stock as well. She'd married him when he was home on leave. Followed him to India thinking it would be a grand adventure. Coming back to England was not part of her plan. Nor was looking after a listless, injured man. I remember Mother as being sad. Angry. Never content. She did her duties, of course. Raised me, clothed me, sent me to the right school in the right uniform. Dad managed some of the lands that belonged to the family estate. I went to boarding school at seven. It was all very formulaic and dull. It was when I came home in the holidays that I discovered Mother had found a way to make her life more interesting.

Caneva: She had an affair?

Hoyer-Wood: She had lots of affairs. Again, I was young, so I don't know how much I imagined and what I saw, but I saw enough. Dad must have known. He must have. But he turned a blind eye. We never talked about any of this. Not after.

Caneva: After what, Seb?

Hoyer-Wood: Mother met somebody different. Before him, it was farmhands and blokes from the village. It was knee-tremblers behind the pigsty. Then there was this man. He entered our lives and nothing was ever the same again.

Caneva: Explain, Seb. You're doing so well . . .

Hoyer-Wood: He wasn't a big man. Nothing special to look at. He did a bit of work at the garage in the village, as far as I can recall. I spotted him at the house often enough for it to become remarkable. I could sense something different between Mother and Dad. I think she was considering leaving him. For this man, this exciting, virile, alpha male with his dirty hands and oil on his overalls. He wanted her to leave me, to leave Dad, to abandon the big house and go rut in poverty for the rest of her life with him.

Caneva: The atmosphere must have been unbearable. I'm so sorry, Seb. How old were you?

Hoyer-Wood: I was eight. Maybe seven. I don't remember the conversations. Just the shouting. The way the air felt. I just rattled around in the big house, wondering what the hell was going on.

Caneva: Did she leave him?

Hoyer-Wood: This is so hard, Lewis.

Caneva: It needs to come out. You know better than anybody, secrets just eat away . . .

Hoyer-Wood: If she'd left him, it wouldn't have happened.

Caneva: What?

Hoyer-Wood: She told him no. Said she couldn't leave me, though in all honesty I think it was the house and the money that twisted her arm. He didn't take it well. The man. Came to the house.

Caneva: To confront her? To confront your father?

Hoyer-Wood: I don't know what his intentions were. But it was late at night and I was reading in bed and suddenly there was this commotion in the hallway. I went downstairs and there he was: this angry ball of venom in a donkey jacket and flat cap. Mother was crying. Father was standing there in his dressing gown and pyjamas, leaning on the banister like he was going to fall down. Mother was in her nightdress. They were all screaming at one another, but somehow they heard me. Mother told me to go to bed, but the man didn't want that. He looked at me, then at Father, and told me to stay where I was. He wanted Mother to see the kind of man she had chosen. Then he hit Dad. He just punched him in the stomach and Dad doubled over. I couldn't move. Just stayed there on the stairs. And then he grabbed Mother by the hair. Forced her down and kicked her legs apart.

Caneva: Oh Seb, I'm so—

Hoyer-Wood: He raped her right there. Kept his eyes on me the whole fucking time. Dad wasn't tied up. Wasn't even that hurt. He just didn't do anything. He froze. Stayed there a few feet away from where this animal was raping his wife. And he just sat there with this look on his face.

Caneva: And you?

Hoyer-Wood: I couldn't move. Couldn't take my eyes off what was happening either.

Caneva: You can't blame yourself. You were a child, and that kind of trauma—

Hoyer-Wood: I don't blame myself. I blame her.

Caneva: How so? I don't—

Hoyer-Wood: Even as it was happening, this thought kept hammering away in my head. The thought that even though she was crying and telling him to stop, it was the same cock she'd loved before.

Caneva: No, Seb, you can't—

Hoyer-Wood: I remember when he finished, he walked over and took the hem of Dad's dressing gown and wiped himself on it. Then he spat on him and walked out the door.

Caneva: Did they phone the police?

Hoyer-Wood: No. They went back to bed. By breakfast, we were all wearing our masks again. Nothing had happened. We went back to living. Mother started having a few extra shots in her morning Bloody Mary. Started having longer naps during the day. By the time I was in my teens she was drunk most of the time. She died when I was twenty.

Caneva: But I knew you when we were twenty. We were friends. You never—

Hoyer-Wood: Never said anything? No. It didn't matter, did it? I had a new life. I'd escaped. I had friends and people liked me.

Caneva: But you must have had so much you wanted to say. So much inside.

Hoyer-Wood: I'm English, Lewis. English going back

hundreds of years. We don't say anything. We keep it all in.

Caneva: But the effects of what you saw . . .

Hoyer-Wood: Oh it took its toll, Lewis. That was my introduction to sex. That was when I saw real control. I saw a nobody, a man in a flat cap, scare my rich, army-officer dad into sitting mute while he fucked his wife. That went in, Lewis. It took root. When I had my first sexual encounters in my teens it was nothing but a disappointment. A disaster, even. I didn't get hard over the same things as other kids. When I got a chance with a girl, I wanted her friends to be watching. Her mum. Her bloody dad. I knew what I wanted to do. I just didn't do it. Honestly, Lewis, it was just that one time, when the demons in my head took over and I found myself in that room in Bridlington, staring down at this woman, and the next thing her husband was throwing me through a window and I was waking up barely able to move. I was in this chair. Lewis, I know you must have had your doubts about the stories you heard. I know they said I did more. But I'll never forget what you did for me. To be here. To be getting better, with your family, in your care, able to talk about it. I'll always be grateful . . .

McAvoy stops reading. The transcript of the counselling session ends shortly afterwards. The next page in the envelope is a photocopy of a report sent to the Home Office by Caneva, using Hoyer-Wood as an example of the good work the new facility was continuing to do. There are no more transcripts of their sessions. McAvoy leafs through the other pages, in case they have been sent out of order. He checks the dates. This was the last session, a week before the breakout and the fire. He checks the time on the document. Cross-references with previous sessions. They all took place on Tuesdays, 4 p.m. He flicks through his notes. Checks the date of the fire and discovers that it happened on a Tuesday. The escape was noticed late afternoon. He bites his lip. Caneva had told the truth. Hoyer-Wood would have been involved in another counselling session, over at Caneva's private residence, at the moment the other patient disappeared.

McAvoy frowns. Wonders if it changes what he already knows. He knew Hoyer-Wood was over there. Why else would he have been there but for counselling? Does it matter? Does it help him catch a killer of three innocents . . .

He holds the documents, loose, in his hands. Sees himself leave damp fingerprints on their pages and smudge the ink. They have only been printed recently. He raises one of the pages and examines the tiny row of black digits in the bottom right-hand corner. They were printed yesterday evening. Could they have made the last post? He looks at the envelope. Examines the postmark. He swallows, unsure what to think. The letter was posted to him in Bradford; an hour or more from Caneva's home in Chester. Why Bradford? He wonders at the significance of it. Grows frustrated. He curses the fact he is clever enough to know he is no genius.

McAvoy pushes himself off from the wall. The sweat on his back has cooled on his skin and his shirt feels cold and damp on his flesh. He feels uncomfortable and strangely angry. He can see fragments of something but cannot even conceive of how the finished picture will look. He starts to walk back towards the station, Hoyer-Wood's words tumbling in his mind like dice in a cup.

McAvoy thinks of himself at seven years old. His mother had been gone four years, disappearing with a man who offered more wealth, more excitement. He, his brother, his father and grandfather were living a simple life in their croft, halfway up a heather-clad hillside in Aultbea. They had a few cattle. Some sheep, on a nearby pasture. They ate well and laughed a lot. They told stories and watched old movies on a black and white TV with a poor picture. Those experiences formed him. His was a childhood of unspoken love and safety. At eight years old, Sebastien Hoyer-Wood saw a father he barely knew sit mute as a stranger raped a mother who didn't give a damn about him. McAvoy finds himself beginning to pity the child. But then he thinks of him as a man. Thinks of what he did. Thinks of the creature who, even yesterday, managed to assert power over a bigger, more able man, by simply mentioning his wife. He cannot pity the rapist Hoyer-Wood became. And he does not believe a word of his denials. Even through the dry black-and-white of the typed sessions, he can smell the lie of Hoyer-Wood's words. Can see when his tone changes, from the raw honesty of his childhood confession to the subtle manipulation of his friend in the closing paragraph. McAvoy doubts much about himself, but he knows he is good at reading people.

A dull headache is starting to form behind McAvoy's eyes. He feels wretched suddenly. Wonders what would make him feel well. He imagines lying on a rug in the back garden of his new home. Imagines Lilah asleep on his belly, Fin kicking a football at the bottom of the garden, Roisin sitting on the new designer swing she has ordered, reading a magazine. He finds himself drifting into maudlin thoughts. Finds himself beginning to over-analyse. Thinks of his days spent with the dead, and his nights trying to be the silly, capable, strong protector that his wife and children adore. Whether Lewis Caneva still thinks he did right by his friend in writing a report that declared Sebastien Hoyer-Wood mentally unfit to stand trial. Whether he would do the same. Whether he has a best friend. Any friends at all . . .

As he crosses the car park and heads for the back door of the police station, he stops short. Somebody has called his name. He turns, and sees a woman standing by a beaten-up old Fiesta in the car park. She looks tired. More than that.

Warily, McAvoy crosses to where she stands.

'Can I help you?'

He takes her in. Short, unnaturally red hair. Blackheads across her nose. Scarring to her hairline and below her ear. One of her teeth is markedly whiter than the others and clearly false. She's wearing a plain, round-neck T-shirt and there are home-made iodine tattoos on arms that bear scars. She has lived, this woman. Lived almost unto death.

'You're McAvoy?'

He nods. Extends a hand. She looks at it, and seems to recoil.

'I'm Ashleigh,' she says. She opens her mouth to speak again, then closes it.

McAvoy waits, then gestures at the police station. 'Would you like to come inside? We could get a coffee . . .'

'You're looking into the deaths, yes? Yvonne. Philippa. Allan.'

McAvoy stops speaking. Holds her gaze. 'I'm on that team, yes.'

She nods. 'You know about Hoyer-Wood, yeah? You know how they're connected?'

McAvoy wants to get her inside. Doesn't want this chat to take place in a car park, with sweat on his clothes and the broken glass and dog shit of the city streets on his shoes.

'We're investigating several lines of enquiry. Could I ask you to come inside, Miss . . .'

She pulls a face. Waves a hand, telling him to be quiet. She takes a breath, and he can see her shoulders shake. 'Is he doing it again? Is he well again?'

'I'm sorry, could you explain . . .?'

She puts her hands in her hair and scratches her face, leaving white lines among the broken blood vessels and acne.

'I think I know who's doing this.' She pauses, and her hand makes a tight fist. 'He tried to do it to me.'

McAvoy freezes. Then he reaches out to take her elbow. She lets him do it. Turns her face to his and lets him look into her brown eyes. Then she speaks again.

'That bastard raped me. That night in Bridlington when he nearly died. It was my bloke who nearly killed him. It was that night I got these scars. And whoever's killing these poor sods wanted to start with me.'

15

11.40 a.m.: fifty feet away.

Helen Tremberg sits in the front seat of her blue Citroën and tries not to let the tears that fall from her eyes bleed into her voice.

She's not touching the mobile phone to her ear, and she is holding it with the cuff of her blouse. It's an unconscious thing. The phone is her own. She's not trying to reduce the chances of leaving evidence. She just somehow doesn't want her skin to be tainted by this phone call. She wants as little of herself as possible to be involved.

She speaks again. Wants to bite her tongue in half as she does so.

'So, you can see why I thought you should be told.'

The young woman at the other end of the line sounds confused and afraid. Helen can't blame her. She should be.

'The other officer made it clear that I was really helping out by making a statement. I didn't want to. I just wanted it to be over and done with. It was horrible, y'know? My dad warned me about setting up my own place but I thought nobody would want to rob a place like this. And I didn't go through the pockets. I don't do that. I'm trying to run a professional business and . . .'

Helen lets her talk. Melanie Langley seems a nice girl. Helen finds it hard to imagine her kicking a robber in the bollocks. Reckons she has a friend she can rely on for that sort of thing.

'The thing is, there have been some complications. Legal issues. I won't bore you with the details, but the thing is,' Helen tries not to stumble over her words, 'Adam Downey has been released on bail. Obviously we are very keen to secure a conviction in this matter and I shouldn't even be calling you but I feel I have a duty to your safety. Adam Downey is a very dangerous man with dangerous friends. I'm deeply concerned that if you don't withdraw your statement, he may take it upon himself to ensure that you do.'

Mel stays silent for a moment, then there is a snuffling noise. 'How can this be happening? I didn't . . . I mean, it wasn't even . . . please, what should I do?'

Helen presses her lips together. She feels tears drip onto her collarbone. She is disgusting herself more every second she stays on the line. She knows she should confess all to Pharaoh. To McAvoy. She knows that she did nothing wrong. Not until now. But she cannot bear the thought of that video being seen. And more, the man who called her had known so much. He had seemed so absolutely certain when he told her how easily her career could be smashed. In the past couple of days she has told herself that perhaps she is doing Mel a favour by persuading her to withdraw her statement. She has no doubts that Downey's employers will stop her from talking one way or another. Yet she still finds herself abhorrent. She can smell the stench of corruption on her skin. It is choking her. Inside the little car, with its misted windows, her senses are full of her own vile lies and it makes her want to gasp for air.

'Miss Langley, I would get in a great deal of trouble if it was discovered I was making this call. My advice would be to call the investigation team and simply tell them you are no longer sure what you saw. Then perhaps you should spend a few days somewhere else. Do you have a friend you could stay with? Your parents?'

Mel just snivels. She doesn't deserve this.

'Miss Langley, I have to go. I hope you understand that if the situation changes, we will of course require you to tell a court what you saw. But at this moment, your safety is paramount. I hope I won't need to be in touch again.'

She ends the call, then opens the car door and throws up all over the rutted concrete. She's barely eaten, so the vomit is just acid and water. She sticks her fingers down her throat and tries to bring up more.

Through tears, with the taste of acid and lies on her tongue, Tremberg looks across the car park. Between two vehicles, she can see Aector McAvoy talking to a short, hard-faced woman beside a little car. McAvoy is leading her into the station. He has an arm on her elbow, as if she is a refined old lady who needs a little help with the steps. Looking at him, the smell of vomit in her nostrils, she realises how much she wants to be like him. He doesn't manipulate. Doesn't strategise. He won't have thought to ingratiate himself with the woman by taking her arm. He won't be trying any psychological tricks. He'll have taken her arm because it's the right thing to do. It's what she needs, in this place, at this time. Helen wouldn't have thought to do that, and if she had, she'd have been too unsure of herself to see it through. She wants to be a good policewoman. She wants to catch villains. But nothing feels as clear as it used to. Her own investigation is currently stalled, Ray's suspension leaving her small team of detectives with little or no direction. Shaz Archer looks like a lost puppy without her mentor. She's spending most of her time on her mobile phone, talking to Colin and trying to find out what is going on.

As she heaves spittle onto her dowdy shoes and feels the hot emptiness in her belly, Helen is suddenly overcome with a need to prove her worth. She suddenly needs to remind herself that she is a good person who has simply been trapped into doing a terrible thing. She wipes her mouth and pops a piece of chewing gum onto her tongue, then checks her reflection in the rear-view mirror and manages to take some of the darkness from under her eyes with a stick of concealer. She sniffs, then steps over the vomit and crosses the now empty car park. She uses her electronic card to open the doors then heads for the major incident room.

Keep it together, keep it together, keep it together . . .

As she enters, Ben Nielsen is in the middle of an extravagant stretch. His shirt is riding up to reveal a belly with a Hollywood six-pack. He's a keen sportsman who hits the gym twice a day, though his stamina seems to be used for bedroom athletics rather than anything on a playing field. He's very good with the ladies. Helen looks at him and has to swallow down spittle and bile as she realises that such a man could easily be put to use by Downey's employers. She has begun to think of them as talent spotters. Businessmen adept at spotting rising stars. Without realising it, she has mentally christened them Headhunters.

'All right Hell's-Bells? You bored?'

Helen manages a smile. Nielsen looks a little wide-eyed, as if he's been staring too long at a computer screen.

'We're a rudderless ship, Ben,' she says, sarcastically. 'Without Colin's example and leadership, we're lost in a fog. I thought I'd see if I could be of any use to you.'

Nielsen raises a suggestive eyebrow, then laughs. Nothing will ever happen between him and Helen. They're friends, and she knows too many of the places that his penis has been to want to go near it herself.

Nielsen smiles, sitting forward in his chair. He leafs through the pile of papers on his desk then hands a list of names to Helen.

'The big man's asked me to look into those buggers. The family of the shrink who looked after Hoyer-Wood. You know where we're at with that, do you?'

'I'm in the dark, Ben.'

Nielsen quickly fills her in. She nods as he outlines McAvoy's theory.

'And the pathologist says that's feasible, yes? That her chest could have been caved in by repeated compressions? Like CPR? Fuck, that's awful.'

Nielsen nods. 'Aye, our killer's not squeamish. So, can I leave those names with you? It would be a big help.'

Helen nods, already jotting down important names, dates, times and places from the brief synopsis Nielsen has just given her. She needs this. Needs to work. Needs to atone. She crosses to her own workstation and starts bringing up databases. For the next forty minutes, the incident room is silent, save for the occasional groan or muttered phone call from Nielsen.

Soon, Helen is lost in work, her face lit by the glow of the computer monitor. She acquaints herself with Caneva's children. His daughter, Maria, is now twenty-eight years old and lives in West Yorkshire, alone. She has one police caution to her name, having been involved in a protest about the building of an incinerator in a Holderness village. A Google search shows that she has been active in several campaign groups for environmental issues and is a registered nurse. She has a Facebook page, but has not used it for several months and only has a dozen friends on it. Her profile picture is a photograph of a cat. Helen makes a note of her discoveries but fancies she has drawn a dead end. She turns her attention to Maria's younger brother, Angelo.

A moment later, Helen is nervously jigging her legs and tapping a pen on her teeth. She wonders if she has struck gold. Angelo Caneva was sentenced at sixteen years old to a stretch in a young offender institute in North Wales, half an hour from Chester, where his father now lives. He was sentenced for petrol-bombing a minibus, but had been getting into steadily worse trouble with the police over the previous eighteen months. The family lived in London at that point. His worsening behaviour coincided with his mother's suicide.

Helen pulls up a web browser and tries to find any reports on the inquest into his mother's death. She finds only a few *In Memoriams* that mention her name, and one paragraph in a London freesheet that said a verdict of suicide had been recorded.

Helen pulls a face. She wants more. The details of the court case are sketchy and she can't find any newspaper reports on it because Angelo's name would not have been mentioned in any press cuttings due to his status as a minor. She examines the date of the sentence. Notes that it was passed at a Crown Court rather than a Youth Court. She alters the boundaries of her web search. Finds the local paper for that region. Keys in a few choice words and waits for something to happen.

Helen lets herself smile for the first time in days. Angelo Caneva was jailed almost a decade ago for petrol-bombing a minibus carrying patients from a local private medical facility for physiotherapy at a nearby spa. It does not take Helen long to ascertain that Hoyer-Wood was a patient at that facility at that time. Nobody was hurt in the incident, which occurred more than a hundred miles from Angelo's London home, but the charge was arson with intent to endanger life. The boy's solicitor offered little mitigation. He said his client had refused to cooperate in the preparation of reports, and could only tell the court that Angelo had been slowly unravelling since the death of his mother. He told the court the boy had been a clever and diligent pupil at a high-class boarding school before his expulsion for continued misbehaviour, and that his father was struggling with business debts and the responsibility of raising two teenagers alone. The judge had given him six years.

Helen feels hungry, suddenly. She nips to the vending machine and comes back with two packets of crisps and a can of pop. She has almost forgotten the phone call to Mel. Has almost put Mark and Downey and the Headhunters from her mind. She suddenly feels like a detective.

Her mouth full of crisps, Helen punches a phone number into the landline on her desk and finds herself speaking to the hassled receptionist at the young offender institute near Wrexham where Angelo Caneva was an inmate. After introducing herself and stressing that she is part of a murder enquiry, she manages to get the governor on the line. He has a Liverpool accent and sounds less busy than his colleague. Helen tells him what she wants. Who she is. Asks him if he remembers Angelo Caneva.

'Posh lad? Yes, I remember Angelo. Didn't really fit in. We had problems.'

Helen tries to keep the excitement from her voice. 'Were you governor then?'

'No, senior warden. Angelo was nice enough, though he looked proper soft compared with some of the lads we get. He had the hard time you'd expect, really. He liked books and drawing and just being left alone. Took him a while to warm up but he got the hang of doing time. Served just over three years, I think. Never went to mainstream prison. Is he in bother again?'

Helen bites her lip, not knowing whether she should give too much away. 'We would love to speak to him in connection with the current enquiry. He's not a suspect, you understand. He just might be able to shed some light on a few things.'

The governor makes a noise that suggests he's thinking. 'I wish I had more to tell you. His file won't have that much more in it. He did a couple of courses while he was with us. Took his GCSEs, now I remember. Got good grades, considering. Earned his stripes with the lads in a couple of scraps. Was popular by the time he left. I thought he'd probably go into something useful. He did a City and Guilds course in something or other. Might have been plastering. I'll check and get back to you. I do remember he was always in a world of his own. Always had his mind somewhere else. I hope he's got himself sorted out, Constable. We always expect the worst but Angelo seemed to have more about him . . .'

Helen leaves her contact details and hangs up. She rubs her nose and it makes a squeaking sound. In her bag, she notices her phone is ringing, but decides to ignore it. She doesn't want to be distracted from this feeling. She clicks back to the Police National Computer and looks into the eyes of Angelo Caneva's mugshot. He's young. Small. Dark-haired and frightened. But there is something else in his eyes. Something that could be called determination.

Helen prints the image. She is about to cross to the printer when the phone on her desk begins to ring. Impatiently, she snatches up the receiver and barks her name.

'Constable Tremberg,' comes a familiar voice. 'Please don't ignore my calls. I could be in distress and require your assistance.'

The joy of the previous moment dissipates as the colour drains from Helen's face. She sinks into her chair.

'I did what you asked,' she hisses, spittle hitting the receiver.

'Indeed you did, and your services are hugely appreciated. I understand that Miss Langley is busy recanting her calumnies as we speak. No, I am seeking your assistance in one more matter. You may not be currently aware, but one of my well-informed young uniformed constables told us some days ago that when he was apprehended, Mr Downey was spitting and cursing with regard to having had his money taken by a girl of decidedly Romany appearance. I am not of the opinion that Miss Langley could be described in said terms. No, I require a little clarification from yourself regarding the identity of this unknown creature.'

Helen feels herself begin to shake. Jesus, no . . .

'I am not a great believer in happy accidents. I don't find the idea of serendipity to be reliable. But sometimes the universe does play along. I'm referring to McAvoy. Like yourself, Detective Constable, he will soon become a little more manageable. And it would seem Sergeant McAvoy has a wife who caused considerable embarrassment and distress to our Mr Downey.'

Helen leans forward. Rests her head on the cool corner of the desk. She can feel herself coming apart.

'Don't,' she says, softly. 'Whatever you're doing, whatever you're planning, don't go near her. You don't have any idea what you would be starting.'

From the other end of the line comes a faint laugh.

'So, you concur. The young Mrs McAvoy is indeed the person to whom we should be addressing our petition for recompense. Thank you, Detective Constable. Now, please do not trouble yourself any further. I can assure you that your contributions to our cause have been appreciated. The funds deposited in your bank account will remain there as a gesture of gratitude. Do not be foolish enough to warn your superior about the information we have in our possession. The fates have actually succeeded in saving Mrs McAvoy from our original plan. Mr Downey will not be pleased but Mrs McAvoy will be grateful her identity has become known to us. I am an adaptable man. But I guarantee you that our plans will become more severe in execution should you go running to her husband with your stories. I thank you for your time.'

Helen holds the phone to her ear long after the call is terminated. She feels part of herself leave her body and die in the hot, static-laden air. Then she wipes her face with the heel of her hand, and manages to stand up. She needs to find McAvoy. She needs to help him catch a killer. She just hopes that she can look him in the eye.

It's cold in the interview suite. Although it's a small, airless space, the walls have shielded the little room from the heat of the day. The walls are damp and the air cool. The hairs on Ashleigh Cromwell's arms rise as she crosses them on the chilly rubber surface of the desk.

McAvoy sits down opposite her and hands her the can of fizzy pop she had asked for, along with a see-through plastic cup. She takes it gratefully and pours herself a drink. She watches the bubbles bounce on the surface, then drains it. She closes her eyes, trying to compose herself. McAvoy lets her take her time. He sits back in the chair, content to wait.

Ashleigh Cromwell had been living with her husband and children for more than ten years when Sebastien Hoyer-Wood had taken a shine to her that winter day in Bridlington fourteen years ago. She was no holidaymaker. The house where he tried to rape her was the family home, on a quiet street near the seafront. She'd seen him looking at her a few hours before the attack. She and her husband, Johnny, were having a drink in one of the boozers off the promenade. He'd stared. Stared until her husband had asked him what he was looking at.

'He seemed out of place,' says Ashleigh. 'Everybody knew Johnny. He was a bit of a character. He was a tough man and everybody knew we were a couple. The way he was looking . . . it just wasn't . . . Johnny gave him a look to say clear off and he did. We just laughed about it. It didn't matter. He was just a bloke. It didn't seem to matter.'

It had mattered that night, though. Sebastien Hoyer-Wood had got into their house.

Ashleigh plays with the empty cup. She'd told him on the way in that she didn't like coppers, didn't like police stations or telling tales. She seems uncomfortable here, as though she is being interviewed under caution. McAvoy is trying to put her at her ease. She looks at him before she speaks again, as if to thank him for his patience. Then she takes a breath, and stumbles on.

'I reckon he sneaked in when Johnny was having a fag with the back door open. They found his clothes later on. He'd been naked when he came in. Must have hidden somewhere in the house till we went to bed. My kids were there. That's the bit that I can't get past. My kids . . .'

Shortly before midnight, Ashleigh and Johnny Cromwell were woken by Sebastien Hoyer-Wood pouring petrol over their sleeping bodies. The bedroom light was switched on and a naked man in a surgical mask told them to take a deep breath. To sniff the air. To look at what he had in his hand.

'We were half asleep and wide awake at the same time,' says Ashleigh. 'You know when a light goes on and you sort of can't see properly? But we smelled the petrol. And we saw the lighter. And you only had to look between his legs to know what he wanted.'

Hoyer-Wood had ordered Johnny back against the bedroom wall. He told him he was going to do him a good turn. He was going to let the children carry on sleeping.

'He pulled the covers back,' says Ashleigh, eyes closed. 'I had a nightie on, and he poured more petrol on me. It stung. Stung my eyes. Then he told Johnny that if he moved, we would both go up like fireworks. The house would burn down. His kids would die. He told him to stay still like a good boy, and enjoy the show.'

Johnny Cromwell had never been the type to apply logic to a situation. He was a straight-ahead kind of man who had taken his fair share of beatings but handed out plenty more. He had looked at the naked man lying on top of his wife, parting her thighs, and he had reacted instinctively. He'd moved. He'd hit Sebastien Hoyer-Wood so hard in the face that he broke his own hand. And then Hoyer-Wood had dropped the lighter.

'He got himself more than me,' says Ashleigh, her fingers brushing the scarring at her hairline. 'I went up, like. My nightie caught fire. There was a whoosh of flame. I don't know how I knew to do it but I flung myself on the floor and rolled, like they do on the movies. I put myself out. Then I looked up and the curtains were blowing and there was glass everywhere and he'd gone out of the fucking window . . .'

McAvoy looks across at Ashleigh Cromwell. She's probably in her early forties but looks ten years older. She looks wrung out. It is as if a pretty, vivacious woman has been dehydrated. All of the moisture has gone from her flesh. Her softness has been burned away.

There is silence in the room as Ashleigh wipes her fist across her nose. A low, insistent buzz has started to penetrate McAvoy's consciousness, and as he looks for the source, a wasp lands on the table between them. Instinctively, he takes Ashleigh's empty cup and drops it over the creature. It knocks, ineffectually, against the plastic.

'Johnny went after him. I ran to see the kids were okay. They were still sleeping. Then I went out onto the street. Johnny had caught up with him. He was smashing his head on the pavement. I don't know why I told him to stop. I guess I thought that with Johnny's record he would do time. I don't even know if I was thinking at all. I was sore and scared and there was this naked man all bloody and burned in the snow on Bridlington seafront and the next thing there are all these people and somebody is putting a coat around me and Johnny is being held back and the police are there . . .'

On the table, the wasp has begun to beat against the plastic. Its tiny tinfoil wings are breaking as it fights, pathetically, in the sticky syrup that pools on the table. McAvoy cannot stand it. He lifts the cup and watches, gratified, as it buzzes angrily away.

'I didn't save him,' says Ashleigh. 'Other people saved him. The people who died.'

She seems to get smaller. Takes her face in her hands.

McAvoy reaches across, his arms rubbing the drips of orange soda into the tabletop. He puts his hand on her bare forearm and she raises her eyes to his.

'You said you thought the killer wanted you, Mrs Cromwell. Could you tell me what you meant by that?'

Ashleigh sniffs, noisily, and raises her eyes to the ceiling. She rubs at her arms.

'Johnny and me broke up not long after it all happened,' she says. 'I don't know if it was because of that night or all the other stuff. Johnny was always hard work. He had other women, but I usually forgave him. I had a few other men, though they were usually too shit-scared of Johnny to be tempted. I was a bit more of a catch then, as well. Johnny got himself into more bother. He stopped coming home. We split up then he got sent down for glassing some bloke. I don't even know what it was about. The kids and me moved away. The oldest has her own place but my son and me are doing okay.'

'You live locally?' asks McAvoy.

'Scunthorpe,' she says. The steel town is half an hour away, over the bridge. Not too far from Barton, where Yvonne Dale died. McAvoy wonders if it is significant.

'I have a sister there,' explains Ashleigh. 'We wanted a fresh start. She runs a newsagent's and I work there with her. We're doing okay.'

McAvoy nods. He licks his lips, unsure how to ask. 'Hoyer-Wood,' he says, gently. 'He wasn't sent to prison. He could be said to have got away with it . . .'

Ashleigh looks as if she has just cracked an out-of-date egg onto her tongue. She looks like she wants to spit.

'Me and coppers have never got on,' she says. 'I never expect much of them but I thought he'd have done a stretch. The copper in charge, George Goss – he said the bastard had been doing it for years. He reckoned they'd put him away for nigh-on life. Then his posh mates got involved and next thing he was living it up in some plush mental asylum. I don't know how I felt, really. I know he was suffering, so that was something. I sometimes wondered if Johnny would have got sent down if he'd killed him. I sometimes wonder why I told him to stop. I wonder a lot of things, but I keep it all inside, most of the time. Then something brings it back. Like now.'

McAvoy waits. He rubs at the sticky patch on his skin and watches the wasp as it crawls up the pale green wall.

'How did you know to ask for me?' asks McAvoy.

'George Goss,' says Ashleigh, looking at the floor. 'When I heard about the murders I rang for him. They told me he was retired. They put me through to CID and some bloke said he could get a message to George if it was important. I said it was and George rang me. Told me that I should speak to you. Said you were okay.'

McAvoy nods, embarrassed. 'The murders,' he says. 'What do you know about the victims?'

Ashleigh gives him an angry look, and for an instant, McAvoy sees the animated features of the woman she once was. There is a light in her eyes and a flame appears to have been lit behind her pale skin.

'I didn't know the paramedic, but I remember the two women and it doesn't take a genius to work out that they're all connected.' She says this with an accusing tone. 'I work in a newsagent's. I read the *Scunthorpe Telegraph*. I don't watch the news. But you hear, don't you? Somebody told somebody else and then my sister told me to read one of the other papers. I can't believe you haven't told people they're linked. I thought you might not know, but George says you already know about Hoyer-Wood and what happened . . .'

McAvoy raises defensive hands. 'That decision was made at a senior level,' he says, neutrally. 'Myself and the senior investigating officer are trying to change the thinking on that. We're trying to get in touch with anybody who may be at risk. I'm sure an officer would have been in touch with yourself at some point . . .'

Even as he says it, he senses that his words will not give Ashleigh much new faith in the police.

'Too late for me, Mr McAvoy. He already bloody got to me. That's why I'm here.'

McAvoy looks at her, trying to make sense of her words. Behind her, the wasp appears to lose its grip on the wall. It tumbles and lands on the cold floor, where it twitches and spins until, finally, the soft buzzing comes to a halt.

'I don't understand,' he says, and wonders if he should have it etched on his gravestone.

Ashleigh takes the can of drink and raises it to her lips. It shakes in her hand. The can is empty, but she makes a show of swallowing.

'A year ago,' she says, quietly. 'Maybe a little more. It happened again. I woke up with a fucking man sitting in my bedroom.'

The room suddenly seems smaller. The chill of this desolate, enclosed space seems to wrap itself around McAvoy like a damp shroud. He has to fight not to openly shiver.

'I'm not some wimpy lass,' says Ashleigh, as if this is an important point. 'I can punch my weight. I don't cry all the bloody time like a baby. I've been through stuff, but I've done my best to put it behind me. But when I woke up and there was a man in my bedroom I thought my heart was going to stop. It was like it had never gone away.'

McAvoy closes his eyes. Tries to imagine what went through her mind and then stops himself when it becomes too painful to endure.

'Was he . . .?'

'Naked? No. Didn't have the light on either. He was just a shape at the end of the bed. A weight. I'm not tall and I sleep with my feet drawn up but I stretched out and felt this lump. I thought I might have left the laundry basket at the foot of the bed or something daft like that, but then the weight shifted. I opened my eyes and could tell there was somebody there. Looking back, I suppose I might have thought it was my son, but it didn't feel like that. He felt wrong, somehow. I knew. Knew it was happening again.'

McAvoy scratches his head, hard enough to hurt. 'What happened?'

'I'm not a screamer,' she says. 'I shout, if I do anything. But I didn't even do that. I just sat up and asked if there was somebody there, and then he spoke. Just sitting there, on the end of the bed. He spoke, like we were friends or family and he wanted a chat.'

McAvoy can find no better way to express his feelings than by swearing. 'Fucking hell.'

'He said it was my fault. People like me. We'd saved him. Hoyer-Wood could have died that night but people like me had saved his life. He said he wanted to punish me. People like me.'

'Did he have a weapon? Fuel? A flame?' asks McAvoy.

'I don't think so,' she says. 'It was dark and I was trying not to wet myself. But even though I was bloody terrified, I was angry at him for what he said.'

'What did you say to him?' McAvoy asks.

'I told him that I'd suffered at that bastard's hands more than anyone. That if he thought I had somehow saved his life out of fear or compassion, he was out of his mind. I told him that I wished him dead every fucking day and that if he had the chance, he should find the crippled bastard and kill him – not me. Not people who had suffered enough.'

McAvoy pictures it. Pictures Ashleigh, scared yet defiant, talking to a voice in the darkness.

'Did he hurt you?'

Ashleigh gives what could be called a laugh. 'He started to snivel,' she says, eyes wide. 'Started to fucking shake. Said he was lost. Said he wanted to put things right but didn't know what to do. He even started to say sorry . . .'

McAvoy rubs at his eyebrow. Licks his teeth and tastes elderberry cordial and chocolate on his tongue.

'What happened, Ashleigh?'

'I put the light on,' she says, eyes closed again. 'And he ran.'

'You saw him?' asks McAvoy, sitting forward. 'You saw his face?'

Ashleigh shrugs. 'Maybe. A shape. Half a face.'

'And you never called the police?'

She shakes her head. 'I never told anybody. Not until now. I thought whoever it was had changed their mind. They were confused. Upset. They could have killed me as I slept but they didn't. Then all this started. I knew you had to know. So I'm telling you.'

McAvoy is about to speak when a knock on the interview room door breaks the silence. A moment later, Helen Tremberg enters, holding a sheet of paper. To McAvoy, she looks ill. She's pale and there is darkness under her eyes. She looks like she has been vomiting and there are sweat patches under the arms of her white blouse.

'A word, Sarge?'

McAvoy gestures at Ashleigh. Tries to suggest with his gaze that now is not a good time. He looks across the table at the short, red-headed woman who has endured more than anybody should have to. She is not looking at him. She is looking at the piece of paper trailing loosely from Helen Tremberg's hand.

Suddenly, Ashleigh stands and darts towards the door. She grabs the paper from Helen's hand and seems to crumple. She reaches out to the table, and McAvoy grabs her before she can fall.

She looks at him, uncertainty and confusion in her eyes. She brandishes the piece of paper; the print-out of a ten-year-old mugshot.

'Him,' she says, stabbing a finger onto the page. 'It was fucking him!'

McAvoy looks at the page and then up at Helen, who is opening and closing her mouth, wordlessly.

He takes the page. Looks at the image of a teenage boy.

Locks eyes with Angelo Caneva.

16

Sodium street lights, the neon of a kebab shop and the faint cigarette glow of an unfamiliar sun.

A taxi office, just off Hull's Hedon Road. Knackered cars parked on double-yellow lines and a drunk pissing against the graffiti and chipboard of the boarded-up convenience store next door.

Inside the office, Adam Downey is leaning forward to snort a line of high-quality cocaine off the glossy front cover of a porno magazine. He's laid out the line on the thigh of a black woman. He likes the effect. Better yet, he likes the sudden rush that is thumping up his nose and eyeballs and into his brain, filling him with a sudden fervour and fury and causing him to emit a strange, animal growl as he raises his head to the ceiling and feels the drugs fill his system.

Downey has never been the sort of drug pusher to sample too much of his own product. He likes to smoke a spliff while watching a movie, and one of the girls he sees regularly has pretty toes that look extra special when holding a nice fat joint out for him to take a puff upon. But he hasn't taken much cocaine. Truth be told, he's a little frightened of it. Despite making his living by selling the white powder in bulk, he's seen too many people come to depend upon it to want to start sticking too much of it up his nose. Besides, the product that passes through his hands is a little too pure. Once it's been through a few dealers and been cut with glucose and a little bicarbonate of soda, he might consider the occasional line to help him stay awake or better enjoy a night out. But the idea of waking up and reaching for a cellophane wrap of the stuff makes him feel uncomfortable.

Adam Downey has decided to make an exception tonight.

Half an hour ago, the telephone rang in the taxi office. It was the voice that Downey has come to fear. He'd told him the name of the woman who had taken his money. Told him she was a copper's wife. Told him what he had to do. Downey had agreed, even as his insides turned to water. He'd thought he was just dealing with some pikey bitch. He'd thought that his boys could have a fun time with her and that would be the end of it. He'd entertained visions of sticking a few extra quid in her knickers when they were done, so she knew there were no hard feelings save the one in his pants. Now the evening's entertainment has become overloaded with risk. He's heard about the copper she's married to. Heard the rumours.

Downey is worried, even though he has three good men to lend a hand. Two Turks and Big Bruno are going to watch his back. They are each formidable and reliable. Bruno, in particular, is an intimidating specimen. He's a black guy with a Hull accent. He has long dreadlocks and wears shorts all year round. He has muscles on top of muscles, rippling like storm clouds across his skin, and Downey knows that despite his deep laugh and playfulness with the other drivers, Bruno has a violent side. He's killed before. Downey saw it happen. Saw Bruno smash a fifteen-kilo dumb-bell over the head of an enforcer who made the mistake of inviting him into his home to discuss a peaceful resolution to their differences.

As he stares up at the ceiling and fully opens his jaws, Downey feels the drugs fill his system. He bounces his legs, feeling tightness in his toes. He stands and looks at himself in the mirror that covers one full wall of the tiny space. It faces a desk that carries an old computer and a stack of unread paperwork. He examines himself. He's dressed for the occasion, in a baggy white T-shirt with a designer tattoo pattern across the chest. He's wearing tight jeans that sag, fashionably, at the arse, with slip-on shoes and no socks. He's accessorised effectively, with diamond earring and expensive watch. He looks good, and the bruises add an air of menace to the pop-star image he tends to affect. He stares into his own eyes. Tells himself he can do this. He has men at his disposal. He just beat a serious charge.

You're beautiful, mate. You're the prince of the fucking city . . .

As the drugs course through his system, he begins to feel untouchable. Begins to question his orders. He's been told to give Roisin McAvoy a message, but not in the way he had wanted to. He is under instructions not to hurt her. The voice had told him that the organisation has other plans for McAvoy. He's not to hurt her. Not to make a scene.

Fuck them!

The cocaine emboldens him. He had been looking forward to making that bitch cry. He'd been dreaming about closing his hand around that tiny throat, crushing those full lips until they burst like ripe fruit. He turns and spits on the floor. He looks at his hands and sees that they are trembling. He closes them into fists. His nose is running so he rubs it with the back of his hand. His movements are frantic. He is surprised to find that his dick has gone hard. He wants to do this. Wants it to happen now. Wants her in front of him, begging . . .

Downey pushes open the door to the main office, where Bruno and the Turks are sitting in mismatched chairs. He grunts. Tells them it's time. They stand up without saying a word. The Turks had signed up for the job even before learning what it was. He'd just told them he needed back-up and there was cash in it for them. They're a curious pair. Memluk is the taller of the two at just over six feet. Tokcan is a quiet lad who has fallen in love with Fruit Pastilles since arriving in England and always seems to be chewing. Neither is over thirty. They're tanned and unshaven, dark-haired and fit. They both liked Hakan. They know that, somehow, the woman they are going to visit tonight was responsible for his disappearance, and are looking forward to taking out their frustrations. Downey realises he should tell them the plan has changed. They're not to hurt her. Not to make a fuss. But he finds himself unable to.

'Time to play,' says Downey, and is rewarded with a trio of smiles.

They head outside, into air that feels baking hot despite the hour. The sky reminds him of a white towel that has been mixed in with a dark wash.

Downey and his men climb, wordlessly, into a large American 4x4. Bruno had turned up in it tonight and nobody has questioned him about its origins. It's large, comfortable and stylish, and Downey feels very much at home as he slides, dizzily, into the leather passenger seat and hears the throaty hum of the engine turning over.

'We good, Boss?'

Bruno asks the question quietly. The two Turks are on their team, but there is an unspoken agreement that the men in the front of the car are in charge.

Downey nods. His head is spinning. His eyes are open but he's struggling to take in much about the scene before him. He shakes his head and slaps his cheeks. Focuses. Sees . . .

The car is cruising down Hedon Road, past the entrance to the docks; the cemetery; the prison. He watches the landscape change as they approach the flyover. To his left is Sammy's Point, where the glass-panelled city aquarium sits on a jutting spit of land. They cross the River Hull, its muddy banks curving down to chocolate-coloured water. They pass through a city that Downey thinks of as his own. He finds himself giggling as he waves a hello to the statue at the crossroads. It's a man on a golden horse. It might be a king. It's stood there for as long as he can remember. Downey once heard a rumour that the sculptor killed himself because he got the stirrups wrong. It's outside a pub that used to be run by a local rugby legend called Flash Flanagan, a good old bloke who wore Elvis glasses and became a fixture in the Old Town after he retired from the game. Played on a Lions tour, apparently. The story goes that he turned up for the flight without a passport and carrying his clothes in a carrier bag . . .

My city, my people, my city, my people . . .

Downey's mind feels alive.

Wired.

Memories are fizzing inside his skull. The lights on the dual carriageway seem to be blurring and forming shapes. He wants to talk to Bruno. Wants to tell him that he's on top of everything and that this is just another step down a road he's already mapped out. But his mouth feels dry and his heart is beating too hard, so he says nothing. Just closes his eyes and lets the car drift towards the Humber Bridge. Enjoys a fantasy or two and lets his brain become a pan of popping corn.

You're the man, Downey. The man!

He feels powerful. A fucking king! Feels tired, too. Feels his eyes closing even as his blood fizzes with excitement.

Minutes later, Bruno's hand is on his shoulder, shaking him awake. The vehicle is parked on a nondescript side street in the small town of Hessle. He vaguely remembers telling Bruno this was the plan.

'This way.'

He points and sets off up the road, looking in the windows of the large, three-storey townhouses. Nice place. Decent folk. Could kill them all with a point and a nod . . .

He crosses a main road then down a little back alley, leaves and branches sticking out from the slats in the old fence, dead leaves crinkling and turning to dust underfoot. They emerge on the foreshore. Downey looks up at the Humber Bridge. He's walked across it plenty of times. His mam did some sort of charity jog for breast cancer across it a few years back. It's a familiar, comforting thing.

The Turks are muttering between themselves. He gives them a nod and they smile back, all teeth and stubble.

'Oh, we're going to have such fun . . .'

Downey checks his phone. Double-checks the address. Walks on, softly, until he finds the house. Four cottages, side by side. White paint and a pale blue trim. Picket fence and dainty eaves. Welcoming lights and herbs in a window box, freshly labelled, the soil a rich brown.

Cautiously, urging the others to stay back, Downey walks to the front of the property. The small fence shields a front yard of no more than two metres by three, and he can see straight into the front room.

'Bingo.'

She's there. The gypsy bitch. She's unpacking some cardboard boxes and turning to talk to somebody on the sofa. He angles his head and is surprised to see the seamstress. She's wearing a hooded jumper and is hugging a cushion, feet drawn up. Cross-legged on the floor is a young lad with red hair. He's drawing in a colouring book, his tongue sticking out of the corner of his mouth in concentration.

It's a nice scene.

There's no sign of the copper.

Downey wonders if he should just knock on the door. The orders are clear enough. He's to hold a phone to McAvoy's ear and play him a message. That's it. Roisin is not to be harmed. Not now. Not yet. But the bitch had hurt *him*. She'd kicked him in the balls and took his money. She'd made him doubt himself and reminded him what a pathetic little weakling he really is. He wants to hurt her.

Downey chews his cheek with his back teeth. Rubs a hand across the scabs on his chest. He begins to consider the consequences. His employers have indulged him this far. He's proven his usefulness several times and they moved mountains to get the charges against him dropped. Would they lose patience if he were to slap the bitch around a little? After all, it's his crew. His patch. It's his city . . .

He feels Bruno approach him. Smells marijuana and clothes dried in a damp room. He turns and looks into the big man's face. Downey looks at him, questioningly, and Bruno gives a nod that could mean anything.

'Playtime, Boss?'

With coke coursing through his veins, Downey takes it as an affirmation. Takes it as agreement that they should kick the door in and drag the bitch to the ground by her hair.

'That's them,' he says, pointing. 'It's the right house. There's a kid, but . . .'

'A kid?' says Bruno. 'Fuck.'

'Take him in another room. There's no need for him to see.'

Bruno presses his lips tight together. He sniffs. Turns to the Turks and tells them they're to follow him inside. Then he turns back to Downey.

'You sure, Boss? I'm game, but you're going to have to stuff something in his mouth not to wake the neighbours.' Bruno leers. 'Try his mum's knickers.'

Downey considers the adjacent houses. None of them seem occupied. While there are people strolling past and enjoying the warm air down by the water's edge, the area is quiet enough for him and his team to do what they want.

'She needs to learn her lesson,' says Downey. 'They all need to see.'

He opens the garden gate.

One step.

Two.

Three.

Fuck, fuck, fuck . . .

Before he can talk himself out of it, Downey bangs on the painted wood of the front door. A moment passes in which a part of him begins to hope that nobody will answer. Then Roisin McAvoy opens the door, smiling wide, halfway through enquiring whether he has lost his key . . .

It all happens fast and loud.

Bruno pushes past Downey, causing him to stumble against the doorframe. He hears Roisin let out just the quickest of shrieks and then Bruno's hand is around her mouth. He's dragging her down the hall, knocking a photograph from the wall so that it smashes on the cord carpet.

'Keep her quiet, keep her quiet!'

The Turks run past him too. Downey finds himself staggering, one arm on the wall to keep himself upright. He hears a door bang, then there are cries and shouts.

Christ, what are we bloody doing?

He slides along the wall, his mind racing, heart thudding like two rams butting heads. Then he staggers into the living room.

One of the Turks has Roisin against the wall. Her feet are off the floor and her face is turning purple. The other is pressing Mel's face into the sofa, yanking down her jogging trousers as he does so. There's a tattoo at the base of her spine. He suddenly wants to cut the thing off. Wants to stick her with pins. Sew her bloody lips together.

'Little bastard bit me!'

Downey turns to see Bruno, sucking a wound on his hand, kicking a sideboard over in front of a small door beneath the staircase. The muffled cries and screams within suggest that the boy inside is fighting to get out.

'Close the fucking curtains,' says Downey, and Bruno does as he is commanded.

Downey crosses to where Memluk is throttling Roisin.

'You like that, sweetie?'

He looks into her eyes. Sees nothing but fear. Sees frothy spittle pop from between her lips and land on her chin. The sight reminds him of an earlier fantasy, and he lashes out with his right fist, hitting her hard in the mouth. The blow bursts her lips and smashes her head back against the wall.

'Aw, did that sting?'

Behind him, he can hear Mel kicking and biting, and then mumbled foreign curses.

'Drop her,' says Downey to Memluk, and Roisin tumbles to the floor. Rather than lying there as he had expected, she scrambles to her feet, looking around for her child.

She fixes her eyes on Downey.

'He'll kill you,' she says, and blood sprays out to spill on the exposed skin above her vest.

Downey laughs, hoping Bruno will join in. But nobody does. The only noises are of violence and fear and there is nothing fun about any of it. He loses his temper. Fixes his venom on Roisin then lashes out with a kick. She's tiny and tries to dodge but he still connects where he had intended. She falls forward, both hands between her legs, as Downey finds himself giggling and pointing, excited, like a child . . .

As Downey turns to seek Bruno's approval, a figure appears in the doorway. Bruno senses him too and turns, just as a fist the size of a boiled ham takes him in the jaw. Bruno's head snaps back as if he has been struck under the chin with a golf club and he falls like a tree.

The Turks both move towards the new threat and Downey watches, entranced and motionless, as the giant flame-haired figure in the doorway lunges forward and hits them like a train.

'Stop, stop . . .'

Before Downey can finish the sentence, he feels pain screaming through his left leg. He looks down and locks eyes with the gypsy girl as she sinks her teeth into his skin. He opens his mouth to scream but before he can do so, a giant, pale, freckled hand closes around his lower jaw and he is pushed back across the living room and slammed into the wall.

A face is in front of his.

Broad.

Handsome.

Scarred.

Furious beyond words.

'A message,' says Downey, desperately. 'I've got a message . . .'

He winces, waiting for the fist to slam into his jaw, but the big man suddenly drops him as one of the Turks hits him with a punch to the lower back.

Downey's mind clears for a second.

Her husband.

The copper.

He watches as McAvoy turns. Watches as the big man grabs Memluk by his shirt and throws him at the wall so hard that a crack appears from floor to ceiling, the fresh plaster splitting like dry wood. Tokcan grabs him by the knees and the two of them go down in a melee of arms and legs.

Downey gasps for air. He reaches down and feels the blood on his leg and the sensation clears his senses for a moment. He looks down and sees Tokcan on McAvoy's back, his arm around his throat. Sees McAvoy stand, the weight upon him unimportant.

Downey wants to run. He wants to push his way free and run

into the warm air. He wants to be somewhere else. Someone else . . .

Without knowing why, without even realising he is doing it, Downey pulls the phone from his pocket. He fumbles with the buttons. Finds the message on his answering service and turns the volume up as far it will go. Then he lurches forward and presses the phone to the big man's ear.

McAvoy can't see. There is too much rage and fury in his eyes. But he can hear.

And he can hear his own voice, dribbling out of the telephone that is being held to his ear by some pretty boy in jeans and a T-shirt.

He stops. Shrugs the foreign man off his back and hears him swear as he crashes to the floor.

McAvoy listens.

Hears the words he sobbed at Sabine just yesterday.

'They would have died. All three of them. Roisin thinks they did. She's never asked. Never checked. I beat them unconscious and left them for dead. I don't know how the fire started but it would have cooked them and any evidence. But I couldn't leave them. I put Roisin somewhere safe and went and dragged them out of there. Then I left. I've lived with that ever since. Lived with her thinking one thing, and me knowing another. I let her down. Even now, I know that if it happened again, I couldn't have killed them. I'm not that man. It's not in me. She's married to the wrong man . . .'

McAvoy falls back. Looks up at Adam Downey. Feels the strength go out of him. Feels the man below him scrambling free. Hears them dragging the unconscious men away and the front door banging against the wall.

He feels Roisin's arms around him and hears Mel's cries.

'Fin,' he says, suddenly. 'Lilah.'

He finds himself tangled in a collection of limbs. Feels small arms hugging his knees and kisses from a bloodied mouth upon his forehead.

Through it all, one thought, over and over.

She taped me. She fucking taped me.

And then he is wrapping himself in the people he loves, trying to insulate himself with their caresses. He wants to hurt somebody. He wants answers.

He wants to be a different man.

17

Gnarled fingers of cloud are slowly closing over a nearly full moon. It is the only light in this ebony sky and seems to sit vulnerably on an open palm; a communion wafer waiting to be crushed.

'Stupid,' says McAvoy, again, through thin lips. 'Stupid, stupid.'

He has one hand on the wheel. The other is striking his forehead, the heel of the hand rhythmically hitting his sweaty skin.

It's gone midnight and the road to Beverley is quiet. He could press the accelerator to the floor if he wanted to, but despite his anger he knows where the speed-cameras are and can't afford the bump to his insurance premiums if he got caught doing more than sixty.

'Mouth shut, mouth shut, mouth shut . . .'

He beats the words into his brain, furious with himself for daring to believe there was any benefit to sharing the secret agony that has sat in his chest for a decade.

'I'm so sorry, so sorry, so sorry . . .'

For the past few hours, Roisin has been apologising. Telling him everything.

He thinks about it now. Pictures the scene. Sees himself, growing pale, shaking his head and scratching blood from his arms as she told him why Adam Downey was in their home, and why he shouldn't report the incident to his colleagues.

McAvoy hadn't lost his temper. He'd refused to shout at her. He wanted to shout, of course. Wanted to tell her she had been bloody stupid and demand to know what the hell she had been thinking. But the words got nowhere near his mouth. Besides, his own betrayal far outstrips her moment of weakness. Instead of shaking her until her false nails fell off, he'd sat her on the toilet seat in the bathroom and used a warm flannel to remove the blood from her skin. He had stroked her face and pushed her hair behind her ears. He'd hugged the children, straightened up the living room, and made Mel a hot chocolate. Then he'd led Roisin to their bedroom and told her to explain again. Told her he needed to hear it again so he could fully understand.

She'd been there, she said. Been in Mel's shop when Downey came in demanding the coat that contained the drugs. Downey had offered Mel money but she had refused. So he'd got tough. And Roisin had stood up to him. She'd phoned the police in her pocket and she'd kicked him in the bollocks. Then she'd seen the wedge of cash. It had been instinct. She'd picked it up and run. It had come to just under £600. She'd felt bad straight away and had offered it to Mel, but Mel didn't want it. So she'd spent it. Bought him a watch and some furniture for the garden. She was sorry. She hadn't expected this. She hadn't wanted to cause trouble. It was just a mistake . . .

McAvoy had held her. He said he understood. Told her he would fix it. Told her that the bad men wouldn't come back and then softly kissed her bruised mouth. At that moment he had been so damn relieved that she hadn't heard the message on Downey's phone, he would have forgiven her anything. Relieved, too, that he had arrived home when he did. He thinks about what would have happened had Pharaoh not told him to go get some sleep. Feels pitifully grateful that he hadn't stopped in at a takeaway or a supermarket on the way home for some snacks and a bottle of wine. He makes a squeezing motion with his hand and feels the pain in his fingers where his knuckles had connected with Bruno's jaw. He wonders how badly he hurt the man. Whether his jaw broke. Whether he snapped a vertebra as his head went back. Whether there will be repercussions.

McAvoy follows the road into Beverley. Passes down quiet streets and through the deserted town centre. He doesn't blink. Just follows the road until he sees the sign.

The village of Molescroft doesn't stop before it runs into Beverley. It's a conurbation rather than a suburb, but most people who live here think of the shops in Beverley as being the centre of their community. It's a pretty place, with a good junior school and neatly tended semi-detached homes, spread out around a playing field and a small row of stores.

Sabine Keane lives here. The shrink. The counsellor who betrayed him.

McAvoy bares his teeth as he thinks of it. He sees her, now. Sitting in her chair with her handbag open. She must have left her phone on the entire time. Must have called her other employers at the start of each session and let them listen in as he bared his soul.

It has occurred to McAvoy that perhaps the room itself was

bugged. Perhaps Sabine is an innocent party who will be as appalled and disgusted as he to learn that his confessions had been taped. But he fancies not.

McAvoy turns the car to the right, onto a silent side road, then quickly right again onto Finch Park. Sabine's bungalow is the first house on the left, a small, neat property with a separate garage and unusually petite windows that make the building look as if it was designed by a child with crayons and graph paper.

He sees her even before he has parked the car. She's sitting on the front step, lit by the light that spills out from her open front door. She's holding a glass and wearing a dressing gown, and even in this light, McAvoy can see tears on her bruised cheeks.

McAvoy steps from the car. Sees her recognise him. Sees her drop her head.

'You taped me,' he says, softly, as he walks up the drive. 'You taped our sessions.'

Sabine raises her head. She looks exhausted, like she's been slapped. Her cheeks are red and there is a dark patch above one eye.

Sabine just nods. Takes a sip from the glass.

McAvoy stands over her.

'You know you're finished,' he says. 'You must know that.'

She shrugs. Implies that she truly couldn't give a damn. Sniffs, noisily, and raises the glass again with a hand that shakes.

'Was it money?'

Sabine says nothing. Then she mutters something that might be an apology.

'Sabine, please . . .'

'My husband,' she says, at last. She raises her head. Looks at him with eyes that swim in salt water. 'He knocked a cyclist off their bike last year. Got sent to prison.'

295

McAvoy looks confused. 'I don't understand . . .'

'He's a teacher,' she says. 'He's not strong. He's got another year to go. At least.'

McAvoy rubs a hand through his hair. He slides down to a seated position, his backside on the cold paving stones, his back against the wall. He takes the glass from Sabine and takes a sip. It's vodka. He hates the stuff, and hands it back.

'When did they get in touch?'

'Not long ago,' she says, her voice cracking. 'Not long after you were referred to me. They showed me pictures. Emailed me photos of Graham. That's my husband. Well, we're not really married. That's why I got cleared to provide services for the police. He didn't show up on the background checks.'

'They wanted you to tape me?'

'Not at first,' she says. 'They just wanted to know what made you tick. Then they told me I had to call a certain number at the start of our sessions. To ask you about your secrets. What you felt guilty about. What you loved.'

McAvoy scrapes his boot along the stone. Kicks a pebble and watches it disappear into a flower bed. He draws his knees up, hugging them to his chest. He shivers, despite the clammy warmth of the night.

'You did as you were told?'

'I didn't push,' she says. 'I sort of hoped you wouldn't speak. You'd kept quiet . . .'

'And then I just blurted it out,' he says, so softly he can barely hear his own voice. 'I gave them everything.'

Sabine nods. 'They called tonight. Told me I'd done my bit. Said Graham would be left alone. They said you were getting your message tonight.'

She sounds as if she is about to say more, but she closes her mouth and looks away.

'Do you still have the numbers?' he asks. 'The pictures they sent you?'

She shakes her head. 'They told me to destroy them, delete everything.'

'And the person you spoke to?'

She frowns. 'Well-spoken. Quite wordy, like a solicitor or a politician. Very calm. Not old but not young.'

McAvoy stares up at the sky. The moon has disappeared, throttled by the fist of cloud.

'We could get your phone records. See what numbers you called. We could keep Graham safe . . .'

Sabine shakes her head again.

'I just want this to stop,' she says. 'I thought they might have hurt you. I can't think straight. Couldn't sleep. Couldn't look at the kids . . .'

'They hurt my family,' says McAvoy. 'I can't allow that. How do I begin to allow that?'

Sabine looks sick. Looks like she wants to smash the glass and draw one of the shards across her wrist.

They sit in silence for a time. McAvoy's anger is now just a hot rock in his guts. He's trying to think clearly. He has no doubts that the people who did this are the same outfit that Colin Ray has been chasing. He knows they are well connected, powerful and dangerous. They think they have him in their pocket. They have dirt on Roisin, and dirt on him. With a phone call they could end his career. With a call to Roisin, they could end his marriage. She believes he killed her tormentors. Married him in that belief. Fears, above all, that such a truth would drive her from his arms.

But he doesn't know what they will use their leverage for. He's not actively investigating them. He's not on Colin Ray's team. He's hunting a killer and hasn't thought of organised crime in months. He fancies he has time on his side. He needs to keep Roisin out of harm's way until he can find Angelo Caneva. He needs to stop a killer before he can make sense of tonight's events.

McAvoy makes a decision. In the morning, he will tell Roisin and Mel to take the kids and return to the old house on Kingswood. It's not much of a hiding place but they still have a few days before they have to give the keys back and he'll feel happier knowing they are somewhere they will take a little more finding and where there are plenty of neighbours to shout for help. Caneva is priority. Pharaoh has taken over the reins of the investigation once more and declared him prime suspect. He was released from custody a few years back and is no longer under the supervision of the probation service. The last place he was registered as living was in a flat in Coventry, but that was some time ago and since then he has dropped off the grid. His father is refusing to answer his phone. Tomorrow, McAvoy hopes to visit Angelo's sister, Maria. Nielsen is trying to get a current address, and Pharaoh will alert the media to the fact they are trying to find him. Things are going the right way. McAvoy's intuition and detective work have provided the breakthrough and he should be feeling proud of himself. But all he can see is the blood on Roisin's face and the terror in his son's eyes as he hugged his daddy.

'Did they tell her?' asks Sabine. 'Your wife?'

McAvoy shakes his head. 'They just let me know they knew. I might have to tell her.' He corrects himself. 'I am going to tell her.'

'She sounds a strong woman. You didn't do anything wrong.'

'There are different types of wrong,' he says, the words hanging in the air.

Sabine manages a little smile. 'Do the police really believe that?'

McAvoy looks at her, and then inside himself. Sees what he is becoming.

'I don't know what I believe. I don't know what I am.'

It is just gone 2 a.m. Dr Olivia Pradesh can smell antiseptic and rubber on her long dark hair as the wind blows it across her pale, delicate features. The storm that will soon engulf Hull has already broken here and a fine rain drives at an angle across the car park on a sharp breeze.

She fumbles in her bag for car keys. The bag may be designer but she treats it like a canvas sack, dumping everything in the same central compartment. She rummages inside it as she winces into the rain, turning her head so her dark hair billows behind her. She closes her hand around her phone and takes a quick glance at the screen. A couple of missed calls and a text asking her if she fancies the trip to Prague that some of her old university friends are planning over the next Bank Holiday weekend. She remembers that she was supposed to call some detective constable from East Yorkshire but fancies he will have gone to bed by now. She'll do it in the morning. She'll reply about Prague, too. She needs to recharge her batteries. Needs a toasted sandwich and a glass of milk then a few hours on the sofa under a crocheted blanket.

Dr Pradesh is forty-four years old. She's fit and slim, and though her mother is of Indian descent, her colouring does not proclaim her heritage the way her name does. She's an attractive woman. Her hair has always been jet-black but these days she has to use a dye to mask the grey roots. She's wearing a tweed jacket over a purple blouse, with a short, fawn-coloured skirt and soft leather boots. A string of pearls bounces around in her cleavage as she crosses the car park. They feel cold on her skin and she reaches inside her blouse to pull them free. Her hands betray her profession. Her skin is scrubbed painfully clean, her nails short and neatly trimmed.

As the rain plasters her hair to her face she plunges her hand back into the bag and closes her fist around the keys. She moves around to the far side of her unassuming Audi and reaches out to open the passenger door.

As she closes her fingers around the handle, something slams into her back. She feels the wind go out of her at the same moment as her middle and index fingers dislocate and mangle upon impact with the cold, wet metal of the car.

Dr Pradesh manages to shout but something strikes her left cheek.

In a moment she is semi-conscious; her face in a puddle, one ear and eye submerged.

For a moment there is utter blackness. Dead air. She raises herself, unsteadily, on one arm. Suddenly she hears tyres, squealing across the concrete. Sees a dark vehicle slam to a halt in front of her. Then she is being dragged up by her coat collar.

She hears her string of pearls snap.

Sees them dance as hailstones on the ground.

The doors of the van are pulled open. She feels a clump of hair come loose as she is slammed against something hard and the impact wakes her instincts. She shouts. Lashes out. Tries to turn so she can see who is doing this to her. Then there is a fist in her gut and she is being pushed back onto a patch of dirty grey carpet that masks the hardboard floor of the vehicle. She kicks out again. Feels pain as the van doors slam against her ankle. She draws them up and starts to shout afresh.

For a moment, her screams ring out, loud despite the whistling wind and driving rain. Somebody must have heard! Somebody must see!

She looks around, frantic now. Tries to get a sense of her bearings. Then a scream is ripped from her throat. At her side is a corpse. The skin has taken on a greenish tinge, like moss on an alabaster statue. The eyes are sunken, the mouth locked in a grimace of pain. She throws herself backwards, desperate to get her face away from the body before the stench crawls into her nose, but she is too late.

She smells decay.

Corruption.

Dead flesh.

Sobbing now, she wriggles onto her side and kicks at the corpse, trying to push it as far away as she can. Her booted feet go through the dead creature's torso as if she is stamping on a cardboard box.

And then she is thrown forward. The van is moving, fast and reckless. She tumbles, hits the van doors and one swings open with the impact.

She glimpses fresh air.

The dark, rain-lashed night.

She takes a step, as if to throw herself through the door, but a sudden jolt pitches her back. Her head hits wood. She tastes blood in her mouth. And then her eyes see nothing but gold stars and spinning blackness.

The body beside her slides on the wooden floor as the van slews left. The vehicle hits a speed bump and the doors swing open afresh.

Slowly, unseen by the driver, watched only by the street lights and the stars, the corpse slithers towards the exit.

The vehicle's wheels hit a pothole, and the rotten body teeters over the lip of the van.

And as the driver accelerates, the dead thing finally slips free.

Organs and innards and compressed gases explode in a damp spray as the long-dead sack of rancid meat collides with the unyielding ground.

Angelo Caneva's dead, staring eyes watch the vehicle disappear into the distance.

Steam rises from his ruptured guts, disappearing into the air like a cartoon ghost.

Part Four

18

5.05 a.m. Great Horton Road in Bradford.

It's too early to knock on a stranger's door, so McAvoy sweats and shivers in his car outside a row of grubby shops, waiting for the sun to come up. He hopes that when it does, the windows of the vehicle will stop reflecting his features back at him. He doesn't like what he sees. He's wearing yesterday's clothes and Roisin's blood and feels as feverish and pestilent as the skies he left behind when he set off for West Yorkshire two hours ago. He's unshaven and his face looks puffy and sore. His right hand, limp in his lap, is bruised across the knuckles. He's lost a fingernail, grabbing one of the Turks, and his middle finger is throbbing beneath the Elastoplast.

Well-connected.

Powerful.

Ruthless . . .

He can't stop thinking about the outfit that turned Sabine. Can't stop wondering what the hell to do next. He should be concentrating on the investigation. Should be thinking about Hoyer-Wood and Angelo Caneva.

Here, now, he can barely remember their names.

He looks at the clock. Still too bloody early.

The cup of coffee he bought from a petrol station an hour ago has gone cold, but he sips at it anyway, for something to do. He watches a spider industriously building a web around the wing mirror of the car. It's working hard. It's doing its job. It seems to know what it's doing and what's expected of it. He finds himself envying the little bastard.

He flicks on the radio. Starts listening to an early-morning phone-in show on Radio 5 Live, and switches off when he finds himself agreeing with everybody.

McAvoy knows there is nothing to stop him knocking on Maria Caneva's door immediately. He's a policeman looking into three murders and her brother is prime suspect. She hasn't responded to any phone messages. But to McAvoy, waking the poor woman up at this hour just seems too damned obnoxious and uncivilised. He doesn't want to be that kind of man. And besides, he's not ready for it. Doesn't know what noise will come out when he opens his mouth to speak. He doesn't feel like a policeman. He feels like a thug and a coward who has been manipulated and outplayed. There is so much guilt clogging his guts he feels as though he has been stuffed full of mud and stones.

Roisin, I'm so sorry . . .

His wife will wake up this morning with black eyes and bruised lips. His son will have nightmares for days. Mel may take the matter out of his hands entirely and tell his colleagues what happened.

More than that, Adam Downey might come back.

He has no fucking clue what to do.

5.06.

5.07.

5.08 . . .

At just after 6 a.m., McAvoy rubs a hand through his hair and scratches at his crown. His fingernails come away dirty. His patience frays, then snaps, and he steps out of the car into the cool air of the morning. He drops his bag and spills papers and pens on the damp stone of the pavement. Feels sick rise in this throat as he bends forward to start picking things up. Winces as his phone falls from his pocket. He looks at the image on the cracked screen. At Roisin and his children. Two smiles and one wet, pink, baby face. He wants to press the picture to his face. Wants to breathe them all in and be made better by their nearness.

He makes fists. Closes the car door. Locks it. Pulls his bag over his shoulder and sorts himself out. Steps over a cracked paving slab and nearly loses his footing on a discarded kebab.

Maria Caneva lives down Bartle Lane. The electoral register indicates that she lives alone, though given that it's a student neighbourhood he can't rule out that she rents out a room or two to somebody studying at the nearby university.

He turns off the main road and walks softly towards the small, bare-brick property. McAvoy tries not to think anything too derogatory about Bradford. The areas he has seen are dirty, rubbish-strewn and ugly. Most of the shops carry signs written in a language he presumes to be Urdu, but he feels far too Caucasian and guilty when he starts thinking about the socio-economic reasons for the neighbourhood's current state and usually stops himself before he can think anything negative. It's a community of halal butchers and general stores, where watermelons in damaged crates pile up outside graffiti-covered general stores that carry posters for English newspapers long since defunct. He would think of it as a rough neighbourhood if not for the unexpected flashes of class. Halfway up the main road is a glitzy, brightly lit restaurant that would not look out of place in London's West End, and most of the cars parked outside the takeaway shops and budget electrical stores carry Mercedes badges. It's an area McAvoy struggles to understand and he's grateful he's not a policeman here.

McAvoy finds the right door. Composes himself. Licks his palm and smooths his hair down. Rubs his lips. Closes his eyes and concentrates on breathing.

He knocks, politely, on Maria Caneva's door, then begins to count to ten in his head.

After just a few seconds the door is opened by a plump young woman in her middle twenties. She's wearing a pink dressing gown and has a pair of glasses on top of her head. Brown hair is pulled back from a plain but not unattractive face, and though she looks surprised to be answering the door at this hour, her expression is not unwelcoming.

'I thought you were the milkman,' she says, by way of greeting.

McAvoy shows her his warrant card. Gives a courteous, closed-mouth smile, and introduces himself.

'Are you Maria Caneva?'

She nods.

'I would like to talk to you about your brother.'

Her face falls, but an expression that may be relief also flashes over her features.

'What's he done now, silly sod?'

'Could I come in?'

'Please.'

Maria invites him inside. The door opens straight into an

untidy living room. On the sofa that sits beneath the large front window there are pillows and a quilt. In front of it is a coffee table covered in haphazardly opened letters, food wrappers and empty coffee cups. The TV is an old-fashioned and boxy affair that sits on a dusty glass cabinet and the electric fire looks sad and unlit inside a slate-and-breezeblock fireplace. There are books and old newspapers piled in one corner of the room and DVD cases in the other. It's not a nice room, but Maria makes no apologies as she kicks the duvet behind the sofa and waves McAvoy to sit down.

'Did I wake you?' asks McAvoy, indicating the pillow and trying not to mention how much of her fleshy thighs he can see as she sits down and draws her legs up underneath her.

She looks puzzled, then realisation dawns. 'Oh, I sleep down here most nights. There've been burglaries. I haven't got much to take but I don't like sleeping up there. Every time I hear a noise I think there's somebody in the living room.'

McAvoy looks around him.

'Have you lived here long?'

'A few years. I've never really got round to doing it up the way I want. I just rent, so if I spent too much tarting it up it would just be money down the drain.'

'And you live alone?'

Maria makes a show of sticking out her lower lip. 'Young, free and single. Apart from the "young". Or the "free".'

McAvoy plays with his collar. He's suddenly very aware of how he looks. He gets out his notebook, putting his warrant card down on the sofa beside him as he does so. Maria looks at it again and her mouth opens wide.

'Oh, you're McAvoy? I'm sorry, I was half asleep. Didn't twig . . .'

McAvoy takes his card and looks at it himself, as if for confirmation. 'I'm sorry?'

'You got the transcripts okay, yes? I wasn't sure I'd spelled it right.'

McAvoy feels a little lost, but he suddenly understands how Hoyer-Wood's psychologist sessions ended up in his hands and why the envelope was postmarked West Yorkshire.

'You sent them?'

Maria nods, innocently. She seems to be waking up a bit now. She reaches down beside her and finds a can of pop. She sips at it and smiles.

'I spoke to Dad after you visited him,' she says. 'He called me. He doesn't very often, but I think talking to you had shaken him up a bit. He said what you wanted. What was happening.'

McAvoy looks at her. She seems utterly without guile. She's a bright, open person and McAvoy feels himself warming to her. As she comes alive, she seems to examine him more closely. He feels her looking at the bruises on his knuckles. The Elastoplast. The blood and bruises. 'I'm sorry, have you been trying to get me on the phone?' she asks, raising a hand to her mouth. Her hands are cleaner than the room, with short, clipped nails. 'I'm only on a pay-as-you-go phone and it's off most of the time. I'm a nurse, you know that, yes? My bosses play merry hell with me because I'm such a bugger to get hold of. Dad does too.'

She says it all brightly. McAvoy wants to push.

'You and your dad are close?'

Maria shrugs. She seems about to speak and then stops herself. She closes her eyes and then suddenly stands. 'I'm going to make a coffee. Do you want one?'

McAvoy doesn't know what to say. He just looks down at his

notebook and stays quiet as she rolls her large rear end off the sofa and plods into the kitchen. He hears cupboards opening and a kettle boiling. Hears a fridge opening and closing and then she is back in the room, carrying two glasses of steaming brown coffee.

'No cups,' she says, apologetically. 'Hold it by the top or you'll burn your fingers.'

She hands McAvoy the glass of hot liquid and he sips it, scalding his tongue. He puts it down as Maria plonks herself back on the sofa next to him. She spills coffee on her bare leg but doesn't seem to notice. Then she looks at him so hard that he wonders if she is trying to imprint a thought on the inside of his skull.

'Angelo,' she says, at last. 'He's in trouble again, yeah? I know what you're thinking. You're wrong.'

McAvoy licks his thumb and dabs at a spot of blood on the back of his hand. 'What am I thinking?'

'You're thinking Angelo has killed these people, aren't you?'

McAvoy spreads his hands. 'We're open-minded. But he has questions to answer. This is a murder investigation that is very closely linked to Sebastien Hoyer-Wood. I feel like I'm swimming through treacle, but the one thing I'm certain of is that somebody is punishing the people who saved Hoyer-Wood's life. Yesterday I spoke to a lady who was there the night Hoyer-Wood should have died and who tells me that Angelo broke into her house with plans to kill her. Angelo has spent time inside. He has a record. The picture we're getting is of a dangerous man . . .'

Maria pulls the band from her hair as McAvoy talks and places it over her wrist. She pushes her hair back from her face and rearranges it into the same style it was before. She doesn't look worried. Just distracted.

'He's not dangerous,' she says. 'Not really. He's just been through a lot.'

McAvoy sighs. 'Do you know where he is?'

Maria considers him. 'You've read what I sent you, yes?'

McAvoy nods. 'How did you get the transcripts, Miss Caneva? And why did you send them to me?'

For a time, the small, untidy room is quiet save for the sound of the city coming to life beyond the glass. Steel shutters are being drawn up. Car engines are beginning to purr. A letter box bangs noisily as a newspaper is pushed through it too hard.

Maria finishes her drink. She pulls her legs up afresh. She scratches at her face and makes all the little adjustments that seem to help her decide what to say.

'You know what happened, yeah? You've read them properly?'

'All of them. Every word.'

'You believe him? Sebastien?'

It's a strange question, but McAvoy answers it. 'They helped me put some of the pieces together.'

She nods. 'I've had those transcripts for years, Sergeant. That man had an effect on all our lives. When you're young you ask questions. You need explanations. There was all sorts on Dad's computer, growing up. Angelo and me could quote you most of those sessions word for word.'

McAvoy shakes his head. Decides to be honest. 'Maria, I'm lost . . .'

She gives him an indulgent smile. 'I do prattle, don't I? The funny thing is, I've often wondered what I'd do if I ever had to tell a policeman about this. I didn't imagine I'd be in my dressing gown in a place like this. It's funny. The whole thing's just funny.'

As McAvoy looks into Maria's cheerful, pleasant face, he realises he is talking to somebody damaged. She is too light-hearted. Too sparkly. She's suffered and endured. She's survived, but at a cost to some part of herself. He wonders what she allows herself to feel. He's suddenly too hot, and yet the hairs on his arms are rising and he feels himself about to shiver.

'Angelo went off the rails when Mum was poorly,' she says. 'Got into trouble more and more often. Our lives were different then. We had money, for a start. We were very London in our outlook. We weren't exactly happy, having spent so much time at that bloody place.'

'You mean your dad's hospital?'

She snorts. 'Hospital? It was a factory. A money-making machine. The government was throwing money at private healthcare in those days. Dad always did have an eye for a few quid.'

'Living there must have been hard . . .'

'We never really lived there,' she says, looking at the dirty sole of one foot. Her actions are childlike, and put McAvoy in mind of Fin's schoolfriends.

'No?'

'Weekends and holidays,' she says, licking her finger and rubbing the dirt from the knuckle of her big toe. 'It was pretty, but Mum was never mad keen on us going up there too often. There was plenty of security and there really shouldn't have been any risks, but Mum said it was no place for kids. Even so, Dad got his way. He usually did. It was okay, to be honest. Mum would take us shopping or down to Hull or over to York or wherever. We didn't mind too much.'

McAvoy wonders what she is trying not to blurt out. He decides to steer the conversation.

'Sebastien Hoyer-Wood,' he says, gently. 'Tell me.'

Maria gives a high, girlish laugh. It's a near-hysterical sound, but there are no tears. She just giggles, as if the name is funny.

'We knew that him and Dad were friends at university. We knew he'd got into trouble because he was ill. We knew Dad was helping him get better and we didn't have any reason to doubt it when Dad said there was nothing to be scared of about having him in the house from time to time.'

'How did your mum feel about your father having these sessions in the family home?'

Maria flashes her teeth then shrugs. 'She never said.'

McAvoy waits for more. When nothing comes, he moves closer to her. Tries to hold her gaze.

'Maria, what is it you want me to know? You sent me those transcripts . . .'

She turns around on the sofa, kneeling up, and pulls the curtains aside to look at the street. McAvoy can no longer see her expression, but he can hear her words.

'When we met Sebastien he was in a wheelchair. He couldn't talk very well. He was in a lot of pain. He was a cripple, though you couldn't use that word around Dad. I'm a couple of years older than Angelo, you know that, yes? We'd do impressions of him. It's cruel, isn't it? But Dad would have him in his study and they'd be talking and sometimes Angelo and me would go and listen at the door or go outside and look through the window. Sebastien saw us, once. He was in his wheelchair, looking out the window. Dad had his back to us. He couldn't see what we were doing. Angelo was pulling this face and being silly and I was laughing and we saw that Sebastien was watching. We were so embarrassed. We felt really bad. He didn't look sad, though.

Not Sebastien. He looked like he was smiling. Like he found it funny. It was creepy, but it stopped us watching the sessions any more . . .'

McAvoy wishes he could see her face, wishes he could better read this strange young woman.

'After it all happened, our family was never the same,' she says, quieter now. 'It affected us all. Mum got sick. Angelo closed down. I don't know what happened to me. Dad started to lose everything. I needed answers. So did Angelo. It wasn't hard to get Dad's transcripts off his computer. I think he knows I took them, but at least it spared him having to talk to us about any of what happened. When he told me you wanted to see them I think he was trying to wriggle out of breaking the rules. I think he knew I would send them to you. I'm pleased I did. You seem nice.'

McAvoy just stays silent.

'You know what Angelo got sent down for, don't you? He was in a dark place. He'd started getting high. Sniffing glue, if you can believe that. It was easier for him to get his hands on than the hard stuff. He always looked young. Nobody would sell to him. He was a bit of a softy, really. Didn't make friends very easily. And he was an angry sod in his teens. He blamed Sebastien for what was happening to us. The money. The way he felt. Mum. He must have found out which hospital Sebastien was in from some of Dad's paperwork. Either way, he disappeared from home for a few days and then Dad got a call to say he'd been arrested. He'd thrown a milk bottle full of petrol and rags at a hospital minibus. Petrol-bombed it. We knew straight away which patient he'd been aiming at. The first question I asked wasn't whether Angelo was okay. It was whether he'd got him.'

Maria turns back, smiling.

'In a way, he did get him. The stress of it brought on a massive stroke. Hoyer-Wood ended up worse than he had been before. Proper vegetable.'

She bursts out laughing and McAvoy finds himself smiling out of politeness. He wants to put a hand on hers and make her tell him the bit that matters most, but there is something so brittle about the mask she wears that he fancies any contact would break her.

'The last transcript,' he says, as kindly as he can. 'It was missing from the bundle you sent me.'

Maria nods. She looks serious for a moment. 'I couldn't send that. I wanted to. I wanted you to understand about Sebastien. I wanted to help you. But I couldn't just send that to a stranger. That was where our lives changed. It would be like posting somebody a broken heart . . .'

McAvoy stays silent. Just looks at her and hopes she'll choose to help him.

'He wasn't crippled by the end,' she says, quietly. 'Sebastien.'

'I'm sorry?' says McAvoy, as he feels his heart begin to race.

'When he was first arrested and they nearly killed him and those interfering bastards saved his life. He was hurt. He was crippled. But you have to remember, he was a medical man. A physiotherapist. He knew just what to do and how much to show the people who were looking after him. He was months ahead of where he should have been, but we didn't know that until he stood up and put a knife to Dad's throat.'

McAvoy closes his eyes.

'That last session,' says Maria, into the cloth of the sofa. 'The alarm went off over in the main hospital while Sebastien was still at our house in Dad's office. We don't know if Sebastien set it up or just took advantage of the situation. Either way, Angelo and Mum and me were in the living room watching TV when the door of Dad's office burst open and Sebastien came out with a knife to Dad's throat. We screamed. We didn't know what to do. He was *the cripple*. He couldn't walk. Couldn't talk in much other than grunts and dribble. And now he had a knife to Dad's throat and was standing in our living room.'

McAvoy rubs his hand across his forehead, pushing the sweat back into his hair.

'What happened?'

'You know what happened.'

There is no gentle way to ask the question, but McAvoy still manages to drop his voice to a whisper. 'He raped your mother, didn't he?'

Maria gives a little snort.

'He'd have liked to take his turn with all of us. The way he looked at us . . .'

She stops and looks away.

'He'd have fucked Dad if it wasn't that he seemed to get so much pleasure from ripping his heart out.'

There is silence in the room. McAvoy tries not to picture the scene she has placed in his head but the image is too vivid, the colours and shapes in his mind too intense. He sees it all too clearly.

'Jesus,' he breathes.

'He knew how to play us all,' says Maria, softly. 'Knew we wouldn't move. He made us sit there. Made his wife and children watch as he held a knife to Dad's throat. He just laughed in Dad's face. He'd have started doing star-jumps if he thought it would have helped him make his point. Dad just seemed to deflate. It was like we saw something leave his body. He just seemed to crumble, there in front of us, when he realised he had been played all along. We just sat there crying as he told Dad everything. The names. The places. All his victims. And Dad, open-mouthed and wet-eyed and pitiful, losing all faith in himself and knowing, in his soul, just what he had exposed his family to.'

McAvoy says nothing. Just listens to his own breathing.

'It was the fire that ended it,' says Maria, pulling at the flesh below her chin and staring up at the ceiling. 'We smelled smoke. Saw flames. We heard people banging on the door. Sebastien reacted first. Dropped to the floor like he'd fallen from his wheelchair. And then there were people in the room and we were being evacuated to safety and Dad was telling us not to talk.'

'Why didn't he say anything?'

Maria looks at him kindly. 'His reputation. The reputation of the hospital. He'd said Sebastien was ill. Said he could make him well. He would have been exposed as a fucking idiot.'

'But after all these years . . .' begins McAvoy, before a sudden flash of temper takes him. 'I went to see him. Your father. He stuck to his story. Told me Sebastien had been ill . . .'

Maria rubs her cheeks. 'He's taught himself to believe what he wants to. We don't talk about it. Nobody ever talked about it. Not even Mum, when she was dying. That's probably why Angelo and me had to do our own digging. We were so angry. Our whole lives seemed so broken and it was all Hoyer-Wood's fault. We dug up everything we could on him. Found Dad's files. When we learned that he should have died that night in Bridlington it was like our hearts had been ripped out. What happened to us shouldn't have happened. Sebastien should have died. He should never have entered our lives.'

'But the people who saved him . . .'

Maria waves McAvoy's protests away. 'I know, they were innocent. When I heard about their deaths I was sad. This was never supposed to happen. It was just a fantasy. A way to make ourselves feel better.'

'But Angelo made it real.'

Maria sucks the inside of her cheek, then slowly shakes her head. 'Angelo was sent to a young offender institute. It was rough for him. Really rough. He was a posh boy. He suffered. Suffered torments you wouldn't believe. We didn't exactly lose contact, but when I went to see him it was so hard for both of us that the visits got less and less. When he was released I didn't even know about it. Then he turned up on my doorstep. I barely recognised him. He was scarred and tattooed and looked like death. He had a baby with him, if you can believe that. He came in and we talked and he told me he was trying to sort his life out. Said the baby was his brother's, then giggled. I think he was high again. We talked some more and I gave him some money and my phone number and he went away. I know you think he killed these people, but I remember him as a kid and he just wouldn't have that in him. I sent you those transcripts so you'd know more about the man responsible for everything. Responsible for our lives . . .'

McAvoy is about to speak again when his mobile rings. He looks anguished, but pulls it from his pocket, and is pleased to see that it's a call from Pharaoh rather than any bad news from home.

'Guv? I'm with Maria Caneva—'

'I know you are, Hector,' she says, and she sounds snappy and tired. 'You can tell her that her brother has just abducted the surgeon who saved Sebastien Hoyer-Wood's life. You can tell her he's dropped off a rotting corpse at the fucking scene.'

McAvoy presses his teeth together until he can taste blood and he hears something pop in his ear.

Another one.

He listens for a few more moments then hangs up, telling her he'll be as quick as he can. Then he turns to Maria. She's heard it all.

'If you know where he is . . .'

She shakes her head.

'Who he might be with . . .'

She shrugs.

He feels like crying.

'Please . . .'

Impulsively, she reaches out her hand and takes his. She looks at the bruised knuckles. Up past his blood-speckled shirt to his red-rimmed eyes.

'It can't be Angelo,' she says, though her voice quavers. It seems as though some part of her is waking up for the first time in years.

'Please, Maria. Does he have friends? How did he leave when he left here? Was he in a car? And the baby? Whose was the baby?'

Maria stares at the bruises on McAvoy's skin. Then she stands and crosses to the fireplace. She pulls one of the slates from the ugly construction and pulls out a scrap of paper. She hands it to him.

'That's where he was staying a year ago. Some mate. I never rang it.'

McAvoy turns the paper over in his hands. It's a phone number with a Hull code.

He holds the paper up to the light.

Sees. Sees it all.

He's up and out the door before he can say thank you. Before he can express his gratitude to the strange, broken girl, who took comfort in fantasising about the deaths of those who saved a rapist's life.

The echo of the slamming door is still reverberating in the room when she reaches under the sofa and pulls out her phone. She punches a number.

'Hi. Chamomile House? I was wondering whether . . .'

19

The path is thick mud and dead leaves, a tangle of stinging nettles and brambles. Thorns whip at Helen Tremberg's bare legs as she slips and slithers over the uneven ground, red welts and white spots appearing on her exposed skin.

It's just gone 7 a.m. and she is a little over a mile from her home. She's changed the route of her morning run and is regretting it. The path is almost impassable. The mud thrown up by her running shoes is halfway up her back and her ankle is starting to throb. Changing the route was a bad decision. She took a wrong turn, somewhere. Made a mistake. It's becoming a habit.

Helen focuses on her breathing and the music. Tries to inhale in time with the beat. Holds the oxygen in her lungs for two bars, then releases it.

'. . . and it feels just like . . .'

In Helen's earphones, Annie Lennox is screeching about walking on broken glass. As Helen loses her footing once more, she considers offering the singer a straight swap. She'd happily take the broken glass over the weeds and horse shit of Caistor's Canada Lane.

Helen used to walk up this overgrown bridleway with her grandad when she was a kid. They would pick elderberries in late summer. Pluck sloes from the hedgerows in early autumn. It's an overgrown and boggy track where the treetops lean in to form a natural steeple at various points. The light is never the same two days in a row as the shifting branches and leaves flicker on the constant breeze. It leads up to the broad green pasture where Helen used to go sledging with her friends when the snows would fall and cut Caistor off from the rest of the world for a blissful few days each winter. It's a place of happy memories and where the rich, earthy scents of the countryside combine to form a deep perfume that feels almost healing as she gulps it down.

But Helen did not fall asleep feeling proud of herself. She doubts she ever will again.

Her thoughts keep returning to the man on the end of the phone.

To Roisin.

To McAvoy.

They were her first thoughts as she woke She keeps telling herself not to be so silly. Tells herself that nobody would be fool enough to attack a policeman's wife. Tells herself that Roisin knew what she was doing when she took that bloody money. Why the hell did she do it? She tries to harden her thoughts against her. But she cannot swallow her own lies. Cannot persuade herself there is anybody lower than herself.

As she runs, she finds her mind filling with pictures of McAvoy. She remembers their first meeting. Remembers that agonising walk from Queen's Gardens to Hull Crown Court. It had rained the night before and the damp pavements were patterned with the crushed shells of snails that had not got out of the way as the city's commuters began their walks to work. McAvoy had kept stopping every five or six steps to pick up any snail he thought was in harm's way. He filled his pockets with them then ran back to Queen's Gardens to put them safely on the grass. Then he had run back to her, red-faced and embarrassed, while she had just stared up at him, open-mouthed, and wondered whether she should write the incident down in her notebook to be used as evidence should he ever go off the rails and shoot up a school.

The path begins to dip and the ground becomes more solid underfoot. Helen focuses on where she is placing her feet. Hears the music. Hears her own blood, pumping in her ears . . .

Two terriers run out from the driveway of the only house that stands on this stretch of the bridleway. It's a large white property, with apple and pear trees standing invitingly in the centre of an overgrown garden. Helen stumbles as a Jack Russell jumps at her legs. The shaggy-looking Yorkshire terrier barks loud enough to drown out the music, and Helen feels a sudden stabbing pain in her chest as she swallows her own shout of surprise. She starts to cough, and kicks out at the nearest dog as they jump excitedly up at her.

'Sorry, sorry, they think the whole path belongs to them . . .'

Helen whips off her headphones. A sixty-something woman with a healthy complexion and two too many teeth in the top row is crunching over the gravel. She's smiling broadly, exposing so many incisors that her grin looks like it should be used by Druids as a place of worship. Helen recognises her from the pub. She tries to smile back, to say it's okay, but can't seem to remember how to do it. She just ends up waving both hands around her face as though warding off a wasp, and then she gets flustered and pushes herself off from the gatepost at a sprint.

The dogs bark louder but are called to heel.

Over Annie Lennox's voice, Helen fancies she can hear herself being referred to as a 'stroppy cow'.

Helen staggers down the sloping path. She feels her ankle turn again as she slips on the old bricks that have been used to patch up the many gaps in the rubble and earth. She wants to be at home, suddenly. Wants to shower the dirt and the shame from her skin. Wants to slip into her plain work clothes and hide herself away behind a computer monitor. Wants to pretend. Wants to be somebody else, or perhaps a different version of herself. She's no good at this. No use at introspection and analysis. No good at thinking about right and wrong . . .

The music in her ears switches unexpectedly. Her phone is ringing.

Helen slows and pulls the phone from the clip on her running shorts.

It's from a withheld number.

Helen feels her hands tremble, as if she needs sugar or sleep. She feels a sudden desire to throw the phone into the nearby field. To change her number. To just keep running.

'Helen Tremberg,' she says, breathless and shaky, as she takes the call.

'Good morning, Detective Constable. I trust you slept well?'

Helen closes her eyes. Leans both arms against the trunk of a tree and waits for her breathing to slow down.

'You said you wouldn't call . . .'

'Indeed, indeed. And for that, may I express my sorrow and regret. You have been of considerable service to our organisation and to further impose ourselves upon you is not something I undertake lightly. However, I do believe that the information I am about to impart to you is of considerable importance.'

Helen presses her finger and thumb to her eyes so hard that brightly coloured spots of light seem to explode behind her eyelids.

'Just tell me what you want,' she says, and her voice sounds childlike and weak.

'Last night,' comes the reply. 'The young gentleman whom you have had in custody. He made an error of judgement. He has caused great distress to your sergeant and his family. Distress we had not intended. For this reason, the young man in question is no longer under our protection. More than this, he is yours to do with as you will, should you find him before one of my associates does. However, I am advised that Mr Downey has not taken kindly to the indignities he suffered. More than that, he feels that the lady who took his money and embarrassed him is personally accountable for all of the inconveniences he has endured. I have every faith in my associates' ability to locate him and bring this situation to resolution, but you may be well advised to keep Mrs McAvoy somewhere safe. I do not think her husband would respond to this communication in the same manner as you. Having done so, I feel a lightening of my conscience. For this reason alone, I am grateful to you, and can guarantee that there will be no further communications from myself or my associates. I thank you for your time, and hope that you enjoy the rest of your morning jog. Goodbye.'

As Helen stares at the phone, it returns to playing her music.

Helen looks behind her, up the dirt track, through the tunnel of overhanging, interlocking branches. Her world seems to be narrowing. The scent in her nostrils is suddenly thick and overpowering. She can smell dead creatures in the hedgerows. Can hear the sound of spiders chewing on desiccated corpses in their webs. She can hear the screams of dragonflies and ladybirds and the crunch as sloes are squashed beneath careless feet.

Helen is no longer jogging.

She wants to run for her life.

The sky seems to be moving in a series of freeze-frames. As McAvoy looks up, the dragon he had previously spotted in the skies becomes a cliff face, then jerks, unsteadily, into a choir congregation.

He turns back to the road. Watches as the first spots of rain begin to kiss the glass.

Looks up again.

Now the heavens are a snapshot of a storm-lashed ocean. The clouds broil as waves, curling and crashing in upon themselves in an explosion of black and grey.

McAvoy looks at his phone. It may be due to the fall from his pocket or a consequence of the storm clouds that block out the light, but he is struggling to get a signal. He has managed to call Pharaoh and update her, but was halfway through a garbled conversation with Ben Nielsen when he lost his phone signal, and he cannot seem to get it back. Thankfully, he had already received most of the information he needed. Got the address. The name. The next piece of a puzzle that's turning his brain to paste.

The car comes to a lazy halt in a parking space on Rufforth Garth. He's on the edge of Hull's Bransholme estate. It used to be Europe's biggest council estate, though nobody ever took the time to write that on the marketing materials or 'Welcome to Bransholme' signs. The area has had a lot of money spent on it in recent years, and while it has not exactly become an address to boast about, living on Bransholme is no longer a tick in the 'against' column when applying for a job. It's a sprawling community of small, near-identical houses. Most are crammed into cul-de-sacs that branch off from main roads sporting so many speed-bumps they look corrugated.

McAvoy takes a deep breath, steps from the vehicle.

Wincing into the fine rain that has begun to blow in on a harsh wind from the east, McAvoy looks around at the nearby vehicles for one that matches the registration plate he has scrawled on his notepad. He can't see it. Can't see the van that screeched away from a hospital in Norfolk with Hoyer-Wood's surgeon in the back, and then deposited a rotting corpse on the tarmac. It's all Volkswagen Golfs and old BMWs – their suspensions lowered so they give off a pretty shower of sparks as they scrape the speed bumps.

McAvoy rubs some colour into his cheeks then heads for the address Ben had shouted down the phone at him over the sound of static and rushing wind. He pushes open a metal garden gate and walks down a well-tended front path. He finds himself in front of an old-fashioned and single-glazed front door. The two panes of frosted glass at its centre do not look particularly sturdy. Were he to lean on it he fancies it might fall down. He decides this could be useful, so files the information away without allowing himself to think too hard about it.

Three raps on the glass: a policeman's Morse code for 'open the fucking door'.

No answer.

Tries again, louder now.

He opens the letter box and feels cold air against his face as he looks into an untidy kitchen and down at dirty linoleum. He wonders what he expected to see. Feels an urge to giggle as he imagines seeing Angelo Caneva standing over Dr Pradesh with a scalpel and some surgical rib-spreaders. He wonders if he should have uniformed support. Whether he should wait for Pharaoh. Whether he has got the whole fucking thing completely wrong.

'You won't get him during the day, love.'

McAvoy turns. A woman in her late thirties is standing by the front gate. She has a small child on her hip. The woman has a wrinkled, puckered mouth and features; her hair is long, lank and bottle-black and she has a leather jacket on over a small vest top and tight black jeans. She's wearing a lot of make-up and has a vaguely Gothic look about her, though the effect is spoiled somewhat by the tiger-feet slippers.

'You're after Nick, yeah?'

McAvoy turns away from the closed door. Gives the woman his full attention.

'When did you last see him?'

She looks up, her eyes revolving unnaturally, as if she is scanning the inside of her skull.

'You a copper?'

McAvoy isn't sure how to answer. He wants her to talk to him. Wants her to like him.

'He's a bright-looking lad,' says McAvoy, at last, nodding at the child in her arms. 'What's his name?'

The woman smiles, showing smoker's teeth. 'Reebok,' she says, with a laugh.

McAvoy doesn't know what facial expression to pull. 'That's different.'

She shrugs. 'He's not mine, don't worry. I think it's bloody daft, but if she wants to name her kid after a running shoe, who am I to judge? There's a kid in my daughter's class called Pebbles. Could be worse.'

McAvoy walks towards her, ready to show her his warrant card. He is reaching into his pocket when the child fixes him with a piercing look, and then bursts out laughing. McAvoy and the woman look at the boy, who is pointing at McAvoy and giggling hard.

'Am I that funny?' asks McAvoy, trying to look offended.

'Brave, Brave,' says the child, and sets off in another fit of hysterics.

The woman shrugs, good-naturedly. 'He must think you look like someone from the film.'

'Which film?'

'Disney cartoon. Scottish princess, wants to be a warrior. Billy Connolly's the voice of the dad . . .'

She stops herself. Looks him up and down and appears to agree with the child. She sniggers a little, then uses her sleeve to wipe the rain from the child's face.

McAvoy gives in to a little laugh of his own and then closes his fingers around the warrant card. Holds it tight enough to hurt.

'You're a neighbour?'

'Next door,' says the woman, jerking her head. 'I'm Jen.'

McAvoy shakes her hand. It's cold and slim and the palm feels slightly clammy. He introduces himself.

'I was hoping to talk to Nick.'

'He works days. Some nights too. Busy man, but you've got to go where the work is, don't you?'

As they talk, the rain begins to come down harder. There

is a low rumble and the face in the clouds tears itself in two. The sky becomes an ocean, upended and draining onto the city below.

'Jesus, look at this,' says Jen, huddling into her coat. 'Do you want to come inside?'

McAvoy pulls up his jacket collar and follows her into the neighbouring property. In moments he is soaked to the bone, his hair stuck to his face, shirt clinging to the muscles in his chest, arms and back.

McAvoy shakes himself like a damp dog. Looks up. He finds himself in a square kitchen. A small patio table and chairs sit next to a plain white door. The table supports a basket of unwashed laundry, which contains an unfeasible amount of leopard-print underwear and jogging trousers. The heat in the room comes from the far side, beside the metal sink that overflows with pots and pans soaking in a sea of cold water and dissolving bubbles. The door of the oven is wide open and heat emanates like dragon's breath. Three small children and a Dalmatian are sitting in front of it, eating biscuits and playing with blocks.

'I'm a childminder,' says Jen, filling the kettle. 'That's Pauline, Luke, and the little one's Colin.'

McAvoy looks at the toddler, who is sucking on a plastic brick and trying to get his hand into his nappy.

'He looks a Colin,' he says, and then leans himself against the wall. He tries to order his thoughts.

The phone number that Maria Caneva supplied him with is registered at the house next door to this one, on Rufforth Garth. The electoral register shows the occupier to be a Nick Peace. Before he lost the phone signal, McAvoy had instructed Ben Nielsen to dig up anything and everything on Peace, and to cross-reference those checks with Angelo Caneva. Like shapes in the clouds, McAvoy is starting to see fuller pictures.

'Like I said, I was hoping to talk to your neighbour,' says McAvoy, as chattily as he can manage over the sound of the playing children and banging pots. 'Well, his friend, more accurately. Angelo?'

Jen stops what she is doing and turns to him, drying her hands on her trousers.

'You said you were Old Bill, yeah?'

McAvoy nods. 'I'm investigating several murders. It really is important.'

Jen seems to be weighing things up. This is an estate where talking to the police is only acceptable when the community officers are running a tombola at a family fun day, or providing safety checks on your children's bicycles. Jen seems about to clam up.

McAvoy decides to help her see sense.

'You heard about the murder off Anlaby Road, I'm sure . . .'

Jen nods, then drops her voice, as if it's wrong to say 'murder' in front of children.

'I heard he pulled her heart out, or something. Sick bastard.'

McAvoy looks at the children, then gives a gentle jerk of his head to tell her to come closer. She does so. Her head only comes up to his chest and from here he can see her grey roots and smell her perfume. He can breathe in the sunflower oil and fabric softener of her hair.

'He didn't pull her heart out,' says McAvoy, quietly. 'He caved it in. He performed CPR on her body until her ribcage cracked open and he turned her insides to mush. Then he sliced open the femoral artery of a nice mum over the water. Her kids found her.'

Then he battered a bloke to death with a defibrillator machine in a rage because he couldn't electrocute the poor sod to death. Last night he abducted a surgeon and left an unidentified corpse at the scene. All that these people had done wrong was save the life of a man who was far worse than they were. It really is important I speak to Nick, or Angelo. Please, Jen, what can you tell me?'

There is silence in the room, save for the gleeful chatter of the children and the rain beating hard against the glass. The kitchen feels too dark, suddenly, and Jen switches on a light. It breaks the spell. McAvoy recoils from the light like a vampire. He feels too exposed. Too visible. He's aware of his scars and scrapes and creases and knows that Jen must see them too.

Jen looks him up and down.

'Sick bastard,' she says, again, and McAvoy hopes she is referring to the killer.

'Please, Jen . . .'

The woman gives a little shrug, and seems to make a decision. She doesn't seem overly horrified at what she has heard. Just grimly accepting of further proof that the world can be a horrible place.

'I've lived here two years,' says Jen. 'Nick's lived next door the whole time. He has a little girl. Well, I say he has . . .'

McAvoy leans closer, wondering if he should suggest they go into another room or put the kids somewhere else. He does neither. Instead he asks her about Angelo Caneva.

'His friend,' he says, softly. 'Angelo.'

Jen smiles. 'Little chap, yes? Slightly built. Big brown eyes. Very shy. Yeah, he lived there for a bit. Bit of a weird set-up, two grown men and a little girl, but you get all sorts on this estate . . .'

McAvoy wants to pull out his notepad but fears spoiling the moment. He concentrates on breathing and listening.

'What do you know about Nicholas?'

'Nice enough chap,' says Jen. 'Helped me out a couple of times. My boiler went off and he came and fixed the pilot light and I once got locked out and he jimmied the bathroom window. Brought me a bottle of something on New Year. Yeah, nice enough bloke if you could stop him talking about football.'

McAvoy pauses. Thinks hard. 'When did you last see Angelo?'

Jen looks up and to the left. 'Few weeks, maybe? Maybe more. I don't know.'

'And Nick?'

'Oh, just a couple of days back. He always says hello. He tries to stay cheerful but it can't be easy after that bitch waltzed in and took his daughter . . .'

McAvoy looks up at the ceiling. There is a damp patch spreading out from the corner above the sink. In it, if he squints and cocks his head, he fancies he can see the same leering, sunken-eyed face.

'His daughter?' asks McAvoy.

'Nick's ex-wife won custody of little Olivia,' she says, looking as if the information pains her. 'Broke his heart, I reckon. She's such a lovely little girl, too. Big eyes and the cutest smile. She'll get a nicer tan over there, of course, but it was Nick that brought her up . . .'

'Over where?'

'Benidorm, I think,' says Jen. 'Somewhere sunny, anyway.'

McAvoy looks down at the floor, hoping it will give him something more than the ceiling.

'How did Nicholas take that?'

'His world fell apart. He must have been hell to live with because I never saw Angelo much after that . . .'

McAvoy rubs at the bruise on the back of his hand.

'They worked together, yes? Nick and Angelo?'

'Well, it was Nick's business,' says Jen, back to full volume again. 'Builder. That sort of thing.'

Inside McAvoy's mind, images drift together. He sees the new railings outside Philippa Longman's house. The flat roof at Yvonne Dale's. Dimly recalls that Allan Godber's bank statements showed a hefty withdrawal recently that his wife said had gone on repointing the brickwork.

McAvoy purses his lips. Feels water trickle down the back of his shirt.

He suddenly sees it all. Can imagine Philippa bumping into her builder in the street and stopping for a chat in the glare of a lamp post, moments before he dragged her into the darkness and caved in her chest. He sees so many perfect opportunities for surveillance. For near-invisible proximity to victims.

McAvoy pulls out his phone. The screen is blank and, as he curses, Jen hands him her own. He manages a smile and a thank you, then dials Elaine Longman from memory.

'Elaine? Aector McAvoy. Fine. Yeah. Yes, possibly. Look, Elaine, your mum had had some new railings put in, hadn't she? You said somebody had bodged the job . . . Yes? Okay. No, thank you. Thank you.'

McAvoy hangs up. He imagines the tap on Philippa's door. The sudden appearance of a passing tradesman who had noticed the railings in a poor state. Willing to finish them off for a bit of cash in hand . . .

McAvoy apologises and makes another call.

When he hangs up, he looks at his own phone for a while. Tries to smooth out the crack on the display using his thumb. Tries to make the picture whole again.

'I don't suppose you have a photo of Nick or Angelo, do you?' he asks, quietly.

Jen shakes her head.

McAvoy stares some more. Smells baking bread and wonders if a pizza crust is burning at the back of the open oven. Hears the older child ask Jen who the big man is. Hears little Colin shit his pants and sit in it.

Eventually, Jen's phone bleeps. The forensic report he has requested flashes up in her Hotmail account. She had hastily spelled out her email address as he spoke to Ben, and McAvoy had turned crimson as he'd typed in *tygerpants69*.

He scrolls through the report. It's accompanied by a list of Angelo Caneva's associates from his time in the young offender institute. There are no names that sound familiar, but one was incarcerated for crimes committed within the Hull boundary.

McAvoy flicks his fingers across the screen. Finds the section he was looking for. The organic matter, found at the crime scenes. It has been identified as sap from lime trees: the sticky, corrosive substance that eats through the paintwork on expensive cars parked down shaded avenues.

McAvoy breathes in, hard, as if trying to fire more oxygen into his brain.

Where?

Think, you silly fucker, think!

He sees the name of the gamekeeper's cottage, written in bright letters across the shifting cloudscape of his thoughts.

Tilia Cottage. *Tilia.* Latin for *lime*.

He flicks back to the list of Caneva's associates. Returns to the name of the lad sent down in Hull. He has a sudden flash of recognition.

He turns to Jen. Gabbles something almost unintelligible and nearly steps on Colin as he begins to pace the small room.

'I'm sorry, just one more call . . .'

For the next ten minutes, McAvoy watches the rain run down the glass and listens to the thunder grow closer.

He waits for a call that could mean everything.

Finally, Ben connects him to a sleepy, angry woman in Benidorm.

'No, of course not,' she snaps, in answer to McAvoy's question. 'She's with her dad in Hull. Bastard won't let me see her. Why, what's . . .?'

As lightning tears through the sky, McAvoy throws the phone to Jen.

He blunders through the door and into a day turned to midnight by cloud that hangs as sackcloth over a city that fears the rain.

20

Roisin's face is sore and tender to the touch, but she still makes the effort with her lipstick. She flinches a little as the frosted pink gloss bites into the wound on her mouth, but she will feel better when she looks better, if her mother's wisdom is to be believed.

'He'll come back,' says Mel, gently, from the doorway. 'He adores you. He's just gone to work.'

Roisin slept with her face on a black bin-liner full of old clothes, with her children curled up in her arms. Aector was not here when she woke. His phone won't connect. Her stomach is climbing up her ribcage and all she wants to do is hold him and say sorry a thousand times.

He'd said he forgave her. He'd held her and kissed her sore places and wiped her tears with his bruised fists, and then he'd left her to a fitful sleep, peopled with dreams of loneliness and violence.

'I don't know why I took it, Mel. I'm so sorry.'

Roisin has apologised endlessly to her friend and Mel has told her it's okay. She is still a little shaky after what happened last night, but despite the violence she witnessed and endured, she seems to feel safer with Roisin than anywhere else and has shown no desire to return to her own home. She would rather be here, in an empty house on the Kingswood estate, with its crying children and echoing rooms.

'It was just there,' says Roisin, again. 'He'd offered it to you. He'd made you sad. It was your money. I just picked it up . . .'

'Ro, it's fine, I understand.'

Roisin falls silent. She finishes applying her make-up and checks her reflection in the small compact mirror she has plucked from her handbag. They are sitting on the floor in the living room of the empty house. Fin is playing a game of football in his head, passing an imaginary ball to himself and scoring goals at the far end of the room. Lilah is asleep in her carry cot.

'Why won't he answer his phone?' asks Roisin, despairingly.

Mel gestures at the living-room window. The rain is coming in off the Humber in waves and it's dark enough for the street lights to come on. 'He probably can't get a signal. And he's a murder policeman, Ro. He's up to his eyes. He'll be sorting it all out. You said that's what he does.'

Roisin touches her fingertips to her bruised face. She wants to know what was said to him. What the voice at the other end of the phone had whispered in his ear. She wants to know if McAvoy would have killed her attackers had the voice not stopped him first.

'He went through them like they were made of paper,' says Mel, blankly, as if examining a memory. 'He looked like he was from another time. Like an old king, or something. I don't know. I'm talking shit, aren't I?'

Roisin smiles, then shivers at the pain. She gives her friend a little hug.

'Will you come with me?' she asks. 'To the new house? I don't want him to see it in a state when he gets back. There'll be blood. Mess. I want to put this behind us. All of it.'

Mel looks uncertain. 'He said to stay here. To keep our heads down.'

Roisin points at the scene beyond the window. 'It's chucking it down. Nobody who's going to do anything will do it in weather like this. We'll only be an hour. We're fine. It's important, Mel.'

Mel sighs and smiles and together they begin getting the kids ready for the short journey across the city to the new house on Hessle Foreshore.

They fleetingly appear in the large, curtainless window at the front of the house.

A few feet away, an angry young man spits on the misted windscreen inside the stolen car.

Bitches!

Despite the rain and the darkness and the water that slashes diagonally across the windscreen, Adam Downey recognises the two women who have fucked it all up.

He lowers his head. Sniffs another line from the mountain of cocaine in his lap.

Feels himself filling with fire and rage and sunlight.

He looks at the hammer on the passenger seat. At the grenade that rolls in the coffee holder.

Downey watches the women load the children into the car and reverse out of the driveway in the driving rain.

He turns the key.

Drifts along behind them, his vision marbled and opaque, his quarry a blue blur beyond the cascading water on the glass.

This is his chance.

His last opportunity.

He's going to show them who he is and what he can do. He's going to make the gypsy bitch pay.

11.14 a.m. Courtland Road Police Station. An incident room buckling under the weight of paper, people, bustle and noise. A long, unwelcoming office, painted in puke and buttermilk, that stinks of sweat, fast food and fly spray.

Leaning her head against the cool glass, Trish Pharaoh watches the light die.

Sees the clouds swallow the pale halo of the sun. Sees rain fall like the blade of a guillotine. The dying light puts her in mind of an old halogen bulb, covered in dust and dead flies, that seems to be giving out precious little illumination up until the point it gives out none.

'Bloody hell . . .'

Wind tears in through the open windows. Wind and water and the dirt of the city, and in a moment the incident room is a storm of billowing paper. Officers hang up phone calls to lunge for errant forensics reports and witness statements. A carton of milk tips over on a civilian officer's desk and spills across keyboard, lap, chair and floor. Trish's hair tangles in her earrings, and as she runs to the window the rain plasters loose strands across her features and dampens her breastbone and neck.

'Ben! Ben, Christ, get that one. Fucking hurry up . . .'

A row of harsh lights flicker into life overhead and the last sash window slams down.

'Jesus, it's bloody biblical out there!'

The officers crowd around the glass, watching the tempest beat upon the city. The darkness beyond the window turns the glass into a mirror and each man and woman has to squint through themselves to make sense of the furious scene. Already gutters are being turned into streams and waterfalls by the deluge and the few cars that had been negotiating this quiet area of the Orchard Park estate have slowed and then stopped. It is as if the sea is trying to reclaim the land.

'Come on, come on, it's only rain,' she says, turning away and clapping her hands. 'Killer, yes? That's what we're here for. Nasty man, killing nice people. Remember him? Could we catch him, please? It would be such a help. Thanks.'

Muttering and apologising, the team disperse back to their individual desks. Somebody begins mopping up spilled milk with a tea towel and DC Andy Daniells has his head in his hands after trying to put the papers that have blown from his desk back into some semblance of order.

'Ben,' says Pharaoh, looking around. 'Helen? Word.'

Pharaoh's office is up the stairs, near the head of CID, but she is happier here, in the engine room. She remains by the window and is joined by Ben Nielsen and Helen Tremberg. Ben looks fit and wide awake, though he has likely spent the night engaged in one of his sexual marathons. He's wearing the same shirt as yesterday and hasn't shaved, but still looks stylish and presentable. Helen looks worn out. Her eyes are red, there are crumbs of chocolate on the lapel of her dowdy blazer and she seems to be limping as she walks.

'You okay, Helen?'

Pharaoh looks up into Helen's swollen eyes. This is how she leads. How she inspires. In this moment, the killer is forgotten. She cares, here and now, whether her constable is okay.

Tremberg nods. Seems about to speak and then clams up again.

'I wish you'd been on this from the start,' says Trish, softly. 'Nice that Everett noticed you, though, eh? You must have been doing something right. Bloody good to have you with us though. We wouldn't have got to this stage without you. You should feel proud of yourself.'

Pharaoh hopes for a smile or a thank you but gets neither. Helen just looks down at her feet. Pharaoh reaches out and strokes her arm. 'We'll talk later, yeah?'

Helen nods. Swallows, and closes her eyes.

Pharaoh turns her attention to Ben. 'Talk to me, Handsome.'

Nielsen gives his face a slap on both cheeks, then shakes his head back and forth. His lips wobble a little, then he slaps his face again. Trish has no idea why he does this. He seems to be awake enough already.

'Well,' says Ben, animatedly. 'Caneva may as well have a big sign around his neck with the word "killer" on it. We've got his description to all units within the force boundary and beyond. The vehicle seen leaving the hospital has fake plates but the description has still been sent out for all to see. We've contacted Dr Pradesh's relatives and apprised them of the situation and Andy is using every resource to warn everybody who was in the operating theatre with her when she operated on Hoyer-Wood. The operations she performed on him are bloody complicated, but let's just say that if Caneva is planning to carry them out on her, there won't be any happy ending.'

Pharaoh takes it all in.

'Caneva,' she says, then lets her thoughts drift to the information McAvoy had blurted down the phone before he lost his signal. 'Nick Peace,' she says, turning to Helen. 'You've been back onto the facility where Caneva was an inmate, yeah?'

Helen takes a breath and keeps her voice even.

'I've asked the governor if there were any other inmates that Caneva was especially close with. He didn't recognise the name Nicholas Peace but did mention that Caneva had a very hard time fitting in at first. He was a little bloke, not much about him, with this posh London accent. Read a lot of books. Did drawings. Wrote short stories. He's sending us the lot on the inmate you flagged up. The one who got sent down in Hull.'

'Crime?' asks Pharaoh.

'Attempted murder,' she says. 'Kicked some bloke half to death outside a bingo hall. Was the latest in a long line of escalating crimes. He was thirteen when he was sent down. Spent almost six years at the facility and became mates of sorts with Caneva. Governor remembers bits and bobs.'

Pharaoh licks her lips. Absent-mindedly, she reaches into the pocket of her biker jacket and pulls out her black cigarettes. She places one to her lips and though she doesn't light it, rolling it on her damp lips seems to help her concentrate.

'So we're thinking Caneva went to stay with him when he was released. Got a job working for him. Used the cover to take his revenge on the people who saved his family's tormentor. How am I doing?'

Helen nods her assent and the three fall silent. They turn to watch the storm.

'His phone's still off, yeah?' asks Pharaoh.

Ben grunts an answer.

'And have we any bloody idea who *tygerpants69* is?'

Ben starts to laugh.

Together, the three of them watch the rain make the city into a whorl of dribbled shapes and half-formed slabs. They look, for a moment, as though they are trapped inside an unfinished painting.

'Norfolk CID,' says Pharaoh, at last. 'They know what we know?'

Ben shrugs. 'They know our angle. They're still treating it as a local crime. Belt and braces. They've promised to call when they have an ID on the body.'

'And we're thinking that it's going to be his mate, aren't we? Nick Peace, or whatever he used to be called.'

'Makes sense,' says Helen. 'He must have found out what Caneva's been doing. Confronted him, maybe. If you watch the CCTV of the doctor's abduction, the body fell from the van. It wasn't dumped on purpose. It was a mistake.'

Helen seems about to say something more when a shout from halfway across the room interrupts them. There's a phone call for Ben.

'Is it McAvoy?' asks Pharaoh, and is greeted with a shake of the head from the civilian officer holding out Ben's phone.

Ben crosses the room. Pharaoh watches as he jots down some details and pulls a face. Then he sighs, looking angry and lost. He hangs up and comes back to where they stand.

'The ID is through on the body left at the hospital,' says Nielsen, and he seems to be struggling to keep the anger from creasing his features.

'And?'

'And if we're looking for Angelo Caneva we can fucking relax. He's on a slab. Been dead for weeks, rotting away in a warm, dry space.'

Pharaoh closes her eyes.

'The name,' she says, softly. 'The bloke who was arrested in Hull. Angelo's friend. The lad who might have become Nick Peace. What did he use to be called?'

Helen crosses back to her desk. She sifts through a pile of papers and finds a rain-spattered document. She brings it back to Pharaoh.

'Him,' she says, pointing.

Pharaoh looks at the name. Something in the back of her mind fizzes for an instant, like the last breath of light in the filament of a dying bulb.

And then she sees him. Sees his fillings as he laughs. Hears his voice. Hears him talking football and handing her and McAvoy a business card. Sees McAvoy on the phone in the great hall of an abandoned stately home.

She sees the contractor.

She sees Gaz.

21

Gary Reeves watches the lightning through the gaps in the red tiles. He is soaked to the bone. His blue overalls stick to his skin. His hair hangs lank, touching the back of his collar. His eyes are open, wide and staring; the very image of the dead man in whose name he has become a killer.

He stares.

Doesn't blink as the raindrops bounce off his face.

Watches the patterns in the sky.

The dark sky is a raven, the clouds its feathers. Each fork of brilliant white is a paper dart, thrown by some celestial hand. Reeves isn't sure he believes in God, but he sees the shapes above him quite clearly. Sees the bird's eye, beady and perfectly circular, fix itself upon him. It seems to approve. Seems to like the scene, far below.

He sees himself in its gaze.

Sees a fit young man, lying motionless on an old operating table.

Sees the woman at his side.

Naked.

Bound.

Sobbing and drooling into the stuffed toy wedged in her bleeding mouth.

Gary Reeves has answered to many names. He enjoyed being Nick Peace. It was the name he'd chosen when they let him out. He didn't bother changing it legally but he felt that it fitted him. The 'Nicholas' had honoured the flamboyant Arsenal striker whom one of his foster fathers had always admired. The 'Peace' was a nod to one of his psychologists. She'd told him to find the peace within himself. To find a calm, soothing place in his soul, and try and live within it.

Gary has never really managed to follow her advice. He has spent most of his life in trouble. Doesn't remember his mother or father. Has a birthday that was given to him by Social Services. He has had more foster homes than he can remember. He has spent time in children's homes and on the streets. The only stability he has ever experienced was when he was sent to the young offender institute at fourteen. He'd been living in Hull at that time, a fireball of rage and resentment. He wanted solitude and he wanted company. He wanted silence and chaos. He interpreted every action through a filter that hung behind his eyes like a side of rotting pork. Whatever was given to him was given with spite and the things he needed were absent because nobody loved him. His mind was a ball of wool, pulled apart by warring thoughts and desires. He spat when he talked. He twitched and swore and struggled to make himself understood. He would spend days making himself as filthy as he could before scrubbing his skin until he bled. He had headaches. He masturbated until he was sore. He stole then wept when nobody believed his denials. He took the possessions of those who were kind to him and then used them to violate himself. His education came at a variety of pupil referral units and schools for children unable to be taught in mainstream education. He spent time at a residential school for bad lads, where he found a way to get past the Internet security restrictions and spent a few months with access to every kind of pornography he could imagine. And he could imagine a lot.

Reeves's run-ins with the police led to cautions and community service orders. He didn't mind the community work. Liked getting his hands dirty. Painting old ladies' fences and sweeping streets. He'd go back later, of course. He'd go and graffiti the same fence he had spent the day painting white. He couldn't seem to help it. Nor could he help the calling of his blood. Couldn't help what it told him to do when he saw that perfect fucking family with their perfect house, having their perfect picnic and perfect game of badminton on their perfect front lawn.

Gary Reeves had been as much a witness to his early crimes as he had been a perpetrator. He had not really been in control of his body. He was a passenger in a vessel piloted by some other, unstoppable, force. He had been as surprised as anybody to see himself walk into the front garden of the house. Had simply watched, entranced, as Gary Reeves had kicked over the barbecue, grabbed a hot coal from the glowing pile and pressed it into the face of the portly accountant who'd been standing grilling sausages in his perfect fucking apron with its stupid fucking picture on the front. By then, Gary's blood was in control of his actions. He took lighter fluid and set fire to the smouldering coals. His hand hadn't hurt, despite the ugly flap of burned skin that hung from it. Then he'd begun to shovel the coals through the letter box of the perfect fucking house, where the rest of the perfect family cried and cowered while Dad writhed on the grass as a teenage boy kicked his ribs, rhythmically, purposefully, until they snapped.

Gary arrived in the young offender institute determined not to be bullied. He had three fights on his first day. He smashed a pool cue into the face of one of the prison officers, giving him a scar that he reckons is probably still there. For the first few months he spent most of his time on lockdown in his room. He was sixteen before he began to control himself. The counselling sessions helped. It was nice to talk to somebody who was paid to listen. He didn't think they cared, but the fact they were paid to be there meant they had no choice but to pay attention as he told them how it felt to be him. How his blood called to him. How he sometimes saw things that weren't there and often left his own body and watched it all from above, like an angel.

As he grew older and more physically capable, Gary began to take advantage of some of the courses offered at the centre. He learned metalwork and woodwork with a retired schoolteacher who didn't mind letting him use the more deadly-looking equipment. He made a spice rack for the old bloke's missus. Gave it to him with a grunt but was pleased to see it meant something to him. And then he met Angelo Caneva.

Angelo was a feeble little thing. He was scared and flighty and reminded Gary of a baby rabbit, shivering and ready to bolt. Gary hadn't thought much about him at all, other than the fact he didn't fit in. He had little to do with him. But he saw another side to Angelo when one of the older lads took the physicality too far.

The facility was short-staffed. There weren't enough wardens to cope with so many teenagers. So there was nobody around when Byron Alexander dragged Angelo to the reading room and started smashing his face in. Gary had gone along to watch. So had some of the other lads. The show they were expecting never took place. Instead Angelo turned into the devil. As soon as he realised what Byron was going to do he seemed to come alive. He unleashed a strength that nobody knew he possessed. He got on top of the bigger lad and punched Byron until he was unrecognisable. Instinct made Gary react. He wasn't saving Byron when he dragged Angelo away. He was saving the kid. Saving him from a murder charge. It was a profoundly moving moment for Gary Reeves. He found himself fascinated by the younger boy.

Nobody ever told the screws who had left Byron like that. Nor did anybody ever try it on with Angelo again. They left him alone. Left him to his books and his drawings. Gary wanted to know more about him. Wanted to talk to him. But he didn't know how to. He tried making him something in his woodwork lessons, but he smashed up the toy aeroplane he'd made for him out of balsa wood when he imagined himself giving it to the younger lad.

In the end, Angelo did the hard work for him. One day, out of nowhere, Angelo presented him with a book of short stories. Told Gary he might enjoy it. Said there was a yarn in there about a bloke in solitary confinement who tunnelled his way to freedom behind a big poster of some Hollywood pin-up. Said it was a classic and that the movie version was amazing. Gary was not a comfortable reader but had taken the book anyway. Gave it a go. Asked Angelo for more. Their friendship developed. They began to share stories. Secrets. Despite their different backgrounds and the age difference, they became more than friends. They told one another about what had led them to the facility. They unburdened themselves and each found somebody who understood.

Gary had felt sick when he heard what had happened to Angelo's father. When he'd heard about the rich prick with the double-barrelled name who'd fooled everybody into thinking he was a cripple. He'd laughed when Angelo told him about fire-bombing the bus and the posh wanker suffering a stroke that left him shitting in his pants and unable to move. He'd held Angelo whenever he cried and Angelo had done the same for him. Angelo had told him his fantasy. Told him his dreams. Told him what he and his sister were going to do some day. Told him the people he was going to kill. Told him about the cunts who'd saved the posh prick's life. Gary had liked the plan.

When he was older, Gary was sent to serve the remainder of his sentence in adult prison. He had never felt loneliness like it. His separation from Angelo was the most excruciating sensation he had ever endured. He tried to find a new friend. Ended up in fights. Grew frustrated and began to seek out fresh violence. Had time added to his sentence. Only the letters from Angelo kept him going. They spoke of what it would be like when they were both free. About getting a place for themselves. They would start a business, maybe. Gary would take him to the football. They'd drink beer and watch movies on a Saturday night. They'd get girlfriends but tell them they were for the chop if they ever came between them.

Gary was released first. He headed for Hull, purely because he knew the streets better than he did in any other city. Social Services had found him a flat and a job as a labourer. He stuck it out. Kept his head down. Saved his money. Even got himself a girlfriend. Mandy, she was called. Bit older than him and twice as streetwise. Gave him the eye in a McDonald's and opened her legs for him an hour later, sitting on a pile of wooden pallets and blowing the smoke from her cigarette over his shoulder as he emptied himself inside her. He hadn't expected her to get pregnant. She hadn't wanted the baby but he was delighted when she told him. He imagined being a dad. Imagined being a strong and noble influence on a child. Imagined Angelo and himself raising it together. He'd told her he would take care of her. Of the child. She'd given him a daughter, then fucked off to Spain with somebody else. Gary had written to Angelo. Told him they were parents. And Angelo had told him he was happy.

The day Angelo left the institute, Gary picked him up in his new blue van. It had been a couple of years since they had seen one another and Gary was struck at the change in Angelo. He had fresh scars. His skin clung to his small, birdlike frame. He was quiet and uncommunicative. It seemed in those two years the fight had left him. Bad things had happened to him. He had not always been able to fight people off. He was tired and his voice did not sound like his own. Gary soon discovered that Angelo had started using drugs while inside. He'd started sniffing glue again. Got one of the staff in the kitchens to start bringing in LSD and ecstasy. Gary wanted his friend to be happy so he scored him some drugs. Watched him became his old self again as the high took him in its embrace. Watched Angelo cuddling their daughter, and for a time he felt anything was possible. He moved them to the house on Rufforth Garth. Angelo had to stay in a flat Social Services had got him, but after a few months he was able to slip through the cracks in the system and come home to Gary. Sometimes he'd go and visit his father for money. Once, they went to see Angelo's sister, though the fat cow had changed and wanted nothing to do with the murderous fantasy they had both enjoyed in their teens and which had sustained Angelo through his incarceration. But Gary stuck to his word. He thought the plan was a good one. He thought revenge would help his friend. Angelo wanted it to happen, so he said he would help him. Even drove him to the house of the slag who'd been raped by Hoyer-Wood up in Bridlington the night he should have died. Had sat in the darkness with the engine running and watched Angelo break in.

When Angelo returned, it was clear something had changed. He just didn't have it in him. Didn't have the strength to kill. He saw the people on his list as innocents. They didn't know what they were doing. They'd made a mistake but didn't deserve to die. The fight went out of him. He began to take more drugs. He closed down. Stopped talking. Wouldn't play with their daughter. Wouldn't come out of his room.

A month ago, Angelo took his own life. He parked their blue van in a lock-up they had rented. Turned on the engine and opened the windows. Breathed in blue smoke until his lungs gave out and his eyes closed.

He couldn't have known, Gary told himself, when he found the bodies. *Couldn't have known their daughter was in the back. She just climbed in. Snuggled down in a place she felt comfortable. Angelo couldn't have seen her. The fumes would have reached her first as she lay with her toys in the back. She'd have slipped away as if to sleep. Angelo would never have known, as he sat and waited to die in the front seat, that their daughter was dead.*

Until then, Gary had been Nick Peace. He'd found that peaceful place, within him and without. He'd begun to imagine a future. He'd stopped listening to his blood. As he found the bodies of his friend and their child, he felt himself drifting out of himself in a way he had not done for years. And his blood told him what to do next.

Told him that Angelo was another victim of Hoyer-Wood.

Told him his daughter was too.

Told him they needed to be avenged.

He couldn't bring himself to get rid of the bodies. Drove around with them in the van, even when the stench made him feel sick.

It hadn't been difficult to find the do-gooders who had spoiled all of their lives. Philippa Longman. Yvonne Dale. Allan Godber. Hadn't been hard to get to know them. He was an odd-job man, after all, a contractor. He'd fixed Philippa's railings. Yvonne's roof. Done some pointing work at Allan's place. Got to know them. Became invisible. Peered into their lives as he planned their deaths.

Philippa had been the hardest. Despite what she cost him, she had seemed a nice lady. She'd given him a big smile that night as she spotted him on the street on her walk home from work. Chatted to him about the weather and her grandkids and told him he'd done a grand job on her railings. But Gary's blood wasn't listening, and Gary hadn't returned to himself until Philippa was dead on the ground with her chest caved in.

It had been the same the next time. Yvonne had died quietly but there had been more blood than he expected.

But he'd made a prat of himself with Allan's death. The defibrillator had been too fucking complicated. Had shown him up. Gary never left his skin that time. Stayed very much awake as he battered the former paramedic to death on the cold floor of the lock-up.

As he looks at Dr Pradesh, he wonders how much of today's work he will actually experience, and how much he will simply watch.

The surgeon is still blubbering. She's got one of Olivia's fluffy toys wedged in her gob and it's turning pink. She's bleeding from the mouth. He can't remember if he punched her in the stomach or not. He wonders if she might have internal bleeding, or has just bitten through her cheek.

He rolls off the table. Brushes himself down.

Looks around.

Gary likes this place. It's a ruin now. There are holes in the roof and the bare brick walls are surrounded by a chain-link fence topped with barbed wire. The remaining internal walls are smoke-blackened and the carpet has turned into something organic and squelchy beneath a covering of lime-tree sap and leaves. Still, it has character. It's quiet. And he likes knowing that Angelo had, for a time, been happy here. He can feel him nearby.

Gary shed a tear this morning when he realised he had lost his friend's body. He blames Dr Pradesh. Blames her for a lot of things. The woman on the table saved Hoyer-Wood's life. She opened him up and stopped the bleeding. Stitched his spleen back together. Repaired a laceration to his kidney. She's going to learn how that feels. And then she's going to bleed into her own exposed abdomen until she drowns and dies.

Gary pushes his hair back from his face. He's a little hungry. In one corner of the room are a few empty tins. He's been living on cold beans and spaghetti. Been kipping in his van some nights and lying here, looking through the holes in the roof, on the nights he knows the security guards won't be patrolling.

It had been more luck than design that he'd landed the job of looking after the mansion house. He'd driven up purely to see the place for himself, having heard Angelo's descriptions so many times without ever laying eyes on it. He'd been parking

up on the gravel when a load of posh blokes in suits and accents
had walked out, looking over blueprints and chattering excitedly
about their big plans. They'd approached him and said something
about serendipity and needing somebody to keep an eye on the
place. They'd hired him on the spot to keep the place clean and
tidy. Given him a business card, and told him to email his details
across. Agreed to pay him cash in hand. It had felt like somebody
was smiling on him.

Angelo had still been alive then. But he wasn't communicating
much. Wasn't coming out of his room. Gary didn't even really
trust him to be left alone with Olivia. He'd taken to bringing her
with him everywhere. She'd sit and chatter and play with her
toys in the back of the van. She liked it in there. It was warm and
dry and smelled of Daddy.

He couldn't have known . . .

Gary looks down at Dr Pradesh. The light isn't very good and
her face is only illuminated when the lightning flashes. She's
quite pretty, and her body is in good shape. She even has a little
heart-shaped tattoo where her pubes should be. He'd expected
more from a surgeon.

Gary looks into Dr Pradesh's eyes. Sees himself reflected in
them. Realises he's forgotten the mask. He stole one from a
dental practice a few weeks ago, along with some latex gloves
and a fistful of scalpels and scrapers. He wants to do this right.
To get it as close to perfection as possible. He hopes the doctor
doesn't think that he's stripped her for any perverted reasons. He
would like to put her in a surgical gown, but he doesn't have one,
and feels uncomfortable using this old pine table to operate on
instead of a gleaming, cold slab of steel. But he has to make do.

Gary tears his gaze away and looks up at the sky. The rain

357

patters onto his face and he closes his eyes to enjoy the sensation. When he opens them again, the jackdaw in the sky is staring again. A black pupil is turned upon him. He realises he has an audience. That time is precious and Dr Pradesh has already been alive too long. At some point, he'll be caught. He's already been stupid enough to give a name to those two coppers who turned up last week. He was trying too hard. Trying to be too friendly. Plucked a name from the air that could be exposed as bullshit with a phone call. He'd wanted to seem helpful so they didn't sniff too hard and breathe in the rotting corpses in his van. He'd phoned security the second he'd got away from them, but they both seemed pretty bright and he knows that he has a limited amount of time left before they begin joining the dots. Before they catch him, he has more work to do. There are the nurses who tended to Hoyer-Wood after his operation. There are those who helped him with his rehabilitation. It struck him recently just how incomplete Angelo's list had been. So many more people could be justifiably killed. He intends to right that wrong . . .

Feet squelching on the carpet and the dirt, Angelo crosses to the back door of the derelict property. His mask is in the van, parked behind the screen of lime trees. The scalpel that will be used to open Dr Pradesh's belly is in his pocket. He hadn't been able to purchase the surgical rib-spreader he had wanted but he has a hydraulic foot-pump in the vehicle that should do a similar job in splitting her ribs and allowing him the freedom to poke around inside her with his blade.

He takes the door with both hands. The wood has expanded over the years and sticks on the uneven floor. He yanks it hard and steps out into the darkened day, rain turning the ground beneath him into a swamp of mud and standing water, its surface bouncing and rippling beneath the deluge.

Gary pushes aside the sagging fence and ducks under the dangling barbed wire. His work boots sink into the soft earth and he feels water up to his shins. Carefully, he pulls one foot free, then the other, and manages to slurp his way onto harder ground. The van is only a few feet away.

A sheet of lightning rolls across the blackness and for an instant the scene before him is illuminated.

A big, broad-shouldered man is climbing out of the back of his van.

He's holding the decaying body of Olivia in his arms.

Gary's blood takes over.

He takes the scalpel in his fist. He throws his head back.

Feels the jackdaw's eye upon him.

The flash of recognition is lost in his rage. Even as he realises that the man who holds his daughter is the policeman who spoke to him a few days ago, the knowledge is swept away on a tide of angry blood.

He runs forward.

And sticks the blade in the big man's back.

McAvoy doesn't hear Gary Reeves approach.

The thunder and the driving rain mask the sound of footsteps on sodden earth and it is only as pain rips down his spine that he realises he is in danger.

He pitches forward. His first thought is not for himself. He just doesn't want to drop the dead girl who he holds in his arms as if rocking her to sleep.

McAvoy places the little girl on the hard floor of the van. Only then does he turn.

Steel flashes past his face. He jerks his head back just as it whistles past his cheek, then does so again as the screeching, howling features of Gary Reeves are lit by another flash of lightning.

McAvoy feels the van at his back. Tries to find somewhere solid to put his feet and looks down for the briefest of instants. It is long enough for Reeves to lunge with the knife again and McAvoy sucks in a gasp of agony as the blade digs into his hip.

He pushes hard with both hands, sending Reeves back and onto his arse. McAvoy looks down, expecting the weapon to still be stuck in him, but there is nothing there save a spreading patch of warmth. He looks back up and sees Reeves pulling himself back to his feet. The blade is still in his hands. McAvoy scrabbles in his jacket pocket for his extendable baton but Reeves runs at him again. Savagely, the smaller man stabs and stabs again, opening wounds in McAvoy's arms as he throws his hands up to protect himself. There is suddenly warm wetness upon his face and his vision turns red as the scalpel slices down to the bone above his eye.

In desperation, McAvoy grabs Reeves around the middle, shouting out as the blade sticks in his left bicep and stays there. They go down together, splashing to the ground in a spray of mud and blood and dirty rain.

Reeves slithers free and kicks out, the steel toe of his boot catching McAvoy in the throat. McAvoy raises his hands to his windpipe, gasping for breath, and suddenly Reeves is on him, kicking his hands away and forcing his head down into the great puddle of rain and leaves.

His mouth and nose are suddenly full of mud and water. He

can't see. Can't speak. Can feel only cold pain in his lungs and the weight of Gary Reeves upon his neck, holding his head below the surface.

McAvoy tries to push himself back but the ground is too slippery and his hands give way, forcing him deeper under the water. The sound of the storm dissipates and he realises his ears are under water too. His lungs feel as though they are bursting. His face is agony.

Despite himself, his mouth opens and filthy rainwater fills him.

Lights dance in his vision. He feels himself growing weak. Feels his limbs shake.

Sees, for the briefest of moments, Roisin's face, picked out like a constellation in the dancing stars of the fading darkness.

McAvoy reaches under himself. Through the dirt and the leaves and the swirling water, his hand closes on the scalpel that sticks in his left arm.

In one movement, he pulls it free and stabs, weakly, desperately at the man on his back.

He feels the blade hit home. Feels a momentary loosening of pressure.

McAvoy throws himself backwards, gasping for air, eyes opening into the rain and the storm.

Gary Reeves is a few feet away, pulling the scalpel from his collarbone. His fingers are slick with the blood and his hair hangs forward across his features. It's black, like a jackdaw's wing over his eyes.

McAvoy puts his whole weight into the punch. Throws it while staggering forward in a half-run.

His right hand connects with Gary Reeves's jaw. McAvoy feels a knuckle break with the impact. Then his feet slip out from under him and he lands on top of the unconscious man, a wave of brown water rolling away from their entwined limbs to break against the chicken wire and brick of Tilia Cottage.

Drowsily, feebly, McAvoy gets back to his feet. He staggers a little and presses a hand to the wound at his hip. He feels the warmth of fresh blood, but keeps his footing long enough to cross the grass and stumble through the lime trees to his car. In the glovebox he finds the tie-wrap cuffs he should have had in his pocket. He takes them in his blood-soaked fist and slithers his way back to where Reeves lies. He's half submerged in a puddle, and his jaw hangs slack to one side. McAvoy tries to stop his hands from shaking and slips the cuffs around Reeves's wrists. He drags him clear of the rising puddle, then climbs back to his feet.

He almost falls: his progress across the grass is that of a man trying to stay on his feet on the deck of a boat in a force nine gale.

He ducks under the barbed wire. Pulls open the door.

Sees.

Dr Pradesh.

Naked.

Bleeding.

Alive.

He crosses to her quietly. Begins untying the blue ropes that lash her to the table.

Blood-soaked and mud-spattered, he knows he looks terrifying and fearsome. He talks to her as he would to a startled horse.

Locks eyes with her for a moment.

And then her arms are around him and she is sobbing into the soaked cloth of his jacket, her body heaving as she holds him tight.

He strokes her hair, leaving blood upon her crown. Looks around at the ruin of Lewis Caneva's old home. Imagines, for the briefest of moments, what Angelo witnessed here.

And then he is pulling out his broken phone.

'It's okay,' he whispers, disentangling himself from Dr Pradesh and putting his jacket around her shoulders.

And then he falls to the ground.

Before he loses consciousness, he repeats it.

'It's okay.'

And then, as blackness washes over him: 'I'm a policeman.'

22

Hessle Foreshore. 1.26 p.m.

Downey hadn't expected to see this place again. He wishes she had gone somewhere else. This was the scene of his humiliation. The place where his revenge turned sour. He'd nearly pissed himself when the husband came home.

He lowers his head and snorts up another line. Feels it blast through his system. Feels as if he has opened a window at 35,000 feet.

Bitch!

He watches her climb from the car, rain coming in sideways to patter against her attractive face. He watches her arse as she leans over and into the back seat of her friend's stupid little car. She emerges with her baby in her arms. It's crying, and she hushes it, cooing and singing, as the pouring rain turns her white top see-through, and her mate stands there gormlessly huddled inside a waterproofed coat.

He sees the lights of another car, further up the road. Sees them as the eyes of something powerful and monstrous moving towards him. Has to shake his head to turn the lights back into something safe and unthreatening.

The women run through the rain to the front door of the house. There is some complicated fumbling with keys and then they are pushing inside.

Downey has to time it just right. He wants the door to be closing as he puts his weight behind it. Wants to see her face as she realises who she has dared to cross.

He pulls himself free of the car and splashes through the fast-moving water that covers the road. He hears thunder above and looks up, past the Humber Bridge and into a pewter sky that rolls and twists as if pregnant with a belly full of snakes.

Stumbles.

Curses.

Charges hard.

He puts his shoulder to the door and hears the squeal of surprise.

'Bitch!'

Downey doesn't hesitate as Mel slams into the wall. Just jabs his right fist into the seamstress's face and watches her crumple, falling in a tangle of arms and legs in the doorway.

'Where are ya!'

He's bawling and screaming, his own voice alien to his ears.

The bitch appears from the living-room door. Her eyes widen in surprise as she sees him and then she turns her back on him, moving fast. The baby is over her shoulder, bobbing comically, and Downey almost giggles at the silliness of it all.

Roisin bangs at the back door, desperately rattling the handle, then looks around for a weapon. Her eyes are furious. If she had a blade she would stick it through his heart.

'I'll blow you fucking up!'

Downey hadn't rehearsed the line. Had planned to say something else entirely. But it erupts from his lips unbidden.

'He'll kill you,' she says, turning on him, hissing through bared teeth.

Downey pulls the grenade from his pocket. Looks at her and laughs.

'He wouldn't kill a fly for you, you bitch. Couldn't even kill those blokes who whipped you bloody you when you were a kid. Let them go with a big bunch of flowers and an apology. Move and I'll blow you and your baby into a million fucking bits.'

Roisin looks at the object in his hand. At the cocaine-fuelled hysteria in his eyes. Feels her world tilt as his words slide into her consciousness.

'Please, I'll get you more money. I'll give you everything—'

Downey giggles, high-pitched and effeminate.

'Too fucking late. You've spoiled it. I was supposed to be prince of the city, you know that? Supposed to get some fucking respect. And some pikey bitch just waltzes in and it's over? You have to pay. Have to!'

Downey steps forward. He doesn't know if he's going to throw the grenade or not. He just likes the look in her eyes. He wonders what she'll do if he pulls the pin out and holds it in front of her. It won't detonate unless he throws it. He could have fun. Could make her piss her fucking pants . . .

Downey pulls the pin from the grenade at the exact moment Helen Tremberg clatters into the room.

She has her phone in one hand, her baton in the other. She'd arrived outside just as Downey ran from his vehicle and smashed through the door. She hadn't hesitated. Knew the right thing to do. Knew she would rather be shot or stabbed or have her heart squeezed in a fist than stand back while somebody hurt McAvoy's wife.

Helen lashes out with the baton. It cracks across Downey's arm.

The grenade tumbles onto the floor.

Four pairs of eyes turn to watch the object rolling in a lazy semicircle on the carpet.

Then there is a flash.

The explosion can be heard even above the sound of the thunder.

There is silence for a moment.

And then nothing but the sizzle of rain falling on flame, and the rumble of falling stones.

EPILOGUE

2.06 a.m.

A small hatchback, quiet and dark on a cold country lane.

Chamomile House sits brooding and silent beneath light rain and a half-full moon.

Maria Caneva whistles something she can't quite place. The news is on the radio but she's not really listening. The evening bulletin had been full of reports from East Yorkshire. The doctor who operated on Hoyer-Wood has been found alive. A 25-year-old man was arrested at the scene on suspicion of three murders and abduction. The body of a child was also recovered from a vehicle at the remote former medical facility in Driffield. A police officer has been taken to hospital with life-threatening injuries . . .

Maria had tuned herself out. She reckons she knows who the policeman is. Reckons that the man arrested at the scene is either her brother, having given a false age, or some mate he met inside. She can't think about that. Can't open that door in her head. There are too many screaming ghosts inside.

No, all she can do is this.

She can do what somebody should have done years ago.

The boss of the care home had been friendly. Had told her they tended to use agency staff but would be delighted to take on somebody with her experience and obviously caring demeanour. Told her she could see her fitting right in and that they had one particular patient who would be delighted to hear about her fondness for the arts and interest in poetry. She'd apologised for the smell and told her the septic tank had just been emptied a couple of days ago. It would be years before it would need to be done again, she reckoned. Could she start straight away?

Maria steps out of her car. She's still dressed in her smart interview clothes. She locks the car and crosses the quiet country road. She throws one leg over the low stone wall and painfully climbs over and into a small copse of trees. Then she heads to the back of the building.

She pulls out the swipe card she has stolen from the receptionist and lets herself in, as quietly as she can. The facility is in half-darkness, with only a couple of bulbs in the corridor proving any illumination. She crosses to his door. Turns the handle and steps inside.

Sebastien Hoyer-Wood is on his back. His eyes are shut and he's sleeping soundly. Maria would like to look at him for a while. Would like to savour the physical humiliation and degradation he has endured since their last meeting. But it's not important.

He wakes as she pulls him from the bed. He isn't heavy. Weighs less than a child. He begins to thrash and a low, whinnying sound emerges from his slack mouth, but Maria clamps her hand on his lower jaw. It feels as if he is trying to bite her, so she sticks a thumb on his windpipe, then silently carries him from the room, down the corridor and into the night.

Maria's footsteps sound loud on the leaves and gravel, but nobody comes running. Through the trees she can see moonlight bouncing off standing water.

She follows her nose.

Lays Hoyer-Wood down on the cold ground.

She has no torch or phone, so has to find the lid of the septic tank by touch alone. She feels around amid rotting leaves and damp moss, sharp stones and mud. Feels two plastic handles. Puts her back into it, and pulls.

The smell hits her. The tank may have been emptied but it still stinks of accumulated gases and shit. She looks down into the darkness. Almost vomits at the stench. Sees a stagnant pool of brown, scummy liquid, about a foot above the bottom of the tank.

Without a word, Maria turns her head back to Hoyer-Wood.

He seems to understand. Tries to get away. Tries to stand. Tries to scream.

She doesn't give him the chance.

'Not today, Sebastien,' she says, quietly. 'But some day. I want you to keep the thought of this moment in your head tomorrow when I'm introduced to you. I'm your new nurse, Seb. I've got myself a contract and living accommodation and I'm going to be here at your beck and call for as long as I can stand it. And believe me, Sebastien, we are going to have some fun.'

Maria closes the cover over the fetid blackness and turns back to Sebastien. She picks leaves from his pyjama top and smiles into his terrified eyes. 'They said there was no way to punish you. They said that letting you live as you are is punishment enough. Let's see if they were right, eh?'

Maria scoops Sebastien up and carries him back towards his

room. As she lays him back in his bed she feels his body trembling like a frightened puppy's.

'See you tomorrow,' she says, and switches off the light.

As she slips out of the room and into the cool of the night, a shaft of moonlight spears through from the hazy clouds. She looks at her hands. They are covered in dirt and leaves and filth that makes her want to gag.

She has never felt as clean.

Acknowledgements

Thanks, as ever, to the Quercus team and Oli Munson – agent and friend.

Thanks too, to the crime writers who have influenced, inspired and welcomed me. Stav, Mari, Martyn, Steve, Peter, Tom, John, Mark and Val, you are owed more drinks than I can afford.

Special thanks to Dave and Babs Watson, who allowed me to use their computer to write this damn book when burglars took mine.

Love, gratitude and a look of perennial bewilderment go the way of Nik, George and Elora. I couldn't do any of this without you. And I'd have nobody to do it for.

Finally, thanks to the burglars. You really helped me imagine a whole new raft of gruesome deaths.

NO GRAVES AS YET

In Cambridge, in 1914, the golden June days seem timeless. But for Joseph Reavley, a university don, the idyllic summer is shattered by his parents' deaths in a car accident. Bringing the terrible news, his brother reveals that their father, a retired MP, had been travelling to see him about a sinister plot he had discovered. Matthew's job in the Secret Service means that he would understand the mysterious document their father possessed, but when the brothers hunt for it, the document is nowhere to be found. As their suspicions grow, the brothers visit the scene of the crash and examine their parents' ruined car, and find subtle evidence that their deaths may not have been accidental after all.

ANNE PERRY

NO GRAVES AS YET

Complete and Unabridged

CHARNWOOD
Leicester

First published in Great Britain in 2003
Headline Book Publishing
London

First Charnwood Edition
published 2003
by arrangement with
Headline Book Publishing
a division of Hodder Headline
London

British Library CIP Data

Perry, Anne
    No graves as yet.—Large print ed.—
Charnwood library series
    1. World War, *1914 – 1918* —Fiction
    2. Detective and mystery stories
    3. Large type books
    I. Title
    823. 9'14 [F]

    ISBN 1–84395–072–3

Published by
F. A. Thorpe (Publishing)
Anstey, Leicestershire

Set by Words & Graphics Ltd.
Anstey, Leicestershire
Printed and bound in Great Britain by
T. J. International Ltd., Padstow, Cornwall

This book is printed on acid-free paper

Dedicated to:
MY GRANDFATHER,
Capt. Joseph Reavley
who served as chaplain
in the trenches during
the Great War

And they that rule in England,
In stately conclave met,
Alas, alas for England
They have no graves as yet.

G. K. Chesterton

1

It was a golden afternoon in late June, a perfect day for cricket. The sun burned in a cloudless sky and the breeze was barely sufficient to stir the slender, pale skirts of the women as they stood on the grass at Fenner's Field, parasols in hand. The men, in white flannels, were relaxed and smiling.

St John's were in to bat. The bowler from Gonville and Caius turned, the ball in his hand, and ran slowly up to the crease. The ball flew, and Elwyn Allard hit it with a hard, satisfying crack, sending it far enough for a comfortable four.

Joseph Reavley joined in the applause. Elwyn was one of his students, rather more graceful with the bat than with the pen. He had little of the scholastic brilliance of his brother, Sebastian, but he had a manner that was easy to like, and a sense of honour that drove him like a spur.

St John's still had four more batsmen to play, young men from all over England who had come to Cambridge and, for one reason or another, were remaining at college through the long summer vacation.

Elwyn hit a modest two. The heat was stirred by a faint breath of wind from across the fenlands, with their dykes and marshes, flat under the vast skies stretching eastward to the sea. It was old land, quiet, cut by secret

1

waterways, Saxon churches marking each village. It had been the last stronghold of resistance against the Norman invasion eight and a half centuries ago.

On the pitch one of the fielders just missed a catch. There was a gasp, and then a letting out of breath. All this mattered. Such things could win or lose a match, and they would be playing against Oxford again soon. To be beaten would be catastrophic!

Across the town behind them the clock on the north tower at Trinity struck three, each chime on the large A flat bell, then followed the instant after on the smaller E flat. Joseph thought how out of place it seemed, to think of time on an eternal afternoon like this. It was an irrelevance, a man-made thing against the changeless tide of life. A few feet away Harry Beecher caught his eye and smiled. Beecher had been a Trinity man in his own years as a student and it was a long-standing joke that the Trinity clock struck once for itself, and once for St John's.

A cheer went up as the ball hit the stumps and Elwyn was bowled out with a very respectable score of eighty-three. He walked off with a little wave of acknowledgement, and was replaced at the crease by Lewis Foubister, dark-haired, a little too bony, though Joseph knew his awkwardness was deceiving. He was more tenacious than many gave him credit for, and he had flashes of extraordinary grace.

Play resumed, the sharp crack of a strike, the momentary cheers, the burning blue of the sky, and the scent of grass.

Aidan Thyer, Master of St John's, stood motionless a few yards from Joseph, his hair flaxen in the sun, his thoughts apparently far away. Beside him his wife, Connie, glanced across and gave a little shrug of her shoulders. Her dress was white broderie anglaise, falling loosely in a flare below the hip, and the fashionable, slender skirt reached to the ground. She looked as elegant and feminine as a spray of daisies, even though it was the hottest summer in England for years.

At the far end of the pitch Foubister struck an awkward shot, elbows in all the wrong places, and sent the ball right to the boundary. There was a shout of approval and everyone clapped.

Joseph was aware of a movement somewhere behind him, and half-turned, expecting a grounds official, perhaps to say it was time for lemonade and cucumber sandwiches. But it was his own brother, Matthew, who was walking towards him, his shoulders tight, no grace in his movement. He was wearing a light grey city suit, as if he had newly come from London.

Joseph started across the green, anxiety rising quickly, almost shivering. Why was he here in Cambridge, interrupting a match on a Sunday afternoon?

'Matthew! What is it?' he said as he reached him.

Matthew stopped. His face was so pale it seemed almost bloodless. He was twenty-eight, seven years the younger, broader-shouldered, and fair where Joseph was dark. He was steadying himself with difficulty and he gulped

3

before he found his voice. 'It's . . . ' he cleared his throat. There was a kind of desperation in his eyes. 'It's Mother and Father,' he said hoarsely. 'There's been an accident.'

Joseph refused to grasp what he had said. 'An accident?'

Matthew nodded, struggling to govern his ragged breathing.

'In the car. They are both . . . dead.'

For a moment the words had no meaning for Joseph. Instantly his father's face came to his mind, lean and gentle, blue eyes steady. It was impossible that he could be dead.

'The car went off the road,' Matthew was saying. 'Just before the Hauxton Mill Bridge.' His voice sounded strange and far away.

Behind Joseph they were still playing cricket. He heard the sound of the ball and another burst of applause.

'Joseph . . . ' Matthew's hand was on his arm, the grip tight.

Joseph nodded and tried to speak, but his throat was dry.

'I'm sorry,' Matthew said quietly. 'I wish I hadn't had to tell you like this. I — '

'It's all right,' Joseph cut across him. 'I'm . . . ' He changed his mind, still trying to grasp the reality. 'The Hauxton Road? Where were they going?'

Matthew's fingers tightened on his arm. They began to walk slowly, close together, over the sun-baked grass. There was a curious dizziness in the heat. Sweat trickled down Joseph's skin, and inside he was cold.

4

Matthew stopped again.

'Father telephoned me late yesterday evening,' he replied huskily, as if the words were almost unbearable for him. 'He said someone had given him a document outlining a plot so hideous it would change the world we know, ruin England, and everything we stand for, for ever.' He sounded defiant now, the muscles of his neck and jaw clenched as if he barely had mastery of himself. 'He said it reaches as high as the royal family.'

Joseph's mind whirled. What should he do? The words hardly made sense, let alone carried a meaning. John Reavley had been a Member of Parliament until 1912, two years ago. He had resigned for reasons he had not discussed, but he had never lost his interest in political affairs, nor his care for honesty in government. Perhaps he had simply been ready to spend more time reading, indulging his love of philosophy, poking around in antique and second-hand shops looking for a bargain. More often he was just talking with people, listening to stories, swapping eccentric jokes and adding to his collection of limericks.

'A plot to ruin England and everything we stand for?' Joseph repeated incredulously.

'No,' Matthew corrected him with precision. 'A plot which would ruin it. That was not the main purpose, simply a side effect.'

'What plot? By whom?' Joseph demanded.

'I don't know. He was bringing the document to me . . . today.'

Joseph started to ask why, and then stopped.

The answer was the one thing that made sense. Suddenly at least two facts cohered. John Reavley had wanted Joseph to study medicine, and when he had left it for the Church, he had then wanted it for Matthew. But Matthew had read modern history and languages here at Cambridge, and joined the Secret Intelligence Service. If there were such a plot, of course John would have taken it to him.

Joseph swallowed, the air catching in his throat. 'I see.'

Matthew's grip eased on him slightly. He had known the news longer and had more time to grasp its truth. He was searching Joseph's face with anxiety for him, trying to think of something to say or do to help him through the pain.

Joseph made an immense effort. 'I see,' he repeated. 'We must go to them. Where . . . are they?'

'At the police station in Great Shelford,' Matthew answered. He made a slight movement with his head. 'I've got my car.'

'Does Judith know?'

Matthew's face tightened. 'Yes. They didn't know where to find you or me, so they called her.'

That was reasonable — obvious really. Judith was their younger sister, still living at home. Hannah, between Joseph and Matthew in age, was married to a naval officer and lived in Portsmouth. It would be at the house in Selborne St Giles that the police would have called. Joseph thought how Judith would be

6

feeling, alone except for the servants, knowing neither her father nor mother would come home again — not tonight, not any night.

His thoughts were interrupted by someone at his elbow. He had not even heard footsteps on the grass. He half turned and saw Harry Beecher standing beside him, his wry, sensitive face puzzled.

'Is everything — ' he began. Then, seeing Joseph's eyes, he stopped. 'Can I help?' he said simply.

Joseph shook his head a little. 'No . . . no, there isn't anything.' He made an effort to pull his thoughts together. 'My parents have had an accident.' He took a deep breath. 'They've been killed.' How odd and flat the words sounded. They still carried no reality with them.

Beecher was appalled. 'Oh, God! I'm so sorry!'

'Please — ' Joseph started.

'Of course,' Beecher interrupted. 'I'll tell people. Just go.' He touched Joseph lightly on the arm. 'Let me know if I can do anything.'

'Yes, of course. Thank you.' Joseph shook his head and started to walk as Matthew acknowledged Beecher, then turned to go across the wide expanse of grass towards the way out. Joseph followed him without looking back at the players in their white flannels, bright in the sunlight. They had been the only reality a few moments ago; now there seemed an unbridgeable space between them.

Outside the cricket ground Matthew's Sunbeam-Talbot was parked in Gonville Place. Joseph climbed over the side and into the

7

passenger seat automatically. It was facing north, as if Matthew had been to St John's first, and come all the way through town to the cricket ground looking for Joseph. Now he turned south-west again, back along Gonville Place and finally on to the Trumpington Road.

There was nothing to say now. The brothers were each cocooned in their own pain, waiting for the moment when they had to face the physical proof of death. The familiar winding road, with its harvest fields shining gold in the heat, the hedgerows, the motionless trees, were like things painted on the other side of a wall that encased the mind. Joseph was aware of them only as a bright blur.

Matthew drove as if it demanded his entire concentration, clutching the steering wheel with hands he had to loosen deliberately now and then.

South of the village they turned left through St Giles, skirted the side of the hill over the railway bridge into Great Shelford and pulled up outside the police station. A sombre sergeant met them, his face tired, his body a little hunched, as if he had had to steel himself for the task.

'Oi'm terrible sorry, sir.' He looked from one to the other of them, biting his lower lip. 'Wouldn't ask it if Oi din't 'ave to.'

'I know,' Joseph said quickly. He did not want a conversation. Now that they were here, he needed to do his task as quickly as possible, while his self-control lasted.

Matthew made a small gesture forward, and the sergeant turned and led the way the short distance through the streets to the hospital mortuary. It was all very formal. It was a routine he must have been through scores of times: sudden death, shocked families moving as if in a dream, murmuring polite words, hardly aware of what they were saying, trying to understand what had happened, and at the same time deny it.

They stepped out of the sunlight into the sudden darkness of the building. Joseph went ahead. The windows were open to try to keep the air cool and the closeness less oppressive. The corridors were narrow, echoing, and they smelled of stone and carbolic.

The sergeant opened the door to a side room and ushered the brothers in. There were two bodies laid out on trolleys, covered decently in white sheets.

Joseph felt his heart lurch. In a moment it would be real, irreversible, a part of his own life ended. He clung on to the second of disbelief, the last, precious instant of 'now', before it all changed.

The sergeant was looking at him, then at Matthew, waiting for them to be ready.

Matthew nodded.

The sergeant pulled back the sheet from the face. It was John Reavley.

The familiar aquiline nose looked a little bigger because his cheeks were sunken, and there was a hollowness about his eyes. The skin on his forehead was broken but someone had cleaned away the blood. His main injuries must be to his chest . . . probably from the steering wheel. Joseph blocked out the thought, refusing to picture it in his mind. He wanted to remember his father's face as it was, looking as if he were no more than asleep after an exhausting day. He might still waken, and smile.

'Thank you,' he said aloud, surprised how steady he sounded.

The sergeant said something but he did not listen. Matthew answered. They went to the other body and the sergeant lifted the sheet, but only partially, keeping it over one side, his own face crumpled with pity. It was Alys Reavley, her right cheek and brow perfect, skin very pale, but blemishless, eyebrows delicately winged. The other side was concealed.

Joseph heard Matthew draw in his breath sharply, and the room seemed to swing and slide off to one side, as if he were drunk. He grasped Matthew, and felt Matthew's hand tighten hard on his wrist.

The sergeant covered her face again, started to say something, then changed his mind.

Joseph and Matthew stumbled outside and along the corridor to a small, private room. A woman in a starched uniform brought them cups of tea. Joseph drank. It was too strong and too sweet, and at first he thought he would gag on it, then after a moment the heat felt good, and he drank some more.

'Oi'm awful sorry,' the sergeant said again. 'If it's any comfort, it must've been very quick.' He looked wretched, his eyes hollow and pink-rimmed.

Watching him, Joseph was taken back, in spite of himself, to his days as a parish priest, before

Eleanor died, when he had had to tell families of tragedy, and try to give them whatever comfort he could, struggling to express a faith that could meet the reality. Everybody was always very polite, strangers trying to reach each other across an abyss of pain.

'What happened?' he said.

'We don't know yet, sir,' the sergeant answered. He had said what his name was, but Joseph had forgotten. 'The car came off the road just afore the Hauxton Mill Bridge,' he went on. 'Seems it was going quite fast — '

'That's a straight stretch!' Matthew cut across him.

'Yes, Oi know, sir,' the sergeant agreed. 'From the marks on the road, it looks as if it happened all of a sudden, like a tyre blowing out. Can be hard to keep a hold when that happens. It could even've bin both tyres on the one side, if there were something on the road as caused it.' He chewed his lip dubiously. 'That could take you right off, no matter how good a driver you were.'

'Is the car still there?' Matthew asked.

'No, sir.' The policeman shook his head. 'We're bringing it in. You can see it if you want, o' course, but if you'd rather not . . . '

'What about my father's things?' Matthew said abruptly. 'His case, whatever was in his pockets?'

Joseph glared at him in surprise. It was a distasteful request, as if possessions could matter now. Then he remembered the document Matthew had said John Reavley had been taking to him. He looked at the sergeant.

'Yes, sir, o' course,' the sergeant agreed. 'You

11

can see them now, if you really want, before we . . . clean them.' That was almost a question. He was trying to save them hurt and he did not know how to do it without seeming intrusive.

'There's a paper,' Matthew explained. 'It's important.'

'Oh! Yes, sir.' The sergeant's face was bleak. 'In that case, if you'll come with me . . . ?' He glanced at Joseph.

Joseph nodded and followed them out of the room and along the hot, silent corridor, their footsteps self-consciously loud. He wanted to see what this document could possibly be that his father had believed to concern a plot so terrible it would change and destroy everything they valued. His first vague thoughts were that it might have something to do with the recent mutiny of British army officers in the Curragh. There was always trouble in Ireland, but this looked uglier than usual; in fact various politicians had warned it could lead to the worst crisis in over two hundred years. He knew most of the facts, as the newspapers reported them, but at the moment his thoughts were too chaotic to make sense of anything.

The sergeant led them to another small room where he unlocked one of the several cupboards and pulled out a drawer. Carefully he took from it a rather battered leather attaché case with the initials J. R. R. stamped just below the lock, and then a woman's smart, dark brown leather handbag heavily smeared with blood. No one had yet attempted to clean it.

Joseph felt sick. He knew the blood was his

12

mother's. She was dead and beyond pain, but it mattered to him. He was a minister of the Church; he should know to value the spirit above the body. The flesh was temporary, only a tabernacle for the soul, and yet it was absurdly precious. It was powerful, fragile, and intensely real. It was always an inextricable part of someone you loved.

Matthew was opening the attaché case and looking through the papers inside, his fingers moving delicately. There was something to do with insurance, a couple of letters, a bank statement.

Matthew frowned and tipped the case upside down. Another paper slithered out, but it was only a receipt for a pair of shoes — '12/6'. He ran his hands down inside the main compartment, then the side pockets, but there was nothing more. He looked across at Joseph and, with fingers trembling, he put down the case and reached for the handbag. He was very careful not to touch the blood. At first he just looked inside, as if a paper would be easy to see, then when he found nothing, he began very carefully to move things around.

Joseph could see two handkerchiefs, a comb . . . He thought of his mother's soft hair with its gentle, natural curl, and the way it lay on her neck when she had it coiled up. He had to close his eyes to prevent the tears, and an ache in his throat so fierce he could not swallow.

When he mastered himself and looked down at the handbag again, Matthew was staring at it in confusion.

'Perhaps it was in his pocket?' Joseph suggested, his voice hoarse, jolting the silence.

Matthew looked at him, then turned to the sergeant.

The sergeant hesitated.

Joseph glanced around. The room was bare except for the cupboards — more a storeroom than an office. A simple window faced a delivery yard, and then rooftops beyond.

Reluctantly the sergeant opened another drawer and took out a pile of clothes resting on an oilskin sheet. They were drenched with blood, dark and already stiffening. He did his best to conceal the gore, handing Matthew only the man's jacket.

His face blanched even whiter, Matthew took it and with fingers clumsy now, searched through one pocket after another. He found a handker-chief, a penknife, two pipe cleaners, an odd button and some loose change. There was no paper at all. He looked up at Joseph, a frown between his brows.

'Maybe it's in the car?' Joseph suggested.

'It must be.' Matthew stood still for a moment. As if he had spoken it, Joseph knew what he was thinking: he would have to look through the rest of the clothes — just in case. It would be so much easier not to. He was startled how fiercely he did not want to intrude into the intimate, the familiar smell, as if they were still alive. Death was not real yet, the pain of it only just beginning, but he knew its path; it was like the loss of Eleanor all over again. But they must look, otherwise they would have to come back

14

and do it later, if the document were not in the car.

But of course it was in the car! It had to be. In the glove compartment, or one of the pockets at the side. But how odd not to have put it in the briefcase along with the other papers. Isn't that what anyone would do automatically?

The sergeant was waiting.

Matthew blinked several times. 'May we have the others, please?' he requested.

The clothes were passed over, and Joseph helped him, trying to distance his mind from what his hands were doing. There were no papers there except one small receipt in his father's trouser pocket, soaked with blood and illegible, but there was no way in which it could be called a document. It was barely two or three inches square.

They folded the clothes again and set them in a pile on top of the oilskin. It was an awkward moment. Joseph did not know what to do with them. The sight and touch of them knotted up his stomach with grief. He wished he had never had to see them at all — he certainly did not want to keep them. And yet standing here beside them, neither did he want to pass them over to strangers as if they did not matter.

'May we take them?' he asked haltingly.

Matthew jerked his hand up, then the surprise died out of his face as if he understood.

'Yes, sir, o' course,' the sergeant replied. 'I'll just wrap 'm up for you.'

'If we could see the car, please . . . ?' Matthew asked.

15

But it was still on the way back from Hauxton and they had to wait another half-hour. Two more cups of tea later they were taken to the garage where the familiar yellow Lanchester sat gashed and crumpled. The whole of the engine was twisted sideways and half-jammed into the front of the passenger area. All four tyres were ripped. No human being could have remained alive inside it.

Matthew stood still, struggling to keep his balance.

Joseph reached out to him, glad to break the physical aloneness.

Matthew righted himself and walked over towards the far side of the car where the driver's door was hanging open. He took off his jacket and rolled up the sleeves of his shirt.

Joseph went to the windowless frame of the passenger door, keeping his eyes averted from the blood on the seat, and banged the glove compartment to make it open.

There was nothing inside except a small tin of barley sugar, and an extra pair of driving gloves. He looked across and saw Matthew's face, wide-eyed, confused, his fair skin almost grey. There was no document in the side pocket. He held the road atlas and riffled the pages, but nothing fell out.

They searched the rest of the car as well as they could, forcing themselves to ignore the blood, the torn leather and the twisted metal and shards of glass, but there was no document of any sort.

Joseph stepped back at last, elbows and

shoulders bruised where he had caught himself on the jutting pieces of what had been seats, and the misshapen frames of the doors. He had skinned his knuckles and broken a fingernail trying to prise up a piece of metal.

He looked across at Matthew. 'There's nothing here,' he said aloud.

'No . . . ' Matthew frowned. His right sleeve was torn and his face dirty and smeared with blood.

A few years ago Joseph might have asked him if he were certain of his facts, but Matthew was beyond such brotherly condescension now. The seven years between them were closing fast.

'Where else could it be?' he said instead.

Matthew hesitated, breathing in and out slowly. 'I don't know,' he admitted. He looked beaten, his eyes hollow and his face shadowed with fatigue from battling the inner shock and grief, trying to keep it from overwhelming him. Perhaps this document was something to cling on to over which he could have some control.

Joseph understood how it mattered to him. John Reavley had believed passionately that medicine was the noblest of callings. He had seen the wasting of pain and disease in his youth and cared intensely that it should be helped. Joseph had started medical studies to please his father, and then found himself drowned by his inability to affect all but the smallest part of the suffering he witnessed. He knew his limitations, and he saw what he thought was his strength and his true vocation. He answered the call of the Church, using his gift for languages to study the

17

original Greek and Hebrew of the Scriptures. Souls needed healing as well as bodies. John Reavley was content with that, and deferred his dream to his second son.

But Matthew had refused outright, and turned his imagination, his intellect and his eye for detail towards the Secret Intelligence Service. John Reavley had been bitterly disappointed, too deeply so to hide. He despised espionage and all its works, and equally those who occupied themselves with it. That he had called Matthew in his professional capacity to help him with a document he had found was a far more powerful testimony of his judgement of it than anyone else would understand.

It would have been a chance for Matthew to give his father a gift from his chosen calling, and it had slipped away for ever.

Joseph lowered his eyes. Perhaps understanding was intrusive at this raw moment.

'Have you any idea what it is?' he asked, investing his voice with urgency, as if speed could matter.

'He said it was a conspiracy,' Matthew replied, straightening his back. He moved away from the door, coming round the back of the car to where Joseph was, keeping his voice very low. 'And that it was the most dishonourable thing he had ever seen, a total betrayal.'

'Of whom?'

'I don't know. He said it was all in the paper.'

'Had he told anyone else?'

'No. He didn't dare. He had no idea who was involved.' He stared at Joseph, searching for a

18

response, an answer.

Joseph waited a moment too long.

'You don't believe it!' Matthew's voice was hoarse; he himself was not sure if it was an accusation or not, for it was in his eyes that his own certainty was wavering.

Joseph wanted to save something out of the confusion. 'Did he say he was bringing it, or that he would tell you about it? Could he have left it at home? In the safe, perhaps?'

'I would have to see it,' Matthew argued, rolling his shirtsleeves down and fastening the cuffs again.

'To do what?' Joseph pursued. 'Wouldn't it be better for him to tell you what it was — and he was perfectly capable of memorizing it for you — and then decide what to do, but keep it in the meantime?'

It was a sensible suggestion. Matthew's body eased, the stiffness draining out of it. 'I suppose so. We'd better go home, anyway. We ought to be with Judith. She's alone. I don't even know if she's told Hannah. Someone will have to send her a telegram. She'll come, of course. And we'll need to know her train, to meet it.'

'Yes, of course,' Joseph conceded. 'There'll be a lot of things to do.' He did not want to think of them now. They were intimate, final things, an acknowledgement that death was real, and the past could never be brought back. It was the locking of a door.

★ ★ ★

19

They drove back from Great Shelford through the quiet lanes. The village of Selborne St Giles looked just the same as it always had in the soft gold of the evening. They passed the stone mill, walls flush with the river. The pond was flat as a polished sheet, reflecting the soft enamel blue of the sky. There was an arch of honeysuckle over the lich-gate to the churchyard, and the clock on the tower read just after half-past six. In less than two hours evensong would be held.

There were half a dozen people in the main street. Matthew drove past the doctor with his pony and trap, going at a brisk pace. He waved cheerfully. He could not have heard the news yet.

Joseph stiffened a little. That was one of the tasks that lay ahead: telling people. He was too late to wave back. The doctor would think him rude.

Matthew swung the car left along the side road to the house. The drive gates were closed and Joseph got out to open them, then close them again as Matthew pulled up to the front door. Someone had already drawn the curtains downstairs — probably Mrs Appleton, the housekeeper. Judith would not have thought of it.

Matthew climbed out of the car just as Joseph reached him, and the front door opened. Judith stood on the step. She was fair-skinned like Matthew, but her hair waved heavily, and was a warmer brown. She was tall for a woman, and even though he was her brother, Joseph could see that she had a uniquely fierce and vulnerable kind of beauty. The strength inside her had yet to

20

be refined, but it was there in her bones and her level, grey-blue eyes.

Now she was bleached of all colour and her eyelids were puffy. She blinked several times to hold back the tears. She looked at Matthew and tried to smile, then took the few steps across the porch on to the gravel to Joseph, and he held her motionless for a moment, then felt her body shake as she let the sobs wrench through her.

He did not try to stop her, or find any comforting words to say. There was no reason that made any sense, and no answer to the pain. He tightened his arms around her, clinging as much to her as she was to him. She was nothing like Alys, not really, yet the softness of her hair, the way it curled, choked the tears in his throat.

Matthew went in ahead of them. His footsteps faded along the wooden floor of the hall, and then they heard his voice murmuring something, and Mrs Appleton replying.

Judith sniffed hard and pulled back a little. She felt in Joseph's pocket for his handkerchief. She took it out and blew her nose, then wiped her eyes, screwing up the linen and clenching it in her hand. She turned away and went inside also, talking to him without looking back.

'I don't know what to do with myself. Isn't it stupid?' she gulped. 'I keep walking round from room to room, and going out again, then coming back — as if that would make it any different! I suppose we'll have to tell people?'

He went up the steps behind her.

'I sent Hannah a telegram, but that's all,' she

went on. 'I don't even remember what I said.' Inside she swivelled round to face him, ignoring Henry, the cream-haired retriever who came out of the sitting room at the sound of Joseph's voice. 'How do you tell people something like this?' she asked. 'I can't believe it's real!'

'Not yet,' he agreed, bending to touch the dog as it pushed against his hand. He stood in the familiar hallway with its oak staircase curving upwards, the light from the landing window catching the watercolours on the wall. 'It'll come. Tomorrow morning it will begin.' He could remember with sickening clarity the first time he had woken up after Eleanor's death. There was an instant when everything was as it had always been, the whole year of their marriage. Then the truth had washed over him like ice, and something inside him had never been warm again.

There was a fleeting pity in Judith's face, and he knew she was remembering also. He made an effort to force it away. She was twenty-three, almost an afterthought in the family. He should be protecting her, not thinking of himself.

'Don't worry about telling people,' he said gently. 'I'll do that.' He knew how hard it was, almost like making the death itself happen over again each time. 'There'll be other things to do. Just ordinary housekeeping, for a start, practical things.'

'Oh, yes.' She jerked her attention into focus. 'Mrs Appleton will deal with the cooking and the laundry, but I'll tell Lettie to make up Hannah's room. She'll be here tomorrow. And I suppose there's food to order. I've never done that! Mother always did.' She looked puzzled and a little wry. Judith was quite unlike either her mother or Hannah, who loved their kitchens, with the smells of cooking, clean linen, beeswax polish, lemon soap. For them, to run a house was an art. To Judith it was a distraction from the real business of living, although to be honest she was not yet certain for herself what that would prove to be. But she knew it was not domesticity. To her mother's exasperation, she had turned down at least two perfectly good offers of marriage.

But this was not the time for such thoughts.

'Ask Mrs Appleton,' he told her. He steadied his voice with an effort. 'We'll have to go through the diaries and cancel any appointments.'

'Mother was going to judge the flower show,' she said, smiling and biting her lip, tears flooding her eyes. 'They'll have to find somebody else. I can't do it, even if they were to ask me.'

'And bills,' he added. 'I'll see the bank, and the solicitor.'

She stood stiffly in the middle of the floor, her shoulders rigid. She was wearing a pale blouse and soft, green narrow skirt. She had not yet thought to put on black. 'I suppose somebody'll have to sort . . . clothes and things. I — ' she gulped — 'I haven't been into the bedroom yet. I can't!'

He shook his head. 'Too soon. It doesn't matter, for ages.'

She relaxed a fraction, as if she had been afraid he was going to force her. 'Tea?'

'Yes.' He was surprised how thirsty he was. His mouth was dry.

Matthew was in the kitchen with Mrs Appleton, a square, mild-faced woman with a stubborn jaw. Now she was standing at the table with her back to the stove on which a kettle was beginning to whistle. She wore her usual plain blue dress and her cotton apron was screwed up at the right-hand corner as if she had unthinkingly used it to wipe the tears from her eyes. She sniffed fiercely as she looked first at Judith, then at Joseph, for once not bothering to tell the dog not to come in. She drew in her breath to say something, then decided she could not trust herself to keep her composure, and clearing her throat loudly, turned to Matthew.

'Oi'll do that, Mr Matthew. You'll only scald yourself. You weren't never use to man nor beast in the kitchen. Do nothing but take my jam tarts, as if there was no one else in the house to eat 'em. Here!' She snatched the kettle from him and with considerable clattering and banging, made the tea.

Lettie, the general housemaid, came in silently, her face pale and tear-stained. Judith asked her to make up Hannah's room, and she departed to obey, glad to have something to do.

Reginald, the only indoor manservant, appeared and asked Joseph if they would want wine for dinner, and if he should lay out black clothes for him, or for Matthew.

Joseph said no, they did not want wine, but accepted the offer to lay out black for both of them, and Reginald left. Mrs Appleton's

24

husband, Albert, was outside working off his grief alone, digging in his beloved garden.

In the kitchen they sat around the scrubbed table in silence, sipping the hot liquid, each sunk in his or her own thoughts. The room was as familiar as life itself. All four children had been born in this house, learned to walk and talk here, left through the front gate to go to school. Matthew and Joseph had driven from here to go to university, Hannah to go to her wedding in the village church. Joseph could remember the endless fittings of her dress in the spare bedroom, she standing as still as she could while Alys went around her with pins in her hands and in her mouth, a tuck here, a lift there, determined the gown should be perfect. And it had been.

Now she would never be back. He could remember her perfume, always lily-of-the-valley. The bedroom would still smell of it.

Hannah would be devastated. She was so close to her mother, so like her in a score of ways, she would feel robbed of the model for her life. There would be nobody to share with her the small successes and failures in the home, the children's growth, the new things learned. No one else would reassure her anxieties, teach her the simple remedies for a fever, a sore throat, or the easy way to mend, to adapt, to make do. It was a companionship that was gone for ever.

For Judith it would be different, an open wound of things not done, not said, and now unable ever to be put right.

Matthew had set his cup down and looked

across the table at Joseph.

'I think we should go and sort some of the papers and bills.' He stood up, scraping his chair on the floor.

Judith seemed not to notice the tremor in his voice, or the fact that he was trying to exclude her.

Joseph knew what he meant: it was time to look for the document. If it existed then it should be here in the house, although why John would have set out to show it to Matthew and then not taken it with him was hard to understand. But it seemed the last place left for it to be.

'Yes, of course,' he agreed, rising as well. They had better give Judith something to do. She had no need to know anything about this yet, and perhaps not at all. He turned to her. 'Would you go through the household accounts with Mrs Appleton and see if there is anything that needs doing? Perhaps some orders need to be cancelled, or at least reduced. And there may be invitations to be declined, that sort of thing.'

She nodded, not trusting herself to speak.

'You'll be staying?' Mrs Appleton said with another sniff. 'What'll you be wanting for dinner, Mr Joseph?'

'Nothing special,' he answered. 'Whatever you have.'

'Oi've got cold salmon and summer pudding,' she said a little truculently, as if she were defending Alys's choice. If it was good enough for the master and mistress, it was certainly good enough for the young master, whatever had happened in the world. 'And there's some good Ely cheese,' she added.

'That would be excellent, thank you,' he accepted, and followed Matthew, who was already at the door.

They went along the passage and across the hall to John Reavley's study overlooking the garden. The sun was still well above the horizon and bathing the tops of the orchard trees in gold. The leaves shimmered in the rising wind and a swirl of starlings rose into the sky, black against the amber and flame, turning in wide, spiral arms against the sunset.

Joseph looked around the familiar room, almost like an earlier pattern of his own in Cambridge. There was a simple oak desk, shelves of books covering most of two walls — all sorts, dating back to John's own university days. Some were in German. Many were leather-bound, a few well-thumbed cloth or even paper. There was a folio of drawings on the table by the window, a recent acquisition.

The Bonington seascape hung over the fireplace, exquisitely lovely, colour neither blue nor green, but that kind of luminous grey that holds both at its heart. Looking at it one could draw a cleaner breath and almost feel the sting of the salt in the wind. John Reavley had loved everything in this room — each object marked some happiness or beauty he had known — but the Bonington was special.

Joseph turned away from it. 'I'll start over here,' he said, taking the first book out of the shelf nearest the window.

Matthew began with the desk.

They searched for half an hour before dinner, and all evening afterwards. Judith went to bed, but midnight found the brothers still sifting through papers, looking in books a second or third time, even moving furniture. Finally they admitted defeat and forced themselves into the master bedroom to look with stiff fingers through drawers of clothes, shelves where toiletries and personal jewellery were kept, pockets of the clothes hung in wardrobes. There was no document.

At half-past one, head throbbing, eyes stinging as if hot and gritty, Joseph came to the end of places to try. He straightened up, moving his shoulders carefully to ease the ache. 'It's not here,' he said wearily.

Matthew did not answer for several moments; he kept his eyes on the drawer he had been going through for the third time. 'He was very clear,' he repeated stubbornly. 'He said the effect of it, the daring, was so vast it was beyond most men's imagination. And terrible.' He looked up at last, his eyes red-rimmed, angry, as if Joseph were attacking his judgement. 'He couldn't trust anyone else because of who was involved.'

Joseph's imagination was too tired and too full of pain to be inventive, even to save Matthew's feelings. 'Then where is it?' he demanded. 'Would he trust it to the Bank? Or the solicitor?'

Denial was in Matthew's face, but he clung on to the possibility for a few seconds, because he could think of nothing else.

'We'll have to speak to them tomorrow

anyway.' Joseph sat down on the chair by the desk, where lay a separated pile of documents that would need attention. Matthew was sitting beside the drawers on the carpet.

'He wouldn't give it to Pettigrew.' Matthew pushed his hair back off his forehead. 'They're just family solicitors, wills and property.'

'Then quite a safe place to hide something valuable and dangerous,' Joseph reasoned.

Matthew glared at him. 'Are you trying to defend Father? Prove that he wasn't imagining it out of something that was really perfectly harmless?'

Joseph was stung by the accusation. It was exactly what he was doing — defending, denying, confused and dizzy with loss, his head aching. 'Do I need to?' he demanded.

'Stop being so damn reasonable!' Matthew's voice cracked, emotion raw. 'Of course you need to! It wasn't in the car! It isn't in the house.' He jerked his hand sharply towards the door and the landing beyond. 'Doesn't it sound wild enough to you, unlikely enough? A document that proves a conspiracy to ruin all we love and believe in — and that goes right up to the royal family — but when we look for it, it vanishes into the air!'

Joseph said nothing. The tag end of an idea pulled at his mind, but he was too exhausted to grasp it.

'What is it?' Matthew said roughly. 'What are you thinking?'

'Could it be obvious?' Joseph frowned. 'I mean something we are seeing, but not recognising?'

Matthew looked round the room. 'Like what? For God's sake, Joe! It's a conspiracy that will change the world we know and dishonour England for ever! It's not going to be hung up on the wall along with the pictures!' He put the papers in the drawer, climbed to his feet and carried it back to the desk. He replaced it in its slots and pushed it closed. 'And before you bother, I've taken the backs off all the drawers and looked.'

'Well, there are two possibilities.' Joseph was driven to the last conclusion. 'Either there is such a document, or there isn't.'

'You have a genius for the obvious!' Matthew said bitterly. 'I had worked that out for myself.'

'And you concluded that there is? On what basis?'

'No!' Matthew snapped. 'I just spent the evening ransacking the house because I have nothing better to do!'

'You don't have anything better to do,' Joseph answered him. 'We had to go through the papers anyway to find what needs attending to.' He gestured towards the separated pile. 'And the sooner we do it, the less bloody awful it is. We can think of a conspiracy while we look, which is easier than thinking that we are performing a sort of last rite for both our parents, because yesterday everything was as usual, with years ahead of us of love and safety and good, familiar things — and today they are both dead — '

'All right!' Matthew cut in. 'I'm sorry.' Again he pushed the thick fair hair off his face. 'But honestly, he sounded so certain of it! His voice

30

was charged with emotion, not a bit dry and humorous as it usually is.' His mouth pulled a little crooked, and when he spoke again his voice cracked. 'I know what it must have cost him to call me about something like that. He hated all the secret services. He wouldn't have said anything if he hadn't been certain.'

'Then he put it somewhere we haven't thought of yet,' Joseph concluded. He stood up also. 'Go to bed now. It's nearly two, and there's a lot we have to do later.'

'There was a telegram from Hannah. She's coming on the two fifteen. Will you go and meet her?' Matthew was rubbing his forehead sore. 'She's going to find this pretty hard.'

'Yes, I know. I'll go for her. Albert will drive me. May I take your car?'

'Of course.' Matthew shook his head. 'I wonder why he didn't drive Father yesterday?'

'Or why Mother went?' Joseph added. 'It's all odd. I'll ask Albert on the way to the station.'

⋆ ⋆ ⋆

The next day was filled with small, unhappy duties. The formal arrangements had to be made for the funeral. Joseph went to see Hallam Kerr, the vicar, and sat in the tidy, rather stiff vicarage parlour watching him trying to think of something to say that would be of spiritual comfort, and finding nothing. Instead they spoke of the practicalities: the day, the hour, who should say what, the hymns. It was a timeless ritual that had been conducted in the old church

31

for every death in the village over nearly a thousand years. The very familiarity of it was comfortable, a reassurance that even if one individual journey was ended, life itself was the same, and always would be. There was a kind of certainty in it that gave its own peace.

Just before lunch Mr Pettigrew came from the solicitors' office, small and pale and very neat. He offered his condolences, and assured Joseph and Matthew that everything legal was in order, but no, he had been given no papers to keep recently, in fact not anything this year. A couple of bonds in August of 1913 were the last things. He did not yet mention the will, but they knew it would have to be dealt with in time.

The bank manager, the doctor and other neighbours called in or left flowers and cards. Nobody knew what to say, but it was done in kindness. Judith offered them tea, and sometimes it was accepted and awkward conversations followed.

In the early afternoon Albert Appleton drove Joseph to the railway station at Cambridge to meet Hannah's train from London. Joseph sat beside him in the front of Matthew's Sunbeam-Talbot as they followed the lanes between the late wild roses and the ripening fields of corn already dappled here and there with the scarlet of poppies.

Albert kept his eyes studiously on the road. He looked tired, his skin papery under its dark sunburn, and he had missed a little grey stubble on his cheek when he had shaved this morning.

He was not a man to give words to grief, but he had come to St Giles at eighteen, and served John Reavley all his adult life. For him this was the ending of an age.

'Do you know why Father drove himself yesterday?' Joseph asked as they passed into the shade under an avenue of elms.

'No, Mr Joseph,' Albert replied. It would be a long time before he called him 'Dr Reavley', if he ever did. 'Except there's a branch on the old plum tree in the orchard hanging low, and tossled in the grass. He wanted me to see if Oi could save it. Oi propped it up, but that don't always work. Get a bit o' wind an' it goes anyway, but it tears it off rough. Leaves a gash in the trunk, an' kill the whole thing. Get a bit parky an' the frost'll have it anyway.'

'I see. Can you save it?'

'Best to take it off.'

'Do you know why Mother went with him?'

'Jus' liked to go with him, mebbe.' He stared fixedly ahead.

Joseph did not speak again until they reached the station. Albert had always been someone with whom it was possible to sit in amicable silence, ever since Joseph had been a boy nursing his dreams in the garden or the orchard.

Albert parked the car outside the station and Joseph went in and on to the platform to wait. There were half a dozen other people there, but he studiously avoided meeting anyone's eye in case he encountered someone he knew. The last thing he wanted was conversation.

The train was on time, belching steam and

grinding to a halt at the platform. The doors clanged open. People shouted greetings and fumbled with baggage. He saw Hannah almost immediately. The few other women were in bright summer colours or delicate pastels. Hannah was in a slim travelling suit of unrelieved black. The tapered hem at her ankles was smudged with dust and her neat hat was decorated with black feathers. Her face was pale, and with her wide brown eyes and soft features she looked so like Alys that for a moment Joseph felt his emotions lurch out of control and grief engulfed him unbearably. He stood motionless as people pushed past him, unable to think or even focus his vision.

Then she was in front of him, a little leather case clutched in her hand and the tears spilling down her cheeks. She dropped the bag on the platform and waited for him.

He put his arms around her and held her as close to him as he could. He felt her shivering. He had already tried to work out what to say to her, but now it all slipped away, sounding hollow and predictable. He was a minister, the one of all of them who was supposed to have the faith that answered death and overcame the hollow pain that consumed everything from the inside. But he knew what bereavement was, sharply and recently, and no words had touched more than the surface for him.

Please God, he must find something to say to Hannah! What use was he if, of all people, he could not?

He let go of her at last and picked up her bag,

34

carrying it out to where Albert was waiting with the car.

She stopped, staring at the unfamiliar vehicle, as if she had expected the yellow Lanchester, then with a gasp that caught in her throat, she realised why it was not there.

Joseph took her by the elbow and helped her into the back seat, straightening the slender black skirt around her ankles before closing the door and going round to the other side to get in next to her.

Albert got back in and started the engine.

Hannah said nothing. It was up to Joseph to speak, before the silence became too difficult. He had already decided not to mention the document. It was one more thing to worry about, and there was no way in which she could help.

'Judith will be glad to see you,' he started.

She looked at him with slight surprise, and he knew immediately that her thoughts had been inward, absorbed in her own loss. As if she read his perception, she smiled very slightly, an admission of guilt.

He put out his hand, palm upward, and she slid hers across and gripped his fingers. For several minutes she was silent, blinking back the tears.

'If you can see sense in it,' she said at last, 'please don't tell me now. I don't think I could bear it. I don't want to know a God who could do this. Above all I don't want to be told I should love Him. I don't!'

Several answers rose to his lips, all of them

rational and scriptural, and none of them answering her need.

'It's all right to hurt,' he said instead. 'I don't think God expects any of us to take it calmly.'

'Yes, He does!' she choked on the words. '"Thy will be done"!' She shook her head fiercely. 'Well, I can't say that. It's stupid and senseless and horrible. There's nothing good in it.' She was fighting to make anger conquer the fearful, consuming grief. 'Was anyone else killed?' she demanded. 'The other car? There must have been another car. Father wouldn't simply have driven off the road, whatever anyone says.'

'Nobody else was hurt, and there's no evidence of another car.'

'What do you mean "evidence"?' she said furiously, the colour flooding her face. 'Don't be so pedantic! So obscenely reasonable! If nobody saw it, there wouldn't be!'

He did not argue. She needed to rage at someone, and he let her go on, until they were through the gates and drew up at the front door and she took several long, shuddering breaths, then blew her nose and said she was ready to go inside. She seemed on the edge of saying something more, something gentler, looking steadily at him through tear-brimmed eyes. Then she changed her mind and stepped out of the door as Albert held it for her and gave her his hand to steady her.

★   ★   ★

They ate supper quietly together. Now and again one of them spoke of small, practical things that had to be done, but nobody cared about them. Grief was like a fifth entity in the room, dominating the rest.

Afterwards Joseph went to his father's study again and made certain that all the letters had been written to friends to inform them of John and Alys's deaths, and tell them the time of the funeral. He noticed that Matthew had written the one letter he had considered most important, to Shanley Corcoran, his father's closest friend. They had been at university together — Gonville and Caius. He would be one of the hardest to greet at the church because his pain would be so deep, and the memories were so long, woven into so many of the best days right from the beginning.

And yet there were ways in which the sharing would also help. Perhaps afterwards they would be able to talk about John in particular. It would keep some part of him alive. Corcoran would never become bored with it, never say, 'That's enough now', or let the memory sink into some pleasant region of the past where the sharpness did not matter any more.

About half-past nine the village constable came by. He was a young man of about Matthew's age, but he looked tired and harassed.

'Oi'm sorry,' he said, shaking his head and pursing his lips. 'We'll all miss 'em terrible. I never knew better people.'

'Thank you,' Joseph said sincerely. It was good to hear, even though it twisted the pain. To have

37

said nothing would be like denying they mattered.

'Sunday was a bad day all round,' the constable went on, standing uncomfortably in the hall. 'Did you hear what happened in Sarajevo?'

'No?' Joseph did not care in the slightest, but he did not wish to be rude.

'Some madman shot the Archduke of Austria — and the Duchess too.' The constable shook his head. 'Both dead! Don't suppose you've had time to look at the papers.'

'No.' Joseph was only half-aware of what he was saying. He had not given the newspapers a thought. The rest of the world has seemed removed, not part of their lives. 'I'm sorry.'

The constable shrugged. 'Long way from here, sir. Probably won't mean nothin' for us.'

'No. Thank you for coming, Barker.'

The constable's eyes flickered down. 'I'm real sorry, Mr Reavley. It won't be the same without 'em.'

'Thank you.'

2

The funeral of John and Alys Reavley was held on the morning of 2 July, in the village church at Selborne St Giles. It was another hot, still day and the perfume of the honeysuckle over the lich-gate hung heavy in the air, making one drowsy even before noon. The yew trees in the graveyard looked dusty in the heat.

The cortège came in very slowly, two coffins borne by young men from the village. Most of them had been to school with either Joseph or Matthew, at least for the first few years of their lives, played football with them or spent hours on the edge of the river fishing or generally dreaming away the summers. Now they shuffled one foot in front of the other, careful to look straight ahead and balance the weight without stumbling. The tilted stones of the path had been worn uneven by a thousand years of worshippers, mourners and celebrants from Saxon times to the present day, and the modern world of Victoria's grandson, George V.

Joseph walked behind them, Hannah on his arm, barely keeping her composure. She had purchased a new black dress in Cambridge, and a black straw hat with a veil. She kept her chin very high, but Joseph had a strong feeling that her eyes were almost closed, and she was clinging on to him to guide her. She had hated the days of waiting. Every room she went into reminded her of her loss. The kitchen was worst: it was full of memories, cloths Alys had stitched, plates with the wildflowers painted on them that she had loved, the flat, woven basket she used to collect the dried heads from the roses, the corn dolly she had bought at the Madingley fair. The smell of food brought back memories of her shopping, cooking, especially local things like crumpets and lardy cakes, and, in the winter, hot savoury onion clangers with suet crust. She had liked to buy the blue-veined Double Cottenham cheese, and butter by the yard, instead of the modern weights.

It was the smallest things that hurt Hannah the most, perhaps because they caught her unaware: Lettie arranging flowers in a jug Alys would never have chosen; Horatio the cat sitting in the scullery where Alys would not have permitted him; the fish delivery boy being cheeky and answering back where he would not have dared to before. It was all the first marks of irrevocable change.

Matthew walked with Judith a few steps behind, both of them stiff and staring straight ahead. Judith too had a new black dress with sleeves right down to the backs of her hands, and a skirt so slender it obliged her to walk daintily. She did not like it, but it was actually dramatically becoming to her. Naturally her hat also was veiled.

Inside the church the air was cooler, musty with the smell of old books, stone, and the heavy scent of flowers. Joseph noticed them

40

immediately with a gulp of surprise. The women of the village must have stripped their gardens of every white bloom there was: roses, phlox, old-fashioned pinks, and bowers of daisies of every size, single and double. They were like a pale foam breaking over the ancient carved woodwork towards the altar, gleaming where the sunlight came in through the stained-glass windows. He knew they were for Alys. She had been all the village wanted her to be: modest, loyal, quick to smile, able to keep a secret, proud of her home and pleased to care for it. She was willing to exchange recipes with Mrs Worth, garden cuttings with Tucky Spence, who never stopped talking, patient with Miss Anthony's endless stories about her niece in South Africa.

John had been more difficult for them to understand: a man of intellect far above the usual, who had studied deeply and often travelled abroad. But when he was here his pleasures were simple enough: his family and his garden; old artefacts; watercolour pictures from the last century, which he enjoyed cleaning and reframing. He delighted in a bargain and searched through antique and curio shops, happy to listen to tales of quaint, ordinary people, and always ready to hear or pass on a joke, the longer and shaggier the more he relished it.

Joseph thought of those things as the service began, and he stared at all the long, familiar faces, sad and confused now in their hasty black. He found his throat too tight to sing the hymns.

41

Then it was time for him to speak, just briefly, as representative of the family. He did not wish to preach; it was not the time. Let someone else do that — Hallam Kerr, if he had a mind to. Joseph was here as a son to remember his parents. This was not about praise, it was about love.

It was not easy to keep his voice from breaking, his thoughts in order and his words clear and simple. But this, after all, was his skill. He knew bereavement intimately, and he had explored it over and over in his mind until it had no more black corners for him.

'We are met together in the heart of the village, perhaps the soul of it, to say goodbye for the moment to two of our number who were your friends, our parents — I speak for myself, and for my brother, Matthew, and my sisters, Hannah and Judith.'

He hesitated, struggling to maintain his composure. There was no movement or rustle of whispering among the upturned faces staring at him.

'You all knew them. You met in the street day by day, at the post office, at the shops, over the garden wall. And most of all you met here. They were good people, and we are hurt and diminished by their going.'

He stopped for a moment, then began again. 'We shall miss my mother's patience, her spirit of hope that was never just easy words, never denial of evil or suffering, but the quiet faith that it could be overcome, and the trust in the future that it would be bright. We must not fail her by forgetting what she taught us. We should be grateful for every life that has given us happiness, and gratitude is the treasuring of the gift, the nourishing of it, the use, and then to pass it on bright and whole to others.'

He saw a movement, a nodding, a hundred familiar faces turned towards him, sombre and bruised with the suddenness of grief, each person hurt by his or her own private memory.

'My father was different,' he continued. 'His mind was brilliant, but his heart was simple. He knew how to listen to others without leaping to conclusions. He could tell a longer, funnier, more rambling joke than anyone else I know, and they were never grubby or unkind. For him, unkindness was the great sin. You could be brave and honest, obedient and devout, but if you could not be kind, then you had failed.'

He found himself smiling as he spoke, even though his voice was so thick with tears it was hard to make his words clear. 'He did not care for organised religion. I have known him fall asleep in church, and wake up applauding because he thought for an instant that he was in a theatre. He could not bear intolerance, and he thought those who confessed religious faith could be among the worst at this. But he would have defended with his life St Paul for his words on love: 'Though I speak with the tongues of men and of angels, and have not charity . . . I am nothing.'

'He was not perfect, but he was kind. He was gentle with others' weaknesses. I would gladly labour all my life that you would be able to say the same of me, when I too come to say goodbye.'

He was shaking with relief as he returned to his seat beside Hannah, and felt her hand close over his. But he knew that under her veil she was weeping, and she would not look at him.

Hallam Kerr took the pulpit and thanked Joseph, his words sonorous and sure, but curiously lacking in conviction, as if he too had been swept out of his depth. He continued the service in the familiar way, the words and music woven like a bright thread through the history of life in the village. It was as certain and as rich as the passing seasons, barely changing from year to year down the centuries.

Afterwards Joseph again chose the part that was in a way the most harrowing, standing by the church door and shaking hands with people as they fumbled for words, trying to express their grief and support, and few of them knowing how to. In some way the service had not been enough; something was still unsaid. There was a hunger, a need unmet, and Joseph was aware of it with a hollowness within himself. Now, when he needed it most, his words had lost their consuming power. The last shred of certainty in himself melted in his grasp.

Judith and Hannah stood together, still in the shadow of the arched doorway; Matthew had not yet come out. Joseph moved into the sun to speak to Shanley Corcoran, who waited a few yards away, black-suited, his prematurely white hair like an aureole around his head in the dazzling morning sun. He was not a tall man, and yet the power of his character, the vitality within him, commanded a respect so that no one crowded to him, although most did not even know who he was, let alone the brilliance of his achievements, nor would they have understood had they been told. The word 'scientist' would have had to suffice.

He came forward to Joseph now, holding out both his hands, his face crumpled in grief.

'Joseph,' he said simply.

Joseph found the warmth of touch and the emotion it evoked almost unbearable. The familiarity of such a close friend was overwhelming. He was unable to speak.

It was Orla Corcoran who rescued him. She was a beautiful woman with a dark, exotic face, and her black silk dress with its elegant waist, and flowing jacket to below the hip, and skirt slender beneath, were the perfect complement to her delicate bones.

'Joseph knows our grief, my dear,' she said, laying her gloved hand on her husband's arm. 'We should not struggle to say that for which there can be no words. The village is waiting. This is their turn, and the sooner this duty is accomplished, the sooner the family can go back home and be alone.' She looked at Joseph. 'Perhaps in a few days we may call and visit you for a little longer?'

'Of course,' Joseph answered impulsively. 'Please do. I shall not go back to Cambridge until the end of the week, at least. I don't know about Matthew, we haven't discussed it. We just wanted to get today over.'

45

'Naturally,' Corcoran agreed, letting go of Joseph's hand at last. 'And Hannah will go back to Portsmouth, no doubt.' There was a pucker of anxiety between his brows. 'I assume Archie is at sea, or he would be here now?'

Joseph nodded. 'Yes. But they may grant him compassionate leave when he is next in port.' There was nothing he could do for Hannah. She must now face the ordeal of helping her children recover from the pain of their grandparents' deaths. It was the first big loss in their lives, and they would need her. She had already been away for the larger part of a week.

'Of course, if it's possible,' Corcoran acquiesced, still looking at Joseph with the slight frown, his eyes troubled.

'Why should it not be possible?' Joseph said a trifle sharply. 'For heaven's sake, his wife has just lost both her parents!'

'I know, I know,' Corcoran said gently. 'But Archie is a serving officer. I dare say you have been too busy with your own grief to read much of the world news, and that is perfectly natural. However, this assassination in Sarajevo is very ugly.'

'Yes,' Joseph agreed uncomprehendingly. 'They were shot, weren't they?' Did it really matter now? Why was Corcoran even thinking about it, today, of all days? 'I'm sorry, but . . . '

Corcoran looked a little stooped. It was so slight as to be indefinable, but the shadow in him was more than grief; there was something yet to come that he feared.

'It wasn't a single lunatic with a gun,' he said.

'It's far deeper than that.'

'Is it?' Joseph said without belief or comprehension.

'There were several assassins,' Corcoran said gravely. 'The first did nothing, the second threw a bomb, but the chauffeur saw it coming and managed to speed up and around it.' His lips tightened. 'The man who threw it took some sort of poison, then jumped into the river, but he was pulled out, and survived. The bomb exploded and injured several people. They were taken to hospital.' His voice was very low, as if he did not want the rest of the people standing in the graveyard to hear, even though it must be public knowledge. Perhaps they had not grasped the meaning of it.

'The Archduke continued with his day's agenda,' he went on, ignoring Orla's frown. 'He spoke to people in the town hall, and later he decided to go and visit the injured, but his chauffeur took a wrong turning, and came face to face with the final assassin, who leaped on the running board of the car and shot the Archduke in the neck, and the Duchess in the stomach. Both died within minutes.'

'I'm sorry.' Joseph winced. He could picture it, but the moment he did, their faces changed to those of John and Alys, and the deaths of two Austrian aristocrats a thousand miles away melted into unimportance.

Corcoran's hand gripped his arm again and the strength of him seemed to surge through it. 'It was chaotically done, but it comes from a groundswell of feeling, Joseph. It could lead to

47

an Austro-Serbian war,' he said quietly. 'And then Germany might become involved. The Kaiser reasserted his alliance with Austria-Hungary yesterday.'

It rose to Joseph's lips to argue that it was too unlikely to consider, but he saw in Corcoran's eyes how intensely he meant it. 'Really?' he said with puzzlement. 'Surely it will just be a matter of punishment, reparation, or something? It is an internal matter for the Austro-Hungarian Empire, isn't it?'

Corcoran nodded, withdrawing his hand. 'Perhaps. If there is any sanity in the world, it will.'

'Of course it will!' Orla said firmly. 'It will be miserable for the Serbs, poor creatures, but it doesn't concern us. Don't alarm Joseph with such thoughts, Shanley.' She smiled as she said it. 'We have enough grief of our own without borrowing other people's.'

He was prevented from replying to her by the arrival of Gerald and Mary Allard, close friends of the family whom Joseph had known for many years. Elwyn was their younger son, but their elder, Sebastian, was a pupil of Joseph's, perhaps his best, a young man of remarkable gifts. He seemed to master not only the grammar and the vocabulary of foreign languages, but the music of them, the subtlety of meaning and the flavour of the cultures that had given them birth.

It was Joseph who had seen the promise in him and encouraged him to seek a place at Cambridge to study ancient languages, not only Biblical but the great classics of culture as well.

48

Sebastian had grasped his opportunity, worked with zeal and a remarkable self-discipline for so young a man, and became first one of the brightest of the students, taking first-class honours, and now was doing post-graduate studies, before moving on, Joseph hoped, to a golden career as a scholar and philosopher, perhaps even a poet.

Mary caught Joseph's eye and smiled at him, her face full of pity.

Gerald came forward. He was a pleasant, ordinary-seeming man, fair-haired, good-looking in a benign, undistinguished way. Brief introductions were made to the Corcorans, who then excused themselves.

'So sorry,' Gerald murmured, shaking his head. 'So sorry.'

'Thank you,' Joseph accepted, wishing there were something sensible to say, and longing to escape.

'Elwyn is here, of course.' Mary indicated very slightly over her shoulder where Elwyn Allard was talking to Pettigrew, the lawyer, and trying to escape to join his contemporaries. 'But unfortunately Sebastian had to be in London,' she went on. 'A prior commitment he could not break.' She was thin, with fierce, striking features, dark hair and a fine olive complexion. 'But I am sure you know how deeply he feels.'

Gerald cleared his throat as if to say something — from the shadow in his eyes, possibly a disagreement — but he changed his mind.

Joseph thanked them again, and excused himself to speak to someone else.

The occasion seemed to stretch interminably, the kindness, the grief, the awkwardness, but eventually it was over. He saw Mrs Appleton, sombre and pale-faced, say goodbye to the vicar and start back to the house. Everything was already prepared to receive their closest friends. There would be nothing for the staff to do but take the muslin cloths off the food already laid out on the tables. Lettie and Reginald had been given time off also, but they would both be back to help with the clearing-away.

The house was a mere six hundred yards from the church, and people straggled slowly under the lich-gate, along the road through the village in the quiet sunlight, and turned right towards the Reavley home. They all knew each other and were intimately concerned in each other's lives. They had walked to christenings, weddings and funerals along these quiet roads, quarrelled and befriended, laughed together, gossiped and interfered for better or worse.

Now they grieved, and few needed to find words for it.

Joseph and Hannah welcomed them at the front door. Matthew and Judith had already gone inside, she to the drawing room, he presumably to fetch the wine and pour it.

The last person was ushered in and Joseph turned to follow. He was crossing the hall when Matthew came out of John's study ahead of him, his face puckered with concern.

'Joseph, have you been in here this morning?'

'The study? No. Why? Have you lost something?'

'No. I haven't been in since last night, until just now.'

Had he looked any less concerned Joseph would have been impatient with him, but there was an anxiety in his face that held his attention. 'If you haven't lost anything, what's the matter?' he asked.

'I was the last one out of the house this morning,' Matthew replied, keeping his voice very low so it would not carry to anyone in the dining room, 'after Mrs Appleton, and she didn't come back — she was at the funeral all the time.'

'Of course she was!'

'Someone's been in here,' Matthew answered quietly, but with no hesitation or lift of question in his voice. 'I know exactly where I left everything. It's the papers. They're all on the square, and I left some of them poking out a fraction, to mark my place.'

'Horatio?' Joseph said, thinking of the cat.

'Door was closed,' Matthew answered.

'Mrs Appleton must have — ' Joseph began. Then, seeing the gravity in Matthew's eyes, he stopped. 'What are you saying?'

'Someone was in here while we were all at the funeral,' Matthew replied. 'No one would have noticed Henry barking, and he was shut in the garden room. I can't see anything gone . . . and don't tell me it was a sneak thief. I locked up myself, and I didn't miss the back door. And a thief wouldn't go through Father's papers, he'd take the silver and the ornaments that are easy to move. The silver-rimmed crystal bud vase is still on the mantelpiece, and the snuff boxes are on

51

the table, not to mention the Bonington, which is quite small enough to be carried.'

Joseph's mind raced, wild ideas falling over each other, but before he could put words to any of them, Hannah came out of the dining room. She looked from one to the other of them.

'What's wrong?' she said quickly.

'Matthew's mislaid something, that's all,' Joseph replied. 'I'll see if I can help him find it. I'll be in in a moment.'

'Does it matter now?' There was an edge to her voice, close to breaking. 'For heaven's sake, come and speak to people! They're expecting you! You can't leave me there alone! It's horrible!'

'I'd be happier to look first,' Matthew answered her before Joseph found the words. His face was miserable and stubborn. 'Have you been upstairs since you came home?'

She was incredulous, her eyes wide. 'No, of course I haven't! We have half the village in the house as our guests, or haven't you noticed?'

Matthew glanced at Joseph, then back at Hannah. 'It matters,' he said quietly. 'I'm sorry. I'll be down in a minute. Joe?' He took a deep breath, walked to the foot of the stairs, and went up.

Joseph followed after him, leaving Hannah standing in the hall, fuming. When he reached the landing, Matthew was in the doorway to their parents' bedroom, staring around as if to memorise every article there, every line and shadow, the bright bars of light through the window across the floorboards and the carpet. It was so achingly familiar, exactly as it had been as long as he could remember: the dark oak tallboy with his father's brushes and the leather box Alys had given him for cufflinks and collar studs, her dressing table with the oval mirror on a stand, which needed a little piece of paper wedged to keep it at the right angle, the cut-glass trays and bowls for hairpins, powder, combs; the wardrobe with the round hat box on top.

He had stood here to tell his mother that he was going to leave medicine, because he could not bear the helplessness he felt in the face of pain he could do nothing to ease, knowing how disappointed his father would be. John had wanted it so fiercely. He had never explained why. He would say very little, but he would not understand, and his silence would hurt more than accusation or demand for explanations.

And Joseph had come here later to tell Alys that he was going to marry Eleanor. That had been a winter day, rain spattering the window. She had been putting up her hair after changing for dinner. She always had beautiful hair . . .

He forced his mind to the present.

'Is there anything gone?' he said aloud.

'I don't think so.' Matthew did not move to go in yet. 'But there might be, because it's different somehow.'

'Are you certain?' It was a stupid question because he knew Matthew was not certain. He simply wanted to deny the reality settling more and more firmly in his mind with each second. 'I don't see anything,' he added.

'Wait a minute.' Matthew put up his hand as if

53

to stop Joseph from passing him, although Joseph had not moved. 'There is something . . . I just can't put my finger on it. It's . . . tidy. It doesn't look as if someone just left it.'

'Mrs Appleton — ' Joseph began.

'No. She won't come in here yet. It still feels like an intrusion, as if she were doing it behind Mother's back.'

'Judith? Or Hannah?'

'No.' He sounded quite certain. 'Hannah might look, but she wouldn't touch anything, not yet. And Judith won't come in here at all. At least . . . I'll ask, but I don't think so.' He drew in a deep breath. 'It's the pillows. That's not how Mother had them, and no one here would rearrange them that way.'

'Isn't that how most people have them?' Joseph looked over at the big bed with its handmade coverlet and the matching pillow-shams just touching. It all looked completely usual, like anyone's room. Then a tiny memory prickled as he deliberately brought back the image of telling his mother that Eleanor was expecting their first child. She had been so happy. He pictured her face, and the bed behind her, with the pillows at an angle, one overlapping the other. It looked comfortable, casual, not formal like this.

'Someone has been in here,' he agreed, his heart beating so hard he felt out of breath. 'They must have searched the house while we were all at the funeral.' His pulse was knocking in his ears. 'For the document — just as we did?'

'Yes,' Matthew replied. 'Which means it's real.

Father was right — he really did have something.' His voice was bright and hard, shaking a little, as if he were expecting to be contradicted. 'And they didn't get it from him.'

Joseph swallowed, aware of all the multitude of meaning that lay beyond that statement. He took it a step further. 'They still didn't, because it wasn't here. We searched everywhere. So where is it?'

'I don't know!' Matthew looked oddly blank. Now his mind was racing past his words, with excitement, vindication. 'I don't know what he did with it, but they don't have it, or they wouldn't be still searching, and neither do we.'

'Who are 'they'?' Joseph demanded.

Matthew looked back at him, puzzled, still charged with emotion. 'I have no idea. I've told you everything Father said to me.'

The sound of voices drifted up the stairs. Somewhere towards the kitchen a door closed with a bang. He and Matthew should be down with the guests as well. It was unfair to leave Judith and Hannah to do all the receiving, the thanking, the accepting of condolences. He half turned.

'Joe!'

He looked back. Matthew was staring at him, his eyes dark and fixed, his face gaunt in spite of the high cheekbones so like his own.

'It isn't only what happened to the document, and what it's about,' he said quietly, as if he were concerned someone in the hall below could overhear them. 'It's who it implicates. Where did Father get it? Obviously whoever they are, they

55

know he had it, or they wouldn't have been here searching.' He let the words hang between them, his hand white-knuckled on the doorframe.

The thought came to Joseph only slowly. It was too vast and too ugly to recognise at once. His mouth was dry. 'Was it an accident?'

Matthew did not move; he seemed scarcely to be breathing. 'I don't know. If the document was all he said it was, and whoever it implicated learned he was coming to me with it, then probably not.'

There was a footstep at the bottom of the stairs.

Joseph swivelled around. Hannah was standing with her hand on the newel, her face white, struggling to keep her composure.

'What's the matter?' she said abruptly. 'People are beginning to ask where you are! You've got to talk to them; you can't just run away. We all feel like — '

'We're not,' Joseph cut across her, beginning to come down the stairs. There was no point in frightening her with the truth, certainly not now. 'Matthew lost something, but he's remembered where he put it.'

'You must speak to people,' she said as he reached her. 'They'll expect us all to. You don't live here any more but they were Mother's neighbours, and they loved her.'

He slipped his arm lightly around her shoulder. 'Yes, of course they did. I know that.'

She smiled, but there was still anger and frustration in her face, and too much pain to be held within. Today she had stepped into her

56

mother's shoes, and she hated everything that it meant.

★   ★   ★

Joseph did not see Matthew alone again until just before dinner. Joseph took Henry into the garden, in the waning light, watching it fade and deepen to gold on the tops of the trees. He stared upwards at the massed starlings that swirled like dry leaves, high and wide across the luminous sky, so many dark flecks, storm-tossed on an unseen wind.

He did not hear Matthew come silently over the grass behind him, and was startled when the dog turned, tail wagging.

'I'm going to take Hannah to the station tomorrow afternoon,' Matthew said. 'She'll catch the three fifteen. That'll get her to Portsmouth comfortably before it's dark. There's a good connection.'

'I suppose I should get back to Cambridge,' Joseph responded. 'There's nothing else to do here. Pettigrew will call us if he needs anything. Judith's going to stay on in the house. I expect she told you. Anyway, Mrs Appleton's got to have someone to look after.' He said the last part wryly. He was concerned for Judith, as John and Alys had been. She showed no inclination to settle to anything, and seemed to be largely wasting her time. Now that her parents were no longer here, circumstances would force her to address her own future, but it was too early now to say so to her.

'How long can she run the house on the finances there are before the will is probated?' Matthew asked, pushing his hands into his pockets and following Joseph's gaze across the fields to the copse outlined against the sky.

They were both avoiding saying what they really thought: how would she deal with the hurt; who would she rebel against now that Alys was not here; who would see that she did not let her wild side run out of control until she hurt herself irretrievably? How well did they know each other, to begin the love, the patience, the guiding that suddenly was their responsibility?

It was too soon, all much too soon. None of them was ready for it yet.

'From what Pettigrew said, about a year,' Joseph replied. 'More, if necessary. But she needs to do something other than spend time with her friends, and drive around the countryside in that car of hers. I don't know if Father had any idea where she goes, or how fast!'

'Of course he knew!' Matthew retorted. 'Actually he was rather proud of her skill . . . and the fact that she is a better mechanic than Albert. I'll wager she'll use some of her inheritance to buy a new car,' he added with a shrug. 'Faster and smarter than the Model T. Just as long as she doesn't go for a racer!'

Joseph held out his hand. 'What will you bet on it?'

'Nothing I can't afford to lose!' Matthew responded drily. 'I don't suppose we can stop her?'

'How?' Joseph asked. 'She's twenty-three.

58

She'll do what she wants.'

'She always did what she wanted!' Matthew retorted. 'Just as long as she understands the realities! The financial ones, I mean.' It was not what he meant, and both of them knew it. It was about far more than money. She needed purpose, something to manage grief.

Joseph raised his eyebrows. 'Is that a backwards way of saying it is my responsibility to tell her that?' Of course it was his! He was the eldest, the one to take their father's place, quite apart from the fact that he lived in Cambridge, only three or four miles away, and Matthew was in London. He resented it because he was unprepared. There was a well of anger inside him he dared not even touch, a hurt that frightened him.

Matthew was grinning at him. 'That's right!' he agreed. Then his smile faded and the darkness in him came through. 'But there's something we have to do before you go. We should have done it before.'

Joseph knew what he was going to say the instant before he did.

'The accident.' Matthew used the word loosely. Half of his face was like bronze in the dying light, the other too shadowed to see. 'I don't know if we can tell anything now, but we need to try. There's been no rain since it happened. Actually it's the best summer I can remember. Shearing remarked on it too when he telephoned.'

'Who's Shearing?' Joseph was trying to place a family friend, someone calling with apologies for

59

not being here. He ran his hand gently over the dog's head.

'Calder Shearing,' Matthew replied. 'My boss at Intelligence. Just condolences, and of course he needs to know when I'll be back.'

Joseph looked at him again. 'And when will you?'

Matthew's eyes were steady. 'I'll drive back on Sunday. We can't stay here indefinitely. We all have to go on, and the longer we leave it, the harder it will be.'

But Joseph's thoughts were back on the accident on the Hauxton Road. The idea of such violence being deliberate was horrible. Joseph could not bear to imagine someone planning and carrying out the murder of his parents. Yet the alternative was that John Reavley's sharp and logical mind had slipped out of his control and sent him running from a threat that was not real, dreaming up horrors. That was worse. He refused to believe it.

'And if it wasn't an accident?'

Matthew stared at the last light as the sun kindled fire in the clouds on the horizon, vermilion and amber, tree shadows elongated across the fields. The smell of the twilight wind was heavy with hay, dry earth and the sweetness of mown grass. It was almost harvest time. There were a handful of scarlet poppies like a graze of blood through the darkening gold. The hawthorn petals were all blown from the hedgerows and in a few months there would be berries.

'I don't know,' Matthew answered. 'That's the thing! There's nobody to take it to, because we have no idea who to trust. Father didn't trust the police with this, or he wouldn't have been bringing the information to London. But I still have to look at the scene. Don't you?'

Joseph thought for a moment. 'Yes,' he admitted. 'Yes. I have to know.'

★ ★ ★

The following afternoon, 3 July, Matthew and Joseph stopped by the police station at Great Shelford again and asked if they could be shown on the map exactly where the accident had happened. Reluctantly, the sergeant told them.

'You don't want to go looking at that,' he said sadly. 'Course you want to understand, but there ain't nothing to see. Weren't no one else there, no brangle, no buck-fisted young feller drunk too much an' going faster than he ought. Let it go, sir, that's moi advoice.'

'Thank you,' Matthew replied with a forced smile. 'Just like to see it. There, you said?' He put his finger on the map.

'That's right, sir. Going south.'

'Had accidents there before?'

'Not as Oi know of, sir.' The sergeant frowned. 'Can't say what happened. But then sometimes that's just how it is. Them Lanchesters is good cars. Get up quite a bit of speed with them. Fifty miles an hour, Oi shouldn't wonder. A sudden puncture could send you off the road. Would do anyone.'

'Thank you,' Joseph said briskly. He wanted to end this and face looking at the scene, get it over

61

with. He dreaded it. Whatever they found, his mind would create a picture of what had happened there. The reality of it was the same, regardless of the cause.

He turned away and walked out of the police station into the humid air. Clouds were massing in the west and there were tiny flies settling on his skin, black pinpricks, thunder flies.

He walked to the car and climbed in, waiting for Matthew to follow.

They drove west through Little Shelford through Hauxton and on towards the London road, then turned north to the mill bridge. It was only a matter of three or four miles altogether. Matthew held his foot on the accelerator, trying to race the storm. He did not bother to explain; Joseph understood.

It was only a matter of minutes before they were over the bridge. Matthew was obliged to brake with more force than he had intended in order not to overshoot the place on the map. He pulled in to the side of the road, sending a spray of gravel up from the tyres.

'Sorry,' he said absently. 'We'd better hurry. It's going to rain any minute.' He swung out and left Joseph to go after him.

It was only twenty yards, and he could see already the long gouge out of the grass where the car had ploughed off the paved road, over the verge and the wide margin, crushing the wild foxgloves and the broom plants. It had torn up a sapling as well, and scattered a few stones before crashing into a clump of birch trees, scarring the trunks and tearing off a hanging branch, which lay a few yards further on, its leaves beginning to wither.

Matthew stood beside the broom bushes, staring.

Joseph caught up with him and stopped. Suddenly he felt foolish and more vulnerable with every moment. The police sergeant was right: they should not have come here. It would have been far better to leave the scene in the imagination. Now he could never forget it.

There was a low rumble of thunder around the western horizon, like the warning growl of some great beast beyond the trees and the breathless fields.

'We can't learn anything from it,' Joseph said aloud. 'The car came off the road. We won't ever know why.'

Matthew ignored him, still staring at the broken wake of the crash.

Joseph followed his gaze. At least death must have been quick, almost instantaneous, a moment of terror as they realised they were out of control, a sense of insane, destructive speed, and then perhaps the sound of tearing metal and pain — then nothing. All gone in seconds, less time than it took to imagine it.

Matthew turned and walked back to the road, beside the churned-up wake, careful to avoid stepping on it — not that there was anything more than broken plants. The ground was too dry for wheel tracks.

Joseph was on the edge of repeating that there was nothing to see, when he realised that Matthew had stopped and was staring at the ground. 'What is it?' he said sharply. 'What have you found?'

'The car was weaving,' Matthew answered. 'Look there!' He pointed to the edge of the road where ten yards further on, there was another clump of foxgloves mown down. 'That's where it came off the road first,' he said. 'He tried to get it back on again, but he couldn't. A puncture wouldn't do that, not that way. I've had one, I know.'

'It was more than one,' Joseph reminded him. 'All the tyres were ripped.'

'Then there was something on the road that caused it,' Matthew said with conviction. 'The possibility of getting four spontaneous punctures at the same moment isn't even worth considering.' He started to run until he was level with the first broken foxgloves, then he slowed and began to search the ground.

Joseph followed after him, looking from right to left and back again, and then beyond. It was he who first saw the tiny scratches on the tarmacadam surface. He glanced sideways and saw another less than a foot away, and then another beyond that.

'Matthew!'

'Yes, I see them.' Matthew reached the line and bent to his knees. Once he had found them it was easy to trace the marks right across the road, each less than the width of a car tyre from the next. They were only slight scars, except in two places about axle-width apart, where they were deeper, actual gouges in the surface. In the heat of this summer, day after day of sun, the tar would have been softer than usual, more easily marked. In winter there might have been nothing.

'What were they?' Joseph asked, racking his mind for what could have torn tyres on a moving car and left this track behind, and yet not be here now, nor have been found embedded in the tyres themselves. Except that, of course, no one had been looking for such things.

Matthew stood up, his face white. 'It can't be nails,' he said. 'How could you put nails on a road to stay point upwards, and catch only the car you wanted, and not leave them in the tyres for police to find if they looked?'

'Wait for them,' Joseph answered, his heart knocking in his chest so violently his body shook. A cold, hurting rage engulfed him that anyone could cold-bloodedly place such a weapon across the road, then crouch out of sight, waiting for a car with people in it, and watch it crash. He could hardly breathe as he imagined them walk over to the wreck, ignoring the broken and bleeding bodies, perhaps still alive, and search for a document. And when they did not find it, they left, simply went away, carefully taking with them whatever had caused the wreck.

He hated them, and for a moment the heat of his hatred poured over his skin in sweat. Then he found himself shivering uncontrollably, even though the air was hot and still, damp on the skin. More thunder flies settled on his face and hands.

Matthew had gone back to the side of the

65

road, but opposite from the place where the car had swerved off. On this side there was a deeper ditch, thick with primrose leaves. There was a thin, straight line where they were torn, as if something sharp had ripped through them right from the tarmacadam edge all the way across to the ditch and beyond.

Dizzily, his vision blurred except for a crystal clarity at the centre, Joseph saw a birch sapling next to the hedge. A frayed end of rope hung from the trunk, biting into the bark about a foot from the ground. He could imagine the force that had caused that — he could see it — the yellow Lanchester with John Reavley at the wheel and Alys beside him, possibly at something like fifty miles an hour, striking it . . . striking what?

He turned to Matthew, willing him to deny it, wipe away what he imagined.

'Caltrops,' Matthew said softly, shaking his head as if he could rid himself of the idea.

'Caltrops?' Joseph asked, puzzled.

'Twists of iron prong,' Matthew replied, hooking his fingers together to demonstrate. 'Like the things they put in barbed wire, only bigger. They used them in the Middle Ages to bring down knights on horseback.'

Thunder rumbled again, closer to them. The air was almost too clammy to breathe.

'On a rope,' Matthew went on. He did not look at Joseph, as if he could not bear to. 'They must have waited here until they heard the car coming, then when they knew it was the Lanchester, sprinted across the road to the far side, and pulled it tight.' He bowed his head for a moment. 'Even if Father saw it,' he said hoarsely, 'there would be no way to avoid it.' He hesitated a moment, taking a deep breath. 'Then afterwards they cut the rope, hacked it by the look of it, and took the whole thing away with them.'

It was all clear. Joseph said nothing. It was hideously real now, no more possibility of doubt. John and Alys Reavley had been murdered — he, to silence him and retrieve the document; she, because she happened to be with him. It was brutal, monstrous! Pain ran through him like fire inside his head. He could see the terror in his mother's face, his father struggling desperately to control the car, and knowing he couldn't, the physical destruction, the helplessness. Had they had time to know it was death and they could do nothing for each other, not even time for a touch, a word?

And he could do nothing. It was over, complete, beyond his reach. There was nothing left but blind, bright red fury. They would find whoever had done this. It was his father, his mother, it had happened to. People who were precious and good had been destroyed, taken from him. Who had done it? What kind of people — and why? They must find them, stop them. This must never happen again.

He would do what he should. He would be kind, obedient, honourable — but never hurt like this again. He could not endure it.

'Is Judith safe?' he said abruptly. 'What if they go back to the house?' The thought of having to tell her the truth was ugly, but how could they avoid it?

'They won't go back.' Matthew straightened up, unsteadily. 'They know the document's not there. But where the hell is it? I'm damned if I know!' His voice was breaking, threatening to go out of control. He stared at Joseph, willing him to help, to find an answer where he could not.

Thunder cracked across the sky above them and the first heavy spots of rain fell, splashing large and warm on them, and on the road.

Joseph seized Matthew's arm and they turned and ran to the car, sprinting the last few paces and scrambling in, struggling with the roof as the heavens opened and torrential rain swirled across the fields and hedges, blinding the windscreen and drumming on the metal of the car body. Lightning blazed and vanished.

Matthew started the engine, and it was a relief to hear it roar to life. He put the car into gear and inched out on to the swimming road. Neither of the brothers spoke.

When the cloudburst had passed and they could open the windows, the air was filled with the perfume of fresh rain on parched earth. It was a fragrance like no other, so sharp and clean they could hardly draw enough of it. The sun returned, gleaming on wet roads and dripping hedges, every leaf bright.

'What did Father say, exactly?' Joseph asked when at last he had control of himself enough to speak almost levelly.

Matthew kept his eyes ahead on the road. 'He

68

said he was bringing the document, but since they didn't find it, and they must have looked, and so did we, the only alternative seems to be that he hid it somewhere.' He was almost calm, addressing the problem as though it were an intellectual one he had to solve, and the passion of the reality had never existed.

'We have to tell Judith,' Joseph said, watching his brother's face for his reaction. 'Apart from keeping the house locked if she's ever in it alone, she has a right to know. And Hannah . . . but perhaps not yet.'

Matthew was silent. There was another flare of lightning far away, and then thunder off in the distance to the south.

Joseph was about to repeat what he had said when Matthew spoke again.

'I suppose we must, but let me do it.'

Joseph did not argue. If Matthew imagined Judith would allow him to evade any of the issues, then he did not know his sister as well as Joseph did.

★   ★   ★

When they reached St Giles it started to rain again. They were both glad to leave the car and use getting soaked as an excuse to avoid immediate conversation. It was emotional enough saying goodbye to Hannah as Albert put her luggage into the Ford. She decided in the end that she did not want anyone to go to the station with her.

'I'd rather not!' she said quickly. 'If I'm going

to burst into tears, at least let me do it here, not on the platform!'

No one argued with her. Perhaps they preferred it this way too. She hugged each of them, not able to find words, or a steady voice to say anything. Then holding her head so high she all but tripped on the step, she followed Albert out to the car. Joseph, Matthew and Judith stood in the doorway watching her until the car was out of sight, and Joseph walked over the grass to close the gate.

* * *

'I know what you're going to say,' Judith retorted defensively when they were sitting in the dining room after dinner, Henry asleep on the floor. It was barely dark outside and clear again, the storm long since passed.

'I don't think you do.' Matthew set his coffee cup down and regarded her gravely.

She looked at Joseph. 'Shouldn't you be the one doing this?' she challenged, anger hard in her voice and her eyes. 'Why aren't you telling me what to do? Haven't you the stomach for it? Or do you know it's a waste of time? You're a priest! It's cowardly not even to try! Father always tried!'

It was an accusation that he was not Father, not wise enough, not patient or persistent enough. He knew it already, with a deep ache inside him and, as with her, an anger, because no one had equipped him to do this. John Reavley had gone leaving a task half done, and no one to

70

replace him, as if he did not care.

'Judith — ' Matthew began.

'I know!' She swung round to face him, cutting across his words. 'The house is Joseph's, but I can live here as long as he doesn't need it, and he doesn't. We've already discussed that. But I can't go on wasting my time. That's a condition. I've either got to get married, or find something useful to do, preferably something that pays me enough at least to feed and clothe myself.' Her eyes were red-rimmed, full of tears. 'Why haven't you the courage to say that to me? Father would have! And I don't need a gardener, a cook, a manservant and a housemaid to look after me.' She stared at him furiously. 'I worked that out for myself.' She flicked a glance sideways at Joseph, contempt in it.

Joseph felt the sting, but he had no defence. It was true.

'Actually I wasn't going to say anything of the sort!' Matthew said to her tartly. 'Joseph told me you were perfectly aware of the situation. I was going to tell you why Father was coming to see me on the day he was killed, and what we have learned since then. I would rather have protected you from it, but I don't think we can afford to do that, and Joseph thinks you have a right to know anyway.'

Apology flashed across her face, then fear. She bit her lip. 'Know what?' she said huskily.

Briefly Matthew told her about John Reavley's call on the telephone. 'And when we were at the funeral, someone searched the house,' he

71

finished. 'That is why Joseph and I were late into the dining room.'

'Well, where is it?' she said, looking at one, then the other, her anger added to by confusion and the beginning of sick, urgent fear.

'We don't know,' Matthew answered. 'We've looked everywhere we can think of. I even tried the laundry, the gun room and the apple shed this morning, but we haven't found anything.'

'Then who has it?' She turned to Joseph. 'It is real, isn't it?'

It was a question he was not prepared to face; it challenged too much of the belief in his father, and he refused to be without that. 'Yes, it's real,' he said with biting certainty. He saw the doubt in her eyes, her struggle to believe and understand. 'We went to the stretch of road where it happened,' he said in harsh, measured words, like incisions. 'We saw where the car began to swerve, and where it finally ploughed over the verge and into the trees . . . '

Matthew started to speak, and stopped, blinking rapidly. He turned away.

Judith stared at Joseph, waiting for him to justify what he was telling her.

'Once we understood what had happened, it was quite clear,' Joseph continued. 'Someone had used a kind of barb, tied to a rope — the end of it was still knotted around a sapling trunk — and stretched them across the road deliberately. The marks were there in the tarmacadam.'

He saw the incredulity in her face. 'But that's murder!' she exclaimed.

72

'Yes, it is.'

She started to shake her head, and he thought for a moment she was not going to get her breath. He put out his hand and she gripped on to it so hard it bruised the flesh.

'What are you going to do?' she said. 'You are going to do something, aren't you?'

'Of course!' Matthew jerked up his head. 'Of course we are. But we don't know where to start yet. We can't find the document, and we don't know what's in it.'

'Where did Father get it from?' she said, trying to steady her voice and sound in control. 'They would know what it was about.'

Matthew gave a little gesture of helplessness. 'No idea! It could be almost anything: government corruption, a financial scandal — even a royal scandal, for that matter. It might be political or diplomatic. It could be some totally dishonourable solution to the Irish Question.'

'There is no solution to the Irish Question, honourable or otherwise,' she replied with an edge of hysteria to her voice. 'But Father still kept up with quite a few of his old parliamentary colleagues. Maybe one of them gave it to him.'

Matthew leaned forward a little. 'Did he? Do you know anyone he was in touch with recently? He'd only had the document a few hours when he called me.'

'Are you certain?' Joseph asked. 'If you are, then that would mean he got it on the Saturday before he died. But if he thought about it a while before calling you, it could have been

Friday, or even Thursday.'

'Let's start with Saturday,' Matthew directed, looking back to Judith. 'Do you know what he did on Saturday? Was he here? Did he go out, or anyone come to see him?'

'I don't know,' she said miserably. 'I was in and out myself. I can hardly remember now. Albert was supposed to be doing something in the orchard. The only one who would know would be . . . Mother.' She swallowed and took a ragged breath. She was still clinging on to Joseph's hand, her knuckles white with the strength of her grip. 'But you can't let it go! You're going to do something? If you aren't, then I will! They can't get away with it!'

'Yes, of course I am,' Matthew assured her. 'Nobody's going to get away with it! But Father said it was a conspiracy, that means there are several people involved, and we have no idea who.'

'But — ' she started, then stopped. Her voice dropped very low. 'I was going to say it couldn't be anyone we know, but that's not necessarily true, is it? The document had to have been given to Father by someone who trusted him, but he could have been killed by someone who knew them both.'

He did not answer.

Her rage and misery exploded. 'You are in the Secret Intelligence Service! Isn't this the sort of thing you do? What damn use are you if you can't catch the people who killed our family?' She glared at Joseph. 'And if you tell me to forgive them I swear to God I'll hit you!'

74

'You won't have to,' he promised. 'I wouldn't tell you to do something I can't do myself.'

She searched his face as if seeing him more clearly than ever before. 'I've never heard you say that in the past, no matter how hard it's been.' She leaned forward and buried her head in his shoulder. 'Joe! What's happening to us? How can this be?'

He put his arms around her. 'I don't know,' he admitted. 'I don't know.'

Matthew rubbed his eyes, pushing his hair back savagely. 'Of course I'm going to do something!' he repeated. 'That's why Father was bringing the document to me.' There was pride and anger in his voice. His face was pinched with loss of what was irretrievable now. He was still struggling to be reasonable. 'If it were something the police could deal with he'd have taken it to them.' He looked at Joseph. 'We dare not trust anyone,' he warned them both. 'Judith, you must make sure the house is locked every night, and any time you and the servants are all out — just as a precaution. I don't think they'll come back, because they've already looked here, and they know we haven't got it. But if you'd rather go and stay — '

'With a friend? No, I wouldn't!' she said quickly.

'Judith — '

'If I change my mind, I'll go to the Mannings,' she snapped. 'I'll say I'm lonely. They'll understand. I promise! Just don't push me, I'll do what I want.'

'There's a novelty!' Matthew said with a

sudden, bleary smile, as if he needed to break the taut thread of emotion.

She looked at him sharply, then her face softened and her eyes filled with tears.

'I'll find them,' he promised, his voice choking. 'Not only because they killed Mother and Father, but to stop them doing whatever it was in the document — if we can.'

'I'm glad you said 'we',' she answered his smile now. 'Tell me what I can do.'

'When there is anything, I will,' he said. 'I promise. But call me if there's anything at all! Or Joseph — just to talk if you want. You must do that!'

'Stop telling me what to do!' But there was relief in her voice. A shred of safety had returned, something familiar, even if it was a restriction to fight against. 'But of course I will.' She reached out to touch him. 'Thank you.'

3

Joseph found his first day back at St John's even more difficult than he had anticipated. The ancient beauty of the buildings, mellow brick with castellated front and stone-trimmed windows, soothed his mind. Its calm was indestructible, its dignity timeless. His rooms closed around him like well-fitting armour. He looked with pleasure at the light reflected unevenly on the old glass of the bookcases, knowing intimately every volume within, the thoughts and dreams of great men down the ages. On the wall between the windows overlooking the quadrangle were paintings of Florence and Verona. He remembered choosing them to keep in his heart those streets worn smooth by the footsteps of his heroes. And of course there was the bust of Dante on the shelf, that genius of poetry, imagination, the art of story, and above all, the understanding of the nature of good and evil.

Even Bertie, the college cat, lean, and black as soot, slid in through the window and welcomed him, deigning to accept a small piece of chocolate.

Joseph had been away for long enough for an amount of work to have collected, and the concentration needed to catch up was also a kind of healing. The languages of the Bible were subtle and different from modern speech. Their very nature necessitated that they refer to everyday things common to all mankind: seed time and harvest; the water of physical and spiritual life; slow-walking men in sandals who knew their sheep by name. The rhythms had time to repeat themselves and let the meaning sink deep into the mind; the flavour and the music of it removed him from the present, and so from his own reality.

It was friends who brought him the sharp reminder of loss. He saw the sympathy in their eyes, the uncertainty whether to speak of it or not, what to say that was not clumsy. Every student seemed to know at least of the deaths, if not the details.

The Master, Aidan Thyer, had been very considerate, asking Joseph if he were sure he were ready to come back so soon. He was valued, of course, and irreplaceable, but nevertheless he must take more time if he needed it.

Joseph answered him that he did not. Everything had been done that was required, and his responsibilities to work were a blessing, not a burden. He thanked him, and promised to take his first tutorial the following morning.

It was difficult picking up the threads after an absence of over a week, and it required all his effort of mind on the subject to make an acceptable job of it. He was exhausted by the end of the day, and happy after dinner to leave the dining hall, the stained-glass windows scattered with the coats of arms of benefactors dating back to the early 1500s, the magnificent timbered ceiling, with its carved hammer beams touched with gold, the oak-panelled walls carved in linen-fold, and, above all, its chattering, well-meaning people. He longed to escape towards the river.

He started across the narrow arch of the Bridge of Sighs with its stone fretwork like frozen lace, a windowed passageway to the fields beyond. He would walk across the smooth grass of the 'Backs' stretching all the way from the Magdalene Bridge past St John's, Trinity, Gonville and Caius, Clare, King's College Chapel towards Queens' and the Mathematical Bridge. Perhaps he would go as far as the Mill Pond beyond, and over the Causeway to Lammas Land. It was still warm. The long, slow sunset and twilight would last another hour and a half yet, perhaps more.

He was on the slow rise of the bridge, glancing out through the open lattice at the reflections on the water below, when he heard footsteps behind him. He turned to see a young man in his early twenties. His face was beautiful, strong-boned, clear-eyed, his brown hair bleached gold across the top by the long summer.

'Sebastian!' Joseph said with pleasure.

'Dr Reavley! I . . . ' Sebastian Allard stopped, his fair skin a little flushed with consciousness of his inadequacy to say anything that matched the situation, and perhaps also that he had missed the funeral. 'I'm so sorry. I can't tell you how badly I feel.'

'You don't have to,' Joseph said quickly. 'I would far rather talk about something else.'

Sebastian hesitated, indecision clear in his half-turned shoulder.

Joseph did not want to press him, yet he felt Sebastian had something to say, and he could not rebuff him. Their families had lived in neighbouring villages for years, and it was Joseph who had seen the promise in young Sebastian and encouraged him to pursue it. He had been his mentor for the last year while they had both been at St John's. It had become one of those friendships that blossomed so naturally he could not believe there was ever a possibility it would not have happened.

'I'm going for a walk along the Backs,' Joseph said. 'If you want to join me, you are welcome.' He smiled and began to turn away, so as not to place an obligation on the younger man, as if it were a request.

There were a few moments of silence, then he heard the footsteps quickly and lightly on the bridge after him, and he and Sebastian emerged into the sunlight, almost side by side. The air was still warm and the smell of cut grass drifted on the slight breeze. The river was flat calm, barely disturbed by three or four punts along the stretch past St John's and Trinity. In the nearest one a young man in grey flannel trousers and a white shirt stood leaning on the pole with effortless grace, his back to the sun, casting his features into shadow and making an aureole around his head.

A girl with red hair sat in the back looking up at him and laughing. Her muslin dress looked primrose-coloured in the fading glow, but in the daylight it could have been ivory, or even white. Her skin was amber where she had defied convention and allowed the long, hot season to touch her with its fire. She was eating from a basket of cherries, and dropping the stones into the water one by one.

The young man waved and called out a greeting.

Joseph waved back, and Sebastian answered as well.

'He's a good fellow,' Sebastian said a moment later. 'He's at Caius, reading physics. All terribly practical.' He sounded as if he were about to say something more, then he pushed his hands into his pockets and walked silently on the grass.

Joseph felt no need for speech. The slight splash of punt poles and the current of the river slurping against their wooden sides, the occasional burst of laughter, were a kind of music. Even grief could not entirely mar its timeless peace.

'We have to protect this!' Sebastian said suddenly and with such fierce emotion his voice was thick, his shoulders tense as he half turned to stare across the shining water at the buildings beyond. 'All of it! The ideas, the beauty, the knowledge . . . the freedom to think.' He drew in his breath. 'To discover the things of the mind. We are accountable to humanity for what we have. To the future.'

Joseph was startled. He had been letting himself sink into a sort of vacancy of thought where emotion was sufficient to carry him. Now he was jerked back by Sebastian's words. He

81

deserved a considered answer, and it was apparent from the passion in his face that he needed one. 'You mean Cambridge specifically?' Joseph asked, puzzled by the heat in him. 'It's been here for over half a millennium, and it seems to be growing stronger rather than weaker.'

Sebastian's eyes were grave. His skin had been caught by the sun and in the burning amber light now he looked almost made of gold. 'I don't suppose you've had time to read the news,' he answered. 'Or the inclination, for that matter.' He turned his head away, not wanting to intrude into Joseph's feelings, or else hiding his own.

'Not much,' Joseph agreed. 'But I know about the assassinations in Sarajevo, and that Vienna is unhappy about it. They want some sort of reparation from the Serbs. I suppose it was to be expected.'

'If you occupy somebody else's country, it is to be expected that they won't like it!' Sebastian responded savagely. 'All sorts of things come to be *expected*,' he repeated the word with sarcastic emphasis. 'Strike and counterstrike, revenge for this or that — justice, from the other point of view. Isn't it the responsibility of thinking men to stop the cycle and reach for something better?' He swung his arms wide, gesturing towards the exquisite buildings on the further bank, their western façades glowing pale in the light. 'Isn't that what all this is for, to teach us something higher than 'you hurt me so I'll hurt you back'? Aren't we supposed to be leading the way towards a higher morality?'

There could be no argument. Not only was it the aim of philosophy but of Christianity as well, and Sebastian knew Joseph would not deny that.

'Yes,' he agreed. He sought the supreme comfort of reason. 'But there have always been conquests, injustices and rebellions — or revolutions, if you prefer. It has never endangered the heart of learning.'

Sebastian stopped. A burst of laughter came up from the river where two punts were almost colliding as young men drinking champagne tried to reach across and touch glasses in a toast. One all but overbalanced and was perilously close to falling in. His companion grasped him by the back of his shirt, and all he lost was his straw boater, which floated for a moment or two on the shining surface before someone from the other punt caught it on the end of his pole. He presented it to its owner, who took it, dripping wet, and put it back on his head, to shouts of approval and a loud and hilarious guffaw.

It was so good-natured, a celebration of life, that Joseph found himself smiling. The sun was warm on his face and the smell of the earth and grass were sweet.

'It's not easy to imagine, is it?' Sebastian replied.

'What?'

'Destruction . . . war,' Sebastian answered, looking away from the river and back at Joseph, his eyes dark with the weight of his thoughts.

Joseph hesitated; he had no ready answer. He had not realised Sebastian was so deeply troubled.

'You don't think so?' Sebastian said. 'You're mourning a loss, sir, and I am truly sorry for it. But if we get drawn into a European war, every family in England will be mourning, not just for those we loved, but for the whole way of life we've nurtured for a thousand years. If we let that happen, we would be the true barbarians! And we would be to blame far more than the Goths or the Vandals who sacked Rome. They didn't know any better. We do!' His voice was savage, almost on the point of tears.

Joseph was frightened by the note of hysteria in him. 'There was revolution all over Europe in 1848,' he said gently, choosing his words with care and unarguable truth. 'It didn't destroy civilisation. In fact it didn't even destroy the despotism it was supposed to.' This was reason, calm history of fact. 'Everything went back to normal within a year.'

'You're not saying that was good?' Sebastian challenged him, his eyes bright, assured at least of that. He knew Joseph far too well to suppose he did.

'No, of course not,' Joseph denied it. 'I'm saying that the order of things is set in very deep foundations, and it will take far more than the assassination of an archduke and his duchess, brutal as it was, to cause any radical change.'

Sebastian bent and picked up a twig and hurled it towards the river, but it was too light, and fell short. 'Do you think so?'

'Yes,' Joseph replied with certainty. Private griefs might shake his personal world, tear out the heart of it, but the beauty and the reason of

84

civilisation continued, immeasurably greater than the individual.

Sebastian stared across the river, but unseeingly, his eyes clouded by his vision within. 'That's what Morel said too, and Foubister. They think the world won't ever change, or not more than an inch at a time. There are others, like Elwyn, who think that even if there is war, it will all be quick and noble, a sort of rather more dramatic version of a good Rider Haggard story, or Anthony Hope. You know *The Prisoner of Zenda*, and that sort of thing? All high honour and clean death at the point of a sword. Do you know much of the truth about the Boer War, sir? What we really did there?'

'A little,' Joseph acknowledged. He knew it had been ruthless, and there was a great deal for Britain to be ashamed of. But perhaps there was for the Boers too. 'But that was Africa,' he said aloud. 'And perhaps we've learned from it. Europe would be different. But there's no reason to think there'll be war, unless there's more trouble in Ireland, and we let it get completely out of hand.'

Sebastian said nothing.

'Sarajevo was the isolated act of a group of assassins,' Joseph went on. 'Europe is hardly going to go to war over it. It was a crime, not a — '

Sebastian turned to him, his eyes astonishingly clear in the waning light. 'Not an act of war?' he interrupted. 'Are you sure, sir? I'm not. The Kaiser restated his alliance with Austria-Hungary last Sunday, you know.'

The twilight breeze rippled faintly across the surface of the river. It was still warm, like a soft touch to the skin.

'And Serbia is on Russia's back doorstep,' Sebastian continued. 'If Austria demands too much reparation, they could get drawn in. And there's always the old enmity between France and Germany. The men who fought the Franco-Prussian War are still alive, and still bitter.' He started to walk again, perhaps to avoid the group of students coming towards them across the grass. It was clear he did not want to be caught up in their conversation and interrupted in his infinitely more serious thoughts.

Joseph kept pace with him, moving into the shadow of the trees, their leaves faintly whispering. 'There may be an unjust suppression of the Serbs,' he tried to return to the safety of reason again, 'and the people in general may be punished for the violent acts of a few, which is wrong — of course it is. But it is not the catastrophe to civilisation that you are suggesting.' He too spread his hands to encompass the fading scene in front of them, with its sudden dashes of silver and blue on the water. 'All this is safe.' He said it with unquestioning certainty. It was a thousand years of unbroken progress, towards even greater humanity. 'We shall still be here, learning, exploring, creating our own beauty, adding to the richness of mankind.'

Sebastian studied him, his face torn with conflicting rage and pity, almost a tenderness. 'You believe that, don't you?' he said with incredulity verging on despair. Then he continued to walk again without waiting for the answer. Somehow the movement suggested a kind of dismissal.

Joseph had to try to make reality, an understanding of proportion, heal the fear he could sense so powerfully.

'What is it you think will happen?' he asked firmly.

'Darkness,' Sebastian answered. 'Complacency without the vision to see, or the courage to act. And it takes courage! You have to see beyond the obvious, the comfortable morality everyone else agrees with, and understand that at times, terrible times, the end justifies the means.' His voice dropped. 'Even when the cost is high. Otherwise they'll lead us blindly down the path to a war like nothing we've ever even imagined before.' His words were cutting, and without the slightest hesitation. 'It won't be a few cavalry charges here and there, a few brave men killed or injured. It'll be everyone, the ordinary man in the street, sucked into endless mind-and-body-breaking bombardment by even bigger guns. It'll be hunger and fear and hatred until that's all we know.' He squinted a little as the sun blazed level with the treetops to the west and painted fire on the top of the walls of Trinity and Caius. 'Think of the towns and villages you know — St Giles, Haslingfield, Grantchester, all the rest — with black on every window, no marriages, no christenings, only deaths.' His voice dropped and was filled with a hurting tenderness. 'Think of the countryside, the fields with no men to plant them or to reap. Think of the woods in April with no one to see the blossom. Schoolboys won't dream of this.' He gestured towards the rooftops. 'Only of carrying guns. Their only ambition will be to kill, and to survive.'

He turned to face Joseph again, his eyes clear as seawater in the long light. 'Isn't it worth any price to save us from that? Isn't it what human beings are here for, to nourish and protect what we've been given and add to it before we pass it on? Look at it!' he demanded. 'Don't you love it almost more than you can bear?'

Joseph did not need to look to know his answer. 'Yes, I do,' he said with the same depth of absolute knowledge. 'It is the ultimate sanity of life. In the end, it is all there is to hold on to.'

Sebastian winced, his face looking suddenly bruised and hollow. 'I'm sorry,' he said in a whisper. He moved his hand as if to touch Joseph's arm, then withdrew. 'But this is a universal sanity, isn't it? Bigger than any one of us, a purpose, a healing for mankind?' His voice was urgent, begging for assurance.

'Yes, it is,' Joseph agreed gently. As had happened so many times in their friendship, Sebastian put it in exactly the words that framed his own belief. 'And yes it is our duty, who have seen it and become part of it, to protect it with all our power.'

Sebastian smiled very slightly, and turned away as they started back again. 'But you don't fear war, do you, sir? I mean real, literal war?'

'I would fear it horribly if I thought it were a real danger,' Joseph assured him. 'But I don't think it is. We've had many wars before, and we've lost many men. We've faced invasion more than once, and beaten it off. It hasn't broken us irreparably; if anything, it's made us stronger.'

'Not this time,' Sebastian said bitterly. 'If it happens, and we can't stop it, it'll be pure, blind destruction.'

Joseph looked sideways at him. He could see in his face the love for all that was precious and vulnerable, all that could be broken by the unthinking. There was a pain in him that was naked in this strange, fierce light of dusk which cast such black shadows.

Time and again they had talked of all manner of things — no boundaries of time or place had held them: the men half human, half divine in the epic legends of Egypt and Babylon; the God of the Old Testament, who was creator of worlds, yet spoke face to face with Moses, as one man talks with another. They had basked in lean, golden classicism of Greece, the teeming magnificence of Rome, the intricate glories of Byzantium, the sophistication of Persia. All had been the furniture of their dreams. Wherever Joseph had led, Sebastian had followed eagerly, grasping after each new experience with insatiable joy.

The light was almost gone. The colour burned only on the horizon, the shadows dense on the Backs. The water was pale and polished like old silver, indigo under the bridges.

'We could disappear into the ruins of time, if there's war,' Sebastian resumed. 'One day, in a thousand years' time, scholars from cultures we haven't even imagined, young and curious, could dig up what's left of us, and from a few shards, scraps of writing, try to work out what we were really like. And get it wrong,' he added bitterly. 'English would become a dead language, lost, like Aramaic, or Etruscan,' he went on with quiet misery. 'No more wit of Oscar Wilde, or grandeur of Shakespeare, no more thunder of Milton, music of Keats, or . . . God knows how many more . . . and worst of all, the future culled. All that this generation might do. We have to prevent that — whatever it cost!'

'It is impossible to care too much,' Joseph said gently. 'It is all infinitely precious.' He must bring back reason, ground this fear in the lasting realities. 'There is nothing you or I can do to affect the quarrels of Austria and Serbia,' he went on. 'There will always be fighting somewhere, from time to time. And as inventions like telephones and wireless get better, we will know of them sooner. A hundred years ago it would have taken weeks for us to learn about what happened in Sarajevo, if we did at all. By which time it would all have been over. Now we read about it the day after, so we feel it to be more immediate, but it's only a perception. Hold on to the certainties, the things that endure.'

Sebastian looked at him, his back to the last of the light so Joseph could not make out his expression. His voice was rough-edged. 'You don't think this is different? A hundred years ago we were nearly conquered by Napoleon.'

Joseph realised he had made a tactical error in choosing a hundred years as an example. 'Yes, but we weren't,' he said confidently. 'No French soldier set foot in England, except as a prisoner.'

'As you said, sir, things have changed in a hundred years,' Sebastian pointed out. 'We have steamships, aeroplanes, guns that can shoot further and destroy more than ever before. A west wind won't keep the navies of Europe locked in harbour now.'

'You are letting your fears run away with your reason,' Joseph chided him. 'We have had other, far more desperate times, but we have always prevailed. And we have grown stronger since the Napoleonic wars, not weaker. You must have faith in us — and in God.'

Sebastian gave a little grunt, ironic and dismissive, as if there were some deeper fear he could not explain, and which it seemed Joseph refused or was incapable of understanding. 'Why?' he said bitterly. 'Israel were the chosen people, and where are they now? We study their language as a curiosity. It matters only because it is the language of Christ, whom they denied, and crucified. If the Bible didn't speak of Him, we wouldn't care about Hebrew. We can't say that of English. Why should anyone remember it, if we were conquered? For Shakespeare? We don't remember the language of Aristotle, Homer, Aeschylus. It's taught in the best schools, to the privileged few, as a relic of a great civilisation of the past.' His voice choked with sudden, uncontrollable anger and his face was twisted with pain. 'I don't want to become a relic! I want people a thousand years from now to speak the same tongue I do, to love the same beauty, understand my dreams and how they mattered to me. I want to write something, or even do something, that preserves the soul of who we are.'

The last of the light was now only a pale wash low across the horizon. 'War changes us, even if we win,' he turned away from Joseph, as if to hide a nakedness within, 'too many of us become barbarians of the heart. Have you any idea how many could die? How many of those left would be consumed by hate, all over Europe, everything that was good in them eaten away by the things they had seen, and worse, the things they had been forced to do?'

'It won't happen!' Joseph responded, and the moment the words were gone from his lips he wondered if they were true. He was speaking blindly, using reason because it was all he had, and even as he did it, at last he accepted that it could not answer the fear of the heart. 'If you can't have faith in people, the leaders of nations, then have faith that God will not allow the world to plunge into the kind of destruction you are thinking of,' he said aloud. 'What purpose of His could it serve?'

Sebastian's lip curled in a tiny smile. 'I've no idea! I don't know the purposes of God! Do you, sir?' The softness of his voice, and the 'sir' on the end, robbed it of offence.

'To save the souls of men,' Joseph replied without hesitation.

'And what does that mean?' Sebastian turned back to face him. 'Do you suppose He sees it the same way I do?' Again the smile touched his lips,

92

this time self-mocking.

Joseph was obliged to smile in answer, although the sadness jolted him as if the fading of the light were in some terrible way a permanent thing. 'Not necessarily,' he conceded. 'But He is more likely to be right.'

Sebastian did not reply, and they walked slowly along the grass as the breeze rose a little. All the punts were gone to their moorings and the spires of stone in the arched top of the Bridge of Sighs were barely darker than the sky beyond.

★ ★ ★

Matthew returned to London, going first to his flat. It was exactly as he had left it, except that the maid had tidied it, but it felt different. It should have had the comfort of home. It was where he had lived for the last five years, ever since he had left university and come to work for the Secret Intelligence Service. It was full of his books, the modern history, biography, adventure, drawings and paintings he had collected. His favourite, hanging over the fire, was of cows in the corner of a field. For him their gentle rumination, their calm eyes and slow generosity seemed the ultimate sanity in the world. On the mantel was a silver vase his mother had given him one Christmas, and a Turkish dagger with a rich ornamental scabbard.

But the flat was oddly empty. He felt as if he were returning not to the present but to the past. When he had last sat in the worn, leather armchair or eaten at this table, his family had been whole, and he knew of no vanishing document that was at the heart of conspiracy, violence, and secrets that brought death. The world had not been exactly safe, but whatever dangers there were lay in places far distant, and only the periphery of them touched England, or Matthew himself.

He spent a long evening deep in thought. It was the first time he had been alone more than to sleep since he had walked across the grass at Fenner's Field to break the news to Joseph. Questions crowded his mind.

John Reavley had called him on the Saturday evening, not here at his flat, but at his office in the Intelligence Services. He had been working late, on the Irish problem, as usual. The Liberal Government had been trying to pass a Home Rule bill to give Ireland autonomy since the middle of the previous century, and time after time the Protestants of Ulster had blocked it, refusing absolutely to be forcibly separated from Britain and placed in Catholic Ireland. Their religious freedom and their economic survival depended upon remaining free from such a forced integration and, ultimately, subjection.

Government after government had fallen on the issue, and now Asquith's Liberal Party required the support of the Irish Parliamentary Party in order to retain power.

Shearing, Matthew's superior, shared the view of many others that there was a great deal of political manoeuvring in London behind the mutiny of British troops stationed in the

Curragh. When the men of Ulster, solidly backed by their women, had threatened armed rebellion against the Home Rule Bill, the British troops had refused to take up arms against them. General Gough had resigned, with all his officers, whereupon Sir John French, Chief of General Staff in London, had resigned also, immediately followed by Sir John Seely, Secretary of State for War in the Cabinet.

Little wonder Shearing and his men worked late. It threatened to become a crisis as grave as any in the last three hundred years.

Matthew had been in his office when the call came from John Reavley telling him of the document, and that he was going to drive to London with it the following day, expecting to arrive between half-past one and two o'clock. He would bring Alys with him, ostensibly for an afternoon in the city, but in truth to make his trip unremarkable.

How had anyone else known that he even had the document, let alone that he was taking it to Matthew, and the time of his journey? If he came by car, the route was obvious. There was only one main road from St Giles to London.

Matthew cast his mind back to that evening, the offices almost silent, hardly anyone there, just half a dozen men, perhaps a couple of clerks. He remembered standing at his desk with the telephone in his hand, the disbelief at what his father had said. He had repeated the words after him, to make certain he had heard correctly.

The cold ran through him. Was that it? In the quiet office someone had overheard him? That had been enough. Who? He tried to clear his mind and think back to who else had been there, but it was indistinct. One late night blended into another. He had heard footsteps, muttered voices, deliberately kept low not to disturb others. He might not have recognised them then; he certainly could not now.

But he could find out, discreetly. He could trace it, learn at least the possibilities. That was what John Reavley had said, a conspiracy that went as high as the throne, and it was now clear that it was also deep through even his own colleagues, whom a few days ago he would have trusted without hesitation.

★ ★ ★

When he went in in the morning everything was familiar, the cramped spaces, the echoing wooden floor, the harsh desk lamps, unnecessary now in the sunlight through the windows, the black telephones, the dust motes in the air and the worn surfaces. Clerks bustled back and forth, shirtsleeves grimy from endless papers and ink, collars stiff and often a trifle crooked.

They wished him good morning, and offered their condolences, shy and awkward, and from all he could see, intensely sincere. He thanked them, and went to his own small room where books were wedged into too small a case and papers were locked in drawers. The inkwell and blotting papers were just as usual, not quite straight on his desk, two pens lying beside them. The blotting paper was clean. He never left anything that might be decipherable.

He fished for his keys to unlock the top drawer. At first the key did not slide in easily; it took a moment of fiddling. He bent to look more closely, and that was when he saw the finest of scratches on the metal around the keyhole. It had not been there when he left. So someone had searched here too.

He sat down, thoughts racing in his mind, clouded and skewed by emotion, and guilt now there was no doubt that it was his words overheard that had sent the assassin after John and Alys Reavley.

By mid-morning, Matthew's desk was piled with information on the Curragh mutiny, and it was imperative that he read through it, organise it and begin to assess its validity, but he could not dismiss from his mind the knowledge that someone in the office had overheard his conversation, and begun the chain of murder. The guilt for his own part weighed on him. He had been stupid beyond belief, he had allowed surprise to rob him of care for the most elementary precautions.

Over the next days anger with himself turned outwards and it required all his self-control to keep his temper. People took his erratic moods for grief, and forgave him. Possibly it was that which made him ashamed of his injustice to all but the one, and allowed him to let go of the rage and concentrate his mind.

Even so, the best he could do was establish the innocence of most. He could not even indicate, far less prove, which of the remaining four had betrayed him. Unless chance delivered him a gift, he realised with some bitterness that he never would.

It was Thursday, 9 July before Calder Shearing sent for him and Matthew reported to his office a little after four o'clock. Like all rooms in the Intelligence Service building, it was sparsely furnished — nothing more than the necessities, and those as cheap as possible — but unlike others, Shearing had added nothing of his own, no pictures to speak of his home, no personal books or mementoes. His papers and volumes for work were untidily stacked, but he knew the precise place of every one of them.

Shearing was not a tall man but he had a presence more commanding than mere size. His black hair was receding considerably but one barely noticed it because his brows were heavy and expressive, and his eyes, thick-lashed, were so dark as to seem almost black. His jutting nose was a perfect curve and his mouth grave and sensitive.

He regarded Matthew thoughtfully, assessing his recovery from bereavement, and hence his fitness for duty. His question was only a matter of courtesy.

'How are you, Reavley? All matters taken care of?'

'For the time being, sir,' Matthew answered, standing to attention.

'Again, are you all right?' Shearing repeated.

'Yes, sir, thank you.'

Shearing looked at him a moment longer, then was apparently satisfied. 'Good. Sit down. I expect you have caught up with the news? The King of the Belgians is on a state visit to Switzerland, which might be of significance, but is more probably a routine affair. Yesterday the Government said it might accept the Lords' amendment to the Home Rule Bill excluding Ulster.'

Matthew had heard the news, but no details. 'Peace in Ireland?' he asked, slightly sarcastically.

Shearing looked up at him, his expression incredulous. 'If that's what you think then you'd better take more leave. You're obviously not fit for work!'

'Well, a step in the right direction?' Matthew amended.

Shearing pulled his mouth into a thin line. 'God knows! I can't see a partition in Ireland helping anyone. But neither will anything else.'

Matthew's mind raced. Was that what the conspiracy document was about — something to do with dividing Ireland into two countries, one independent Catholic, the other Protestant and still part of Britain? Even the suggestion of it had already brought British troops to mutiny, robbed the army of its commander in chief, the Cabinet of its Secretary of State of War, and taken Ulster itself to the brink of armed rebellion and civil war. Was that not the perfect ground in which to sow a plot to lead England to ruin and dishonour?

But it was now July and there had been relative peace for weeks. The House of Lords was on the verge of accepting the exclusion of Ulster from the Home Rule Bill, and the Ulstermen would be permitted to remain a part of Britain, a right for which they were apparently not only prepared to die themselves, but to take with them all the rest of Ireland, not to mention the British Army stationed there.

'Reavley!' Shearing snapped, startling Matthew back to the present. 'For God's sake, man, if you need more time, take it! You're no use to me in a daydream!'

'No, sir,' Matthew said tartly, feeling his body stiffen, the blood rush warm in his face. 'I was thinking about the Irish situation, and what difference it will make whether the Government accepts the amendment or not. It's an issue that arouses passion far beyond reason.'

Shearing's black eyes widened. 'I don't need you to tell me that, Reavley. Every Englishman with even half his wits has known that for the last three hundred years.' He was watching Matthew intently, searching for the thought behind his words, trying to judge whether they could possibly be as empty as they sounded. 'Do you know something that I don't?' he asked.

Matthew had kept silent on a few occasions, but he had never lied to Shearing. Now, for the first time, he considered the possibility that he might need to. His father had said the conspiracy went as high as the royal family, and Matthew had no idea who was involved, though certainly at least one person here in his office. But he could not tell Shearing that until he had proof. Perhaps not even then!

Who was Catholic, who was Anglo-Irish, who had loyalties or vested interests one way or the

100

other? Rebellion in Ireland would hardly change the world, but perhaps John Reavley had felt it would his world. And England's honour would affect the Empire, which was the world, as far as he was concerned. Of course there were tens of thousands of Irishmen and women in the United States who still felt passionate loyalty to the land of their heritage. Other Celtic peoples might also sympathise — in Wales, Scotland, Cornwall. It could tear Britain apart, and spread to other colonies around the world.

'No, sir,' Matthew said, judging his words carefully. 'But I hear whispers from time to time, and it helps to know the issues, and whose loyalty lies where. I'm always hearing mention of conspiracies.' He watched for any shadow of change in Shearing's eyes.

'To do what?' Shearing's voice was low and very careful.

Matthew was on dangerous ground. How far dared he go? One slip, and if Shearing were aware of the conspiracy, even sympathetic to it, then Matthew would have betrayed himself. He was uniquely alone. Joseph would not be able to help him, and he could not trust Shearing or anyone else in SIS, especially those near his own room.

'To unite Ireland,' he answered boldly. That was certainly radical enough. Considering the Curragh circumstances, it would rip Britain apart, and possibly sacrifice both army and government in the process, which would provide an interesting opportunity for all Britain's enemies everywhere else — Europe, Asia or

Africa. Perhaps John Reavley was not exaggerating after all. It could be the first domino to topple of many, the beginning of the disintegration of the Empire, which would unquestionably affect all the world.

'What have you heard, precisely?' Shearing demanded.

Better to avoid mentioning his father at all, but he could still be accurate about the details. 'Odd words about a conspiracy,' Matthew said, trying to pitch his tone to exactly the right mixture of caution and concern. 'No details, only that it would have very wide effects, all over the world — which might be an exaggeration — and that it would ruin England's honour.'

'From whom?'

It was on the tip of his tongue to be honest. If he said it was his own father, that would explain so easily and naturally why he had been unable to pursue it any further. But it would also take it a step too close to the truth, if Shearing himself could not be trusted, or might repeat it to whoever it was in the office who had betrayed John Reavley. Far wiser to keep that back.

'Overheard it in a club,' he lied. It was the first time he had deliberately misled Shearing, and he found it extraordinarily uncomfortable, not only for the deceit to a man he respected, but also because it was dangerous. Shearing was not someone to treat lightly. He had a powerful, incisive mind, an imagination that leaped from one thing to another as fast and as easily as his instinct drove it. He forgot almost nothing, and forgave very little.

102

'Said by whom?' Shearing repeated.

Matthew knew that if he gave an unsatisfactory answer, such as that he did not know, Shearing would be certain he was lying. It would be the beginning of distrust. Eventually it would lead to his losing his job. Since he actually was lying, his story would have to be very good indeed. Was he equal to that? Would he ever know if he had succeeded or failed? The answer came even before the question was finished in his mind. No — he would not. Shearing would betray nothing in his eyes, his face, the positioning of his body, the tensions in the neat, strong hands resting on the surface of the desk.

'An army officer, a Major Trenton,' Matthew named a man from whom he had actually obtained information some weeks ago, and who did occasionally attend the same club.

Shearing was silent for several moments. 'Could be anything,' he said at last. There was a very slight twist to his lips. 'There are always Irish conspiracies; it's in the nature of life. It's a society divided by religion. If there is a solution to it, we haven't found it in three hundred years, and God help us, we've never stopped trying. But if there is anything specific at the moment, I think it is more likely to lie in politics than any personal plot. And something personal would not dishonour the nation.'

'If not Ireland, then what?' Matthew asked. He could not let go. His father had died, broken and bleeding, trying to expose a plot and prevent the tragedy he foresaw.

Shearing stared back at him. 'The shootings in

103

Sarajevo,' he replied thoughtfully. 'Was this before then, or after? You didn't say.'

It was like a shaft of light cutting the darkness. 'Before,' Matthew said, surprised to find his voice a little husky. Was it conceivable his father had somehow got word of that — too late! He must have been killed himself almost as it had happened. 'But that doesn't affect England!' he said almost before he had weighed the meaning of it. His throat tightened. 'Or is there more . . . something else yet to happen that we don't know of?'

A shadow of dark humour crossed Shearing's face, then vanished. 'There's always more that we don't know of, Reavley. If you haven't learned that yet then there isn't much hope for you. The Kaiser reasserted his alliance with Austro-Hungary four days ago.'

'Yes, I heard.' Matthew waited, knowing Shearing would go on.

'What do you know about the 'All-Highest'?' Shearing asked, a faint flicker of light dancing in his eyes.

Matthew was lost for words. 'I beg your pardon?'

'The Kaiser, Reavley! What do you know about Kaiser Wilhelm the Second of the German Empire?'

'Is that what he calls himself?' Matthew asked incredulously, scrambling together his thoughts, stories he could repeat about the Kaiser's tantrums, his delusions that first his uncle, Edward VII, and now his cousin George V were deliberately snubbing him, ridiculing and belittling him. There were a great many it might be unwise to retell.

'He's the King's cousin, and the Czar's,' he began, and instantly saw the impatience in Shearing's face. 'He's been writing to the Czar for some time, and they have become confidants,' he went on more boldly. 'But he hated King Edward, and was convinced he was plotting against him, that he despised him for some reason, and he has transferred that feeling to the present King. He's a very temperamental man, very proud and always looking for slights. And he has a withered arm, which is possibly why he is rather bad on horseback. No balance.' He waited for Shearing to respond.

Shearing's mouth flickered, as if he thought of smiling, and decided against it. 'His relationship with France?' he prompted.

Matthew knew what he was expecting. He had read the reports. 'Bad,' he replied. 'He has always wanted to go to Paris, but the French President has never invited him, and it rankles with him. He's — ' he stopped again. He had been going to say 'surrounded by awkward relationships', but perhaps that was a bit presumptuous. He was uncertain of Shearing's regard for royalty, even foreign. The Kaiser was closely related to George V.

'More importantly,' Shearing pointed out, 'he perceives himself to be surrounded by enemies.'

Matthew let the weight of that observation sink into his mind. He saw the reflection of it in Shearing's face. 'A conspiracy to start a war, beginning in Serbia?' he asked tentatively.

'God knows,' Shearing replied. 'There are Serbian nationalists who will do anything for freedom, including assassinate an Austrian archduke — obviously — but there are radical socialists all over Europe as well — '

'Against war,' Matthew cut in. 'At least international war. They are all for class war. Surely that couldn't be . . . ?' He stopped.

'You overheard the remark, Reavley! Could it or not?' Shearing asked tartly. 'What about a pan-European socialist revolution? The whole continent is seething with plots and counterplots — Victor Adler in Vienna, Jean Jaurès in France, Rosa Luxemburg everywhere, and God knows who in Russia. Austria is spoiling for a fight and only wants the excuse, France is afraid of Germany, and the Kaiser is afraid of everyone. And the Czar doesn't know a damn thing about any of it. Take your pick.'

Matthew looked at Shearing's dark, enigmatic face filled with a kind of despairing humour, and realised that he had worked with him for over a year, and he knew almost nothing about him. He knew his intellect and his skills, but his passions he had not even guessed at. He had no idea where he came from, his family or his education, his tastes or his dreams. He was an intensely private man, but he guarded his inner self so well no one was aware he was doing it at all. One thought of him only in connection with his work, as if he walked out of the entrance of the building and ceased to exist.

'Perhaps I had better forget it, unless something else develops,' Matthew said, aware that he had learned nothing, and very possibly made himself look vague to Shearing. 'It doesn't seem to tie in with anything.'

'On the contrary, it ties in with everything,' Shearing answered. 'The air is full of conspiracies — fortunately most of them nothing to do with us. But go on listening, and bring to me anything you hear that makes sense.'

'Yes, sir.'

They discussed other projects for a further twenty minutes, particularly who might replace the Minister of War who had resigned over the mutiny. There were two primary candidates, Blunden, who was in favour of peace, even at a high price, and Wynyard who was far more belligerent.

'We need details,' Shearing said pointedly. 'All the details you can, Reavley. Weaknesses. Where is Blunden vulnerable? It's our job to know. You can't protect a man until you know where he can be hurt.'

'Yes, sir,' Matthew agreed. 'I know that.'

He left, forgetting the Minister of War for a moment and turning over in his mind what Shearing had said about conspiracy. Nothing he had spoken of touched national honour or would change the world, except with the slow evolution of one social system into another, which was going to happen anyway. None of the evangelists for radical reform was English, none of the fighters for national freedom. The closest was the mutiny in the Curragh, and even that was hardly a problem in any way new.

Would anyone kill to hide Irish nationalism, or

Ulster determination not to be torn off the edge of Protestant Britain and forced into being part of Catholic Ireland? There had been plots and counterplots on that issue since the time of Elizabeth I and Sir Francis Walsingham's secret service, the distant ancestor of the present intelligence service.

He walked the quiet corridors back to his own office, nodding to this person, wishing a good evening to that one. He felt extraordinarily alone because he realised suddenly that he was still deeply and profoundly angry. Shearing had in effect damned John Reavley's perception of truth.

Yet John Reavley was dead! And there had been the rope on the tree and marks on the road, scars where a row of caltrops had ripped all four tyres and sent the car veering one way and the other until it crashed into the copse. Where did one buy caltrops in the modern world? Or had they been home-made? It might be simple enough, with strong fence wire, wire-cutters and pliers. Any man could do it, with a few hours to spare and a knack with his hands.

Someone had searched the house in St Giles, and his office.

But he could not prove it. The crushed foxgloves would grow back, the marks would be obliterated by rain and dust and other traffic. The rope end tied to the tree could have been put there for any of a dozen reasons. And no one else could say whether things in the study or the bedroom had been moved or not. The evidence was in memory, a sense of disturbance, minute

108

things not as they should be, marks round a lock that he could have made himself.

They would say that John Reavley was a man out of office and out of touch, who dreamed up conspiracies. Matthew and Joseph were deluded by grief. Surely the violent loss of both parents was enough to cause, and to excuse, disjunction of reason in anyone?

It was all true. And the anger inside him turned to a dull, inward ache of confusion. In his mind's eye he could see his father's keen face. He was an eminently reasonable man, his mind so quick, so very sane. He was the one who curbed Judith's excesses; was patient with Hannah, less fluent to express herself; a man who hid his disappointment that neither of his sons had followed the career he'd so longed for them to pursue.

He had loved the quaint and eccentric things in life. He was endlessly tolerant of difference — and lost his temper with arrogance, and too often with fools who stifled others with petty authority. The real fools, the simple-minded, he could forgive in an instant.

It hurt Matthew almost beyond bearing to think that his father had utterly misunderstood one stupid, minor conspiracy that would make not even a mark in history, never mind turn the tide of it to ruin a nation and alter the world!

The irony was that he would not have found it as hard to be wrong as Matthew found it for him. Matthew knew that, and it did not help. He stood in the centre of his office and had to fight to stop himself from weeping.

In a quiet house on Marchmont Street, a man who liked to be known by those he trusted as 'the Peacemaker', stood near the mantel shelf in his upstairs sitting room and stared with unconcealed fury at the rigid figure opposite him.

'You searched his office and found nothing!' he said between his teeth.

'Nothing of any interest to us,' the other man replied. He spoke English with complete ease, but without colloquialisms. 'They concerned things which we already know. The document was not there.'

'Well, it wasn't in the Reavley house,' the Peacemaker said bitterly. 'That was searched thoroughly.'

'Was it?' the other asked sceptically. 'When?'

'During the funeral,' the Peacemaker replied, a dangerous temper audible in his voice. He did not like being challenged, particularly by someone considerably his junior in rank. It was only his respect for his cousin that made him tolerate this man to the degree he did. He was, after all, his cousin's ally.

'But you have the copy Reavley was carrying,' the man pointed out. 'I'll follow the son. If he knows where it is, I'll find it.'

The Peacemaker stood elegantly, looking to anyone who glanced only casually as if he were at ease. More careful judgement would have seen the tension in his body so great the fabric of his jacket was straining across his shoulders, and his knuckles were white.

'There is no time,' he said in a hard, very level voice. 'Events will not wait. If you can't see that, you're a fool! We must use it within the next few days, or it will be too late. A week, maybe two at the most.'

'One copy — '

'I have to have both! I can hardly offer him one!'

'I'll get another,' the man offered.

The Peacemaker's face was white. 'You can't!'

The other man straightened as if to leave immediately. 'I'll go back tonight — '

'It won't help.' The Peacemaker held up his hand. 'The Kaiser is in a rage. You'll get nothing. You might even lose what we have.' This was spoken with the unmistakable tone of a command.

The other man breathed in and out slowly several times, but he did not argue. There was anger in his face, and frustration, but they were not with the man known as the Peacemaker, rather with the circumstances he was forced to accept.

'You dealt with the other matter?' the Peacemaker asked, his voice little more than a whisper. There was pain in his face.

'Yes,' the man replied.

'How did he get hold of it, anyway?' the Peacemaker asked, sharp frown lines between his brows.

'He was the one who wrote it,' the other man answered.

'Wrote it?' The demand was peremptory.

'Such things have to be written by hand,' the man explained. 'It's the law.'

'Damn!' the Peacemaker swore, just one word, but it carried a weight of passion as if it were torn out of him with physical pain. He bent forward a little, his shoulders high, his muscles tight. 'It shouldn't have happened this way! We shouldn't have let it! Reavley was a good man, the sort we need alive!'

'Can't be helped,' the other explained with resignation.

'It should have been!' the Peacemaker grated, hard bitterness undisguised. 'We've got to do better.'

The other man flinched a little. 'We'll try.'

4

Joseph slipped back into the routine of teaching again and found the old pleasure in knowledge easing a little of the pain inside him. The music of words to the ear and the mind closed out the past, creating their own immediate world. Not only could he build an armour for himself, he could extend it to others as well. Surely that was his calling: to find the divine in the reasoning, creating man that would make sense out of the chaos of emotion, and eventually mould it into a purity of heart capable of coming closer to God?

He stood in the lecture room and saw the earnest faces in front of him, different in features and colouring, but all touched with the shadows of anxiety. Only Sebastian had voiced his fear concerning the possibility of war in Europe, but Joseph heard the echoes of it in them all. There were reports of a French airship making reconnaissance flights over Germany, speculation as to what reparation Austro-Hungary would demand of Serbia, and even who might be assassinated next.

Joseph had spoken once or twice on the subject to the other students. He had no knowledge beyond the newspaper reports available to everyone else, but since the Dean was on a short sabbatical, and therefore unavailable, he felt that he should fill his place with the spiritual resources that would have met just such a need as this. There was nothing better than reason with which to answer fear. There was no cause to believe that there would be a conflict involving England. These young men would not be asked to fight, and perhaps to die.

They listened to him politely, waiting for him to answer their needs for assurance, and he knew from their eyes, the tension still there in their voices, that the old power to comfort was not enough.

On Friday evening he called by at Harry Beecher's rooms and found him reclining in his armchair reading the current edition of the *Illustrated London News*. He looked up, laying the paper flat immediately. Joseph could see, even upside down, a picture of a theatre stage.

Beecher glanced at it and smiled. '*Eugene Onegin*,' he explained.

Joseph was surprised. 'Here?'

'No — St Petersburg. The world is smaller than you think, isn't it? And *Carmen*.' Beecher indicated the picture at the bottom of the page. 'But apparently they've revived Boito's *Mefistofele* at Covent Garden, and they say it's very good. The Russian Ballet has *Daphnis and Chloé* at Drury Lane. Not really my kind of thing.'

Joseph smiled. 'Nor mine,' he agreed. 'How about a sandwich or a pie, and a glass of cider at The Pickerel?' It was the oldest public house in Cambridge, just a few yards along the street, across the Magdalene Bridge. They could sit outside in the fading light and watch the river, as Samuel Pepys might have done when he was a

114

student here in the seventeenth century, or anyone else over the last six hundred years.

'Good idea,' Beecher agreed immediately, rising to his feet. The room was a pleasant clutter of books. Latin was his subject, but his interest lay in the icons of faith. He and Joseph had spent many hours talking, arguing, putting up theory after theory — serious, passionate or funny — as to what was the concept of holiness. Where did it move from being an aid to concentration, a reminder of faith, into being the object of reverence itself, imbued with miraculous powers?

Beecher picked up his jacket from the back of the old leather chair, and followed Joseph out, closing the door behind them. They went down the steps and across the quad to the massive front gate with its smaller door inset, and then out into St John's Street, and left to the Magdalene Bridge.

The terrace outside The Pickerel was crowded. It was the perfect place for a drink and a long conversation on a summer evening. As usual there were punts on the river, drifting along towards the bridge, silhouetted for a moment beneath its arch, then gone as they turned and followed the stream.

Joseph ordered cider and cold game pie for both of them, then carried it over to a table and sat down.

Beecher regarded him steadily for a moment or two. 'Are you all right, Joseph?' he asked gently. 'If you need a little more time, I can take some of your work. Really — '

Joseph smiled. 'I'm better working, thank you.'

Beecher was still watching him. 'But?' he questioned.

'Is it so obvious?'

'To someone who knows you, yes.' Beecher took a long draught of his cider then set the glass down. He did not press for an answer. They had been friends since their own student years here, and spent many holidays walking together in the Lake District, or along the ancient Roman wall that stretched across the mouth of the Tyne on the North Sea coast to the Solway Firth opening on to the Atlantic. They had imagined the legionaries of the Caesars who had manned it when it was the outer edge of Empire against the barbarian.

They had tramped for miles, and sat in the sun staring over the moors in the light and shadow, eaten crusty bread and cheese, and drunk cheap red wine. And they had talked of everything, and nothing, and told endless jokes, and laughed.

Joseph wondered whether to say anything to Beecher about his father's death, and the fear of a conspiracy of the magnitude he had suggested, but he and Matthew had agreed not to speak of it even to the closest friends.

'I was thinking of the ugly situation in Europe,' he said instead. 'And wondering what sort of future lies ahead for the men who graduate this year. A darker one than for us at that age.' He looked at his cider, sparkling a little in the long, amber light. 'When I graduated the Boer War was over, and the world had all the excitement of a new century. It looked as if nothing would ever change except for the better: greater wisdom; better, more liberal laws; travel; new art . . . '

Beecher's humorous, slightly crooked face was grave. 'There are shifts of power all the time, and socialism is a rising force I don't think anything can stop,' he said. 'Nor should it. We're moving to a real enlightenment — even votes for women in time.'

'I was thinking more of the crisis in the Balkans,' Joseph said thoughtfully, taking another bite at his pie, and talking with his mouth full. 'I think that's what many of our students are worried about.' He said 'many', but he was thinking primarily of Sebastian. It was he whose sharp, urgent fears he had failed to reassure.

'I can't see any of our students joining the army.' Beecher spoke just before swallowing the last mouthful of his pastry. 'And no matter how heated it gets between Austria and Serbia, it's a long way from us. It's not our concern, unless we want to make it so. Young men always worry before leaving university and stepping out into the world.' He smiled broadly. 'In spite of the competition, there is a kind of safety here, and multitudes of distractions. The whole college is a hotbed of ideas most of them had never even imagined before, and the first temptations of adulthood — but the only real yardstick is your own ability. You may not get a first, but the only person who can prevent you succeeding is yourself. Outside it's different. It's a harder, colder world. The best of them know that.' He finished his cider. 'Let them worry, Joseph. It's part of growing up.'

Again Joseph thought of Sebastian's tortured face as he had stared with such intensity across the burnished water towards the dark outlines of the college. 'The young man I'm thinking of wasn't anxious for himself, it was for what war in Europe would do to civilisation in general.'

Beecher's face split into a good-natured grin. 'Too much poring over dead languages, Joseph. There's always something ineffably sad about a culture whose people have vanished when an echo of their beauty remains, especially if it is part of the music of our own.'

'He was thinking of our language being overtaken and our way of thought lost,' Joseph told him.

Beecher's eyebrows rose. 'Who do you have in mind?'

'Sebastian Allard . . . ' Joseph had barely finished speaking when he saw a shadow in Beecher's eyes. The still, evening light was unchanged, the sound of laughter from a group of young men drifted on the twilight breeze from the green swathe of the Backs, but inexplicably the air seemed colder. 'He's more aware than the others,' he explained.

'He's got a better intellect,' Beecher agreed, but he did not look at Joseph, and there was something withheld in his voice.

'It's more than intellect.' Joseph felt the need to defend himself, and perhaps Sebastian. 'You can have a brilliant brain without delicacy, fire . . . vision . . . ' There was no other word to describe what he knew in Sebastian. In his translations he had caught the music and understood not only what the poets and philosophers of the past had written, but the whole regions of passions and dreams that lay beyond it. To teach such a mind as his was the wish of all those who wanted to pass on the beauty they themselves had seen. 'You know that!' he said with more force than he had intended.

'We're not in any danger of going the way of Carthage or Etruria.' Beecher smiled, but it did not reach his eyes. 'There are no barbarians at the gates. If they exist, then they are here among us.' He looked at his empty glass, but did not bother to catch the barman's eye. 'I think we are equal to keeping them at bay, at least most of the time.'

Joseph heard a note of pain in his voice, the tip of something he had not seen before. 'Not all the time?' he asked gently.

Then into his mind burst back the crushed foxgloves on the verge of the road, the scars of the caltrops on the tarmacadam, and the screaming of metal in his imagination, and the blood. And he understood violence and rage completely, and fear.

'Of course not all of it,' Beecher replied, his gaze beyond Joseph's head, unaware of the emotion all but drowning him. 'They are young minds full of energy and promise, but they are also morally undisciplined now and then. They are on the edge of learning about the world, and about themselves. They have the privilege of education in the best school there is, and being taught, forgive the immodesty, by some of the best mentors in the English language. They live in one of the most subtle and tolerant cultures in Europe. And they have the intellect and the ambition, the drive and the fire to make something of it. At least most of them have.'

He turned to meet Joseph's eyes. 'It's our job to civilise them as well, Joseph. Teach them forbearance, compassion, how to accept failure as well as success, not to blame others, nor blame themselves too much, but go on and try again, and pretend it didn't hurt. It will happen many times in life; it's necessary to get used to it and put it in its place. That's hard, when you are young. They are very proud, and they haven't much sense of proportion yet.'

'But they have courage,' Joseph said quickly. 'And they care — intensely!'

Beecher looked at his hands on the table. 'Of course they do. Good God, if the young don't care, there isn't much hope for the rest of us! But they're still selfish at times. More, I think, than you want to believe.'

'I know! But it's innocent,' Joseph argued, leaning forward a little. 'Their generosity is just as powerful, and their idealism. They are discovering the world and it's desperately precious to them! Right now they are frightened they're going to lose it. What can I tell them?' he pleaded. 'How can I make that fear bearable?'

'You can't,' Beecher shook his head. 'You can't carry the world, and you'd only rip a muscle trying — and still probably drop it. Leave it to Atlas!' He pushed his chair back and stood up.

'Do you want another cider?' And without waiting for an answer, he took Joseph's glass as well and walked away.

Joseph sat surrounded by murmuring voices, the clink of glass and the occasional burst of laughter, and felt alone. He had never realised before that Beecher did not like Sebastian. It was not only the dismissive words, it was the coldness in his face as he said them. Joseph felt distanced by it, cut off from a warmth he had expected.

He did not stay long after that, but excused himself and walked slowly back through the near darkness to St John's.

★ ★ ★

He was tired, but he did not sleep well. He woke finally a little before six and decided not to waste any more time lying thinking. He got up and dressed in old clothes, then went outside and down to the river. It was a breathless morning, even the topmost leaves of the trees were still against the blue of the sky. The clear, pale light was so sharp every blade of grass shone with the dew and there was no mark at all on the shining surface of the water.

He untied one of the small boats and sat in it, unlashed the oars and rowed out past Trinity and on eastwards into the spreading light, feeling the warmth on his back. He threw his weight into it, pulling steadily. The rhythm was soothing and he picked up speed all the way to the Mathematical Bridge before turning to come back. His mind was empty of every thought but the sheer physical pleasure of the effort.

He was back in his rooms, stripped to the waist and shaving when there was an urgent, almost hysterical banging on his door. He padded barefoot over and opened it wide.

Elwyn Allard was standing on the threshold, his face contorted, his hair flopped over his brow, his right hand raised in a fist ready to hammer on the closed wood again.

'Elwyn!' Joseph was horrified. 'Whatever's happened? Come in.' He stepped back to make room for him. 'You look terrible. What is it?'

Elwyn's body was shuddering. He gasped for breath and started speaking twice before managing to get the words out coherently.

'Sebastian's been shot! He's dead! I'm sure he's dead. You've got to help!'

It took a moment for Joseph to realise the meaning of what he had said, but he refused to accept it. It was impossible!

'Help me!' Elwyn begged. He was leaning on the doorpost, needing it to support himself.

'Of course.' Joseph reached for his dressing gown from the back of the door and ignored his slippers. To think of bothering with clothes would have been ridiculous. Elwyn must be wrong. There might be time to salvage something — everything. Sebastian was probably ill . . . or . . . or what? Elwyn had said he had been shot. People did not shoot each other in Cambridge. Nobody had guns! It was unthinkable.

He ran down the steps behind Elwyn and

across the silent, early morning courtyard, the dew on the grass nearly dry except where the buildings shadowed it. They went in at another door and Elwyn started to scramble up the stairs, lurching from side to side. At the top he turned right and at the second door, hurled his shoulder at it as if he could not turn the handle, although his hands grasped after it.

Joseph passed him and opened it properly.

The curtains were drawn back and the scene was bathed in the hard, clear light of the early sun. Sebastian sat in his chair, leaning back a little. The low table beside him was spread with books, not littered but lying carefully piled on top of each other in a neat stack, here and there a slip of paper in to mark a place. One book was open in his lap and his hands, slender and strong, brown from the sun, lay loosely on top of it. There were a couple of deep scratches on one of them. His head was fallen back, his face perfectly calm, no fear or pain in it. His eyes were closed. His fair hair seemed barely disturbed. He could have been asleep, but for the scarlet wound on his right temple and the blood splattered on the chair arm and floor beyond from the gaping hole at the other side. Elwyn was right: with an injury like that he had to be dead.

Joseph went over to him instinctively, as if even the futile gesture of help were in some way still necessary. Then he stood still, the cold seeping through his body as he stared in sick dismay at the third person he had cared for shatteringly destroyed within the space of two

123

weeks. It was as if he had awoken from one nightmare, only to plunge into another.

He reached down and touched Sebastian's cheek. It was colder than life, but not yet chill.

A choked gasp from Elwyn tore Joseph out of his stupor. With an intense effort he submerged his own horror and turned to look at the younger man. He was ashen-skinned, the sweat standing out on his lip and brow, his eyes hollow with shock. His whole body trembled and his breath came raggedly as he struggled to retain some control.

'There's nothing you can do to help him,' Joseph said, surprised how steady his voice sounded in the silence of the room. There was still no one down in the quad, no feet on the stairs outside. 'Go and fetch the porter.'

Elwyn stood still. 'Who . . . who could have done this?' he said, gulping air. 'Who would . . . ?' he stopped, his eyes filling with tears.

'I don't know. But we must find out,' Joseph replied. There was no gun in Sebastian's hand, nor did it lie on the floor where it would have slipped from his fingers. 'Go and fetch the porter,' he repeated. 'Don't speak to anyone else.'

He glanced around the room. His mind was beginning to regain some clarity. The clock on the mantel said three minutes to seven. They were one floor up from the ground. The windows were closed and locked, every pane whole. Nothing was forced or broken, nor had the door any marks on it. Already the hideous knowledge

124

was on the edge of his mind that this had been done by someone inside the college, someone Sebastian knew, and he must have let that person in.

'Yes . . . ' Elwyn said obediently. 'Yes . . . ' Then he turned on his heel and stumbled out, leaving the door open behind him, and Joseph heard his feet loud and clumsy, going down.

Joseph went over and closed the door, then turned and stared at Sebastian. His face was peaceful, but very tired, as though he had at last shed some terrible burden and allowed sleep to overtake him. Whoever had stood there with a gun in his hand, Sebastian had not had time to realise what he was going to do, or perhaps to believe that he meant it.

Pain was too crippling for anger yet. His mind could not accept it. Who would do such a thing? And why?

Young men were intense, just at the beginning of life, and everything was larger to them, more acute: first real love; the brink of ambition realised; triumph and heartbreak were so sharp; the power of dreams incalculable; the soaring mind tasting the joy of flight. Passion of all kinds was coming into its own, but violence was only of the occasional fist fight; a brawl when someone had had too much to drink.

This had a darkness to it that was alien to everything Joseph knew and loved of Cambridge, to the whole of life here and all it meant. Like a blow, he remembered what Sebastian had said about the heart being changed by war, the beauty and the light of it being destroyed by those who did not understand. It was as if he had in those brief words written his own epitaph.

The door opened behind him and he turned to see the porter standing in the entrance, his hair ruffled and his face puckered with alarm. He glanced at Joseph, then stared past him at Sebastian and the colour drained from his skin. He made a gagging sound in his throat.

'Mitchell, will you please lock the room here, then take Mr Allard . . . ' he nodded to indicate Elwyn a couple of steps behind him on the landing, 'and get him a cup of hot tea with a good stiff drop of brandy. Look after him.' He took a shivering breath. 'We'll have to call the police, so no one else should go up or down this stair for the time being. Will you tell the other gentlemen who use this way to remain in their rooms until informed otherwise? Tell them there's been an accident. Do you understand?'

'Yes, Dr Reavley.' Mitchell was a good man who had served at St John's for over twenty years and was up to meeting most crises appropriately, from drunken brawls, and the odd dislocated or broken bone, to the occasional overzealous student stuck up on the roof. But the worst crimes had been the theft of a few pounds and, once, cheating at an examination. This was of a different nature, something intruding from outside his world.

'Thank you,' Joseph accepted, stepping on to the landing himself. He looked beyond Mitchell to Elwyn. 'I'll go and see the Master and do everything else that's necessary. You go with Mitchell, stay with him.'

'Yes . . . yes . . . ' Elwyn's voice tailed off and he remained motionless until Mitchell locked the door. Then Joseph took the young man gently by the arm, forcing him to turn away, guiding him to the stairs and down them a step at a time.

Once outside in the quad Joseph walked briskly across the path to the next quad, which was smaller and quieter, with one slender tree asymmetrically planted to the left. At the further side was the wrought-iron gate leading through to the Fellows' Garden. At this hour it would be locked, as usual. The Master's lodgings had two doors, one from the Fellows' Garden, one from this quad.

He passed into the shadow where the dew still lay, and suddenly remembered he was barefoot. His feet were cold. He had not even thought to go back to his own room for slippers. It was too late to matter now.

He knocked on the door and ran his fingers through his hair to push it back off his face, suddenly conscious of how he looked if Connie Thyer should answer, not the Master himself.

As it was he had to knock twice more before he heard footsteps. Then the lock turned, and Aiden Thyer stood blinking at him.

'Good God, Reavley! Do you know what time it is?' he demanded. His long, pale face was still dazed with sleep and his fair hair flopped forward over his brow. He looked at Joseph's dressing gown and his bare feet, then up again quickly, a flicker of alarm shadowing his eyes. 'What is it? What's wrong?'

'Sebastian Allard has been shot dead,' Joseph

127

replied. The words somehow gave the nightmare a sickening reality. The very act of sharing it increased those for whom it was true. He saw from Thyer's confusion that he had not grasped that Joseph meant violence of the mind as well as of the hand. He had not used the word 'murder', but it was what he meant. 'Elwyn just came and told me,' he added. 'I need to come in.'

'Oh!' Thyer jerked to attention, embarrassed. 'Yes, of course. I'm sorry.' He pulled the door wide and moved back.

Joseph followed him, relieved to step on to carpet after the cold stone of the pathway. He had not realised it, but he was shivering.

'Come into the study.' Thyer led the way.

Joseph closed the front door and followed. He sat down in one of the big chairs while Thyer poured him a stiff brandy from the tantalus on the sideboard and passed it to him, then he turned back and poured a second one for himself.

'Tell me what happened,' he directed. 'Where were they?' He glanced at the mahogany clock on the mantel. It was quarter past seven. 'Poor Elwyn must be in a state. What about the others who were there?' He shut his eyes for a second. 'For God's sake, how did they manage to shoot anyone?'

Joseph was not sure what he was imagining — target shooting practice somewhere, a tragic piece of carelessness?

'In his room,' he answered. 'He must have got up very early to study. He's . . . he was one of my best students.' He tried to steady himself. He

128

must think of the practical, put from his mind the wider meaning. 'He was in his chair, alone, apart from whoever shot him. The windows were closed and locked and there are no marks of forced entry on the door. It was just one shot, to the side of the head, but the gun is not there.'

Thyer's face stiffened and his hands clasped the arm of his chair. He sat a little forward. 'What are you saying, Joseph?' Unconsciously he slipped into familiarity.

'That someone else shot him and then left, taking the gun with him,' Joseph answered. 'I can't think of any way to explain it except that.' How had he come in the space of two weeks to speak of murder as if he understood it?

Thyer sat without moving for several moments. There was a rustle behind him and Joseph turned to see Connie standing in the open doorway, her dark hair loose around her shoulders and a pale satin wrap covering her from neck to foot.

Both men rose to their feet.

'What is it?' she said quietly. Her face was full of concern, making her look younger and far more vulnerable than the beautiful, self-assured woman she usually was. It was the first time Joseph had seen her when she was not aware, before anything else, of being the Master's wife.

'Dr Reavley, are you all right?' she asked anxiously. 'You don't look well. I'm afraid this has been a terrible time for you.' She came into the room, ignoring the fact that she was really not dressed suitably to greet anyone. 'If I am intruding, please tell me. But if there is anything

129

I can do to help . . . at all?'

Joseph was conscious of the warmth of her, not just her physical nearness, the slight perfume of her hair and skin and the slither of silk as she moved, but of a softness in her face, an understanding of what it is to be hurt.

'Thank you, Mrs Thyer,' Joseph said with an attempt at a smile that failed. 'I am afraid something dreadful has happened. I — '

'There is nothing you can do, my dear,' Thyer cut across him, leaving Joseph feeling as if he had been clumsy. And yet there was no point in protecting her from the truth. Within a few hours everyone in St John's would have to know.

'Nonsense!' she said abruptly. 'There are always things to do, even if it is only seeing that the domestic arrangements continue. We still need to eat, to have clean clothes, and it doesn't help anyone to have the staff in a turmoil. What is it that has happened?'

Thyer's face tightened. 'Sebastian Allard has been killed. Apparently it could not have been an accident.' He looked at her apologetically, seeing the colour drain from her skin.

Joseph stepped towards her, all but losing his own balance as he put out his hands to steady her, and felt the muscles in her arms lock with surprising strength.

'Thank you, Dr Reavley,' she said very quietly but with almost complete control. 'I am quite all right. How very dreadful. Do you know who is responsible?'

Thyer moved towards her as well, but stopped short of touching her. 'No. That is rather what

Joseph expects us to do, I imagine — call the police? Isn't it?'

'It is unavoidable, Master,' Joseph answered, dropping his hands to his sides. 'And if you will excuse me, I must go and see what I can do to help Elwyn. The Dean . . . ' he did not finish.

Thyer walked from the room to the hall where there was a telephone on the small table. He lifted it, and Joseph heard him asking the operator to get the police station for him.

Connie looked at Joseph, her dark eyes searching his, trying to find some answer to the fear that was already beginning inside her. What could he say to comfort her, and make some bearable sense out of it? What was the core of faith in him that took one back to sanity when something one loved was snatched away and broken for no reason? If he had known that, he could have eased the rage burning inside him over his parents' murders.

'I . . . ' he began, and realised he had no idea how to go on. She was expecting him, as a man professing a faith in God, to explain it to her in some terms that at least made sense to him. Idiotic phrases came into his mind that people had said to him after Eleanor's death — things about God's will being beyond the human mind to grasp, that obedience lay in accepting. They had been meaningless to him then, and were even more so now when the violence was deliberate and personal.

'I don't know,' he admitted. He saw the confusion in her face. That was not good enough. 'You are right,' he forced himself to sound certain. 'We need to do the ordinary things to help each other. I appreciate your good sense. The students who are here are going to be distressed. We shall need to keep our heads, for their sakes. It will be unpleasant having the police here asking questions, but we must endure it with as much dignity as we can.'

Her face ironed out and she smiled very slightly. 'Of course. If such a hideous thing had to happen, I am so glad you were here. You always grasp the core of things — some other people only ever seem to touch the edges.'

He was embarrassed. She had seen more in him than had been there. But if it comforted her, he would not indulge in the honesty of denying it at her expense.

'It is good to have something to do, isn't it?' she said wryly. 'Someone else to help, to concentrate on their pain and not your own. How wise you are. It will at least get us through the worst of it with some kind of honour. I had better get dressed. I dare say the police will be here almost immediately. The Master will inform the poor young man's family, but I should prepare their accommodation here in college, in case that is what they would like. Fortunately at this time of year there are plenty of rooms.' She gave a choking little laugh. 'The practical and domestic again. I cannot imagine what to say to a woman whose son has been . . . murdered!'

Joseph thought of Mary Allard and how her grief would consume her. No mother can bear the death of her child, but Mary had loved Sebastian with a fierce, all-enveloping pride. She saw in him everything that fed her ambition and her dreams.

He could understand it so easily. Sebastian had possessed an energy of the spirit that lit not only his own vision, but that of others as well. He had touched the lives of so many at the college, whether they wished it or not. Although how could anyone not wish to have their inner hungers awoken, new adventures opened up, the love of every kind of beauty shared: laughter, hope, the whole magnitude of thought scattered like stars in front of them?

It was impossible to believe that his mind did not exist any more; how could Mary Allard ever bear it?

'Yes,' he said, turning to her with sudden urgency. 'You will have to look after them . . . and not be hurt or dismayed if they are in the kind of pain which unintentionally wounds others carelessly, or . . . or even on purpose. Sometimes when we are drowning in our own loss we lash out. Anger is momentarily easier to cope with . . . ' That was hideously true, and yet he was not speaking from his own passion but in the accustomed platitudes he had used for years. He was ashamed of himself, but he did not know what else to say. If he laid open his own feelings he would allow her to see the rage and confusion inside him, and he could not afford that. She would be repelled by its savagery — and frightened.

'I know,' she smiled with great sweetness. 'You don't need to tell me . . . or to worry about them.' She spoke as if he had answered her need.

'Thank you.' He had to escape before he broke the grace of her judgement. 'Yes . . . thank you. I must see what else I can do.' And he excused himself and left, still barefoot and now feeling ridiculous in the broad daylight. He had given no answers at all, not from faith. He had simply given the advice of common sense. Deal with what you can. At least do something.

He went under the archway into his own quad. Two students returning from early exercise, stared at him in amusement and smothered laughter. Did they imagine he was coming back in his pyjamas after an assignation? At another time he would have corrected them and left them in no doubt, but now the words died on his tongue. It was as if there were two realities side by side, glittering, bright as shattered glass: one in which death was violent and terrible, the smell of blood was in the throat and images floated before the eyes, even when they were closed, and he would give anything to forget it; and another in which he merely looked absurd, wandering around in his dressing gown.

He did not trust himself to speak to them in case he screamed the dreadful truth. He could hear his own voice inside his head, wild and soaring out of control.

He ran awkwardly across the last few yards to the door, then up the stairs, tripping and stumbling, until he threw open the door to his own room and slammed it behind him.

He stood still, breathing heavily. He must get control of himself. There were things to do, duties — duty always helped. First of all he should finish shaving, and get dressed. He must make himself look respectable. He would feel better. And eat something! Except that his stomach was churning and his throat ached so abominably he would not be able to swallow.

He took off his dressing gown. It was a flat, baking summer in Cambridge and he was cold. He could smell blood, and fear, as if he were coated with it.

Very carefully, because his hands were stiff, he ran hot water and washed himself, then stared at his face in the glass. Black eyes looked back at him above high cheekbones, strong slightly aquiline nose and highly individual mouth. His flesh looked grey, even beneath the dark stubble of his half-shaved beard. There was something waxen about him.

He finished shaving very carefully, and still cut himself. He put on a clean shirt, and his fingers could not find the buttons or get them through the holes.

It was all absurd, idiotic! The students had thought he was off on some amorous encounter. Looking like this? He was a man walking through a nightmare. And yet he had been so aware of Connie Thyer — the warmth of her, the sweet smell, her closeness. How could he even think of such a thing now?

Because he was blindingly, desperately alone! He would have given anything at all to have had Eleanor here, to take her in his arms and cling to her, have her hold him, take some of this unbearable loss from him.

His parents were dead, crushed and tossed

aside, for a document! That said . . . what? All the warmth and beauty, the intelligence and laughter and giving of their lives just snuffed out. The hole gaped wide, hollow with pain, unfillable.

And now Sebastian! His brain destroyed, blasted into wreckage by a bullet. Everything was slipping away, all that was good and precious and gave light and meaning. What was there left that he dared love any more? When would God smash that and take it away?

This was the last time he was ever going to let it happen. There was going to be no more pain like this! He could not open himself up to it.

Habit told him that it was not God's fault. How many times had he explained that to other people who were screaming inside because of something they could not bear?

Yes it was! He could have done something! If He couldn't manage that, why was He God?

And the ice-cold voice of reason said — 'There is no God. You are alone.'

That was the worst truth of all — alone. The word was a kind of death.

He stood still for several minutes, no coherent thoughts in his head. The coldness didn't stay. He was too angry. Someone had killed John and Alys Reavley, and he was helpless to find out who, or why. There was a conspiracy out there in the world, who knew how big.

Memories flooded back of pottering quietly in the garden, John telling long, rambling jokes, the smell of lily-of-the-valley, Hannah brushing Alys's hair, Sunday dinner.

136

He leaned against the mantel and wept, letting go of the self-control at last and freeing the grief to wash over him and take hold.

★ ★ ★

By mid-morning he was still ashen-faced, but composed. His bedder, the elderly woman who tidied and cared for all the rooms on this stair, had been in, shaking and tearful, but completed her duty. The police had arrived, led by an Inspector Perth, a very ordinary-seeming man of barely average height with receding hair sprinkled with grey, and crooked teeth, two missing. He spoke quietly but he moved with unswerving purpose, and although he was gentle with the grieving and severely rattled students, he allowed none of his questions to go unanswered.

As soon as he discovered that the Dean was absent in Italy, but that Joseph was an ordained minister, he asked him to stay at hand. 'Might help,' he said with a nod. He did not explain whether it was to make it more likely that people would then tell the truth, or for the comfort of their distress.

'Seems nobody came nor went during the night,' Perth said, looking at Joseph with sharp grey eyes. They were alone in the porter's lodge, Mitchell having been sent on some errand. 'No break-in. My men've bin all over. Sorry, Reverend, but it looks loike your young Mr Allard — the dead one, that is — must've bin shot by someone inside the college here. Police

137

surgeon might be able to tell us what time, but it doesn't make no difference for who could've bin there. He was up an' dressed an' sitting at his books — '

'I touched his cheek,' Joseph interrupted him. 'When I went in. It wasn't cold. I mean it was . . . cool.' He shuddered inside at the memory. That had been three hours ago. He would be cold now, the spirit, the dreams and the hunger that made him unique dissolved into — what? He knew what the answer was supposed to be, but he had no inner fire that affirmed it to him.

Perth was nodding, biting his lip. 'Sounds right, sir. Looks loike he knew whoever did it, from what Oi've bin told. You knew him, Reverend — was he the sort of young gentleman to let in someone he didn't know, at that time — which looks to've bin about half-past five — and while he was studying?'

'No. He was a very serious student,' Joseph replied. 'He would resent the intrusion. People don't normally call on anyone before breakfast, unless it's an emergency.'

'What Oi thought,' Perth agreed. 'And we've searched all over the room, and the gun's not there. We'll be going over the whole college for it, of course. Don't look loike he put up any sort of a fight. Took by surprise, by all we can see. Someone he trusted.'

Joseph had thought the same thing, but until now he had not put it in those words. The idea was indescribably ugly.

Perth was staring at him. 'Spoken to a few of the young gentlemen, sir. Asked if anyone heard a shot, seeing as there must've bin one. One young gentleman said he heard a bang, but he didn't take notice. Thought it was just something in the street, car mebbe, and he doesn't know what time it was. Went back to sleep again.' Perth chewed his lip. 'And no one has any thoughts as to why, least none as how they'll own to. All seem took by surprise. But it's early days. D'you know of anyone who had a brangle with him — jealous, mebbe? He was a very good-looking young man. Clever too, by accounts, good scholar, one of the best. First class honours, they say.' His expression was carefully unreadable.

'You don't kill people because they outshine you academically!' Joseph said with too much of an edge to his voice. He was being rude and he could not help it. His hands were shaking and he felt dry-mouthed. It was hard to breathe normally.

'Don't you?' Perth left it as a question unanswered. He sat on the edge of the porter's desk. 'Why do you kill someone then, Reverend? Young gentlemen like these,' his body was stiff, 'with every advantage in the world, and their whole lives to look forward to?' He waved at the chair for Joseph to sit down. 'What would make one o' them take a gun an' go into someone's rooms afore six in the morning, and shoot him in the head? Must've bin a powerful reason, sir, something for which there weren't no other answer.'

Joseph's legs were weak and he sank into the chair.

'An' it weren't spur of the moment, like,' Perth

139

continued. 'Someone got up special, took a gun with 'em, and there was no quarrel, or Mr Allard wouldn't've bin sitting back all relaxed, with not a book out of place.' He stopped and waited, staring curiously at Joseph.

'I don't know.' The full enormity of what had happened was settling on him with a weight so heavy he could scarcely fill his lungs with air. His mind flickered over the students closest to Sebastian. Who could he have let in at that hour, and remained seated, talking to him, instead of getting up and fairly robustly telling him to come back at a more civilised time? Elwyn, of course. And why had Elwyn gone to see him so early? Joseph had not asked him, but no doubt Perth would.

Lewis Foubister. He and Sebastian had shared an interest in Greek poetry. Foubister was the better language scholar — he had the vocabulary — but he had less feeling for the music and the rhythm of it, or for the subtlety of the culture than Sebastian had. They collaborated well, and both enjoyed it, often publishing their poems in one of the college magazines. If Foubister had also been up early studying, and found a particularly good line or phrase, one that he almost gripped but not quite, he would have disturbed Sebastian, even at that time.

But Joseph would not tell Perth that, at least not yet.

And there were Eardslie and Morel, good friends to each other, with whom Sebastian and Peter Rattray often made a four for tennis. Rattray was keen on debate, and he and

140

Sebastian had indulged in many all-night arguments, to the intense pleasure of both of them. Although that did not seem a reason for going to anyone's rooms so early.

Who else was there? At least half a dozen others came to his mind, all of whom were still here in college, for one reason or another, but he could not imagine any of them even thinking of violence, let alone acting it out.

Perth was watching him, content to wait, patient as a cat at a mouse-hole.

'I have no idea,' Joseph reiterated helplessly, aware that Perth would know he was being evasive. How could any man who was trained in the spiritual care of people, living and working with a group of students, be totally blind to a passion so intense it ended in murder? Such terror or hatred does not spring whole into being in a day. How was it that he had not seen it?

'How long've you bin here, Reverend?' Perth asked.

Joseph felt himself blushing, the heat painful in his face. 'A little over a year.' He had to have seen it, merely refused to recognise it for what it was. How stupid! How totally useless!

'And you taught Mr Sebastian Allard? What about his brother, Mr Elwyn? Did you teach him too?'

'For a while, for Latin. He dropped it.'

'Why?'

'He found it difficult and he didn't think it was necessary for his career. He was right.'

'So he weren't so clever as his brother?'

'Very few were. Sebastian was remarkably

141

gifted. He would have . . . ' The words stuck in his throat. Without any warning, the reality of death engulfed him again. All the golden promise he had seen ahead for Sebastian was gone, as if night had obscured daylight. It took him a moment to regain control of himself so he could continue speaking. 'He had a remarkable career ahead of him,' he finished.

'Doin' what?' Perth raised his eyebrows.

'Almost anything he wanted.'

'Schoolmaster?' Perth frowned. 'Preacher?'

'Poet, philosopher. In government if he wanted.'

'Government? Learning old languages?' Perth was utterly confused.

'A lot of our greatest leaders have begun with a degree in classics,' Joseph explained. 'Mr Gladstone is the most obvious example.'

'Well, I never knew that!' Perth clearly found it beyond his comprehension.

'You don't understand,' Joseph went on. 'At university there are always those who are more brilliant than you are, more spectacularly gifted in a particular area. If you didn't know that when you came, you would certainly learn it very quickly. Every student here has sufficient talent and intellect to succeed, if they work. I know of no one foolish enough to carry anything more than a passing moment of envy for a superior mind.' He said it with absolute certainty, and it was only when he looked at Perth's expression that he realised how condescending he sounded, but it was too late to retrieve it.

'So you didn't notice anything at all?' Perth

observed. It was impossible to tell if he believed that, or what he thought of a teacher and minister who could be so blind.

Joseph felt like a new student chastised for a stupid mistake. 'Nothing I thought could lead to more than a passing stiffness . . . a distance,' he defended himself. 'Young men are emotional, highly strung sometimes. Exams . . . ' He tailed off, not knowing what else to add. He was trying to explain a culture and a way of life to a man for whom it was totally foreign. The gulf between a Cambridge student and a policeman was unbridgeable. How could Perth possibly understand the passions and dreams that impelled young men from backgrounds of privilege, and in most cases a degree of wealth, men whose academic gifts were great enough to earn them places here? He must come from an ordinary home where learning was a luxury, money never quite enough, necessity a constant companion on the heels of labour.

A cold breath touched him of fear that Perth would inevitably come to wrong conclusions about these young men, misunderstand what they said and did, mistake motives, and blame innocence, simply because it was all alien to him. And the damage would be irretrievable.

And then the moment after, his own arrogance struck him like a blow. He belonged to the same world, he had known all of them for at least a year, and seen them almost every day during term time, and he had not had even the faintest idea of hatred slowly building until it exploded in a lethal violence.

There must have been signs; he had ignored them, misinterpreted them as harmless and misread everything they meant. He would like to think it had been charity, but it wasn't. To have been blind to the truth was stupidity at best, at worst it was also moral cowardice. 'If I can help you, of course I will,' he said much more humbly. 'I . . . I am as . . . shocked — '

'Of course you are, sir,' Perth said with surprising gentleness. 'Everybody is. No one expects anything like this to happen to them. Just tell me if you remember anything, or if you see anything now. And no doubt you'll be doing what you can to help the young gentlemen. Some of 'em look pretty frangled.'

'Yes . . . naturally. Is there — '

'Nothing, sir,' Perth assured him.

Joseph thanked him and left, going outside into the bright, hard sunlight of the quad. Almost immediately he ran into Lewis Foubister, his face white, his dark hair on end as if he had run his hands through it again and again.

'Dr Reavley!' he gasped. 'They think one of us did it! That can't be true. Someone else must've . . . ' He stopped in front of Joseph, blocking his way. He did not know how to ask for help, but his eyes were desperate. He was a northerner from the outskirts of Manchester, used to rows of brick houses back to back with each other, cold water and privies. This world of ancient, intricate beauty, space and leisure had stunned and changed him for ever. He could never truly belong here, neither could he return to who he had been before. Now he looked

144

younger than his twenty-two years, and thinner than Joseph had remembered.

'I am afraid it appears that it was,' Joseph said gently. 'We may be able to find some other answer, but no one broke in, and Sebastian was sitting quite calmly in his chair, which suggests he was not afraid of whoever it was.'

'Then it must have been an accident,' Foubister said breathlessly. 'And . . . and whoever it was is too scared to own up to it. Can't blame him, really. But he'll say, when he realises the police are thinking it's murder.' He stopped again, his eyes searching Joseph's, begging to be reassured.

It was an answer Joseph longed to believe. Whoever had done such a thing would be devastated. To run away was a coward's act, and he would be ashamed, but better that than murder. And it would mean Joseph had not been blind to hatred. There had been none to see.

'I hope that's true,' he answered with as much of a smile as he could manage. He put his hand on Foubister's arm. 'Wait and see what happens. And don't leap to judgement yet, good or bad.'

Foubister nodded, but he said nothing. Joseph watched as he hurried away across to the opposite side of the quad. As clearly as if he had been told, Joseph knew he was going straight to see his friend Morel.

★ ★ ★

Gerald and Mary Allard arrived before noon. They had only to come from Haslingfield, about four miles to the south-west. The first shock of the news must have reached them after breakfast, perhaps leaving them too stunned to react immediately. There may have been people to tell, perhaps a doctor or a priest, and other members of the family.

Joseph dreaded meeting them. He knew Mary's grief would be wild and savage, she would feel all the pent-up, wounding rage that he did. The comforting words that she had said so sincerely to him at his parents' funeral would mean nothing repeated back to her now, just as they meant nothing to him at the time.

Because he was afraid of it, he went straight away, within minutes of their car pulling up at the front gate on St John's Street. He saw Mitchell taking them solemnly, dazed and stiff with the new wounds of loss, through the first quad and the second towards the Master's house. Joseph met them a dozen yards from the front door.

Mary was dressed in black, her skirt stained with dust at the hem, her hat wide, shading her veiled face. Beside her Gerald looked like a man struggling to stand the morning after a drunken binge. His skin was pasty, his eyes bloodshot. He took a moment or two to recognise Joseph, then he lurched towards him, momentarily seeming to forget his wife.

'Reavley! Thank God you're here! What happened? I don't understand — it doesn't make sense! Nobody would . . . ' He tailed off helplessly, not knowing what else he meant to say. He wanted help, anyone who would tell him it was not true, and release him from a grief he could not bear.

Joseph gripped his hand, and steadied his other arm, taking some of his weight as he staggered. 'We don't know what happened,' he said firmly. 'It seems to have been around half-past five this morning, and the best thing I can say at the moment is that it was very quick, a couple of seconds, if that. He didn't suffer.'

Mary was in front of him, her black eyes blazing even through her veil. 'Is that supposed to comfort me?' she demanded, her voice hoarse. 'He's dead! Sebastian's dead!'

Her passion was too fierce for him to touch, and yet he was standing here in the middle of the quad in the July sun, trying to find words that would be something more than a statement of his own futility. He did not know how to ease the loss for her, or for himself. Where was the fire of his faith when he needed it? Anyone could believe on a calm Sunday in a church pew, when life was whole and safe. Faith is only real when there is nothing else between you and the abyss, an unseen thread strong enough to hold the world.

'I know he's dead, Mary,' he answered her. 'I can't tell you why, or how. I don't know who did it, or whether they meant to or not. We may learn everything except the reason, but it will take time.'

'It's the reason I want!' Her voice shook with fury. 'Why Sebastian? He was . . . beautiful!'

He knew what she meant — not only his face but the brilliance of his mind, the strength of his

147

dreams. 'Yes, he was,' he agreed.

'So why has your God let some stupid, worthless . . . ' She could not think of a word big enough to carry her hatred. 'Destroy him?' she spat. 'Tell me why, Reverend Mr Reavley!'

'I don't know. Did you think I would be able to tell you? I'm just as human as you are, just as much in need of learning faith, walking with trust, not — '

'Trust in what?' she cut across him, slicing her thin, black-gloved hand in the air. 'A God who takes everything from me and lets evil destroy good?'

'Nothing destroys good,' he said, wondering if it were true. 'If good were never threatened, and even beaten sometimes, then there would be no good, because it would eventually become no more than wisdom, self-interest. If — '

She turned away from him impatiently, snatching her arm back as if he had been holding her, and stalked over the grass towards Connie Thyer, standing at the doorway of the Master's house.

'I'm sorry,' Gerald muttered helplessly. 'She's taking it . . . I . . . I really . . . '

'It's all right.' Joseph stopped his fumbling embarrassment. It was painful to see and he wanted it ended for both their sakes. 'I understand. You had better go and be with her. She needs you.'

'No, she doesn't,' Gerald said with an instant's extraordinary bitterness. Then he caught himself, blushed and walked away after her.

Joseph started back towards the first quad and

was almost there when he saw a second woman, also veiled and in black. She was apparently lost, looking through the arch tentatively. She seemed young, from the grace of her posture, yet there was a dignity and natural assurance to her, suggesting that in other circumstances she would have been very much in command of herself.

'May I help you?' Joseph asked, startled to see her. He could not imagine what she could be doing here in St John's, or why Mitchell had ever let her in.

She came forward with relief. 'Thank you, that is very kind of you, Mr . . . ?'

'Reavley, Joseph Reavley,' he introduced himself. 'You seem uncertain which way to go. Where is it you wish to be?'

'The Master's house,' she replied. 'I believe his name is Mr Aidan Thyer. Is that correct?'

'Yes, but I am afraid he is engaged at present, and likely to be for some considerable time. I am very sorry, but an unexpected event has changed everyone's arrangements.' There was no need to tell her of the tragedy. 'I shall convey any message to him when he is free, and perhaps you can make an appointment to call at another time?'

She stood even straighter. 'I am aware of the 'event', Mr Reavley. You are referring to the death this morning of Sebastian Allard. My name is Regina Coopersmith. I was his fiancée.'

Joseph stared at her as if she had spoken in an alien language. It was not possible! How could Sebastian, the passionate idealist, the scholar whose mind danced to the music of language,

149

have fallen in love and contracted himself to marriage, and never even mentioned it?

Joseph looked at Regina Coopersmith, knowing he should be telling her how sorry he was, offering her some sympathy, even if comfort was beyond any of them to give or receive, but his mind refused to accept what she had said.

'I'm sorry, Miss Coopersmith,' he said awkwardly. 'I didn't know.' He must add something. This superficially composed young woman had lost the man she loved in the most appalling circumstances. 'I'm deeply sorry for your bereavement.' He meant it. He knew how it felt to face that gulf of loneliness suddenly, without any warning at all. One day you had everything, the next day it was gone. He also knew that no words were going to help in the slightest.

'Thank you,' she replied with the ghost of a smile.

'May I accompany you to the Master's house? It is through there.' He gestured behind him. 'I expect the porter has your bags?'

'Yes. Thank you. That would be most courteous,' she accepted.

He turned and walked with her back into the sunlight again and along the path. He glanced sideways at her. Her veil hid only part of her face; her mouth and chin were clearly visible. Her features were strong, but pleasant rather than pretty. She had dignity, resolve, but it was not a face of passion. What had made Sebastian fall in love with her? Could she have been Mary Allard's choice for her son, rather than his own?

Perhaps she had money, and good connections with county families? She would give Sebastian the security and the background he would need for a career in poetry or philosophy, which might not immediately provide such things itself.

Or perhaps there were whole areas of Sebastian's nature that Joseph had assumed, and he had been wrong.

The midday sun was hot and sharp, casting the shadows with hard edges, like the cutting realities of knowledge.

5

The Peacemaker heard the footsteps coming up the stairs, then the tap on the door.

'Come,' he said tersely, turning away from the window and standing with his back to the light. He knew already that the news would not be good. It was in the man's tread, the weariness, the lack of energy.

The door opened and the visitor came in. He had been to Germany and returned since the previous time they had spoken.

'Well?' the Peacemaker said.

The man's face was calm, but there was a bleakness about his eyes. 'We need to think further,' he said simply. 'In case we fail. Just as a precaution.' The faintest smile crossed his lips, irony without pleasure. 'I know there is still time, and it would be infinitely the greater good, but we are dealing with fools.'

The Peacemaker raised his eyebrows. 'Did you come here to tell me that?' he said with disbelief so cold it shivered in the air.

The muscles in the man's face tightened. 'I came to find out what realistic plans you have, should we fail, so that I can be of whatever assistance is possible from Berlin.'

The Peacemaker relaxed his shoulders a little and moved away from the window towards the centre of the room. 'Of course I have alternative plans,' he agreed. 'Should they become necessary to implement, the groundwork has already been laid, in America, in Mexico, and in Japan. There are also other possibilities. But they are all wasteful in comparison.' His fists tightened till his knuckles were white. 'God knows how many human lives will be thrown away — uselessly!' He leaned forward a little. 'Find it!' he said between his teeth. 'Find the document!'

The visitor breathed in and out slowly, steadying himself. 'What message do I take back?'

'None!' the Peacemaker replied. 'Do your job here. I have people in place where they are needed. Go.'

The visitor stood to attention for a moment, then turned and left, closing the door behind him with a click.

★   ★   ★

Late on Saturday afternoon Matthew drove from London back to St Giles. It had been an unpleasant day, not from any cause that he had expected, such as news from Ireland or the Balkans, but an increasingly immediate domestic problem. A bomb had been found in a church in the heart of Westminster, with the fuse lit. Apparently it had been the work of a group of women who were agitating in increasingly violent ways to be given the right to vote.

Fortunately no one had been hurt, but the possibility of the destruction it could have caused was deeply disturbing. It had meant

153

Matthew had been drawn from his investigation of Blunden, and the political weapons that might have been used against him. Instead he had been busy all day with increasing the security in London itself, and had had to ask Shearing for permission to leave, which would not ordinarily have been the case on a weekend.

His sense of relief as he drove out of the heat and enclosure of the city was like an escape from captivity. It was exhilarating, he felt almost drunk as he put his foot down hard on the accelerator and the Sunbeam-Talbot sped forward on the open road.

The weather was fine, another golden evening with great puffball clouds piling up in the east, with the sun blazing on them till they drifted like white galleons in the shimmering air, sails full set to the horizon. Beneath them the fields were already ripe with harvest.

The light deepened across the broader skies of the fenland, almost motionless in the amber of sunset.

Matthew drove into St Giles, along the main street past the shining millpond, and turned down the road to the house. Mrs Appleton met him at the front door and her face lit with pleasure.

'Oh, Mr Matthew, it's good you're here. An' you'll be staying?' She stepped back to allow him in, just as Judith came down the stairs, having heard the crunch of car tyres on the gravel. She ran down the last couple of steps, Henry at her heels, tail aloft. She threw her arms around Matthew, giving him a quick, fierce hug. Then

154

she pulled back and looked at him more carefully.

'Yes, of course I'm staying,' he said to Mrs Appleton over Judith's shoulder. 'At least until lunchtime tomorrow.'

'Is that all?' Judith demanded. 'It's Saturday evening now! Do they expect you to work all the time?'

He did not bother to argue. It was a discussion they had had before, and they were unlikely to agree. Matthew had a passion for his work that Judith would probably never understand. If there were anything that fired her will and her imagination enough to give all of herself to it, then she had not yet discovered what it was.

He acknowledged the dog, then followed her into the familiar sitting room with its old, comfortable furniture and slightly worn carpet, colours muted by time. As soon as the door was closed she asked him if he had discovered anything.

'No,' he said patiently, reclining in the big chair that used to be his father's. He was self-conscious about sitting in it. He had always taken it when his father was not there, but now it seemed like a statement of ownership. Yet to have sat somewhere else would have been awkward also, a break with habit that was absurd, another difference from the past that had no purpose.

She watched him, a tiny frown on her face.

'I suppose you are trying?' There was a flash of challenge in her eyes.

'That's part of why I came up this weekend

155

'. . . and to see you, of course. Have you heard from Joseph?'

'A couple of letters. Have you?'

'Not since he went back.' He looked at her, trying to read her feelings from her expression. She sat a little sideways on the couch, with her feet tucked up, the way Alys had criticized and told her was unladylike. Was she as much in control as she looked, with her hair swept back from her calm brow, her smooth cheeks and wide, vulnerable mouth?

Or was the emotion bottled up inside her, too raw to touch, but eating away at her will? She was the one of them who was still living here in the house. How often did she come down the stairs and find herself startled that there was no one else here to say 'good morning' to, except Mrs Appleton? Did she hear the silence, the missing voices, the footsteps? Did she imagine the familiar touch, the smell of pipe tobacco, the closed study door to indicate that John must not be interrupted? Did she listen for the sound of Alys singing to herself as she arranged flowers, and did the dozens of small things that showed someone in the house loved it, and was happy here?

He could escape. Life in London was exactly the same as before, except for the very occasional telephone call and the visits home. The difference was all inside. It was knowledge he could set aside when he needed to.

It would be like that for Hannah also, and for Joseph. He was worried about them as well, but differently. Hannah had Archie to comfort her,

156

and her children to need her and fill her time.

Joseph was different. Since Eleanor's death something within him had retreated from emotions to hide in reason. Matthew had grown up with Joseph, who was seven years older and always seeming cleverer, wiser, and quicker. He had imagined he would catch up, but now, in adulthood, he began to think that perhaps Joseph had an intellect of extraordinary power. Understanding for which other people laboured came to him with ease. He could climb on wings of thought into regions most people only imagined.

But this was also a retreat from the realities of certain kinds of pain, and in the last year he had escaped more completely. Matthew had seen in his eyes, and in fleeting, unguarded moments, an awareness of it in Joseph himself.

Judith was watching him, waiting for him to continue.

'I've been pretty busy lately,' he said. 'Everyone's preoccupied with Ireland and, of course, with the Balkan business.'

'Ireland I can understand, but why the Balkans?' She raised her eyebrows. 'It doesn't really have anything to do with us. Serbia is miles away, the other side of Italy, for heaven's sake. It's a pretty revolting thought, but won't the Austrians just go in and take whatever they want in reparation, and punish the people responsible? Isn't that what usually happens with revolutions — either they succeed and overthrow the government, or they get suppressed? Well, anyone who thinks a couple of Serbian assassins are going to overthrow the Austro-Hungarian

Empire has to be crazy.' She shifted her feet around the other way and settled further into the cushions, hugging one in front of her as if it would escape were she to let it go.

Henry got up from where he had been lying and rearranged himself closer to her.

'It's not they who would do it,' Matthew said quietly, wondering as he spoke if he should tell her this. It was only speculation, a fear of the worst possibilities.

'Who then?' She frowned. 'I thought it was just a few lunatic young men? Is that not true?'

'It seems as if it was,' he agreed. 'War is just the last in a chain of events that could happen . . . but almost certainly someone will step in with enough sense to stop it. The bankers, if no one else. War would be far too expensive!'

She looked at him very levelly, her grey-blue eyes unflinching. 'So why did you mention it?'

He forced himself to smile. 'I wish I hadn't. I just wanted you to know I'm not making excuses. I don't know where to begin. I thought I'd go over and see Robert Isenham tomorrow. I expect he'll be at church — I'll see him afterwards.'

'Sunday lunch?' she said with surprise. 'He won't thank you a lot for that! What do you want to ask him, anyway?'

He shook his head with a slight smile. 'Nothing so blunt as that. You wouldn't make a detective, would you!'

Her face tightened a little. 'All right! What do you think he knows?'

He became serious again. 'Maybe nothing, but

158

if Father confided anything at all, it would probably be to Isenham. He might even have mentioned where he was going, or who he was expecting to see. I don't know where to start, other than going through everyone he knew.'

'That could take for ever.' She sat quite still, her face shadowed in thought. 'What do you think it could be, Matthew? I mean . . . what would Father have known about? People who plot great conspiracies don't leave documents lying around for anyone to find by chance.'

A chill touched him. Then he saw in her eyes a fear she could not put words to.

'I know he didn't find the document by accident,' he answered her. 'It was given to him — maybe by someone he knew very well — '

'Like Robert Isenham,' she finished the thought for him. 'Be careful!' Now the fear was quite open.

'I will,' he promised. 'There's nothing suspicious in my going to see him. I would do anyway, sooner or later. He was one of Father's closest friends, geographically, if nothing else. I know they disagreed about a lot of things, but they liked each other underneath it.'

'You can like people and still betray them,' Judith said, 'if it were to a cause you believed in passionately enough. Maybe father took the document rather than was given it. You have to betray other people rather than betray yourself — if that's what it comes to.' Then seeing the surprise in his face, she added, 'You told me that.'

'I did? I don't remember.'

'Yes, you do. It was last Christmas. I didn't agree with you. We had quite a row. You told me I was naïve, and idealists put causes before anything else. You told me I was being a woman, thinking of everything personally rather than in larger terms.'

'So you don't agree with me, but you'll quote my own words back at me in an argument?' he retorted.

She bit her lip. 'Actually, I do agree with you, I just wasn't going to say so then. You're cocky enough.'

'I'll be careful.' He relaxed into a smile and leaned forward to touch her for a moment, and her hand closed tightly around his.

★ ★ ★

The morning was overcast and heavy with the clinging heat of a storm about to break. Matthew went to church, largely because he wanted to catch up with Isenham as if by chance.

The vicar caught sight of him in the congregation just before he began his sermon. Kerr was not a natural speaker, and the presence of overwhelming emotion in a member of his audience, especially one for whom he felt a responsibility, broke his concentration. He was embarrassed, only too obviously remembering the last time he had seen Matthew, which had been at his parents' funeral. He had been unequal to the task then, and he knew he still was.

Sitting in the fifth row back, Matthew could

almost feel the sweat break out on Kerr's body at the thought of facing him after the service, and scrambling for something appropriate to say. He smiled to himself, and stared back expectantly. The only alternative was to leave, and that would be even worse.

Kerr struggled to the end. The last hymn was sung and the benediction pronounced, and row by row the congregation trooped out into the damp, motionless air.

Matthew went straight to Kerr and shook his hand. 'Thank you, Vicar,' he said courteously. He could not leave without speaking to him, and he did not want to get waylaid and miss the chance to bump into Isenham. 'Just came home to see how Judith is.'

'Not at church, I'm afraid,' Kerr replied dolefully. 'Perhaps you could talk to her. Faith is a great solace at times like these.'

It was clumsy. There were no other 'times like these'. How many people have both their parents murdered in a single, hideous crime? But then, of course, Kerr did not know it was murder. But given Judith's character, the last thing poor Kerr needed was an encounter with her! He would attempt desperately to be kind, to say something that would be of value to her, and she would grow more and more impatient with him, until she let him see how useless he was.

'Yes, of course,' Matthew murmured. 'I'll convey your good wishes to her. Thank you.' As he turned and left he felt that was exactly what his mother would have said — or Joseph. And

161

they would not have meant it any more than he did.

He caught up with Isenham in the lane just beyond the lich-gate. He was easily recognizable even from behind. He was of average height, but barrel-chested, with close-cropped fair hair greying rapidly, and he walked with a slight swagger.

He heard Matthew coming, even though his footsteps were light on the stony surface. He turned and smiled, holding out his hand. 'How are you, Matthew? Bearing up?' It was a question, and also half an instruction. Isenham had served twenty years in the army and seen action in the Boer War. He believed profoundly in the Stoic values. Emotion was fine, even necessary, but it should never be given in to, except in the most private of times and places, and then only briefly.

'Yes, sir.' Matthew knew what was expected and he meant this encounter to earn him Isenham's confidence and to learn from it anything John Reavley might have told him, even in the most indirect way. 'The last thing Father would have wanted would be for us to fall apart.'

'Quite! Quite!' Isenham agreed firmly. 'Fine man, your father. We'll all miss him.'

Matthew fell in step beside him as if he had been going that way, although as soon as they came to the end of the lane he would turn the opposite direction if he were to go home.

'I wish I'd known him better.' He meant that with an intensity that showed raw through his voice, more than he wanted. He meant to be in control of this conversation. 'I expect you were probably as close as anyone?' he continued more briskly. 'Funny how differently family see a person — until you're adult, anyway.'

Isenham nodded. 'Yes. Never thought of it, but I suppose you're right. Funny thing, that. Look at one's parents in a different light, I suppose.' Unconsciously he increased his pace.

Matthew kept up with him easily, as his legs were an inch or two longer. 'You were probably the last person he really talked with,' he went on. 'I hadn't seen him the previous weekend, nor had Joseph, and Judith was out so often.'

'Yes . . . I suppose I was.' Isenham dug his hands deep into his pockets. 'It's been a very bad time. Did you hear about Sebastian Allard? Dreadful business.' He hesitated an instant. 'Joseph will be very upset about that too. Did a lot for him. In fact I dare say he wouldn't even have gone up to Cambridge if it weren't for Joseph's encouragement.'

'Sebastian Allard?' Matthew was confused.

Isenham turned to look at him, stopping in the road where it had already changed into the long, tree-lined avenue down towards his own house. 'Oh dear. No one told you.' He looked a trifle abashed. 'I dare say they felt you'd had enough to get over. Sebastian Allard was murdered, in Cambridge. Right in college — St John's. Devilish thing. Yesterday morning. I only heard from Hutchinson. He's known the Allards for years. Dreadfully cut up, of course.' He pursed his lips. 'Can't expect you to feel the same, naturally. I imagine you've got all the grief you

163

can manage at the moment.'

'I'm very sorry,' Matthew said quietly. There was no sound here in the shelter of the trees and not a breath in the air. He felt as if Isenham must hear the shock in his voice, the control slipping away from him, and helplessness to do anything for those he loved. 'What an appalling tragedy,' he said to fill the silence. 'I must call in on Joseph before I go back to London. He'll be very grieved. He's known Sebastian for years.' He was aware of the numbing pain Joseph would feel, and later he must think what to say to him, but now he wanted to ask Isenham about John Reavley. He forced all other thoughts out of his mind and kept pace with him in the shade of the ancient elms that closed out the sky above them.

Again the tiny thunder flies were hovering, irritating the eyes and face. He swatted at them, even though he knew it was useless. If only it would hurry up and rain! He did not mind getting wet, and it would be a good excuse to stay at Isenham's house longer. 'Actually it's been a pretty rotten time altogether,' he continued. 'I know a good few people are worried about this Balkan business.'

Isenham took his hands out of his pockets. 'Ah! Now there you have a real cause for anxiety.' His broad, wind-burned face was intensely serious. 'That's very worrying, you know? Yes, I expect you do know . . . I dare say more than I do, eh?' He searched Matthew's eyes intently.

Matthew was a little taken aback. He had not realised that Isenham knew where he worked.

Presumably John had said something. In pride, or confiding a shame? The thought stung with all the old sharpness, multiplied by the fact that now Matthew would never be able to prove to his father the value of his profession, and that it was not devious or grubby, full of betrayals and moral compromise.

The charge was unjust, and he fought hard to suppress the anger of it in his mind. He must think. The very least he could do was learn the truth of his parents' deaths. And he was the only one who could do that. It was his intelligence training that would work now, not the medicine his father had wanted him to study, and not Joseph's intellect or his ministry.

'Yes,' he acknowledged. 'Yes, it's pretty ugly. Austria has demanded reparation, and the Kaiser has reasserted Germany's alliance with them. And, of course, the Russians are bound to be loyal to Serbia.'

The first heavy drops of rain fell on the leaves above, spattering loudly, and far in the distance thunder rattled like a heavy cart over cobbles, jolting and jarring around the horizon.

'War,' Isenham said succinctly. 'Drag us all in, damn it! Need to get ready for it. Prepare men and guns.'

'Did Father know that, do you think?' Matthew asked.

Isenham pursed his lips, frowning very slightly. 'Not sure, honestly.' It was an unfinished remark, as if he had stopped before he said too much.

Matthew waited.

Isenham looked unhappy, but he apparently

165

realised he had to continue. 'Seemed a trifle odd lately. Nervous, you know? He . . . er . . . ' He shook his head. 'The day before he died he expected war.' He was puzzled. 'Not like him, not at all.' He increased his pace, his body stiff, shoulders very straight. The rain was beating on the canopy of leaves above them and beginning to come through. 'Sorry, Matthew, but there it is. Can't lie about it. Definitely odd.'

'In what way?' Matthew asked, the words coming automatically as his mind raced to absorb this new information, and at the same time defend himself from what it meant. There was a darkness, a coldness about it.

He was relieved that the weather made it so easy to stay with Isenham, although at the same time it allowed him no excuse to avoid asking still more searching questions. Thank goodness the house was no more than sixty yards away or they would get very wet indeed. Isenham bent forward and began to run. 'Come on!' he shouted. 'You'll get soaked, man!'

They reached the gate of his garden and dashed through to open the front door. The path was already swimming in water and the smell of hot, wet earth filled the air. Plants drooped under the fierceness of the storm as it drummed on the leaves.

Matthew turned to close the gate behind him, and saw a man walking across the lane, coat collar turned up, dark face shining wet, then he disappeared through the trees.

Matthew found Isenham inside and stood dripping in the hallway, surrounded by oak panelling, hunting prints and leather straps with horse brasses in dozens of different designs.

'Thank you.' Matthew accepted the towel Isenham offered him, drying his hands and his face on it and pushing back his wet hair. The rain could not have come at a better time if he had designed it. 'I think there were certain groups, interests, Father was worried about,' he went on, picking up the conversation before their dash to the gate.

Isenham lifted his shoulders in a gesture of denial and took back the towel, dropping it on the floor by the cloakroom door along with his own. 'He said something about plots, but frankly, Matthew, it was all a bit . . . fanciful.' He had struggled to find a polite word for it but the real meaning was plain in his face. 'From what he said to me, he was imagining grand schemes behind things.' He shook his head. 'Not so, you know. Most of our disasters came from good, old-fashioned British blunders. We don't plot our way into wars, we trip over our own feet and fall into them by accident.' He winced, looking apologetic, and rubbed his hand over his wet hair. 'Win in the end, on the same principle that God looks after fools and drunkards. Presumably He has a soft spot for us as well.'

'You don't think Father could have found something?'

Isenham's face tightened. 'No. He lost the thread a bit, honestly. He rambled on about the mutiny in the Curragh, at least that's what I think he was talking about. Wasn't very clear, you know. Said it would get a lot worse, hinted that it would end in a conflagration to engulf all England, even Europe.' He coloured with embarrassment. 'Nonsense, you see? War Minister resigned, and all that, I know, but hardly Europe in flames. Don't suppose anyone across the Channel gives a damn about it one way or the other. Got their own problems. You'd better stay for a bite of lunch,' he said, looking at Matthew's sodden shoulders and feet. 'I've got a telephone. Call Judith and let her know. You'll be wet to the skin if you go back in this.'

He turned and led the way to the dining room where his housekeeper had laid out cold meat, pickles, fresh bread and butter, a newly baked pie, which had barely cooled, and a jug of thick cream.

'Sufficient for two, I think,' he pronounced. He ignored his own wet clothes because he could do nothing about Matthew's. It was part of his code of hospitality that he should sit to dine in dripping trouser legs because his guest was obliged to do so.

'You don't think the Irish situation could escalate?' Matthew said when they were halfway through the excellent cold lamb, and he had taken the edge off his hunger.

'To involve Europe? Not a chance of it. Domestic matter. Always has been.' Isenham took another mouthful and swallowed before continuing. 'I'm sorry, but poor old John was a bit misled. Ran off with the wrong end of things. It happens.'

It was the note of pity in his voice that Matthew could not bear. He thought of his father and saw his face as vividly as if he had left the room only minutes before, grave and gentle, his eyes as direct as Judith's. He had a quick temper at times and he suffered fools badly, but he was a man without guile. To hear him spoken of with such condescension hurt with a fierce, hot pain, and he was instantly defensive.

'What do you mean, 'it happens'?' he demanded. 'What happens?' He heard the anger inside himself and knew he had to control it. He was sitting in Isenham's house, eating his food and, more important than that, he needed his help. 'What was it he was afraid of?'

'Best leave it,' Isenham replied, looking down at his plate and very carefully balancing a piece of pickle on the crust of his bread.

'Are you saying he was deluded?' The instant it was out Matthew wished he had chosen a word less pejorative. He was betraying his own hurt, as well as leaving himself unguarded. It sabotaged his purpose. He was angry with himself. He had more skill than that!

Isenham raised his eyes, hot and miserable. 'No, no, of course not. He was just . . . a little jumpy. I dare say we all are, what with the army mutinying, and then all this violence in the Balkans.'

'Father didn't know about the Archduke,' Matthew pointed out. 'He and Mother were killed that day themselves.'

'Killed?' Isenham asked.

Matthew amended it instantly. 'When the car went off the road.'

'Of course. I'm — I'm sorrier than I can say.

Look, wouldn't you rather — '

'No. I'd like to know what he was worried about. You see, he mentioned it to me, but only briefly.' Was that a risk? It was a deliberate one. He watched Isenham's face minutely for even a flicker, the slightest shadow or movement of the eyes that would give away more than he had said, but there was none. Isenham was merely embarrassed. 'I don't know what to tell you. I don't want to let down an old friend. Remember him as he was, Matthew . . . '

'Was it really so bad?' Matthew said between his teeth. He was shaken by how angry Isenham's implication made him, and how that hurt. It was barely within his control not to lash back.

Isenham flushed. 'No, of course not! Just . . . just a misinterpretation of facts, I think. A touch overdramatic, out of proportion. After all,' he was trying to repair the damage, and failing, 'we've always had wars, here or there, over the last thousand years or so. It's our national spirit, our destiny, if you like.' His voice lifted with his own belief. 'We'll survive it. We always do. It'll be nasty for a while, but I dare say it won't last more than a few months.'

He tried to smile, but it was thin, but not because he did not mean what he said. He was still aware of having revealed his friend's weakness to the man's own son, and when he was not here to defend himself. 'I'm sure in a little while he would have seen that,' he added lamely.

Matthew leaned forward, elbows on the table.

170

'What was it he thought?' He felt his heart hammering. The muscles of his arms and chest were knotted so hard they hurt. It was not that he might be about to learn what the conspiracy was that mattered, it was that his father would be vindicated or not.

'That's it,' Isenham said, shaking his head from side to side. 'He wasn't clear. Honestly, Matthew, I don't think he knew! I think — I didn't want to say this, but you force me to.' He looked resentful, his face red even under his windburn. 'I think he got hold of half an idea, and imagined the rest. He wouldn't tell me what it was because I don't think he could. But it had something to do with honour . . . and he wanted war. There! I'm sorry. I knew it would hurt you, but you insisted.'

It was preposterous. John Reavley would never want war, no matter what anyone had done. It was barbaric, revolting! It was utterly unlike anything he believed in and had fought for all his life, against all the decency he had treasured, nurtured, every human faith he had professed! The very reason at the heart of his hatred of the intelligence services was what he saw as their dishonesty, then manipulation of people to serve nationalist ends, and ultimately to make war more likely.

'He wouldn't want war!' Matthew said aloud, his voice shaking. He had demanded to know, and yet he wished Isenham had not told him this. It could not be true. It made his father someone he did not know, alien and frightening.

But then, how well had he known him? His

face was as familiar as his own, more so. It came from the past so far back it lay before awareness of himself. But that was one side of him! How many children know their fathers as men, as fighters, lovers, friends? Matthew thought. Do we ever become old enough to see beyond the tie of love, the knowledge that we are part of each other's existence? When do we become separate, and able to see clearly?

Perhaps it was that blind, driving instinct to protect that kept children alive, and protected the parent when the positions were reversed and the younger became the stronger.

'He wouldn't ever want war!' Matthew repeated intensely, fixing Isenham with a glare.

'That's what I said,' Isenham nodded. 'He had half a story and he wasn't making sense of it. He was a good man. Remember that, Matthew, and forget the rest.' He took another bite of bread and pickle, then helped himself to more meat, speaking with his mouth full. 'This kind of tension makes everyone a bit jumpy. Fear does different things to people. Some run away, some go forward to meet it before it's there, sort of try to provoke it to happen! Can't bear the suspense. Seems John was one of those. Seen it out on the hunting field sometimes; more in the army. Takes a strong man to wait.'

Matthew felt the accusation of weakness scald with a pain almost physical. Father was not weak! He drew in his breath in a gasp, longing to retort with something that would crush this injustice out of existence, but he could not find even an idea, let alone words.

172

'There are no grand conspiracies, only nasty little plots now and then,' Isenham continued, as if he were unaware of the emotions raging inside Matthew. 'He wasn't in government any more and I think he missed it. But look around you.' He waved his free hand. 'What could be going on here?'

The truth of it sank in on Matthew with a slowly crushing weight: Isenham was probably right, and the harder he struggled against the realisation, the tighter it coiled around him.

'You should remember the best in him, Matthew,' Isenham said. 'That was what he was really like.'

He did not add 'but a fool', yet Matthew heard it in his head as clearly as if he had. He did not answer.

Isenham deliberately changed the subject, and Matthew allowed the conversation to move to other trivial matters: the weather, people in the village, an upcoming cricket match, the daily minutiae of a safe and gentle life in the peace of a perfect summer.

★　★　★

He walked home again when the rain had stopped. The elms were still dripping and the road steamed in glittering drifts like silken gauze, too faint to catch, and yet weaving brightness around him. The perfume of the earth was almost overpowering. Wet leaves and flowers shone as the sunlight caught them.

Birdsong was sudden and liquid, a beauty of

173

sound, and then gone again.

As he passed the church he saw a man move very quickly into the shadow of the lich-gate, the thick honeysuckle completely hiding him. When Matthew drew level and looked sideways, he was gone. He was certain from his height and the oddly sloping angle of his shoulders that it was the same man he had seen earlier on his way to Isenham's house. Was he going somewhere, and had taken shelter from the rain? Without having any reason he could name, Matthew went under the lich-gate and into the churchyard.

There was no one there. He walked a few paces between the gravestones and looked towards the only place where anyone could be concealed. The man had not gone into the church; the door had been in Matthew's sight all the time.

He walked two or three yards further on, then to the right, and saw the outline of the man half concealed by the trunks of the yew trees. He was standing motionless. There was nothing ahead of him but the churchyard wall, and he was not looking down as if at headstones, but out across the empty fields.

Matthew bent his head as if reading the gravestone in front of him. He remained motionless for several moments. The man behind the yew tree did not move either.

Finally Matthew walked over to his parents' grave. There were fresh flowers. Judith must have put them there. There was no stone yet. It looked very raw, very new. This morning two weeks ago they had still been alive.

The world looked just the same, but it wasn't. Everything was altered, as a golden day when suddenly the clouds mass across the sun. All the outlines are the same, but the colours are different, duller, something of the life gone from them.

The caltrop marks on the road had been real, the rope on the sapling, the shredded tyres, the searching of the house, and now this man who seemed to be following him.

Or was this exactly what his father had done, added together little pieces that had no connection with each other, and made of them a whole that reflected no reality? Maybe the marks were not caltrops but something else, put there not at the time of the crash but any time that day? Perhaps an agricultural vehicle of some sort stopped and left scars from the blades of a harrow?

Had there really been anyone in the house, or was it just things rearranged wrongly in the shock of tragedy, a reversal of habit, along with everything else?

And what was to prove the man behind the yews had anything to do with Matthew? He might not want to be seen for a dozen reasons, something as simple as an illicit Sunday afternoon assignation? A grave to visit privately, to conceal his emotion? Was this how delusion started? A shock, too much time to think, a need to feel as if you understood, so you find yourself weaving everything together, regardless of wherever it fits?

For a moment he considered speaking to the

175

man, a comment on the rain, perhaps, then decided not to intrude on his contemplation. Instead he straightened up and walked back through the lich-gate and out into the lane without looking towards the yews again.

6

A few miles away in Cambridge the Sunday was also quiet and miserable. Thunder threatened all morning, and by the afternoon it rolled in from the west with heavy rain. Joseph spent most of the day alone. Like everyone else he went to chapel at eleven, and for an hour drowned all thought in the glory of the music. He ate luncheon in the Dining Hall; in spite of its magnificence, it was claustrophobic because of the heat and the oppressive weather outside. With an effort he joined in casual conversation with Harry Beecher regarding the latest finds in Egyptology, about which Beecher was wildly enthusiastic. Afterwards he went back to his rooms to read. The *Illustrated London News* lay on the table in his study, and he glanced at the theatre and arts sections, avoiding the current events, which were dominated by pictures of the funeral of the great statesman, Joseph Chamberlain. He had no desire whatever to look at pictures of mourners, whoever they were.

He considered scriptures, then instead lost himself in the familiar glory of Dante's 'Inferno'. Its imagery was so sharp it carried him out of the present, and its wisdom was timeless enough, at least for the moment, to lift him above personal grief and confusion.

The punishments for sin were not visited from outside, decided by a higher power; they were the sins themselves, perpetuated eternally, but stripped of the masks that had made them seductive once. Those who had given in to the selfish storms of passion, regardless of the cost to others, were now battered and driven by unceasing gales, forced to rise before them without rest. And so it was, down through the successive circles, the sins of indulgence that injured self, the sins of anger that injured others, to the betrayal and corruption of the mind that damaged all mankind. It made infinite sense.

And yet beauty was there. Still Christ 'walked the waters of Styx with unwet feet'.

Joseph lost himself in the healing of the poetry. If Inspector Perth were working, he did not see him that day. Nor did he see Aidan Thyer, nor any of the Allard family.

Matthew called in briefly on his way back to London, simply to say how sorry he was about Sebastian. He was gentle, full of tacit compassion.

'It's rotten,' he said briefly, sitting in Joseph's rooms in the last of the twilight. 'I'm very sorry.'

Hundreds of words turned in Joseph's mind, but none of them seemed important, and certainly none of them helped. He remained in silence, simply glad that Matthew was there.

However, Monday was entirely different. It was 13 July. It seemed that on the previous day the Prime Minister had spoken at length about the failure of the present army methods of recruitment. It was a sharp and unpleasant reminder that if the Balkan situation were not resolved and there were indeed war, then Britain might be unable to defend itself.

Far more immediate to Joseph was Perth's presence in St John's, moving about discreetly, speaking to one person after another. Joseph caught glimpses of him, always just going, leaving behind him a wake of deeply troubled young men.

'I hate it!' Elwyn said as he and Joseph met crossing the quad. Elwyn was flustered and unhappy, as if he were being harried on all sides, trying to do something for everyone and desperate to be alone and deal with his own grief. He stared after Perth's disappearing figure, determined and ordinary, with none of the ease of students familiar in such surroundings.

'He seems to think it's one of us!' Elwyn said exasperatedly; the disbelief in his voice made it high and a little shrill, as if he were losing control. 'Mother's watching him like a hawk. She thinks he's going to produce an answer any minute. But even if he did, it wouldn't bring Sebastian back.' He looked down at the ground. 'And that's the only thing that would make her happy.'

Joseph could see in his face all that he did not say, and imagine it only too easily: Mary Allard wild with pain, lashing out at everyone without realising what she was doing to her other son, while Gerald offered ineffectual and comforting remarks that only made her worse, and Elwyn tried desperately to be whatever they expected of him.

'I know it's wretched,' he replied. 'Do you feel like leaving college for a while? Take a walk into

179

town? I need a couple of new pairs of socks. I left some of mine at home.'

Elwyn's eyes widened. 'Oh God! I forgot about your parents. I'm so sorry!'

Joseph smiled. 'It's all right. I forget about it myself at times. Do you feel like a walk?'

'Yes, sir. Yes, I do. Actually I need a couple of books. I'll go to Heffers, you can try Eaden Lilley. They're about the best for haberdashery around here.'

They walked together back across the quad and out of the main gate into St John's Street, then right into Sydney Street. It was fine and dry after the rain, and the Monday morning traffic included at least half a dozen motor cars, along with delivery vans, drays and wagons. Cyclists and pedestrians wove in and out of them at practised speed. It was quieter than term time because the usual gowned figures of students were absent.

'If they don't find anyone, what will happen?' Elwyn said when they had the chance to speak and be heard.

'I suppose they'll give up,' Joseph answered. He looked sideways at him, seeing the anxiety in his face. He could imagine Mary Allard's fury. Perhaps that was what Elwyn was thinking of too, and afraid of. 'But they will.' The instant the words were out he knew they were a mistake. He saw the bleak pain in Elwyn. He stopped on the footpath, reaching for Elwyn's arm and swinging him round to a standstill also. 'Do you know anything?' he asked abruptly. 'Are you afraid to say it, in case it would give somebody a motive for killing Sebastian?'

'No, I don't!' Elwyn retorted, his face flushed, his eyes hot. 'Sebastian wasn't anything like as perfect as Mother thinks, but he was basically pretty decent. You know that! Of course he said some stupid things, and he could cut you to bits with his tongue, but so can lots of people. You have to live with that. It's like being good at rowing, or boxing, or anything else. You win sometimes and sometimes you lose. Even those who didn't like Sebastian didn't hate him!' His emotion was overwhelming. 'I wish they . . . I wish they didn't have to do this!'

'So do I,' Joseph said sincerely. 'Perhaps it will turn out to be more of an accident than deliberate.'

Elwyn did not dignify that with an answer. 'Do you think there'll be war, sir?' he asked instead, beginning to walk again.

Joseph thought of the Prime Minister's words in the newspaper. 'We have to have an army, whether there's war or not,' he reasoned. 'And the mutiny in the Curragh has shown a few weaknesses.'

'I'll say!' Elwyn pushed his hands into his pockets, his shoulders tense. He was broader, more muscular than Sebastian, but there was an echo of him in his sun-bleached hair and fair skin. 'He went to Germany in the spring, you know?' he continued.

Joseph was startled. 'Sebastian? No — I didn't know. He never mentioned it.'

Elwyn shot a glance at him, pleased to have known first. 'He loved it,' he said with a little

181

smile. 'He meant to go back when he could. He was reading Schiller, when he had time. And Goethe, of course. He said you'd have to be a barbarian not to love the music! The whole of human history has produced only one Beethoven.'

'I knew he was afraid, of course,' Joseph answered him. 'We spoke of it just the other day.'

Elwyn's head jerked up, his eyes wide. 'You mean worried, not afraid! Sebastian wasn't a coward!' The last word was said with anger, and challenge.

'I know that,' Joseph said quickly, and honestly. 'I meant that he was afraid for the beauty that would be destroyed, not for himself.'

'Oh.' Elwyn relaxed again. In that single gesture Joseph could see a wealth of Mary's passion, her pride and brittleness, her identification with her sons, especially the elder. 'Yes, of course,' Elwyn added. 'Sorry.'

Joseph smiled at him. 'Don't think of it. And don't spend your time trying to imagine who hated Sebastian, or why. Leave it to Inspector Perth. Look after yourself . . . and your mother.'

'I am doing,' Elwyn answered him. 'All that I can.'

'I know.'

Elwyn nodded unhappily. 'Goodbye, sir.' He turned away towards the book shop, and left Joseph to continue on his way to the department store to look for socks.

Once inside Joseph wandered around the tables, and between the shelves, which went right up to the ceiling, stacked neatly with all manner of goods. He was outside again, with a pair of black socks and a pair of dark grey, when he bumped into Nigel Eardslie.

Eardslie looked flustered. 'Sorry, sir,' he apologized, stepping aside. 'I . . . I was miles away.'

'Everyone's upset,' Joseph responded, and was about to move when he realised that Eardslie was still looking at him.

A young woman passed them. She was dressed in a navy and white dress, her hair swept up under a straw hat. She hesitated an instant, smiling at Eardslie. He coloured, seemed about to say something, then averted his eyes. The young woman changed her mind and quickened her step.

'I hope she didn't go on my account?' Joseph asked.

'No!' Eardslie said too vehemently. 'She . . . she was really more Morel's friend than mine. She knew Sebastian too. I expect she just wanted to give her condolences, or something.'

Joseph thought that was less than the truth. She had looked at Eardslie as if she had wished to say more than polite conventions.

'Did he know her well?' he asked. She had seemed an attractive girl, perhaps a little under twenty, and she carried herself with grace.

'I don't know,' Eardslie replied, and this time Joseph was certain it was a lie. 'Sorry for banging into you, sir,' he went on. 'Excuse me.' And before Joseph could say anything further, Eardslie moved very quickly to the doorway of

Eaden Lilley and disappeared inside, leaving Joseph to walk on further into the town alone.

★ ★ ★

Tuesday was much the same: a routine of small chores. Joseph saw Inspector Perth coming and going busily, but he managed to put Sebastian's death out of his mind most of the time, until Nigel Eardslie caught up with him crossing the quad early in the afternoon. It was hot and still again; the windows of all the occupied rooms were wide open, and every now and then the sound of music or laughter drifted out.

'Dr Reavley!'

Joseph stopped.

Eardslie's rather square face was puckered with anxiety, hazel eyes fixed on Joseph's. 'That policeman's just been talking to me, sir, asking a lot of questions about Allard. I really don't know what to say.' He looked awkward and unhappy.

'If you know something that could have bearing on his death, then you'll have to tell him the truth,' Joseph answered.

'I don't know what the truth is!' Eardslie said desperately. 'If it's just a matter of 'Where were you?' or, 'Did you see this, or that?', then of course I can answer. But he wanted to know what Allard was like! And how do I answer that decently?'

'You knew him pretty well,' Joseph said. 'Tell him about his character, how he worked, who his friends were, his hopes and ambitions.'

'He didn't get killed for any of those,' Eardslie

184

replied, a slight impatience in his voice. 'Do I tell him about his sarcasm as well? The way he could cut you raw with his tongue, and make you feel like a complete fool?' His face was tight and unhappy.

Joseph wanted to deny it. This was not the man he had known. But then no student would dare exercise his pride or cruelty on a tutor. A bully chooses the easy targets, even a young man not consciously using his superior weight or talent to build his own power, but simply because it was there!

He was making excuses again to deny the pain, which was futile. He did not even know how to balance the shock against reality in order to gain some proportion. He was only conscious of a shattering of something bright — leaving behind a coldness.

'I could tell him how funny he was,' Eardslie was continuing. 'He made me laugh sometimes till I couldn't get my breath, and my chest hurt, but it could be at someone else's expense, especially if they'd criticized him lately.'

Joseph did not reply.

'Do I tell him that he could forgive wonderfully, and that he expected to be forgiven, no matter what he'd done, because he was clever and beautiful?' Eardslie rushed on. 'And if you borrowed something without asking, even if you lost it or broke it, he could wave it aside and make you think he didn't care, even if it was something he valued.' His mouth pinched a little and the light faded in his eyes. 'But if you questioned his judgement, or beat him at one of the things that mattered to him, he could carry a grudge further than anyone else I know! He was generous — he'd give you anything! But God, he could be cruel!' He stared at Joseph helplessly. 'I can't tell the police that . . . He's dead.'

Joseph felt numb. That was not the Sebastian he knew. Was Eardslie's the voice of envy? Or was he speaking the truth Joseph had refused to see?

'You don't believe me, do you?' Eardslie challenged him. 'Perth might, but the others won't. Morel knows Sebastian took his girl, Abigail something, and then dumped her. I think he did it simply because he could. She saw Sebastian and thought of him as this sort of young Apollo and he let her believe it. It flattered him . . .'

'You can't help it if someone falls in love with you,' Joseph protested, but he remembered the characteristics attributed to the Greek gods: the childishness, the vanity, the petty spite, as well as the beauty.

Eardslie looked at him with barely concealed anger. 'You can help what you do about it!' he retorted. 'You don't take your friend's girl. Would you?' Then he blushed, looking wretched. 'I'm sorry, sir. That was rude, and I had no right to say it.' He jerked his chin up. 'But Perth keeps asking. We want to be decent to the dead, and we want to be fair. But someone killed him, and they say it had to be one of us. I keep looking at everyone and wondering if it was them.

'I met Rattray along the Backs yesterday evening, and I started remembering quarrels he'd had with Sebastian, and wondering if it could be him. He's got a hell of a temper.' He blushed. 'Then I remembered a quarrel I'd had, and wondered if he was thinking the same thing of me!' His eyes pleaded for some kind of reassurance. 'Everybody's changed! Suddenly I don't feel as if I really know anyone . . . and even worse than that in a way, I don't think anyone trusts me either. I know who I am, and that I didn't do it, but no one else knows!' He took a deep breath. 'The friendships I took for granted aren't there any more. It's done that already! People are talking about rivalries. Perth's even got it into his head that Foubister could have cheated! It's sickening.'

'Get a grip on your imagination, Eardslie,' Joseph said firmly. 'Of course everyone is upset over Sebastian's death, and frightened. But in a day or two I expect Perth will have it solved, and you'll all realise that your suspicions were unfounded. One person did something tragic and possibly evil, but the rest of you are just what you were before.' His voice sounded flat and unreal. He did not believe what he was saying himself — how could Eardslie? He deserved better than that, but Joseph did not have anything to give that was both comforting and even remotely honest.

'Yes, sir,' Eardslie said obediently. 'Thank you, sir.' And he turned and walked away, disappearing through the arch into the second quad, leaving Joseph alone.

★   ★   ★

The following morning Joseph was sitting in his study again, having written to Hannah, which he had found difficult. It was simple enough to begin, but as soon as he tried to say something honest, he saw her face in his mind and he saw the loneliness in her, the bewilderment she tried to hide, and failed. She was not accustomed to grief. The gentleness she had for others was rooted in the certainties of her own life; first her parents and Joseph, then Matthew and Judith, younger than she and relying on her, wanting to be like her. Later it had been Archie, and then her own children.

She reminded him so much of Alys, not only in her looks but in her gestures, the tone of her voice, sometimes even the words she used, the colours she liked, the way she peeled an apple or marked the page in a book she was reading with a folded spill of paper.

She and Eleanor had liked each other immediately, as if they had been friends who had simply not seen each other for a while. He remembered how much pleasure that had given him.

Hannah had been the first one to come to him after Eleanor's death, and she had missed her the most, even though they had lived miles apart. He knew they had written every week, long letters full of thoughts and feelings, trivial details of domestic life, more a matter of affection than of news. Writing to Hannah now was difficult, full of ghosts.

He had finished, more or less satisfactorily, and was trying to compose a letter to Judith, when there was a discreet tap on the door.

Assuming it was a student, he simply called for them to come in. However, it was Perth who entered and closed the door behind him.

'Morning, Reverend,' he said cheerfully. He still wore the same dark suit, slightly stretched at the knees, and a clean, stiff collar. 'Sorry if Oi'm interrupting your letters.'

'Good morning, Inspector,' Joseph replied, rising to his feet, partly from courtesy, but also because he felt startled and at a disadvantage still sitting. 'Do you have some news?' He was not even sure what answer he wanted to hear. There had to be a resolution, but he was not yet ready to accept that anyone he knew could have killed Sebastian, even though his brain understood that it had to be true.

'Not really what you'd call news,' Perth replied, shaking his head. 'Oi've bin talking to your young gentlemen, o' course.' He ran his fingers over his thin hair. 'Trouble is, if a man says he was in bed at half-past foive in the morning, who's to know if he's telling the truth or not? But Oi can't afford to take his word for it, you see? Different for you, 'cos Oi know from Dr Beecher that you was out rowing on the river.'

'Oh?' Joseph was surprised. He did not remember seeing Beecher. He invited Perth to sit down. 'I'm sorry, but I don't know how to help. There would be no one around in the corridors or on the stairs at that time.'

'Unfortunately for us.' Perth sat in the large chair opposite the one Joseph had risen from, and Joseph sank back into his own. 'No witnesses at all,' Perth said dolefully. 'Still, people ain't often obliging enough to commit murder when they know someone else is looking at 'em. Usually we can write off a goodly number because o' their bein' able to show they was somewhere else.' He studied Joseph gravely. 'We come at a crime, particularly a murder, from three sorts of angles, Reverend.' He held up one finger. 'First, who had the opportunity? If somebody weren't there at the time, that cuts them out.'

'Naturally,' Joseph nodded.

Perth regarded him steadily. 'Second,' he continued, putting up the next finger, 'there's the means, in this case a gun. Who had a gun?'

'I have no idea.'

'That's a shame, you see, because no one else 'as neither, leastways not that they're telling of.' Perth still had a pleasant air about him, as if he were a lecturer with a bright student, leading him through the points of a piece of logic. 'We know it was a small gun, a revolver of some sort, because of the bullet — which we got, by the way.'

Joseph winced at the horrible thought of its passage through Sebastian's torn brain, presumably into the wall of the room. He had not looked. Now he was aware of Perth's eyes watching him, but he could not keep the revulsion from his face, or the slight feeling of sickness from his stomach.

'And o' course it would be awkward, loike, to be carrying a rifle or a shotgun around with you

190

in a place loike this,' Perth went on, his voice unemotional. 'Nowhere to hide it from being seen, except in a case for a trumpet or something like that. But what would anybody be doing with a trumpet at foive o'clock in the morning?'

'Cricket bat,' Joseph said instantly. 'If — '

Perth's eyes widened. 'Very clever, Reverend! Oi never thought o' that, but you're right. A nice early practice out on that lovely grass by the river — or even one o' those cricket fields — Fenner's or — what's the other one? — Parker's Piece?'

'Parker's Piece belongs to the town,' Joseph pointed out. 'The university uses Fenner's. But you can't practise cricket by yourself.'

'O' course — Town and Gown — separate,' Perth nodded, pursing his lips. The difference was a gulf between them, uncrossable, and Joseph had inadvertently just reminded him of it. 'But then you see our fellow might not 'ave bin sticking to the rules,' he said stiffly, his expression tight, defensive. 'In fact he might not even have practised at all, seeing as he would have had a gun in his case, not a bat.' He leaned forward. 'But since we're having a lot o' trouble finding this gun, which could be anywhere by now, that means we got just the last thing left on which to catch him — doesn't it? Motive!' He held up his third finger.

Joseph should have realised it from the moment Perth had come in. He knew Joseph would have nothing to give him on means or opportunity, and Perth knew it. He would hardly be here simply to keep Joseph informed. 'I see,' he said flatly.

191

'Oi'm sure as you do, Reverend,' Perth agreed, a gleam of satisfaction in his eyes. 'Not easy to find that out. Not even countin' the fact that no one wants to incriminate 'emselves, they don't want to speak ill o' the dead neither. It ain't decent. People talk the greatest rubbish Oi ever heard about a person just because they're dead. Why do you think that is, Reverend? You must come across a lot of that in your line o' work.'

'I don't have an active ministry now,' Joseph explained, surprised by the pang of guilt it caused him, like a captain having left his ship in bad weather, and before his crew. That was ridiculous; what he was doing here was just as important a job, and one to which he was far better suited.

'Still ordained, though, aren't you.' Perth made it a statement.

'Yes . . . '

'You must be a good judge o' folk, an' Oi dare say as they trust you more'n most, tell you things?'

'Sometimes,' Joseph said carefully, and aware with a biting hollowness that he had been confided in very little, or he would not be as totally confused as he was by this eruption of violence. 'But a confidence is precisely that, Inspector, and I would not break it. But I can tell you that I have no idea who killed Sebastian Allard, or why.'

Perth nodded slowly. 'Oi took that for granted, sir. But you know these young men mebbe better'n anyone else. And you understand Oi can't leave here until Oi know what happened.

192

An' for that, Oi have to learn why. If Oi find something as don't have nothing to do with the murder, Oi'll tear up my notes and forget all about it.'

'I don't know of any reason!' Joseph protested. 'Being a minister means that people tend not to tell you their uglier thoughts!' He realised with dismay how profoundly that was true. How many things had he been blind to? For how long? Years? Had his own pain made him retreat from reality into uselessness? Then without grasping the fullness of what he said, he spoke with sudden intensity. 'But I shall find out! I ought to have known!' He meant it, savagely, with the intensity of a drowning man's need for air. There had been too much violence and pain that destroyed all the old certainties in him, and he had to find sanity again if he were to survive. Perth might need to solve this for his professional reputation, or even to prove that 'Town' was as good as 'Gown' any day, but Joseph needed to do it for his belief in reason and the power of men to rise above chaos.

Perth nodded slowly, but his eyes were wide and unblinking. 'Very good, Reverend.' He drew in his breath as if about to add something more, then just nodded again.

After Perth had gone Joseph began to appreciate the enormity of what he had promised himself. There was no point in waiting for people to come to see him and confide some anger or resentment against Sebastian. They had not done it before, when it was comparatively innocent; they certainly would not now. He had to go and seek it. Perhaps if he had been braver, more honest all along, he would have seen the danger before the violence had erupted. There was nothing he could have done for his mother or father, but he might have saved Sebastian.

The first person he spoke to was Aiden Thyer. He found him at home finishing a late breakfast. He looked tired and flustered, his fair hair more faded by grey than had been apparent at a glance, his face unrefreshed by sleep. He looked up at Joseph in surprise as the maid showed him into the dining room.

'Good morning, Reavley. Nothing wrong, I hope?'

'Nothing new,' Joseph replied a trifle drily.

'Tea?' Thyer offered.

'Thank you.' Joseph sat down, not because he particularly wanted tea, but it obliged the Master to continue the conversation. 'How are Gerald and Mary?'

Thyer's face tightened. 'Inconsolable. I suppose it's natural. I can't imagine what it is like to lose a son, let alone in such a way.' He took another bite of his toast. 'Connie's doing everything she can, but nothing makes the slightest difference.'

'I suppose one of the worst things is realising that someone hated him so much they resorted to murder. I admit, I had no idea there was such a passion in anyone.' Joseph poured himself tea from the silver pot and sipped it tentatively. It was very hot; obviously someone had refilled it. 'Which shows that I was paying far too little attention.'

194

Thyer looked at him with surprise. 'I had no idea either! For God's sake, do you think if I had, that — '

'No! Of course not,' Joseph said quickly. 'But you might at least have been more aware than I of an undercurrent of emotion, a rivalry, an insult, real or imagined, or some kind of a threat.' The truth embarrassed him and it was hard to admit. 'I had my head so buried in their academic work I paid too little attention to their other thoughts or feelings. Perhaps you didn't?'

'You're an idealist,' Thyer agreed, picking up his tea, but the sharp perception in his eyes was not unkind.

Joseph accepted it without argument, but it was a harsher criticism of him than Thyer meant. 'And you can't afford to be,' he replied. 'Who hated Sebastian?'

'That's blunt!'

'Yes.' Joseph smiled very slightly. 'I think it would be better if we knew before Perth did, don't you?'

Thyer put down his cup again and regarded Joseph very steadily. 'Actually, more people than you would care to think. I know you were very fond of him, knowing the family, and perhaps he showed you the best of himself, for that reason.'

Joseph took a long breath. 'And who saw the other side?' Unwittingly Harry Beecher's wry, familiar face came to his mind, sitting on the bench in The Pickerel, watching the boats on the river in the evening light, and the sudden tightness in his voice.

Thyer considered for a moment. 'Most people,

195

one way or another. Oh, his work was brilliant, you were right about that, and you perceived it long before anyone else. He had the potential to be excellent one day, possibly one of the great poets of the English language. But he had a long way to go to any kind of emotional maturity.' He shrugged. 'Not that emotional maturity is any necessity for a poet. One could hardly claim it for Byron or Shelley, to name but two. And I rather think that both of them probably escaped murder more by luck than virtue.'

'That is not very specific,' Joseph said, wishing he could leave it all to Perth, and never know more than simply who had done it, not why. But it was already too late for that.

Thyer sighed. 'Well, there's always the question of women, I suppose. Sebastian was good-looking, and he enjoyed exercising his charm, and the power it gave him. Perhaps in time he would have learned to govern it, or on the other hand it might have grown worse. It takes a very fine character indeed to have power, and refrain from using it. He was a long way from that yet.' His face tightened until it was curiously bleak. 'And of course there is always the possibility that it was not a woman, but a man. It happens, particularly in a place like Cambridge. An older man, a student who is full of vitality and dreams, hunger . . . ' He stopped. Further explanation was unnecessary, or words to spell out the dangers of it.

Joseph heard a slight sound in the doorway and swivelled around to see Connie standing behind him, her face grave, a flash of anger in her dark eyes.

'Good morning, Dr Reavley.' She came in and closed the door behind her with a snap. She was wearing a deep lavender morning dress, suitable both for the heat, and for the tragedy of her houseguests. The sweeping lines of it, impossibly slender at the knees, became her rich figure, and the colour flattered her complexion. Even in these circumstances it was a pleasure to look at her.

'Really, Aiden, if you have to be so candid, you might at least do it with more discretion!' she said sharply, coming further into the room. 'What if Mrs Allard had overheard you? She can't bear to hear anything but praise for him, which I suppose is natural enough, in the circumstances. I don't suppose the boy was a saint — few of us are — but that is how she needs to see him at the moment. And apart from unnecessary cruelty to her, I don't want a case of hysteria on my hands.' She turned away from her husband, possibly without seeing the shadow in his face, as if he had received a blow he half expected.

'Would you like some breakfast, Dr Reavley?' she invited. 'It won't be the least difficulty to have Cook prepare you something.'

'No, thank you,' Joseph declined, feeling discomforted for having wanted Thyer to be candid, and a degree of embarrassment at having witnessed a moment of personal pain. 'I am afraid the Master's comments were my fault,' he said to Connie. 'I was asking him because I feel we need to have the truth, if possible before the police uncover every mistake of judgement by a student — or one of us, for that matter. And every petty rivalry becomes an enormity too deep to forget.' He was talking too much, explaining unnecessarily, but he could not stop. 'People are already nervous, protective of themselves and suspicious of everyone else. I have seen half a dozen discussions descend into quarrels over the last few days, and at least two people I know of have told stupid lies, not to conceal crime but because they are embarrassed. I hadn't admitted to myself, until Perth came to see me this morning, but it will only get worse until the truth is known.'

She sat down at the head of the table, managing the restriction of her skirts with extraordinary grace, and he was aware of the faint lily-of-the-valley perfume she wore. He felt a wave of loss for Alys, which was momentarily overwhelming.

If Connie noticed it she was delicate enough to speak as if she had not. 'I suppose you are right,' she conceded. 'Sometimes fear is worse than the truth. At least the truth will destroy only one person. Or am I creating a fool's paradise?'

A flicker of awareness crossed Thyer's face, and he drew in his breath, then changed his mind and did not speak.

This time Joseph was honest. 'Yes . . . I'm sorry, but I think you are,' he said to her. 'Students have asked me whether they should tell the inspector what they know about Sebastian, or be loyal to his memory and conceal it. I told them to tell the truth, and because of it Foubister and Morel, who have been friends ever since they came up, have quarrelled so bitterly, both feel betrayed. And we have all learned things about each other we were far happier not knowing.'

Still not looking at her husband, she reached across and touched her fingers to Joseph's arm. 'I am afraid it seems ignorance is a luxury we can no longer afford. Sebastian was very charming, and he was certainly gifted, but he had uglier sides as well. I know you would prefer not to have seen them, and your charity does you great credit.'

'No, it doesn't,' he contradicted her miserably. 'It was a matter of self-protection, not generosity of spirit. I rather think cowardice is the correct name for it.'

'You are too hard on yourself.' Connie was very gentle. There was a softness in her face he had always liked. Now he thought briefly, and with a respect that surprised him, how fortunate a man Aiden Thyer was.

Joseph smiled at her. 'Thank you. That is generosity which speaks, but let us have the truth about ourselves as well. I think we can't afford anything less now.'

In the evening, Joseph went as usual to the Senior Common Room for a few moments' quiet companionship and time to relax before going in to dinner. Almost as soon as he entered he saw Harry Beecher sitting in one of the big, comfortable chairs near the window, nursing a glass of what looked like gin and tonic.

199

Joseph walked over towards him with a sudden lift of pleasure. He had shared many years of friendship with Beecher and never found in him meanness of spirit or that self-absorption that makes people blind to the feelings of others.

'Your usual, sir?' the steward asked, and Joseph accepted, sitting down with a deep sense of ease at the sheer, luxurious familiarity of the surroundings, the people he had known and found so congenial over the last, difficult year. They thought largely as he did. They had the same heritage and the same values. Disagreements were minor, and on the whole added interest to what might otherwise have become flat. The challenge of ideas was the savour of life. Always to be agreed with must surely become an intolerable loneliness in the end, as if anchored by endless mirrors of the mind, sterile of anything new.

'Looks as if the French President is going to Russia to speak to the Czar,' Beecher remarked, sipping at his glass.

'About Serbia?' Joseph asked, although it was a rhetorical question. The answer was assumed.

'What a mess.' Beecher shook his head. 'Walcott thinks there'll be war.' Walcott was a lecturer in modern history they both knew moderately well. 'I wish to hell he'd be a bit more discreet about his opinions.' A flicker of distaste crossed his face. 'Everyone's unsettled enough without that.'

Joseph took his glass from the steward and thanked him, then waited until the man was out of earshot. 'Yes, I know,' he said unhappily.

'Several of the students have spoken about it. You can hardly blame them for being anxious.'

'Even at the worst, I don't suppose it would involve us,' Beecher dismissed the idea, taking another sip of his gin. 'But if it did, say we were drawn in to help, I don't know whom?' His eyebrows lifted with faint humour. 'I can't see us being overly concerned with the Austrians or the Serbs, but, regardless, we don't conscript to the army. It's all volunteer.' He smiled lopsidedly. 'I think they are rather badly upset about Sebastian Allard's death, and that's what they are really worried about. Someone killed him.' His mouth tightened momentarily. 'And unfortunately, from the evidence, it has to have been someone here in college.' He looked at Joseph with sudden, intense candour. 'I suppose you haven't got any idea, have you? You wouldn't consider it your religious duty to protect them?'

Joseph was startled. 'No, I wouldn't!' The hot anger still welled up inside him at the thought of Sebastian's vitality and dreams obliterated. There was an emptiness where he should have been, and he imagined the ache of it would always be there, forgotten for a while, and then returning again and again like a phrase from an old song, surprising the mind with pain. 'I don't know anything.' He looked at Beecher earnestly. 'But I feel I need to. I've gone over everything I can remember of the last few days I saw Sebastian, but I was away, because of my parents' deaths, for a good while right before he was killed. I couldn't have seen anything.'

'You think it was foreseeable?' There was

surprise and curiosity sharp in Beecher's eyes. He ignored his unfinished drink.

'I don't know,' Joseph admitted. 'But it can't have happened without some cause which built up over a while, unless it was an accident — which would be the best possible answer, of course! But I can't imagine how that could happen, can you?'

'No,' Beecher said with quiet regret. The evening light through the long windows picked out the tiny lines around his eyes and mouth. He was more tired than he was admitting, and perhaps a lot more deeply worried. 'No, I'm afraid that's wishful thinking,' he added. 'Someone killed him because they meant to. And I don't know whether we should have been aware of it or not.' He reached out and picked up his drink again, sipping it and rolling it around his mouth, but it obviously gave him no pleasure. His expression was tense, inward. 'Certainly his work was falling off over the last few weeks. And to be honest,' he looked up at Joseph apologetically, 'I've seen a certain harder edge to it, and a lack of delicacy lately. I thought it might be a rather uncomfortable transition from one style to another, made without his usual grace.' That was half a question.

'But?' Joseph prompted. He knew Beecher did not like Sebastian, and he was not looking forward to what he would say, but the truth could no longer be overlooked, however precious the illusions it broke.

'But on looking back, it was more than just his work,' Beecher said. 'His temper was fragile, far more so than it used to be. I don't think he was sleeping well, and I know of at least a couple of rather stupid quarrels he got involved in.'

'Quarrels about what? With whom?'

Beecher's lips pulled tight in the mockery of a smile. 'About war and nationalism, false ideas of honour. And with several people — anyone fool enough to get involved in the subject.'

'Why didn't you mention it?' Joseph was startled. He had not seen anything of the sort. Had he been totally blind? Or had Sebastian hidden it from him deliberately? Why? Kindness, not to concern him? Self-protection, because he wanted to preserve the image of him Joseph had, keep one person seeing only the good? Or had he simply not trusted him, and it was only Joseph's imagination and vanity that they had been friends?

Beecher was embarrassed. Joseph could see it in his face, the way he wished to avert his eyes, and was deliberately avoiding doing so, because he knew it would betray the truth in him. 'I assumed that Sebastian confided in you,' he said. 'I realised only the other day that he hadn't. I'm sorry.'

'You didn't say anything at the time,' Joseph pointed out. 'You noticed something was wrong with him, but you didn't ask if I had seen it also, and if I knew what it was. Perhaps together we could have done something to help.'

Beecher looked a little beyond Joseph; it was not an evasion this time but a concentration within himself. 'I didn't like Sebastian nearly as much as you did,' he said slowly. 'I saw his charm, but I also saw how he used it. I considered asking you if you knew what was causing him such distress, and I believe it was profound. Actually I did approach it once, but you didn't take me up. We were interrupted by something, and I didn't go back to it. I didn't want to quarrel with you.' He raised his eyes, bright and troubled, and for once the humour in him totally absent.

Joseph was stunned. He had been expecting pain, but this blow hurt far more than anything he had foreseen. Beecher had tried to protect him because he thought Joseph was not strong enough to accept or deal with the truth. He had thought that he would turn aside from a friend rather than look at it honestly.

How could he? What had Joseph ever said or done that even Beecher believed him not only so blind, but such a moral coward?

Was that why Sebastian had not told him? He had spoken of the fear of war and its destruction of the beauty he loved, but surely that was hardly sufficient to disturb him the way Beecher had implied. And it had obviously started weeks before the assassination in Sarajevo.

Elwyn had turned on him instantly when Joseph had said something about fear, denying hotly that Sebastian was a coward, a charge that had never crossed Joseph's mind. Should it have? Had Sebastian been afraid and felt unable to confide it to Joseph, who was supposed to be his friend? What was friendship worth, if one had to wear a mask over the thoughts that really hurt, and felt the need to present a more comfortable face for Joseph's own sake?

Not a great deal. Without honesty, compassion, the will to understand, it was no more than an acquaintanceship, and not even a good one at that.

And Beecher's forbearance was no better. There was pity in it, even kindness, but there was no equality, and certainly no respect.

'I wish I had known,' he said bitterly. 'Now all we are left with is that somebody hated him so uncontrollably they went to his room early in the morning and shot him in the head. That's a very deep hatred, Harry. Not only did we not see it before, we can't even see it now, and God knows, I'm looking!'

Beecher drew in his breath, held it a moment, then let it out in a sigh without speaking. He stared out of the window at the birds on the grass.

★   ★   ★

The next day, late in the morning, Joseph called on Mary and Gerald Allard, still at the Master's house, at least until the funeral, which the police had held up because of the investigation. They had been acquaintances a long time. He could think of nothing to say that would ease their pain, but that did not excuse the need at least to express some care. Apart from that, he must learn anything from them he could that would help him to know Sebastian better, if possible to gain any sense of the fears the young man might have shared with his parents. Perhaps Sebastian

205

had confided something they did not yet see as important. Possibly they had not told Perth, feeling him an outsider who would not understand or sympathise with what they feared might be perceived as weakness. Perth was of a different class, a different background. Joseph knew Mary well enough to know how she would recoil from any intrusion into the life of her son.

'Come in,' Connie said as soon as the maid took him from the front hall into her quiet sitting room. He saw immediately that none of the Allards was there still. The moment could be put off a little longer, and he was ashamed of being so relieved.

'Do sit down, Dr Reavley,' she invited. She looked at him with a smile and a shred of humour in her eyes, as if she read his thoughts and sympathised with them.

He accepted. The room was wildly eclectic. Of course it was part of the college, and could not be fundamentally altered, but Thyer's taste was conservative, and most of the house was furnished accordingly. However, this room was hers, and a Spanish flamenco dancer whirled in a glare of scarlets in the painting over the mantelpiece. It burst with vitality. It was crudely painted and really rather bad taste, but the colours were gorgeous. Joseph knew Thyer loathed it. He had given her a modern, expensive impressionist painting that he disliked himself, but he thought it would please her, and at least be fit to hang in the house. She had accepted it graciously, and put it in the dining room. Perhaps Joseph was the only one who knew that

206

she did not like it either.

Now he sat down next to the Moroccan blanket in rich earth tones, and made himself comfortable, disregarding a tall brass hookah on the table beside him. Oddly, he found the mood of the room both unique and comfortable.

'How is Mrs Allard?' he asked.

'Plunging between grief and fury,' Connie answered with wry honesty. 'I don't know what to do for her. The Master has to continue with his duties to the rest of the college, of course, but I have been doing what little I can to offer some physical care to her at least, but I confess I feel totally helpless.' She gave him a sudden, candid smile. 'I'm so glad you've come! I'm at my wits' end. I never know if what I'm saying is right or wrong.'

He felt vaguely conspiratorial; it eased the moment. 'Where is she?' he asked.

'In the Fellows' Garden. That policeman was questioning her yesterday and she was berating him for his failure to arrest anyone yet.' Her eyes became serious and the soft lines of her mouth pulled a little tighter with pity. 'She said there couldn't be more than one or two people who hated Sebastian, so it should be a simple enough thing to find them.' Her voice dropped. 'I'm afraid that's not really true. He was not always a comfortable person at all. I look at that poor girl Miss Coopersmith, and I wonder what she is feeling. I can read nothing in her face, and Mrs Allard is too consumed in her own loss to spare her anything but the most perfunctory attention.'

Joseph was not surprised, but he was sorry.

207

'Poor Elwyn is doing all he can,' Connie went on, 'but even he cannot console his mother. Although I think he is a considerable strength to his father. I am afraid he is in a private hell of his own.' She did not elaborate, but her eyes met Joseph's with the ghost of a smile.

He understood perfectly, but he was not prepared to let her see that, not yet. He had a wrenching pity for Gerald's weakness, and it forced him to conceal it, even from Connie.

He rose to his feet. 'Thank you. You have given me a few moments to collect my thoughts. I think I had better go and speak to Mrs Allard, even if it doesn't do much good.'

She nodded and walked with him through to the passage and the side door into the garden. He thanked her again and went out into the sun and the motionless, perfumed heat where the flowers blazed in a profusion of reds and purples, and billowed across the carefully paved walks between the beds. Flaming nasturtiums spilled out of an old terracotta urn left on its side. Spires of blue salvia made a solemn background to a riot of pansies, faces jostling for attention. Delphiniums towered almost to eye level, and ragged pinks cast up a giddy perfume. A butterfly staggered by like a happy drunkard, and the droning of bees was a steady, somnolent music in the background.

Mary Allard was standing in the centre looking at the dark burgundy moss roses. She was dressed entirely in black and Joseph could not help thinking how insufferably hot she must have been. In spite of the sun, she had no parasol, and she was also unveiled. The harsh light exposed the tiny lines in her skin, all dragging tight and downwards, betraying the pain eating inside her.

'Mrs Allard,' he said quietly.

Judging from the sudden rigidity of her body under the silk, she had obviously not been aware of his presence. She swivelled round to face him. 'Dr Reavley!' She did not add anything else, but there was a challenge in her bearing and the directness of her eyes.

It was going to be even harder than he had thought.

'I came by to see you,' he began, knowing he was being trite. But then to ask her how she was would be equally useless. She was tormented with grief, and anyone could see it at a glance.

'Do you know anything more about who killed Sebastian?' she demanded. 'That policeman is useless! I'm beginning to think he doesn't want to find out. He doesn't seem to understand anything.'

Joseph changed his mind. Any attempt at comfort was doomed to failure. Instead he would pursue his own need, which was also hers.

'What does he think?' he asked her.

She was startled, as if she had expected him to argue with her and insist that Perth was doing his best, or at the very least defend him by pointing out how difficult his task was.

'He's going around looking for reasons to hate Sebastian,' she answered witheringly. 'Envy, that's the only reason. I told him that, but he doesn't listen.'

'Academic?' he asked. 'Personal? Over anything in particular?'

'Why?' She took half a step towards him. 'Do you know something?'

'No, I don't,' he said. 'But I want very much to find out who killed Sebastian, for a lot of reasons.'

'To cover your own failure!' She spat the word. 'That's all that's left. We sent him here to learn. That was your idea! We trusted you with him, and you let some . . . creature . . . kill him. I want justice!' Tears filled her eyes and she turned away from him. 'Nothing can bring him back,' she said hoarsely. 'But I want whoever did it to suffer.'

Joseph could not defend himself. She was right, he had failed to protect Sebastian because he had seen only what he wanted to see, not any of the darker envies or hatreds that had to have been there. He had thought he was dealing with reality, a higher, saner view of man. In truth he was looking for his own comfort.

It was also pointless to argue about justice, or to tell her that it would ease nothing. It was morally wrong, and she would almost certainly never know all the truths of what had happened. It would only add to her anger to tell her that mercy was the better part, just as she herself would need mercy when her own judgement should come. She was not listening. And if he were honest, his own rage at violence and senseless death was so close beneath the surface of his words that he would have been a hypocrite to preach to her. He could not forget how he had felt when he stood on the Hauxton Road and realised what the caltrop marks meant, and pictured it in his mind.

And whoever had killed Sebastian had destroyed a vitality and hope, a passion for beauty that amazed with its depth of loss. Sebastian had embodied all that was best in the fire of youth, and perhaps some of the failings as well — the occasional thoughtlessness, and the arrogance. But if he did his job properly then the weaknesses would have passed, leaving only the worth.

'I want them to suffer too,' he confessed quietly.

She lifted her head and turned slowly back to him, her eyes wide.

'I apologize,' she whispered. 'I thought you were going to come and preach at me. Gerald tells me I shouldn't feel like that. That it's not really me speaking, and I'll regret saying it later.'

'Maybe I will too,' he smiled at her. 'But that's how I feel now.'

Her face crumpled again. 'Why would anyone do that to him, Joseph? How can anyone envy so much? Shouldn't we love beauty of the mind and want to help it, protect it? I've asked the Master if Sebastian was in line for any prizes or honours that might have excluded someone else, but he says he doesn't know of anything.' She drew her black eyebrows together. 'Do you . . . do you suppose that it would have been some woman? Someone who was in love with him, obsessed with him, and couldn't accept rejection? Girls can be very hysterical. They can imagine that a

211

man has feelings for them when it is only a passing admiration, no more than good manners, really.'

'It could be over a woman — ' Joseph began.

'Of course it could!' she interrupted eagerly, seizing on the idea, her face lighting up, the rigid line of her body relaxing a little. He could see in the sun the sheen on the silk of her gown and how it pulled over her thin shoulders. 'That's the one thing that makes sense! Raging jealousy because a woman was in love with Sebastian, and someone felt betrayed by her!' She put out her hand tentatively and laid it on his arm. 'Thank you, Dr Reavley. You have at least made sense out of the darkness. If you came to comfort me, you have succeeded, and I am grateful to you.'

It was not how he had intended to succeed, but he did not know how to withdraw. He remembered the girl in the street outside Eaden Lilley, and what Eardslie had said about Morel, and wished he did not have to know about it.

He was still searching for an answer when Gerald Allard came from the quad gate of the garden, walking very carefully along the centre of the path between the tumbles of cat mint and pinks. It was a moment before Joseph realised that his considered step was due to the fact that he had already partaken more refreshment than he could absorb. He looked curiously at Joseph, then at his wife.

Mary's eyes narrowed at the sight of him.

'How are you, my dear?' he enquired solicitously. 'Good morning, Reavley. Nice of

212

you to call. However, I think we should speak of other things for a little while. It is — '

'Stop it!' Mary said between her teeth. 'I can't think of other things! I don't want to try! Sebastian is dead! Someone killed him! Until we know who it was, and they are arrested and hanged, there are no other things!'

'My dear, you should — ' Gerald began.

She whirled around, catching the fine silk of her sleeve on a stem of the moss rose. She stormed off, uncaring that she had torn the fabric, and disappeared in through the door to the sitting room of the Master's house.

'I'm sorry,' Gerald said awkwardly. 'I really don't know . . . ' He did not finish. He had started without any idea what to say, and that was clear in his face.

'I met Miss Coopersmith,' Joseph said suddenly. 'She seems a very pleasant young woman.'

'Oh . . . Regina? Yes, most agreeable,' Gerald replied. 'Good family, known them for years. Her father's got a big estate a few miles away, in the Madingley direction.'

'Sebastian never mentioned her.'

Gerald pushed his hands deeper into his pockets. 'No, I don't suppose he would. I mean . . . ' Again he stopped.

This time Joseph waited.

'Well, two separate lives,' Gerald went on uncomfortably. 'Home and . . . and here. Man's world, this.' His arm swept around in a wide, slightly unsteady circle. 'Not the place to discuss women, what?'

'Is Mrs Allard fond of her?'

Gerald's eyebrows shot up. 'No idea! Yes! Well, I suppose so. Yes, must have liked the girl.'

'You put that in the past,' Joseph pointed out.

'Oh! Well, Sebastian's dead now — God help us.' He gave a little shrug. 'Next Christmas will be unbearable. Always spend it with Mary's sister, you know. Fearful woman. Three sons. All successes one way or another. Proud as Lucifer.'

Joseph could think of nothing to say. Gerald would probably wish later that he had never made such a remark. It was better not to acknowledge it now. Joseph made the heat an excuse to leave Gerald wandering aimlessly between the flowers, and go back into the house.

He went into the sitting room to thank Connie and take his leave, but the figure standing by the mantel, though roughly the same height and build as Connie, was someone else. The words died on his lips when he saw the black dress, which was very fashionable, with a broad sash at the waist and a sort of double tunic in fine pleats over the long, tapering skirt.

She turned round, and her eyes widened with something like relief. 'Dr Reavley! How agreeable to see you.'

'Miss Coopersmith. How are you?' He closed the door behind him. He would like the opportunity to speak to her. She had known a side of Sebastian that he had been totally unaware of.

She gave a little shrug, slightly self-deprecatory. 'This is difficult. I don't really know what I am doing here. I hoped I could be of some comfort to Mrs Allard, but I know I'm not succeeding. Mrs Thyer is very kind, but what do you do with a fiancée who isn't a widow?' Her strong, rather blunt face were touched with self-mocking humour to hide the humiliation. 'I'm an impossibility for a hostess.' She gave a little laugh, and he realised how close she was to losing her self-control.

'Had you known Sebastian long?' he asked her. 'I have, but only the academic side of his life.' It was odd to say that aloud; until very recently he had not imagined it to be true, but now it was unquestionable.

'That was the biggest side,' she replied. 'He cared about it more than anything else, I think. That's why he was so terrified there'd be a war.'

'Yes. He spoke to me about it a day or two before he . . . died.' He remembered that long, slow walk along the Backs in the sunset as if it were yesterday. How quickly a moment sinks into the past. He could still see quite clearly the evening light on Sebastian's face, the passion in it as he spoke of the destruction of beauty that he feared.

'He travelled a lot this summer,' Regina went on, looking at the distance, not at Joseph. 'He didn't talk about it very much, but when he did you could feel how strongly he cared. I think you taught him that, Dr Reavley — how to see the loveliness and the value in all kinds of people, how to open his mind and look without judgement. He was so excited by it. He wanted intensely to live more . . . ' she hunted for the word, 'abundantly than one can being buried by

215

the confines of nationalism.'

As she said it Joseph remembered other things Sebastian had said about the richness and diversity of all Europe, but he did not interrupt her.

She went on, controlling her trembling voice with difficulty. 'For all his excitement at the different cultures, especially the ancient ones, he was terribly English at heart, you know?' She bit her lip to gain a moment's hesitation, trying to control herself before she went on. 'He would have given anything he had to protect the beauty of this country, the quaint and funny things, the tolerance and the eccentricity, the grandeur and the small, secret things one discovers alone. He'd have died to save a heath with skylarks — or a bluebell wood.' Her voice was trembling. 'A cold lake with reed spears in it, a lonely shore where the light falls on pale sand bars.' She gulped. 'It's hard to believe they are all still just the same, and he can't see them any more.'

He was too full of emotion himself to speak, and his thoughts included his father as well, and all the multitude of things his mother had treasured.

'But lots of people love things, don't they?' She was looking intently at him now. 'And there were parts of him I didn't know at all. A terrible anger sometimes, when he thought of what some of our politicians were doing, how they were letting Europe slip into war because they are all so busy protecting their own few square miles of territory. He hated jingoism, I mean, really hated it. I've seen him white to the lips, almost so choked with it that he couldn't speak.' She took a deep, shuddering breath. 'Do you think there will be war, Dr Reavley? Are we heading for a catastrophe bigger than anything we've ever seen before? That's what he was afraid of, you know? He wanted peace . . . so much!'

Joseph saw Sebastian's face in the fading light again, as clearly as if he had been in the room with them.

'Yes, I know.' He found his own voice shaking. 'I know he did.'

'I wonder if he would be surprised to see how much turmoil he's left behind.' Regina gave a tiny little laugh, almost like a hiccup. 'We are tearing ourselves apart trying to find out who killed him and, you know, I'm not sure if I want to succeed. Is that wicked of me, irresponsible?'

'I don't think we have a choice,' Joseph answered. 'We are going to be forced to know.'

'I'm afraid of that!' She stared at him, searching his face.

'Yes,' he agreed. 'So am I.'

7

On the evening of Friday, 17 July, Matthew again left London and drove north towards Cambridge. It was a fine evening with a slight wind piling clouds into bright towers of light high up in a cobalt sky. It was a perfect time to be on the road, once he had left the confines of the city. Long stretches opened up ahead of him, and he increased speed until the wind tore at his hair and stung his cheeks, and in his imagination he thought what it would be like to fly.

He reached Cambridge, and at about quarter-past seven was obliged to slow down to what now felt little better than the pace of a good saunter. He came in on the Trumpington Road with the river on his left and the Lammas Land beyond, past the Fitzwilliam, Peterhouse, Pembroke, Corpus Christi, and up the broad elegance of King's Parade with shops and houses to the right, and intricate wrought-iron railings to the left. He passed the ornate spires of the screen that walled off the Front Court of King's College, then the classical perfection of the Senate House, Great St Mary's opposite, and the beautiful towers of Gonville and Caius, Trinity, then St John's.

He pulled up at the main gate and climbed out of the seat. He was a little stiff, and it felt good to stand up at last. He went to the porter's lodge and was about to tell Mitchell who he was, and that he had come to see Joseph, when Mitchell recognised him.

Within a quarter of an hour his car was safely parked and he was sitting in Joseph's rooms. The sun made bright patches on the carpet and picked out the gold lettering on the books in the case. The college cat, Bertie, sat with his eyes closed in the warmth, and every now and again his tail gave a slight twitch.

Joseph sat in shadow; even so, Matthew could see the weariness and the pain of uncertainty etched in his face. His eyes looked hollow in spite of his high cheekbones. His cheeks were thin and there were shadows that had nothing to do with the darkness of his hair.

'Do they know who killed Sebastian yet?' Matthew asked.

'No,' Joseph shook his head very slightly. 'I don't honestly think they have any idea at all.'

'How's Mary Allard? Someone told me she came here.'

'Yes. She and Gerald are staying at the Master's house. The funeral was today. It was ghastly.'

'They haven't gone home?'

'They're still hoping the police will find something any day.'

Matthew looked at his brother with concern. He seemed to lack all vitality, as if something inside him were exhausted. 'Joe, you look bloody awful!' he said abruptly. 'Are you going to be all right?' It was a pointless question, but he had to ask. He had some idea how fond Joseph had been of Sebastian Allard, and his acute sense of responsibility, perhaps taken too personally. Was this additional blow too much for him?

Joseph raised his eyes. 'Probably.' He rubbed his hand over his forehead. 'It just takes a day or two. There doesn't seem to be any sense in this. I feel as if everything is slithering out of my grasp.'

'Joe,' Matthew said gently, leaning forward a little, 'Sebastian Allard was extraordinarily gifted, and he could be more charming than anyone else I can think of, but he wasn't perfect. I hate to say this, but you've got to let go of some of your dreams, because they're going to hurt you even more if you don't! There are no easy answers — you've told me that often enough. And nobody is entirely good — or bad. Someone killed Sebastian, and it's a tragedy, but it's not inexplicable. There'll be an answer which makes as much sense as most things ever do . . . when we know it.'

Joseph straightened up. 'I expect so. Do you suppose reason is going to be any comfort?' Then before Matthew could answer he went on, 'The Allards brought Regina Coopersmith with them.'

Matthew was lost. 'Who is Regina Coopersmith?'

'Sebastian's fiancée,' Joseph replied.

That explained much. If Joseph had not known of her he would feel excluded. How odd that Sebastian should not have told him. Usually when a young man was engaged to marry he told everyone. A young woman invariably did.

'His idea, or his mother's?' Matthew asked bluntly.

Joseph made a slight grimace. 'I don't know. I've talked with her a little. I should think it's his mother's. But it's probably irrelevant to his death.' He changed the subject. 'Are you going home?'

'For a day or two,' Matthew replied, feeling a sense of darkness inside him as he recalled the anger he had felt listening to Isenham the previous week. The wound was far from healed. He thought of his father and the interpretation Isenham had had of his actions, and it felt like an abscessed tooth. He could almost ignore it until he accidentally touched it, then it throbbed with all the old pain, exacerbated by a new jolt.

Joseph was waiting for him to go on.

'I went to see Isenham when I was up last weekend,' he said thoughtfully. He'd said on Sunday only that he'd come to see Judith. He did not want to tell Joseph lies, but sooner or later he would ask. Better to approach it himself. Also he needed to share the weight of the realisation towards which he was being pushed step by step. 'I thought Father might have confided his fears to him, and he would be able to tell me at least in which direction to look.'

Something in Joseph tightened, a moment so slight it was barely noticeable, but it betrayed his fear of what he was going to hear. He watched Matthew guardedly.

'He thinks Father read more into things than there was any basis for,' Matthew told him. He heard the sinking in his own voice and could not control it. He looked down, away from Joseph's eyes and the question in them. 'I talked to him for quite a long time, to see if he had any idea what it was Father thought, but all he told me that was specific was that Father wanted war — '

'What?' Joseph's voice was angry and incredulous. 'That's ridiculous! He was the last man on earth to want war. Isenham must have misheard him. Perhaps he said he thought war was inevitable! The question is, was it Ireland or the Balkans?'

'How would Father know anything about either of them?' Matthew was playing devil's advocate, and hoping Joseph could beat him. At least argument, and the use of reason, made Joseph more like his old self.

'I don't know,' Joseph answered. 'But that doesn't mean he didn't. You said he was very specific that he had been given a document which outlined a conspiracy that would be totally dishonourable, and change — '

'I know,' Matthew cut across him. 'I didn't tell Isenham that, but he said Father had been there, and was — '

'What? Losing control of his imagination?' Joseph demanded.

'More or less, yes. He was kinder about it than that, but it comes to the same thing. Let's say 'exaggerated rather wildly, possibly out of boredom'.'

'And a chance to be important again,' Joseph said with surprising venom. 'Does that sound like Father to you? If it does, then you didn't know him very well!'

'I know you're angry,' Matthew said quietly. 'So was I, and I still am. But what is the truth,

Joe? No one wants to think someone they love is mistaken, losing their grip. But wanting doesn't alter reality.'

'Reality is that he and Mother are dead,' Joseph said a little unsteadily. 'That their car hit a row of caltrops on the Hauxton Road and crashed, killing them both, and whatever document he had, whatever it said, wasn't with him. So presumably whoever killed him searched the car and the bodies, and found it.'

Matthew was forced to carry on the logic. 'Then why did they search the house for it?' he asked.

'We only *think* they did,' Joseph said unhappily, then with a very slight smile he added, 'But if they did, then they must have thought it important enough to take the risk of one of us coming back early and catching them. And don't tell me it was a petty thief. None of the valuables was taken, and the silver vase, the snuff boxes, the miniatures were all in plain sight.'

'You're right.' Matthew felt the first easing of the knots inside himself. 'But it could still have been a small scandal rather than a major espionage affecting the world.'

'It was major enough to murder two people in order to hide it,' Joseph said between his teeth, his jaw tight. 'And apart from that, Father didn't exaggerate.' He made it a simple statement, no additions, no emphasis.

Images raced through Matthew's mind: his father standing in the garden in old clothes, trousers a trifle baggy, mud-stained at the knees,

223

watching Judith picking blackberries; sitting in his armchair in the winter evening by the fire, a book open on his lap as he read them stories; at the dining-room table on a Sunday, leaning a little forward in his chair as he argued reasonably, refusing to lose his temper, or to be pushed into overstating his case. His father reciting absurd limericks and smiling, singing the Gilbert and Sullivan patter songs as he drove along the road with the top of the old car down in the wind and the sun.

The pain of loss was sweet for all he had been, and almost too sharp to bear because it no longer existed except in memory. It was a moment before he could control his voice enough to speak. 'I'll go and see Shanley Corcoran.' He took a deep breath. 'He was Father's closest friend. I can at last tell him the truth, or most of it. If Father trusted anyone, it would be he.'

Joseph hesitated a moment or two. Matthew had no way of knowing where his thoughts had been, if they ran as deep.

'Be careful,' was all he said.

★ ★ ★

Matthew spent the evening at home in St Giles, and he telephoned Corcoran to ask if he could call the next day. He received an immediate invitation to dinner, which he accepted unhesitatingly.

He was glad of a lazy morning, and he and Judith dealt with a number of small duties. Then in the hot, still afternoon they took Henry and walked together to the churchyard, and on through the lanes, Henry scuffling happily in the deep grasses on either side. The wild rose petals had mostly fallen.

Matthew changed for dinner early, and was glad to be able to put the top down on the car and drive the ten or twelve miles to Corcoran's magnificent home. As he passed through Grantchester a dozen or more youths were still practising cricket in the lengthening sun, to the cheers and occasional shouts of a handful of watchers. Girls in pinafore dresses dangled hats by their ribbons. Three miles further on children were sailing wooden boats in the village duck pond, entirely ignored by the ducks, who were apparently used to it. A hurdy-gurdy man cranked out music, and an ice-cream seller was packing his barrow to go home, his wares gone, his purse heavy.

Matthew crossed the main road between Cambridge and the west, then a mile and a half further along he swung off just short of Madingley, and in through the gates of Corcoran's house. He had barely stepped out of the car when the butler appeared, solemn-faced and punctilious.

'Good evening, Captain Reavley. How pleasant to see you, sir. We have been expecting you. Have you anything you wish carried, sir?'

'No, thank you.' Matthew declined with a smile, reaching into the car to pick up the box of Orla's favourite Turkish delight from the passenger seat. 'I'll manage these myself.'

'Yes, sir. Then if you leave your keys, I'll see that Parley puts your car away safely. If you would like to come this way, sir . . . ?'

Matthew followed him under the portico and up the shallow steps, through the door and into the wide, stone-flagged hallway, black and white squared like a chessboard. A full suit of medieval armour stood beside the carved newel post at the right hand of the mahogany staircase, its helmet catching the sun through the oval window on the landing.

Matthew dropped the car keys on to the tray the butler was holding, then turned as the study door opened and Shanley Corcoran appeared. A wide smile lit his face and he came forward, extending both his hands.

'I'm so glad you could come,' he said enthusiastically, searching Matthew's face. 'How are you? Come in and sit down!' He indicated the study doorway, and without waiting for a reply he led the way in.

The room was typical of the man: exuberant; the books and artefacts were highly individual and there were also scientific curiosities and exquisite works of art. There was a Russian icon, all golds and umber and black, solemn-faced and gentle. Above the fireplace hung an Italian old master drawing of a man riding a donkey, probably Jesus entering Jerusalem on Palm Sunday. An astrolabe made of silver, polished bright, stood on the mahogany Pembroke table by the wall, and an illustrated copy of Chaucer on the drum table in the centre of the room. Corcoran had read to him from it once, long ago. It was bawdy, vital and funny. They had laughed aloud, enriched by his love of it.

'Sit down, sit down,' Corcoran invited, gesturing towards the other chair.

Matthew sank back into it, at ease already in the familiar room, memories crowding back, all of them good. It was quarter-past seven and he knew dinner would be served by eight. There was no time to waste on a preparatory conversation. 'Thank you. Did you hear about the death of Sebastian Allard? His family is devastated. I don't suppose their grief will begin to heal until they find out what happened. I know how they feel.'

Corcoran's face darkened. 'I understand your grief.' His voice was very gentle. 'I miss John. He was one of the kindest, most honest men I knew. I can't begin to imagine how you must feel.' A frown of puzzlement creased his brow. 'But what more is there to know about his death? No one was responsible. Perhaps it was a slick of oil on the road, or something wrong with the steering of the car. I don't drive, personally. I know nothing about the mechanics.' He smiled at the irony of it. 'I understand aeroplanes a little, and submarines a lot, but I imagine there are considerable differences.'

Matthew attempted to smile in answer. Being here with Corcoran brought back memories with an intensity he had been unprepared for. The veil between past and present was too thin. 'Well, neither aeroplanes nor submarines are going to crash off the road, if that is what you meant. But I don't believe that was what happened. In fact

227

I'm sure it wasn't.' He saw Corcoran's eyes widen very slightly. 'Joseph and I went to the place,' Matthew explained. 'We saw the skid marks exactly where the car veered off. There was no oil.' He hesitated, then took the plunge. 'Only a line of scratches, as if made by a row of iron caltrops across the tarmacadam.'

The silence was so heavy in the room he could hear the ticking of the long-case clock against the far wall as if it were beside him.

'What are you saying, Matthew?' Corcoran spoke at last, his eyes steady, his face creased with concern.

Matthew leaned forward a little. 'Father was on his way to see me in London. He called me up to arrange it the night before. I've never heard him more serious.'

'Oh? About what?' If Corcoran already had any idea, there was no indication of it in his face. Matthew searched for it, and he eased a little inside when he failed to see fear, suspicion, or anything that might be foreknowledge.

'He said he had learned of a conspiracy which was highly dishonourable, and would eventually affect the whole world,' Matthew replied. 'He wanted my advice on it.'

Corcoran's vivid blue eyes were unblinking. 'Your professional advice?' he said cautiously, something in his voice close to disbelief.

'Yes.'

'I suppose you are certain of that? You couldn't have misunderstood it?'

'No.' Matthew was not going to elaborate and perhaps put words into Corcoran's mouth.

Suddenly the conversation was no longer easy, or simply between friends. The room was silent, prickly, as if waiting for something startling to happen.

'I knew he was concerned about something,' Corcoran said, looking at Matthew over the top of his steepled fingers. 'But he didn't tell me what it was about. In fact he was politely evasive, so I didn't pursue it.'

'You have no idea what it was?' Now, unaccountably, Matthew was disappointed. He did not know what he had been expecting, but it had been more than this. Was Corcoran being deliberately evasive, or did he really know nothing? 'What did he say to you . . . exactly?' he pressed.

Corcoran blinked. 'Very little: only that he was worried about the pressure in the Balkans — which we all are, but he seemed to think it were more explosive than I did.' Corcoran's expression tightened, his lips a thin line, taking the imagination and the humour out of his face. 'It seems he was right. The assassination of the Archduke is very ugly. They'll demand reparation, and of course Serbia won't pay. The Russians will back the Serbs, and Germany will back Austria. That's inevitable.'

'And us?' Matthew asked. 'That's still a long way from Britain, and has nothing to do with our honour.'

Corcoran was thoughtful for a moment. The ticking of the clock measured the silence.

'The alliances are a web right across Europe,' he said at last. 'We know some of them, but perhaps not all. It's fears and promises that could be our undoing.'

'Do you think Father could possibly have known about the assassination before it happened?' It was a wild thought, but Matthew was reduced to desperation.

Corcoran lifted his shoulders very slightly, but there was no incredulity in his face, and no ridicule. 'I can't think how!' he answered. 'If he had any connections with that part of the world, he didn't mention them to me. He knew France and Germany well, and Belgium too, I think. He had some relative who married a Belgian, I believe, a cousin he was fond of.'

'Yes, Aunt Abigail,' Matthew confirmed. 'But what has Belgium to do with Serbia?'

'Nothing, so far as I know,' Corcoran answered. 'But what puzzles me far more is that he should want to involve you professionally.' He looked apologetic. 'I'm sorry, Matthew, but you know as well as I do that he hated all secret services.'

'Yes, I do know!' Matthew cut in sharply. 'He wanted Joseph to go into medicine; and when he didn't, he wanted me to. He never really said why — ' He stopped, seeing surprise and a swift tenderness in Corcoran's face. He was blinking as if to hold back sudden tears.

'He didn't tell you?' he asked.

Matthew shook his head. It was a place inside him that still hurt too much to explore. He had always believed that one day he would have the chance to show his father the value of what he did. Discreetly, it also saved lives, it saved the peace in which people could go about their ordinary, open business without fear. It was one of those professions that, if practised with great enough skill, one was unaware of. It was visible only when it failed. But John's death had made that proof impossible, and it was an unresolved pain he had no way to deal with.

He resented Corcoran's probing it now, of all times. Had he liked him less, were there not the ties of common love that were so precious to him, he would have refused to permit it. It would be easy enough to retreat, to close all the emotional doors and be polite but cold. They could easily talk of trivialities until it was time for him to leave. But to lose Corcoran's warmth, his laughter, his common memories, would be like a tiny death all over again.

'It was a long time ago,' Corcoran began thoughtfully. 'When he and I were both young. Perhaps it was even something to do with me, I don't know. It was in our first year at Cambridge — '

'I didn't know you were in the same year!' Matthew interrupted.

There was the very faintest flush on Corcoran's fair skin. 'I was a year older than he. I was there on my father's money, he was on a scholarship. He started in medicine, you know?' Even without Matthew's amazement, it was obvious in Corcoran's face that he knew Matthew had not known. 'I was reading physics. We used to spend hours talking and dreaming about what we could do . . . after we graduated.'

Matthew waited, trying to visualise it — the

231

two young men, minds full of the future, of hopes and ambitions. Had John Reavley been happy with what he had achieved? It hurt like a slow grinding pain in the pit of the stomach to think that perhaps he had not, that he had died a disappointed man.

'Don't,' Corcoran said gently, his eyes searching Matthew's face. 'He changed his mind because he wanted to go into politics. He thought he could achieve more there, so he read classics instead. That's where most of our leaders come from, the men who learned the discipline of the mind and the history of thought and civilisation in the West.' He let out his breath slowly. 'But there were times when he regretted it. He found politics a hard and often graceless master to serve. In the end he preferred the individual to the mass, and he thought it would give you greater happiness, and far more security.'

'But you went on with physics . . . ' Matthew said.

Corcoran gave a downwardly twisted smile, self-mocking, but also evasive. 'I was ambitious in a different way.'

Matthew voiced the knowledge he was more afraid of. 'He hated the intelligence services. He thought we were underhand, essentially betrayers; that we deliberately used people and had no loyalties ahead of the gaining of information, no personal compassion or judgement of our own. He didn't even seem to understand that not all battles can be fought face to face. He . . . ' He hesitated, not because he had not the words, but he was loath to use them.

Corcoran nodded slowly, the sunlight behind him lighting his hair like a halo, but his face was sad. Even if he knew what Matthew was going to say, he did not finish his sentence for him.

'He had no patience with deviousness,' Matthew went on. 'He couldn't be bothered to be indirect, to play to people's vanities or use their weaknesses. I don't think he understood how to. And he thought that was what we do.'

Corcoran's smile was sweet and warm. 'Isn't it?' he asked with a kind of wry regret.

Matthew sighed, and leaned back in his chair again, crossing his legs. 'Sometimes. Mostly it's just collecting as much information as possible and fitting it together so we see a picture. I wish I could have shown him that.'

'Matthew,' Corcoran said earnestly, 'if he was coming to you for your professional advice, then whatever he had discovered, he must have believed it was profoundly serious, and that only one of the secret services could help.'

'But you have no idea what it was? What did he say to you? Anything? Names, places, dates, who would be affected . . . anything at all?' Matthew pleaded. 'I don't know where to start, and I don't trust anyone, because he said important people were involved.' Even to Corcoran he held back that his father had spoken of the royal family. He had no idea how distant the royalty implicated might be: a cousin, someone connected by marriage, or higher? That was a peculiarly repulsive thought. But then remembering how large Queen Victoria's family had been, the net spread very wide indeed.

Corcoran nodded. 'Of course,' he agreed. 'If he could have trusted the ordinary services then he would have.'

There was a slight sound outside the door, then a knock, and Orla Corcoran came in. She was dressed in a bluish-green gown of silk Charmeuse with Venetian lace draped around her shoulders. The dress had the easy grace of something very simple that has required brilliant design to fall so perfectly, and yet seem to have taken no trouble at all. In the fashion of the moment, the waist was high and soft, and the full drape came almost to the ankle before sweeping back to be caught up behind, revealing only a few inches of a plainer skirt beneath. The gown was decorated with two crimson roses, one just under the bosom, the other on the skirt. Orla's dark hair was curled loosely and had only a few streaks of grey at the temples, and they made her the more striking.

'Matthew, my dear,' she said with a smile. 'How good it is to see you.' She regarded him more closely. 'But you are looking a little tired. Have you been working too hard with all this wretched business in Eastern Europe? The Austrians don't seem to manage their affairs very well. I do hope they don't draw us all into their mess.'

'I'm in good health, thank you,' he said, taking her hand and touching it to his lips. 'Unfortunately they haven't given me anything so interesting to do. I fear I may be picking up the domestic duties of others who are sent off to exotic parts.'

'Oh, you really don't want to go to Serbia!' she said instantly. 'It would take you ages to get there, and then you wouldn't understand a word they said.' She turned to Corcoran. 'Dinner is about to be served. Do come through, and talk about pleasanter things for a while. Have you been to the theatre lately? Last week we saw Lady Randolph Churchill's new play at the Prince of Wales.' She led the way across the hall, passing a maid dressed in black with a crisp white lace-edged apron, without apparently seeing her. 'Very mixed, I thought,' she went on. 'Lots of drama, but a bit thin on skill here and there.'

'You are repeating exactly what the reviewers say, my dear,' Corcoran remarked with amusement.

'Then perhaps for once they are right!' she retorted, leading the way into the splendid rose and gold dining room.

The long mahogany table was very simple, in the classic style of Adam. The mahogany chairs whose high, tapered backs echoed the lines of the windows. The curtains were drawn, hiding the view across the garden and the fields beyond.

They took their seats and the first course was served. Since it was high summer, and in the nature of a family meal rather than a formal one, a cold collation was quite acceptable. The second course was grilled trout and fresh vegetables, with a light German wine, dry and very delicate.

Matthew passed the natural compliments to

235

the cook, but he meant them with great sincerity.

The conversation meandered over a dozen subjects: the latest novels published, accounts of travel in North Africa, more local gossip of Cambridgeshire families, the likelihood of a cold winter after such a glorious summer, anything but Ireland or Europe. Eventually they touched on Turkey, but only as a possible site for the ruins of what was once the great city of Troy.

'Wasn't that where Ivor Chetwin went?' Orla asked, turning to Corcoran.

Corcoran glanced at Matthew, then back to his wife. 'I don't know,' he answered.

'Oh, for goodness' sake!' she said impatiently, spearing a slice of nectarine with her fork. 'Matthew knows perfectly well that John quarrelled with Ivor. You don't have to tiptoe around it as if it were a hole he would fall into.' She turned to Matthew, the fork still in her hand. 'Ivor and your father used to be very good friends, nine or ten years ago. They both knew a man called Galliford, or Galliard, or something like that. He was doing something serious that he shouldn't, I don't know what. They never tell you.' She ate the last of the nectarine quickly. 'But Ivor told the authorities about it and the man was arrested.'

Corcoran drew in his breath to interrupt, then changed his mind. The damage was done.

'John never really forgave him for it,' Orla continued. 'I don't know why, after all Galliford, or whatever his name was, was guilty of doing it. That was Ivor's chance to join some branch or other of the secret services, and he took it. After

236

that he and John never really spoke to each other, except to be polite. It was a great shame, because Ivor was a lovely man and they used to enjoy each other's company.'

'It wasn't that he caught Gallard,' Corcoran said quietly. 'It was the way in which he did it that John couldn't forgive. John was a very candid man, almost innocent, you might say. He expected a certain standard of honesty from other people. He couldn't bear guile, and the secret services depend upon it.' He glanced at Matthew. 'I suppose they have to. It is the weapon our enemies use against us.'

'He must have known that,' Orla protested. 'He was not foolish, Shanley. He understood reality.'

'He didn't like that element of it.' There was a note of warning in Corcoran's voice. 'He didn't want to be part of it.'

'You don't have to be careful for me,' Matthew said a little abruptly. 'He didn't want me part of it either, although he never told me about Ivor Chetwin. Did he go to Turkey?'

'Of course he did!' Orla responded. 'But he came back.'

'Do you think Father would have seen him again, recently?' Matthew asked. 'In the last week or so before he died?'

Orla looked surprised.

Corcoran understood immediately. 'I don't know,' he admitted. 'It's possible.'

Orla had no such hesitation. 'Of course it's possible,' she said with a smile. 'I know Ivor is at home because he lives in Haslingfield, and I saw him only a couple of weeks ago. I'm sure if your father visited him he'd be happy to tell you about it.'

Corcoran looked at her, then at Matthew, uncertain.

Matthew could not afford to care about old quarrels. High in his mind was the possibility that Ivor Chetwin could be the man behind the conspiracy John Reavley had learned of. It was suddenly very important to know if they had met, but he would have to be extremely careful. Whoever it was did not hesitate to kill. Again he was overwhelmed with anger for his father for having been so naïve as to trust someone, to think the best of them when it so agonizingly was not true!

'Matthew . . . ' Corcoran began, his face earnest, the lamplight now accentuating the warmth in his features.

'Yes!' Matthew said instantly. 'I shall be extremely careful. Father and I are quite different. I trust no one.' He wanted to explain to them what he intended to do. However, he did not know yet, and he needed the freedom to change his mind. But above all, he did not want his father's friend watching over his shoulder to see his weaknesses, or his pain if what he found was sad and vulnerable — and private.

'That's not what I was going to say,' Corcoran chided him, with a slight smile intruding across his thoughts. 'Ivor Chetwin was a decent man when I knew him. But I doubt your father would have confided anything in him before telling you.

Have you considered that this issue your father was so concerned about may have been a piece of politicking which he felt was dishonourable, rather than anything you or I would consider a conspiracy? He was a little . . . idealistic.'

'Conspiracy?' Orla looked from Matthew to her husband, and back again.

'Probably nothing.' Corcoran smiled very slightly. 'I dare say he would have found that out, if he had had the chance.'

Matthew wanted to argue, but he had no weapons. He could not defend his father, he had nothing but remembered words, which he had repeated so often he was hearing his own voice saying them now. There was nothing tangible except death, the awful absence of those he loved, the jolting surprise of the empty rooms, the telephone call no one would answer from the study.

'Of course,' he said, not meaning it, nor looking at Corcoran's face. He was agreeing for Orla's sake, so as not to alarm her. 'I wish I didn't have to go back to London so soon. It is so timelessly peaceful here.'

'Have a glass of port?' Corcoran offered. 'I have some real vintage stuff.'

Matthew hesitated.

'Oh, it's excellent!' Corcoran assured him. 'No cork in it, no crust or sediment, I promise.'

Matthew gave in gracefully.

The butler was sent for, and dispatched to fetch one of the best bottles. He returned with it cradled in a napkin.

'Right!' Corcoran said enthusiastically. 'I'll

open this myself! Make sure it's perfect. Thank you, Truscott.'

'Yes, sir.' The butler handed it over with resignation.

'Really . . . ' Orla protested, but without any belief she would make a difference. 'Sorry,' she said ruefully to Matthew. 'He's rather proud of this.'

Matthew smiled. It was obviously a ritual that mattered to Corcoran, and he was happy to observe as Corcoran led them to the kitchen, heated the tongs in the kitchen stove, then grasped the bottle with them, closing them around its neck. Truscott handed him a goose feather and held out a dish of ice. Corcoran passed the feather through the ice, then carefully around the neck of the Port.

'There!' he said triumphantly as the glass cracked in a perfect circle, cutting the corked top off cleanly. 'You see?'

'Bravo!' Matthew laughed.

Corcoran was grinning widely, his face alight with triumph. 'There you are, Truscott! Now you can decant it and bring it to us in the dining room. Mrs Corcoran will have a Madeira. Come . . . ' And he led the procession back to the rose and gold room.

*   *   *

It was late on Sunday afternoon when Matthew drove over to Haslingfield and called on Ivor Chetwin. It had taken him a long time to decide what to say to him. Whether it was actually true

240

or not was irrelevant; all that mattered was that it should be believable. It was taking a liberty with his father's intent, but it was in a cause he would have approved.

Chetwin did not live in the magnificent manner of the Corcorans, but his home was still extremely agreeable. It was a Georgian manor a mile outside Haslingfield and the long drive from the road swept around a gracious curve with a stand of silver birches, their leaves shimmering delicately in the slight breeze, their white trunks leaning with exaggerated grace away from the prevailing wind.

A parlour maid welcomed Matthew, but Chetwin himself appeared almost immediately, an enthusiastic spaniel puppy at his heels.

'I'd have recognised you,' Chetwin said without hesitation, holding his hand out to Matthew. His voice, unusually deep, still had the echo of music in it from his native Wales. 'You resemble your father . . . about the eyes.'

The loyalty hardened even more deeply inside Matthew, memory catching him again.

'Thank you for agreeing to see me at such short notice, sir,' he replied. 'I'm just up for the weekend. I spend most of my time in London now.'

'I'm afraid I only get occasional weekends here myself at the moment,' Chetwin agreed. Then, followed by the puppy, he turned and led the way into a very casual sitting room opening on to a highly unusual paved and gravelled garden, largely shaded by overhanging trees. It was full of blossom from bushes and shrubs at the sides, and low-growing silvery-grey-leaved plants in clumps in the paving. The extraordinary thing about it was that every flower was white.

Chetwin noticed Matthew staring.

'My white garden,' he explained. 'I find it very restful. Sit down. Oh, move the cat.' He gestured towards a black cat that had settled itself in the middle of the second chair and looked very disinclined to shift.

Matthew stroked the cat gently and felt rather than heard it begin to purr. He lifted it up, and when he had taken the seat, put it down again on his lap. It rearranged itself slightly, and went back to sleep.

'My father intended to come and see you,' he said smoothly, as if it were true. 'I never had the chance to ask him if he actually did.' He had considered adding to it that John Reavley had regretted losing the friendship, but it was possible that if he had visited Chetwin, that would very obviously be a lie.

He watched Chetwin's face. It was dark-eyed, with a strong, round jaw, black hair greying and receding from a high brow. Matthew could read nothing in it. It was a face that could give away exactly what its owner wished it to. There was nothing whatever naïve or easily misled in Ivor Chetwin. He was full of imagination and subtlety. Matthew had been here only a few minutes, yet already he had a sense of Chetwin's inner power.

'I'm sorry he didn't,' Chetwin replied, and there was sadness in his voice. If he were acting, he was superb. But then Matthew had known men who betrayed their friends, even their families, and profoundly though they regretted what they saw as the necessity, it had not stopped them.

'He didn't contact you at all?' Matthew pressed. He should not have been disappointed, and yet he was. He had hoped Chetwin would have an idea, a thread, however fine, that would lead somewhere. He realised now that hope was unreasonable. John Reavley would have come to Matthew first, before trusting anyone else, even the far more experienced Chetwin.

Or was it that he knew Chetwin too well to trust him? An old disillusion unforgiven, or a new betrayal feared? Or he had met Chetwin somewhere else, and Chetwin was lying?

'I wish he had.' Chetwin's face still showed the same sadness. 'I would have called on him, but I doubted he would see me.' A new bleakness shadowed his eyes. 'That's one of the deepest regrets of death: the things you thought of doing and put off, and then suddenly it's too late.'

'Yes, I know,' Matthew agreed with more emotion than he had meant to expose. He felt as if he were laying a weapon down with the blade towards himself and the handle to a potential enemy. And yet had he shown less, Chetwin would have sensed it, and known he was guarding himself. From what? A natural desire to preserve his own dignity, or a suspicion of the fact that John Reavley was murdered? A guilty man would think the latter.

Chetwin was watching him closely, his bright, dark eyes seeing every nuance. If he were good at his job, he would miss nothing. Matthew watched with equal care, just as casually. He wanted to study the room and learn from it what he could of the man, but Chetwin would see, and understand exactly what he was doing, and why. It did not fit in with the casual call of friendship he had professed. What he had observed so far told him nothing. The furniture was traditional, and probably inherited from at least one previous generation. There were the characteristics of long family use on it: the worn patches, unmatched chairs, pieces from different periods, but nothing individual to Chetwin himself. He was a man who lived here, but if his personality, his mind and his tastes were imprinted on anything, it was somewhere other than this comfortable room. Matthew could not help wondering why. What was there so vulnerable to hide?

Chetwin was waiting for him to continue.

Matthew smiled self-deprecatingly. 'I think of something every day I would like to have said to him. I suppose that's really why I called. You knew him during a time when I was so young I thought of him only as my father, not as a person who led any life beyond St Giles.'

'A natural blindness of youth,' Chetwin dismissed it. 'But I think most of what you would have heard about your father you would have liked.' He smiled, which momentarily softened his face. 'He was stubborn at times; he had an intellectual arrogance he was not even aware of. It sprang from an effortless intelligence, and yet he had untiring patience for those he perceived as genuinely limited. It was the lazy he could not bear, and the dishonest. And, I suppose, the cowards who would not face unpalatable truths.'

He looked upward, retreating further into memory. 'He was a gentle man, naturally courteous. He treated the old, the poor, the unlearned with dignity. To him the great sin was unkindness.' He continued to stare at some place within his own memory. He was revisiting the past before their quarrel had bled the pleasure from their association.

Matthew forced himself from the balm it gave him back to the reasons for his visit. He needed information, not affection, however good it was to hear it. He took the risk of probing. 'I remember him as being completely without guile,' he said. 'Was that true, or just what I wanted to think?'

Chetwin gave a sharp, self-mocking little laugh. 'Oh, that was true! He couldn't tell a lie to save himself, and he wasn't about to change what he was to please anyone, or to deceive them, even to gain his own ends.'

His face shadowed again, but his black eyes were unreadable. If there was pain, he concealed it. 'I think quite often that was his weakness as well as his strength. He was one of the most intelligent men I ever knew, and probably the nicest, but it prevented him from being an effective politician, except when he could gain a consensus because the idea was so patently good no one could justify voting against him. He was incapable of deviousness, and that is a

245

politician's main weapon.'

That was not true, however, of Chetwin. He was a chameleon, changing colour to suit his needs, the core of him elusive.

Matthew hesitated, wondering if he should admit to being in the intelligence services, and knowing that Chetwin was also. It might be a short cut to gaining confidences. It would save time, take him nearer the truth. Or should he guard the little ammunition he had? Where were Chetwin's loyalties? He was easy to like, and the ties of the past were strong. But perhaps that was exactly what had cost John Reavley his life! Matthew must be wiser than that: use his brain, not his emotions.

'He was very worried about the present situation in the Balkans,' he said instead. 'Even though he died the day of the assassination, so he didn't hear of it.'

'Yes,' Chetwin agreed, his face losing the pleasure of memory, and becoming totally serious. 'I know he used to have a considerable interest in German affairs, and had many German friends. He climbed in the Austrian Tyrol now and then when he was younger. He enjoyed Vienna, its music and its culture, and he read German, of course.'

'He discussed it with you?'

'Oh yes. We had many friends in common, in those days.' There was sadness in his voice and a gentleness that seemed entirely human and vulnerable. But if he were clever, it would do!

Matthew knew he was learning nothing. He could not stay here much longer. He was behaving like an amateur. How much time was there until the conspiracy that his father feared came into fruition, and it would be too late to do anything to prevent it? He had heard urgency in his father's voice, a need to drive down immediately to London, not wait until the next time Matthew should come up to St Giles for a weekend, as he did every month or so. John had begun his drive the next morning!

Matthew must take a risk now. Dangerous as it might be, it was still better than being so cautious he lost by default, doing nothing until it was too late.

'Did he keep up with them, do you know?' he asked. He was going to trail a faint thread of the truth in front of Chetwin to see if he picked it up, or if he even noticed it.

There was nothing guarded in Chetwin's clever face. 'I should imagine so. He was a man who kept his friends . . . ' he gave a little grimace, 'except in my case, of course. But that was because he did not approve of my change in career. He felt it was immoral, deceitful, if you like.'

Matthew drew in his breath. It was like jumping into melted ice. 'The intelligence services . . . yes, I know.' He saw Chetwin flinch so minutely it was no more than a shadow. 'I think it was because of you that he was so disappointed when I joined them as well,' he went on, and this time there was no mistaking the surprise. But then if he were behind John Reavley's death, he could have checked on Matthew any time he wished to. Within the service it would be easy enough to find out. 'You didn't know?' he added.

Chetwin breathed out very slowly. 'No . . . I didn't.' An expression flashed in his eyes. It could have been amusement, or any of a dozen things.

Matthew was in the presence of a master of guile, and he knew it. But he could play the game too. 'Yes. He didn't approve of it, of course,' he said, smiling ruefully. 'But he knew that we have our uses. Sometimes there is no one else to turn to.'

This time Chetwin hesitated.

Matthew smiled.

'Then he'd changed,' Chetwin said slowly. 'He used to think there was always a better way. But I suppose you know that too?'

'Something like that,' Matthew said noncommittally. He struggled for something else to pursue. He could not leave Chetwin, possibly the best source of hidden information about his father, without trying every avenue there was. Yet he was always aware that Chetwin could so easily be the source of the document, and everything he said a lie.

'Actually, I think he had changed,' he said suddenly. 'Something he said to me not long ago made me think he had begun to appreciate the value of discreet information.'

Chetwin's eyebrows rose. 'Oh?' He did not conceal the interest in his face.

Matthew hesitated, acutely aware of the danger of what he was doing. His father had once been a close friend of Chetwin, and the break in the relationship had been final, as far as he knew. Was he being totally ridiculous in trusting him with anything now? Damn Father for telling him so little! He had left him knowing enough to be aware of the danger, to be afraid of all its possibilities, and to realise he had nothing with which to fight them.

He had Corcoran's version of the quarrel that had driven John Reavley to loathe all secret intelligence, but was it the truth? If he could have asked his father now, would he say the same? He had been a tolerant man, slow to judge. Why had this been beyond his nature or his power to overlook? Was there far more to it than Corcoran had said? Perhaps it had been such a betrayal, its ramifications so wide and so dangerous still, that John Reavley could not afford to ask.

Then how much dare Matthew say now? He must give away nothing, and he could not back out, or Chetwin would instantly suspect him. Nor must he look as if he were being less than frank. Chetwin was trained in sensing nervousness, let alone deceit.

'Just the value of information,' he said lightly, smiling and leaning back a little in his chair. 'I never heard the rest of it. I thought it might matter. Who would he have taken it to?'

'Information about what?' Chetwin asked.

Matthew was very careful. 'I'm not sure. Possibly the situation in Germany.' That was probably far enough from the troubles in either Ireland or the Balkans to be safe.

Chetwin thought for a moment or two, his lips

pursed in thought. 'Best to go to the man at the top,' he said finally. 'If it was important, it would reach Dermot Sandwell eventually.'

'Sandwell!' Matthew was surprised. Dermot Sandwell was a highly respected minister in the Foreign Office. Then as he thought about it, he realised it made excellent sense. Sandwell was an outstanding linguist, well-travelled, a classicist and scholar. 'Yes, I suppose it would. Thank you,' he accepted.

He stayed a little longer. Conversation moved from one thing to another: politics, memories, small gossip about Cambridgeshire. Chetwin had a vivid and individual turn of phrase describing people, and a sharp wit. Matthew could see very clearly why his father had liked him.

Half an hour later he rose to go, still uncertain whether John Reavley had confided anything about the document to Chetwin or not, and if he had, if doing so had been the catalyst for his own death.

Matthew drove back to London that evening in heavy, thundery weather, wishing the storm would break and release the grey, choking air into rain to wash it clear.

Thunder rolled menacingly around the western rim of the clouds at about half-past six as he was twenty miles south of Cambridge, gliding between deep hedges in full leaf. Then ten minutes later the lightning forked down to the ground and the rain dashed torrentially, bouncing up again from the smooth, black road till he felt as if he were drowning under a

250

waterfall. He slowed up, almost blinded by it.

When it was gone, steam rose from the shimmering surface, a silver haze in the sun, and it all smelled like a Turkish bath.

★　★　★

On Monday morning the newspapers told the public that the King had reviewed two hundred and sixty ships of the Royal Navy at the Spithead base, and that the naval reserves had been called up on orders from the First Lord of the Admiralty, Winston Churchill, and the First Sea Lord, Prince Louis of Battenberg. There was no word whatever of Austria's ultimatum to Serbia on the reparations demanded for the death of the Archduke. Shearing sat at his desk staring grimly ahead of him into the distance. Matthew stood, not yet given permission to sit.

'Means nothing,' Shearing said to Matthew darkly. 'I'm told there was a secret meeting in Vienna yesterday. I wouldn't be surprised if they push it to the limit. Austria can't be seen to back down. If they did, then all their territories would think they could assassinate people. That's the damn shame of it.' He muttered something else under his breath, and Matthew did not ask him to repeat it. 'Sit down!' he said impatiently. 'Don't hover like that as if you were about to go. You aren't! We've all these reports to go through.' He indicated a pile of papers on his desk.

Even the room's functionality was anonymous, clever rather than personal. An Arabic brass dish

251

and bowl were beautiful, but of no meaning. Matthew had asked him about them once. Similarly the watercolour paintings of a storm blowing up over the South Downs, and another of dying winter light over the London Docks, the black spars of a clipper sharp and straight against the sky, carried no personal significance.

The conversation moved to Ireland and the situation in the Curragh, which was still a cause of anxiety. It was far from resolved.

Shearing swore softly and imaginatively, more to himself than for Matthew's benefit. 'How could we be so bloody stupid as to get ourselves into this mess?' he said, his jaw tight till the muscles stood out in his neck. 'The Protestants were never going to let themselves be absorbed by the Catholic south. They were bound to resort to violence, and our men would never have fired on them. Any damn fool knows they'll not shoot their own — and so you've got a mutiny!' His dark face was flushed. 'And we can't let mutiny go unpunished, so we've painted ourselves into an impossible corner! How stupid do you have to be not to see that coming? It's like being caught by surprise when it snows in January!'

There was no point in arguing; there was nothing to disagree with. 'I thought the Government were consulting the King?' Matthew replied.

Shearing looked up at him. 'Oh, they are! They have! And what happens if the King sides with the Ulster Loyalists? Has anybody thought of that?'

Matthew clenched inside. He had been too consumed with the murder of his father, and the question of the document and what might be in it, to give deeper thought to such an idea. Now he did, and it was appalling. 'He can't! Can he?' he demanded.

The anger in Shearing's face was so sharp its power filled the room. 'Yes, he damned well can!' he spat, glaring at Matthew.

'When will they reach a decision and tell us?'

'Today . . . tomorrow! God knows. Then we'll see what real trouble is.' He saw the question in Matthew's eyes. 'Yes, Reavley,' he said with level, grating calm. 'The assassination in Serbia is bad, but believe me, it would be nothing compared with one at home.'

'An assassination!' Matthew exclaimed.

Shearing's eyebrows rose. 'Why not?' he challenged.

Matthew started to speak, then stopped, uncertain what he wanted to say.

'Why not?' Shearing repeated. 'What's the difference? Serbia is a subject part of the Austro-Hungarian Empire and some of its citizens think assassination of a royal duke is the way to freedom and independence. Ireland is part of the British Empire. Why shouldn't some of its subjects assume that the assassination of a king might earn them the freedom they want?'

'Protestant Northern Ireland wants to remain part of the British Empire,' Matthew replied, keeping his voice level with difficulty. 'That's what the term 'Loyalist' means! They don't want to be swallowed up in Roman Catholic Ireland!'

But even as he was saying it he knew the words were empty.

'Very rational,' Shearing said sarcastically. 'I'm sure if you say that a little louder all the madmen with glory in their brains will put their guns away and go home again.' He pulled a thin sheaf of papers out of the drawer in his desk and held it out. 'Go and look at those, see what you make of them.'

Matthew took them from him. 'Yes, sir,' he accepted, and went back to his own office with his fingers numb, his head singing with ideas.

Matthew attempted to work on the papers all day. They were the usual notes on intelligence information intercepted, reports of the movement of men either known or suspected of Irish Independence sympathies. He was still looking for any threat to Blunden, and his possible appointment to the War Ministry, with the obvious effect it would have on further military action in Ireland, the need for which seemed almost certain.

If the position went to Wynyard, with his robust opinions and more volatile judgement, it might not only hasten the violence, but make it worse, possibly even spreading it to England itself.

He found it difficult to keep his mind on the subject; it was too nebulous to grasp, the connections too remote. And one name occurred a number of times: Patrick Hannassey. He had been born in Dublin in 1861, the second son of a physician and Irish patriot. His elder brother had gone into law, and died young in a boating disaster off the County Waterford coast. Patrick also had studied law for a while, married and had a daughter. Then tragedy had struck again. His wife had been killed in a pointless exchange of violence between Catholic and Protestant, and Patrick, in his grief, had abandoned the slow-moving workings of the law in favour of the swifter struggle of politics, even of civil war.

It would suit his avowed purpose very well for Blunden to succeed to the War Minister's post, where he could be taunted, defied and mocked into action that would seem to justify armed retaliation, and the beginning of open warfare. He preached uprising, but he did it subtly, and he was a hard man to catch; elusive, clever, never overreaching himself with arrogance, never betraying those who trusted him, not looking for personal power and certainly not for money.

A little before six Matthew went back to Shearing's office, knowing he would find him still there.

'Yes?' Shearing looked up. His eyes were red-rimmed, his skin colourless.

'Patrick Hannassey,' Matthew replied, placing the papers on the desk in front of him. 'I'd like your permission to go after him. He is the most serious threat to Blunden, because frankly he's far cleverer. Blunden doesn't react instinctively, but Hannassey's capable of making him look like a coward, compared with Wynyard.'

'Denied,' Shearing answered him.

'But he's — ' Matthew began.

'I know,' Shearing cut him off. 'And you're right. But we don't know where he is, and his

255

own men will never betray him. For the time being he's disappeared. Learn what you can about him, but discreetly, if there's time. Go after Michael Neill, his lieutenant. You'll get plenty of co-operation on that.'

There was a flatness in his voice that alarmed Matthew, a sense of defeat. 'What is it?' he asked edgily.

'The King has backed the Loyalists,' Shearing answered, watching Matthew, bleak misery in his eyes. 'Go and see if you can find out what Neill is up to, and if there's anyone willing to betray him. Anything that will help.'

'Sir . . . '

'What?'

Should he mention John Reavley's document? Was this what it was about, and he had the chance now to make it matter? Perhaps even to save the country from plunging into civil war? But Shearing might be part of the conspiracy.

'Reavley, if you've got something to say, then say it!' Shearing snapped. 'I haven't got time to play nursemaid to your feelings! Get on with it, man!'

What could he say? That his father knew there was a conspiracy of some sort, involving people in the royal family? That was not exactly what he had said. His words were that it went as high as the royal family. A plot to assassinate the King? To provoke England into crushing Ireland in a manner intolerable to honour, perhaps even to humanity, in a bloodbath that would stain England in the eyes of the world — infinitely more importantly, that would corrupt it beyond

256

redemption in its own eyes — or anyone else's.

Shearing drew in his breath sharply, with a little hiss between his teeth, impatient, scratchy.

'Only that I think you're right, sir,' Matthew said aloud. 'One of my informants believed there was a conspiracy.'

'Then why the hell didn't you mention it?' Shearing's eyes were hot and black.

'Because he had no facts,' Matthew retorted with equal tartness. 'No names, no dates, places, nothing but a belief.'

'Based on what?' Shearing glared at him, challenging him for a reply.

'I don't know, sir. He was killed before he could tell me.' How hard the words were to say, even in anger. He found his voice thick, his throat aching. His fists were clenched at his sides, and it was rage that John Reavley had tried to get involved in things he was incompetent to deal with, and got himself killed, leaving the questions all unanswered, and everyone behind to grieve for him.

'Killed?' Shearing said softly, his face changed. Death of one of his own men, however indirectly he was involved in the service, always hurt Shearing more than Matthew expected. 'How? Are you saying he was murdered for this piece of information?' His fury exploded in a snarl, full of helplessness he could not longer conceal. 'What the hell's the matter with you that you didn't tell me?' he accused. 'If your parents' deaths have robbed you of this much of your wits, then — ' He stopped.

In that instant Matthew knew that Shearing

257

understood. Had he gone too far? Had he done precisely what his father had warned him against?

'Was it your father, Reavley?' Shearing asked, regret in his face now, something that might even have been pity.

There was no purpose in lying. Shearing would know, if not now then later. It would destroy his trust, and make Matthew look a fool, and it would gain nothing.

'Yes, sir,' he admitted. 'But he was killed in a car accident on his way to see me. All I know is that he spoke of a conspiracy that would dishonour England.' It was ridiculous — he had trouble keeping his voice steady. 'And it went as high as the royal family.' That was not all of the truth. He omitted the involvement of the world. That was only his father's opinion, and perhaps he put too much importance on England's place in things. He said nothing of the scars on the road, and his certainty that the car crash had been murder.

'I see.' In the low, slanting sunlight through the windows the tiny lines in Shearing's skin were etched clearly. His emotion and his weariness were naked, but his thoughts were as hidden as always. Matthew wondered if there were anyone he trusted, or if the lifetime habit had become a shell that could not be broken into, or out of. 'Then you'd better follow it up, find out all you can.' His lips tightened. It was impossible to imagine his thoughts. 'I presume you will anyway. Do it properly.'

'And Neill?' Matthew asked. 'Blunden?'

Shearing's eyes were bright, as though with amusement he could not share. 'I have other men who can do that, Reavley. You are not indispensable. You will be more use to me doing one job properly than half-doing two.'

Matthew did not allow his gratitude to show. Shearing should not think him too much in his debt. 'Thank you, sir.' He let out his breath slowly. 'I'll report when I have something.' He turned on his heel before Shearing could add anything, and went out, closing the door behind him. He felt a curious sense of freedom, and of danger.

★ ★ ★

Matthew began immediately and his first call was exactly as Chetwin had suggested, to Dermot Sandwell. Matthew asked if he might see him as a matter of urgency, to do with the King's announcement today of his support for the Ulster Loyalists. He gave his name and rank, and that he was on assignment to the Secret Intelligence Service. There was no point in hiding it because Sandwell could very easily find out, and would be extremely unlikely to receive him at all otherwise.

He had to wait only fifteen minutes before he was taken into first the outer office, and then the inner. It was a handsome room overlooking Horse Guards Parade, furnished with an extremely individual and pleasing mixture of classical and Middle Eastern styles. A burr walnut desk was flanked by Queen Anne chairs.

259

Turkish brassware sat on an Italian petra dura table. Persian miniatures painted on bone decorated one wall, and above the fireplace was a minor Turner of exquisite beauty, and probably worth as much money as Matthew would earn in a decade.

Sandwell himself was tall and very slight but there was a wiry grace to him that suggested strength. His hair and skin were fair and his eyes were a uniquely vivid blue. There was an intensity to his face that would have made him unusual even were the rest of him ordinary. It would have held the attention of anyone who had been in his company for more than a few moments.

He came forward and shook Matthew's hand, his grip firm, then he stepped back.

'How do you do, Reavley? What can I do for you?' He waved at the chair to indicate Matthew was to sit, then sat back again in his own, his eyes not leaving Matthew's face. He continued to create a life and a tension in the room while remaining perfectly motionless. Matthew noticed that there was a mosaic ashtray on the desk, with at least half a dozen cigarette ends in it.

He had given great thought to what he was going to say, depending upon what Sandwell was able to tell him.

'As you know, sir, His Majesty has expressed his support for the Ulster Loyalists,' he began, 'and we are concerned that in doing so he may have placed himself in a certain amount of danger from Nationalists.'

'I should think that is beyond doubt,' Sandwell

agreed with only the smallest flicker of impatience across his face.

'We have cause to believe — insubstantial but sufficient to concern us — that there may be a plot to assassinate him,' Matthew went on.

Sandwell was motionless, but something inside him became even more rigid. He let out his breath very slowly. 'Have you, indeed? I admit that in itself does surprise me, but I had no idea they were so . . . daring! Do you know who is behind it?'

'That's what I'm working on,' Matthew answered. 'There are several possibilities, but the one that seems most likely so far involves a man named Patrick Hannassey.'

Sandwell nodded very slowly. 'A Nationalist with a long history of activity,' he agreed. 'I've had slight dealings with him myself, but not lately.'

'No one has seen him for over two months,' Matthew said drily. 'Which is one of the facts that concerns us. He has dropped out of sight so completely that none of our contacts knows where he is.'

'So what is it you want from me?' Sandwell asked.

'Any information you might have on Hannassey's past contacts,' Matthew replied. 'Anything about him we might not know — foreign connections, friends, enemies, weaknesses . . . anything at all.' He had decided not to mention Michael Neill. Never pass on information you do not have to.

Sandwell thought in silence for so long

261

Matthew was afraid he was not going to answer. He began to wonder why Chetwin had suggested he came to Sandwell for information that John Reavley might have confided. Suspicion flickered in his mind, and then flared up, that Chetwin had been deliberately misdirecting him.

Suddenly he wished he had not come. He was not answering Shearing's need here, and certainly not his own.

Then finally Sandwell spoke. His voice was very quiet, rough-edged with a startling depth of emotion.

'Hannassey fought in the Boer War . . . on the Boer side, of course.' He was staring at Matthew. 'He was captured by the British and held in a concentration camp for some time. I don't know how long, but several months at least. If you'd seen that . . . ' His voice cracked. 'War can rob men of their humanity,' he went on so softly that Matthew instinctively leaned forward to catch his words. 'Men you would have sworn were decent, and they were before fear, pain, hunger, and the propaganda of hatred stripped away that decency and left only the animal will to survive.'

His blue eyes flashed up and held Matthew's with a storm of feeling that his casual, easy elegance had completely masked. 'Civilisation is thin, Captain Reavley, desperately thin, a veneer like a single coat of paint, but it is all we have between us and the darkness.' His long-fingered, almost delicate hands were clenched, the knuckles pale where the skin stretched. 'We must hold on to it at any cost, because if we lose it we face chaos — and I don't mean the unthinking

262

way we use the word to speak of a certain amount of disorder.'

His voice was soft, but there was fury in it, and a contempt he could not control. 'I've heard men say there was chaos on the roads when they meant too many horses and carts all going at different speeds, from a brewer's dray to a gig, and now automobiles as well, faster than any of them.' He took a breath. 'I mean the loss of that primal decency which stops us from raping women, from killing other human beings and eating them when we're starving, which gives us reverence for age, gentleness with the wounded and the vulnerable, which makes us protect a child, marvel at the miracle of birth, and acknowledge the obsequies of death — to grasp the concept of a universal morality.' Sandwell leaned even further forward. 'Believe me, Captain Reavley,' now his voice was little more than a whisper, 'it can all be swept away and we can turn into savages so hideous it is a horror you can never wipe from your soul. You wake up sweating in the night, your skin crawling, but the nightmare is inside you, for the possibility that this is what we are all like . . . underneath the smiling masks.'

Matthew could think of nothing to say. Certainly he could offer no argument. Sandwell was speaking about something of which he had no knowledge. He had heard only fragments of accusation and denial, rumours of ugliness that belonged to another world, and other, far different people.

Sandwell smiled, but it was a grimace, an

attempt to conceal again a little of the passion he had allowed to show too nakedly. 'We must grasp civilisation, Reavley, pay any price to keep it for ourselves and those who come after us. Guard the gates of sanity so madness does not return. We can do that for each other . . . we must. If we can't, there is nothing else worth doing. You want to find Hannassey, I'll help you. If he assassinates the King, God only knows what hatred will follow! We could even end up with martial law, the persecution of thousands of totally innocent Irish people, simply by association. As it is, it's going to take the effort of every good man in Europe to keep the lid on this Austro-Serbian affair, after the assassination of the Archduke. Neither side can afford to back down, and they are both gathering allies everywhere they can: Russia for the Serbs, Germany for the Austrians — naturally.'

He reached for a black leather cigarette case and took out a cigarette so automatically he seemed unaware of doing it. He lit it and drew in a deep draught of smoke. 'As well as the Irish, you might look towards some of the socialist groups,' he continued. 'Men like Hannassey take their allies anywhere they find them. Socialist aspiration is far greater than many people think. There's Jaurès, Rosa Luxemburg, Adler, unrest everywhere. I'll give you what help I can, all the information this office has is at your disposal, but time is short — desperately so.'

'Thank you, sir,' Matthew said simply. He was profoundly grateful. Suddenly he was lurching forward with a frightening speed. From being alone he too had moved to having one of the most discreetly powerful men in foreign affairs willing to listen to him and to share information. Perhaps the truth was only just beyond sight. In days, a week at most, he would face the truth of his parents' deaths. John Reavley had been right: there was a conspiracy.

'Thank you, sir,' he repeated, rising to his feet. 'I appreciate that very much.' Small words to convey the excitement and the apprehension inside him.

8

On Monday, 20 July Joseph spent the morning in a lively and rather erratic discussion with half a dozen students in which he doubted anyone learned very much.

He found himself tired by it as he walked back across the quad towards his own room, eager for the peace of familiar books and pictures, and above all the silence. He was fourteen or fifteen years older than most of the young men he had been with, but today it seemed more than a generation. They were frightened, perhaps of the thought of war in Europe, even though it was distant and problematical.

Far more immediate was the continuing police investigation of Sebastian Allard's murder. That could not be escaped. He was dead; his grieving mother walked the Fellows' Garden in black, waiting for justice, her rage and misery consuming her. She seemed in a self-chosen isolation from the rest of the world. Inspector Perth moved from one person to another, asking questions and telling no one what he had concluded from their answers. And always was the knowledge that one of these gilded scholars, studying the collected thoughts of the ages, had fired the deliberate shot. What emotion had cracked the shell of reason and burst through with such barbarity?

Joseph was almost at the door when he heard

266

the light, rapid footsteps behind him and turned to find Perth a couple of yards away. As always he wore a neat, very ordinary suit that fitted without elegance or grace. His hair was combed back straight and his moustache trimmed level. He was carrying a pipe by the bowl, as if he were undecided whether to light it or not.

'Oh! Good. Reverend Dr Reavley . . . glad to catch up wi' you, sir,' he said cheerfully. 'Are you going inside?'

'Yes. I've just finished a debate with some of my students.'

'Oi never thought you gentlemen worked so hard, even in holiday times,' Perth observed, following Joseph in through the carved stone doorway and past the oak stairs, almost black with age, the middle of the steps hollowed by centuries of feet.

'Quite a few students choose to remain here and do some extra study,' Joseph replied, turning the bend and going on up. 'And then there are always the undergraduates pursuing other studies.'

'Oh, yes, the undergraduates.' Perth was only a step behind him.

They reached the landing and Joseph opened his own door. 'Is there something I can do for you, Inspector?' He meant it to be off-putting and place Perth in a position where casual conversation would be impossible.

Perth smiled appreciatively. 'Well, since you ask, sir, there is.' He stood expectantly on the step.

Joseph surrendered and invited him inside.

'What is it?' he asked.

'Oi think it'd be true to say, sir, that you knew Mr Allard better than any o' the other gentlemen here?'

'Possibly,' Joseph agreed.

Perth put his hands in his pockets. 'You see, Reverend, Oi've bin talking to Miss Coopersmith, Mr Allard's fiancée, as was, if you see what Oi mean? Nice young lady, very collected, no weeping and wailing, just a quiet sort o' grief. Can't help admiring it, can you?'

'No,' Joseph agreed. 'She seems a fine young woman.'

'Did you know her before, sir? Seeing as you know the Allard family, and Mr Sebastian especially. People tell me you were very close, gave him lots of advice in his studies, watched over him, as you might say.'

'Academically,' Joseph pointed out, acutely aware how true that was. His personal ignorance was a darkness eating into him. The trust he had imagined was a daydream built on his own vanity. 'I knew very little of his personal life,' he added. 'I have a number of students, Inspector. Sebastian Allard was one of the brightest, but he was certainly not the only one. I would be deeply ashamed if I had neglected any of the others because they were less gifted than he. And to answer your question, no, I did not know Miss Coopersmith.'

Perth nodded, as if that corroborated something he already knew. He closed the door behind him but remained standing in the middle of the floor, as if the room made him

268

uncomfortable. It was alien territory, with its silence and its books. 'But you know Mrs Allard?' he asked.

'A little. What is it you are looking for, Inspector?'

Perth smiled apologetically. 'Oi'll come to the point, sir. Mrs Allard told me what time Sebastian left home to come back to college on Sunday, the twenty-eighth o' June. He'd been up in London on the Saturday, but he came home in the evening.' His face became very sombre. 'That were the day of the assassination in Serbia, although of course we didn't know that then. And Mr Mitchell, the porter at the gate, told me what time he got here.'

'The purpose . . . ?' Joseph reminded him. Since Perth did not, he felt unable to sit down.

'Oi'm coming to that,' Perth said unhappily. 'He told his mother as he'd got to come back for a meeting here, and so he had. Six people as'll confirm that.'

'He wasn't killed on the twenty-eighth,' Joseph pointed out. 'It was several days after that, in fact two weeks. I remember because it was after my parents' funeral, and I was back here.'

Perth's face registered his surprise, and then his sympathy. 'Oi'm sorry, sir. A dreadful thing. But my point is, like yourself, Mr and Mrs Allard live close by, not more'n ten miles. How long would you say it'd take to drive that far, for a young man with a fast car like his?'

'Half an hour,' Joseph replied. 'Probably less, depending on the traffic. Say twenty minutes. Why?'

'When he left home he told his parents he was going to see Miss Coopersmith for a couple of hours,' Perth replied. 'But she says that he stayed barely ten minutes with her. He went, going through your village o' St Giles, and on towards Cambridge, about three o'clock.' He shook his head. He was still holding the pipe by its bowl. 'That means he should've bin here by quarter to four, at the outside. Whereas he didn't actually get here, Mr Mitchell says, until just after six.'

'So he went somewhere else,' Joseph reasoned. 'He changed his mind, met a friend, or stopped in the town before coming on to college. What does it matter?'

'Just an example, sir,' Perth said. 'Bin asking around a bit. Seems he did things like that quite regular, couple of hours here, couple there. Oi thought as you might know where he spent that time, and why he lied to folks about it.'

'No, I don't.' It was an unpleasant thought that Sebastian had regularly done something he had wanted or needed to hide from his friends. But it was drowned in Joseph's mind by another thought, sharp and clear as a knife in sudden light. If Perth were accurate about the time Sebastian had left his home, and that he had driven south to Cambridge through St Giles, which was the natural and obvious way, then he would have passed the place on the Hauxton Road where John and Alys Reavley were killed, within a few minutes of it happening.

If it had been just before, then it meant nothing; it was merely a coincidence easily explained by circumstance. But if it had been

270

just after, then what had he seen? And why had he said nothing?

Perth was staring at him, bland, patient, as if he could wait for ever. Joseph forced himself to meet his eyes, uncomfortably aware of the intelligence in them; Perth was far more astute than he had appreciated until now. 'I'm afraid I have no idea,' he said. 'If I learn anything I shall tell you. Now if you will excuse me I have an errand to run before my next tutorial.' That was not true, but he needed to be alone. He must sort out the turbulence of thought in his mind.

Perth looked a little surprised, as if the possibility had not occurred to him. 'Oh. You sure you have no idea what he was doing? You know students better'n Oi do, sir. What might it've bin? What do these young men do when they ain't studying and attending lectures and the loike?' He looked at Joseph innocently.

'Talk,' Joseph replied. 'Go boating sometimes, or to the pub, the library, walk along the Backs. Some go cycling, or practise cricket at the nets. And, of course, there are papers to write.'

'Interesting,' Perth said, chewing on his pipe. 'None of that seems worth lying about, does it?' He smiled, though it was not friendliness so much as satisfaction. 'You have a very innocent view o' young men, Reverend.' He took the pipe out again, as if suddenly remembering where he was. 'Are those the things you did when you was a student? Maybe divinity students are a great deal more righteous-living than most.' If there was sarcasm in his voice it was well concealed.

Joseph found himself uncomfortable, aware

271

not only that he sounded like a prig, but that perhaps he had been as deliberately blind as that made him sound, and that Perth was not. He could remember his own student days perfectly well, and they were not as idealized as the picture he had just painted. Divinity students, along with medical, were among the heaviest drinkers of all, not to mention other, even less salubrious, pursuits.

'I started in medicine,' he said aloud. 'But as I recall none of us appreciated being obliged to account for our free time.'

'Really?' Perth was startled. 'A medical student? You? Oi didn't know that. So you know some o' the less admirable kinds of youthful carry-ons, then?'

'Of course I do,' Joseph said a trifle sharply. 'You asked me what I know of Sebastian, not what I might reasonably suppose.'

'Oi see what you mean,' Perth replied. 'Thank you for your help, Reverend.' He nodded several times. 'Then Oi'll just keep on.' He turned and went out of the door, at last pulling out a worn, leather tobacco pouch and filling the pipe as he went down the stairs, slipping a bit on the last and most uneven one.

Joseph left a few moments later and walked briskly across the quad and out of the main gate into St John's Street. But instead of turning right for the town, he went left for a few yards along Bridge Street, across it, along the main road and eventually on to Jesus Green, looking over to Midsummer Common.

All the time his mind was struggling with the

fact that Sebastian had passed by the place in the Hauxton Road where John and Alys Reavley had been killed, almost certainly within minutes of its happening. The question that burned in his head was, had he witnessed it and known that it was not an accident, possibly even seen whoever was responsible waiting, emerge from the ditch and go over and search the bodies? If so, then he had known too much for his own safety.

Since he too was in a car he must have been seen by them, and they had to have realised he knew what had happened. Had they tried to follow him?

No, if they were on foot, their car hidden, then they would be unable to go after him. But with any intelligence at all, a few questions and they could have found who owned the car and where he lived. From there on it would be simple enough to trace him to Cambridge.

Had he been aware of that? Was that why he had been so tense, so full of dark thoughts and fears? It had not really been anything to do with Austria or the destruction that a war in Europe would bring, but the knowledge that he had seen a murder?

Joseph walked across the grass. The sun was hot on his right cheek. There was no traffic on the Chesterton Road, and only a couple of young men in white trousers and cricket sweaters walking side by side a hundred yards away, probably students from Jesus College. They were involved in heated conversation with each other, and oblivious of anyone else.

Why had Sebastian said nothing? Even if he

273

had not known at the time that it was John and Alys Reavley who had been killed, he must have known afterwards. What was he afraid of? Even if he had weighed the chance of the murderers tracing his car, since he had not recognised them, what threat was he?

Then the answer came to Joseph, ugly and jagged as broken glass. Perhaps he had known them!

If they were responsible for his death, then there was only one hideous and inescapable conclusion: it was someone here in college! No one had broken in. Whoever murdered Sebastian was one of those already here, someone they all knew and whose presence was part of daily life.

But why had Sebastian told no one? Was it somebody so close, so unbelievable, that he dared not trust anyone with the truth, not even Joseph, whose parents were the victims?

The sun burned in the silence of the mown turf. The traffic seemed to belong to another world. He walked without sense of movement, as if caught in an eddy of time, separate from everyone else.

Was it fear for himself that had kept Sebastian silent? Or defence of whoever it was? Why would he defend them?

Joseph came to the edge of Jesus Green and crossed the road on to Midsummer Common, walking south into the sun.

But if Sebastian thought it was an accident, and he had been the one who had reported it, why hide that fact? If he had simply run away, why? Was he such a coward he would not go to the wreck, at least to see if he could help?

Or had he recognised whoever it was who had laid the caltrops and pulled them away afterwards, and kept silent because it was someone he knew? To defend them? Or had they threatened him?

And had they killed him afterwards anyway?

Was that why he had not come straight to college that day — fear?

But what about all the other occasions Perth spoke of? Joseph felt a strange sense of disloyalty even thinking such things. He had known Sebastian for years, met his straight-eyed, passionate gaze as they spoke of dreams and ideas, beauty of thought, music of rhythm and rhyme, the aspirations of men down the ages from the first stumbling recorded words in history. Surely they had trusted each other better than this? Had they been no more than children playing with concepts of honour, as real children built towers of sand to be crashed away by the first wave of reality?

He had to believe it was more than that. Sebastian had come even earlier than Regina Coopersmith said, and passed along the Hauxton Road before the crash. Or he had gone somewhere else altogether, by another route. Whoever had killed him had done so for a reason that had nothing to do with John and Alys Reavley's deaths. That was the only answer he could bear.

Then he must prove it!

He turned back towards St John's, increasing his pace. There were specific places to begin.

275

Enough had been said about Sebastian and the injuries people felt they had suffered at his hands that a closer look at some of them would lead either to proving them trivial — merely the irritation that weaves into any group of people living and working together — or, if followed to the very end, to the reason for his death.

One that came to his mind first was the curious exchange with Nigel Eardslie when they were standing outside Eaden Lilley, and the young woman who walked with such grace had appeared about to speak to them, and then changed her mind. Then it had been suggested by Eardslie that Sebastian had intentionally taken Morel's girl simply to show that he could, and then cast her aside. Was that true, not a tale motivated by envy?

Joseph would rather not have had to know the answer, but that kind of cowardice was something he could no longer justify, even with the gentlest words. The retreat from judgement that allowed him to blur the edges of reality and call it kindness had disappeared.

It took him half an hour to find Eardslie, who was sitting on the grass on the Backs, leaning against the trunk of a tree with books spread out around him. He looked up at Joseph in surprise and made as if to stand up.

'Don't,' Joseph said quickly, sitting down on the ground opposite him, crossing his legs and making himself comfortable. 'I wanted to talk to you. Do you remember the young woman who passed us outside Eaden Lilley the other day?'

Eardslie drew in his breath to deny it.

'Perhaps I shouldn't make that a question,' Joseph amended. 'It was quite obvious that you did know her, whether it was well or slightly, and that seeing me there, she decided not to speak to you.'

Eardslie looked uncomfortable. He was a serious young man, the oldest son of whom his family expected a great deal, and the weight of it frequently lay rather heavily on him. Now in particular he seemed conscious of obligation. 'Probably a matter of tact, sir,' he suggested.

'No doubt. What would she need to be tactful about?'

Eardslie coloured very slightly. He was not good at evasion. He looked at Joseph's dark face and steady eyes, and realised he could not escape the truth. 'Her name is Abigail Trethowan,' he said unhappily. 'She was more or less engaged to Morel, but she met Sebastian, and sort of . . . ' He was at a loss to put into words what he meant. It was not that he did not know them, but that he could think of no way to make them sound as he wished.

'Fell in love with Sebastian,' Joseph finished for him.

Eardslie nodded.

'And you are suggesting that Sebastian brought that about deliberately?' Joseph asked, raising his eyebrows.

Eardslie's colour deepened and he looked down. 'Yes, it certainly looked that way. And then he dropped her. She was very upset.'

'And Morel?'

Eardslie raised his eyes, wide, golden-flecked

and burning with anger.

'How would you feel, sir?' he said furiously. 'Somebody takes your girl from you, just to show you, and everybody else, that he can? And then he doesn't even want her, so he just dumps her, as if she were unwanted baggage. You can't take her back or you look a complete fool, and she feels like . . . like a . . . ' He gave up, unable to find a word savage enough.

Joseph realised how much Eardslie himself had cared for the young woman, possibly more than he was admitting.

'Where does she live?' Joseph asked.

Eardslie's eyes widened. 'You're not going to say anything to her!' He was horrified. 'She'd be humiliated, sir! You can't!'

'Is she the kind of woman who would conceal the truth of a murder, rather than face embarrassment?' Joseph asked.

Eardslie's struggle was clear in his face.

Joseph waited.

'She's at the Fitzwilliam, sir. But please . . . ' he stopped. 'Do you have to?'

Joseph stood up. 'Yes, of course I have to. Would you rather I ask Perth to do it?'

'No!' Eardslie scrambled to his feet, something like desperation in his face. 'I'll — '

'No you won't,' Joseph put out his hand and grasped Eardslie's arm. 'I can find the Fitzwilliam myself, and I can ask for Miss Trethowan.'

Eardslie stood still. Joseph turned and walked away.

★ ★ ★

He found Abigail Trethowan in the Fitzwilliam library. He introduced himself and asked if he might speak to her. With considerable apprehension she accompanied him to a tea shop around the corner, and when he had ordered for both of them, and before the waitress brought the tea and scones, he broached the subject.

'I apologize for speaking of what must be painful, Miss Threthowan, but the subject of Sebastian's death is not going to rest until it is solved.'

She was sitting very straight in her chair, like a schoolgirl with a ruler at her back. Joseph could remember Alys reminding both Hannah and Judith of the importance of posture, and poking a wooden spoon through the spokes of the kitchen chairs to demonstrate, catching them in the middle of the spine. Abigail Trethowan looked just as young, and as proud and vulnerable as they had. It would be hard to forgive Sebastian if he had done what Eardslie believed.

'I know,' she said quietly, her eyes avoiding his.

How could he ask her without being brutal?

All around them was the clatter of china and the murmur of conversation as ladies took tea, exchanged gossip, in many cases bags and boxes of shopping piled near their feet. No one was vulgar enough to look at Joseph and Abigail openly, but he knew without doubt that they were being examined from head to foot, and speculation was rich and highly inventive.

279

He smiled at Abigail, and saw by the flash of humour in her eyes that she was as aware of it as he.

'I could ask you questions,' he said frankly. 'But wouldn't it be better if you simply told me?'

The colour burned up her cheeks, but she did not look away from him. 'I'm ashamed of it,' she said in little above a whisper. 'I'd hoped I wouldn't ever have to think of it again, much less tell anyone.'

He hated having to press her, and he was going to hate even more what she would tell him, but he was already halfway there in his imagination. He still could not grasp how blind he had been. He seemed to walk through the whole of his life seeing only what fitted his dreams. 'I'm sorry, but I'm afraid there is no escape,' he said aloud. 'We owe it to everyone else involved.'

The waitress brought their tea, scones crumbly and still warm, the butter, cut off in chunks about an inch square from the yard it had been bought in, and blackcurrant jam and clotted cream. Joseph thanked her.

She poured the tea, but it was too hot yet to drink.

'I met Edgar Morel,' she began, her concentration steady, as if she were swallowing medicine. 'I liked him very much, and gradually it turned into love — at least I thought it did. I had never really been in love before, I didn't know what to expect.' She glanced up at him, and then down at her hands again. She held them clasped in front of her, strong, well-shaped and bare of rings. 'He asked me to marry him, and I was wondering whether to accept. It seemed a little soon.' She drew in her breath. 'Then I met Sebastian. He was the most beautiful person I had even seen.' She raised her eyes to meet Joseph's and they were bright, swimming in tears.

He wanted to help her, but there was nothing he could do except listen. If he did not interrupt it would be over more quickly.

'He was so clever, so quick to understand everything,' she went on, rueful now, obviously curious of the irony of it. 'And he was funny. I don't think I've ever laughed so much in my life.' She looked at him again. 'I never really laughed, not just a little giggle but the sort of aching, uncontrollable laughter my mother would think was totally indecent. And it was such fun! We talked about all sorts of things and it was like being able to fly — in your mind. Do you know what I mean, Dr Reavley?'

'Yes, certainly I do,' he said with a catch in his voice, partly for Sebastian, partly for Eleanor, perhaps most of all for inner loneliness for something he needed, and did not have.

She sipped her tea.

He took one of the scones and put butter, jam and cream on it. It was delicious.

She reached a decision. 'I was in love with Sebastian. I realised it. It wouldn't matter what Edgar did, I could never feel like that about him. I couldn't marry him. It would have been an impossible lie. I told him, and he was very upset. It was awful!'

'Yes, I'm sure it was,' he agreed. 'There is not much that hurts as deeply as rejection, when you are in love.'

'I know,' she whispered.

He waited.

She sniffed a little and sipped her tea again, then set down the cup. 'Sebastian rejected me. Oh, very nicely. He was quite kind about it. He said he liked me very much, but he liked Edgar also, and he couldn't do what amounted morally to stealing his girl.' She took a shivery breath. 'I never saw him alone after that. I was mortified. For ages I didn't want to see anyone. But I suppose it passes. We all survive.'

'No we don't,' he corrected her. 'Sebastian is dead.'

The blood drained from her face, and she stared at him in horror. 'You don't . . . you don't think Edgar . . . Oh no! No! He was upset, but he would never do that! Besides, it really wasn't Sebastian's fault. He didn't do anything to encourage me!'

'Would that make you feel any better, if you were in Edgar's place?' he asked. 'It wouldn't comfort me to know somebody had taken the woman I loved, without even having to try.'

She closed her eyes and the tears ran down her cheeks. 'No . . . ' she said huskily. 'No, I think I'd feel worse. I still don't believe Edgar would kill him. He didn't love me that much, not to commit murder for. He's a nice man, really nice, just not — not alive as Sebastian was.'

'It isn't always the value of what is taken that makes us hate,' he pointed out. 'Sometimes it's just the fact that we've been robbed. It's pride.'

It was a bitter thing to say, and he understood Morel's pain, but there was a warmth flowing through him that at least in one thing Sebastian had been just, even generous. He had been the man Joseph believed.

'Edgar wouldn't,' she repeated. 'If you think he did, then you don't know him.'

Perhaps she was right, but Joseph wondered if she were defending Edgar Morel because she carried such a burden of guilt for having hurt him. It would be a way of paying some of that debt.

And yet the man Joseph knew would not have killed for such a reason. He could easily see him fighting, perhaps punching Sebastian hard enough to kill him by accident, but not deliberately with a gun. For one thing, the sheer physical release of violence would not be in it. It would leave him still empty, and consumed not only with guilt but with fear also.

'No, I don't think he would either,' he agreed.

'Do you have to tell that policeman?'

'I won't unless something happens to change things,' he promised. 'Unfortunately there are many other possibilities, and very few of us can prove we didn't. Please have one of these scones, they really are excellent.'

She smiled at him, blinking hard, and reached out to accept.

★　★　★

283

On Tuesday afternoon, Joseph took the train to London and was waiting for Matthew when he came home to his flat.

'What are you doing here?' Matthew demanded, coming into the sitting room and seeing Joseph lounging in his own favourite chair. Matthew was in uniform, and he looked tired and harassed, his fair hair untidy and uncharacteristically in need of cutting, his face pale.

'The doorman let me in,' Joseph replied, climbing to his feet to leave the chair free. 'Have you eaten?' It was past dinner time. He had found bread and a little cheese in the kitchen and some Belgian pâté, and opened a bottle of red wine. 'Can I get you something?'

'Like what?' Matthew said a little sarcastically, but easing himself into the chair and relaxing slowly.

'Bread and pâté? I finished the cheese,' Joseph replied. 'Wine or tea?'

'Wine, if you haven't finished that too! Why have you come? Not for dinner!'

Joseph ignored him until he had cut three slices of the bread, which was fresh and very good, and brought it along with butter, pâté and the bottle of wine and a glass.

'Thank you,' Matthew accepted. 'You didn't answer my question. You look like hell. Has something else happened?'

Joseph heard the edge to his voice. 'So do you,' he said, sitting in the other chair and crossing his legs. 'How are you progressing?'

Matthew smiled, half ruefully, and a little of

284

the weariness ironed out of his face. 'I know more. I'm not sure how much of it is relevant. The British and Irish parties met at the Palace and failed to reach any agreement. I suppose no one is surprised. The King supported the Loyalists yesterday, but I expect you know that.'

'No, I didn't,' Joseph said. 'But I meant to do with Father's death and the document.'

'I know you did. Let me finish! I've spoken to several people — Shanley Corcoran; Chetwin, who used to be a friend of Father's; my boss, Shearing; and Dermot Sandwell from the Foreign Office,' Matthew answered. 'Sandwell was actually the most helpful. From everything I can gather, an Irish plot to assassinate the King seems most likely . . . ' He stopped, having seen Joseph's face. 'It answers all Father's criteria,' he said very quietly. 'Think of what the British reaction would be.'

Joseph closed his eyes for a moment. Views of rage, bloodshed, martial law, oppression filled his mind, sickening him. He had wanted his father to be right, to be justified rather than foolish, but not at this cost. He looked up at Matthew, seeing the greyness in him with an overwhelming understanding. 'Is there anything we can do?' he asked.

'I don't know. At least Sandwell is aware of it. I imagine he will warn the King.'

'Will he? I mean, would he even be able to get access to see him without alarming — '

'Oh, yes. I think they're distantly related somewhere along the line. One of Victoria's umpteen children's marriages. I just don't know

285

if he can make him believe it. No one has ever assassinated a British monarch.'

'Not assassinated, perhaps,' Joseph agreed. 'But we've certainly had a good few murdered, deposed, executed or otherwise got rid of. But the last was bloodless, and a long time ago: 1688 to be precise.'

'Rather beyond living memory,' Matthew pointed out. 'Did you come to ask what I'd found so far?' He took another bite of his bread and pâté.

'No. I came to tell you that the police have discovered that Sebastian lied about when he left home to go back to college the day Mother and Father were killed. He actually left a couple of hours earlier.'

Matthew was puzzled. 'I thought he was killed nearly a fortnight later. What difference does that make? It seems stupid to lie, but when he comes or goes is really nobody else's business, is it?'

Joseph shook his head. 'The point is that he lied about it, and why do that, unless there was something he wanted to conceal? As you said, where he was is nobody else's affair.'

Matthew shrugged. 'So he had a secret,' he said with his mouth full. 'Probably he was seeing a girl his parents wouldn't approve of, or who was involved with someone else, possibly even someone's wife. Sorry, Joe, but he was a remarkably good-looking young man, which he was well aware of, and he wasn't the saint you like to think.'

'He wasn't a saint!' Joseph said a trifle abruptly. 'But he could behave perfectly decently where women were concerned, even nobly. And he was engaged to marry Regina Coopersmith, so obviously any involvement with someone else would be something he wouldn't want known. But that isn't why I'm telling you about it. What does matter is that to drive from Haslingfield to Cambridge he would pass along the Hauxton Road, going north, and it now seems at pretty much the same time as Father and Mother were going south.'

Matthew stiffened, his hand with the bread in it halfway to his mouth, his eyes wide. 'Are you saying he could have seen the crash? In God's name, why wouldn't he say so?'

'Because he was afraid,' Joseph replied. He felt the tightness knot inside him. 'Perhaps he recognised whoever it was, and knew they had seen him.'

Matthew's eyes were fixed on Joseph's. 'And they killed him because of what he had seen?'

'Isn't it possible?' Joseph asked. 'Someone killed him! Of course he may have passed before the crash, and known nothing at all about it.'

'But if he did see it, that would explain his death.' Matthew ignored his supper and concentrated on the idea, leaning forward in his chair now, his face tense. 'Have you come up with any other motive for what seems to be a pretty cold-blooded shooting?'

'Cold-blooded?'

'Do your students usually call on each other at half-past five in the morning carrying guns?'

'They don't have guns,' Joseph replied.

'Where did it come from?'

'We don't know where it came from, or where it went to. No one has ever seen it.'

'Except whoever used it,' Matthew pointed out. 'But I presume no one left the college after Elwyn Allard found the body, so who left before? Don't they have to pass the porter's lodge at the gate?'

'Yes. And no one did.'

'So what happened to the gun?'

'We don't know. The police searched everywhere, of course.'

Matthew chewed on his lip. 'It begins to look as if you've got someone very dangerous indeed in your college, Joe. Be careful. Don't go wandering around asking questions.'

'I don't wander around!' Joseph said a little tartly, stung by the implication not only of aimlessness, but of incompetence to look after himself.

Matthew was deliberately patient. 'You mean you are going to tell me this about Sebastian, and leave it for me to investigate? I'm not in Cambridge and I don't know those people anyway.'

'No, of course I don't mean that!' Joseph retorted, keeping his anger and frustration under control with difficulty. 'I'm just as capable as you are of asking intelligent and discreet questions, and deducing a rational answer without annoying everybody and arousing their suspicions.'

'And you're going to do it?' That seemed to be a question.

'Of course I am! As you pointed out, you are not in a position to. And since Perth knows nothing about it, he won't. What else do you suggest?' He realised just how profound was his obligation. He really had no other choice.

'Just be careful,' Matthew warned, his voice edgy. 'You're just like Father. You go around assuming that everyone else is as open and honest as you are. You think it's highly moral and charitable to think the best of people. So it is. It's also damn stupid!' His face was angry and tender at the same time. Joseph was so like their father: he had the same long, slightly aquiline face, the dark hair, the kind of immensely reasonable innocence, totally unprepared for the deviousness and cruelty of life. Matthew had never been able to protect him and probably never would. He would go on being logical and naïve. And the most infuriating thing about it was that he would not really have wished him different, not if he were honest.

'And I can't afford for you to get yourself killed,' he went on. 'So you'd better just get on with teaching people, and leave the questions to the police. If they catch whoever shot Sebastian, we'll have a lead towards who's behind the conspiracy in the document.'

'Very comforting,' Joseph replied sarcastically. 'I'm sure the Queen will feel a lot better.'

'What has the Queen to do with it?'

'Well, it'll be a trifle late to save the King, don't you think?'

Matthew's eyebrows rose. 'And you think finding out who shot Sebastian Allard is going to save the King from the Irish?'

'Frankly, I think it's unlikely anything will save

289

him if they are determined to kill him, except a series of mischances and clumsiness, such as nearly saved the Archduke of Austria.'

'The Irish falling over their own feet?' Matthew said incredulously. 'I'm not happy to rely on that! I imagine rather more is expected of the SIS.' He looked at Joseph with a mixture of misery and frustration. 'But you stay out of it! You aren't equipped to do this sort of thing.'

Joseph was stung by the condescension in him, whether it was intentional or not. Sometimes Matthew seemed to regard him as a benign and other-worldly fool. Part of him knew perfectly well that Matthew was aching inside from the loss of his father just as much as he was himself, and would not admit that he was afraid of losing Joseph as well. Perhaps it was something he would never say aloud.

But Joseph's temper would not be allayed by reason. 'Don't be so bloody patronizing!' he snapped. 'I've seen just as much of the dark side of human nature as you have. I was a parish priest! If you think that just because people go to church that they behave with Christian charity, then you should try it some time, and disabuse yourself. You'll find reality there ugly enough to give you a microcosm of the world. They don't kill each other, not physically anyway, but all the emotions are there. All they lack is the opportunity to get going with it.' He drew in his breath. 'And while you're at it, Father wasn't as naïve as you think. He was a Member of Parliament, and if you don't think that's a display case for the grubbier side of human nature, then you haven't been there. He didn't get killed because he was a fool, he discovered something vast and — '

'I know!' Matthew cut across him. He did it so sharply Joseph realised that he had hit a nerve; it was precisely what Matthew feared and could not bear. He recognised it because it was within himself as well: the need to deny, and at the same time protect. He could see his father's face as vividly as if he had left the room minutes ago.

'I know,' Matthew repeated. He looked away. 'I just want you to be careful!'

'I will.' This time the promise was made sincerely, with gentleness. 'I've no particular desire to get shot. Anyway, one of us has got to keep Judith in some kind of check — and you aren't going to!'

Matthew grinned suddenly. 'Believe me, Joe, neither are you!'

Joseph picked up the wine bottle and for a few moments did not speak. Then: 'If Father was bringing the document to you in London, and whoever killed him took it from the car, what were they searching the house for?'

Matthew thought for a while. 'If it really is a plot of some sort to kill the King, or some conspiracy on that scale, as Father said, perhaps there are at least two copies of it,' he replied. 'They took the one Father was bringing, but maybe they need the other as well. It's far too dangerous to leave it where someone else might find it — especially if they actually put it into effect.'

It made perfect sense. At last there was

something about the conspiracy their father had
spoken of that fell into place. Intellectually this
explanation was a comfort, finally something
reason could grasp. Emotionally it was a
darkening of the shadows and a waking of a
more urgent fear.

9

Joseph returned to Cambridge the following morning, 22 July. The train pulled away from the streets and rooftops of the city and into the open country northwards.

He felt an urgency to be back in college again, and to look with fresh and far more perceptive eyes at the people he knew. He was aware that he would see things he would prefer not to: weaknesses that were impinging on his consciousness; Morel's anger and perhaps jealousy because Abigail had been in love with Sebastian. Had he taken his revenge for that, storing it up until it became unbearable? Or was it the insult to Abigail he avenged? Or was it nothing to do with either of them, but one of the other cruelties? Had someone cheated, and been caught? Would a man kill to save his career? To be sent down for cheating was certainly ruin of all future hope in a profession or society.

Matthew's question about the gun came back again. Where had it come from? Perth had said it was a handgun. Joseph did not know a lot about guns; he disliked them. Even in the open countryside where he lived, close to woods and water, he knew of no one who kept handguns. There was a deliberateness about having one that chilled him.

As soon as he reached the college he went to his rooms, washed and changed, then started to look again at all he knew so far. It was like taking the concealing bandages off a wound to find where the infection was, the unhealed part, and how deep it went. If he were honest, he knew it was to the bone.

And it was time he addressed the next issue he knew of. Had someone cribbed from Sebastian or he from them? The suggestion had been that it was Foubister, and Joseph knew why. Foubister came from a working-class family in the suburbs of Manchester. He had studied at Manchester Grammar School, one of the best in the country, and came to Cambridge on scholarship. His parents must have saved every penny simply to afford his necessities such as clothes and fare. The shock of coming from the narrow, back-to-back houses of the northern industrial city, to the broad countryside of Cambridge, the ancient city steeped in learning, the sheer wealth of centuries of endowment, was something he could not hide.

His mind was outstanding, quick, erratic, highly individual, but his cultural background was of poverty not only in material surroundings but in art, literature, the history of Western thought and ideas. The leisure to create what was beautiful, but essentially of no immediate practical use, was as alien an idea to everyone he had known before coming here. It strained the imagination that he should have found the same felicitous phrase to translate a passage from the Greek or Hebrew as Sebastian Allard, whose background was so utterly different, nurtured in the classics from the day he started school.

Joseph stood up with a weariness inside, and went to look for Foubister. It must be faced. He found him coming down the stairs from his own rooms. They met at the bottom, just inside the wide oak door open on to the quad.

'Morning, sir,' Foubister said unhappily. 'That wretched policeman doesn't know anything yet, you know?' His face was pale, his eyes defiant, as if he had already read Joseph's intent. 'He's ferreting around in everyone's affairs, asking questions about who said what. He's even gone into past exam results, would you believe?'

So Perth was already pursuing the thought of a cheat! Did he understand that such a charge would follow a man all his life? The whisper of it would deny him a career, blackball him from clubs, even ruin him in society. Was that something a man like Perth would grasp?

Someone had killed Sebastian. If it were not for that, then it was something else equally ugly. Perhaps it would be even worse if it were for a trivial reason?

He looked at Foubister's miserable face, the anger in it, the desperation. He had such a burden of trust, hope and sacrifice on his shoulders. It would have crushed many young men. And added to that, even coming here had opened a world to him he would never forget. The family and the home that had nurtured him, and loved him so selflessly, was already somewhere to which he could never fully return. The gulf widened every day. He had already lost most of his Lancashire accent; only the odd vowel sound appeared now and then. He must have worked terribly hard to achieve that.

As if he had spoken it aloud, Foubister sensed Joseph's thought. 'I didn't crib!' he said furiously, his face white, his eyes hurt and angry.

'It would be very foolish,' Joseph replied. 'Your style is nothing like his.' Then in case it seemed like an insult he added, 'You are quite individual. But do you think it is possible someone has cribbed, and Sebastian knew it?'

Slowly Foubister's anger drained away. He looked embarrassed. 'I suppose it is,' he admitted reluctantly, shifting from one foot to the other. 'But it would be stupid. You'd have known one style from another, the pattern of thinking, the words, the phrases, the kind of ideas. Even if you weren't sure, you'd suspect.'

It was true. Joseph knew each voice as uniquely as the brush stroke of an artist or the musical phrase of a composer.

'Yes, of course,' he agreed. 'I'm just looking for a reason.'

'We all are,' Foubister said tensely, holding the book in his hand more tightly. 'We're all wandering around tearing ourselves to pieces. He doesn't understand!' He jerked his arm backwards to indicate Perth, somewhere in the college behind him. 'He doesn't really know anything about us! How could he? He's never been in a world like this.' He said it without condescension, but with impatience for those who had placed Perth out of his depth, a feeling he himself must taste every day, even if it was lessening, at least on the surface. But surely deeper into thought, he must have understood that the thread of it ran through everything: class, manner, words chosen, even dreams?

Joseph drew breath to interrupt, then silenced himself. He should listen. Unguarded talk was exactly what he needed to hear, and weigh. He forced himself to relax and lean a little against the door jamb.

'Someone mentions an argument, and he thinks it's a fight!' Foubister went on, his wide eyes on Joseph's, expecting understanding. 'That's what university is all about! Exploring ideas. If you don't question it, try to pick it to pieces, you never really know whether you believe it or not.'

Joseph nodded.

'We don't argue to prove a point!' Foubister went on, his voice rising in desperation. 'We argue to prove that we exist! Not to think, not to try to reason, is the same thing as being dead! Differences of opinion don't mean hate, for heaven's sake — exactly the opposite! You can't be bothered to waste time arguing with someone you don't respect. And respect is about the same thing as liking, isn't it?'

'Almost,' Joseph agreed, thinking back to his own college days.

They heard a clatter of feet on a stairway above them, and a student excused himself and ran past, clutching a pile of books. He glanced at Joseph and Foubister. His eyes were wide with question, and suspicion. It was clear in his expression that he thought he understood something. He turned away and sprinted across the quad and through the archway.

'You see!' Foubister challenged, fear rising sharply in his voice. 'He thinks I cheated and you're calling me out on it!'

'You can't stop people leaping to conclusions. If you deny it, you'll make it worse,' Joseph warned. 'He'll find out he's wrong.'

'Will he? When? What if they never find out who killed Sebastian? They're not doing very well so far!'

'You said people were arguing and Perth didn't understand,' Joseph said levelly. 'Who was he thinking of in particular?'

'Morel and Rattray,' Foubister answered. 'And Elwyn and Rattray, because Rattray doesn't think there'll be war, and Elwyn does. Sometimes he sounds as if he almost looks forward to it! All heroic sort of stuff, like the Charge of the Light Brigade, or Kitchener at Khartoum.' His voice betrayed not only fear but disgust. 'Sebastian thought there would be,' he went on. 'Unless we prevented it, and it would be catastrophic, which seems to be what Perth thinks. Got a face like an undertaker! Elwyn is only afraid it'll all be over before he has a chance to do his bit! But it was just argument!'

He stared at Joseph, his eyes begged for agreement. 'You don't kill someone because they disagree with you! Might kill myself if nobody did!' A smile flashed across his face and vanished. 'That would be a sure sign I was talking such rubbish nobody cared enough about it, or me, to be bothered contradicting. Either that — or I was in hell.' He stood motionless, his cotton shirt hanging limply on his body.

'Imagine it, Dr Reavley! Total isolation — no other mind there but your own, echoing back to you exactly what you said! Oblivion would be better. Then at least you wouldn't know you were dead!'

Joseph heard the note of hysteria in his voice.

'Foubister,' he said gently, 'everyone is frightened. Something terrible has happened, but we have to face it, and we have to learn the truth. It won't go away until we do.'

Foubister steadied a little bit.

'But you should have seen some of the things people have come up with!' He shivered in spite of the breathless heat in the sheltered doorway. His face was pinched. 'Nobody looks at anyone the way they used to. It's a sort of poison. One of us here actually took a gun, walked into Sebastian's room and, for some dreadful reason, shot him in the head. It's a mad, horrible thing to do.' He shrugged his shoulders, and Joseph noticed how much thinner he was than a month ago.

'We have our faults, and I've seen that in the last couple of weeks more than I ever wanted to.' Foubister's face was white with misery and he hunched himself as if even in this dazzling summer he could be cold. 'I look at fellows I've worked with, sat with at the pub all evening and talked about all kinds of things, profound ideas and absolute rubbish, laughed with, done silly things like climbing on to the roof and leaving a scarecrow up there. Do you remember that? And it comes into my mind: 'Was it you'?' He rubbed his hand across his eyes and blinked several

299

times. 'And then I'm ashamed. I feel like a traitor because the idea even entered my head. I want to apologize, but what is there to say?'

Joseph did not interrupt him.

'And even worse than that,' he went on, speaking more and more rapidly. 'People look at me — all sorts of people, even Morel — and I can see the same thoughts in their eyes, and the same embarrassment afterwards, and they don't know what to say either. It's like a disease, and it's getting to all of us. What's going to happen when it's over and we know who it was? Are we ever going to be able to go back to how we were before? I won't forget who thought it could be me! How can I feel the same about them as I used to? And how could they forgive me, because I have wondered . . . about lots of people!'

'It won't be the same,' Joseph said frankly. 'But it may still be bearable. Friendships change, but that doesn't have to be bad. We all make mistakes. Think how much you would like your own buried and forgotten, and then do the same for others — and for yourself.' He was afraid he sounded trite, because he dared not say what was really in his mind: what if they never found who had shot Sebastian? What if the suspicion and the doubt remained here, working their erosion forever, dividing, spoiling, tearing apart?

'Do you think so?' Foubister asked earnestly. He shrugged and pushed his hands into his pockets. 'I doubt it. We're all too damned scared to be idealistic.'

'Did you like Sebastian?' Joseph said impulsively, just as Foubister had turned to walk away.

300

He had no idea why he had asked, and instantly he wished he had not.

Foubister's dark face was blank with surprise for a moment. He searched Joseph's eyes. 'I'm not sure,' he replied with painful honesty. 'I used to be certain I did. I wouldn't even have questioned it. Everyone liked him, or it seemed that way. He was funny, and clever, and he could be extraordinarily kind. And . . . ' He gave a slight shrug. 'Once you start liking someone, it becomes a habit, and you don't change, even if they do.' He stopped.

'But?' Joseph prompted, tensing himself against what must come. It was going to hurt.

'He had such charm,' Foubister said ruefully. 'He could dazzle people and he pretended he didn't know it, but he did. He could listen to every word you said one day, and then cut you dead the next. He made people feel things.' He looked uncomfortable. 'The way he spoke you couldn't help admiring him, catching sight of his dreams. They were so vivid, they mattered so much. When you were with him you saw something good, and believed you could do something that mattered too. But then sometimes he'd just forget you, or go ahead and do something so much better you felt crushed.'

Joseph tried to ignore his own feelings. Sebastian had still needed him, but one day when he didn't, would he have treated Joseph with the same off-hand arrogance? He would never know. It was all a matter of belief, and he ought to be able to have some control over that.

'Anyone in particular?' he said aloud.

Foubister's eyes widened. 'If you mean, do I know who killed him — no, I don't. You don't get a gun and shoot someone because they hurt you or make you feel like a fool, not unless you're mad! You might punch him, or — ' he bit his lip, blushing a little — 'no, you wouldn't even do that, because you'd be showing everyone how much you hurt. You'd just wear a nice smile as long as anyone was looking at you, and wish you could find a place to hide. Depending on who you are, you either look for something spectacular to do yourself, to show you are just as good, or you take hell out of someone else. I don't know, Dr Reavley, maybe you do kill. I wish I did know, because it would mean at least that I could stop suspecting everyone else.'

'I understand,' Joseph said gently.

'Yes — I suppose you do. Thank you at least for saying that.' Foubister gave a tiny smile, then turned and walked away, shoulders still tight, his body angular, yet moving with a certain grace.

It was unavoidable now. Joseph must go back to the translations that gnawed at the back of his mind, the occasions when Foubister and Sebastian had struck the same brilliant and unexpected phrase. He hated the thought that Foubister had cheated, but it seemed more and more likely. Was it really only other people's whispers that made Foubister so conscious of suspicion, and so afraid, or was it guilt?

He might never know, but he was compelled to look. There were papers he could reread, compare, do all he could to satisfy his own mind. He knew Foubister's work, and he knew

Sebastian's. If he had any skill at all, any feeling for the cadence of language, he would know if one man were copying another. If not, then he was no more than a mechanic.

He went back inside and climbed slowly back up the stairs, fingers touching the dark oak of the banister. The first floor up was cooler, airy with its higher ceiling and open window.

Inside his room was newly tidy from the bedder's ministrations. She was a good woman, neat and quick, pleasant, said no more than 'good morning' and 'goodbye'. He really should appreciate her more.

He pulled out the appropriate papers. He knew exactly which ones to begin with; there was only the one instance where the exact, inventive phrase had caught his attention. Looking back, he should have questioned it at the time.

He found Sebastian's paper and read it through. It was a translation from the Greek, lyrical, full of metaphor and imagery. He had made a beautiful thing of it, keeping the rhythm swift and light, an excellent mixture of words, long and short, complex and simple, all blending into a perfect whole. And there was the one phrase he remembered: 'the bent-limbed trees crowding along the mountain ridge, bearing the burden of the sky upon their backs'.

He put it down on the desk and searched for Foubister's translation of the same original. It was in the middle of the page: 'the hunch-limbed trees, crawling along the mountain's rim, carrying the sky upon their backs'.

The Greek poet had described them only as

misshapen, silhouetted against the sky. The idea of bearing or carrying was not there, nor the suggestion of human intent. The translations were too alike for coincidence.

He sat still, the cold grief hardening inside him. He could not ask Sebastian how he had allowed his work to be imitated so closely, and surely there was little point in confronting Foubister. He had just sworn that he had never cheated. If Joseph faced him now with this, would he still deny it? Swear it was just chance? Joseph winced at the thought. He liked Foubister, and could only imagine what grief it would bring his parents if he were sent down in shame.

But if he had killed Sebastian that was something that could not possibly be overlooked. He realised with surprise that using those words, even to himself, meant that he had considered ignoring the cheating.

He did not feel like lunch. His stomach churned with a sick unhappiness. What other explanation was there? Where could he look for it, who was there to ask?

His thoughts went immediately to Beecher. He could at least depend on him to be both honest and kind. Perhaps he would even honour Joseph's silence, if he were asked to.

He caught up with Beecher on his way across the quad towards the Dining Hall.

Beecher squinted at him. 'You look awful,' he said with a half-smile. 'Anticipating something disgusting in the soup?'

Joseph fell into step beside him. 'You've been

teaching far longer than I have,' he began without ceremony. 'What explanation might there be for two students coming up with the same highly individual translation of a passage, other than cheating?'

Beecher looked at him with a frown. 'Has this something to do with Sebastian Allard?' he asked as they walked into the shadow of the archway and turned into the Dining Hall. Bright patterns of coloured light danced on the walls from the coats of arms on the windows. There was a buzz of conversation and expectancy. It should all have been infinitely comforting.

Beecher sat down, nodding to one or two other people, but giving nothing to his glance to suggest he wished their company.

'Possibly a conversation,' he said at last, just as a steward appeared at his elbow to offer him soup. 'An experience shared, which began a train of thought. They might even have read the same source book for something.' He declined the soup, picking up bread instead and breaking it apart.

Joseph also declined the soup. He leaned forward a little across the table. 'Have you ever had that happen?'

'You mean is it likely?' Beecher added. 'Who are we talking about?'

Joseph hesitated.

'For heaven's sake!' Beecher said exasperatedly. 'I can't give you an opinion if you don't tell me the facts.'

Was Joseph willing to put it to the test? Was

it even inevitable now? 'Sebastian and Foubister,' he said miserably.

Beecher chewed his upper lip. 'Unlikely, I agree. Except that Sebastian didn't need to cheat, and I can't see Foubister doing it. He's a decent chap, but he's also not a fool. He's been here long enough to know what it would cost if he were caught. And if he did want to cheat, he'd pick someone less idiosyncratic than Sebastian.'

'How do I find out?'

'Ask him! I don't know of anything else.' Beecher grinned suddenly. 'Logic, my dear fellow! That rigid goddess you admire so much.'

'Reason,' Joseph corrected. 'And she's not rigid — she just doesn't bend very easily!'

★ ★ ★

He went back to Foubister, carrying the paper with him.

'That's an excellent line,' he said, disliking the duplicity. 'What made you think of it? It's quite a long way from the original.'

Foubister smiled. 'There's a line of trees a good bit like that,' he answered. 'Over there in the Gog Magog Hills.' He gestured roughly to the south. 'Several of us went up that way one Sunday and we saw them, outlined against a clear sky, and then a summer storm came up. It was rather dramatic.'

'Good use of opportunity,' Joseph observed. 'Do it when you can, as long as it doesn't destroy the spirit of the author. The way you have it here, I think it adds to it. It has the right feel.'

Foubister beamed, it lit up his dark face, making him suddenly charming. 'Thank you, sir.'

'Who else was there and saw it?'

Foubister thought for a moment. 'Crawley, Hopper and Sebastian, I think.'

Joseph found himself smiling back, an easy, genuine feeling full of warmth. 'I should have told you earlier,' he said. 'It's very good.'

★　★　★

In the middle of the afternoon Connie sent Joseph a note inviting him to join Mary Allard and herself for a cold lemonade. He recognised it as a plea for help, and steeled himself to respond. He closed his book and walked across the quad.

He was beginning to accept that because of Sebastian's charm, his promise as a poet, even his grace and physical beauty, Joseph had seen in him only what he wanted. And because he had not seen the faults he had done nothing to check them. That was a dereliction of duty whose gravity he was only just beginning to understand. It was his task, as a teacher, to instruct, to praise what was good, to make the student feel the passion to learn and the belief that they can succeed. But it was also his duty to correct what was ugly, false, selfish, in the end destructive of others.

You cannot help what you have refused to see. Like many of the others, he had basked in Sebastian's friendship, and he had not wanted to forfeit it. It was a kind of cowardice. Perhaps that

307

was also what had kept him out of medicine: the turning away from other people's dislike, their pain, their loss of trust in you because you could not keep the promises they had understood you'd made, even though you had not.

He went in through the Fellows' Garden and found Mary Allard alone there.

She turned as she heard his footsteps on the path. 'Dr Reavley . . . ' she acknowledged him, but there was no welcome in her eyes or her voice. Had she heard the whispers about Sebastian, and was expecting him to repeat the same accusations of cruelty and manipulation.

'Good afternoon, Mrs Allard,' he replied. 'I wish I had something helpful to tell you, but I'm afraid I know nothing of comfort.'

'There is nothing,' she said, her tone very slightly softening the abruptness of the words. 'Unless you can stop them saying such things about my son. Can you do that, Reverend? You knew him as I did!' That was almost an accusation, as if he had already been derelict in failing to prevent the ugliness and the doubts. And perhaps he had! If he had been braver, more honest to see Sebastian's faults and to curb them, maybe he would be alive now.

'I didn't know him as you did,' he reminded her. 'For example, I did not know that he was engaged to be married. He never mentioned it.'

She looked up at him defiantly. 'That is a personal matter. It had been arranged for some time, but obviously he would have completed all his studies first. It was not imminent. What I meant was that you, of all people, knew his quality! You know he had a clarity of mind, of heart, that he was honest in a way most people do not even understand.' The anger and the hurt burned through her words. 'You knew that he was nobler than ordinary men, his dreams were higher and filled with a beauty they will never see.' She looked him up and down as if seeing him clearly for the first time, and finding him incomprehensible. 'Doesn't it hurt you unbearably that they are questioning his very decency now? How can you be here and endure it without fighting to defend him?' Her contempt was raw and absolute. 'Coward' lay behind every word, the worst and ugliest charge she could name. It stung, because it was true — not now, but in the past when he had run away from telling Sebastian the truth when he deserved it, and before it was too late.

What could he say to her that was of any comfort? He had, in his own way, been as blind as she, because he wanted to be. It was far more comfortable to believe what you wish, and call it love, when it is really the safeguarding of your own dreams.

Elwyn came out of the sitting room and walked towards them. Mary Allard did not turn.

'When you love someone, surely you must also find the courage within yourself to see them with honesty, the light and the darkness as well?' Joseph said to her. He saw her anger gathering to explode. 'He was good, Mrs Allard, and he had amazing promise, but he was not perfect. He had much growth of spirit yet to accomplish, and by refusing to see the shadows in him we reinforced them, instead of helping him to overcome them. I am guilty as well, and I wish it were not too late to mend the fault.'

Mary's face held no forgiveness. 'Dr Reavley — '

Elwyn took her by the arm, his eyes meeting Joseph's. He knew his mother was wrong, but her weakness was something he did not know how to face, let alone to overcome. His eyes pleaded with Joseph not to be forced to.

'Let go of me, Elwyn!' Mary said sharply, leaning away from him.

He kept hold of her, pulling a little more strongly. 'Mother, we can't help what people are saying! Why don't you come inside? It's hot out here, especially in black.'

She whirled on him. 'Are you suggesting I shouldn't wear black for your brother? Do you imagine a little discomfort matters a jot to me? Perhaps you'd like me to wear white, like all the young girls in the town, as if I hadn't a care in the world?'

Elwyn looked as if he had been slapped, but also as if he were used to it. He did not let go of her. 'I'd like you to come inside where it is cooler,' he replied. 'I'll ask for tea for you, if you wish?'

She snatched her arm away. She was hurting too deeply to be kind, absorbed in her own pain and careless of his.

Joseph was suddenly angry with her. Her grief was unbearable, but it was also selfish. He turned to Elwyn. 'Some pain is intolerable,' he said gently. 'But it is generous of you to be more

310

concerned for your mother than for yourself, and I admire you for it.'

Elwyn flushed deeply. 'I loved Sebastian,' he said huskily. 'We weren't much alike — he was cleverer than I'll ever be — but he always made me feel he respected what I could do, sports, and painting. He said my painting was good. I think a lot of people cared for him.'

'I know they did,' Joseph agreed. 'And I know he admired you, but more than that, he loved you also.'

Elwyn blushed and turned away, embarrassed by his emotion.

Joseph looked steadily at Mary until a deep stain of colour worked up her cheeks. With a look of fury at him for having seen her weakness, she went after her younger son and caught up with him as he reached the steps to the garden door.

Joseph followed her inside, but she barely hesitated in the sitting room. Offering the briefest apology to those there, she hurried after Elwyn through the other door into the hall.

Joseph looked at Thyer, Connie and Harry Beecher standing uncomfortably in the silence. 'I can't think of anything helpful to say,' Joseph confessed.

Thyer was standing by himself, nearest the garden doors, Connie and Beecher at the other side of the room, closer to each other, glasses of lemonade in their hands.

'No one can,' Connie said with a very faint smile. 'Please don't blame yourself.'

Thyer smiled very slightly. 'Particularly her

311

husband, poor devil, and he's trying the hardest.' There was pity in his face, and a degree of irritation. 'Strange how in times of severest grief some people move further from each other, not closer.' His eyes flickered towards Connie, and then back to Joseph. 'I would like to remind her of her husband's loss as well as her own, but Connie says it would only make it worse.'

'Everything makes it worse,' Connie answered him. 'It's Elwyn I'm sorriest for. Mr Allard is old enough to look after himself.'

'No, he isn't,' Beecher contradicted her quietly, the usual humour gone from his face. 'No one is ever old enough to hurt alone. A little tenderness would help him face it, and then begin to recover enough to start again with something like normality.'

Connie smiled at him, the warmth filling her eyes, her face. 'I don't think Mary is going to see that for a long time,' she said sadly. 'It's a pity. In grieving for what she has lost, she risks forfeiting what she still has.'

Beecher's face tightened.

Connie saw it, blushed a little, and looked away.

Joseph heard Thyer draw in his breath, and glanced across at him, but his face was expressionless.

Connie plunged into the silence, talking to Joseph. 'We'll do what we can, but I don't think we're going to make much difference. I've tried to reassure Elwyn, but I know a word or two from you now and then would matter to him more.'

'He's in an impossible situation,' Thyer added. 'Neither of them seems to give a damn about him.'

Connie put her glass down. Her face was hot. 'Sometimes what people are is so much woven into their nature and their lives, that no outside force, however great, can change them. They were like this long before Sebastian was killed. It's only that his death is making it easier to see, not that it created it in the first place.'

'Well . . . ' Beecher began, then changed his mind.

'There's not much point in philosophizing about it.' Thyer straightened up. 'Can I get you a lemonade, Reavley? The day is suffocating.'

'Yes, please,' Joseph accepted. 'Do you think Mrs Allard — '

'Duty done,' Thyer cut across him. 'You are acquitted, for the time being.'

Joseph smiled a little awkwardly, and accepted the cool glass Connie offered him.

★   ★   ★

It was later the same afternoon that he caught up with Edgar Morel walking on the path along the river.

The conversation began badly.

'I suppose you think I killed him over Abigail!' he challenged Joseph as soon as he caught up with him.

Joseph felt pressed to find the truth before it did any more damage. 'I hadn't thought it,' he replied.

313

Morel's face was hard, defensive, almost as if he were close to tears. The weight of suspicion was obviously cutting him very deep. 'Of course, if Sebastian was killed, it has to have been because he knew something foul about someone else, doesn't it?' he said bitterly. 'It has to be envy of his brilliance, or his charm or some bloody thing! It couldn't be that he was cheating someone, or stealing, or anything so grubby!' The sarcasm was too overwrought to be truly cutting. 'He's far too good for that.' Unconsciously he was mimicking Mary Allard's voice. 'Nothing's ever his fault. To listen to his mother you'd think he'd been martyred in some holy cause, and the rest of us were heretics dancing on his grave.'

'Try to have patience with her,' Joseph urged, smiling in spite of himself. 'She has no means of coming to terms with her loss.' He did not know what else he wanted to say, but Morel cut him off before he had the chance to search for it.

'No one has,' he said with sudden fury. 'My mother died last year, just about the time Abigail dumped me for Sebastian. I didn't go around saying everybody else was heartless because they didn't care! The world doesn't stop for anyone's death! And it doesn't excuse making yourself a pain in the arse to everybody else!'

'Morel!' Joseph said sharply, putting out his hand to steady him.

Morel misunderstood the gesture and swung his arm back and let fly with a punch. It caught Joseph glancingly on the cheek, but it knocked him off balance, at least as much with surprise as from the weight of it. He staggered backwards and just saved himself from falling.

Morel stood aghast.

Joseph straightened up, feeling painfully foolish. He hoped no one else had seen. He did not wish to pursue the matter, but it would be the end of his authority, and of Morel's respect for him, if he simply let it go. Then the answer came to him instinctively. He took a step forward, and to Morel's total stupefaction, he hit him back. Not very hard, but sufficiently to make him stagger. He was surprised by the skill he showed; a little more weight and he would have knocked him over.

'Don't do that again,' he said as levelly as his pounding heart would allow. 'And pull yourself together. Somebody shot Sebastian, and we need to keep our heads and find out who it was, not run around like a lot of schoolgirls getting hysterical.'

Morel took a shaky breath, rubbing his jaw. 'Yes, sir,' he said obediently. 'Yes, sir!'

★   ★   ★

Joseph knew he had handled the situation well, but he felt like a long walk and a drink by himself in some quiet pub where he could be surrounded by the warmth of laughter and friendship, without having to participate in it. He was exhausted by other people's emotions. He had more than sufficient burden of his own. It was not yet a month since both his parents had been killed and the loss was still raw.

315

Added to that, since Eleanor's death had shattered his emotional world, taking the energy, the drive out of his faith, he had carefully rebuilt a strength out of reason, impersonal order, the sanity of the mind. It had seemed good, proof against the injuries of grief, loneliness, doubts of all kinds. It had cost him a great deal to create it, but the truth of it was a beauty sufficient to sustain him through anything.

Except that it wasn't working. Everything he knew was still there, still true, it just had no soul. Perhaps hope is unreasonable? Trust is not built on facts. Dealing with man it is wise not to leap where you cannot see. Dealing with God, it is the final step without which the journey has no purpose.

He dismissed the thoughts and returned to the present, more earthbound troubles. He seesawed between fear that his father had been right — there was some hideous conspiracy about to burst on them — and the nagging, aching doubt that perhaps he had been deluded, losing his grip on reality. That thought hurt with an amazing fierceness. He had not realised he was so vulnerable.

Added to that, his cheek where Morel had hit him was scratched and definitely a little tender. He did not want to have to explain that to anyone, especially Beecher. Somehow or other the conversation would get around to the subject of Sebastian, and end unpleasantly.

So instead of going to The Pickerel, with its familiar tables by the river, and people he knew, he went along the Backs in the opposite direction, almost as far as the Lammas Land. He found a small pub overlooking the fields and the Mill Pond, and went into the bar. It was panelled with oak worn dark with time, and pewter tankards hung along the rail above the bar itself, gleaming in the sunlight through the open door. The floor was broad, rough beams that not long ago would have had sawdust over them.

It was early and there were only a couple of elderly men sitting in the corner, and a pretty, fair-skinned barmaid with a wealth of wavy hair tied in a careless knot on the back of her head. It was the colour of faded wheat and when she bent to draw a pint for one of the men, the light shone pale gold like an aureole around her.

She handed the foaming mug to the man, who thanked her for it with ease of habit, then she turned to Joseph.

'Afternoon, sir,' she said cheerfully. She had a soft, pleasing voice, but distinctly broadened with a Cambridgeshire accent. 'What can Oi get for you?'

Joseph did not like ale very much. 'Cider, please,' he answered. 'Half a pint.' He'd begin with a half, and perhaps have another half later. It was a pleasant place and the sense of solitude was exactly what he wanted.

'Right y'are, sir.' She poured it for him, watching the clear, golden liquid till it stopped just short of the top of the glass. 'Haven't seen you here before, sir. We do a fair enough meal, if you'd loike a boite? Just plain, but it's there if you fancy it.'

He had not thought he was hungry, but

317

suddenly the idea of sitting here gazing at the flat water of the Mill Pond, and the sun setting slowly behind the trees, was a far better prospect than going back to the Dining Hall. There he would have to make polite conversation, while knowing perfectly well everyone was wondering what on earth he had done to his face, and making guesses. Sometimes tact was so loud it deafened one. 'Thank you,' he said. 'I probably will.'

'You'll be from one of the colleges?' she asked conversationally as she handed him a card with a list of the possibilities for supper.

'St John's,' he replied, reading down the menu. 'What sort of pickle?'

'Green tomato, sir. It's home-made, an' if Oi say so when maybe Oi shouldn't, it's the best Oi've ever had, an' most folks agree.'

'Then that's what I'll have, please.'

'Roight, sir. What sort of cheese? We got Ely cheese, or a good local half an' half.' She was referring to the half-milk cheese, white and hard, half soft, yellow cream cheese. 'Or do you like the French?' she added. 'We moight have a bit o' Brie.'

'Half and half sounds good.'

'It is. All fresh. Tucky Nunn brought it in this morning,' she agreed. She hesitated, as if to add something, but uncertain if she should.

He waited.

'Did you say St John's, sir?' There was a faint colour in her cheeks and her soft face was suddenly a little tighter.

'Yes.'

'Did . . . ' she swallowed, 'did you know Sebastian Allard?'

'Yes, quite well.' What could she know of him? She was a very pretty girl, her face was wholesome and charming, and not unintelligent. She kept a bland exterior behind the bar, but that was her job. Perhaps if she felt free to, she might have more courage and opinion than her professional manner indicated. If she knew anything at all of Sebastian, even if it were nothing more than observation of him with friends, he should learn it. 'You did too?' Joseph asked.

She nodded, her eyes flooding with tears.

'I think I'll have my meal outside,' he said with a slight smile. 'Perhaps you'd be kind enough to bring it to me?'

'Yes, sir, course Oi'll do that,' and she turned away quickly, hiding her face.

He walked out into the sun again and found a table set for two. Less than five minutes later she came with a tray and put it down in front of him. The bread was thick-cut with sharp crusts, which were cracked where they had broken under the knife. The butter was cut in small chunks off the yard, with a bright sprig of parsley on it, the cheese rich and fresh. The pickle was not one he had seen before, but the pieces were large and the juice of it a dark, ripe colour.

'Thank you,' he said, taking a moment to appreciate it before he looked up and met her eyes. She was still troubled, hesitant.

'Have they — do they know what happened yet?' she asked.

319

'No.' He gestured to the other chair. 'I'm sure the men inside will manage without you for a few minutes. Sit and talk to me. I liked Sebastian very much, but I think I may not have known him as well as I imagined. Did he come along here often?'

She blushed very slightly, lowering her eyes for a moment before looking up at him with startling candour. 'Yes, this summer.' She did not add that it was to see her; it was unnecessary. It needed no explaining; any young man might well have. Joseph wondered with a coldness that still hurt, in spite of his growing acceptance of the facts, if Sebastian had used her completely selfishly, without her having any idea of his engagement to Regina Coopersmith. But surely this charming barmaid could never have imagined she could marry Sebastian Allard? Or could she? Was it possible she had no real idea of the world he came from?

'I am Joseph Reavley,' he introduced himself. 'I lecture at St John's in Biblical languages.'

She smiled shyly. 'Oi thought that was who you must be. Sebastian talked about you a lot. He said you made the people o' the past, and their ideas and dreams into a whole life that really happened, not like just a lot of words on paper. He said you made it matter. You joined up the past and the present so we're all one, and that makes the future more important too.' She blushed a little self-consciously, aware of using someone else's words, although she so obviously understood and believed them herself. 'He told me you showed him how beauty lasts — real beauty, the sort of thing that's inside you.' She took a ragged breath, controlling herself with difficulty. 'And it really matters what you leave behind. He said as it's your thanks to the past, your love of the present, and your gift to the future.'

He was surprised, and far more pleased than he wanted to be, because it awoke all the old emotions of friendship, the trust and the hope in Sebastian's integrity that he feared now was slipping out of his hands into something greyer and more mundane.

'My name's Flora Whickham,' she went on, suddenly aware of not having introduced herself.

'How do you do, Miss Whickham?' Joseph replied. The formality was intended to signify she was equal, another friend of Sebastian, not merely a barmaid who happened to have served him.

She registered it with a moment's surprise, and something that might have been pleasure, then her face became sombre as she returned to the subject. 'Do you think it was summink to do with the war?' she asked.

He was mystified. 'War?'

Her face darkened with fear.

'He was terribly scared there was going to be a war in Europe,' she explained. 'He said everyone was on the edge of it. O' course they still are, only it's worse now since those people were shot in Serbia. But Sebastian said as it would come anyway. The Russians and the Germans want it, and so do the French. Oi hear people in there,' she moved her head slightly to indicate the bar

321

inside, 'saying that the bankers and factory owners won't let it happen, there's too much to lose. And they 'ave the power to stop it.'

She lowered her eyes, and then looked up at him quickly. 'But Sebastian said it would, 'cause it's the nature o' governments, and the army, and they're the ones who have the power. Their heads are stuffed with dreams about glory, and they haven't any idea how it would be for real. He said they were loike a bunch o' blind men tied together, runnin' towards the abyss. He thought millions would die . . . ' She searched his face, longing for him to tell her it would not happen.

'No sane person wants war,' he said carefully, but with the earnestness that her passion and intelligence deserved. 'Not really. A few expeditions here and there, but not out-and-out war. And nobody would kill Sebastian because he didn't either.' He knew as soon as the words were out of his mouth that they were of little use. Why could he not speak to the heart?

'You don't understand,' she argued, embarrassed to be contradicting him, and yet her feeling was too strong to be overridden. 'He meant to do something about it. He was a pacifist. Oi don't mean he just didn't want to foight, he was going to do something to stop it happening.' Her face pinched a little. 'Oi know his brother didn't loike that, and his mother would have hated it. She'd think it was cowardice. For her you're loyal and you fight, or you're disloyal, and that means you betray your own people. There's no other way. At least that's what he said.'

She looked down at her hands. 'But he'd grown away from them. He knew that. His oideas were different, a hundred years after theirs. He wanted Europe to be all one and not ever to foight each other again like the Franco-Prussian War, or all the wars we've had with France.'

She raised her eyes and met his with intense seriousness. 'That meant more to him than anything else in the world, Dr Reavley. He knew summink about the Boer War and the way everybody suffered, women and children as well, horrible things. And not only the victims, but what it did to people when they fight like that.' Her face was tight and bleak in the soft light. The sunlight shimmering on the Mill Pond made of it an old mirror tarnished by the weeds. Dragonflies hovered above it on invisible wings. The evening was so still a dog barking in the distance seemed close enough to touch.

'It changes them inside,' she went on, still searching his face to see how much he really understood. 'Can you think how you'd feel if it was your brother, or husband, someone you loved, who killed people, like a butcher — all sorts, women, children, the old, just like your own family?'

Her voice was soft and a little ragged with the pain she could see. 'Can you think o' trying to feel like a good person again afterwards? Sitting over the breakfast table talking, just as if it all happened to somebody else, and you'd never done all those things? Or telling your children a story, putting flowers in a jug, thinking what to make for dinner, and you were the same person who'd driven a hundred women and children into a concentration camp, and let them starve. Sebastian would have done anything at all to stop that happening again — ever. But Oi can't tell that to anybody else. His parents'd hate it; they wouldn't understand at all. They'd see him as a coward.' Even saying the word hurt her, the hurt naked in the soft, sad lines of her face.

'No . . . ' Joseph said slowly, knowing without question that she was right. He could imagine Mary Allard's reaction to such a concept. She would have refused to believe it. No son of hers, especially her beloved Sebastian, could have espoused anything so alien to the kind of patriotism she had believed in all her life, with its devotion to duty, sacrifice, and the innate superiority of her own way of life, her own code of honour. 'Did his brother know how he felt?' he added.

Flora shook her head. 'Oi don't think so. He's idealistic, but in a different kind o' way. For him war is all about great battles and glory, and that kind of thing. He doesn't think o' being so tired you can't hardly stand up, an' hurting all over, and killing other people who are just like you are, and trying to break up their whole life.'

'That's not what the Boer War was about,' he said quickly, and then the moment the words were out of his mouth, he wondered if he were being as naïve as Elwyn, seeing only what he could bear to see . . . again. 'Is that what Sebastian really believed?' he asked.

324

'More'n anything else in the world,' she said simply.

He looked at her calm, tear-filled eyes, her mouth with jaw closed hard to control herself, her lips trembling, and he understood that she had known Sebastian better than he had, and immeasurably better than Mary Allard, or Regina Coopersmith, who probably knew nothing about him at all.

'Thank you for telling me,' he said honestly. 'Perhaps Sebastian's death does have something to do with that, I really don't know. It seems to make as much sense as anything else.' He did not tell her any of the malice, the jealousy that was being whispered in the college. It would hurt her for no purpose, and he did not know how much was simply people's fear corroding the better part of their natures.

He stayed in the westering sun and ate his supper, had another glass of cider and a slice of apple pie with thick, clotted cream, spoke again with Flora, remembering happy things. Then in the dusk he walked back along the pale river's edge to St John's. Perhaps he had discovered where Sebastian went in his unaccounted hours, and it was very easy to understand. He smiled as he thought how simple it was, and that given the same mother, the same imprisoning worship, he would have done so too.

10

Matthew did not immediately tell Shearing of his intent to continue pursuing Patrick Hannassey as well as Neill. There were too many uncertainties to make a justifiable case for using his time, and he still did not know whom he trusted. If there were a conspiracy to assassinate the King, he could not believe Shearing would be party to it.

And if it were something else — although the more he thought of this, the more did it seem to possess all the qualities of horror and betrayal — then he would be wasting time. He would have to abandon his investigation instantly, and change course to pursue whatever new threat loomed. There was no time to waste in explanations.

Special Branch had been set up in the previous century, at the height of the Fenian violence, specifically to deal with Irish problems. Since then it had become involved in every area of threat to the safety or stability of the country — threats of anarchy, treason or general social upheaval — but the Irish problem remained at the core. Therefore Matthew made one or two discreet enquiries among professional friends, and Wednesday lunchtime saw him walking casually across through Hyde Park beside a Lieutenant Winters, who had expressed himself willing to give him all the assistance he could.

However, Matthew knew perfectly well that each branch of the intelligence community guarded its information with peculiar jealousy, and it would be easier to pry the teeth out of a crocodile than shake loose any fact they would rather keep to themselves. He cursed the necessity for secrecy, which prevented him from telling them the truth. But his father's voice rang in his ears with warning, and he dared not yet ignore it. Once given away, his own secret could never be taken back.

'Hannassey?' Winters said with a grimace. 'Remarkably clever man. Sees everything and seems to have a memory like an elephant and, what is more important, relate one thing to another and deduce a third.'

Matthew listened.

'An Irish patriot,' Winters went on, staring at the cheerful scene in the park ahead of them: couples walking arm in arm, women in high summer fashion, much of it nautical in theme. A hurdy-gurdy man played popular ballads and music-hall tunes, smiling as passers-by threw him pennies and threepences. Several children, boys in dark suits, girls in lace-edged pinafores, threw sticks for two little dogs.

'Educated by the Jesuits,' Winters continued. 'But the interesting thing about him is that to the eye or ear he is not obviously Irish. He has no accent, or at least when he wishes to he can sound like an Englishman. He also speaks fluent German and French, and has travelled very considerably over a great deal of Europe. He is reputed to have good connections with international socialists, although we don't know if he sympathises with them, or merely uses them.'

'What about other nationalist groups?' Matthew asked, not sure in which direction he was driving, but thinking primarily of the Serbians, because of their recent resort to assassination as a weapon.

'Probably,' Winters answered, his lean, rather cadaverous face a little furrowed in thought. 'Trouble is, he's very difficult to trace because he's so unremarkable to look at. I don't know that he deliberately disguises himself.' He glanced at Matthew, his face lopsided with amusement. 'No, nothing so melodramatic as wigs or false moustaches, but a change of clothes, parting the hair on the other side, a different walk, and suddenly you have a different person. No one remembers him or can describe him afterwards.'

A young man in Guard's uniform walked past them whistling cheerfully, a smile on his face.

'So he has a sense of proportion, no theatrics,' Matthew observed, referring to Hannassey. 'Clever.'

'He's in it to win,' Winters affirmed. 'He never loses sight of the main purpose, and that is unusual. He has no personal vanity.'

'And the main purpose is?'

'Independence for Ireland, first, last and always. Catholics and Protestants together, willing or not.'

'Obsessive?'

Winters thought for a moment. 'Not so as to

lose balance, no. Why are you asking?'

In spite of Winters' light, even casual tone, Matthew knew he was anything but. Matthew had placed questions in that way himself, with the one that mattered surrounded by all the others that were predictable, and to which he probably already knew the answers.

How much dare he say? He knew that Winters professed to be no more than a junior officer, a sort of civil servant, but that might be less than the truth. Matthew was realising more bitterly each day how little he did know beyond doubt. How much of it was simply a comfortable assumption he was intended to make? That was the worst of suspicion: one ended by distrusting everyone. Sometimes it was a weapon in itself, as destructive as an actual betrayal. Was that what this was — not a real conspiracy, just the fear, the doubt, the mistrust eventually crippling them, until they in effect betrayed each other?

Winters was waiting. Matthew must answer.

'I've heard rumours of a plot,' he said equally casually. The sun was hot on his cheek, the breeze a faint rustle in the leaves overhead. The grass was soft and springy under his feet. A dozen yards away a group of young people sat on the ground, the bright dresses of the girls spread out around them. Some had brought a picnic basket and they were sharing out sandwiches and lemonade.

'Wondered if he could be involved,' Matthew added.

Winters stiffened very slightly. 'I assume, from

the fact that you don't tell me, that you can't?' he remarked.

'Large, very vague, but with considerable ramifications,' Matthew said evasively.

There were horses cantering gently down Rotten Row, riders immaculately turned out, ladies sitting side-saddle, of course. He would have liked Winters' view on John Reavley's fears, but he would have no control over who else Winters might tell. He dare not risk saying more yet. He still had no idea who the conspirators were, or how many there were of them. Even Hannassey was only a guess. John Reavley had spoken of what he knew as if it were a betrayal, and for an Irishman to fight for his country, whatever means he used, might technically be treason against the Crown, but it was not morally a betrayal, the stabbing in the back by a supposed friend. Hannassey, and the men like him, had never portrayed themselves as anything but what they were.

'If it's an Irish plot, you'd better tell me,' Winters said, keeping up his steady, easy pace as they passed an elderly gentleman stopping to light his cigar, cupping his hands around the flame of his match. The breeze was very slight, only a whisper, but it was sufficient to blow out a match.

The hurdy-gurdy man changed to a love song, and some of the young people started to sing with him.

'I don't know that it is.' Matthew was sorely tempted to tell Winters all he knew. He desperately needed an ally. The loneliness of

330

confusion and responsibility weighed on him almost suffocatingly. What if there were an attempt on the King's life, and he could have prevented it by speaking? What was there to lose if he were wrong? If there were no plot he would look a fool, even hysterical, a man not to be relied on. It could cost him his job; certainly any chance of promotion.

But that was self-concern at a time when he was playing with the possibility of national catastrophe, and he would have despised another man for such pettiness.

And if Winters were part of the conspiracy? He would know it was uncovered. But then whoever was behind it knew that anyway, or they would not have killed John Reavley, and be following Matthew himself when he was in St Giles.

The worst possibility was that the plot was as powerful and far-reaching as he feared, and that Winters had information and did not give it to him.

'It could be any of several things,' he said aloud.

Winters' face was bleak. He was still looking straight ahead and avoiding Matthew's eyes. 'How much do you really know what you're talking about, Reavley?'

It was the moment of decision. Matthew took the plunge. 'Only that someone uncovered a document outlining a conspiracy that was profoundly serious, and he was killed before he could show it to me,' he answered. 'The document disappeared. I'm trying to prevent a disaster without knowing what it is. But it seems to me that with the Curragh mutiny, the failure to get any Anglo-Irish agreement, and now the King coming out on the side of the Loyalists, that a plot against him fills the outline too well to ignore.'

Winters walked in silence for at least fifty yards, which took them around the end of the Serpentine. The sun was hot, baking the ground. The air was still, carrying the sounds of laughter from the distance, and a thread of music again.

'I don't think so,' he said at last. 'It wouldn't serve Irish purposes. It's too violent.'

'Too violent!' Matthew said in amazement. 'Since when has that stopped the Irish Nationalists? Have you forgotten the Phoenix Park murders? Not to mention a score of other acts of terror since! Half the dynamiters in London have been Fenians.' He barely refrained from telling him he was talking nonsense.

Winters seemed unperturbed. 'The Catholic Irish want self-government, independence from Britain,' he said patiently, as if it were something he had been obliged to explain too many times, and to men who did not wish to understand. 'They want to set up their own nation with its parliament, foreign office, economy and so on — '

'That's impossible without violence,' Matthew cut across him. 'In 1912 over two hundred thousand Ulstermen, and even more women, signed the Solemn League and Covenant to use all means which may be found necessary to defeat the present conspiracy to set up a Home Rule Parliament in Ireland! If anyone thinks they're going to suppress Ulster without violence they've never been within a hundred miles of Ireland!'

'Very much my point,' Winters said grimly. 'To have any hope at all of succeeding, the Irish Nationalists will have to win the co-operation of as many other countries outside Britain as they can. If they assassinate the King they will be seen as merely criminals, and lose all support everywhere — support they know that they need.'

They passed an elderly couple walking arm in arm, and nodded politely to them, raising their hats.

'Hannassey is not a fool,' Winters continued when they were out of earshot. 'If he didn't know that before the assassination in Sarajevo, he certainly knows it now. Europe may not approve of Austria's subjugation of Serbia, and they may get into such a violent and ill-balanced tangle of diplomatic fears and promises that it ends in war. But the one group who will not win will be the Serbian Nationalists, that I can promise you. And one thing Hannassey is not is a fool.'

Matthew wanted to argue, but even as he drew breath to do so, he realised it was to defend his father rather than because he himself believed it. If Hannassey were as brilliant as Winters said, then he would not choose assassination of the King as a weapon . . . unless he could be certain it would be attributed to someone else.

'The Irish wouldn't be blamed for it, if it appeared to be — ' He stopped.

Winters raised his eyebrows curiously. 'Yes?

Who did you have in mind, who wouldn't be traced back, or betray them, intentionally or not?'

There was no one, and they were both aware of it. It did not really even matter whether the Irish were behind it or not, they would still be blamed. The whole idea of such a public crime was one they would abhor. They might be even as keen to prevent it as Matthew himself. He was at a dead end.

'I'm sorry,' Winters said ruefully. 'You're chasing a ghost with this one. Your informant is overzealous.' He smiled, perhaps to rob his words of some of their sting. 'He's an amateur at this, or he's trying to make himself more important than he is. There are always whispers, bits of paper floating around. The trick is to sort out the real ones. This one's trivial.' He gave a bleak little gesture of resignation. 'I'm afraid I've got enough real threats to chase. I'd better get back to them. Good day.' He increased his pace rapidly and within a few moments he was lost to sight among the other pedestrians.

Matthew stood alone, anger boiling up inside him, wordless because he did not know what to say or do. He wanted passionately to show to Winters that John Reavley was not confused or amateurish. He had had a supreme clarity of intelligence, unbiased by intolerance or bigotry — almost always. A little arrogant at times, but who was there without such a weakness? He had not been chasing illusions, or self-importance! He had died to defend something of intense and lasting value. It had not been a mistake.

But how could he prove it? He could see his father's face in his mind, the mild blue eyes, which had become a little short-sighted lately. He used to push his glasses up and hold important things closer to him, things like old watercolours, a set of carved chessmen he had found in a curiosity shop, an unusual and pleasing triangular postage stamp from some island no one could place.

Why the hell had John trusted someone who must then have betrayed him? Why couldn't he have taken more care? His blind naïvety had cost Alys her life as well.

Matthew turned on his heel and walked rapidly back the way he had come, tears stinging his eyes. He ignored the sun, the wind in the trees, the sounds of laughter, and a dog barking at a man with a furled umbrella. He had started with almost a conviction that he was right. Now with half an hour of reasoning it had unravelled into nonsense and he was left with nothing at all.

★ ★ ★

Shearing called him into his office the next day, his face grave.

'Sit down,' he ordered. He looked tired and impatient, his voice very carefully under control, but the rough edge to it was still audible. 'What's this Irish assassination plot you're chasing after?' he demanded. 'I told you I had other men to work on that. Drop it! Do you understand me?'

'I have dropped it,' Matthew said tersely. It was the truth, but not all of it. If it was not Irish then it was something else, and he would go on until he found it. He felt acutely uncomfortable lying to Shearing, and he did everything he could to keep it from showing in his face. But whatever disillusion it brought, he had to learn the truth of the document. He was forced to concede that Winters was right as far as Hannassey was concerned. It would not be a Fenian conspiracy to kill George V. 'I assume you didn't wish me to do so before I investigated it in the light of the document my father saw?' he added with more sarcasm than he had ever used to Shearing before.

Shearing blinked very slowly. 'There are strikes in Russia,' he said. 'Over a hundred and fifty thousand men out in St Petersburg alone. And apparently on Monday there was another attempt to murder the Czarina's mad monk, Rasputin. We haven't got time to chase after private ghosts and goblins.' He was still staring at Matthew. 'I don't consider you to be a glory-seeker, Reavley, but if I find I am mistaken, you'll be out of here so fast your feet will barely touch the ground on your way.' There was challenge in his face, and anger. Matthew was overcome for a moment by the chill realisation that there was also a shred of fear in it as well, a knowledge that things were out of control.

'The situation in the Balkans is getting worse almost by the day,' Shearing went on harshly, glaring at him. 'There are rumours that Austria is preparing to invade Serbia. If it does, there is a very real and serious danger that Russia will act to protect Serbia. They are allied in language, culture and history.' His face was tight, his hands, dark-skinned, immaculate, were clenched on the desk until the knuckles shone white. 'If Russia mobilizes it will be only a matter of days before Germany follows. The Kaiser will see himself as ringed around by hostile nations, all fully armed, and growing stronger every week and, unbalanced as he is, to a degree he is right. He will face Russia to the east, and inevitably France to the west. Europe will be at war.'

'But not us,' Matthew said, hearing his own words not entirely as a statement; there was doubt in his voice too, and an edge of fear because he was beginning to see the enormity of the situation. 'We are no threat to anyone, and it's hardly our concern.'

'God knows,' Shearing replied.

'Isn't that exactly the time the Irish National-ists would strike?' Matthew could not forget the document, and the outrage in his father's voice. He could not let go. 'It would be if I were their leader.'

'I dare say God knows that too,' Shearing said waspishly. 'But you will leave it to the Special Branch. Ireland is their problem. Concentrate on Europe. That is an order, Reavley!' He picked up a small bundle of papers from the top of his desk and held it out. 'By the way, 'C' wants you in his office — in half an hour.' He did not look up as he said it.

Matthew froze. Sir Mansfield Smith-Cumming had been head of the Secret Intelligence Service since 1909. He had begun his career as a sub-lieutenant in the Royal Navy, serving in the East Indies, until he was placed in the inactive list, for chronic sea-sickness. In 1898 he had been recalled and undertaken many highly successful espionage duties for the Admiralty. Now the agency he led served all branches of the military, and the high-level political departments.

'Yes, sir,' Matthew said hoarsely, his mind racing. Before Shearing could look up, he turned on his heel and went out into the corridor. He was shaking.

Precisely thirty minutes later Matthew was shown into Smith-Cumming's inner office, a Spartan room he had no time to look at. He stood to attention, waiting.

Smith-Cumming looked up at him, his face unsmiling.

'Captain Reavley, sir,' Matthew said. 'You sent for me.'

'I did,' C agreed.

Matthew waited, his heart pounding, his throat tight. He knew that his entire professional future lay in what he said, or omitted to say, in this interview. Perhaps far more depended on it: his father's reputation, whether he was right or wrong, might affect the honour of England and the ability to prevent ruin to the rest of the world.

'Sit down,' C ordered. 'You are going to remain until you tell me all you know about this conspiracy you are chasing.'

Matthew was glad to sit. He pulled the nearest chair around to face C's desk and sank into it.

'Obviously you do not have the documentary

proof,' C began. 'Neither, apparently, did the men who have been following you, and occasionally me.'

Matthew sat motionless.

'You did not know that?' C observed.

'I knew he was following me, sir,' Matthew said quickly, swallowing hard. 'I did not know he had followed you.'

C's eyebrows rose, softening a little of the sternness of his face. 'Do you know who he is?'

'No, sir.' He thought of offering excuses, and decided instantly against it.

'He is a German agent named Brandt. Unfortunately we don't know much more about him than that. Where and when did you first hear of this document, and from whom?'

Matthew did not even consider the possibility of lying. 'From my father, sir, on the telephone, on the evening of June the twenty-seventh.'

'Where were you?'

'In my office, sir.' He felt his face hot as he said it. The image of the crumpled car was sharp in his mind, his father's face, the scream of tyres. For a moment he felt sick. It was his fault.

C's face softened. 'What did he say to you?'

Matthew kept his voice level with difficulty, but he could not control the hoarseness in it. 'That he had been given a document in which was outlined a conspiracy that would ruin England's honour for ever, and change the world irreparably for the worse.

'Had you heard anything of this before?'

'No, sir.'

'Did you find it hard to believe?'

'Yes — almost impossible.' That was the truth. He was ashamed of it, but it was still difficult.

'Did you repeat it, to make sure you had understood him?'

'No, sir.' Matthew felt the heat burn up his face. 'But I did repeat the fact that he was bringing it to me the following day.' The admission was damning. The only thing more completely guilty would have been to lie about it now.

C nodded his head very slowly. There was compassion in his eyes. 'Interesting,' he said thoughtfully. 'So whoever overheard you already knew that the document was missing, and that it was your father who had it. That tells us a great deal. What else do you know?'

'My father's car was deliberately ambushed and sent off the road, killing both my parents,' Matthew answered. He saw the flash of pity in C's face. He took a deep breath. 'When I heard about the car crash from the police I went to Cambridge to pick up my elder brother, Joseph — '

'He didn't know?' C interrupted. 'He was closer, and you say older than you!'

'Yes, sir. He was at a cricket match. He lost his wife about a year ago. I don't think they wanted someone from college telling him. The Master was at the match as well, and most of his friends.'

'I see. So you drove to Cambridge and told him. What then?'

'We identified our parents' bodies, and I searched their effects and then the wreckage of the car to find the document. It wasn't there. Then when we got home I searched there also, and asked the Bank, and our solicitor. When we returned from the funeral, the house had been searched by someone else.'

'Unsuccessfully,' C added. 'They appear to be still looking for it. Presumably a second copy, which would suggest it is some kind of agreement. Your father indicated no names?'

'No, sir. He was very brief.'

C stared at him, frowning. For the first time Matthew sensed the depth of his anxiety. 'You knew your father, Reavley — what was he interested in? Who did he know? Where could he have been given this document?'

'I've thought about it very hard, sir, and I've spoken to several of his closest friends that I'm aware of, and as far as I can tell, none of them knows anything. When I mentioned plots, they all said Father was naïve and out of touch with reality.' He was surprised how much that still hurt to say. He heard the defensiveness in his voice, the underlying anger ready to attack.

C smiled very slightly, the amusement reaching all the way to his eyes.

'It seems they did not know your father very well.' Then his face hardened. 'Resist the temptation to prove to them that they are wrong, Reavley, whatever it costs you!'

Matthew swallowed. 'Yes, sir.'

'So you have no idea what this is about?'

'No, sir. I did think it might be an Irish plot to assassinate the King, but — '

'Yes!' C waved his hand briefly, dismissing it. 'I

341

know that. Pointless. Hannassey is not a fool. It is European, not Irish. Mr Brandt is not interested in the independence or otherwise of Ireland, except as it might affect our military abilities. But that is something to consider. If we are involved in civil war in Ireland our limited resources will be strained to the limit.'

He leaned forward a few inches. 'Find the document, Reavley. Find out who is behind it. Where did it come from, for whom was it intended?' He pushed a piece of paper across the top of his desk. 'This is a list of names of German agents in London that we know of. The first is at the German Embassy, the second is a carpet manufacturer, the third is a minor member of the German royal family presently living in London. Be extremely discreet. You should be aware by now that your life depends on it. Confide in no one at all.' He met Matthew's eyes in a cold, level gaze. 'No one! Not Shearing, not your brother — no one at all. When you have an answer, bring it to me.'

'Yes, sir.' Matthew stood up, reached for the paper, read it, and passed it back.

C took it and put it in a drawer. 'I'm sorry about your father, Captain Reavley.'

'Thank you, sir.' Matthew stood to attention for a moment, then turned and left, his mind already racing.

* * *

In the upstairs sitting room of the house on Marchmont Street, the Peacemaker stood by the window. He watched as a younger man walked briskly along the pavement, glancing occasionally at the houses to this side. He was reading the numbers. He had been here before, twice to be exact, but on both occasions brought by car, and at night.

The man in the street stopped, glanced up, and satisfied himself that he had found what he was looking for.

The Peacemaker stepped back, just one pace. He did not wish to be seen waiting. He had recognised the man below even before he saw his thick, dark hair, or the broad brow and wide-set eyes. It was a powerful face, emotional, that of a man who follows his ideals regardless of where they led him . . . over the cliffs of reason and into the abyss, if need be. He knew his easy walk, the mixture of grace and arrogance. He was a northerner, a Yorkshireman, with all the pride and the aggressive stubbornness of the land from which he came.

The doorbell rang, and a moment later it was opened by the butler. There followed a short silence, then footsteps up the stairs — soft, light, those of a man used to climbing the fells and dales — then a tap on the door.

'Come,' he answered.

The door opened and Richard Mason came in. He was almost six feet tall, an inch or two less than the Peacemaker, but he was more robust, and his skin had the wind and sunburn of one who travels.

'You sent for me, sir?' he said. His voice was unusual, his diction perfect, as if he had been trained for drama and the love of words. It had a sibilance so slight one was not certain if it was there or not, and one listened to catch it again.

'Yes,' the Peacemaker assured him. They both remained standing, as if to be seated were too much a sign of ease for the situation that brought them together. 'Events are moving very rapidly.'

'I am aware of that,' Mason said with only the merest touch of asperity. 'Do you have the document?'

'No.' That was a tight, hard word carrying a burden of anger in it so great one expected to see the man's shoulders bend under it. But the Peacemaker remained upright, his face pale. 'I've had men searching for it, but we have no idea where it went. It wasn't in the car or on the bodies, and we've tried the house twice.'

'Could he have destroyed it?' Mason asked dubiously.

'No.' The answer was immediate. 'He was a . . . ' he gave the merest shrug, a gesture so small it could have been overlooked, 'an innocent man in some ways, but he was not a fool. He knew the meaning of it, and he knew no one would believe him without it. Under his calm manner, he was as stubborn as a mule.' His face tightened in the sunlight through the bay windows. 'He would never deliberately have defaced it, let alone destroyed it.'

Mason stood still, his pulse beating hard. He had some idea of how much was at stake, but the enormities of it stretched into an unimaginable future. The sights of war still haunted his nightmares, but the blood, the pain and the loss of the past would be no more than a foretaste of what could happen in Europe, and eventually the world. Any risk at all was worth the price to prevent that, even this price.

'We can't waste any more time looking,' the Peacemaker went on. 'Events are overtaking us. I have it from excellent sources that Austria is preparing to invade Serbia. Serbia will resist, we all know that, and then Russia will mobilize. Once Germany enters France it will be over in a matter of days, weeks at the most. Schlieffen has drawn up a plan of absolute exactitude, every move timed to perfection. The German army will be in Paris before the rest of the world has time to react.'

'Is there still a chance we will remain out of it?' Mason asked. He was a foreign correspondent. He knew Austria and Germany almost as well as the man who stood opposite him. His background, his aristocratic connections, stretching as high as the junior branches of the royal family, on both sides of the North Sea, his brilliance with languages — these made him valuable. They shared a rage at the slaughter and destruction of war. The highest goal a man could achieve would be to prevent that from ever happening again, by any means at all.

The Peacemaker chewed his lip, his face strained with tension. 'I think so.' There was doubt in his voice; his hands were stiff. 'But there are difficulties. I've got an SIS man breathing down my neck. Not seriously,' he added. 'Reavley's son, actually. He's not important, just a nuisance. I doubt it will be

345

necessary to do anything about him. Don't want to draw attention. Fortunately, he's looking in the wrong direction. By the time he realises it, it won't matter any more.'

'Another copy of the document?' Mason asked.

The plan was brilliant, more daring than anything he could have imagined. The sheer enormity of it dazzled him. When the Peacemaker had first told him of it, it had taken his breath away. They had been walking slowly along the Thames Embankment, the lights dancing on the water, the smell of the incoming tide, the sounds of laughter across the river, the pleasure boats making their slow way upstream towards Kew. He had stood rooted to the spot, lost for words.

Slowly the plan had moved from a dream, lightly touched on, into a wish, and finally a reality. He still felt a little like a man who had created a unicorn in his imagination, only to walk his garden one day and find one grazing there, milk white, with cloven hoofs and silver horn — a living and breathing animal.

'We haven't found a second copy,' the Peacemaker answered grimly. 'At least not yet. I've done a certain amount to discredit John Reavley.' His face tightened with anger again. 'I hated that!' he said between his teeth. 'I wish it hadn't been necessary.' He looked sharply at Mason as he saw the alarm in his eyes. 'Nothing overt!' he snapped. 'We need to give the dust time to settle.' His mouth pinched unhappily, a shadow in his eyes. 'Sometimes the sacrifice is heavy,' he said softly. 'But if he had understood, I think he would have paid it willingly. He was not an arrogant man, certainly not greedy, and not a fool, but he was simplistic. He believed what he wanted to, and there is no use arguing with a man like that. A pity. We could have used him otherwise.'

Mason felt a heaviness settle on him too, an ache of regret eat inside him. But he had seen the devastation of war and human cruelty in the Balkans only a year ago, between Turkey and Bulgaria, and the memory of it still soaked his nightmares in horror and he woke trembling and drenched in sweat.

Before that, as a younger man he had gone east and reported the eyewitness accounts of the Japanese sinking of the entire Russian fleet in 1905. Thousands of men were buried in steel coffins under the trackless water, nothing remaining but the stunned loss, the grief of families from half a continent.

Earlier still, on the first foreign assignment of his career, he had watched the farmers on the Veldt in Africa, the stubborn dispossessed, wending their slow way across the endless open plains, angry, sometimes cruel, bitter, arrogant on occasion, but unbreakable. He had watched the women and children die.

None of it must happen again. One might speak of honour, of England's name among nations, or the integrity of its own heart, and make a good argument. Mostly he thought simply of humanity. One should not permit such a thing to happen to other human beings.

'A statesman has to think of individuals,' he said.

The Peacemaker said nothing, but his shoulders eased a fraction and he walked over to the middle of the room and reached for a cigarette. He lit it without offering one to Mason. He knew he would not want it. 'We have other things to consider,' he continued. 'Without the document war may be inevitable. We must do what we can to make sure that it is quick and clean. There are many possibilities, and I have plans in place, at least on the home front. We can still have tremendous effect.'

'I imagine it will be brief,' Mason concurred. 'Especially if Schlieffen's plan works. But it will be bloody. Thousands will be slaughtered.' He used the word bitterly and deliberately.

The Peacemaker's smile was thin. 'Then it is even more important that we ensure it is as short as possible. I have been giving it a great deal of thought over the last few days — in fact since the document was taken.' A sudden fury gripped him, clenching his body and draining the blood from his face until his skin was pallid and his eyes glittered. 'Damn Reavley!' his voice choked on the name. 'Damn him to hell! If he'd just kept out of it we could have prevented this! Lives! Tens of thousands of lives are going to be lost! For what?' He flung his hand out, fingers spread wide enough to have played over an octave on a keyboard with ease. 'It didn't have to happen!' He gulped in air and very carefully steadied himself, breathing in and out several times until his colour returned and his shoulders relaxed.

'I'm sorry,' he said with a catch in his voice, as if he were still close to losing control. 'But I can't bear to think of it — the ruin of a way of life that is the culmination of millennia of civilisation, all unnecessary! That's what it is, Mason . . . all unnecessary!' His voice was close to a sob. 'How many widows will there be? How many orphans? How many mothers waiting for their sons who will never come home, weeping for the rest of their lives, perhaps not even knowing where they are buried in some future bloody battlefield, in a war that they didn't ask for and didn't want?'

'I know that,' Mason said almost under his breath. 'Why do you think I'm doing this? It's like drinking poison . . . but the only alternative is a slow journey into hell . . . from which we won't come back.'

'You're right,' the Peacemaker responded, turning towards the light streaming in through the window. 'I know! I'm heartsick that we came so close, and lost it through an idiotic piece of mischance — a German philosopher with good handwriting, and an inquisitive ex-politician, who was damned useless at it anyway, and all our plans are jeopardized. But it's too early to despair.

'We must prepare for war, if it comes. And I have several ideas, with the groundwork already done, just in case. We must never give up, Mason, never. We cannot afford to. Everything we value depends on our success: the progress in science and art, stability and the rule of law, international trade and the freedom to travel. I admit, I hadn't thought it would come to this.' He rubbed his hand over his brow. 'God damn it! The Germans are our natural allies. We come from the same blood, the same language, the same heritage of nature and character!'

He stopped for a moment, regaining his composure. 'But perhaps it is no more than a setback. We don't have the document, but neither do they. If they did, Matthew Reavley wouldn't still be looking for it and asking questions. But don't worry, he's no danger to us. He's well within control, and I'll see that he remains so. Without the document he's thrashing around in the dark, a nuisance, but no more.' His face hardened again. 'We have to see at all costs that he doesn't get it! If it fell into the wrong hands it would be disastrous!'

'Is he the only one?' Mason asked.

'Oh, there's another brother, Joseph, but he's totally ineffectual,' the Peacemaker replied with a smile, his whole body easing, the tension released now. 'A scholar, idealist, retreated from life and responsibility. Teaches at Cambridge — Biblical languages, of all things! He wouldn't acknowledge the truth if it leaped up and bit him. He's a dreamer. Nothing is going to waken him, because he doesn't want to be disturbed. Reality hurts, Mason, and the Reverend Joseph Reavley doesn't like pain. He wants to save the world by preaching a good, carefully thought out and well-reasoned sermon to them. He doesn't realise that nobody's listening — not with their hearts or their guts — or willing to pay the price for it. It's up to us.'

'Yes,' Mason said. 'I know that.'

'Of course you do.' The Peacemaker pushed his hands through his hair. 'Go back to your writing. You have a gift. We may need it. Stay with your newspaper. If we can't prevent it, and the worst happens, get them to send you everywhere you can! Every battlefield, every advance or retreat, every town or city that's captured, or where there are negotiations for peace. Become the most brilliant, the most widely read war correspondent in Europe . . . in the world. Do you understand?'

'Oh yes,' Mason said with a soft hiss of breath between his teeth. 'Of course I understand.'

The Peacemaker nodded, a tight, thin smile on his face. 'Good. Then you'd better go, but keep in touch.'

Mason turned and walked slowly to the door, then out of it, and his footsteps barely sounded on the stairs.

11

In Cambridge Joseph felt that he was achieving something in his pursuit of the truth about Sebastian Allard, but it was all a matter of exclusion. He was no nearer to knowing what had happened, as opposed to what had not. And if Inspector Perth had made progress then he kept it to himself. The tension and unhappiness were increasing with every day that passed. Joseph was determined to continue in whatever way he could to discover more about Sebastian and who had had reason to hate or to fear him.

An opportunity came to him when he was discussing a problem of interpretation with Elwyn, who was finding a particular passage of translation difficult.

They began by talking of the use of language in certain situations, particular forms of rhetoric. They had walked from the lecture rooms together and, rather than go inside, had chosen to cross the bridge to the Backs. It was a quiet afternoon. As they turned on the gravel path to go towards the shade, bees drifted lazily among the spires of delphiniums and late pinks by the wall of the covered walk. Bertie was rolling on the warm earth in between the snapdragons.

Elwyn was still showing signs of the shock and grief of loss. Joseph knew better than others how one can temporarily forget a cataclysm in one's life, then remember it again with surprise and the renewal of pain. Sometimes one floated in a kind of unreality, as if the disaster were all imagination, and in a little while would disappear and life be as it was before. One was tired, without knowing why, concentration slipped from the grasp and slithered away.

It was not surprising Elwyn was wandering off the point, again, unable to keep his mind in control.

'I ought to get back to the Master's house,' he said anxiously. 'Mother may be alone.'

'You can't protect her from everything,' Joseph told him.

Elwyn's eyes opened abruptly, then his lips tightened and the colour flooded his face. He looked away. 'I've got to. You don't understand how she felt about Sebastian. She'll get over this anger, then she'll be all right. It's just that — ' He stopped, staring ahead at the flat, bright water reflecting the light as if it were some liquid resin, too thick to see through.

Joseph understood, but he wanted to hear Elwyn's words. Surely if anybody knew something deeper about Sebastian it would be he. He must have heard phrases, some expressions, caught nuances others hadn't.

He finished the sentence for him. 'If she knew who did it, and saw them punished, her anger would be satisfied.'

'I suppose so,' Elwyn conceded, but there was no conviction in his voice.

Joseph broached the subject he least wanted to. 'But perhaps not?'

Elwyn said nothing.

'Why?' Joseph persisted. 'Because to do so would force her to see something in Sebastian that she would not wish to?'

Again Elwyn said nothing, but the misery in his face was unmistakable.

'We might be able to protect her from some of it,' Joseph went on, angry with Mary Allard for being so dependent on illusions that she made her younger son feel he needed to protect her regardless of the cost to himself, and robbing him of the time and the freedom to do his own grieving. It was natural that he should want to protect his brother's memory against the prying eyes of the police, or the envy of his peers, but not to place himself, and his own feelings in all their raw pain, as a shield between his mother and the truth.

'I don't know how we can,' Elwyn said miserably, pushing his hands deeper into his pockets. 'Everyone sees a different side of people. She doesn't have any idea what he was like away from home, or even in it, really.'

Joseph felt intrusive, and certain he too wanted to keep his illusions intact, but that was a luxury he could no longer afford. He was being offered a chance to learn and he dared not turn away from it.

'Did she know about Flora Whickham?' he asked.

Elwyn stiffened, for an instant holding his breath. Then he let it out in a sigh. 'He told you?'

'No. I discovered for myself, largely by accident.'

Elwyn swung around. 'Don't tell Mother! She

354

wouldn't understand. Flora's a nice girl, but she's . . . '

'A barmaid,' Joseph supplied for him.

Elwyn gave a rueful smile. 'Yes, but what I was going to say was that she's a pacifist, I mean a real one, and Mother wouldn't begin to understand that.' There was confusion and distaste in his face, and a hurt too tender to probe. He looked away again towards the river, shielding his eyes from Joseph's gaze. 'Actually, neither do I. If you love something, belong to it and believe in it, how can you not fight to save it?' His face was miserable and confused. 'I mean . . . what kind of a man wouldn't?'

Perhaps he suspected Joseph of that same incomprehensible betrayal. If he did, there would be some truth in it. But then Joseph had read of the Boer War and his imagination could recreate the unreachable pain, the horror that could not be eased or explained, and never, with all the arguments on earth, be justified.

'He was not a coward,' Joseph said aloud. He was not sure why he needed to say that. No one had accused Sebastian of cowardice. Perhaps it was defence of himself, because for him the question was there, sharp as a spur, digging into his mind. 'He would fight for what he believed in,' he added.

'Probably.' There was no certainty in Elwyn's voice or his face.

'Who else knew about her?' Joseph asked.

'Flora? I don't know.'

'Regina Coopersmith?' Joseph asked.

Elwyn froze. 'God! I hope not!'

'But you're not certain?'

Elwyn thought for a moment. 'I suppose I don't know,' he said at length. 'I'd have imagined she'd be furious, maybe even break off the engagement. But maybe I don't really know her. I suppose,' he chewed his lip and looked awkwardly at Joseph, 'I don't know women very well. I would feel dreadful — but maybe . . . ' He did not finish.

There were a few moments of silence as they walked side by side over the grass and on to the path under the trees.

'Sebastian had a row with Dr Beecher,' Elwyn went on.

'When?' Joseph felt a sinking inside himself.

'A couple of days before he died.'

'Do you know what it was about?'

'No, I don't.' He turned to face Joseph. 'I thought it was odd, actually, because Dr Beecher was pretty decent to him.'

'Wasn't he to everyone?'

'Of course. I meant more than to the rest of us.'

Joseph was puzzled. He remembered Beecher's dislike of Sebastian. It had surprised him, but at the time he had been more conscious of his own hurt. It had been incomprehensible then, because he was seeing Sebastian as he wanted him to be. Now it was still something he did not understand, but he accepted that it was necessary he should. Had Beecher always felt dislike, or was it recent, provoked by some knowledge or event within the last few weeks of Sebastian's life?

'In what way?' he asked. He had meant to be casual, but he heard the harder edge in his voice, and Elwyn must have heard it also.

Elwyn hesitated, uncomfortable. He moved his feet very slightly on the gravel of the path.

'I would rather ask you than someone else,' Joseph said grimly.

Elwyn sighed. 'We all behave badly sometimes, come to a lecture late, turn in sloppy work — you know how it is?'

'I do.'

'Well, usually you get disciplined for it, ticked off and made to look an ass in front of the others, or get privileges revoked, or something like that. Well, Dr Beecher was easier on Sebastian than on most of us. Sebastian sort of took advantage of it, as if he knew Dr Beecher wouldn't do anything. He could be an arrogant sod at times. He believed in his own image.' He stopped. Guilt was naked in his face, the stoop of his shoulders, the fidgeting of his right foot as it scuffed the stones. He had said only what was true, but convention decreed that you spoke no ill of the dead. His mother would have seen it as betrayal. 'I never thought he liked Sebastian very much,' he finished awkwardly.

'Yet he favoured him?' Joseph pressed.

Elwyn stared at the ground. 'It makes no sense to me, because it isn't a favour in the long run. You've got to have discipline, or you have nothing. And other people get fed up if you keep on getting away with things.'

'Did other people notice?' Joseph asked.

'Of course. I think that's what the row was

about with Beecher, a day or two before Sebastian's death.'

'Why didn't you mention it before?'

Elwyn stared at him. 'Because I can't see Dr Beecher shooting Sebastian because he was arrogant at times, and played on his popularity. It's stupid, and it's irritating as hell, but you don't kill someone for it!'

'No,' Joseph agreed, but that thought was not what rushed into his mind, filling him with coldness. 'Of course you don't.' He tried to think of the need to bring Mary Allard towards reality in a way she could manage. He wanted to help, but he could see her fragility, and nothing was going to ease the blow for her if something ugly were exposed in Sebastian. She might even refuse to believe it and blame everyone else for lying. 'Try to be patient with your mother,' Joseph added. 'There is little on earth that hurts more than disillusion.'

Elwyn gave a twisted smile and, blinking rapidly to fight his emotion, he nodded and walked away, too close to tears to excuse himself.

Joseph went back to St John's to look for anyone who could either substantiate or deny what Elwyn had told him. The first person he ran into was Rattray.

'Favour him?' Rattray said curiously, looking up from the book he was reading where he sat on one of the benches near the bridge. 'I suppose so. Hadn't thought about it much. I got rather used to everyone thinking Sebastian was the next golden poet, and all that.' The wry, almost challenging look in his eyes very much included

358

Joseph within that group, and Joseph felt the heat burn up his face.

'I was thinking of something rather more definable than a belief,' he said rather tartly.

Rattray sighed. 'I suppose he did let Sebastian get away with more than the rest of us,' he conceded. 'There were times when I thought it was odd.'

'Didn't you mind?' Joseph was surprised.

It was Rattray's turn to blush. 'Of course I minded!' he said hotly. 'Once or twice taking advantage of Beecher was clever, and we all thought it would make it easier for the rest of us to skip lectures if we wanted, or turn in stuff late, or whatever. Even came in blotto a couple of times, and poor old Beecher didn't do a damn thing! Then I began to see it was all rather grubby, and in the end stupid as well. I told Sebastian what I thought of it, and that I wasn't playing any more, and he told me to go to hell. Sorry. I'm sure that isn't what you wanted to hear. But your beautiful Sebastian could be a pain in the arse at times.'

Joseph said nothing. Actually it was Beecher he was thinking of, and afraid for.

'When he was good, he was marvellous,' Rattray said hastily, as if he thought he had gone too far. 'Nobody was more fun, a better friend, or honestly a better student. I didn't resent him, if that's what you think. You don't, when somebody's really brilliant. You see the good, and you're happy for it — just that it exists. He just changed a bit lately.'

'When is 'lately'?'

Rattray thought for a moment. 'Two or three months, maybe? And then after the Sunday of the assassination in Sarajevo he got so wound up I thought he was going to snap. Poor devil, he really thought we were going to war.'

'Yes. He talked to me about it.'

'Don't you think it's possible, sir?' Rattray looked surprised. 'A quick sort of thing, in and out. Settle it?'

'Perhaps,' Joseph said uncertainly. Had Sebastian been killed out of some stupid jealousy here after all, nothing to do with the document, or John Reavley's death?

Rattray gave a sudden grin. It lit his rather ordinary face and made it vivid and charming. 'We don't owe the Austrians anything, or the Serbs either. But I wouldn't find a spell in the army so terrible. Could be a wheeze, actually. Spot of adventure before the grind of real life!'

All kinds of warnings came into Joseph's mind, but he realised he actually knew no more than Rattray did. They were both speaking in total ignorance, fuelled only by other men's experiences. He made some innocuous reply, and started to walk towards the bridge.

* * *

Before dinner, when he was almost certain to find him alone, Joseph went to Beecher's rooms, bracing himself for a confrontation that could break a friendship he had long valued.

Beecher was surprised to see him, and evidently pleased.

360

'Come in,' he invited warmly, abandoning his book and welcoming Joseph, offering him the better chair. 'Have a drink? I've got some fairly decent sherry.'

That was typical of Beecher's understatement. 'Fairly decent' actually meant 'absolutely excellent'.

'Thank you,' Joseph accepted, embarrassed that he was going to take hospitality in what might prove to be a false understanding.

'I could do with one myself.' Beecher went to the sideboard and took the bottle out of the cupboard, and set two elegant engraved crystal glasses on the table. He was fond of glass and collected it now and then, when he found something quaint or very old. 'I feel as if I've been dogged by that wretched policeman all week, and God knows, the news is bad enough. I can't see any end to this Irish fiasco. Can you?'

'No,' Joseph admitted honestly, sitting down. The room had grown familiar over the time he had been here. He knew every book on the shelves, and had borrowed many of them. He could have described the view out the window with his eyes closed. He could have named the various members of the family in each of the silver-framed photographs. He knew exactly where the different scenic paintings were drawn, which valley in the Lake District, which castle on the Northumberland coast, which stretch of the South Downs. Each held memories they had shared or recounted, one time or another.

'The police are not getting anywhere, are they?' he said aloud.

'Not so far as I know.' Beecher finished pouring the sherry and returned with it, offering one to Joseph and holding up the other. 'Here's to an end to it, although I'm not sure if we'll like it.'

'What do you think Perth will find?' Joseph asked, then sipped at the sherry. As Beecher had implied, it was superb, an exquisite dryness without being too sharp.

Beecher studied Joseph for some time before replying. 'I'm sorry,' he said at last, 'but I think we'll discover that somebody had a thoroughly good motive for killing him, even though they may be hideously sorry now.'

Suddenly Joseph was cold, and the aftertaste of the sherry was bitter in his mouth. He spoke with difficulty, trying to keep the emotion from his voice. 'What do you think a 'good motive' could be?' he asked. 'The killing was in cold blood. Whoever did it took a gun to his room at six in the morning.'

Beecher frowned. 'Earlier than that. You found him a little after six, didn't you? Was he dead just moments before?'

With a jolt of memory so violent it turned his stomach, Joseph recalled exactly the feel of Sebastian's skin, already cool.

Beecher must have been watching him and seen his colour bleach. 'Sorry,' he apologized ruefully, his eyes gentle. 'That was clumsy.' He breathed out slowly. 'I'd like to let you go on in your belief that he was as good as you wanted him to be, but he wasn't. He had promise, but he had threat as well. He was on the verge of being

362

spoiled. Poor Mary Allard was at least in part responsible.'

Now was the moment. 'I know,' Joseph conceded. 'I was responsible as well.' He ignored Beecher's look of amusement and compassion. 'Elwyn protected him partly for his own sake, partly for his mother's,' he went on. 'And apparently you let him get away with being late with work, rude, and sometimes sloppy. And yet you didn't like him. Why did you do that?'

Beecher was silent, but the colour had paled from his face and his hand holding the sherry glass was trembling very slightly; the golden liquid in it shimmered. He made an effort to control it, and lifted it to his lips to take a sip, perhaps to give himself time.

'It was hardly in your interest,' Joseph went on. 'It was bad for your reputation and your ability to be fair to others and maintain any kind of discipline.'

'You favoured him yourself!' Beecher said very quietly, his voice a little hoarse.

'I liked him,' Joseph pointed out. 'I admit my judgement was flawed. It would have been better for everyone, but principally for him, if I had been more realistic. One cannot correct faults one refuses to see. And we are here, at least in part, to do that, as well as to teach facts and the love of learning. You didn't like him and you know the rules as well as I do. Why did you break them for him?'

'I didn't know you had such tenacity,' Beecher said drily. 'You've changed.'

'Rather past time, isn't it?' Joseph said with

regret. 'But as you said, there is no point in dealing with anything less than the truth.'

'No.' Beecher looked down for a moment, studying the glass in his hands. 'But I don't propose to discuss it with you.' He raised his eyes, clear and seemingly candid. 'I did not kill Sebastian, and I don't know who did. You'll have to believe that or not, as you wish.'

It was not as Joseph wished, it was as he could, and that was a difference that dug into his mind like a blade. He had liked Beecher profoundly almost since they had met. This was another painful awakening. He wondered with a bite of fear how many people he was mistaken in. Should he include even himself?

Did he believe Beecher? Everything he knew about him, or thought he knew, was decent. He was the ideal professor, learned without being pompous. He taught for the love of his subject, and his students knew it. His pleasures seemed to be mild: old buildings, especially those with quaint or unusual history, odd dishes from around the world. He had the courage and the curiosity to try anything: mountain climbing, canoeing, pot-holing, small boat sailing. Joseph smiled in spite of himself at the recollection of some of their more lurid adventures in that direction, particularly the first. They had spent some magnificent, starlit nights on Ben Nevis, and some bitterly wet and miserable ones.

Beecher loved old trees, the more individual the better. He had jeopardized his reputation campaigning to save them, to the great annoyance of local authorities. He liked old people and their memories, and odd irrelevant facts.

He had spoken of his family now and then. He was particularly fond of certain aunts, all of whom were marvellously eccentric creatures who espoused lost causes with passion and courage, and invariably a sense of humour. He was sufficiently like them to understand effortlessly exactly what they felt.

Joseph realised with surprise, and sadness, that Beecher had never spoken of love. He had laughed at himself over one or two youthful fancies, but never anything you could call a commitment, nothing truly of the heart. It was a gaping omission, and the longer Joseph considered it the more it troubled him.

Guardedly he looked at Beecher now, sitting only a few feet away from him, affecting to be relaxed. He was not handsome, but his humour and intelligence made him unusually attractive. He had grace and he dressed with a certain flair. He took care of himself like a man who was not averse to intimate involvement.

And yet he had never spoken of women. If there was no one, why had he not ever mentioned that, perhaps regretted it? The most obvious answer was that had such an attachment existed, it was illicit. If so, he could not afford to tell even his closest friends.

The silence in the room, which would usually have been warm and comfortable, was suddenly distressing. Joseph's thoughts raced in his head. Had Sebastian either stumbled on a secret, or gone looking for it and unearthed it deliberately

— and then used it? It was a thought Joseph would much rather have put away as unworthy, but he could no longer afford to do that.

Who was it Beecher loved? If he were telling the truth, and he had not killed Sebastian, nor did he know who had, then surely the natural person to consider after that would be whoever else was involved in the illicit romance? Or whoever was betrayed by it, if such a person existed?

At last he faced the ultimate ugliness — what if Beecher were lying? What if his illicit lover were Sebastian himself? The thought was extraordinarily painful, but it fitted all the facts he knew — the undeniable ones, not the dreams or wishes. Perhaps Flora Whickham was merely a friend, a fellow pacifist, and an escape from the inevitable demands of his family?

There were people who could love men and women with equal ease. He had never before considered Sebastian as one such, but then he had not thought deeply about him in that regard at all. It was a private area. Now he was obliged to intrude into it. He would do it as discreetly as possible, and if it led nowhere with regard to Sebastian's death, he would never speak of it. He was used to keeping secrets; it was part of the profession he had chosen.

Beecher was watching him with his character-istic patience until Joseph should be ready to talk again.

Joseph was ashamed of his thoughts. Was this what everyone else was feeling — suspicion: ugly ideas racing through the mind, refusing to be

366

banished, and then embarrassment, and shame?

'Sebastian had a friendship with a local girl, you know?' he said aloud. 'A barmaid from the pub along near the Mill Pond.'

Beecher grinned. 'Well, that sounds healthy enough!' Then his face darkened with something very close to anger. 'Unless you're suggesting he misused her? Are you?'

'No! No, I really mean a friend!' Joseph corrected him. 'It seems they shared political convictions.'

'Political convictions!' Beecher was amazed. 'I didn't know he had any.'

'Very deep! He was passionately against war.' Joseph remembered the emotion shaking Sebastian's voice as he had spoken of the destruction of conflict. 'For the ruin it would bring,' he went on. 'Not only physically, but culturally, even spiritually. He was prepared to work for peace, not just wish for it.'

The contempt in Beecher's face softened, ruefully, as if it surprised him that he should discover such a change within himself. 'Then perhaps he was better than I supposed,' he said generously.

Joseph smiled, the old warmth returning. This was the friend he knew. 'He saw all the fear and the pain,' he said quietly, 'the glory of our entire heritage drowned in a sea of violence until we became a lost civilisation, and all our wealth of beauty, thought, human wisdom, joy and experience as buried as Nineveh or Tyre. No more Englishmen, none of our courage or eccentricity, our language or our tolerance left.

He loved it intensely. He would have given everything he had to preserve it.'

Beecher sighed and leaned backwards, gazing up at the ceiling. 'Then perhaps he is in some ways fortunate that he won't see the war that's coming,' he said softly. 'Inspector Perth is sure it will be the worst we've ever seen. Worse than the Napoleonic Wars, make Waterloo look tame.'

Joseph was stunned.

Beecher sat up again. 'Mind, he's a miserable devil,' he said more cheerfully. 'A regular Jeremiah. I'll be glad when he finishes his business here and goes to spread alarm and despondency somewhere else. Would you like another glass of sherry? You didn't take much.'

'It's enough,' Joseph replied. 'I can escape reality nicely on one, thank you.'

Beecher grinned.

Joseph remained a little longer, then excused himself to prepare for dinner.

★　★　★

The following day he began his investigation into the worst of all possibilities.

He must start by learning all he did not already know about Beecher. And surely in this case discretion was the better part of honesty. Candour would ruin Beecher's reputation, and unless it exposed Sebastian's murderer, it was no one else's concern.

The easiest thing to check without speaking to anyone else was a record of all Beecher's classes, lectures, tutorials and other engagements for the last six weeks. It was time-consuming, but simple enough to do, and easily concealed by finding the same information for everyone and simply extracting that which related to Beecher.

Correlating times and figures was not Joseph's natural talent, but with concentration he compiled a record of where Beecher had been, and with whom, for at least most of the previous month.

He sat back in his chair, ignoring the piles of papers, and considered what it proved, and what he should search for next. How did one conduct a secret relationship? Either by meeting alone where no one at all would see you, or where all those who did would be strangers to whom you would mean nothing. Or else by meeting in plain sight, and with a legitimate reason no one would question.

In Cambridge there was no place where everyone would be strangers, nor in the nearby villages. It would be crazy to take such a risk.

Completely uninhabited places were few, and not easily reached. Beecher might bicycle to them, but what about a woman? Unless she were very young and vigorous she would hardly bicycle far, and a woman who drove a car was very rare. Judith was an exception, not a rule.

That left the last possibility: they met openly, with natural reasons that no one would question. Sebastian knew of their feelings either because he had been more observant than others, he had caught a glance, a touch perhaps, or he had accidentally seen something acutely private. Either thought was distasteful.

Surely it would prove to be nonsense, his own overheated imagination. Perhaps Beecher was simply one of those scholarly men who do not form attachments. Such men existed. Joseph's idea that he was not arose simply from his own nature. He failed to imagine living with no desire for intimacy. Possibly Beecher had loved once, and could not commit himself again, nor speak of it even to someone like Joseph, who would surely have understood.

And yet even as the thoughts were in his mind, he did not believe them. Beecher was too alive, too physical to have removed himself from any of the richness of passion or experience. They had walked too far, climbed too high, laughed too hard together, for him to be mistaken.

★ ★ ★

Joseph had been hoping to avoid Inspector Perth when he almost bumped into him walking along the path in the middle of the quad, his pipe clenched between his teeth.

He took it out: 'Good afternoon, Reverend,' he said, this time not standing aside but remaining in front of Joseph, effectively blocking his way.

'Good afternoon, Inspector,' Joseph answered, moving a little to the right to go around him.

'Any luck wi' your questions?' Perth said, with what looked like polite interest.

Joseph thought for a moment of denying it, then remembered how frequently he had passed Perth coming or going. He would be lying, but, more importantly, Perth would know it and then assume he was hiding something — both of which were true. 'I keep thinking so, and then realising it all proves nothing,' he answered evasively.

'Oi know exactly what you mean,' Perth sympathised, knocking his pipe out on his shoe, examining it to make certain it was empty, then putting it in his pocket. 'Oi come up wi' bits and pieces, then it slips out o' my hands. But then you know these people, which Oi don't.' He smiled pleasantly. 'You'd know, f'r instance, why Dr Beecher seems t've made an exception for Mr Allard, letting him get away wi' all kinds o' cheek, and lateness and the loike, where he'd punish someone else.' He waited, quite obviously expecting an answer.

Joseph thought quickly. 'Can you give me an example?'

Perth replied without hesitation, 'Mr Allard handed in a paper late, and so did Mr Morel. He took a mark off Mr Morel for it, but not off Mr Allard.'

Joseph felt a chill and stared fixedly at Perth, suddenly afraid of him. He did not want him poking around in Beecher's private affairs. 'People can be eccentric in marking sometimes,' he said, affecting an ease he was very far from feeling. 'I have been guilty of it myself, at times. Translation in particular can be a matter of taste as well as exactness.'

Perth's eyes widened. 'Is that what you think, Reverend?' he said curiously.

Joseph wanted to escape. 'It seems probable,' he said, moving a little to the right again, intending to go around Perth and continue on his way. He wanted to end this conversation before Perth led him any further into the morass.

Perth smiled, as if Joseph had met his prejudices exactly. 'Dr Beecher just loiked Mr Allard's style, did he? Poor Mr Morel just ain't in the same class, so when he's late, he's in trouble.'

'That would be totally unfair!' Joseph said hotly. 'And it was not what I meant! The difference in mark would have had nothing to do with being late or early.'

'Or being cheeky, or careless?' Perth persisted. 'Discipline's not the same for the clever students from what way it is for the less clever. You know Mr Allard's family quite well, don't you?'

It was not himself Joseph was afraid for, it was Beecher, and the thoughts that were darkening in his own mind.

'Yes, I do, and I never allowed him the slightest latitude because of it!' he said with considerable asperity. 'This is a place of learning, Inspector, and personal issues have nothing to do with the way a student is taught or the marks given to his work. It is irresponsible and morally repugnant to suggest otherwise. I cannot allow you to say such a thing and be uncorrected. You are slandering a man's reputation, and your office here does not give you immunity to do that!'

Perth did not seem in the least disconcerted. 'Oi've just bin going around asking and listening like you have, Reverend,' he replied quietly. 'And Oi've begun to see that some people thought Dr

Beecher really didn't like Mr Allard very much. But that don't seem to be true, because he bent over backwards to be fair to him, even done him the odd favour. Now why d'yer think that was?'

Joseph had no answer.

'You know these people better'n Oi do, Reverend,' Perth went on relentlessly. 'Oi'd've thought you'd want the truth o' this, because you can see just how hard everybody's taking it. Suspicion's an evil thing. Turns people against each other, even when there's really no cause for it.'

'Of course I do,' Joseph responded, then had no idea what to say next.

Perth was smiling. It was amusement and a faint, rather sad compassion. 'Hard, ain't it, Reverend?' he said gently. 'Discovering that a young man you thought so well of weren't above using a spot o' blackmail now and then?'

'I don't know anything of the sort!' Joseph protested. It was literally true, but already morally a lie.

'Of course not,' Perth agreed. 'Because you stopped before you had any proof as yer couldn't deny. If you did, then you'd have to face it, and maybe even tell. But you're an interesting man to follow, Reverend, and not nearly as simple as you'd have me think.' He ignored Joseph's expression. 'Good thing Dr Beecher was way along the river when Mr Allard was killed, or Oi'd have to suspect him, and of course Oi'd have to find out exactly what it was Mr Allard knew, although Oi can think of it easy enough. A very handsome woman, Mrs Thyer, and mebbe

373

just a little bit lonely, in her own way.'

Joseph froze, his heart racing. Beecher and Connie? Could that be true? Images teemed through his mind, becoming sharper and sharper: Connie's face, beautiful, warm, vivid; he thought of the flamenco dancer, and the passion in it, and Aiden Thyer's cool, pale face as he stood at the side of the room from her; he pictured her face as she turned to Beecher, the laughter in it, and the warmth.

Perth shook his head. 'Don't look at me like that, Reverend. Oi haven't suggested something improper. All men have feelings, and sometimes we don't want 'em seen by others. Makes us feel kind of . . . naked. Oi wonder what else Mr Allard's sharp eyes noticed? You wouldn't happen to know, would you?'

'No, I wouldn't!' Joseph snapped, feeling the heat in his face. 'And as you say, Dr Beecher was at least a mile away when Sebastian was shot. I told you that I can't help you, Inspector, and it is the truth. Now would you be good enough to let me pass?'

'Course Oi would, Reverend. You be about your business.' He regarded Joseph steadily, his eyes hard and bright. 'But Oi'm telling you, all of you here, you can go round and round the houses all you like, Oi'm going to find out who did it, whoever he is, an' no matter what his father paid to have him up here. And Oi'm going to find out why! Oi may not be able to argue all kinds o' fancy logic, like you can, Reverend, but Oi know people, and Oi know why they do things against the law. And Oi'll prove it. Law's

374

bigger'n all of us, and you being a religious man, you oughta know that!'

Joseph saw Perth's antipathy and he understood it. He was out of his depth in surroundings he could never aspire to, or be comfortable in. He was being patronized by a number of men considerably younger than he, and they were probably not even aware of it. The law was both his master, and his weapon, perhaps his only one.

'I do know that, Inspector Perth,' Joseph said with slight embarrassment for his own condescension. 'And we need you to find the truth. The uncertainty is destroying us.'

'Yes,' Perth agreed. 'It does that to people. But Oi will!' At last he stepped aside, nodding graciously for Joseph to proceed.

Joseph walked on rapidly, with the certain knowledge that he had come off second best, and Perth understood him far better than he wished. Once again he had misjudged somebody.

★ ★ ★

Joseph was invited to dine at the Master's lodgings that evening, and accepted because he understood Connie Thyer's desperation to escape the sole responsibility for looking after Gerald and Mary Allard under the weight of their grief. She could hardly offer them anything that could be construed as entertainment, and yet they were her guests. But their unalloyed presence at her table must be almost more than she could bear. Joseph at least was an old family friend, also mourning a close and almost equally recent loss. Also his religious calling made him extremely suitable. He could hardly refuse.

He arrived a little before eight to find Connie alone in the drawing room with Mary Allard. As always Mary was head to toe in black. He thought it was the same dress as he had seen her in last time they met, but one black gown looked much like another to him. She certainly appeared even thinner and there was no doubting the anger in her face. It did not soften in the slightest when she saw Joseph.

'Good evening, Dr Reavley,' she said with polite chill. 'I hope you are well?'

'Yes, thank you,' he replied. 'And you?' It was an absurd exchange. She was obviously suffering intensely. She looked anything but well. One enquired because it was the thing to say.

'I am not sure why you ask,' she answered, catching him off guard. 'Do I tell you how I feel? Not only has some murderer robbed me of my son, but now vicious tongues are fouling his memory. Or would you feel less guilty if I merely tell you that I am perfectly well, thank you? I have no disease, only wounds!'

Neither of them noticed that Gerald Allard had come into the room, but Joseph heard his swift intake of breath and waited for Gerald to make some attempt to retrieve his wife's naked rudeness.

The silence prickled as if on the brink of thunder. Connie looked from one to the other of them.

Gerald cleared his throat.

Mary swung round to him. 'You were going to say something?' she accused. 'Perhaps to defend your son, since he is lying in his grave and cannot defend himself?'

Gerald flushed a dark red. 'I don't think it is fair to accuse Reavley, my dear — ' he started.

'Oh, isn't it?' she demanded, her eyes wide. 'He is the one who is assisting that dreadful policeman to suggest that Sebastian was blackmailing people, and that is why someone murdered him!' She swivelled back to Joseph, her eyes blazing. 'Can you deny it, Reverend?' She loaded the last word with biting sarcasm. 'Why? Were you jealous of Sebastian? Afraid he was going to outshine you in your own field? He had more poetry in his soul than you will ever have, and you must realise that. Is that why you are doing this? God! How he'd have despised you for it! He thought you were his friend!'

'Mary!' Gerald said desperately.

She ignored him. 'I've listened to him talk about you as if you were flawless!' she said, her voice shaking with contempt, tears glistening in her eyes. 'He thought you were wonderful, an unparalleled friend! Poor Sebastian . . . ' She stopped only because her voice was too thick with emotion to continue.

Connie was watching, white-faced, but she did not interrupt.

'Really — ' Gerald tried again.

Joseph cut across him. 'Sebastian knew I was his friend,' he said very clearly. 'But I was not as good a friend to him as I would have been had I tried more honestly to see his faults as well as his

377

virtues. I would have served him better had I tried to curb his hubris instead of being blind to it.'

'Hubris?' she said icily.

'His pride in his own charm, his feeling of invulnerability,' he started to explain.

'I know what the word means, Dr Reavley!' she snapped. 'I was questioning your use of it with reference to my son! I find it intolerable that — '

'You find any criticism of him intolerable,' Gerald managed to make himself heard at last. 'But somebody killed him!'

'Envy!' Mary said with absolute conviction. 'Some small person who could not endure being eclipsed.' She looked at Joseph as she finished.

'Mrs Allard,' Connie said very clearly and with startling firmness, 'we all sympathise with your grief, but that does not excuse you for being both cruel and unjust to another guest in my house, who has also lost his closest family almost as recently as you have. I think perhaps in your own loss you had temporarily forgotten that.' It was calmly said, even gravely, but it was a bitter rebuke.

Aidan Thyer, who had entered the room during the exchange, looked startled, but he did not intervene, and his expression as he glanced at Connie was unreadable, as if of emotions profound and conflicting. In that instant Joseph wondered if he knew that Beecher was in love with his wife, and if it hurt him, or made him fear he could lose what he must surely value intensely. Or did he? What was there really

378

behind the habitual courtesy? He glimpsed with pain the possibility of a world of loneliness and pretence.

But the present hauled him back. Mary Allard was furious, but she was too clearly in the wrong to defend herself. She adopted Connie's offer of escape.

'I'm sorry,' she said stiffly. 'I had forgotten. I dare say your own loss has ... ' She had obviously been going to say something like 'cramped your judgement', but realised it made things no better. She left the sentence hanging in the air.

Normally Joseph would have accepted any apology, but not this time. 'Made me think more deeply about reality,' he finished for her. 'And see that no matter how much we love someone, or regret lost opportunities to have given them more than we did, lies do not help, even when we would find them more comfortable.'

The colour drained out of Mary's face and she looked at him with loathing. Even if she understood anything he said, she was not going to concede it now. 'I have no idea what things you may regret,' she said coldly. 'I do not know you well enough. I have heard no one speak ill of your parents, but if they have, then you should do all within your power to silence them. If you have not loyalty, above all to your own family, then you have nothing! I promise you I will do anything in my power to protect the name and reputation of my dead son from the envy and spite of anyone cowardly enough to attack him in death when they would not have dared to in life.'

'There are many loyalties, Mrs Allard,' Joseph answered, his voice grating with the intensity of his feelings: the misery and loneliness of too many losses of his own, his anger at God for hurting him so profoundly, and at the dead for leaving him with such a weight to bear of responsibilities he was not ready for, and above all the fear of disillusion, the disintegration of the love and beliefs dearest to him. 'It is a matter of choosing which to place first. Loving someone does not make them right, and your family is no more important than mine, or anyone else's. Your first loyalty ought to be to honour, kindness, and some degree of truth.'

The hatred in her face was answer enough without words. She turned to Connie, her skin white, her eyes burning. 'I am sure you will understand if I do not choose to remain for dinner. Perhaps you will be good enough to have a tray sent to my room.' And with that she swept out through the door in a rustle of black silk taffeta and the faintest perfume of roses.

Connie sighed. 'I am sorry, Dr Reavley. She is finding this investigation very hard indeed. Everyone's nerves are a little raw.'

'She idealized him,' Gerald said, as much to himself as to anyone else. 'It isn't fair. No one could live up to that, nor can the rest of us protect her forever from the truth.' He glanced at Joseph, perhaps expecting him to read some apology in it, although Joseph had the feeling he was looking more for acceptance of his own silence. Joseph was sorry for Gerald — he was a man floundering around in a hopeless task

— but he felt far greater pity for Elwyn, trying to defend Sebastian whose flaws he knew, while protecting his mother from truths she could not face, and his father from looking completely impotent and sinking into self-loathing. It was more than anyone should have to do, let alone a young man who was himself bereaved, and who should have been supported by his parents, not made to support them in their self-absorbed grief.

He glanced at Connie and saw a reflection of the same pity and anger in her face. But it was Joseph she was looking at, not her husband. Aidan Thyer was averting his gaze, perhaps in order to hide his distaste at Gerald's excuses.

Joseph filled the silence. 'Everyone's nerves are a little raw,' he agreed. 'We suspect each other of things that in our better moments would not even enter our thoughts. Once we know what happened, we will be able to forget them again.'

'Do you think so?' Aidan Thyer asked suddenly. 'We've pulled off too many masks, and seen what is underneath. I don't think we'll forget.' He looked momentarily at Connie, then back at Joseph, his pale eyes challenging.

'Perhaps not forget,' Joseph amended. 'But isn't the art of friendship very much the selecting of what is important and allowing some of the mistakes to drift away until we lose sight of them? We don't forget, so much as let the outlines blur, and accept that a thing happened, and one can be sorry. This is how we are today, but it does not have to be tomorrow as well.'

'You forgive very easily, Reavley,' Thyer said

coolly. 'I wonder sometimes if you've ever had anything very much to forgive? Or are you too Christian to feel real anger?'

'You mean too anaemic to feel anything with real passion,' Joseph corrected for him.

Thyer blushed. 'I'm sorry, that was irredeemably rude. I do beg your pardon.'

'Perhaps I shouldn't weigh things so much before I speak,' Joseph said thoughtfully. 'It makes me sound pompous, even a little cold. But I am too afraid of what I might say if I don't.'

Thyer smiled, an expression of startling warmth.

Connie looked taken by surprise, and she turned away. 'Please come in to dinner, Mr Allard,' she invited Gerald, who was moving from one foot to the other and plainly at a total loss. 'We will help no one by not eating. We shall need our strength, if only to support each other.'

He offered her his arm, and Joseph walked in behind them with Thyer.

★ ★ ★

Joseph spent a miserable night, twisting himself round and round in his bed, his thoughts preventing him from sleeping. Small recollections came back to his mind: Connie and Beecher laughing together over some trivial thing, but the sound of it so rich, so full of joy; Connie's face as she had listened to him talking about some esoteric discovery in the Middle East. Beecher's concern when she had a summer cold, his fear that it might be flu, or even turn to pneumonia. And other more shadowy incidents, which now seemed out of proportion to the casual friendship they claimed.

What had Sebastian known . . . exactly? Had he threatened Beecher openly, or simply allowed fear and guilt to play their part? Was it possible he had been innocent of anything more than a keener observation than others?

But Beecher had been with Connie and Thyer when the Reavleys had been killed — not that Joseph had ever suspected him of that! And Perth said he had been along the Backs when Sebastian was shot, so he could not be guilty.

What about Connie? He could not imagine Connie shooting Sebastian. She was generous, charming, quick to laugh, just as quick to see another's need or loneliness, and to do all she could to answer it. But she was a woman of passion. She might love Beecher profoundly, and be trapped by circumstance. If she were discovered in an affair with him and it were made public, he would lose his position, but she would lose everything. A woman divorced for adultery ceased to exist even to her friends, let alone to the rest of society.

Would Sebastian really have done that to her?

The young man Joseph had known would have found it a repulsive thought, cruel, dishonour-able, destructive to the soul. But had that man existed, outside Joseph's imagination?

He fell asleep not sure of what was certain about anyone, even himself. He woke in the morning with his head pounding, and deter-mined to learn beyond dispute all the facts that he could. Everything he cared about was slithering out of his grasp. He needed something to hold on to.

It was barely six o'clock, but he would begin immediately. It was an excellent time to walk along the Backs himself and find Carter the boatman, who had apparently spoken with Beecher on the morning of Sebastian's death. He shaved, washed and dressed in a matter of minutes, and set out in the cool clarity of the morning light.

The grass was still drenched with dew, giving it a pearly, almost turquoise sheen, and the motionless trees towered into the air in unbroken silence.

He found Carter down at the mooring, about a mile along the bank.

'Mornin', Dr Reavley,' Carter greeted him cheerfully. 'Yer out early, sir.'

'Can't sleep,' Joseph replied.

'Oi can't these days neither,' Carter agreed. 'Everybody's frettin'. Newspapers flying off the stands. Got to get 'em early to be sure o' one. Never seen a toime loike it, 'cepting when the old Queen were ill.' He scratched his head. 'Not even then, really. Howsoever, we all knew what the end o' that would be, God bless 'er. Sure as for all of us, sooner or later.'

'It's the best time of the morning,' Joseph said, glancing around him at the slow-moving river shimmering in the sun.

'It is that,' Carter agreed.

'I thought I might see Dr Beecher along here. He hasn't been this way already, has he?'

'Dr Beecher? No, sir. Comes occasional, loike, but not very often.'

'He's a friend of mine.'

'Nice gentleman, sir. Friend to a lot o' folk,' Carter nodded. 'Always got a good word. Talked a bit about them ole riverboats. Interested, he is, though between you an' me, Oi think he do it only to be agreeable. He knows Oi get lonely since moi Bessie died, and a bit of a chat sets me up for the day.'

That was the Beecher Joseph knew, a man of great kindness, which he always masked as something else so there was never debt.

'You must have been talking together when young Allard was killed,' he remarked. How bare that sounded.

'Not that mornin', sir,' Carter shook his head. 'Oi tole the police gentleman it were because Oi forgot, but that were the day Oi 'ad the bad puncture. Oi had to fix it, an' it took me an age 'cos it were in two places, an' Oi didn't see it at first. An hour late home, Oi were. O' course, Dr Beecher must've bin 'ere if he said so, but Oi didn't see him 'cos Oi weren't, if you get me?'

'Yes . . . ' Joseph said slowly, his own voice sounding far away, as if it belonged to someone else. 'Yes . . . I see. Thank you.' And he turned and walked slowly along the grass.

Did he have a moral obligation to tell Perth? He had agreed that the law was above them all, and it was. But he needed to be sure. Right now he was certain of nothing at all.

12

On Saturday afternoon Matthew dined with
Joseph at The Pickerel, overlooking the river.
There were just as many people there as always,
sitting around the tables, leaning forward in
conversation, but voices were lower than a week
ago, and there was less laughter. Punts still
drifted back and forth on the water, young men
balancing in the sterns with long poles clasped,
some with grace, others with precarious
awkwardness. Girls, wind catching the gossamer-
like sleeves of their pale dresses, lay half reclined
on the seats. Some wore sweeping hats, or hats
decked with flowers to shade their faces, others
had parasols of muslin or lace, which dappled
the light. One girl, bare-headed, with russet hair,
trailed a slender arm into the river, her skin
brown from the sun, her fingers shedding bright
drops behind her in the golden light.

'One of us ought to go home,' Matthew said,
reaching his knife into the Belgian pâté and
spreading more of it on to his toast. 'It ought to
be you, and anyway, I need to go and see
Shanley Corcoran again. He's about the only
person I dare trust, with things as they are.'

'Are you any further?' Joseph asked, then
immediately wished he hadn't. He saw the
frustration in Matthew's face and knew the
answer. Neither of them was prepared to say,
even to each other, that perhaps John Reavley

had been mistaken. It was childish to want or expect those we love always to be right, but Joseph, at least, was not yet ready to concede defeat, not aloud where someone else would know.

Matthew ate another mouthful before replying. He swallowed and drank the last of his red wine, then poured himself more before replying.

'Only ideas. Shearing doesn't think it is an Irish plot. He seems to be trying to steer me away from it, although I have to admit his logic is pretty sound.' He reached for more butter. 'But then, of course, I don't know beyond any doubt at all that he isn't the one behind it.'

'We don't know that about anyone, do we?' Joseph asked. He was thinking of the illusions he had seen splintered into pieces in the last few days. He had thought nothing would hurt him more than the revelations about Sebastian, but he was still amazed how sharp the pain was that he had ever allowed the possibility into his mind that it could have been Beecher who killed him.

'Not really,' Matthew agreed. 'Except Shanley. That's why I need to speak to him. There's . . . ' He looked across the river, narrowing his eyes against the brilliance of the lowering sun. 'There's a possibility it could be an assassination attempt against the King, although the more I consider it, the less certain I am that anyone would benefit from it. I don't know what I think any more.'

Joseph knew exactly what his brother was thinking — how would he face the fact that John Reavley might have been magnifying something out of all proportion without feeling as if he were betraying him? It mattered that he had been right, to Joseph to whom it would satisfy his fierce, defensive love, and to Matthew who craved a vindication at last of his own profession. By coming to him with the document, John had acknowledged his skill, and asked his help. For him to have been misguided now would be another kind of betrayal, because in the end it would finally prove him deluded, and inept. And it would matter to Judith. She had loved him intensely. All her rebellion, her wilfulness, was against life, against people's expectancy of her. She accused him of being restrictive, yet she wanted the limits he made for her. It was her safety, and the sudden removal of it was the worst thing that had happened in her life. She was filled with anger against whoever had killed him. She could not bear it if it were his own stupidity, if his going were his own fault.

And for all their differences, in a way that was exactly what Hannah would feel, except it would be Alys's death for which she would blame him the most.

But the one reality that remained was that they were dead, and the questions twisted inside Joseph: why? For what?

'There was a document,' he said. 'And whatever was in it, it was sufficient for someone to kill him.'

Matthew looked weary. 'Perhaps it was evidence of a crime,' he said flatly. 'Simply a piece of ordinary greed. Maybe we were looking beyond the mark, for something wildly political, involving the grand tide of history, and it was only a grubby little bank robbery, or fraud.'

'Two copies of it?' Joseph said sceptically.

Matthew lifted his head, his eyes widening. 'It might make sense! Copies for different people? What if it were a stock market scandal, or something of that nature? I'm going to see Shanley tomorrow. He'll have connections in the City, and at least he would know where to start. If only Father had said more!' He leaned forward, his food forgotten. 'Look, Joe, one of us has got to go and spend a little time with Judith. We've both been neglecting her. Hannah's taken it all very hard, but at least she's got Archie some of the time, and the children. Judith's got nothing really.'

'I know,' Joseph agreed quickly, guilt biting deep. He had written to both Judith and Hannah, but since he was only a few miles away from his younger sister, that was not enough.

There was a short burst of laughter from the next table, and then a sudden silence. Someone rushed into speech, something completely irrelevant, about a new novel published. No one responded and he tried again.

'Anything more on Sebastian Allard?' Matthew asked, his face gentle, sensing the slow discovery of ugliness, the falling apart of beliefs that had been held dear for so long.

Joseph hesitated. It would be a relief to share his thoughts, even if as soon as tomorrow he would wish he had not. 'Actually . . . yes,' he said slowly, not looking at Matthew but beyond him. The light was fading on the river and the spill of scarlet and yellow like fire poured out across the flat horizon from the trees over by Haslingfield right across to the roofs of Madingley.

'I've discovered Sebastian was capable of blackmail,' he said miserably. Even the words hurt. 'I think he blackmailed Harry Beecher over his love for the Master's wife. For nothing so obvious as money — just for favour, and I think maybe for the taste of power. It would have amused him to exert just a very subtle pressure, but one that Beecher didn't dare resist.'

'Are you sure?' Matthew asked, his face puckering with doubt. There was not the denial in his voice Joseph hungered to hear. He had overstated the case deliberately, waiting for Matthew to say it was nonsense. Why didn't he?

'No!' he replied. 'No, I'm not sure! But it looks like it. He lied as to where he was. He's engaged to a girl his mother probably picked out for him, but he's got a girlfriend of his own in one of the pubs in Cambridge.' He saw Matthew's look of amusement. 'I know you think that's just natural youth,' he said angrily. 'But Mary Allard won't! And I don't think Regina Coopersmith, the fiancée, will either, if she ever finds out.'

'All right, it's a bit shabby,' Matthew agreed, the flicker of humour still in his eyes. 'A last fling before the doors of propriety close him in for ever with 'Mother's choice'. Why hadn't he the guts to say so?'

'I've no idea! I didn't know anything about it! Anyway, he would never have married Flora, for heaven's sake. She's a barmaid. She's also a pacifist.'

Matthew's eyebrows shot up. 'A pacifist? Or do you mean she agreed with whatever her current admirer happened to say?'

Joseph considered for only a moment. 'No, I don't think I do. She seemed to know quite a lot about it.'

'For God's sake, Joe!' Matthew sat back with a jerk, sliding the chair legs on the floor. 'She doesn't have to be stupid, just because she pulls ale for the local lads!'

'Don't be so patronizing!' Joseph snapped back. 'I didn't say she was stupid. I said she knew more about pacifism, and Sebastian's views on the subject, than to have been merely an agreeable listener. He was drifting away from his roots at a speed which probably frightened him. His mother idolized him. To her he was all she wished her husband could have been — brilliant, beautiful, charming, a dreamer with the passion to achieve his goals.'

'Rather a heavy weight to carry — the garment of someone else's dreams,' Matthew observed a great deal more gently, and with a note of sadness. 'Especially a mother. There'd be no escaping that.'

'No,' Joseph said thoughtfully. 'Except by smashing it, and there would be a strong temptation to do that!' He looked curiously at Matthew to see if he understood. His answer was immediate in the flash of knowledge in Matthew's eyes. 'It's not always as simple as we think, is it?' he finished.

'Is that what you believe?' Matthew asked. 'Somehow Sebastian was making a bid for freedom, and it went wrong?'

'I really don't know,' Joseph admitted, looking away again, across the river. The girl with the bright hair was gone, and the young man who balanced with such grace. 'But very little I've found out so far fits the idea of him I had — which makes me wonder if I was almost as guilty as Mary Allard of building a prison for him to live in.'

'Don't be so hard on yourself,' Matthew said gently. 'He built his own image. It may have been in part an illusion, but he was the chief architect of it; you only helped. And believe me, he was happy to let you. But if he did see what happened on the Hauxton Road, why wouldn't he say something?' His brow furrowed, his eyes shadowed and intense. 'Do you think he was mad enough to try blackmail on someone he knew had already killed two people? Was he really such a complete fool?'

Put like that it sounded not only extreme, but dangerous beyond any possible profit. And surely he would have known the people killed were Joseph's parents? Even if not at the time, then later?

'No,' he answered, but there was no conviction in his voice. Matthew would never have done such a thing, but he was used to thinking in terms of danger. He was only a few years older than Sebastian, in fact, but in experience it was decades. To Sebastian death was a concept not a reality, and he had all the passionate, innocent

392

belief in his own immortality that goes with youth.

Matthew was watching him. 'Be careful, Joe,' he warned. 'Whatever the reason, someone killed him, and someone in college. Don't go poking around in it, please! You aren't equipped!' Anger and frustration flickered in his eyes, and fear. 'You're too hurt by it to see straight!'

Joseph looked at the emotion in Matthew's face and felt the warmth of it like a balm over his own feelings. 'I have to try,' he said, reasserting reason. It was the one sanity to hold on to. 'Suspicion is tearing the college to pieces. Everyone is doubting things, friendships are cracking, loyalties twisted. I need to know for myself. It's my world . . . I have to do something to protect it.'

He looked down. 'And if Sebastian did see what happened on the Hauxton Road, there may be some way of finding out.' He met Matthew's steady blue-grey eyes. 'I have to try. Was he saying something to me that last evening on the Backs, and I wasn't listening? The more I think of it, the more I realise he was far more distressed than I understood then. I should have been more sensitive, more available. If I'd known what it was, I might have saved him.'

Matthew clasped his hand over Joseph's wrist for a moment, then let go again. 'Possibly,' he said with doubt. 'Or you might have been killed as well. You don't know if it had anything to do with that at all. At least for this weekend, go and see Judith. She's our world too, and she needs someone, preferably you.' It was said gently, but it was a charge, not a suggestion.

Matthew offered to drive him, and no doubt Judith would have brought him back, but Joseph wanted the chance to be alone for the short while it would take him to ride there on his bicycle. He needed time to think before meeting Judith.

He thanked Matthew, but declined, then walked briskly back to St John's to collect a few overnight things such as his razor and clean linen, then took his bicycle and set out.

As soon as he was beyond the town the quiet lanes enclosed him, wrapping him in the shadows of deep hedges, motionless in the twilight. The fields smelled of harvest, that familiar dry sweetness of dust, crushed stalks and fallen grain. A few starlings were black dots against the blue of the sky, fading grey already to the east. The long light made the shadows of the hay stooks enormous across the stubble.

There was a hurt in the beauty of it, as if something were slipping out of his grip, and nothing he could do would prevent his losing it. Summer always drifted into autumn. It was as it should be. There would be the wild colour, the falling of the leaves, the scarlet berries, the smell of turned earth, woodsmoke, damp; then winter, stinging cold, freezing the earth, cracking and breaking the clods, ice on the branches like white lace. There would be rain, snow, biting winds, and then spring again, delirious with blossom.

But his own certainties had fallen away. The safety he had built so carefully after Eleanor's death, thinking it the one indestructible thing, the path towards understanding the ways of God, even accepting them, was full of sudden weaknesses. It was a path across the abyss of pain, and it had given way under his weight. He was falling.

And here he was, almost home where he was supposed to be the kind of strength for Judith that his father would have been. He had not watched closely enough, and John had never spoken of it, never shown him the needs, and the words to fill them. He was not ready!

But now he was in the main street. The houses were sleepy in the dusk, the windows lit. Here and there a door was open, the air was still warm. The sound of voices drifted out. Shummer Munn was pulling weeds in his garden. Grumble Runham was standing on the street corner lighting his clay pipe. He grunted as Joseph passed him, and gave a perfunctory wave.

Joseph slowed. He was almost home. It was too late to find any answers to give Judith, or any wiser, greater strength.

He turned the corner and pedalled the final hundred yards. He arrived as the last light was fading, and put his bicycle away in the garage beside Judith's Model T, finding the space huge and profoundly empty where the Lanchester should have been. He walked around the side and went past the kitchen garden, stopping to pick a handful of sharp, sweet raspberries and eat them, then went in through the back door.

Mrs Appleton was standing over the sink.

'Oh! Mr Joseph, you give me such a start!' she

said abruptly. 'Not that Oi in't pleased to see you, mind.' She squinted at him. ' 'Ave you had any supper? Or a glass of lemonade, mebbe? You look awful hot.'

'I cycled over from Cambridge,' he explained, smiling at her. The kitchen was familiar, full of comfortable smells.

'Oi'll fetch you some from the pantry.' She dried her hands. 'Oi dare say as you could eat some scones and butter too? Oi made 'em today. Oi'll fetch 'em to the sitting room for you. That's where Miss Judith is. She in't expecting you, is she? She din't say nothing to me! But your bed's all made up, loike always.'

'Thank you,' he accepted, already feeling the warmth of home settle around him, holding him in a kind of safety. He knew every gleam of the polished wood, just where the dents were, the thin patches worn into carpets by generations of use, the very slight dips in the floorboards, which stairs creaked, where the shadows fell at what time of day. He could smell lavender and beeswax polish, flowers, hay on the wind from outside.

Judith was sitting curled up on the couch with her head bent over a book. Her hair was pulled up hastily, a little lopsided. She looked absorbed and unhappy, hunched into herself. She did not hear him come in.

'Good book?' he asked.

'Not bad,' she replied, uncurling herself and standing up, letting the book fall closed on to the small table, losing her place in it. She looked at him guardedly; she was smiling a little, but it was

396

polite, without any candour. She was keeping her emotions protected in case he hurt her by being less than she needed, by not having the strength or the belief. 'I like my fairy tales with a little more reality,' she added. 'This is too sweet to be believable — or I suppose any good, really. Who cares if the heroine wins, if there wasn't any battle?'

'Only herself, I imagine.' He looked at her more closely. There were shadows of tiredness around her eyes and very little colour in her skin. She was dressed in a pale green skirt, which was flattering because she moved with grace, but very ordinary. Her white cotton blouse was such as most young women choose in country villages: high to the neck, shaped to fit, and with minimum decoration. She was not interested in whether it pleased anyone else or not. He realised with a sense of shock the change in her in a few weeks. The regularity of her features was still there, the gentleness of her mouth, but the vitality that made her beautiful was gone.

'Mrs Appleton's bringing me some scones and lemonade. Would you like any?' he said it to break the silence. He was thinking how badly he had neglected her. He had allowed himself to become swallowed up in his own anger and confusion over Sebastian's murder, perhaps to divert his emotions from his parents' deaths. She had nothing to do with that. And she was alone here in the house where they should have been, reminded every day by the silence, the absence that ached like a tooth eaten out by decay.

'No, thanks,' she replied. 'I've already had

some. Did you come home for anything in particular? I suppose they don't know who killed Sebastian Allard yet? I'm sorry about that.' She met his eyes, trying to read if he was hurting, if there were anything she could say or do to help.

He sat down, deliberately choosing his father's chair. 'Not yet. I'm not even sure if they're getting any closer.'

She sat down also. 'What about Mother and Father?' she said with a slight break in her voice. She was searching his face, her eyes probing. 'Matthew doesn't tell me anything. Sometimes I think he forgets I even know about it being murder, or about the document. We still get the papers, and the news is awful. Everyone in the village is talking about the possibility of war.' She was waiting for him to say something that would comfort her, make sense of it all so she could begin to pick up the broken pieces and start again.

Mrs Appleton brought in his scones and juice and he thanked her. When she had gone he looked at Judith again, and realised how little he knew her inner strengths and weaknesses. Could she bear the truth that they had no idea who had killed John Reavley, or that his whole judgement of the document could be flawed? He might have died for a simple crime of greed. Could she bear to know that war was a real possibility that nobody could measure? The whole future lay ahead clouded and uncertain — perhaps worse than that, even tragic.

Now he was supposed to say to her whatever her father would have said, something to give her courage without frightening her, something for her to rely on and give her strength. Except that he did not know what that was. He did not really know Judith. He had been there all her life. He could have recounted the important dates and events, but he was bitterly aware that he knew nothing of her thoughts except the little she had chosen to tell him. He had been content with that. She was twenty-three now; a woman, not the child he had known.

A hard knot of anger clenched inside him against his father for expecting this of him, without warning. It should not be his job. He was inadequate to it; he had already proved that with Sebastian, and all the other young men at St John's for whom he was supposed to be a spiritual anchor.

He ate the scones; they were crumbly and fresh and piled with butter. The lemonade was sharp, cleaning the mouth.

John Reavley should have had more sense than to be so stupid, telling Matthew he had a document that could rock the world, and then driving unprotected along the road, for someone to kill — and not only him, but Alys as well!

'Well, are they right?' Judith demanded, an edge to her voice. 'Is there going to be a war? You can't be so isolated in your ivory tower that you don't know Austria and Serbia are on the brink!'

'I'm not.' He said it with the sharpness of his own anger and frustration. 'Yes they are, and I expect Austria will march into Serbia and conquer them again.'

'If that happens they're talking about Russia

getting involved as well,' she persisted.

Why couldn't she accept what he had told her? He looked across at her troubled face, and knew there was a long way for him to go before he satisfied her, even if he managed to make her stop asking. It would be an evasion, brought about in order to ease himself. His father would not have done that. It was self-serving, even cowardly.

'It's possible all Europe could be involved,' he said, meeting her eyes. 'It's not likely, but if it does happen then we may be drawn in. It's also possible that they will come back from the brink, seeing what it will cost them.'

'And if they don't?' She struggled to keep her voice level, but her face was white.

He stood up and walked over to the french windows opening on to the garden.

'Then we'll have to conduct ourselves with honour, and do what we've always done — send our armies to the battle,' he replied. 'I dare say it won't last very long. It's not Africa, where there are vast stretches of open country to hide.' She must have risen to her feet also, because she spoke from just behind him. 'I suppose not.' She hesitated a moment. 'Joseph, do you think that was what Father knew about? I mean something to do with the assassination in Sarajevo? Could he have stumbled on to the plan for that?'

Did she want to believe it? It would be far easier than supposing some new danger. It was a moment of judgement. Evasion, or the truth that he did not know? 'Perhaps,' he agreed, walking out on to the grass. She followed him. The early evening was balmy and softly scented with the heavy sweetness of pinks and late lilies. 'Maybe there was no date on it, and he didn't realise it was planned for that day.'

'No, it wasn't,' she said grimly. 'That doesn't have anything to do with England's honour!' He heard the vibrancy in her voice. She was angry, alive again. 'Don't condescend to me, Joseph!' She caught his arm. 'I hate it when you do that! Killing an Austrian archduke has got nothing to do with England.'

'It was your suggestion,' he pointed out, stung by her remark about his condescension, because he knew it was true. Evasion had been a mistake.

'And it was stupid,' she went on. 'Why can't you tell me I'm stupid honestly? Don't always be so damn polite! I'm not your congregation — and you're not my father! But I suppose you're trying to be, and at least you're somebody I can talk to properly.'

'Thank you,' he said drily. It was a back-handed compliment he had not deserved, and he was disturbed by how much it mattered to him.

They passed the border and were snared in the warm, sweet perfume. A barn owl swooped low between the trees and disappeared on soundless wings.

'Don't you want to know what the document was?' she asked.

'Of course I do.'

He stopped at the edge of the lawn and Judith stood beside him. 'Then we ought to be able to find out where he got it, surely?' she said. 'He

401

can't have had it very long, or he would have taken it to Matthew sooner.' Her voice was steady now, some inner resolve asserting itself.

'We've already tried to find out everywhere he went for several days before that,' Joseph answered. 'He saw the bank manager, Robert Isenham, and old Mr Frawley who keeps the curiosity shop up on the Cambridge Road.' He looked at her gently. 'He and Frawley know each other pretty well. If Father had just discovered anything awful, Frawley would have known there was something wrong.'

'Mother went to see Maude Channery the day Father called Matthew,' she said seriously.

'Who is Maude Channery?' If he knew he had forgotten.

'One of Mother's 'good causes',' she answered, struggling for a moment to keep her voice level. 'Father couldn't bear her, said she was a fearful old fraud, but he drove Mother there anyway.'

'He'd have to, if it was far,' he pointed out. 'Unless you did — and Mother would never go to visit anyone important in your Model T! Not if the Lanchester were available.'

'I could have driven her in the Lanchester,' she argued.

'Oh? Since when could you drive that?' he said, surprised. 'Or more to the point, since when would Father have let you?'

'Since he couldn't stand Maude Channery,' she retorted, a tiny flash of humour in her voice. 'But he didn't. He took Mother. And when they came back he went straight to his study, and Mother and I had supper alone.'

402

Joseph hesitated. The idea was absurd. 'Surely you aren't suggesting he got a document of international importance from an old woman who was one of Mother's 'good causes'?'

'I don't know! Can you think of somewhere better to start? You haven't got anything, and neither has Matthew.'

'We'll go and see her tomorrow, if you like,' he offered.

She gave him a wry look, and he knew it was on the tip of her tongue to tell him again not to be so condescending, but instead she simply accepted. She said that they would make it a morning call — before he could change his mind — and she would be ready at ten.

★   ★   ★

Joseph woke up early. It was a warm, blustery day, the wind full of the fine dust of the first crops being gathered. He walked down to the village and collected the Sunday papers from Cully Teversham at the tobacconists, and exchanged the usual pleasantries, a word about the weather, a spot of local gossip, and left to go home again. He passed a few neighbours on the way, and nodded good morning.

He intended not to open the papers until breakfast, but his curiosity overcame him. The news was worse than he had expected. Serbia had rejected Austrian demands and diplomatic relations had been broken off. It seemed like the prelude to war. Russia had declared that it would act to protect Serbia's interests. Who would win the Tour de France seemed like an issue from another era already sliding into the past, almost irretrievable even now, and a visit to Maude Channery was the last thing on his mind.

But he had promised Judith, and at least it would make up for some of the time he had been so absorbed with his own emotions that he had forgotten hers.

They set off at ten o'clock, but it took them until after half-past to drive as far as Cherry Hinton. After making enquiries at the village shop, they found Fen Cottage on the outskirts, and parked the car just around the corner.

They had knocked twice on the front door before it swung open and they were faced by a short, elderly woman leaning heavily on a walking stick. It was not an elegant cane with a silver tip, but a plain, stout wooden affair, such as a man would use to bear his weight. Her face was set in irritation and her frizzy, white hair was pinned up in a style twenty years out of fashion. Her black skirts brushed the floor and looked as if she inherited them from someone at least three inches taller.

'If yer lookin' for the Taylors, they moved six months back, and Oi dunno where to,' she said abruptly. 'And if it's anyone else, ask Porky Andrews at the shop. He knows everything, and'll likely tell you, whether you care or not.' She ignored Judith and looked Joseph up and down curiously.

'Mrs Channery?' he asked. His days as a parish priest came back to his mind with cutting clarity. How often he had called on resentful people who were raw-tongued from pride, guilt, or the need to guard some pain they could neither accommodate nor share. 'I'm Joseph Reavley, and this is my sister, Judith. I believe you were a great friend of our mother's.' He did not make it a question.

'Oh!' She was taken by surprise. The tart remark she had been going to make died on her lips. Something inside her softened. 'Yes . . . well . . . well, Oi suppose Oi were. Terrible thing. I'm rale sorry. We'll all miss her. Not much point in tellin' you my sympathies. Won't do no good.'

'I'd be glad to accept a cup of tea.' Joseph was not going to be put off.

'Then you'd better come on in,' Mrs Channery responded. 'Oi don't serve on the doorstep.' And she turned round and led the way into a remarkably pleasant sitting room, beyond which lay a small, overcrowded garden backing on to the churchyard. He could clearly see a pale carved angel above the hedge, neatly outlined against the dark mass of yew trees.

Mrs Channery followed his glance. 'Humph!' she snorted. 'On good days Oi think he's watching over me . . . most times Oi say as he's just snoopin'!' She pointed to the couch and another chair. 'If you want tea Oi et to put the kettle on, so you'd best sit down whoile Oi do. Oi've got biscuits. Oi'm not cuttin' cake at this toime in the mornin'.'

Judith swallowed her temper with an effort that was visible, at least to Joseph. 'Thank you,' she said meekly. 'May I help you carry anything?'

'Great heavens, choild!' Mrs Channery

exclaimed. 'What d'you think Oi'm bringin'? It's only elevenses.'

Anger flushed up Judith's face, but she bit back her response.

Mrs Channery swivelled on her heel and disappeared into the kitchen.

Judith looked at Joseph. 'Mother deserves to be canonized for putting up with her!' she said in a savage whisper.

'I can see why Father loathed her,' he agreed. 'I wonder why he came?'

'With a sword, in case it was necessary, I should think!' Judith retorted. 'Or a packet of rat poison!'

Joseph's mind worried at the question. Why had John Reavley come here? Judith could quite easily have driven Alys, and Alys would consider it a useful lesson for her in charitable duty. John tended to avoid unpleasant people, his tolerance of rudeness was low, and he admired his wife's patience, but he had no intention of emulating it.

Mrs Channery returned, staggering a little under the weight of a large and very well-set tea tray. She had kept her word that there was no cake, but there were three different kinds of biscuits, and home-made raisin scones with plenty of butter.

Joseph leaped to his feet to help her, taking the tray before she dropped it, and setting it down on the small table next to a floral jug filled with sweet williams. The ritual of pouring, accepting, passing around the food and making appropriate remarks was all observed to the letter. It was several minutes before Joseph could broach the subject for which they had come. He had given it some thought, but now it seemed foolish. The only thing to be gained by this visit was the time spent with Judith. On the way over they had spoken of odd, unimportant things, but she had seemed to be easier, and once or twice she had actually laughed.

'You have a lovely garden,' Joseph remarked conversationally.

'It's all over tossled,' Mrs Channery retorted. 'Oi can't be frabbed doin' the work, and I can't be payin' that daft man what does Mrs Copthorne's. She pays him twice what he's worth . . . the more fool her! And it's still full o' meece! I seen 'em!'

Joseph could sense Judith biting her tongue. 'Perhaps that's why I like it,' he replied, refusing to be put off.

'Makes yours look good, do it?' Mrs Channery demanded.

'Yes, it does,' he agreed, smiling at her. Out of the corner of his eye he saw Judith's expression of disgust. He noticed an enormous borage plant overtaking its neighbours. 'And you have quite a few herbs.'

'Gardener, are you?' Mrs Channery said drily. 'Thought you was an airy-fairy sort o' man up at the university.'

'One can be both,' he pointed out. 'My father was, but I expect you know that.'

'No idea,' she responded. 'Scarce saw 'im. Long enough to be civil, and then 'e were off again like Oi'd bit him.'

Judith sneezed — at least it sounded

something like a sneeze.

'Really?' Joseph said, suddenly his attention held as if in a vice. 'He didn't stay with Mother the last time she was here?'

'Din't even stay for tea,' she shook her head. 'Chocolate cake, Oi 'ad. An' Madeira, both. Looked at it loike 'e 'adn't eaten for a week, then went straight out o' the door and got into that great big yellow car of 'is. Smelly things, cars,' she added. 'An' noisy. Dunno why a civilised man can't use an 'orse an' carriage. Good enough for the Queen, God bless her memory.' Her lips thinned, and she blinked several times. 'Don't get horses going mad an' running all off the road into the trees and killing good folk!'

'Yes, you do!' Judith contradicted her. 'Hundreds of horses have taken fright at something and bolted, taking carriages off the road, into trees, hedges, ditches, rivers even. You can't spook a car. It doesn't take fright at thunder, or lightning, or a flapping piece of cloth.' She drew in her breath. 'And wheels fall off carriages just as often as off cars.'

'Thought you'd lost your tongue,' Mrs Channery said with satisfaction. 'Found it again, 'ave you? Well, nothin' you say'll get me into one of them machines!'

'Then I shan't try,' Judith answered, exactly as if it had been the next thing she had intended. 'Do you know where he went?'

'Who? Your father? Do you think Oi asked him, Miss Reavley? That would be very ill-fatched up o' me, now wouldn't it?'

Judith's eyes widened for a moment. 'Of

course you wouldn't, Mrs Channery. But he might have said. I imagine it wasn't a secret.'

'Then you imagine wrong,' Mrs Channery pronounced with immense pleasure. 'It were a secret. Your dear ma asked him, and he went four wont ways about answerin'. Just said he'd be back for her in an hour . . . an' 'e weren't! Took him an hour and a half, but she never said a word.' She fixed Judith with an accusing eye. 'Good woman, your ma was! No one left like her no more.'

'I know,' Judith said quietly.

Mrs Channery grunted. 'Shouldn't 'ave said that,' she apologized. 'Not that it ain't true. But it don't do no good cryin'. Not what she'd have wanted. Very sensible woman, she were. Lots o' patience with others what was all but useless, but none for 'erself. And she'd 'ave expected you to be like 'er!'

Judith glared at her, angry not only at what she had said, but that she, of all people, should have known Alys well enough to have understood so much about her.

'You were very fond of her,' Joseph observed, to fill the silence more than anything else.

Mrs Channery's lips trembled for a moment. 'O' course Oi were!' she snapped at him. 'She knew how to be kind without lookin' down on folks, and there ain't many what can do that! She never come by without askin' first, and she ate my cake. Never brought any of her own, like needing to keep score. But she brought me jam now and then. Apricot. An' Oi never told her as how the rhubarb jam was 'orrible. Like so much boiled string, it were. Oi gave it to Diddy Warner, 'er with the toddy-grass all up in the air like a gummidge. That surprised 'er. Should have seen the look on 'er face.' She smiled with satisfaction.

'With the hair like a scarecrow?' Judith clarified.

'In't that what I just said?' Mrs Channery asked.

'I can imagine!' Judith said frankly. 'She was the one who gave it to Mother! It was disgusting.'

To Joseph's amazement Mrs Channery burst into laughter. It was a deep, chesty guffaw of delight, and she laughed so hard he was afraid she was going to choke. The sound was so genuine and so infectious, he found himself joining in, and then after a moment, Judith did also. Suddenly he knew why his mother had bothered with Maude Channery.

They stayed another half-hour, and left in surprisingly good spirits, but walking back to the car they were serious again.

'Father went somewhere,' Judith said urgently, catching Joseph's sleeve and forcing him to stop. 'How can we find out where? He was different when he returned, and that night he called Matthew. It has to be where he got the document!'

'Perhaps,' he agreed, trying to keep his thoughts in check.

They started walking again. He wanted intensely to believe that there really had been a document of the importance his father had attached to it. But then, why had no one found it?

They reached the car.

'What are we going to do?' Judith demanded, slamming the door as Joseph cranked up the handle at the front and the engine jumped to life. He took the handle out and climbed in beside her, closing his own door more gently. The car moved away and she changed gear with practised ease.

'We're going home to see what Appleton knows about where the car went,' Joseph replied.

'Father wouldn't have told him.' She steered with panache around the corner and into the main road from Cherry Hinton back towards St Giles.

'Doesn't Appleton still clean the car?' he asked.

She glanced at him sideways, and increased speed.

He put out a hand to steady himself.

'Of course he does,' Judith answered. 'You think he'd have noticed something? Such as what?'

'We'll ask him. And from what Mrs Channery said, Mother was there an hour and a half, so he can only have gone a certain distance. We ought to be able to narrow it down. If we ask, someone will have seen him. The Lanchester was rather noticeable.'

'Yes!' she said exuberantly, pressing her foot down harder on the accelerator and sending the car forward at nearly fifty miles an hour.

Asking Appleton turned out to be a delicate matter. They found him in the garden staking up the last of the delphiniums, which were beginning to sag under their own weight.

'Albert,' Joseph began, admiring the flowers without saying so; their colour was dazzling, 'when my father returned from taking Mother to visit Mrs Channery at Cherry Hinton, did you clean the car afterwards?'

Appleton straightened up, his face dark. 'O' course Oi cleaned the car, Mr Joseph! And checked the brakes and the fuel and the tyres! If you think Oi din't — '

'I want to work out where he went!' Joseph said quickly, realising what accusation Appleton had assumed. 'I thought you might be able to help me, from anything you observed.'

'Went?' Appleton was confused. 'He took Mrs Reavley to Cherry Hinton.'

'Yes, I know. But he left her there, and went somewhere else, then came back for her.'

Appleton tied up the last sky-blue delphiniums absent-mindedly, and stepped out of the flowerbed on to the path. 'You think summin' 'appened to the car?'

'No, I think perhaps he saw someone, and I need to know who it was.' He did not intend to tell Appleton more than that. 'It's about three and a half miles from here to Cherry Hinton. Is there any way you can tell how much further he went?'

'Course Oi can. Just got to look at the

mileometer. That'll tell you pretty exact. Course, it won't say where to, only how far.'

Joseph felt the silence settle into the hot garden with its motionless flowers, gaudy splashes of colour, butterflies pinned like precarious ornaments on to the lilies.

'Did you see anything at all that would help us to know where they went?'

Appleton screwed up his face.

'Dust?' Joseph suggested. 'Gravel? Mud? Clay? Peat, maybe? Or manure? Tar?'

'Loime . . . ' Appleton said slowly. 'There was loime under the wheel arches. Et to wash it off.'

'Lime kilns!' Joseph exclaimed. 'He was gone an hour and a half altogether. How fast does the Lanchester go? Forty . . . fifty-five?'

'Mr Reavley was a very good driver,' Appleton said pointedly, looking at the path where Judith was coming towards them. 'More loike thirty-five.'

'I see.'

Judith reached them and looked enquiringly from Joseph to Appleton and back again.

'Appleton found lime on the car,' Joseph said to her. 'Where are the nearest lime kilns, close enough to the road that the lime itself would be tracked across, so someone would pick it up?'

'There are lime kilns on the roads south and east out of Cherry Hinton itself,' she answered. 'Not west back to St Giles or Cambridge, or north towards Teversham or Fen Ditton.'

'So what lies south or east?' Joseph said urgently.

'Stapleford, Great Shelford,' she said thought-fully, as if picturing the map in her mind. 'To the east there's Fulbourn, or Great and Little Wilbraham. Where shall we start?'

'Shelford's only a couple of miles from here,' he replied. 'We could start there, and work our way north and east. Thank you, Appleton.'

'Yes, sir. Will there be anything else?' Appleton looked puzzled and faintly unhappy.

'No . . . thank you. Unless there's anything my father might have said about where he went?'

'No, sir, not that Oi can think. Will you be taking the car out again, Miss Judith? Or shall Oi put it away?'

'We'll be going straight out, thank you,' she replied firmly, turning back towards the house without waiting for Joseph.

'What shall we say to the people if we find out where he got the document?' she asked when they were on their way out of St Giles again on the road southwards, climbing almost immedi-ately up into the shallow hills. She kept her eyes on the road ahead. 'They'll know who we are, and they have to realise why we've come?' It was a question, but there was no hesitation in her voice, and her hands were strong and comfort-able on the wheel. If there was tension in her, she masked it completely.

Joseph had not thought of that in detail; all that weighed on his mind was the compulsion to know the truth and silence the doubts.

'I don't know,' he answered her. 'Mrs Channery was easy enough; it seemed like following Mother's footsteps. I suppose we could say he left something behind?'

'Like what?' she said with faint derision. 'An umbrella? In the hottest, driest summer we've had in years! A coat? Gloves?'

'A picture,' he answered, the solution coming to him the instant before he spoke. 'He had a picture he was going to sell. Are they the people he was going to show it to?'

'That sounds reasonable. Yes . . . good.' Unconsciously she increased the speed and the car surged forward, all but clipping the edge of the grass on the side of the road.

'Judith!' he cried out involuntarily.

'Don't be stuffy!' she retorted, but she did slow down. She had been almost out of control, and she knew it even better than he did. What it took him longer to realise, and he did it with surprise, was that it was exuberance that drove her, the feeling that at last she was able to do something, however slight the chances of success. It was not fear, either of the process or the discovery of facts she might find painful.

He was looking at the profile of her face, seeing the woman in her and beginning to understand how far behind the child had become when she turned and shot him a glance, and then a quick smile.

He drew breath to tell her to concentrate on the road, then knew it would be wrong. He smiled back, and saw her shoulders relax.

They stopped in Shelford and asked, but no one had seen John Reavley on the Saturday before his death, and the yellow Lanchester was a car they would have remembered.

They had sandwiches and a glass of cider on the village green outside the pub at Stapleford.

Joseph was not quite sure what to say, afraid in case his voice unintentionally carried disappointment. While he was still considering, Judith began the conversation, talking about various things, interesting but inconsequential. He felt himself gradually enjoying it, his mind following hers as she spoke of Russian theatre, then Chinese pottery. She was full of opinions. He did not appreciate how hasty they were until it dawned on him that she was speaking to reassure him, to lend him the strength of normality, and of not being the leader for a little while. It amazed him, and embarrassed him a little, and yet there was a warmth to it that for an instant brought a sharp prickle to his eyes, and he was obliged to turn away.

If she noticed, she affected not to.

Afterwards they drove north again. They turned right on the Works Causeway, past the gravel pits, the clunch pit — named for the peculiar sticky local clay — and into the village of Fulbourn. It was nearly three o'clock, a bright afternoon with the heat shimmering up from the road. Even the cows in the fields sought the shade, and the dogs lying on the grass under the trees and hedges were panting contentedly.

Judith swung the car into the main village street and drew to a stop. It was almost deserted. Two boys of about seven or eight stared at them curiously. One of them had a ball clutched in a grubby hand and he smiled, showing a gap where his front tooth was still growing in. He was obviously more interested in the car than in either of its occupants.

'Ever seen a yellow car?' Joseph asked him casually.

The boy stared at him.

'Do you want to look inside?' Judith offered.

The other boy backed away, but the gap-toothed one was braver, or more curious. He nodded.

'Come on, then,' she encouraged.

Step by step he came towards the car and then finally was persuaded to peer inside the open door, while she explained to him what everything was and what it did. Finally she asked again if he had seen a yellow car.

He nodded slowly. 'Yes, miss. Bigger's this, but Oi never seed inside it.'

'When was that?'

'Donno,' he answered, still wide-eyed. 'Way back.'

And no matter how she tried, that was all he knew. She thanked him and reluctantly he allowed her to close the door. He gave her a beaming smile, then turned and ran away and disappeared into a crack between two cottages, closely followed by his companion.

'Hopeful,' Judith said with more courage than belief. 'We'll ask again.'

They found an elderly couple out walking, and a man with a dog, strolling in a side lane, thoughtfully sucking at his pipe. None of them remembered a yellow car. Neither did anyone else in Fulbourn.

'We'll have to try Great and Little Wilbraham,'

Joseph said flatly. 'Not very far.' He glanced at her, and saw the anxiety in her eyes. 'Are you all right?'

'Of course!' she answered, staring back at him levelly. 'Are you?'

He smiled at her, nodding, then started up the car again and climbed in. They headed back into Fulbourn and from there north across the railway line east to Great Wilbraham. The streets were quiet, towering trees motionless except for the topmost leaves flickering gently in the breeze. A flock of starlings swirled up in the sky. A tabby cat blinked sleepily on top of a flat gatepost. The peal of church bells sounded clear and mellow in the warm air, familiar, gentle as the smell of hay or the sunlight on the cobbles.

'Evensong,' Joseph observed. 'We'll have to wait. Would you like something to eat?'

'It's early for dinner,' she answered.

'Tea?' he suggested. 'Scones, raspberry jam and clotted cream?'

She agreed, meeting his eyes unflinchingly. 'Rather have strawberry!' she replied.

They found a teashop willing to serve them at this hour. Afterwards they went back into the street and walked up towards the church just as the congregation was leaving.

It was not easy to approach someone gracefully, and Joseph was waiting an opportunity when the vicar saw him and walked over, smiling at Judith and then speaking to Joseph.

'Good evening, sir. Another beautiful day. Sorry you're just too late for the service, but if I can be of any help?'

'Thank you.' Joseph looked around with genuine appreciation at the ancient building, the worn gravestones leaning a little crookedly in the earth. The grass between was neatly mowed, here and there fresh flowers laid in love. 'You have a beautiful church.'

'We have,' the vicar agreed happily. He looked to be in his forties, a round-faced man with a soft voice. 'Lovely village. Would you care to look around?' His glance included Judith.

'Actually I think my late father may have come here a little while ago,' Joseph replied. 'His car was rather distinctive, a yellow Lanchester.'

'Oh yes!' the vicar said with obvious pleasure. 'Delightful gentleman.' Then his face clouded. 'Did you say 'late'? I'm so sorry. Please accept my sympathies. Such a nice man. Looking for a friend of his, a German gentleman. I directed him to Frog End, where he had just rented the house.' He shook his head, biting his lip a little. 'Really very sad. Takes a lot of faith sometimes, it really does. Poor gentleman was killed in an accident just after that himself.'

Joseph was stunned. He was aware of Judith beside him drawing in her breath in a gasp. Her fingers dug into his arm. He tried to keep himself steady.

'Out walking about in the evening and must have slipped and fallen into Candle Ditch,' the vicar went on sorrowfully. 'Up where it meets the river near Fulbourn Fen.' He shook his head a little. 'He wouldn't know the area, of course. I suppose he hit his head on a stone or something. And you say your poor father died

419

recently as well? I'm so sorry.'

'Yes.' Joseph found it difficult to gather his feelings in the face of this sudden very real compassion. Indifference woke anger, or a sense of isolation, and that was in some ways easier. 'Did you know this German gentleman?'

An elderly couple passed and the vicar smiled at them, but turned back to Joseph and Judith to indicate he was engaged, and the couple moved on.

'I did not know him closely, I regret to say.' The vicar shook his head. They were still standing out on the road in the sun. 'But it was actually I who rented him the house, on behalf of the owner, you know. An elderly lady who lives abroad now. Herr Reisenburg was a very clever gentleman, so I'm told, a philosopher of some sort — kept largely to himself. Melancholy sort of person.' Grief filled his mild face. 'Not that he wasn't very pleasant, but I sensed a certain trouble within him. At least that's what I thought. My wife tells me I imagine too much.'

'I think perhaps you were correct, and it was sensitivity rather than imagination,' Joseph said gently. 'Did you say his name was Reisenburg?'

The vicar nodded. 'Yes, that's right, Reisenburg. Very distinguished-looking gentleman he was, tall and a little stooping, and softly spoken. Excellent English. He said he liked it here . . . ' He stopped with a sigh. 'Oh dear. So much pain sometimes. I gathered from the gentleman in the yellow car that they were friends. Corresponded with each other for years, he said. He thanked me and drove towards Frog End. That was all I saw of him.' He looked a little shyly at Judith. 'I'm so sorry.'

'Thank you.' Joseph swallowed, the tightness almost choking his throat. 'My father was killed in a car accident the next day . . . and my mother along with him.'

'How very terrible,' the vicar said in little more than a whisper. 'If you would like to be alone in the church for a while I can see that no one disturbs you.' His invitation included both of them, but it was Joseph he reached out to touch, placing his hand on Joseph's arm. 'Trust in God, my dear friend. He knows our path and has walked every step before us.'

Joseph hesitated. 'Did Herr Reisenburg have any other friends that you are aware of? Someone I might speak to?'

The man's face crumpled in regret. 'None that I saw. As I said, he kept very much to himself. One gentleman asked for him, apart from your father, at least so I am told, but that's all.'

'Who was that?' Judith asked quickly.

'I'm afraid I don't know,' the vicar replied. 'It was the same day as your father, and frankly I rather think it was just someone else he must have spoken to. I'm sorry.'

Joseph found himself too filled with grief to answer. But he also believed that in Herr Reisenburg he had found the source of the document, and that he too had paid for it with his life. There was now no possibility whatever that John Reavley was mistaken as to its importance. But where was it now, and who was behind it?

'Don't you have any idea what that document was?' Judith asked when they were in the car again and turning towards home. 'You must have thought about it.'

'Yes, of course I have, and I don't know,' Joseph replied. 'I can't remember Father ever mentioning Reisenburg.'

'Neither can I,' she agreed. 'But obviously they know each other, and it was really important, or he wouldn't have gone looking for him while Mother was with Maude Channery. Why do you think Reisenburg had the document?' She negotiated a long curve in the road with considerable skill, but Joseph found himself gripping on to his seat. 'Do you suppose he stole it from someone?'

'It looks like it,' he replied.

She gave a shudder. 'And they murdered him for it, only he'd already given it to Father — so they murdered Father. What do you suppose they're going to do with it? If they got it back then, it's four weeks ago now, why hasn't anything happened?' Her voice dropped. 'Or has it, and we just don't know?'

He wanted to be able to answer her, but he had no idea what the truth would be.

She was waiting, he knew it by the turn of her head, the concentration in her face.

'Matthew thinks there may have been two copies,' he said quietly. 'It isn't that they need one, so much as they can't let the other one be roaming around, in case it falls into the wrong hands. That's why they're still looking.' Fear for her seized him with an almost physical pain. 'For

God's sake, Judith, be careful! If anyone — '

'I won't!' she cut across him. 'Don't fuss, Joseph. I'm perfectly all right, and I'll stay all right. It isn't in the house, and they know that! For heaven's sake, they've looked thoroughly enough. Are you staying tonight? And I'm not asking because I'm afraid, I'd just like to talk to you, that's all.' She gave a gentle, almost patient little smile and avoided looking at him. 'You're not much like Father, most of the time, but now and then you are.'

'Thank you,' he said as unemotionally as he could, but he found he could not add anything; his throat was tight and he needed to look away from her at the long slope of the fields, and compose himself.

13

Joseph waited up alone for Matthew to return from seeing Shanley Corcoran. It was almost midnight.

'Nothing,' Matthew replied to the unspoken question. He looked tired, his fair hair blown by the wind, but under the brief flush of travel he was pale. 'He can't help.' He sat down in the chair opposite Joseph.

'Want anything to drink?' Joseph asked, then without waiting for an answer, he told Matthew what he and Judith had discovered about Reisenburg.

Matthew seized on it. 'That must be it!' he said, enthusiasm lifting his voice. He sat forward eagerly, his eyes bright, attention suddenly focused again. 'Poor devil! It looks as if they killed him for it as well. No proof, of course.' He rubbed his hand over his face, pushing his hair back. 'It looks as if it must be as dangerous as Father said. I wonder how Reisenburg got it, and where from!'

Joseph had been thinking about that all evening. 'He might have been the courier for it,' he said dubiously. 'But I think it's far more likely he stole it, don't you?'

'But where was he taking it when they caught up with him?' Matthew enquired. 'Not to Father, surely? Why? If he'd been in any sort of intelligence service, I'd know!' He made it a statement, but Joseph could see in his eyes that it was a question. The yellow lamplight cast shadows on his face, emphasizing the uncertainty in him.

Joseph crushed his own doubts with an effort of will. 'I think he just knew Father,' he replied. 'The people he stole it from knew he had it and were after him. He passed it on to the only honourable person he could. Father was here. There was no time to get to London, or to whoever he meant to deliver it to.'

'No more than chance?' Matthew said with a twist of his lips. The irony of it hurt.

'Perhaps he came this way because this was where Father lived,' Joseph suggested. 'It seems he knew Cambridgeshire — he took the house here.'

'Who was he intending to give it to?' Matthew stared ahead of him into the distance. 'If only we could find that out!'

'I don't know how,' Joseph replied. 'Reisenburg is dead and the house is let out to someone else. We drove past.'

'At least we know where Father got it.' Matthew sat back, relaxing his body at last. 'That's a lot. For the first time there's a glimmer of sense!'

They stayed up another half-hour, arguing more possibilities, the chances of finding out more about Reisenburg. Then the brothers went to bed. Matthew had to get up at six and drive early to London, Joseph to go back to Cambridge at a slightly more agreeable hour.

★ ★ ★

Almost as soon as he entered the gate of St John's Joseph ran into Inspector Perth, looking pale, hunch-shouldered and jumpy.

'Don't ask me!' he said before Joseph had even spoken. 'Oi don't know who killed Mr Allard, but, so help me God, Oi mean to find out if Oi have to take this place apart man by man!' And without waiting for a reply he strode off, leaving Joseph open-mouthed.

He had left St Giles before breakfast, and now he was hungry. He walked across the quad in the sun, and under the arch to the Dining Hall. The atmosphere was sombre. No one was in the mood for talking. There were murmurs about Irish rebels in the streets of Dublin, and the possibility of sending in British troops to disarm them, perhaps even as soon as today.

Joseph was busy catching up on essay papers all morning and when he had time for his own thoughts at all, it was for Reisenburg, lying in a Cambridgeshire grave, unknown to whoever loved or cared for him, murdered for a piece of paper. Could the document possibly be to do with some as yet unimagined horror in Ireland that would stain England's honour even more deeply than its dealings with that unhappy country had done already? The more he thought of it, the less likely did it seem. It must be something in Europe, surely. Sarajevo? Or something else? A socialist revolution? A giant upheaval of values such as the revolutions that had swept the continent in 1848?

He did not wish to go to the Hall for luncheon, and bought himself a sandwich instead. Early in the afternoon he was crossing the quad back to his rooms when he saw Connie Thyer coming from the shadow of the arch. She looked harassed and a little flushed.

'Dr Reavley! How nice to see you. Did you have a pleasant weekend?'

He smiled. 'In many ways, yes, thank you.' He was about to ask her if she had also, and stopped himself just in time. With Mary Allard still her guest, still waiting for justice, and vengeance, how could she? 'How are you?' he asked instead.

She closed her eyes for a moment, as if exhaustion had overtaken her. She opened them and smiled. 'It gets worse,' she said wearily. 'Of course this wretched policeman has to ask everyone questions: who liked Sebastian and who didn't, and why.' Her face suddenly pinched with unhappiness, and her eyes clouded. 'But what he is finding is so ugly.'

Joseph waited. It seemed like minutes because he dreaded what she was going to say; he was prolonging the moment of ignorance, and yet he was pretending. He did know.

She sighed. 'Of course he doesn't say what he's found, but one can't help knowing because people talk. The young men feel so guilty. No one wants to speak ill of the dead, especially when his family is so close by. And then they are angry because they are placed in a situation where they can't do anything else.'

He offered her his arm, and they walked very slowly as if intending to go somewhere.

'And because they have been cornered into doing something they are ashamed of,' she went on, 'poor Eardslie is furious with himself, and Morel is furious with Foubister, who must have said something dreadful, because he is so ashamed he won't look anyone in the face, especially Mary Allard.' She glanced at him, and away again. 'And I think Foubister is afraid Morel had something to do with it, or at the very least may be suspected. Rattray is just as afraid, but I think for himself, and Perth won't leave him alone. The poor boy looks wilder every day. Even I am beginning to think he must know something, but whether it is something that matters or not, I have no idea.'

They moved from the temporary shade of the archway out into the next quad.

'What about Elwyn?' he asked. He was concerned for them all, but Elwyn particularly. He was a young man with far too much weight to bear.

'Oh dear,' Connie said softly, but her voice was full of emotion. 'That is the one thing for which I really dislike Mary. I never had children of my own.'

Was it pain in her voice, masked over the years, or simply a mild regret? He did not turn to look at her — that would be unpardonably intrusive — but he thought of her love affair with Beecher with a new clarity. Perhaps there was more to understand than he had imagined.

'I cannot know what her loss is,' she went on, looking at the sunlight on the grass ahead of her, and the castellated roof against the blue of the sky. 'But Elwyn is her son also, and she is indulging her own grief without any thought for him. Gerald is useless! He mopes around, most of the time saying nothing beyond agreeing with her. And I'm afraid he is helping himself to rather too much of Aiden's port! He is glassy-eyed more often than not, and it is not simply out of grief or exhaustion. Although Mary would be enough to exhaust anyone!'

Joseph kept step with her.

'Poor Elwyn is left to try and comfort his mother,' she said, shaking her head. 'He's attempting to shield her from the less pleasant truths that are emerging about Sebastian, who has reached the proportions of a saint in her mind. Anyone would think he had been martyred for a great cause rather than killed by some desperate person, in all likelihood goaded beyond endurance.' She stopped, turning to face Joseph, her eyes wretched. 'It isn't going to last. It can't!'

He was startled.

'She's going to find out one day, she has to!' she said so softly he had to lean towards her to catch the words. Her voice was tight with fear. 'And then what can we do for her?' Her eyes searched his. 'For any of them? She's built her whole world around Sebastian, and it's not real!' Then she sounded surprised at herself. 'Sometimes I feel desperately sorry for him. How could anyone live up to what she believed of him? Do you suppose the pressure of it, his own knowledge of what he was really like, drove him to some of the ugly things he seems to have

429

done? Is that possible?'

'I don't know,' Joseph said honestly. They were walking very slowly. 'Perhaps. He was remarkably gifted, but he had flaws like any of us. Maybe they now look the greater because we hadn't known they were there.'

'Was that our fault?' she asked earnestly. 'I thought he was . . . golden . . . that he was superbly clever, and his character was as beautiful as his face.'

'And his dreams,' he added. His own voice was hoarse for a second as grief overcame him for the loss not only of Sebastian, but for a kind of innocence in himself, for the lost comfort it carried with it. 'And yes, it was my fault, certainly,' he added. 'I saw him as I wanted him to be, and I loved him for that. If I were less selfish, I would have loved him for what he was.' He avoided meeting her eyes. 'Perhaps you can destroy people by refusing to see their reality, offering love only on your own terms, which is that they be what you need them to be — for yourself, not for them.' It was true, gouging out the last pretence inside him, leaving him raw.

She smiled very slightly, and her voice was very gentle. 'You didn't do quite that, Joseph. You were his teacher, and you saw and encouraged the best in him. But you are an idealist. I dare say none of us is as fine as you think.'

Again her love for Beecher rushed into his mind, and the hard, abrasive thought that Sebastian had known of it, and used it to manipulate Beecher into things painfully against his nature.

'No,' he agreed quietly. They had reached the shade of the next archway and he was glad of it. 'I think I have learned that. I wish I could help you with Mary Allard, but I'm afraid she is too fragile to accept the truth without it breaking her. She is a hard, brittle woman who has built a shell around herself, and reality won't intrude easily. But I'll be here. And if that is any help at all, please turn to me whenever you wish.'

'Thank you, I fear I will,' Connie replied. 'I can't see the end of this, and I admit it frightens me. I look at Elwyn and I wonder how long he can go on. Mary doesn't seem even to be aware of his presence, let alone do anything to comfort him! I admit, sometimes I am so angry I could slap her.' She coloured faintly; it made her face vivid and uniquely lovely. He was aware of her perfume, which was something delicate and flowery, and of the depth of colour in her hair. 'I'm sorry,' she said under her breath. 'It's very unchristian of me, but I can't help it.'

Joseph smiled in spite of himself. 'Sometimes I think we imagine Christ to be a lot less human than He was,' he replied with conviction. 'I'm sure He must feel like slapping us on occasions . . . when we bring our grief not only upon ourselves, but upon everyone around us as well.'

She thanked him again with a sudden smile, then turned to walk away back into the sun towards the Master's lodgings.

★ ★ ★

Joseph sensed the tension mounting all afternoon. He saw Rattray carrying a pile of books. He walked quickly and carelessly, tripping on an uneven paving stone at the north side of the quad, and dropping everything on to the ground. He swore with white-lipped fury, and instead of helping him, another student sniggered with amusement, and a third told him off for it sarcastically.

It was left to Joseph to bend down and help.

He met a junior lecturer and encountered several sarcastic remarks to which he replied calmly, and in his annoyance unintentionally snubbed Gorley-Brown.

The ill-feeling finally erupted at about four o'clock the following afternoon, and unfortunately it was in a corridor just outside one of the lecture halls. It began with Foubister and Morel. Foubister had stopped to speak to Joseph about a recent translation he was unhappy with.

'I think it could have been better,' he complained.

'The metaphor was a little forced,' Joseph agreed.

'Sebastian said he thought it referred to a river, not the sea,' Foubister suggested.

Morel came by and had gone only a few steps beyond when he realised what he had overheard. He stopped and turned, as if waiting to see what Joseph would say.

'Do you want something?' Foubister asked abruptly.

Morel smiled, but it was more a baring of the teeth. 'Sounds as if you didn't hear Sebastian's translation of that,' he replied. 'That's the trouble when you only get bits! It doesn't fit together!'

Foubister went white. 'Obviously you got it all!' he retaliated.

Now it was Morel's turn to change colour, only it was the opposite way; the blood rushed to his cheeks. 'I admired his work! I never pretended otherwise!' His voice was rising. 'I still knew he was a manipulative swine when he wanted to be, and I'm not going to be hypocrite enough, now he's dead, to go around saying he was a saint. For God's sake, somebody murdered him!'

There was a roll of thunder overhead and a sudden, wild drumbeat of rain. No one had heard footsteps approach and they were all jolted into embarrassment when they saw Elwyn only a couple of yards away. He looked bowed with exhaustion and there were dark smudges under his eyes as if he were bruised inside.

'Are you saying that means he must have deserved it, Morel?' he asked, his voice tight in his throat and rasping with the effort of controlling it.

Foubister stared at Morel curiously.

Joseph started to speak, then realised that his intervention would only make it worse. Morel would have to answer for himself, if he could make his voice heard above the drumming of the rain on the windows and the gush of water leaping from the guttering.

Morel took a deep breath. 'No, of course I'm not!' He shouted above the roar. 'But whoever

433

did it must have believed they had a reason. It would be much more comfortable to think it was a lunatic from outside who broke in, but we know it wasn't. It was one of us — someone who knew him for at least a year. Face it! Somebody hated him enough to take a gun and shoot him.'

'Jealousy,' Elwyn said hoarsely.

Beecher emerged from the doorway of the lecture room, his face white. 'For God's sake be quiet!' he shouted. 'You've all said more than enough!' He did not appear to see Joseph. 'Go on back to your work! Get out!'

'Rubbish!' Morel exploded, ignoring Beecher completely. 'That's absolute bloody rubbish! He was a charming, brilliant, conspiring, arrogant sod, who enjoyed his power over people, and for once he went too far.' He swung his arm wide, almost hitting Foubister. 'He made you run errands like a boot boy. He took people's girlfriends, just to show everyone that he could.' He glanced at Beecher, and away again. 'He got away with all kinds of things nobody else did!' His voice was almost a scream above the rain.

'Shut up, Morel, you're drunk!' Beecher shouted at him. 'Go and put your head under the cold tap, before you make even more of a fool of yourself. Or go and stand in the rain!' He jerked his hand towards the streaming window.

'I'm not drunk!' Morel said bitterly. 'The rest of you are! You don't have any idea what's going on!' He jabbed his finger viciously in no particular direction. 'Perth does! That miserable little bastard can see through us all. It'll give him a kick to arrest one of us. Can't you see it in his

434

face — the glee? He's positively smacking his lips.'

'Then at least it'll be over!' Foubister yelled it as if it were an accusation.

'No it won't, you fool!' Morel shouted back at him. 'It won't ever be over! Do you think we can just go back to the way we were? You're an idiot!'

Foubister launched himself at Morel, but Beecher had seen it coming and caught him in full flight, staggering backwards to pitch up hard against the wall, Foubister in his arms.

Outside the rain was still roaring and hissing over the rooftops and bouncing back off the ground.

Beecher straightened up and pushed Foubister away. Foubister swung around to face Morel, Joseph and Elwyn. 'Of course we won't be the same!' he choked, his voice a sob. 'For a start, one of us will be hanged!'

Elwyn looked dazed, as if someone had hit him also.

Morel was white to the lips. 'Better than going to war, which is where the rest of us will end up,' he lashed back. 'He was always afraid of that, wasn't he — our great Sebastian! He — '

Elwyn lurched forward and hit Foubister as hard as he could, sending him staggering backwards to strike his head and shoulders on the wall and slither to a heap on the floor.

'He wasn't a coward!' Elwyn gasped out the words, tears streaming down his face. 'If you say that again, I'll kill you!' And he aimed another punch, but Foubister saw it coming and rolled out of the way.

435

Beecher was staring at Elwyn in disbelief.

Elwyn jerked forward again, and Joseph grasped his arms, exerting all his strength to hold him, surprised to find it sufficient. 'That was stupid,' he said coldly. 'I think you had better go and sober up too. If we don't see you again until tomorrow, that will be more than soon enough.' Elwyn went slack and Joseph let him go.

Beecher helped Foubister to his feet.

Elwyn glared sullenly at Joseph, then turned and walked away.

Foubister shook himself and winced, then mumbled something, touching his jaw tentatively and smearing blood across his mouth.

'Maybe that will teach you to keep a wiser tongue in your head,' Joseph said unsympathetically.

Foubister said nothing, but limped away.

'Coward . . . ?' Beecher turned the word over as if he had discovered a new and profound meaning in it.

'Everybody's afraid,' Joseph responded, 'except those who are too arrogant to realise the danger. It's an easy word to fling around, and it's guaranteed to hurt pretty well anyone.'

'Yes . . . yes, it is,' Beecher agreed. 'And I don't know what the hell we're going to do about it. Isn't there anything worth salvaging out of this? God knows what!' He pushed his hair off his forehead, gave Joseph a sudden, bright, gentle smile, and went back the way he had come.

The rain had stopped as suddenly as it had started. The wet stones of the quad steamed, and everything smelled sharp and clean.

436

Joseph continued on to his rooms. But he knew that he needed to face the fact that he was afraid Sebastian might have been morally blackmailing Beecher. He had either to prove it to be true — and perhaps destroy one of the best friends he had ever had — or else prove it untrue — or at least that he was innocent of Sebastian's death — and release them both from the fear that now invaded everything. He must not avoid acting any longer.

He walked across the quad and into the shade of his own stairway. The conclusion that Beecher and Connie Thyer were in love had become inescapable, but without any proof, how could Sebastian have blackmailed Beecher? Was that a delusion, one of the many born of fear? Now was the time to find out.

He turned and walked very slowly back out again and across to the stair up to Sebastian's rooms. The door was locked, but he found the bedder, who let him in.

'You sure, Dr Reavley?' she said unhappily, her face screwed up in anxiety. 'In't nothing in there, as worth seein' now.'

'Please open it, Mrs Nunn,' he repeated. 'It'll be all right. There's something I need to find — if it's there.'

She obeyed, still pursing her lips with doubt.

He went in slowly and closed the door behind him. The room was silent. He drew in a deep breath. The air smelled stale. The windows had been closed for over two weeks and the heat had built up, motionless, suffocating. Yet he could not smell blood, and he expected to.

His eyes were drawn to the wall. He had to look because he could think of nothing else until he did. It was in his mind's eye whichever way he faced, and even if his eyes were closed.

It was there, paler than he had remembered, brown rather than red. It looked old, like something that happened years ago. The chair was empty, the books still piled on the table and stacked on the shelves.

Of course Perth would have been through them, and everything else: the papers, the notes, even Sebastian's clothes. He would have to, searching for anything that would point to who had killed him. Obviously he had found nothing.

Still Joseph's own hands turned automatically through the pages of the notes, held up each book and riffled to find anything loose, anything hidden. What was he expecting? A letter? Tickets to something, or somewhere?

When he found the photograph he barely looked at it. The only reason it caught his attention at all was because it was Connie Thyer and Beecher standing together, smiling at the camera. There were trees close to them, massive, smooth-trunked, autumnal. Beyond them there was a path winding away towards a drop to the river, and up again at the far side. It could be anywhere. A couple of miles away there was a place not unlike it.

He put it down and moved on. There were other photographs, Connie and her husband, even one of Connie and Joseph himself, and several of students and various young women. He thought one was Abigail, standing beside

438

Morel and laughing.

He went back to the picture of Connie and Beecher. Something about it was familiar, yet he was sure he had never seen it before. It must be the place. It was not the same place as in the other pictures. If it was somewhere near here, then he would know it.

He held it in his hand, staring at it, trying to recall the scenery around it, the bank of the river beyond the camera's eye. It went upward steeply. He could remember walking it — with Beecher. They had been eating apples and laughing about something, some long, rambling joke. It had been a bright day, the sun was hot on their backs, the stream rattling loudly below them. Little stones loosened and fell into the pool — splashing. The shadows were cool under the trees. There had been wild garlic. They were heading uphill, towards the open moorland, with huge, wind-raked skies — Northumber-land!

What was Connie doing in Northumberland — with Beecher? Almost before he had finished asking, the answer was whole in his mind. He remembered her taking a holiday late the previous summer, just after he had come to Cambridge. She had gone north to visit a relative, an aunt or something. And Beecher had gone walking alone; Joseph had been mourning Eleanor and refused even to think of such a thing. He needed to be busy, his mind occupied until exhaustion took over. The thought of so much wild, solitary beauty was too powerful to bear.

But where had Sebastian found the photograph? A dozen answers were possible: a visit to Beecher's rooms, a jacket left over a chair and it had slipped out of a pocket, or even Connie's handbag tipped over and the contents fallen out.

Was that what had unnerved Beecher to the point he had so openly criticized Sebastian, and at the same time allowed him to get away with such slipshod, challenging behaviour? He was afraid. This was proof.

He put the photograph into his pocket and turned to leave. The room was stifling now, the air heavy, choking in the throat. He fancied now he could smell the dried blood on the wall and in the cracks of the floorboards. Did one ever really get such things out?

It was time to face Beecher. He went out and closed the door behind him. He felt stiff and weary, dreading what was to come.

It was windless and hot in the late slanting sunlight, as he crossed the quad, and went in through the door on the far side, and up the stairs to Beecher's rooms. He dreaded having to be so blunt about what was a private subject, but nothing was truly private any more.

He reached the landing and was surprised to see Beecher's door slightly ajar. It was unusual because it was an invitation to anyone to interrupt whatever he was doing, and that was completely out of character.

'Beecher?' he called, pushing it a few inches wider. 'Beecher?'

There was no answer. Could he have slipped out to see someone, intending to be back in a moment or two, and simply left the door ajar?

Joseph did not like to go in uninvited. He was going to intrude painfully enough, when it was inevitable. He called out again, and there was still no answer. He stood, expecting to hear Beecher's familiar step any minute, but there was no sound except the far-off call of voices in the distance.

Then at last there were footsteps, light and quick. Joseph spun around. But it was Rattray coming down from the floor above.

'Have you seen Dr Beecher?' Joseph asked.

'No, sir. I thought he was in his rooms. Are you sure he isn't?'

'Beecher!' Joseph called again, this time raising his voice considerably.

Still there was silence. But it would be most unlike Beecher to have gone out and left his door open. Joseph pushed it wider and went inside. There was no one in the study, but the bedroom door beyond was also ajar. Joseph walked over and knocked on it. It swung open. Then he saw Beecher. He was leaning back in the bedroom chair, his head lolled against the wall behind him. He looked exactly as Sebastian had: the small hole in his right temple, the gaping wound on the other side, the blood drenching the wall. Only this time the revolver was on the floor where it had fallen from the dead hand.

For a moment Joseph could not move for horror. It lurched up inside him and he thought he was going to be sick. The room wavered and there was a roar in his ears.

He breathed in deeply and tasted bile in his

throat. Gradually he backed out of the door and through the outer room to find Rattray still waiting on the landing. Rattray saw his face and the words were hoarse on his lips. 'What is it?'

'Dr Beecher is dead.' Joseph's voice sounded strangled, as if his lungs were paralysed. 'Go and get Perth . . . or . . . someone.'

'Yes, sir.' But for several seconds Rattray was unable to move.

Joseph closed the door to Beecher's rooms and stood for a moment gasping for air. Then his legs buckled and he collapsed on to the floor, leaning his back against the door lintel. His whole body was shuddering uncontrollably and the tears ran down his face. It was too much; he could not bear it.

At last Rattray went, stumbling down the first two or three steps, and Joseph heard his feet all the way down, then a terrible silence.

It seemed an eternity of confusion, horror and soul-bruising misery until Perth arrived with Mitchell and, a couple of paces behind him, Aidan Thyer. They went in past Joseph, and a few moments later Thyer came out, grey-faced.

'I'm sorry, Reavley,' he said gently. 'This must be rotten for you. Did you guess?'

'What?' Joseph looked up at him slowly, dreading what he was going to say. His mind was whirling; thoughts slipped out of his grasp, there was no coherence to them, but he knew it was black with tragedy.

Thyer held out his hand. 'Come on. You need a stiff shot of brandy. Come back to the house and I'll get . . . '

Oh God! Joseph was appalled — one thought emerged from the rest — Connie! She would have to be told that Beecher was dead! Who should tell her? It was going to be unbearable for her, whoever it was, but what would be least terrible? Her husband . . . alone? Could she mask her own feelings for Beecher? Was it even conceivable that Thyer knew?

Had Beecher taken his own life, knowing that the truth would come out, and he'd be blamed for Sebastian's murder? Joseph refused even to think that he might actually have done it. Or was it Aidan Thyer who had made it look like suicide, standing there in front of him, with his grave face and pale hair, his hand outstretched to help Joseph to his feet?

The answer was something he could not evade. Yes, he should go to the house, whether it was he or Thyer who told Connie. She would need help. If he did not go, and there were a further tragedy, he would be to blame.

He grasped Thyer's hand and allowed himself to be pulled to his feet, accepting Thyer's arm to steady himself until he found his balance.

'Thank you,' he said huskily. 'Yes, I think a stiff brandy would be very good.'

Thyer nodded and led the way down the stairs, across the quad and through the archway towards the Master's lodgings. Joseph's mind raced as he walked beside him a little dizzily, every step drawing him closer to the moment that would end Connie's happiness. Would she believe Beecher had killed Sebastian? Had she even known of the blackmail? Had Beecher told

443

her, or had he borne it alone? Or had the photograph been his?

And might she think the murderer was Aidan Thyer? If she did, then she might be terrified of him herself. But Joseph could not stay there for ever to protect her. What could he say or do so that she would be safe after he left? It was his responsibility because he was the only one who knew!

Nothing. There was nothing anyone could do to save her from ultimately having to face the husband she had betrayed, at heart, if not more.

They were at the door. Thyer opened it and held it for Joseph, watching him with care in case he staggered and tripped. Did he really look so dreadful? He must. He certainly felt it. He was moving in a nightmare, as if his body did not belong to him.

It seemed interminable moments before Connie appeared. For seconds she did not realise there was anything wrong. She said something pleasant about having tea, then slowly the look on Thyer's face registered with her, and she looked at Joseph.

Thyer was about to speak. Joseph must act now. He stepped forward a couple of paces.

'Connie, I'm afraid something very dreadful has happened. I think you had better sit down . . . please . . . '

She hesitated a moment.

'Please,' he urged.

Slowly she obeyed. 'What is it?'

'Harry Beecher has killed himself,' he said quietly. There was no way to make it any better,

444

or gentler. All he could do now was try to save her from a self-betraying reaction.

There was an instant's terrible silence, then the blood drained from her face. She stared at him.

He stepped between her and her husband, taking her hands in his as if he could hold her together, in some physical fashion bridge the gulf of aloneness. What he really wanted was to shield her from Thyer's sight.

'I'm so sorry,' he went on. 'I know you were as fond of him as I was, and it is the most awful shock, on top of everything else that has happened. It was very quick, a single shot. But no one yet knows why. I'm afraid there is bound to be speculation. We must prepare ourselves.'

She drew in her breath in a stifled little cry, her eyes wide and empty. Did she understand that he knew about them, that he was saying all this to give her whatever protection there was?

Thyer was at his elbow with two glasses of brandy. Joseph straightened up to allow him to give one to Connie. Had he any idea? Looking at his white face and pinched mouth told him nothing. It might as easily have been only the horror of yet another tragedy in his college.

Joseph took the brandy offered to him and drank it, choking on the unaccustomed fire in his throat. Then he felt it blossom inside him with artificial warmth, and it did help. It steadied him, gave him a little strength, even though he knew it was only temporary, and changed nothing.

Thyer took over. 'We don't know what

happened yet,' he was telling Connie. 'The gun was there on the floor beside him. It looks as if it is maybe the end of all this.'

She stared at him and started to say something, but the words died in her throat. She shook her head, whimpering in pain she would always have to conceal. No one would understand; no one would offer her sympathies or make allowances for her grief. She would have to bear it alone, even pretend it did not exist.

That was something Joseph could do for her: he could share his own loss of a friend, recall all the good things about him and let her borrow his grief. Without the embarrassment of saying so, or requiring any confession or acknowledgement from her, he could let her know that he understood.

He stayed a little longer. They made meaningless remarks. Thyer offered them each another brandy, and this time he had one himself as well. After about half an hour, Joseph left and walked in a daze of grief back to his own rooms for one of the worst nights he would ever endure. He sank into sleep at last a little before one, and was engulfed in nightmare. He slipped in and out of it until five, then woke with a tight, pounding headache. He got up, made himself a cup of tea and took two aspirins. He sat in the armchair and read from Dante's 'Inferno'. The passage through hell was vaguely comforting; perhaps it was the power of Dante's vision, the music of the words, and the knowledge that even in the worst pain of the heart he was not alone.

Finally at eight o'clock he went outside. The

weather was exactly as it had been nearly all summer — calm and still, with a slight heat haze on the town — but inside St John's suddenly the pressure seemed to have lifted.

Joseph met Perth, who was setting out across the quad.

'Ah! Morning, Dr Reavley,' Perth said cheerfully. He still looked tired, shadows around his eyes, but his shoulders were squared and his step was lighter. 'Shame about Dr Beecher. Oi know he were a friend o' yours, but mebbe it's the best way. Clean end. No trial. Best for poor Mr Allard's family too. Now the public don't need to have all the details.'

The words, with Perth's unquestioning assurance, crystallized the anger inside Joseph. All Perth knew was that Beecher was dead and the gun was found next to him, yet he was happy, almost gleeful, to take it for granted that he had killed Sebastian, and then himself. Arguments boiled up in Joseph's mind, and fury at Perth's willingness to believe without looking any further. What about the others? They had known Beecher for years. Was all that carried away as if by a single, flash flood? He wanted to shout at Perth to stop, to think, to weigh and measure. These actions were nothing like those of the man Joseph had known! How dare Perth, or anyone, be so certain?

But then Joseph himself had not seen the affair with Connie Thyer, right under his nose! Or that Sebastian had seen it and was using it in subtle blackmail. How well did he know anyone?

And it was all hideously reasonable. The words

died on his lips. He was really only angry because Perth was relieved. Everyone would be. The suspicion had stopped. They would be able to start rebuilding all the old friendships that had been the fabric of their lives.

'Are you so very sure?' he said thickly, his voice strained.

Perth shook his head. 'Makes sense, Reverend. About the only answer what does — when you think on it.'

Joseph said nothing. The courtyard seemed to waver around him, like a picture blurred by rain.

'Looks like the same gun,' Perth went on. 'When we test it, Oi reckon we'll find as it is. Was a Webley that killed Mr Allard. Did Oi ever tell you that?'

Joseph stared into space, trying not to visualise it. Whatever had happened to Beecher, the scholarly, dry-humoured man he had known, the good friend, that he would have killed Sebastian to protect his own reputation? Or was it Connie's? Thyer could have overlooked it if no one knew. Such things happened often enough. But to have made it public would be different. No man could ignore that. Beecher would have lost his position, but he could have found another, even if not in such a prestigious university as Cambridge, if not even in England! Surely better anything rather than murder?

Or was it to protect Connie? Perhaps she would have been divorced by Thyer. But even that was something they could have lived with!

And would Sebastian really have sunk so low as to tell people? It would have ruined Connie

448

and Beecher, and made Thyer the butt of pity. But it would have broken for ever Sebastian's own image as a golden youth. Surely he would not have done that, simply to exercise power?

'I'm sorry, Reverend,' Perth said again. 'Very sad thing, and 'ard to believe it of friends. That's the trouble with a calling like yours. Always reckoning the best o' folk. Comes a shock when you see the other side. Now for me, Oi'm afraid it's no shock at all.' He sniffed. 'Still a shame, though.'

'Yes . . . ' Joseph pulled his thoughts together. 'Yes, of course it is. Good day, Inspector.' Without waiting for a reply he walked away towards the Dining Hall. He did not want to eat, and he certainly did not want company, but it was like getting into cold water — better done quickly.

In the Hall there was the same slightly hysterical air of relief. People burst into conversation, then stopped suddenly and burst into high-pitched, self-conscious laughter. They were not sure whether it was decent to show their happiness that the weight of suspicion was gone, but they dared to look at each other, because words were no longer guarded against hidden meaning. They spoke of the future; they even told jokes.

Joseph found it intolerable. After a couple of slices of toast and a single cup of tea, he excused himself and left. They were behaving as if Beecher had not been one of them, as if they had not lost a friend in the most hideous way imaginable. The moment real friendship was put

449

to the test they cut and ran.

That judgement was unfair, but it would not leave his mind, for all the sensible reasoning he used. The hurt was too great.

Joseph was not certain whether to go back to the Master's lodgings or not. He did not want to intrude on Connie in what must be a time she would bear only because there was no possible alternative. One could not die purely from misery. He had discovered that after Eleanor's death.

But even if he did not go specifically to see Connie, he should speak to Mary now that Beecher's death was generally accepted as the close of the case. The Allards would be leaving to go home, and if he waited it might be too late. Then it would seem as if he were indifferent.

He was shown into the sitting room by the parlour maid, and a few moments later Connie appeared. She might have doubted within herself whether she should wear black or not, but even if she had considered it might be too revealing of her emotions, she had cast aside such caution. She wore a fashionable silk dress with a deep sash and pleated tunic, black from neck to hem, and black shoes. Her face was as white as chalk.

'Good morning, Joseph,' she said quietly. 'I imagine you have come to see Mrs Allard. She has her vengeance now, and she can leave.' Her eyes expressed the fury and the pain she dared not speak aloud. She dropped her voice to a whisper. 'Thank you for coming yesterday evening. I . . . I — '

'You don't need to thank me,' he interrupted.

'I liked him very much. He was my best friend, right from the beginning.' He saw her eyes fill with tears, and it was almost impossible to continue, his own throat was so tight. He could scarcely breathe from the weight constricting his chest.

At that moment Mary Allard came in through the door.

'Oh, good morning, Dr Reavley.' She still looked proud and angry, and she was dressed in unrelieved black. It flattered her olive complexion but not her gaunt body. 'It is good of you to come to wish us goodbye.' There was a faint softening in her voice.

He could not think what to say to her. Nothing in her yielded or offered warmth.

'I hope the resolution of the matter will give you some measure of peace,' he said, and the instant later wished he had not. In saying that he had wished Beecher's death to give her peace, and he felt like a betrayer.

'Hardly,' she snapped. 'And I would not have expected you, of all people, to suggest it!'

Connie drew in her breath.

Joseph was bitterly aware that if he hurt so much out of grief for Beecher, then she must be almost torn apart by it.

Mary Allard stared back at him defensively. Her voice shook when she spoke. 'You have been willing to allow it said that my son blackmailed this wretched man over some sin or other, God knows what — no one will tell me — and that he murdered Sebastian to keep him quiet.' She was trembling with bewilderment and unanswered

451

pain. 'The suggestion is monstrous! Whatever he had done, or Sebastian knew about, Sebastian would never have put pressure upon him, except to persuade him to act honourably.' She gave a little gulp. 'Obviously that failed, and the miserable man murdered Sebastian in order to protect himself. Now not only has this damnable place taken my son's life, but you would like to take from him as well the very memory of who and what he was. You are beneath contempt! If I do not meet you again, Dr Reavley, I shall be much better suited.'

Her words were both arbitrary and unjust. He was angry enough to retaliate, but the words did not come easily.

'People will say what they wish to say, Mrs Allard,' he said stiffly, his mouth dry. 'Or what they believe to be true. I cannot stop them, nor would I, any more than I can stop you saying whatever you wish to about Dr Beecher, who was also my friend.'

'Then you are unfortunate in your choice of friends, Dr Reavley,' she snapped. 'You are naïve, and think too well of many people, but not well enough of others. I think you would be better served by some long and deep contemplation of your own powers of judgement.' She lifted her chin a trifle higher. 'It was civil of you to come to wish us goodbye. No doubt you considered it your duty. Please accept that it is done, and feel no need to call upon us further. Good day.'

'Thank you,' Joseph said with unaccustomed sarcasm. 'That puts my mind greatly at ease.'

She swung round and glared at him. 'I beg your pardon?'

'I shall feel free not to call upon you again,' he answered. 'I am obliged to you.'

She opened her mouth to make some reply, and to her fury the tears flooded her eyes. She swung around and marched out, black silk skirts crackling, shoulders stiff.

Joseph felt guilty, and angry, and thoroughly miserable.

'Don't,' Connie whispered. 'She deserved that. She has been behaving for over two weeks as if she were the only person in the world who has ever been bereaved. My heart aches for her, but I can't like her!' She took in a long, deep breath and let it out in a sob. 'Even less now.'

He looked at her. 'Nor I,' he said gently, and they both stood there, smiling and blinking, trying not to weep.

★　★　★

Joseph spent the rest of the day in a haze of misery. At night he slept poorly and rose late, grief washing back over him like a returning tide. He missed breakfast altogether, and forced himself to go back to the Dining Hall for luncheon. He had expected the conversation still to be about Beecher's death. He was startled to find instead that it was about yesterday's news in the papers, added to by this morning's. Somehow he had not taken any notice until now.

'Troops?' he said, turning from one colleague to another. 'Where?'

'Russia,' Moulton replied to his left. 'Over a million men. The Czar mobilized them yesterday.'

'For the love of heaven, why?' Joseph was stunned. A million men! It was shattering, and absurd.

Moulton stared at him dourly. 'Because two days ago Austria-Hungary declared war on Serbia,' he replied. 'And yesterday they bombed Belgrade.'

'Bombed . . . ' The coldness went through Joseph as if someone had opened a door on to a freezing night. He gulped. 'Bombed Belgrade?'

Moulton's face was tight. 'I'm afraid so. I suppose with poor Beecher's death no one mentioned it. Ridiculous, I know, but the death of someone we know seems worse than dozens, or even hundreds of deaths of people we don't — poor devils. God only knows what'll happen next. It seems we can't stop it now.'

'I'm afraid it looks as if war in Europe is inevitable,' Gorley-Brown said from the other side, his long face very grave, the light shining on his bald head. 'Can't say whether it'll drag us in or not. Don't see why it should.'

Joseph was thinking of a million Russian soldiers, and the Czar's promise to support Serbia against Austria-Hungary.

'Makes our troops in the streets of Dublin look like a very small affair, doesn't it?' Moulton said wryly.

'What?' Joseph did not know what he was referring to.

'On Monday,' Moulton told him, raising his

454

wispy eyebrows. 'We sent the troops in to disarm the rebels.' He frowned. 'You'll have to pull yourself together, Reavley. It seems Allard was a bit of a wrong 'un after all. And poor old Beecher lost his head completely. Woman's reputation, I suppose, or something of the sort.'

'Of the sort,' Addison said sourly from the other side of the table. 'Never saw him with a woman, did you?'

Joseph jerked up and glared at him. 'Well, if it were something worth blackmailing him about, you wouldn't, would you!' he snapped.

Gorley-Brown raised his glass. 'Gentlemen, we have far larger and graver issues to concern ourselves with than one man's tragedy, and a young man who, it appears, was not as good as we wished to believe. It seems that Europe is on the brink of war. A new darkness threatens us, unlike anything we have seen before. Perhaps in a few weeks young men all over the land will be facing a far different future.'

'It won't touch England!' Addison said with a slight smile, which was more of contempt than any kind of amusement. 'It'll be Austria-Hungary and east, or north if you count Russia.'

'Since they've just mobilized over a million men, we can hardly discount them!' Gorley-Brown retorted.

'Still a long way from Dover,' Moulton said with assurance. 'Let alone London. It won't happen. For one thing, think of the cost of it! The sheer destruction! The bankers will never let it come to that.'

Addison leaned back, holding his wine glass in

455

his hand, the light shining through the pale German white wine in it. 'You're quite right. Of course they won't. Anyone who knows anything about international finance must realise that. They'll go to the brink, then reach some agreement. It's all just posturing. We're past that stage of development now. For God's sake, Europe is the highest civilisation the world has ever seen. It's all sabre-rattling, nothing more . . . '

The conversation swirled on around Joseph but he barely listened. In his mind he saw not the oak-beamed Dining Hall, the windows with their centuries of stained-glass coats of arms, the linen, glass and silver, but instead the evening sun shining long and golden across the river. He saw Sebastian staring at the beauty of Cambridge, not just at the architecture, but the dreams, the knowledge, the glories of the mind and the heart treasured down the centuries, and dreading the barbarity of war and all it would break in the spirit of mankind.

It was impossible to believe that he had really been a grubby blackmailer! Vain sometimes, weak enough to use the power of his charm and his intellect just because he could. His ability had been still raw, but surely on the brink of becoming great! His dreams could have been cleaned of their tarnish, refined until the dross was burned away, kindness brought back again. Self-restraint could have been learned, compassion garnered from the pain of his own fears.

Flora had said he would have given anything

at all, even perhaps his life, to preserve what he loved.

And Harry Beecher. Joseph still found it impossible to grasp that he had killed Sebastian, even to save Connie, certainly not to save himself. Had he?

And was any of it tied to the murders of John and Alys Reavley? Had Sebastian seen it, and known who was responsible? Or was that only a hideous coincidence? How could it have anything to do with Reisenburg, and whoever had killed him?

Maybe there was someone else who had taken advantage of Beecher's love affair to hide the fact that it was he whom Sebastian was blackmailing . . . because he had seen him lay that string of caltrops across the road? Getting rid of Sebastian quickly, and then afterwards building a case to place the blame on someone else, closing it all neatly — and walking away?

Or was Joseph simply trying, yet again, to avoid a truth he found too painful to believe? For all his proclaimed love of reason, the faith in God he professed aloud, was he a moral coward, without the courage to test the truth, or the real belief in anything but the facts he could see? Did he trust God at all? Was it a relationship of spirit to spirit? Or just an idea that lasted only until he tried to make it carry the weight of pain or despair?

He laid down his napkin and rose to his feet. 'Excuse me. I have duties I must attend to. I'll see you at dinner.' He did not wait for their startled response, but walked quickly across the floor and out of the door into the sun.

It was time he looked at Sebastian's murder without any evasion or protection for his own feelings. He must have at least that much honesty. Perhaps he had not really accepted it until now. His emotions were still trying to absorb the death of his parents.

He was walking aimlessly, but swiftly enough to distract anyone from speaking to him.

Sebastian had been shot early in the morning before most people were up. According to Perth it had been with a Webley revolver, probably like the one that had killed Beecher. No one had admitted ever seeing such a gun in college. So where had it come from? Whose was it?

Surely the fact of having such a thing indicated intent to kill? Where did one buy or steal a gun? It was certain beyond any reasonable doubt that the same gun had been used both times, so where had it been that the police had not found it?

He walked over the Bridge of Sighs and out into the sun again. He knew St John's better than the police possibly could. Surely if he applied his mind to the problem, he could deduce where the gun had been.

He passed a couple of students strolling, deep in conversation. A man and a young woman in a punt drifted lazily along the river. Three young men sat on the grass, absorbed in conversation. Another sat alone, lost in a book. Peace soaked into the bones, like the heat of the sun. If these people had read the same news as Moulton and Gorley-Brown, they did not believe it.

Where could one hide a gun that it would be retrievable, and in a condition in which it could be used again? Not the river. And not where anyone else would find it, either casually or because they were looking for it.

He stopped on the path and stood facing the college. As always its beauty filled him with pleasure. From the Bridge of Sighs the fine brick was met by white stone sheer down into the water. Further on there was a short stretch of grass sloping to the river. The walls were smooth except for the windows, all the way up to the crenellated edge of the roof with its dormers and high chimneys.

But Perth's men had been up there.

All except the Master's lodgings. In deference to the Allards they had merely looked at it from the next roof over from where they could see everything. The drainpipes down were wide at the neck, to catch the pipes through the castellations with the run-off from the roof behind. An idea stabbed his mind. Was it possible? It was the one place so far as he knew where no one had looked.

Could Beecher have put it there after killing Sebastian? And could he have retrieved it again in time to take his own life with it? But even if Joseph were right, there would be no way to prove it now.

Perhaps he could deduce it, if he tried. Where should he begin? With everyone's movements after the discovery of Sebastian's body. Anyone climbing on the roof of the Master's lodgings would have risked being noticed, even at half-past five in the morning. At this time of the year it was broad daylight.

He started to walk slowly.

Was it possible the gun had been kept somehow concealed temporarily, and then put in a safe place later? Had the hiding place been in the top of the downpipe it would have taken only a few moments to place it: a quick visit to one of the attic rooms with a dormer window, open it wide, lean far out and drop the gun, perhaps wrapped in something. Even a scarf or a couple of handkerchiefs would disguise the outline, then a few leaves.

If that were the answer, then it could only have been done from the Master's lodgings. Joseph could not imagine the person who hid the gun was one of the servants. That reduced the suspects to Aidan and Connie Thyer, Beecher if he had seen Connie there, and whoever else might have visited.

That person had to have concealed the gun very soon after Sebastian's murder was committed, because the police had started the search within an hour of their arrival.

What would Joseph have done were he in that situation? Hidden it in the undergrowth in the Fellows' Garden until he was free to go back and get into the Master's lodgings unobserved.

And to retrieve it again? Perhaps much the same.

It came back to Connie and Aidan Thyer — and perhaps Beecher. He could not believe it was Connie, but the more he thought of it, the more likely did it become that it was Thyer.

Perhaps it was he whom Sebastian had seen on the Hauxton Road? Perhaps it was even he who was behind the plot itself? He was a brilliant man with a position of far more power than most people realised. As Master of a college in Cambridge, he had influence over many of the young men who would, in a generation's time, be the leaders of the nation. He was sowing seeds the world would reap.

Now that the thought was in his mind, Joseph had to test it until it was proved, one way or the other. And there was only one place to begin. He would hate doing it, but he could think of no alternative.

He walked slowly back to the Bridge of Sighs and into St John's, then across the inner quad to the Master's lodgings. Thyer himself would be in the library at this time in the early afternoon. He hoped Connie would be at home.

The parlour maid let him in and he found Connie standing at the window staring out at the bright flowers in the Fellows' Garden. She made an effort to smile at him.

'Thank you for coming yesterday,' she said a little huskily. 'It was kind of you.' She did not explain what she meant, and turned away again almost immediately. 'I'm relieved the Allards have gone home, and Elwyn has moved back to his own rooms. But the house is unnaturally quiet now. It seems like silence rather than peace. Is that absurd?'

'No,' Joseph answered. He hated what he was about to do, the more so because if it proved anything at all, it might be something she would

461

infinitely prefer not to know. 'I need to ask you one or two questions . . . ' He hesitated, not sure how to address her. Her Christian name was too familiar; using it would be taking something of a liberty. And yet to address her as 'Mrs Thyer' was both cold, and bitterly ironic.

She was only mildly curious. 'About what?'

He must do it. He could feel his body stiffen and he was standing awkwardly. 'I found a photograph in Sebastian's rooms.' He hated this. He saw her tense and knew instantly that she was aware of it, and that it meant all that he had supposed. 'You met Harry in Northumberland. I know the place it was taken. He and I walked there.'

The tears filled her eyes. 'He told me,' she whispered, her voice choked. 'I didn't go there to meet him. It was almost by accident.' She gave an awkward, lopsided little shrug. 'I should have stopped myself. I knew it was wrong, and I knew what it would lead to — but I wanted it so much! Just once to have — ' She stopped, looking away from him. It was a moment before she was able to compose herself. 'Some passer-by took the photograph. Harry kept it. It must have fallen out of his pocket when his coat was over the arm of a chair. He was frantic when he discovered it was gone. I didn't know Sebastian had it.' Her face was touched by a rare, terrible anger. It frightened him.

'Connie . . . '

The expression vanished again, drowned in misery.

He had to go on: there were other things that

he had to know, and no more time to spend in patience. 'About the morning Sebastian was murdered, and the day leading up to the time Harry died.'

'I don't know anything useful.' Her voice was flat again, emotion buried far below in a sea of pain too deep to dare touch.

'And about Sunday, the day the Archduke and Duchess were shot in Sarajevo,' he went on.

She swung around. 'Oh God! You can't think Harry had anything to do with that! That's idiotic!'

'Of course I don't!' He denied it vehemently, but his mind went to the yellow Lanchester mangled and broken, and his parents' bodies covered with blood. Until the moment of saying it, the thought had not entered his mind that Beecher could be guilty of that, but now it was there, a tiny shard, like a dagger.

Connie was staring at him incredulously, on the edge of an anger that would last as long as they knew each other.

'No!' he said again, forcing a smile, this time in the face of the absurdity of Beecher being responsible for the assassination in Sarajevo. 'I simply used that event to bring the day to your mind. If you remember, it was also the day my parents were killed?'

'Oh!' She was stunned and utterly contrite, her face crumpled in pity. 'Joseph, I'm so sorry. I had completely forgotten! With . . . ' She took a deep breath and held it a moment. 'With murder,' she forced herself to use the word, 'here in college, an accidental death, even two, seems so much . . . cleaner. What is it you need to know? If I can tell you, of course I will.'

Now was the moment to say what he had to. 'I think someone may have seen what happened. Do you know where Harry was about noon that day?'

The colour swept up her face. She must have felt its heat, because her eyes betrayed her as well. 'Yes. It couldn't have been he,' she said

He could not let it go quite so delicately. 'Are you certain, as a fact, not a belief?'

'Absolutely.' She looked down, away from him.

'And the morning Sebastian was killed?' He chose the slightly softer word, blunting it where he could.

She turned a little to look out of the window again. 'I got up early and walked along the Backs. I was with Harry. I can't prove it because we kept to the trees. We didn't want to be seen, and there are quite often other people around, mostly students, even at five or six.'

'Then it is not possible that Harry could have killed Sebastian,' he said, watching her for the slightest shadow in her eyes, or alteration in the rigidity of her body that would betray that she was lying to protect him, even now that he was dead.

She turned to face him, her eyes wide, brilliant. 'How can you be sure?' she said, not daring yet to grasp the hope. 'We didn't meet until nearly six. He could have been killed before that — couldn't he?' She was very pale now, perhaps wondering if Beecher had come to her straight from having murdered the one man who threatened them both.

'Where did you meet?' Joseph asked.

She was confused. 'Where? I went over the Bridge of Sighs, because it's enclosed so no one would have seen me, then walked to the beginning of the trees. He was there.'

'He didn't come to the lodgings?'

Her dark eyes widened.

'Good heavens, of course not! We're not completely mad!'

'When was the next time he was there?'

'I don't know. Why? About two days later, I think. I had the Allards by then, and everything was a nightmare.'

A warmth began to ease inside him. Beecher had definitely not killed Sebastian, because he had had no time to hide the gun! Not if it had been on the Master's roof — and the more Joseph thought of it, the more certain he became that that was where it had been. 'And before he shot himself?' he asked.

She stiffened again, her face white. 'I saw him in the Fellows' Garden the evening before, just for a little while, almost fifteen minutes. Aidan was due home.'

'Did he go inside?'

'No. Why?'

Should he tell her? Caution said not . . . but she had loved Beecher, the thought that he had committed murder and then suicide was a bleeding wound inside her.

Yet if he explained, then she would work out for herself the only terrible alternative: that it was someone who had access to the roof of her

465

house — her husband. She would be a danger to him then, and would he kill her too?

Would she work it out, even if he did not tell her? No. It all depended upon the gun having been hidden on the roof. He dared not let her deduce it.

'I'm not sure,' he lied. 'When I'm certain, I'll tell you.'

'Did Harry kill Sebastian?' Her voice was trembling, her face ashen.

Would she guess anyway? 'No, he couldn't have,' he answered. 'But say nothing to anyone!' He made the warning sharp, a message of danger. 'If he didn't, Connie, then someone else did! Someone who may kill you. Please, say nothing at all, to absolutely anyone . . . including the Master! I may be wrong.' That too was a lie; he had no doubt he was right. Aidan Thyer might kill, but Joseph was certain in his heart that Harry Beecher had not. And if Connie had been out on the Backs early in the morning, then Aidan Thyer could have been anywhere; certainly he could have been in Sebastian's rooms. And Thyer could have killed Sebastian for the same reason — because he was blackmailing any or all of them over exposing Connie's affair.

Or it could have been Thyer he had seen on the Hauxton Road.

'Say nothing,' he repeated even more urgently, touching her arm. Her wrist was slender under his fingers. His mouth was dry, his hands sweating. 'Please — remember it is murder we are dealing with.'

'Two murders?' she whispered.

466

'Perhaps,' he replied. He did not say it could be four — or if Reisenburg had been murdered also, then five!

She nodded.

He stayed only to give her a few words of assurance, then walked slowly back in the bright sun, cold in his flesh and his bones.

467

14

Joseph walked slowly across the quad. The sun was hot in the early afternoon, but it felt airless. His clothes stuck to his skin. There were no clouds that he could see in the blue distance bounded by the crenellated tops of the walls, but it felt like thunder to come. The electricity of it was already inside him, an excitement and a fear that he was on the brink of the truth. He'd had a day to think it over, but was no nearer the answer.

Where had Aidan Thyer been on the afternoon of Sunday, 28 June? Who could he ask that Thyer would not hear about it? Connie had been in the garden with Beecher. If Thyer had been on the Hauxton Road, where would he have told people he was? And who would remember now, nearly five weeks later?

He could not ask Connie; she would know why he was asking, and then no matter how hard she tried, it would surely be beyond her to conceal that knowledge from Thyer himself.

Joseph was walking more and more slowly as he tried to make up his mind. Thyer had come late to the cricket match. Would Rattray, who had captained the St John's side, know where he had been before that? It was worth asking him. He turned and went rapidly back in through the door at the further side, and up to Rattray's rooms. He was not there.

Ten minutes later Joseph found him in a corner of the library between the stacks, scanning the bottom shelf.

'Dr Reavley! Are you looking for me, sir?' he asked, closing his place in the book in his hands.

'Yes, actually I was.' Joseph bent to the floor, looking along the row curiously. They were on warfare and European history. He regarded Rattray's thin, anxious face.

Rattray bit his lip. 'It looks pretty bad, sir,' he said quietly. 'If Russia doesn't stop within twenty-four hours, Germany will probably mobilize too. Professor Moulton reckons they'll probably close the world stock exchanges pretty soon. Maybe even by Monday.'

'It's a bank holiday,' Joseph replied. 'They'll have all weekend to think about it.'

Rattray sat back on the floor, legs out in front of him. 'Do you think so?' He rubbed the heel of his hand along his jaw. 'God, it would be awful, wouldn't it? Who could imagine four weeks ago that some lunatic in a town in Serbia, of all places, taking a pot-shot at an archduke — and Austria's got loads of them — could blow up into this? Just a short time, barely more than a month, and the whole world's changed.'

'Five weeks ago, nearly.' Joseph found the thought strange too. Then his parents had been alive. Five weeks ago tomorrow would be the Saturday John Reavley had driven the yellow Lanchester to Little Wilbraham and talked to Reisenburg, and been given the document, and that night he had telephoned Matthew in London. The next day he had been killed.

469

'We played cricket at Fenner's Field,' he said aloud. 'You captained the side. I remember being there, and Beecher, and the Master.'

Rattray nodded.

'Sebastian wasn't,' Joseph continued. 'He was late coming back home. I expect the Master wasn't pleased. He was one of our best bats.'

'Rotten bowler, though,' Rattray smiled. He looked close to tears, his voice a little thick. 'No, the Master was pretty cross when he did come, actually. Sort of caught him by surprise that Sebastian wasn't playing.'

Joseph felt cold. 'When he did come?'

'He was late too!' Rattray pulled a slight face. 'Don't know where he'd been, but he arrived in a hell of a temper. He said he'd been stuck on the side of Jesus Lane with a puncture, but I know he wasn't, because Dr Beecher came that way and he'd have seen him.' He sighed and looked away, blinking hard. 'Unless, of course, you can't believe Dr Beecher any more. I just can't — I can't understand that!' He chewed painfully on his lower lip to stop it trembling. 'Everything's sort of . . . slipping apart, isn't it? You know I used to think Sebastian was pretty decent, a bit arrogant at times, but basically all right, you know?' He looked at Joseph. 'He had some odd ideas, used to waffle on about peace, and that war was a sin against mankind, and there wasn't anything in the world worth fighting for if it meant killing whole nations and filling the earth with hate.'

He rubbed his jaw again, leaving a smudge of dust on it. 'A bit too much, but still sane, still all

470

right! I never thought he would do something really squalid, like blackmail. That's what the police say it was. That's filthy! Beecher might have been doing something out of line, but he was a decent chap, I'd have staked anything you like on that.' He pushed his hair back off his forehead in a gesture of infinite weariness. 'I'm beginning to wonder if I really know very much at all.'

Joseph understood his confusion profoundly. He was fighting his own way through the same desperation, trying to make sense of it, and regain his own balance. But there was no time for the long, gentle conversations of comfort now. 'Where do you think the Master was?' he asked.

Rattray shrugged. 'I've no idea. Or why he should say something that wasn't true.'

'But he was in his car?' Joseph persisted.

'Yes, I saw him drive up in it. I was waiting for him.'

'Thank you.'

Rattray looked curious. 'Why? What does it matter now? It's over. We were all wrong — you and me, everyone. Beecher's dead and our quarrels don't amount to much if there's going to be war, and we're all drawn into the biggest conflict in Europe. Do you suppose they'll ask for volunteers, sir?'

'I can't see that we'll be involved,' Joseph replied, not sure if he were speaking the truth. 'It will be Austria, Russia and perhaps Germany. It's still possible they're all just threatening, seeing who'll be the first to back down.'

'Maybe,' Rattray said without conviction.

Joseph thanked him again, and went out of the library and back to the first quad to see Gorley-Brown. There was only one thing to find out now, and he dreaded the answer. He was surprised how deeply it cut into his emotions to believe that Aidan Thyer was guilty of killing John and Alys Reavley. And for what? That was something he still did not know.

He knocked on Gorley-Brown's door and stood impatiently until it was opened. Gorley-Brown looked tired and irritable. His hair was untidy, he had his jacket off and his shirt was sticking to his body. It very obviously cost him some effort to be civil.

'If you came to apologise for your attitude at luncheon yesterday, it really doesn't matter,' he said abruptly, and started to push the door to again.

'I didn't,' Joseph answered him. It was already very clear that there was going to be no opportunity for subtlety. 'Beecher doesn't seem to have left any note, or wishes of any kind . . . '

Gorley-Brown suppressed his momentary annoyance. 'No, I don't suppose he did. Look, Reavley, I know he was a friend of yours, but he was obviously driven beyond his sanity by whatever it was that young Allard was pressuring him over, and I'd really rather not know the details. I don't think we should speculate.' His face was filled with distaste, and anxiety to avoid embarrassment.

Joseph knew what was on his mind. 'I was going to ask you,' he said coldly, 'if you know if he'd had any opportunity to speak to the Master round about that time. He might have some ideas what we should do. As far as I know Beecher had no close family, but there must be someone who ought to be informed as discreetly as possible, in the circumstances.'

'Oh.' Gorley-Smith was taken aback. 'Actually I don't think so. Whatever sent him over the edge must have been rather sudden, and as it so happens, I know the Master was in a meeting for at least two hours before we heard about it, because I was there myself. I'm sorry, Reavley, but you'll have to look elsewhere.'

'You're quite sure?' Joseph pressed. He wanted it to be true, and yet it made nonsense of the only answer he could think of.

'Yes, of course I'm sure,' Gorley-Brown replied wearily. 'Basildon went on interminably about some damned building fund, and I thought we were going to be there all day. It was mostly the Master he was arguing with.'

'I see.' Joseph nodded. 'Thank you!'

Gorley-Brown shook his head in incomprehension, and closed the door.

Joseph went down the stairs and outside slowly. The shadows in the quad were already deep on the western side and the top windows of the rooms to the east were bathed in fire. Once again he made his way over the bridge to the Backs. The air was cooling at last and the light shone through the flowers in rich colours like stained glass. The trees across the grass barely shimmered in the faint sunset wind, and there was no sound but the call of birds. He saw no

473

one else, even on the river. The water was flat and opaque. It could have been as solid as green mercury.

If Aidan Thyer had not killed Beecher, and Beecher had not killed Sebastian, then what was the answer?

He walked slowly, his feet silent on the dry grass. He passed into the shade of the trees. Here it smelled cooler, as if the greenness itself had a fragrance.

Who else could have put the gun on the roof of the Master's lodgings? Or was he wrong about that after all? He went back to the beginning of all that he knew for certain. Elwyn had come to his rooms, almost hysterical with shock and grief, because he had gone to fetch Sebastian for an early morning walk by the river, and found him shot to death. There was no gun there. Anyway, no one had ever suggested Sebastian had any reason on earth to take his own life. No one who knew him had ever imagined such a thing.

The police had been called and had searched everywhere for the gun, but had not found it. Everywhere except the funnel openings to the drainpipes on the Master's roof.

Of course it was always possible there was another answer he simply had not thought of! Maybe someone had quite casually walked out with it, and put it in another college, or given it to somebody?

Except that whoever it was had retrieved it with no difficulty in order to shoot Beecher.

He concentrated on who could have shot

Beecher, and who might have wanted to. Everyone seemed to assume after his death that he had killed Sebastian. But had anyone assumed it before?

Mary Allard? She would have had the fury and the bitterness to kill. But how would she have known where the gun was, or got herself to the roof for it?

Gerald Allard? No, he had not the passion, and he also would not have known where it was.

He was opposite Trinity now. The wind was rising a little, whispering in the leaves above him, and here in their shade the light was fading rapidly.

Elwyn? He could not have killed Sebastian. He was accounted for in his own room at the time. And why would he have! They had been close, even for brothers, and so unalike as to have been rivals in very little. They admired each other's skills without especially wanting to possess them.

Nor could Elwyn have had anything to do with crashing the Lanchester. He had been in Cambridge all day.

But he had been in and out of the Master's lodgings seeing his mother, trying to comfort her and offer her the support his father seemed incapable of giving. He could have retrieved the gun, if he had known it was there!

But how could he have known? Unless he had seen it somewhere? Could Beecher have hidden it there? For whom? Connie? The thought was ugly, and the pain of it sat so tight in his chest he could hardly breathe. Had Beecher been protecting her?

And had Elwyn assumed it was Beecher who had shot Sebastian? That would have been motive enough to have killed him, and deliberately left the gun there to make it seem like suicide, an admission of guilt.

Except that he was wrong.

In the shadows he could hardly see the path at his feet, although there were echoes of light across the sky. He walked on to the grass again. Outside the avenue of trees there was still that tender, airy dusk that seems neither silver nor grey. He looked at the horizon to the east where the depth of the coming night was a veil of indigo.

In the morning he would have to face Connie again and put his theories to the final test.

He slept badly and woke with a nagging headache. He had a hot cup of tea and two aspirins, and then as soon as he knew Aidan Thyer would have begun his college duties, he went across to the Master's lodgings.

Connie was surprised to see him, but there was no shadow in her eyes. If anything, she seemed pleased.

'How are you, Joseph? You look tired. Have you had any breakfast? I'm sure Cook could make you something if you wish?' They were in the sitting room with the light slanting in through the french windows.

'No, thank you,' he declined. His stomach was knotted far too tightly to eat, and the aspirins had not yet had much effect. 'I have been thinking a great deal about what must have happened, and I've asked a few questions.'

She looked puzzled, but there was neither hope nor fear in her face.

'The police never found the gun after Sebastian was killed,' he said. 'Although they believed they searched everywhere.'

'They did,' she confirmed. 'Why do you say 'believed'? Do you know of somewhere they didn't look? They were here. They searched the entire house.'

'When?'

She thought for a moment. 'I . . . I think we were about the last. I suppose they came here only as a matter of form. And at first Elwyn was here, because he was desperately shocked and grieved, and then, of course, his parents.'

'Did they search the roof?'

Would she lie, to protect herself? Even if it were only to leave the matter closed? Was it she who had originally started the very subtle suggestion that the love affair over which Beecher was blackmailed was not with her, but with Sebastian himself? That was a repulsive thought. He pushed it away.

'They were up on the next roof,' she replied thoughtfully, remembering it as she spoke. 'They can see all of this one from there. It's not so big. Anyway, I really don't think anybody could have been up there. We would have heard. How can you hide a gun on a rooftop? It would be obvious.'

'Not if it were poked barrel first into one of the funnels at the top of a downpipe,' Joseph said.

Her eyes widened. 'You could reach those

477

from the dormer windows. It could be anyone who was in this house!'

'Yes . . . '

'Aidan? Harry?'

'No.' He shook his head. 'Neither of them had the opportunity. I told you, I have been asking a few more questions. Harry could not have killed Sebastian, you told me that yourself. Weren't you telling the truth?'

'Yes! Yes, I was!' she assured him. 'You don't think Aidan? But why? Not over . . . ' Again the blood flushed up her cheeks. 'He doesn't know,' she said huskily.

'What about Elwyn? Could he have found the gun there, and taken it to kill Beecher, believing Beecher had killed Sebastian?'

She stared at him, misery and grief swimming in her eyes.

'Could he?' he repeated.

'Yes,' she nodded. 'But how would he know it was there? Who killed Sebastian? I can't believe Aidan would have, and I know I didn't. And it wasn't Harry, so who was it?'

'I don't know,' he admitted. 'I'm right back to the beginning with that. Who else could have put the gun up there? He would have to have come through the house.'

'No one,' she said after a moment. 'It must have been somewhere else. Unless . . . ' she blinked several times, 'unless Aidan were hiding it for someone? Do you think he would have done that, and Elwyn knew?'

'Perhaps, but why would he?' And the moment the words were spoken he knew the answer. It was back to the document again, but he dared not tell her that. 'Of course it depends upon other things,' he added.

She opened her mouth to ask, then changed her mind. 'The police, the whole college, think that Harry killed Sebastian,' she said instead. 'And that when he thought they were about to arrest him, he killed himself.' Her voice was shaking. 'I wish I could prove that wasn't true. I loved him very much, but even if I hadn't, I don't think I could allow anyone to be blamed for something terrible if I could prove they were innocent.'

A little of the old warmth returned inside him. 'Then I think we had better go and tell Inspector Perth. I imagine we can find him at the police station in the town.'

Connie hesitated only a moment. She might never have to do anything that would cost her more than this. Once the words were said, she could not ever return to this privacy, this safety of unknowing. Then she took a step forward, and he followed her out of the room and to the front door.

They walked to the police station. It was less than a mile, and at this hour in the morning it was still cool and fresh. The streets were busy with tradesmen, early deliveries, shoppers seeking bargains. The footpath was bustling with people and the roadway loud with hoofs of horses pulling wagons and drays, delivery carts, and a doctor's gig. There were several cars and a motor van with advertisements printed on the side, and, as always, dozens of bicycles. Only if one listened carefully did one hear a different tone in the voices, or realise that conversations were not about the weather, and there was no gossip. It was all news, carefully disguised anxiety, forced jokes.

Perth was busy upstairs and they were obliged to wait over quarter of an hour in tense, unhappy impatience. When he finally arrived he was less than enthusiastic to see them and only when Joseph insisted did he take them to a small cluttered office where they could speak without being overheard.

'Oi don't know what you want, Reverend,' Perth said with barely veiled impatience. He looked tired and anxious. 'Oi can't help you. Oi'm very sorry about Mr Beecher, but there's an end to it. Oi don't know if you've seen the papers this mornin', but the King o' the Belgians has gone against his own government and mobilized all his armies. There's a whole lot more at stake than any one man's reputation, sir, and that's something we can't tossle about no more.'

'Truth is always worth arguing about, Inspector Perth,' Connie said gravely. 'That's why we fight wars: to keep the right to rule ourselves and make our own laws, to be who we want to be and answer to no one but God. Dr Beecher did not kill himself, and we believe we can prove it.'

'Mrs Thyer — ' Perth began with exaggerated patience.

'You never found the gun, did you!' Joseph cut across him. 'Until it was by Dr Beecher's body.'

'No, we didn't,' Perth admitted reluctantly, anger sharpening his voice. It was a failure he did not like having pointed out to him. 'But he must have known where it was, because he got it back again!'

'Did you search his rooms?'

'O' course we did! We searched the whole college! You know that, sir. You saw us.'

'There must be somewhere you missed,' Joseph said reasonably. 'The gun did not dematerialize, and then reappear.'

'Are you bein' sarcastic, sir?' Perth's eyes hardened.

'No, I am stating the obvious. It was somewhere that you did not look. I have spent some time considering where that could be. You looked on the roof, didn't you? I can remember seeing your men up there.'

'Yes, we did, sir, very thorough, we were,' Perth replied, thin-lipped. 'Not that there's a lot o' places on a roof as you could hide a gun. Quite a big thing, a revolver, and not the same shape as anythin' else. Not to mention that metal shines in the sun. Just did it to be thorough. Long days this time o' the year, and a man climbing around on a roof'd be seen.' Now his tone was also distinctly sarcastic.

'What about the bucket at the top of a drainpipe?' Joseph asked. 'With the barrel pointing down, and the top covered with, for example, an old handkerchief, suitably dusty, and a few leaves?'

'Very good, sir,' Perth conceded. 'That could be. Except we looked.'

481

'How about the downpipes on the Master's lodgings?' Joseph asked. 'Did you look there too?'

Perth stood absolutely still, his face frozen.

Joseph waited, aware of Connie holding her breath beside him.

'No,' Perth said at last. 'We reckoned . . . nobody'd be able to hoide anything there unless they went through the Master's lodgings to do it. Are you sayin' as they did?' The last was addressed to Connie.

'Elwyn Allard was in and out of the house a great deal while his mother and father stayed with us,' she replied, her voice very nearly steady. 'He was there within an hour of Dr Beecher being shot.'

Perth stared at her. 'If you're sayin' that he shot his brother, Mrs Thyer, you got it wrong. We thought o' that. Lots of families don't get on all that well.' He shook his head dismally. 'Brother killing brother is as old as the Bible, if you'll excuse me saying so. But we know where he was, and he couldn't've. You'd not understand the medical evidence, mebbe, but you'll have to trust us in that.'

'And Dr Beecher didn't do it either,' she said, her voice tight as if her throat would barely open. 'He was with me.' She ignored Perth's expression of incredulity. 'I am perfectly aware of what time it was, and of the impropriety of it. I would not admit to it lightly, and I can barely imagine what my husband will feel, if it has to be made public — or what he will do. But I will not allow Dr Beecher, or anyone else, to be branded

482

for a crime they did not commit.'

'Where were you . . . and Dr Beecher, madam?' Perth asked, his face sour with disbelief, and perhaps disapproval.

Connie blushed, understanding his contempt. 'On the Backs along the river, Inspector Perth. At this time of the year, as you say, the daylight hours are long, and it is a pleasant place if you wish to talk unobserved.'

His expression was unreadable. 'Very interestin', Oi'm sure. Why didn't you mention this before? Or has Dr Beecher's reputation suddenly got so much more important to you?'

Her face tightened. She was white about the lips. Joseph could see how intensely she would like to have lashed back at Perth and withered him, but she had already given away her weapons. 'Like others, I'm afraid I thought Sebastian Allard had been blackmailing him over his regard for me, and the indiscretion of it for both of us,' she replied. 'I thought he had killed himself rather than have it exposed, which he believed was going to happen because of the investigation into Sebastian's murder.'

'Then, who did kill Sebastian, Mrs Thyer?' Perth asked, leaning forward a little across the desk. 'And who put the gun down the drainpipe on your roof? You? If you'll excuse me saying so, we only got your word that Dr Beecher was with you. Same as we only got his word that you was with him . . . and he ain't 'ere to back you up.'

She understood perfectly, but her eyes did not waver from his. 'I am aware of that, Inspector. I do not know who killed Sebastian, but it was not

Dr Beecher, and it was not I. But I believe that if you investigate a little further, you will find that Elwyn Allard shot Dr Beecher, and you cannot find it difficult to understand why, since you yourself assumed that Dr Beecher was guilty of killing Sebastian.'

'Oi'm not sure as how Oi do believe it.' Perth bit his lip. 'But Oi suppose Oi'd better go back to St John's and ask around a bit more; leastways find out if anyone saw Elwyn near Dr Beecher's rooms just before he were shot. But Oi still don't see how he could have known where the gun were! If it were in the pipe from the roof of the Master's lodgings!'

'The gun was on the floor, by Dr Beecher's hand,' Joseph said suddenly. 'Did you do any tests to see if that was where and how it would fall if dropped from a man's hand after he was shot?'

'And how would we do that, sir?' Perth asked dourly. 'We can't hardly ask somebody to shoot theirselves to show us!'

'Haven't you ever seen suicides before?' Joseph was thinking rapidly. How on earth could he prove the truth he was more and more certain of with every moment? 'Where do guns fall after the shock of death? A gun is heavy. If you shoot yourself in the head . . . ' he carried on, regardless of Connie's gasp, 'you fall sideways. Does your arm go down as his was, and the gun slither out of your fingers? For that matter, were there any fingerprints on it?'

'Oi dunno, sir,' Perth said sharply. 'It was plain it was suicide to me. We know Sebastian Allard had been blackmailing him into doing all kinds of favours for him, things as he wouldn't do of hisself, and ruining his name as a professor.'

'Yes, I know that,' Joseph said impatiently. 'But I'm talking about proof. Think back on it now, with other possibilities in mind! Was that how a gun would fall?'

'Oi dunno, sir.' Perth looked troubled. 'Oi suppose it were a bit . . . awkward. But that ain't proof of anything. We dunno how he sat, nor what way he moved when he were shot. Begging your pardon, ma'am. Oi'd like to spare your feelings, but you ain't making it possible.'

'I know that, Inspector,' she said quietly, but her face was ashen and Joseph was afraid she might faint. He moved a step closer to her, to hold her if she did.

'Inspector,' he said urgently, his mind racing, 'surely if we could prove that the gun was in the bucket at the top of the drainpipe on the Master's roof, that would also prove that Dr Beecher could not have got it to shoot himself?'

'Yes, sir, it would. But how are we going to prove that? Guns don't leave nothin' behind, and if it were there, likely it were wrapped in a cloth or something, to keep it from being seen, or getting wet.'

Wet. The idea was like a lightning flare. 'We had rain the day Beecher was killed!' Joseph almost shouted the words. 'If there was a cloth around the gun, then the whole thing would have blocked the drain! There are barrels at the bottom of the downpipes in the Fellows' Garden! If one of them is dry, that's your proof!

And he would choose that side, because the other overlooks the quad, where it was far more exposed.'

Perth stared at him. 'Yes, sir, if it's clear now, Oi'd take that as proof.' He started towards the door, barely waiting for them to follow. 'We'd best go and look now, before it rains again, and we've lost it all.'

On the walk back to St John's they did not speak as they dodged between pedestrians on the narrow footpaths. It was already getting warmer as the sun beat down on the stone.

They went in through the front gate past Mitchell, who looked startled and unhappy to see Perth again, then across the first quad, through the archway, and across the second. Then, since the gate was locked, as usual, they hurried through the Master's lodgings into the Fellows' Garden.

Joseph felt his pulse quicken as they passed between the flowers, the perfume of them heavy in the stillness, and stopped in front of the first water barrel.

He glanced at Connie, and she back at him. His mouth was dry.

Perth looked into the barrel. 'About quarter full,' he announced, 'near as Oi can tell.'

Connie reached out and took Joseph's hand, gripping him hard.

Perth moved to the middle barrel and looked in. He stood still, a little bent.

Connie's fingers tightened.

Joseph felt his heart pounding.

'It's dry . . . ' Perth said huskily. He turned to

486

look at Joseph, then Connie. 'Better check the last one,' he said softly. 'Oi think you're right, Reverend. In fact seems like for certain you are.'

'If it's dry,' Joseph pointed out, 'then there was something wrapped around the gun. It might still be there, especially if there's still no water at all.'

Perth stared at him, then very slowly he turned away and bent to peer up the drainpipe. 'Reckon as there is an' all,' he said, pursing his lips. 'Come most o' the way down. Oi'll 'ave to see if Oi can get it the rest.'

'Can I help?' Joseph offered.

'No, thank you, sir. Oi'll do it myself,' Perth insisted. He took his jacket off, reluctantly handing it to Joseph, then rolled his shirtsleeve up very carefully and poked his arm up the drainpipe.

There were several moments of frustrated silence while he wriggled without effort.

Connie walked over to the delphiniums and plucked out one of the canes that held them up. She returned with it and offered it to Perth.

'Thank you, madam,' he said, tight-lipped, and extended a dirty and scratched hand to take it from her. Three minutes later he retrieved a piece of canvas awning like that used on the punts at night. It was almost a foot square and there were smudges of oil near the middle. Perth held it to his nose and sniffed.

'Gun oil?' Joseph asked huskily.

'Yes, sir, I reckon so. Suppose Oi'd better go and have a few words with Mr Elwyn Allard.'

'I'll come with you,' Joseph said without

487

hesitation. He turned to Connie. 'I think you'd better stay here.'

She did not argue. She let Joseph and Perth out of the side gate into the quad, then went back into the house.

Joseph followed Perth across towards Elwyn's rooms. He knew it would be desperately painful, the more so because he could understand the passion of hatred, the compulsion which had drawn Elwyn to defend his mother from grief. And perhaps also the hunger within him to do something sufficiently powerful to make her grateful to him, even if she did not know why. Then she might emerge from her obsession with Sebastian long enough to acknowledge that she still had one live son who was equally worthy of her love.

They found Elwyn in Morel's rooms. They were studying together, discussing alternative translations of a political speech. It was Morel who answered the door, startled to see Perth again.

'Sorry to disturb you, sir,' Perth said grimly. 'Oi understand Mr Allard is here.'

Morel turned just as Elwyn came up behind him.

'What is it?' Elwyn asked, glancing from Perth to Joseph and back again. If he was afraid, there was no sign of it in his face.

Joseph spoke before Perth could answer. 'I think it would be a good idea if you were to come to the police station in the town, Elwyn. There are a few questions you may be able to answer, and it would be better there.'

Perth glanced at him, a flicker of annoyance across his face, but he conceded.

'If you want,' Elwyn agreed, the tension greater in him now too.

Morel looked at him, then at Joseph. Finally he turned to Elwyn. 'Do you want me to come?'

'No, thank you, sir,' Perth cut him off. 'This is a family matter.' He stepped back to block the stairway door. 'This way, sir,' he directed Elwyn.

'What is it?' Elwyn asked halfway down the steps.

Perth did not answer until they had reached the bottom and were outside in the quad.

'Oi'm taking you in for questioning, sir, regardin' the death o' Dr Beecher. Oi thought it easier for you if Mr Morel didn't 'ave to know that, at this point. If you give me your word to come without making a fuss, there'll be no need for handcuffs, or anything like that.'

Elwyn went white. 'Handcuffs!' he stammered. He turned to Joseph.

'If you wish me to come with you, then of course I will,' Joseph offered. 'Or if you prefer me to contact your parents, or a lawyer, then I'll do that first.'

'I . . . ' Elwyn looked lost, stunned, as if he had never considered the possibility of this happening. He shook his head, bewildered.

'Mr Allard's an adult, Reverend,' Perth said coldly. 'If he wants a lawyer, then o' course he can have one, but he don't need his parents, nor you. And strictly speaking, sir, this in't your concern. We're grateful for your help, and all you've done, but Mr Allard ain't going to give no

489

trouble, so you could stay here at St John's. Mebbe you'd be more use if you told the Master what's happened, and sent for Mr and Mrs Allard.'

'Mrs Thyer will already have done that,' Joseph pointed out, and saw the flash of annoyance on Perth's face as he realised. 'I'll come with Elwyn, unless he would rather I didn't?'

Elwyn hesitated, and it was that instant of indecision that made Joseph certain that he was guilty. He was frightened, confused, but he was not outraged.

Perth gave in, and they walked together into the shadow of the front gate, and out into the street on the far side.

At the police station it was a formal matter of charging Elwyn with the murder of Harry Beecher, to which he pleaded not guilty, and on Joseph's advice, refused to say anything further until he had a lawyer with him.

★   ★   ★

Gerald and Mary Allard arrived at St John's an hour after Joseph returned. Mary was beside herself, her face contorted with fury. The moment Joseph walked into the sitting room at the Master's lodgings she swung around from Aidan Thyer, to whom she had been speaking, and glared at Joseph. Her thin body looked positively gaunt in its tight, black silk, like a winter crow.

'This is monstrous!' she said, her voice strident. 'Elwyn couldn't possibly have killed that

490

wretched man! For heaven's sake, Beecher murdered Sebastian! When he knew you were closing in on him, he took his own life. Everybody knows that. Let Elwyn go immediately . . . with an apology for this idiotic mistake. Now!'

Joseph stood still. What could he tell her? One of her sons was dead, and the other guilty of murder, even if he had done it in mistaken revenge.

'I'm sorry,' he said to her — and he meant it profoundly, with a pain that throbbed inside him. 'But they have proof.'

'Nonsense!' she spat. 'It is totally absurd. Gerald!'

Gerald came to stand almost level with her. He looked wretched, his skin was pale and blotchy and his eyes blurred. 'Really, for God's sake, what is going on?' he demanded. 'Beecher killed my son, and now you have arrested my other son, when quite obviously Beecher took his own life.' He put out a hand tentatively as if to touch Mary, but she pulled away from him.

'No,' Joseph said as gently as he could. He could not like Gerald, but he was fiercely sorry for him. 'Beecher did not kill Sebastian. He was seen elsewhere at the time.'

'You are lying!' Mary accused him furiously. Her face was ashen, with scarlet splashes on her cheeks. 'Beecher was your friend, and you are lying to protect him. Who on earth would see Beecher anywhere at five o'clock in the morning? Unless he was in bed with somebody? And if he

491

was, then she is a whore, and her word is worth nothing!'

'Mary . . . ' Gerald began, then faltered under her withering glance.

'He was out walking,' Joseph replied. 'And the gun which killed Sebastian was hidden where only a limited number of people could have placed it, or retrieved it — '

'Beecher!' Mary said with scalding triumph. 'Naturally! It is the only answer which makes sense.'

'No,' Joseph told her. 'He might have been able to hide it there, but he could not have retrieved it. Elwyn could have.'

'It's still ridiculous,' she asserted, her whole body so tense she was shuddering. 'If he had known where it was, he would have told the police! It might have led to the arrest of whoever killed Sebastian. Or are you insane enough to believe he did that too?'

'No. I know he didn't. I don't know who did,' he admitted. 'And I believe that Elwyn sincerely thought it was Beecher, and that the law could not touch him — '

'Then he was justified!' she said savagely. 'He killed a murderer.'

'He killed someone he thought was a murderer,' Joseph corrected. 'And he was mistaken.'

'You're wrong,' she insisted, but she turned away from him, and her voice rose, shrill with desperation, as if the world no longer made sense. 'Beecher must have done it! Elwyn is morally innocent of any crime and I shall see to it that he doesn't suffer.'

Joseph looked past her at Aidan Thyer, and again the darkness filled his mind that it could have been he who was behind the document, and perhaps Sebastian's death. He looked pale and tired today, the lines in his face deeper. Did he know about Connie and Beecher? Had he always known? Joseph stared at him, searching, but there was nothing in Thyer's eyes to betray him.

'Dr Reavley?' Gerald said tentatively. 'Would you . . . would you do what you can for Elwyn? I . . . I mean, I wish he would . . . You are a person of standing here . . . The police will . . . ' He floundered helplessly.

'Yes, of course I will,' Joseph agreed. 'Do you have legal representation in Cambridge?'

'Oh, yes. I meant as a . . . I don't know . . . As a friend . . . '

'Yes. If you wish, I'll go right away.'

'Yes . . . please do. I'll stay here with my wife.'

'I'm going to Elwyn!' Mary shouted at him.

'No, you are not,' Gerald answered, unusually firmly for him. 'You are staying here.'

'I — ' she began.

'You are staying here,' he repeated, catching hold of her arm as she lunged forward, and bringing her to a stop. 'You have done enough harm already.'

She swivelled round and gaped at him in stupefaction, fury and pain struggling in her face. But she did not argue.

Joseph bade goodbye to them, and went out again.

Perth placed no barrier to Joseph seeing Elwyn alone in the police cell. It was late afternoon and the shadows were lengthening. The room smelled stale, of old fears and miseries.

Elwyn sat on one of the two wooden chairs and Joseph on the other, a bare, scarred table between them.

'Is Mother all right?' Elwyn asked as soon as the door was closed and they were alone. He was very pale and the shadows around his eyes looked like bruises.

'She is very angry,' Joseph replied truthfully. 'She found it hard to accept that you could be guilty of Beecher's death, but when she could no longer avoid it, she believed that you had just cause, and were morally innocent.'

The rigidity eased out of Elwyn's shoulders. His skin looked oddly dead, as if it would be cold to touch.

'Your father will engage a lawyer for you,' Joseph went on. 'But is there anything I can do, as a friend?'

Elwyn looked down at his hands on the table. 'Look after Mother, as much as you can,' he answered. 'She cares so much. You wouldn't understand if you hadn't seen Aunt Aline. She is Mother's older sister. She always does everything right, and first. And she boasts about it all the time. Her sons win everything, and she makes us feel as if we'll never be as clever, or as important. I think she's always been like that. She made it — ' He stopped suddenly, realising it was all pointless now. He drew in his breath. And went on more quietly. 'You cared about Sebastian, you saw the best in him. Go on caring, and don't let them say he was a coward . . . ' He looked up quickly, searching Joseph's face.

'I've never heard anyone say he was a coward,' Joseph replied. 'No one has even suggested it. He was arrogant, and at times manipulative. He enjoyed the power his charm gave him. But I think, in time, even that will be forgotten, and people will choose to remember only what was good.'

Elwyn nodded briefly and brushed his hand across his face. He looked desperately weary.

Joseph ached with pity for him. Too much had been asked of him, far too much. His brother had been idolised and Mary, in her grief, had expected Elwyn to ignore his own pain and carry hers for her, defend her from the truth and bear the weight of her emotions. And as far as Joseph knew, she had given him nothing back, not even her gratitude or her approval. Only now, when it was far too late, did she consider him, and prepare to defend him. In a way it was her passion that had driven Elwyn to seek such a terrible revenge and, as it turned out, a mistaken one.

The truth was still to find. Someone else could have put the gun in the drainpipe, after killing Sebastian, someone with access to the Master's lodgings. Connie, in order to protect her reputation, and thus all her marriage gave her? Or Aidan Thyer, because it was he whom Sebastian had seen on the Hauxton Road when the Lanchester crashed? Perhaps this was the last chance for Joseph to ask, and the moment when Elwyn had nothing left to lose, and would tell him, if he knew.

'Elwyn . . . ?'

Elwyn moved very slightly in acknowledgement, but he did not look up.

'Elwyn, how did you find the gun?'

'What? Oh . . . I saw it.'

'Out of the upstairs window?'

'Yes. Why? What does it matter now?'

'It matters to me. You didn't see Dr Beecher put it there. Was it Mr Thyer, or Mrs Thyer?'

Elwyn stared at him in silence, his eyes wide.

Joseph waited. It seemed almost a battle of wills.

'Yes I did, it was Dr Beecher,' Elwyn said at last.

'Then he did it for someone else,' Joseph told him, knowing the blow he was dealing him, but it was a truth he could not hide for ever. 'Dr Beecher did not kill Sebastian. He couldn't have. He was somewhere else, and he has a witness to prove it.'

Elwyn's body was rigid, his eyes hollow, almost black in the fading light of the room. 'Somewhere else?' he whispered in horror — but it was not disbelief. Joseph saw it in him the moment before he tried to mask it, and for an instant they saw in each other that terrible understanding that can never be taken back.

Then Joseph looked away, the knowledge burned into him. Elwyn had known Beecher had not killed Sebastian! Then why had he shot

496

Beecher? To protect whom? Not Connie. Aidan Thyer? Had Sebastian seen Thyer on the Hauxton Road, and told Elwyn before he was killed? Was that why Elwyn would not speak, even now? Was it even conceivable that he had killed Beecher on Thyer's orders, rather than be killed himself? The thoughts whirled in Joseph's mind like leaves in a storm, chaotic, battering. Was this all part of the plot John Reavley had discovered in Reisenburg's document? And was it going to cost Elwyn Allard his life as well?

He closed his eyes. 'I'll help you if I can, Elwyn,' he said softly. 'But so help me God, I don't know how!'

'You can't,' Elwyn whispered, covering his face with his hands. 'It's too late.'

15

Joseph woke up late on Sunday morning, his mind still consumed with Elwyn's last words to him, and the picture in his mind of his utter despair. And yet he was determined to hide some secret of Sebastian's death, even at this cost. Joseph had turned it over and over in his wakeful hours, grasping and losing, finding nothing that made sense.

It was August, and he still did not know who had killed his parents, what the document was or what had happened to it. He had tried, and every answer had evaporated the moment he framed it. But John and Alys Reavley were dead, Sebastian Allard, the German, Reisenburg, and now Harry Beecher. And poor Elwyn might well be, when the fullness of the law had run its course. He knew of no way to help any of it.

Tomorrow was a bank holiday; he should go back to St Giles and spend it with Judith. He had been too overwhelmed in the last few days even to write to her, or to Hannah.

He got up slowly, shaved and dressed, but he did not go down to the Dining Hall for breakfast. He was not hungry, and certainly he did not want to face Moulton, or any other of his colleagues. He was not going to explain about Elwyn or discuss the matter. It was a consuming tragedy, but it was a private one. The Allards had more than enough to bear without the added scourge of other people's speculation.

He spent the morning tidying up various books and papers, writing a long letter to Hannah, which he knew said little of any meaning, it was simply a way of keeping in touch. He went to the eleven o'clock service in the chapel, and found it washed over him without giving him any of the deep comfort he needed. But he had not honestly expected that it would. Perhaps he knew the words so well that he no longer heard them. Even the perfection of the music seemed irrelevant to the world of everyday life, the disillusion and all the loss he knew of around him.

He saw Connie Thyer briefly in the afternoon, but she had only a few minutes to talk. Again she was overtaken by the growing hysteria of Mary Allard, and the futility of attempting to help, and yet she was obliged by circumstances and her own sense of pity to try.

Joseph walked out of the front gate and ambled aimlessly along the nearly deserted streets of the town. All the shops were closed in Sabbath decency. The few people he saw were soberly dressed and merely nodded to him respectfully as they passed.

Without intending to, he found himself on Jesus Lane, and instinctively turned right down Emmanuel Road. He strolled past Christ's Pieces and eventually across St Andrews Street, along to Downing Street towards Corpus Christi and the river again.

He was not really thinking so much as letting things run through his mind. It was still teeming with questions, and he had no idea where to find a thread to begin untangling even one answer. Perhaps it began with who had killed Sebastian, and why?

The longest day of summer was well past, and by half-past six he was tired, thirsty, and the sun was lowering in the west. Maybe he had come to the pub near the Mill Pond intentionally, even if it had not been consciously in his mind. He would be able to sit down here, and have supper and a long, cool drink. In time he could make the opportunity to talk with Flora Whickham again. If Sebastian had known anything about the crash of the Lanchester, then she would be the one person he might have told, other than Elwyn, and there was no chance that Joseph could draw it out of him. He was locked inside his own misery and grief, and perhaps fear as well. If he held that lethal knowledge, it could be the catalyst for his own death if he spoke it aloud, to anyone. And why should he trust Joseph? So far he had succeeded in nothing except proving that Beecher did not kill Sebastian, or take his own life.

The pub was quiet — a few older men sitting over pints of ale, faces grim, voices subdued. The landlord moved among them quietly, filling tankards, wiping tables. Even for Flora there were no jokes.

Joseph had cold game pie with fresh tomatoes, pickle and vegetables, then raspberries and clotted cream. The other tables were empty and the air was already hazed with gold when at last he was able to gain Flora's attention undivided.

500

It was deserted now, and the landlord granted her an early evening.

She seemed quite willing to walk along the Backs under the trees in the fading light. There was no one on the river, at least on this stretch, and the leaves flickered in the barest breeze. One minute they were green and shadowed, the next opaque gold. There was little sound but a whispering of the wind, no voices, no laughter.

'Is it true that Sebastian's brother killed Dr Beecher?' Flora asked him.

'Yes. I'm afraid it is.'

'In revenge over Sebastian?'

'No. Dr Beecher didn't kill Sebastian, and Elwyn knew that.'

She frowned, the golden light making her hair a halo around her troubled face. 'Then why?' she asked. 'He loved Sebastian, you know?' She shook her head a little. 'He din't hero-worship him, he knew his faults; even though he din't understand him much. They was a lot different.' She stared ahead of her at the light across the smooth sweep of the grass, the tiny motes of dust swirling in the air, the sun gilding the flat surface of the water. 'If there's going to be a war, and it seems loike from what people say that there is, then Elwyn would have gone to fight. He would have thought it was his duty, and honour. But Sebastian would have done anything on earth to prevent it.'

'Did Elwyn know that?'

'Oi think so.' She waited a moment or two before she continued. 'He din't understand how much Sebastian cared, though. No one else did.'

501

'Not even Miss Coopersmith?' he asked gently. He did not know if Flora knew of her, but even if she had not, she surely never hoped for more from Sebastian than friendship, at the very most. The least would have been something grubbier and far less worthy.

'Oi think she knew something,' she said, looking away from him. 'But it made her feel bad. She come to me after his death. She wanted me to say nothing, to save his good name, and Oi suppose his family from bein' hurt.' Her mouth pulled a little at the corners, her face soft with pity. 'He din't love her, and she knew it. She thought he might come to in time. Oi can't think how awful that must be. But she still wanted to protect him.'

Joseph tried to imagine the same scene, the proud, almost plain Regina in her elegant mourning black, facing the barmaid with the oval face and the shining, almost pre-Raphaelite hair, and asking her to keep silent over her friendship with Sebastian, to save his reputation. And perhaps something to salvage a little of her public pride, if not privately, to know he had preferred Flora as a confidante.

'Did he care about it so much?' he asked aloud, remembering his own conversation with Sebastian, only a few yards from here. It had been intense, there was no question of that, but was it fears and dreams, or a will to do anything. Flora had spoken of doing. 'Was it really more than words?'

She stared at the grass in the fading light, and her voice was very low. 'It were a passion in him,' she said. 'In the end it were the most important thing in his loife . . . keep the peace, look after all this beauty what's come to us from the past. He was terrified o' war — not just the foighting an' bombing.' She lifted her head a little and gazed across the shining river at the towers of the intricate, immeasurably lovely buildings, and the limpid sky beyond. 'The power to break and smash and burn, but the killing o' the spirit most of all. When we've broke civilisation, what 'ave we got left inside us? The strength and the dreams to start over again? No, we 'aven't. In smashing up all we got left o' what's wise, an' lovely, an' speaks to what's holy inside us, we break ourselves too. We get to be savages, but without the excuses that savages have for it.'

He heard Sebastian's words echoed in hers, exactly as if it had been he again, walking silent-footed in this exquisite evening.

She turned to face him. 'Do you understand?' she said urgently. It seemed to matter to her that he did.

For that reason Joseph needed to answer her honestly. 'That depends upon what you are prepared to do to avoid war.'

'Does it?' she demanded. 'Ain't it worth anything at all?'

'Did Sebastian think so?'

'Yes! Oi . . . ' She seemed troubled, looking away from him. 'What d'you mean, 'it depends'? What could be worse'n that? He told me about some of the things in the Boer War.' She shuddered almost convulsively, hugging her arms around herself. 'The concentration camps, what happened to some o' the women and children,' she said in a whisper. 'If you do that to people, what is there left for you when you come home, even if you won?'

'I don't know,' he confessed, finding himself cold as well. 'But I've come to the point where I can't believe that appeasement is the answer. Few sane people want to fight, but perhaps we have to.'

'Oi think mebbe that was what scared him.' She stood still on the grass. They were opposite Trinity; St John's was dark against the sunset, and there was only a tiny sliver of light on the water under the bridge. 'He was terrible upset over something, the last few days. He couldn't sleep; Oi think he was afraid to. It was as if he had a pain inside him that were so deep he weren't never free of it. After that shooting in Serbia 'e were so close to despair that Oi was scared for him . . . Oi mean real scared! It was as if for 'im there were nothing out there but darkness. Oi tried to comfort him, but Oi din't manage.' She looked back at Joseph, her eyes full of grief. 'Is it a wicked thing to say — sometimes Oi'm almost glad he din't live to see this . . . 'cos we're going to war, aren't we? All of us.'

'I think so,' he said quietly. It seemed a ridiculous conversation with the tremendous sunset dying on the horizon, the evening air full of the perfume of grass, no sound but the murmur of leaves, and a whirl of starlings thrown up against the translucent blue of the sky. Surely this was the very soul of peace, generations mounting to this pinnacle of

504

civilisation? How could it ever be broken?

'He tried so hard!' There were tears of anger and pity in her voice. 'He belonged to a very big sort of club fighting for peace, all over the world. And he would have done anything for 'em.'

Something tugged at his mind. 'Oh? Who were they?'

Flora shook her head quickly. 'Oi dunno. He wouldn't tell me. But they had big ideas he was terribly excited about, that would stop the war that's coming now.' She knotted her hands together, her head bowed. 'Oi'm glad he din't 'ave to see this! His dreams was so big, and so good, he couldn't bear seeing 'em come to nothing. He went almost mad just thinking of it, before they killed him. Oi've thought sometimes if that was why they did it.' She looked up and searched Joseph's face. 'Do you think there's anyone so wicked they'd want war enough to kill 'im in case he stopped it?'

He did not answer. His voice was trapped inside him, his chest so tight it filled him with pain. Was that the plot his father had stumbled on? Did Sebastian know about it all the time? What price was it they were prepared to pay for a peace that John Reavley had believed would ruin England's honour?

Flora was walking again, down over the slope of the grass towards the river, perhaps because the light was fading so rapidly she needed to be away from the trees to see where she was going. She belonged in the landscape, her blemishless skin like gold in the last echoes of the light, her hair an aureole around her head.

505

He caught up with her. 'I'll walk back with you,' he offered.

She smiled and shook her head. 'It ain't late. If Oi can go through the college Oi'll walk along the street. But thank you.'

He did not argue. He must see Elwyn. He was the only one who could answer the questions that burned in his mind, and there was no time to wait. The darkness was not only in the sky and the air, it was in the heart as well.

He did not go back to St John's but cut across the nearest bridge back through Trinity to the street again, and walked as fast as he could towards the police station. His mind was still whirling, thoughts chaotic, the same questions beating insistently, demanding answer.

He had to see Elwyn, whoever he had to waken, whatever reason or excuse he gave them.

The streets were deserted, the lamps like uncertain moons shedding a yellow glare on the paving stones. His footsteps sounded hollow, rapid, slipping a little now and then.

He reached the police station and saw the lights were on. Good. There were people, perhaps still working. The doors were unlocked and he went straight in. There was a man at the desk but Joseph ignored him, hearing the voice calling after him as he strode into the room beyond where Perth was remonstrating with Gerald and Mary Allard, and a man in a dark suit, who was presumably their solicitor.

They turned as Joseph came in. Perth looked harassed and so tired his eyes were red-rimmed. 'Reverend . . . ' he started.

'I need to speak to Elwyn,' Joseph said, hearing a thread of desperation in his voice. If the solicitor got to him first, then he might never hear the truth.

'You can't!' Mary refused savagely. 'I forbid it. You have brought nothing but ill to my family, and — '

Joseph turned to Perth. 'I think he may know something about Sebastian's death. Please — it matters very much!'

They stared at him. There was no yielding in Mary's face, and the solicitor moved half a step closer to her, as if in support. Gerald remained motionless.

'I think Sebastian knew about the death of my parents!' Joseph said, panic coursing through him, threatening to slip out of control. 'Please!'

Perth made a decision. 'You stay here!' he ordered the Allards and the solicitor. 'You come wi' me,' he said to Joseph. 'If 'e wants to see you, then you can.' And without waiting for possible argument he went out of the room with Joseph on his heels.

It was only a short distance to the cells where Elwyn was being held and in a few moments they were at the door. The key was on a hook outside. Perth took it off and inserted it into the lock and turned it. He pushed it open and stopped, frozen.

Joseph was a step behind him, and taller. He saw Elwyn over Perth's shoulder. He was hanging from the bars of the high window, the noose around his neck made from the strips of his shirt plaited together, strong enough to hold his weight and strangle the air from his lungs.

Perth lunged forward, crying out, although barely a sound escaped his lips.

Joseph thought he was going to be sick. Emotion overwhelmed him with a crushing force: pity and relief. He barely felt the tears running down his face.

Perth was scrambling to untie Elwyn, fingers clumsy, tearing at the knots, breaking his nails, his breath rasping in his throat.

Joseph saw the letter on the cot and went to it. There was nothing he or anyone could do for Elwyn. The envelope was addressed to him. He opened it, before Perth or anyone else should tell him he couldn't.

He read it.

Dear Dr Reavley,

Sebastian was dead when I got to his room that morning, the gun was on the floor. I knew he had killed himself, but I thought it was because he was afraid of going to war. He always believed we would do. It looks now as if he was right. But I didn't read his letter until afterwards, when it was too late. All I could think of was hiding his suicide. Mother could not have lived with the knowledge that he was a coward. You know that, because you know her.

I took the gun and hid it in the bucket at the top of the drainpipe in the Master's house. I never meant anyone to be blamed, but it all got away from me.

Dr Beecher must have realised. You heard what he said on the landing, about Sebastian and courage. By then I'd read his letter, but it was too late. I'm so sorry, so terribly sorry. There is nothing left now. At least this is the truth.

Elwyn Allard

Wrapped inside it was another letter, on different paper, and in Sebastian's hand:

Dear Dr Reavley,

I thought I knew the answer. Peace — peace at any price. War in Europe could slaughter millions, what is one life or two to save so many? I believed that and I would have given my own life gladly. I wanted to keep all the beauty. Perhaps it isn't possible, and we'll have to fight after all.

I was in London when I heard the document had been stolen. I came back to Cambridge that night. They gave me a gun, but I made the caltrops myself, out of fence wire. Then it would look like an accident. Much better. It wasn't difficult, just tedious.

I went out on a bicycle the next day, left it in a field. It was all very simple — and more terrible than anything I could have imagined. You think of millions and the mind is devastated. You see two you know, broken, the spirit gone, and it tears the soul apart. The reality of blood and pain is so very different from the idea. I can't live with who I am now.

509

I wish it hadn't been your parents, Joseph.
I'm so sorry, sorrier than anything will heal.
    Sebastian

Joseph stared at the paper. It explained everything. In their own way Sebastian and Elwyn were so alike: blind, heroic, self-destructive, and in the end totally futile. The war would happen anyway.

Perth laid Elwyn on the floor, gently, a blanket under his head, as if it mattered. He was staring up at Joseph, his face was grey.

'It's not your fault,' Joseph said. 'At least this way there doesn't have to be a trial.'

Perth gasped. Tried to say something and ended in a sob.

Joseph put Elwyn's letter back on the cot, and kept Sebastian's.

'I'll go and tell them.' He found his mouth dry. What words could he possibly find? He walked out and back the short distance. Perth could send for somebody to help him.

As soon as he was in the room Mary stepped forward and drew in her breath to demand an explanation, then she saw his face and realised with terror that there was something more hideously wrong.

Gerald moved behind her and placed his hands firmly on her shoulders.

'I'm sorry,' Joseph said quietly. 'Elwyn has admitted to killing Dr Beecher, because Beecher realised the truth of Sebastian's death — '

'No!' Mary said stridently, trying to raise her arms and snatch herself away from Gerald's grip.

Joseph stood still. There was no way to avoid it. He felt as if he were pronouncing sentence of death upon her. 'Sebastian took his own life, no one murdered him. Elwyn did not want you to know that, so he took the gun and made it look like murder — to protect you. I'm sorry.'

She stood paralysed. 'No,' she said quite quietly. 'That isn't true. You are lying. I don't know why, but you are lying. It's a conspiracy!'

Gerald's face puckered slowly as understanding broke something inside him. He let go of Mary and staggered backwards to collapse on to one of the wooden chairs.

The solicitor looked totally helpless.

'No!' Mary repeated. 'No!' Her voice rose. 'No!'

Perth appeared in the doorway. 'I've sent for a doctor . . . '

Mary swung round. 'He's alive! I knew it!'

'No,' he said huskily. 'For you. I'm sorry.'

She stood swaying.

Joseph reached to help her and she lashed out at him as her legs buckled and he helped her to one of the other chairs. She caught his face, but it was only a glancing blow.

'You'd better go, sir,' Perth said quietly. There was no anger in his face, only pity and an immense weariness.

Joseph accepted and walked out into the cool, shrouding darkness and the protection of the night. He needed solitude.

★ ★ ★

511

The next day, 3 August, Mitchell brought Joseph the newspaper early.

'There's going to be war, sir,' he said sombrely. 'No way we can help it now. Russia invaded Germany yesterday, and the Germans have gone into France, Luxembourg and Switzerland. Navy's mobilized, and troops are guarding the rail lines and ammunition supplies and so on. Reckon it's come, Dr Reavley. God help us.'

'Yes, Mitchell, I suppose it has,' Joseph answered. The reality of it choked like an absence of air, heavy and tight in his lungs.

'You'll be going home, sir?' It was a statement.

'Yes, Mitchell. There really isn't anything to do here for the moment. I should be with my sister.'

'Yes, sir.'

Before leaving he called briefly on Connie. There was very little to say. He could not tell her about Sebastian, and anyway, when he looked at her, he thought of Beecher. He knew what it was like to lose the only person you could imagine loving, and exactly how it felt to face the endless stretch ahead. All he could do was smile at her, and say something about the war.

'I suppose many of them will enlist as officers,' she said quietly, her eyes misted over, staring at the sunlight on the walls of the garden.

'Probably,' he agreed. 'The best — if it comes to that.'

She turned to look at him. 'Do you think there's any hope it won't?'

'I don't know,' he admitted.

He stayed only a moment longer, wanting to

say something about Beecher, but she understood it all. She had known Harry perhaps even
better than Joseph had, and would miss him even
more. In the end he simply said goodbye, and
went to find the Master, to say goodbye to him,
for the time being.

Afterwards he had barely reached the centre of
the outer quad when he met Matthew coming in
through the main gate. He looked pale and tired,
as if he had been up most of the night. His fair
hair was a little sun-bleached across the front,
and he was wearing uniform.

'Do you want a lift home?' he asked.

'Yes . . . please.' Joseph hesitated only a
moment, wondering if Matthew wanted a cup of
tea, or anything else before he went on the last
few miles. But the answer was in his face.

Ten minutes later they were on the road again.
It hardly seemed different from any summer
weekend. The lanes were thick with leaf, the
harvest fields ripe, here and there stippled with
the burning scarlet of poppies. The swallows
were gathering.

With a heavy heart Joseph told Matthew what
had happened the previous night. He could
remember Elwyn's letter and he still had
Sebastian's. He read it as they drove. It needed
no explanation, no added comments. When he
had finished he folded it and put it back in his
pocket. He looked at Matthew. His face was
heavy with pain, and anger for the sorrow and
the futility of it. He glanced sideways at Joseph,
for a moment. It was a look of compassion,
wordless and deep.

'You're right,' he agreed quietly, swinging round the curve of the road into St Giles and seeing the street ahead of them deserted. 'There's nothing either of us can do now. Poor devils. All so bloody pointless. I suppose you've still got no idea what happened to the document?'

'No,' Joseph said bleakly. 'I'd have told you.'

'Yes, of course. And I still don't know who's behind it . . . unless it is Aidan Thyer, as you suggest. Damn! I liked him.'

'So did I. I'm beginning to realise how little that means,' Joseph said ruefully.

Matthew shot him a glance as he turned right off the main street towards the house. 'What are you going to do now? Archie'll stay at sea as usual. He won't have a choice. And I'll keep on with the SIS, naturally. But what about you?' His brow was furrowed slightly, concern in his eyes.

'I don't know,' Joseph admitted.

Matthew pulled the car up in front of the house, its tyres crunching on the gravel. A moment later Judith opened the front door, relief flooding her face. She took the steps in two strides and hugged Joseph and then Matthew, before turning to go back inside.

They told her about Elwyn and Sebastian walking out over the soft grass in the garden under the apple trees. She was stunned; rage, pity, confusion washed over her like storm waves, leaving her dizzy.

It was a late and sombre lunch, eaten in an agreed silence, each willing to be alone with their thoughts. It was one of those strange, interminable occasions when time stands still. The sound of cutlery on the china of a plate was deafening.

Today, tomorrow, one day soon, Joseph would have to make his decision. He was thirty-five. He did not have to fight. He could claim all kinds of exemptions and no one would object. Life had to continue at home: there were sermons to be preached, people to be christened, married, buried, the sick and the troubled to be visited.

There were raspberries for dessert. He ate his slowly, savouring the sweetness of them, as if he would not have them again. He felt as if Matthew and Judith expected him to say something, but he had no idea what, and he was saved by Matthew interrupting his indecision.

'I've been thinking,' Matthew said slowly. 'I don't know what armaments we have, not in detail. I do know it's not enough. We may be asked to give up anything we have that works. I don't know if anyone will want them, but they might.'

'It's not going to be that bad! Is it?' Judith looked very pale, her eyes frightened. 'I mean — '

'No, of course it isn't!' Joseph rushed in. He glared warningly at Matthew.

'They may ask us for guns,' Matthew said stiffly. 'I shan't be home, and I don't know whether you will or not.' He looked at Joseph, pushing his chair back as he spoke, and standing up. 'There are at least two shotguns, one new, and an old one which may not be up to much. And there's the punt gun.'

515

'You could stop an elephant with that!' Judith said wryly. 'But only if it was coming at you across the fens, and you just happened to be out punting at the time.'

Matthew pushed the chair back in at the table. 'I'll get it out anyway. It'll probably be of use to someone.'

Joseph went with him, not out of any interest in guns — he loathed them — but for something to do. 'You don't need to frighten her like that!' he criticized. 'For God's sake, use some sense!'

'She's better knowing,' was all Matthew replied.

The guns were kept in a locked cupboard in the study. Matthew took the key from his ring and opened it. Inside were the three guns he had mentioned, and a very old target pistol. He looked at them one by one, breaking the shotguns and examining them.

'Have you decided yet what you're going to do?' he asked, squinting down one of the barrels.

Joseph did not answer. The thoughts in his head had been forming into immovable shapes, far longer than he had realised. They had already cut off every line of retreat from the inevitable. Now he was forced to acknowledge it.

Matthew looked down the other barrel, then straightened the gun again. He picked up the second gun and broke it. 'You haven't much time, Joe,' he said gently. 'It won't be more than another day or two.'

Joseph hoped he might be guessing. It was a last grasp at innocence, and it failed. He understood Sebastian's fear. Perhaps that was what he had seen in him that had found the deepest echo within himself, the helpless pity for suffering he could not reach, even to ease. It overwhelmed him. The anger of war horrified him, the ability to hate, to make your life's aim the death of another . . . for any cause at all. If he became part of it, it would drown him.

Matthew picked up the big punt gun. It was an awkward thing, long-barrelled and muzzle-loaded. It did not break in the middle like a shotgun, but it was lethal over the short distances that it could be aimed and used.

'Damn!' he said irritably, peering up the barrel. 'I can't see a thing! Whoever designed these bloody guns should be made to look after them. I don't know whether it's working or not. Do you remember the last time anybody used it?'

Joseph was not listening. His mind was back in the hospital where he had started his medical training, the injuries, the pain, the deaths he could not prevent.

'Joe!' Matthew said savagely. 'Damn it! Pay attention! Pass that rod and let me see if this is clean or not!'

Joseph passed over the rod obediently and Matthew rammed it up the barrel of the punt gun.

'There's something up here,' he said impatiently. 'It's . . . ' Very slowly he lowered his hands, still holding the gun. 'It's paper,' he said huskily. 'It's a roll of paper.'

Joseph felt the sweat break out on his skin and go cold. 'Hold the gun!' he ordered him, taking the rod from Matthew and beginning to tease very gently. He found his hands were shaking, as was the barrel of the punt gun in Matthew's grip.

It took him nearly ten minutes to prise the paper out without tearing it, and then unroll it and hold it open. It was in German. They read it together.

It was an agreement between the Kaiser and King George V, the terms of which were shatteringly simple. Britain would stand aside and allow Germany to invade and conquer Belgium, France and, of course, Luxembourg, saving the hundreds of thousands of lives that would be lost in trying to defend them.

In return a new Anglo-German Empire would be formed with unassailable power on land and sea. The riches of the world would be divided between them: Africa, India, the Far East, and best of all, America.

The surgery of war would be swift and almost painless, the reward beyond measure. The document was signed by the Kaiser, and obviously on its way to the King for approval and countersignature.

'God Almighty!' Matthew said hoarsely. 'It's . . . it's monstrous! It's . . . '

'It's what Father died to prevent,' Joseph said, tears choking his voice. It was the one thing he had believed that had stood fast and whole through all the loss. His father was right. Nothing had misled or deceived him. He had been right. It spread a peace through him, a kind of certainty at the core. 'And perhaps he succeeded,' he went on aloud. 'There will be war. God knows how many will die, but England gave her word to Belgium, and she will not betray it. That would be worse than death.'

Matthew rubbed his hands over his face. 'Who's behind it?' He was weary, but in him too there was something stronger within — a doubt, a vulnerability gone.

'I don't know,' Joseph said. 'Someone in Germany close to the Kaiser, very clever, with a great deal of vision, and power. And, more importantly to us, someone here in England too, who was going to get it to the King — and damn nearly did.'

'I know,' Matthew shook his head. 'It could be anyone. Chetwin . . . Shearing himself, I suppose. Even Sandwell! I don't know either.'

'Or anyone else we haven't even thought of,' Joseph added.

Matthew stared at him. 'But whoever it is, he's brilliant, ruthless, and he's still out there.'

'But he's failed . . . '

'He won't accept failure.' Matthew bit his lip, his voice tight, his face almost bloodless. 'A man who could dream up this won't stop here. He'll have contingency plans, other ideas. And he's far from alone. He has allies, other naïve dreamers, and wounded idealists, the disaffected, the ambitious. And we never know who they are, until it's too late. But by God I'll put every spare minute I've got into hunting him down. I'll follow every trail, wherever it goes, whoever it touches, until I've got him. If we don't, he'll destroy everything we care about.'

Something in the words crystalized the

knowledge in Joseph's mind, and it became undeniable, sealed for ever. Whatever he felt, regardless of mind or heart, horror or his own weakness to achieve anything of use, he must join the war. If honour, faith, any values, human or divine, were to be kept, then there was no escape. He would do everything he could. He would learn to preserve his emotions apart, not to feel the rage or the pity, then he could survive.

'I'll join the army,' he said aloud. 'As a chaplain.' It was an absolute statement, no question, no alteration possible. 'I won't fight, but I'll be there. I'll help.'

Matthew smiled, his face softening to an extraordinary gentleness, and something in his eyes that Joseph realised with amazement was pride.

'Thought you would,' he said quietly.

Somewhere far away in the house the telephone rang.

The light outside was softening, turning hazy.

'What are we going to do with this?' Matthew asked, looking at the document.

'Put it back in the gun,' Joseph answered without hesitation. 'We may want it one day. No one would believe its existence without seeing it. They didn't find it here before, and they looked. That's as safe as anywhere. Disable the gun where they'll see it, and then no one will think to use it.'

Matthew regarded the old gun ruefully. 'I hate to do that,' he said but, even as he spoke, removing the firing pin.

Joseph rolled up the document again and

pushed it down the barrel, using the rod to jam it as far as possible.

They had just finished when Judith came to the door, her face pale.

'Who was it on the telephone?' Joseph asked.

'It was for Matthew,' she said a little jerkily. 'It was Mr Shearing. Sir Edward Grey said in Parliament that if Germany invades Belgium, then Great Britain will honour the treaty to safeguard Belgian neutrality, and we will be at war. He wants you back as soon as we know.' She took a deep, shuddering breath. 'It will happen, won't it?'

'Yes,' Joseph answered. 'It will.' He glanced at Matthew.

Matthew nodded.

'We found the document Father died for,' he said to Judith. 'You'd better come to the sitting room and we'll tell you about it.'

She stood motionless. 'What is it?' she demanded. 'Where was it? Why didn't we find it before?'

'In the punt gun,' Joseph told her. 'It was every bit as terrible as he said . . . more.'

'I want to see it!' she said without moving.

Matthew drew in his breath.

'I want to!' she repeated.

It was Joseph who went to the gun and very carefully started to lever the paper out again. Matthew held the gun to help him. Finally he had it. He unrolled it and opened it for Judith.

She took it in her hands and read it slowly.

Instead of fear in her face there was a kind of fierce, hurting pride. The tears stood out in her eyes and she ignored them as they slid down her cheeks. She looked up at them. 'So he was right!'

'Oh yes!' Joseph found his own voice choked. 'Typical of Father — he understated it. It would have changed the whole world, and made England the most dishonourable nation in the annals of history. It might have saved lives, or not — but only in the short term. In the end the cost would be beyond counting or measuring. There are things we have to fight for . . . '

Judith nodded and turned away, walking back to the sitting room. The sun was sinking already, casting long shadows.

Joseph and Matthew carefully replaced the treaty yet again, then went after her.

They sat quietly together, speaking a little, remembering, while the light lasted, moments shared, past laughter, times woven into the fabric of memory to shine in the darkness ahead.

Later Shearing telephoned again. Matthew answered it and listened.

'Yes,' he said at length. 'Yes, sir. Of course. I'll be there first thing in the morning.' He hung up and turned to Joseph and Judith. 'Germany has declared war on France, and is massed to invade Belgium. When it happens, we will send Germany an ultimatum, which of course they will refuse. By midnight tomorrow we shall be at war. Grey said, 'The lamps are going out all over Europe; we shall not see them lit again in our lifetime.' '

'Perhaps not.' Joseph took a deep breath. 'We shall have to carry our own light . . . the best we can.'

Judith buried her head in his shoulder, and Matthew reached out around her to take Joseph's hand and grip it.

THE END

We do hope that you have enjoyed reading this large print book.

Did you know that all of our titles are available for purchase?

We publish a wide range of high quality large print books including:
Romances, Mysteries, Classics
General Fiction
Non Fiction and Westerns

Special interest titles available in large print are:
The Little Oxford Dictionary
Music Book
Song Book
Hymn Book
Service Book

Also available from us courtesy of Oxford University Press:
Young Readers' Dictionary
(large print edition)
Young Readers' Thesaurus
(large print edition)

For further information or a free brochure, please contact us at:
Ulverscroft Large Print Books Ltd.,
The Green, Bradgate Road, Anstey,
Leicester, LE7 7FU, England.
Tel: (00 44) 0116 236 4325
Fax: (00 44) 0116 234 0205

Other titles in the
Charnwood Library Series:

LOVE ME OR LEAVE ME

Josephine Cox

Beautiful Eva Bereton has only three friends in the world: Patsy, who she looks upon as a sister; Bill, her adopted cousin, and her mother, to whom she is devoted. With Eva's father increasingly angry about life as a cripple, she and her mother support each other, keeping their spirits high despite the abuse. So when a tragic accident robs Eva of both parents, Patsy, a loveable Irish rogue, is the only one left to support her. Tragedy strikes yet again when Eva's uncle comes to reclaim the farm that Eva had always believed belonged to her parents. Together with Patsy, Eva has no choice but to start a new life far away . . .

COLDITZ: THE GERMAN STORY

Reinhold Eggers

This is the story of the famous German prison camp Colditz — as the German guards saw it. It was a place where every man felt that in spite of the personal tragedy of imprisonment, it was his duty to overcome. The book vividly describes the constant battle of wits between guards and prisoners, the tunnelling, bribery, impersonations, forgery and trickery of all kinds by which brave men sought to return to the war.

CHARLOTTE GRAY

Sebastian Faulks

It is 1942. London is blacked out, but France is under a greater darkness, as the Vichy regime clings ever closer to the Nazi occupier. From Edinburgh, Charlotte Gray, a volatile but determined young woman, travels south. In London she conceives a dangerous passion for an English airman. Charlotte goes to France on an errand for a British organisation helping the Resistance, and for her own private purposes. Unknown to her, she is also being manipulated by people with no regard for her safety. As the weeks go by, Charlotte finds that the struggle for France's soul is intimately linked to her battle to take control of her own life.

AN APRIL SHROUD

Reginald Hill

After seeing Inspector Pascoe off on his honeymoon, Superintendent Andy Dalziel runs into trouble on his own holiday. He accompanies his rescuers back to their rundown mansion, where he discovers that Lake House's owner, Bonnie Fielding, seems less troubled by her husband's tragic death than by the problem of completing the Banqueting Hall. Prompted not only by a professional curiosity — why would anyone want to keep a dead rat in a freezer? — but also by Mrs Fielding's ample charms, Dalziel stays on. By the time Pascoe reappears, there have been several more deaths . . .